寒夜

COLD NIGHTS

中國現代文學中英對照系列

Bilingual Series on Modern Chinese Literature

中國現代文學中英對照系列
Bilingual Series on Modern Chinese Literature

寒夜
Cold Nights

中英對照版
Chinese-English Bilingual Edition

巴金 著
茅國權、柳存仁 英譯

Original Chinese Text by
PA CHIN
Translated by Nathan K. Mao and Liu Ts'un-yan

With an Introduction by Paul G. Pickowicz

The Chinese University Press

《**寒夜**》(中英對照版)
巴金 著
茅國權、柳存仁 英譯

國際統一書號 (ISBN) 978-962-996-013-1

2002年第一版
2010年第二次印刷

出版：中文大學出版社
香港中文大學・香港 新界 沙田
圖文傳真：+852 2603 6692
+852 2603 7355
電子郵遞：cup@cuhk.edu.hk
網　　址：www.chineseupress.com

Cold Nights (Chinese-English Bilingual Edition)
Chinese text by Pa Chin
Translated by Nathan K. Mao and Liu Ts'un-yan

ISBN 978-962-996-013-1

First edition 2002
Second printing 2010

Published by The Chinese University Press,
The Chinese University of Hong Kong,
Sha Tin, N.T., Hong Kong.
Fax: +852 2603 6692
+852 2603 7355
E-mail: cup@cuhk.edu.hk
Web-site: www.chineseupress.com

Printed in Hong Kong

出版人的話

近二十年，中國與外界接觸日趨頻繁，影響所及，華文作家在世界文學圈中益受注目。二○○○年諾貝爾文學獎由高行健先生獲得，或許並非偶然。

中文大學出版社一向秉承促進中西方文化交流的使命，故於年前開始籌劃「中國現代文學中英對照系列」，邀得鄭樹森教授出任編輯委員會主席，及幾位國際著名學者出任成員，挑選中國著名作家之重要作品及現有最好之英譯本，以中英文雙語對照排列出版，計劃每年出版五至六種書目。間或有版權問題未能解決的，則另邀請翻譯界的高手操刀英譯。每位著名作家及其作品亦會由圈內名家作序介紹，以為導讀。

本社謹對編輯委員會及其他曾出力人士之鼎力協助，致以熱切謝忱。

Publisher's Note

The Chinese University Press in Hong Kong is uniquely situated to play an active role in bridging the gap between Chinese and Western cultures. Under the able guidance of Professor William Tay and the other members of the Academic Committee, the *Bilingual Series on Modern Chinese Literature* seeks to present work by seminal authors in a bilingual format for the broadest range of cross-cultural appreciation. For each book in the series the committee either identifies the best existing translation or commissions experts to bring the work into the English language and literary canon. Each title also contains a critical introduction by a noted scholar.

The publisher appreciates the invaluable advice of the Advisory Committee and sincerely thanks everyone who has helped to make this series a reality.

Nathan dedicates this book to all his children

Contents

目 錄

Introduction

Pa Chin's Cold Nights and China's Wartime and Postwar Culture of Disaffection

Paul G. Pickowicz
Department of History
University of California, San Diego

Li Fei-kan (1904–2005), much better known by his pen name, Pa Chin, was one of the most productive and popular writers in China during the tumultuous 1930s and 1940s.[1] He was also a jumble of contradictions. On the one hand, he was a staunch nationalist, who consistently and loudly denounced the exploitation of China by Japan and other imperialist aggressors. Like other proud patriots, he looked forward to a time when the Chinese nation would be powerful, prosperous and, above all, independent. On the other hand, Pa Chin was profoundly cosmopolitan. He lived in France in 1927–28, had a remarkable grasp of world literature, and possessed a sophisticated knowledge of French, English and other foreign languages. An unabashed champion of the French and Russian revolutions, Pa Chin was a dedicated internationalist. From the late 1920s he openly espoused anarchism and enthusiastically embraced the radical writings of Bakunin and Kropotkin. Indeed, according to legend, his pen name, Pa Chin, consists of the first syllable of Bakunin's name and the last

1. The standard biography is Olga Lang's, *Pa Chin and His Writings* (Cambridge: Harvard University Press, 1967).

前 言

巴金的《寒夜》與抗戰時期及戰後的憤懣文化

畢克偉 撰
加州大學聖地牙歌校區
歷史系

陳嘉恩 譯
香港中文大學
翻譯系

李芾甘(1904年生)，以筆名「巴金」廣為人知，在動盪的三、四十年代甚為多產，亦極風行。[1] 巴金是充滿矛盾的作家。一方面，他是堅定的民族主義者，不斷疾聲譴責日本及其他帝國主義的侵略剝削；與其他愛國者一樣，巴金期盼中國終會富強，尤其是獨立自主。另一方面，巴金視野廣闊，放眼世界；一九二七至二八年間，旅居法國，熟悉各國文學，精通法語、英語及其他外語。巴金是熱心的國際主義者，堅定支持法國及俄國革命。一九二零年代末起，公開推崇無政府主義，並贊同巴枯寧(Mikhail Aleksandrovich Bakunin)及克魯泡特金(Pëter Alekseyevich Kropotkin)的激進論述。據說其筆名即由「巴枯寧」的首個音節「巴」及「克魯泡特金」的最

1. 至今通行的巴金傳是 Olga Lang's, *Pa Chin and His Writings* (Cambridge: Harvard University Press, 1967).

syllable of Kropotkin's. Like his namesakes, Pa Chin firmly believed in universal human values. Thus, he saw the struggle to liberate the Chinese nation as part of a world-wide effort to emancipate all individuals from various forms of oppression. A stubborn and principled idealist, some say a dreamer, he longed for the day when all people would be able to enjoy freedom.

The many tensions evident in Pa Chin's social and political thought are beautifully captured in his best known and enormously influential novel, *Family* (*Chia*), published in Shanghai in 1931. This largely autobiographical work is set in the immediate aftermath of World War I at a time when a badly divided China was ruled by a myriad of local warlords and, thus, highly vulnerable to foreign encroachments. The young elites featured in the novel are militantly nationalistic, but, like Pa Chin himself, they are scathingly critical of patriarchal norms and many other bedrock aspects of Chinese culture. His youthful heroes and heroines subscribe to what they regard as universal standards of human liberation. They are fiercely nationalistic in the context of China's painful confrontation with Japanese imperialism, but their patriotism is grounded intellectually in a rejection of key aspects of Chinese culture. Unlike their Japanese adversaries, they do not engage in chauvinistic celebrations of a supposedly ancient, pure and sacred cultural tradition. It is this far more critical approach to indigenous culture that sets early twentieth century Chinese nationalism apart from both its German and Japanese counterparts.

The political logic of *Family* stresses that the Chinese nation cannot win freedom and independence until individual Chinese shake free of oppressive patriarchal structures associated with the family unit. Old moral principles are not only anachronistic, they are local and thus inconsistent with newly recognized universal human values. To Pa Chin, the ideals articulated by Kropotkin and Bakunin are not Western or Russian, they are global. In other words, Pa Chin's

末一個音節「金」所組成。他以巴枯寧及克魯泡特金為名，思想亦與兩人相近，相信人類的普世價值，故此他將解放中華民族的抗爭，視為全球個人解放運動的一部份，要把所有人從各種壓迫中匡救出來。他是一位執着的理想主義者，原則性強，有人甚至會說他是一位夢想家；他冀望有一天，所有的人都得享自由。

巴金社會及政治思想中的各種張力，在小說《家》中充份彰顯。《家》於一九三一年在上海出版，是他作品中最膾炙人口及影響深遠的小說。這部自傳性質甚強的小說，以第一次世界大戰後的中國為背景。當時中國四分五裂，軍閥割據，受外敵侵凌。小說中的精英份子都是激昂的民族主義者，但他們跟巴金一樣，嚴厲批判父權制度的規範與中國文化的其他本質。在巴金筆下，年輕的男女主角認為人類解放有一套世界性的標準。中國與日本帝國主義苦戰時，他們極端愛國，但在理智上，他們的愛國主義是以摒棄中國文化的要義為出發點的。他們不是沙文主義者，與日本人不一樣，不會去誇耀所謂古遠、純粹及神聖的文化傳統。正因為這種批判本土文化的態度，二十世紀初中國的民族主義與德國及日本的民族主義大相徑庭。

《家》的政治邏輯強調，壓抑個人的父權建構與家庭有關，只有當個人從這個建構中擺脫出來，中國方可贏得自由與獨立。舊有道德價值不但過時，而且狹隘，只着眼於中國本土，所以與五四以來認同的人類普世價值並不符合。在巴金而言，巴枯寧與克魯泡特金的理想並非是西方或俄國的，而是屬於全世界的。換句話說，巴金

protagonists are at once nationalists who love the modern Chinese nation and internationalists who reject what they perceive to be anti-modern Chinese values.

In stylistic terms, *Family* is a good example of Pa Chin's lifelong approach to writing. For one thing, like much of the literature produced in twentieth century China, this immensely popular work has an obvious allegorical quality. It focuses narrowly on an individual family unit, but the problems of the dysfunctional and suffocating family are symptomatic of the cultural ills that plague the entire nation. Furthermore, *Family* is exceedingly wet: the characters shed hot tears on practically every page. Pa Chin's addiction to sentimentality makes it extremely difficult for literary critics to consider him to be a genuinely innovative writer. It is hard to deny, however, that Pa Chin had a shrewd understanding of popular tastes. His melodramatic protests against brutal foreign aggressors and sadistic family patriarchs are full of caricatures, but they invariably reduced many of his youthful readers to tears and caused others to take action.

Family is without a doubt the quintessential Pa Chin novel, but it is not his best work. *Cold Nights* (*Han yeh*), published in 1947, is a much stronger candidate for that distinction. At one important level, *Cold Nights* deals with daily life in China toward the end of World War II. It is highly significant that the novel is set in Chungking, China's wartime capital, where Pa Chin resided beginning in the summer of 1944. Although the heroic and largely defenseless people of Chungking successfully resisted countless Japanese air attacks during the course of the war, Pa Chin's novel makes no effort whatsoever to glorify the wartime achievements of the Chinese. On the contrary, *Cold Nights* is a dark and depressing book from start to finish.

Once again, Pa Chin uses a discussion of a single family unit to shed light on China's problems. And, once again, the family is dysfunctional. In Pa Chin's earlier works, including *Family*, there are

筆下的主角既是民族主義者，熱愛現代中國，但也是國際主義者，排斥反現代的中國價值觀。

在風格上，《家》很能代表巴金畢生的寫作取向。一如不少中國二十世紀的文學作品，這部非常風行的小說喻意色彩鮮明。小說集中描述一個家庭，但這個家庭的有乖常態、令人窒息，象徵着折磨整個國家的病疫。然而，《家》也相當煽情：小說人物幾乎每頁都揮淚如雨。巴金濫情成癖，故文學批評家無法將他視為真正具有創意的作家。但毋庸置疑，他洞悉大眾口味，以富於嘲弄的筆觸，控訴殘酷的外敵與施虐成狂的家長，每每令青年讀者熱淚盈眶，激勵人們行動起來。

《家》無疑是最典型的巴金小說，但並非他的最佳作品。相較之下，一九四七年出版的《寒夜》更勝一籌。《寒夜》描述二次大戰末期中國人的日常生活，這是一個重要的層次。以重慶作為背景更別具深義。重慶是中國戰時的首都，亦是巴金一九四四年夏天所居之地。雖然重慶人民大都無力自衞，卻能英勇抗敵，成功抵禦戰時日軍的無數空襲。然而，巴金在小說中完全沒有頌揚中國人抗戰的成就，相反，全書的基調由始至終都灰暗沉鬱。

在《寒夜》中，巴金再度通過個別家庭的描繪，揭示困擾中國的問題，而小說中的家庭也是有乖常態的。巴金早期的作品中，包括《家》，家庭生活時受衝擊，直至破裂（延伸至國家層面亦作如是

definite signs of hope despite all the problems that tear at family (and, by extension, national) life. Youthful and progressive idealists are seen at the end of many of his works rushing off to forge a new path for themselves and for China. In *Cold Nights*, however, the mood is grey and somber. The family simply collapses.

This turn of events is ironic because Pa Chin goes out of his way toward the end of *Cold Nights* to describe Japan's defeat and unconditional surrender in August 1945. In a word, China wins victory. In the wartime capital, however, family members are neither rejoicing nor contemplating solutions to festering social, economic and political problems.[2] Victory does not feel like victory, it feels like defeat. The emphasis in *Cold Nights* is not placed on the patriotic resistance and inspiring wartime sacrifices of ordinary families; the focus is on the cancers of corruption, profiteering, and runaway inflation that are responsible for a depressing environment of wartime disaffection and resignation. By the end of the war, Wang Wen-hsüan, the pathetic anti-hero of *Cold Nights*, is said to have "abandoned all hopes or illusions, reacting with apathy to the news of Germany's surrender. Even the prediction of the forthcoming collapse of Japan did not bring him any pleasure. It seemed that any bright and beautiful prospects for the future had no relationship to him at all." (p. 432) It is quite tempting, therefore, to interpret *Cold Nights* as a bitter indictment of wartime conditions that caused widespread disillusionment and seriously eroded popular confidence in the Nationalist Party and the government of Chiang Kai-shek.

Pa Chin's portrait of family life in Free China during World War II is shocking. At the center of the narrative is a family of refugees from

2. For a stimulating discussion of social change in wartime and postwar China, see Joseph W. Esherick, "War and Revolution: Chinese Society during the 1940s," *Twentieth-Century China*, vol. 27, no. 1 (November 2001), pp. 1–37.

觀），但又明確暗示希望尚存。在很多巴金作品的結尾，年輕進取的理想主義者前仆後繼，為自己、也為中國去開拓新路。然而，《寒夜》的基調灰暗陰鬱，小說中的家庭最終猝然崩潰。

《寒夜》的故事如此劇變不免反諷，因為故事快結束時，巴金特地描述日本於一九四五年八月戰敗，無條件投降。換言之，中國勝利了。不過，重慶的汪家家人並未因此而歡欣，也不去思考如何解決不斷惡化的社會、經濟及政治的問題。[2] 勝利不似勝利，反似戰敗。《寒夜》並沒有強調愛國的抗日戰爭，或是一般家庭於戰時作出激勵人心的犧牲；小說的焦點在於暴露貪污舞弊、牟取暴利、物價飛漲等毒害，在戰時造成一個憤懣與無奈的環境，令人沮喪。戰事結束時，《寒夜》中可悲的反英雄人物汪文宣說：「他對一切都斷念了。他不再敢有甚麼妄想，甚至德國投降也不曾帶給他快樂和安慰。他聽見人說日本在一年內就要崩潰，他也笑不出聲來。那些光明、美麗的希望似乎都跟他斷絕了關係。」（頁433）因此，人們很容易把《寒夜》詮釋為對戰時苦況的尖銳控訴，這些苦況使人人理想破滅，嚴重侵蝕民眾對國民黨及蔣介石政府的信心。

巴金對二次大戰時國統區家庭生活的寫照，實在令人瞠目。小說主要描述一個來自中國沿海的難民家庭，成員包括丈夫（汪文

2. 有關戰時及戰後中國的社會轉變，可參見 Joseph W. Esherick, "War and Revolution: Chinese Society during the 1940s," *Twentieth-Century China*, vol. 27, no. 1 (November 2001), pp. 1–37。文中的討論甚具啟發性。

coastal China consisting of a husband (Wang Wen-hsüan), a wife (Shu-sheng), a teenage son, and an elder (Wang's mother). Pa Chin's characterizations of these people are quite vivid. Wang Wen-hsüan, a sickly, low-level intellectual who labors at a meaningless, low-paying job in the wartime publishing world, is astonishingly weak. Manipulated and dominated by his hopelessly old-fashioned mother, Wang spends most of his time wallowing in self-pity, shedding tears about his plight in the wartime environment, and worrying about his inability to command the affection and even the respect of his stylish common law wife. Page by page, the family disintegrates.

Pa Chin's unsympathetic description of Wang's mother is virtually identical to the many stereotypic accounts of backward family elders contained in *Family* and other early works. Although *Cold Nights* does not deal primarily with the alleged failings of Chinese cultural traditions, Pa Chin simply cannot pass up an opportunity to take critical shots at the ways in which the people of "old China" impede the efforts of the young to create a "new China." In *Cold Nights*, the struggle between old and new culture is waged on the front of medical science. Pa Chin makes it clear that Wang Wen-hsüan has tuberculosis, a disease that claimed many in wartime Chungking. Wang's mother absolutely insists that he does not have tuberculosis and that his illness, whatever it is, can be cured by practitioners of traditional Chinese medicine. Wang's modern wife, Shu-sheng, openly disputes this course of action, demanding, instead, that the family consult a specialist in Western medicine. The mother (tradition) prevails and, thus, the dreaded disease continues to ravage Wen-hsüan (China).

If Wang Wen-hsüan is a portrait of wartime weakness and frailty and his mother is the stuff of cultural conservatism, Shu-sheng, his wife, is the picture of middle-class determination. Bourgeois to the core, Shu-sheng is by no means without faults, but for reasons that are unexplained she adapts much better to wartime privations than her

宣)、妻子(樹生)、一名十來歲的兒子及一名長者(汪母)。這些人物的性格描寫極為生動逼真。汪文宣軟弱不堪，是多病而卑微的知識份子，從事戰時的出版業，為毫無意義且工資微薄的工作營營役役。汪母頑固得無可救藥，在她的操控之下，汪文宣終日沉湎於自憐自傷，為自己在戰時遭受的苦困垂淚，也擔心自己無力博取他時髦的同居人的愛，甚至得不到她的尊重。

巴金並不同情汪母，小說對她的刻劃是很典型的，與《家》及其他早期作品中對家族長輩的描述如出一轍。《寒夜》的首要目標並不是討論中國文化傳統的所謂缺失，但巴金不能錯過這個機會去抨擊「舊中國」的人，因為他們阻礙年輕人努力創造「新中國」。在《寒夜》中，新舊文化的鬥爭在醫學的戰線上展開。小說中汪文宣染上肺癆，是戰時重慶很多人喪生的疾病。汪母卻堅信汪文宣沒有肺癆，無論甚麼病，總能靠傳統中醫治好。汪文宣的妻子樹生是現代女性，公然提出異議，並要求延請西醫專家治病。最後，汪母(傳統)在這場鬥爭中獲勝，凶疾遂繼續蹂躪汪文宣(中國)。

假如說汪文宣是戰時衰頹中國的寫照，而汪母是守舊文化的產物，他的妻子則是中產階層堅毅精神的化身。樹生是徹頭徹尾的布爾喬亞，當然絕非毫無缺點。她比畏縮不前的丈夫更能適應戰時的

shrinking husband. She has a good job and supports the family, she enjoys good health, and she insists upon leading an active social life, including a flirtation with a male coworker. Indeed, *Cold Nights* features a fascinating reversal of customary gender roles. As Wang Wen-hsüan wastes away, haunted by his own ineffectiveness, Shu-sheng is ever more confident and capable. Pa Chin seems to be suggesting that the war brings out the weaknesses in Chinese men and the strengths in Chinese women. Thus, the excruciating demise of the conventional family in *Cold Nights* can easily be read as a metaphor for the unraveling of China during World War II. The weak male figures can be seen as representing incompetent patriarchs in positions of political power; that is, leaders who shamelessly abdicate their responsibilities to society.

In addition to his familiar commentary on the failings of the Chinese patriarchy, Pa Chin makes unflattering remarks about Chinese intellectuals as well. In imperial times self-confident Confucian scholars played a central role in the efficient administration of the realm. With the end of the dynastic system in the early twentieth century, modern intellectuals and students were at the forefront of various path breaking efforts to reform society and build modern political movements. But the intellectuals who appear in *Cold Nights* are petty and self-centered. Worse still, they are irrelevant. They are poorly informed, they get no respect, and, consequently, no one listens to them. "I'm really useless," Wang Wen-hsüan concedes at the very outset of the novel. (p. 18)

However useful it may be to think of *Cold Nights* as a *wartime* novel that discusses family life during the anti-Japanese struggle, it is perhaps even more productive to view this important book as a distinctively *postwar* novel that deals indirectly, but primarily, with the life and death issues that dominated Chinese life in the years following Japan's defeat. True, Pa Chin began the novel in 1944 and worked on it during his sojourn in wartime Chungking, but Pa Chin left Chungking as

苦困（箇中原因小說未有闡明）；她工作穩定，承擔家計，健康良好，堅持活躍的社交生活，又搭上一名男同事。在這方面，《寒夜》中傳統性別角色的調換，更為引人入勝。隨着汪文宣在軟弱無能中逐步枯萎，樹生益發自信能幹。巴金似乎在告訴讀者，戰爭帶出中國男性的弱，以及中國女性的強。因此，《寒夜》中傳統家庭制度的痛苦崩毀，大可視為二戰期間中國的崩潰 —— 軟弱的男性代表當權、無能的家長，亦即無恥地推卸社會責任的領導。

除了慣見的對中國父權體制之缺失的批判，巴金更毫不留情地批判中國知識份子。在君主專制年代，自負的儒者扮演重要的管治角色。二十世紀初王權終結，現代知識份子及學生挺身而出，站在前線，改革社會，推動現代政治運動。然而，《寒夜》中的知識份子心胸狹隘，以自我為中心，更糟的是備受冷落，孤陋寡聞，得不到他人尊重，因此，沒有人聽取他們的意見。男主角汪文宣在小說開始時已承認：「我真沒有用。」（頁19）

《寒夜》當然是「抗戰時期」描繪大後方家庭生活的作品，但若視之為一部重要的「戰後小說」，就着勝利後數年與中國國運生死攸關的課題，進行間接但根本的探討，也許更有意義。不錯，巴金於一九四四年即着手寫這部小說，於戰時旅居重慶時繼續寫作，但戰事一結束，巴金即離開重慶，返回上海，在上海完成《寒夜》，一九四

soon as the war ended and returned to Shanghai where he continued working on *Cold Nights* until it was published in 1947. More than anything else it is a work of literature produced during the bloody Civil War of 1946–1949, a massive conflict that pitted the Nationalist Party against its Communist challengers.

When *Cold Nights* appeared in 1947 Pa Chin and his legions of admiring readers were far more concerned about the Civil War that was raging across the land than about daily life in wartime Chungking. War weary urban dwellers, particularly those who had suffered under the Japanese occupation, wanted to know why, after eight years of agonizing war with Japan, Chinese were now killing each other in such staggering numbers. Why was victory in the war of resistance followed so quickly by an all-out Civil War? Would there ever be an end to the sufferings of the Chinese people?

Cold Nights was popular during the Civil War period because it offered compelling explanations of these and other pressing questions. Indeed, *Cold Nights* makes two major points about the horrific dynamics of the Civil War. First, it shows that the horrors endured by ordinary people after the war — official greed and corruption, commercial speculation and profiteering, run-away inflation, and so forth — are the very same ones that ate away at the fabric of Chinese society in Chungking during the war. Readers see that the damage done by these evils in Chungking during the war is the same as the harm they cause in the present. Second, Pa Chin is arguing that the similarity between present and past is no coincidence. The corrupt officials and unscrupulous merchants responsible for the cancer that infected Chungking society during the war are the ones who spread the dreaded disease throughout coastal China after the war. As a result, the despair that overwhelmed and destroyed Wang Wen-hsüan and his family during the war was now sweeping postwar China and contributing to a widespread sense of hopelessness and disaffection.

七年正式出版。其實，《寒夜》也可視為一九四六至一九四九年國共兩方血腥苦鬥的內戰期間完成的文學作品。

一九四七年《寒夜》問世時，巴金與一眾仰慕他的讀者的注意力，都集中於那場蔓延全國的內戰，多於戰時重慶的日常生活。城市居民都厭戰，尤其是那些在日治時期吃過苦頭的人，他們不禁自問，八年艱苦抗戰之後，為甚麼中國人還要自傷殘殺，弄致死傷無數？為甚麼抗戰勝利後，全面內戰隨即發生？中國人的苦難是否永無終結？

《寒夜》於內戰期間一紙風行，正因為對這類迫切的問題提出令人信服的答案。實際上，《寒夜》就內戰殘酷而多變的戰況提出兩個重要的論點：第一，它展現老百姓要忍受的惡行 —— 官僚既貪婪又貪污、商業投機牟取暴利、物價飆升等不一而足的弊害。在戰時的重慶，同樣的惡行侵蝕中國社會的基礎。讀者可以看到，這些惡行對戰時重慶造成的破壞，與他們眼前所見的禍害一模一樣。其次，巴金認為今昔的情況相似並非偶然。貪官污吏與無良商人的毒瘤，損害戰時的重慶社會，在戰後，也正是這幫人把同樣的凶疾蔓延到整個中國沿岸地區。在這情況下，戰時摧毀汪文宣個人與家庭的頹喪，在戰後席捲全中國，釀成更廣泛的絕望與憤懣。沿岸地區的居

Cold Nights offered to residents of coastal China, who knew little or nothing about the sicknesses of wartime Chungking, an explanation of the source of their postwar problems.[3]

This intimate connection between present and past is spelled out quite explicitly in *Cold Nights*. Noting at the close of the novel that corrupt officials and profiteers scrambled to return to coastal China after the Japanese surrender, a bystander is quoted by Pa Chin as saying, "Now is the time for officials to reclaim their positions, not for common people to return home." "Victory is for them, not for us," he continued. "We haven't made any profit out of the country's misfortune, and it hasn't done us any good. I should have known there was no point in participating in the victory demonstration." (p. 512)

Similarly, readers in 1947 could plainly see that the outrageous lies that rained down on Pa Chin's characters in *Cold Nights* are the same as the lies citizens were being told every day during the Civil War. One of the tasks assigned to anti-hero Wang Wen-hsüan is proofreading government documents that are full of blatant fabrications. Too weak-willed to protest, Wang is nevertheless sickened by what he sees: "Once he coughed up some phlegm which accidently fell on one of the proof-sheets. In wiping it off with a piece of waste paper, he smeared the sheet with his blood-tinged phlegm. Exasperated, he wanted to tear all the sheets to shreds, for they told nothing but lies about improvements in the people's living conditions. But he did not dare." (p. 454)

Cold Nights thus captures not only the mood of profound resignation that characterized wartime society in Chungking, but, perhaps more importantly, it throws light on the malaise that infected

3. For an excellent overview of the dynamics of the Civil War see Lloyd Eastman, *Seeds of Destruction: Nationalist China in War and Revolution, 1937–1949* (Stanford: Stanford University Press, 1984).

民對戰時重慶的病態一知半解，甚至一無所知，《寒夜》正好為他們找出戰後各種問題的根源。[3]

在《寒夜》中，讀者可以看到戰時與戰後的密切關係。小說完結的時候，貪官污吏與投機商人於日軍投降後爭相返回沿岸地區。巴金引述一位旁觀者的話：「現在是官復員，不是老百姓復員。」「勝利是他們勝利，不是我們勝利。」這位旁觀者繼續說：「我們沒有發過國難財，卻倒了勝利楣。早知道，那天真不該參加勝利遊行。」（頁513）

同樣，一九四七年的讀者可以清楚看到，衝着《寒夜》人物身上而來的無數彌天謊言，正與內戰時期老百姓每天聽到的謊言一樣。反英雄人物汪文宣的一項工作是校對憑空捏造的政府文件。雖然汪文宣過於軟弱，無力提出抗議，但是他仍然厭惡眼前所見的一切：「自然他會咳出痰來，痰裏也帶點血……有一次他不小心濺了一點血在校樣上，他用一片廢紙拭去血跡，他輕輕地揩了一下，不敢用力，害怕弄破紙質不好的校樣。他拿出廢紙，在那段歌頌人民生活如何改善的字句中間還留着他的血的顏色……他憤怒地想，他幾乎要撕碎那張校樣，但是他不敢。」（頁455）

《寒夜》不僅捕捉了戰時重慶市民深刻的無奈情緒，也許更重要的是，它使人明白困擾着戰後都市社會的隱憂。一九四七年《寒夜》

3. Lloyd Eastman對內戰戰況的概述甚佳，詳見*Seeds of Destruction: Nationalist China in War and Revolution, 1937–1949* (Stanford: Stanford University Press, 1984).

urban society during the postwar era. When *Cold Nights* was published in 1947, it was still not clear which side, the Nationalists or the Communists, would prevail in the Civil War. But the popularity of *Cold Nights* points to the ways in which postwar urbanites lost confidence in the Nationalist government. The main characters in *Cold Nights*, especially Wang Wen-hsüan and Shu-sheng, are hardly Communist sympathizers. But, like many educated, urban, middle-class people in China in the mid- and late-1940s, they had no faith in the Nationalists. Urban residents knew very little about the Communists, but with the economy in total ruins, corruption everywhere, and morale sagging, it was hard for people to imagine anything worse than the status quo. It is in this sense that *Cold Nights* contributed to the destabilization of the Nationalist regime.

It would be easy to dismiss *Cold Nights* if it was the only work of its sort to appear after World War II. After all, in stylistic terms, it features the same emotionalism and exaggerated characterizations abundantly present in *Family* and other well known novels by Pa Chin. What reason is there to believe that the highly excitable Pa Chin is a credible source of information about the phenomenon of wartime and postwar disaffection?

One can begin to answer this question by referring to another postwar novel, Ch'ien Chung-shu's unsurpassed masterpiece, *Fortress Besieged* (*Wei ch'eng*), published in book form in 1947, the same year as the publication of *Cold Nights*. As a mature work of satire it has nothing in common with the sentimental, weepy, and melodramatic thrusts of *Cold Nights*. But the fact remains that *Fortress Besieged* presents an extremely disparaging picture of intellectual and middle-class life in government controlled portions of China during World War II. Like Wang Wen-hsüan, educated people in Ch'ien Chung-shu's stunning novel are shown to be shallow, self-centered, and without real substance or purpose. Like *Cold Nights*, *Fortress Besieged* is a finely tuned

出版之際，國共內戰究竟鹿死誰手，仍是未知之數。但它一紙風行，這就說明了都市居民對國民政府失去信心的原因。《寒夜》的人物，尤其是汪文宣及樹生，談不上同情共產黨；不過，他們卻與中國一九四零年代中晚期，許多城市裏的中產知識份子一樣，對國民黨沒有信心。他們對共產黨一知半解，但眼見經濟一蹶不振，貪污處處，士氣低落，都覺得現狀實在壞透了。從這個意義來說，國民黨政權不穩，《寒夜》實在起了推波助瀾的作用。

假如《寒夜》是二次大戰後唯一一部採用上述主題的作品，那就根本不值一提。不過，在風格而言，《寒夜》中濃厚的感情主義和誇張的人物塑造，比比皆是，與《家》及巴金其他著名小說別無異致。巴金既是一位激情的作家，我們為甚麼還要相信他，把他當作戰時和戰後憤懣文化的可靠資料來源？

要回答這問題，我們可以引述另一部戰後小說，錢鍾書的傑作《圍城》。《圍城》與《寒夜》同於一九四七年出書發行，比《寒夜》篇幅更長，寫得更好。它是一部成熟的諷刺小說，不像《寒夜》那麼煽情、催淚和誇張，但仍以極度譴責的態度，展示出二次大戰期間國統區知識份子與中產階層的生活。《圍城》震撼人心，小說中的讀書人跟巴金的反英雄人物汪文宣相似，同樣淺薄而自我中心，而且缺

analysis of Chinese society that engages readers at two levels. On the one hand, it accounts for the spiritual and emotional problems that afflicted middle-class people in the wartime environment. On the other hand, it conveys the message to postwar readers that the despair that grips China in the postwar period is linked to wartime abnormalities and distortions.

Narratives dealing with wartime and postwar disaffection were by no means confined to the world of letters. The booming film world of postwar China produced many motion pictures that resonated with the interpretive direction of *Cold Nights*. For example, *Far Away Love* (*Yao-yüan te ai*, d. Ch'en Li-t'ing, 1947), an extremely popular film starring the legendary actor Chao Tan, details the ways in which wartime conditions destroyed the relationship between a husband and a wife. The husband, a weak and cowardly intellectual, becomes ever more corrupt and selfish in the wartime environment, while the wife works tirelessly at the front helping people in need. In the end, the marriage dissolves. The husband does all he can to run away from the enemy, while the wife finds meaning in a commune of selfless patriots.

Another highly successful film was *Heavenly Spring Dream* (*T'ien-t'ang ch'un meng*, d. T'ang Hsiao-tan, 1947), starring matinee idols Shih Yü, Lan Ma, and Shang-kuan Yün-chu. Set in the immediate postwar period, this film describes the destruction of a family that returns to Shanghai from the interior following the defeat of Japan. In this picture the husband, yet another weak male figure, is cruelly denied every one of his dreams for the postwar era. With the economy in ruins, the anti-hero (an architect by profession) is unable to find employment of any sort, and, as a result, cannot secure housing for his wife, mother, and infant son. From the outset, he is forced into a relationship of dependency with an old friend who collaborated with the Japanese invaders during the war. In this film, as in many others, corrupt

乏真材實學，無所用心。《圍城》跟《寒夜》一樣，分析中國社會極為精細，並在兩個層次上吸引讀者：一方面析述戰時困擾着中產階級的精神及情感問題；另一方面向戰後讀者點出，瀰漫戰後中國的絕望情緒，實與戰時的弊端惡行相關。

描述戰時與戰後憤懣文化的作品，並非局限於文學界。戰後中國電影業發展蓬勃，不少製作都與《寒夜》的詮釋方向互相呼應。《遙遠的愛》(導演：陳鯉庭，一九四七年) 正是一例。這齣電影廣受歡迎，由名演員趙丹主演，描述戰時情況如何破壞夫妻關係。戲中的丈夫本已是軟弱復懦弱的知識份子，戰時加倍腐化與自私，妻子則一直在前線工作，幫助別人，從不言倦。最後，他們的婚姻破裂，丈夫扭盡六壬，設法離開敵人，而妻子則在一班無私的愛國者社群中找到生活的意義。

另一部成功的電影是《天堂春夢》(導演：湯曉丹，一九四七年)，由電影偶像石羽、藍馬及上官雲珠主演。故事講述戰爭剛完結，一個家庭於日軍戰敗後由內地返回上海，最後家庭破裂。戲中的丈夫也是軟弱的男人，他戰後的夢想屢屢落空，令人不忍卒睹。當時經濟萎靡不振，這位反英雄人物 (職業是建築師) 找不到工作，因而沒有能力為妻子、母親及稚子找到居住的地方；一開始，他便被迫依靠一名在戰時當上漢奸的舊朋友。跟其他電影一樣，戲中的

businessmen are shown to be thriving after the war while patriotic and law-abiding citizens are unable to survive. After giving away his son to the wealthy businessman, the pathetic architect, his mother and his wife are seen at the end of the film out on the street, looking for shelter.

Because *Far Away Love* and *Heavenly Spring Dream* express extreme anger about wartime and postwar corruption, it is sometimes forgotten that they were produced in government-owned film studios. The fact is that films produced in all types of studios, private and state-owned alike, tended to deliver the same message one finds in Pa Chin's *Cold Nights*. Not only do the most popular and influential films of this period criticize corruption, profiteering, and economic turmoil, they suggest in no uncertain terms that the maladies that crippled society in government controlled areas during the war quickly spread throughout coastal China after "victory" was proclaimed. They argue convincingly that the origins of Civil War era public disaffection and resignation can be traced to the type of wartime despair discussed by Pa Chin in *Cold Nights*.[4]

Popular films of the late 1940s are consistent with *Cold Nights* in other ways as well. Whether the stories deal with wartime despair, postwar malaise, or the connection between the two, the films tell the story from the perspective of a struggling, dysfunctional and disintegrating family unit. In most cases, but not all, the film is sentimental, weepy and melodramatic in stylistic terms.[5] And, with some

4. Paul G. Pickowicz, "Victory as Defeat: Postwar Visualizations of China's War of Resistance," in Wen-hsin Yeh, ed., *Becoming Chinese: Passages to Modernity and Beyond, 1900–1950* (Berkeley: University of California Press, 2000), pp. 365–398.
5. Paul G. Pickowicz, "Melodramatic Representation and the 'May Fourth' Tradition of Chinese Cinema," in Ellen Widmer and David Der-wei Wang, eds., *From May Fourth to June Fourth: Fiction and Film in Twentieth Century China* (Cambridge: Harvard University Press, 1993), pp. 295–326.

奸商於戰後大富大貴，愛國和守法的市民卻要掙扎求存。這可悲的建築師把兒子送給一名富商，自己與妻母卻終致流落街頭，尋找棲身之所。

由於《遙遠的愛》及《天堂春夢》對戰時及戰後的腐敗表達強烈的怨憤，大家或會忽略兩部電影都是由官方的片廠攝製。事實上，不管是民營或官方的電影公司的影片，傳達的信息大抵與《寒夜》相同。當時最為流行及影響人心的電影不但抨擊貪污腐敗、牟取暴利及經濟騷亂，而且毫不含糊指出國統區內不少病態使社會癱瘓，而這些病態於政府宣佈「勝利」後蔓延整個沿岸地區。這些電影言之有據地指出內戰時期民眾的憤懣與無奈，根源可追溯至巴金《寒夜》中所描述的戰時的絕望情緒。[4]

一九四零年代末期的流行電影在其他方面亦與《寒夜》一致。不論電影的故事是描述戰時的絕望情緒、戰後的隱憂，抑或兩者的關係，都是從掙扎、失常及瓦解中的家庭單位出發。在風格而言，大部份電影都濫情催淚，充滿傳奇劇色彩；[5] 此外，儘管劇情略有差

4. Paul G. Pickowicz, "Victory as Defeat: Postwar Visualizations of China's War of Resistance," in Wen-hsin Yeh, ed., *Becoming Chinese: Passages to Modernity and Beyond, 1900–1950* (Berkeley: University of California Press, 2000), pp. 365–398.
5. Paul G. Pickowicz, "Melodramatic Representation and the 'May Fourth' Tradition of Chinese Cinema," in Ellen Widmer and David Der-wei Wang, eds., *From May Fourth to June Fourth: Fiction and Film in Twentieth Century China* (Cambridge: Harvard University Press, 1993), pp. 295–326.

minor variations, these narratives of ordinary families in turmoil feature gender role reversals involving weak, ineffective men, like Pa Chin's Wang Wen-hsüan, and strong, resourceful women, like Pa Chin's Shu-sheng.

It is impossible, therefore, to view *Cold Nights* as an anomaly. It should be seen as part of a coherent body of fiction and film that treats the central social and economic problems of the combined wartime and civil war eras. Many urban people were frightened, disoriented, lonely and depressed in the late 1940s. *Cold Nights* and many other arresting works provided answers to their urgent questions about the disintegration of society. In the process these works of art contributed to the erosion of popular confidence in the Nationalist state.[6]

Cold Nights, it is interesting to note, appealed to people of various political persuasions. Cultural conservatives, lacking confidence in the modern cultural values espoused by modern young people like Shu-sheng, called for a restoration of old-style ethics. Liberals thought that a greater effort should be made to strengthen the small, modern, middle-class family in which both husband and wife work. Radicals envisioned collective units that would replace the family. Few felt that the Nationalist state had much to offer by way of leadership.

Pa Chin did a great deal to undermine the legitimacy of the Nationalist state. It is hardly surprising, therefore, that in 1949 he welcomed the new Communist regime, wished it well, and worked on its behalf in the 1950s, even though his own relationship to the Communist Party was complicated, even troubled. It was common knowledge, for example, that both during and after World War II Pa

6. For a careful analysis of the postwar political scene, see Suzanne Pepper, *Civil War in China: The Political Struggle, 1945–1949* (Berkeley: University of California Press, 1978).

異，這些描繪尋常家庭風波的電影，都出現男女性別角色的顛倒：男的軟弱無能，女的堅定多謀，恰似巴金筆下的汪文宣與樹生。

由此觀之，《寒夜》並非特例。抗戰及內戰時期的一系列描繪主要社會經濟問題的小說及電影，《寒夜》祇是其中之一。一九四零年代末期，不少都市居民驚惶失措，方寸大亂，感到孤寂抑鬱。《寒夜》與其他引人入勝的作品，為市民極度關心的社會崩潰提供了答案。這些藝術作品因而逐步使民眾對國民政府失去信心。[6]

有趣的是，政治取態不同的讀者都受《寒夜》吸引。文化守舊派對樹生般青年所擁護的現代文化價值觀欠缺信心，要求復興舊倫理；自由主義派認為要大力鞏固現代中產小型家庭，夫妻都應各有工作；激進派寄望以集體單位取代家庭；只有少數人認為國民政府尚能有所作為。

國民黨的合法性的動搖，巴金的影響不容忽視。因此，一九四九年歡迎和支持新政權，一九五零年代為其效力，並不教人驚訝，雖然他個人與共產黨的關係複雜困擾。眾所周知，二次大戰後，夏

6. Suzanne Pepper對戰後政局的分析甚為精確，詳見*Civil War in China: The Political Struggle, 1945–1949* (Berkeley: University of California Press, 1978).

Chin was criticized by Hsia Yen and other Communist cultural bureaucrats who were unable to overlook either his humanist proclivities or his strident cosmopolitanism.

Considering that Pa Chin was victimized by Party cultural hacks, it is painful to recall that in the mid-1950s he was involved in the cruel and senseless persecution of others. In the summer and fall of 1957, for example, at the height of the vicious Anti-rightist Campaign that destroyed the lives of hundreds of thousands of urban intellectuals in China, Pa Chin wrote several high profile articles, including one entitled "The Path of Anti-party, Anti-people Individualistic Careerists Is a Blind Alley," denouncing those who had been arbitrarily and recklessly labeled as rightists.[7] When the Party was targeting the famous woman writer Ting Ling (a person who had strong anarchist leanings in the 1920s), Pa Chin assisted her tormenters by writing "Hit Hard at the Rightists, Try Hard to Improve Our Work, and Remold Our Thought." Ting Ling, he insisted, had failed to see that "without the leadership of the Party, literary workers will be lost."[8]

Despite Pa Chin's unique contribution to the overthrow of the Nationalist government, his somewhat masochistic willingness to accept ideologically motivated criticisms of his early writings, and his complicity in the Party's Anti-rightist Campaign, Communist fundamentalists remained suspicious and continued to subject the veteran writer to verbal assaults from time to time. Still, Pa Chin tried to maintain his dual identity as a proud patriot and a cultivated

7. Pa Chin, "Fan tang fan jen-min te ko-jen yeh-hsin-chia te lu shih chüeh-tui tsou-pu-t'ung te," *Jen-min jih-pao*, August 31, 1957.
8. Pa Chin, "Hen-hen te ta-chi yu-p'ai, hen-hen te k'ai-chin kung-tso, hen-hen te kai-tsao ssu-hsiang," *Wenhui pao*, October 8, 1957. A portion of Pa Chin's article is translated in Hualing Nieh, editor and co-translator, *Literature of the Hundred Flowers, Volume II: Poetry and Fiction* (New York: Columbia University Press, 1981), p. 267.

衍及其他共產黨文化官員曾批判巴金人道主義傾向及世界主義情懷。

巴金雖曾受共產黨御用文人攻擊，但於一九五零年代中期，他竟參與一些殘酷而無理的迫害行動，令人痛心。一九五七年夏秋，反右運動正值高峰，摧毀了中國成千上萬的都市知識份子，巴金那時寫了數篇高調的文章，包括《反黨反人民的個人野心家的路是絕對走不通的》，去譴責那些無端被打成右派份子的知識份子。[7] 當共產黨的矛頭指向著名女作家丁玲時(一九二零年代曾相當同情無政府主義)，巴金助紂為虐，寫了《狠狠的打擊右派，狠狠的改進工作，狠狠的改造思想》一文，堅持丁玲不明白「沒有黨的領導，文藝工作者就會迷失路途」。[8]

儘管巴金推翻國民黨政權有功，也近乎自虐地接受共產黨對他早年作品的教條批判，又參加反右，但黨內教條派對這位老作家始終不信任，不時撻伐。不過，巴金依然努力維持驕傲的愛國者及富

7. 巴金：〈反黨反人民的個人野心家的路是絕對走不通的〉，《人民日報》，一九五七年八月三十一日。
8. 巴金：〈狠狠的打擊右派，狠狠的改進工作，狠狠的改造思想〉，《文匯報》，一九五七年十月八日。巴金這篇文章節譯於聶華苓編輯及合譯的*Literature of the Hundred Flowers, Volume II: Poetry and Fiction* (New York: Columbia University Press, 1981), p. 267.

internationalist. His patriotism caused him to support the Communist Party, but his anarchist humanism tugged him in other directions. His life-long aversion to hierarchies of power and his vision of the Chinese people united in harmony rather than tearing each other apart in periodic spasms of violent class struggle often put Pa Chin at odds with rigid party purists.

During the Cultural Revolution that erupted in 1966, Pa Chin was abused and physically assaulted for his anarcho-humanist tendencies and other transgressions. His writings were removed from bookstores and libraries, his home in Shanghai was invaded and ransacked, and he was forced to kneel on broken glass and confess his crimes at a mass rally. Humiliated and degraded, Pa Chin was placed under house arrest for approximately ten years.

It was not until the death of Mao Tse-tung, the arrest of Mao's wife Chiang Ch'ing and other zealots, and the launching of the reform policies of the late 1970s that Pa Chin was allowed to resurface in public life. Before long new editions of his writings were published. Indeed, *Cold Nights* was one of the many Republican-era novels that enjoyed a revival in the early 1980s, a time when there was little else to read. In 1984 the Beijing Film Studio went so far as to make a movie version of *Cold Nights* (*Han yeh*, d. Ch'üeh Wen). Unfortunately, the film is a truly dreadful work that utterly fails to appreciate the many contributions of the original novel. One can only hope that Pa Chin has never taken the time to see the movie.

Pa Chin was admitted to Shanghai's Hua-tung Hospital in the spring of 1999 for treatment of Parkinson's disease and other serious illnesses. From the early 1980s Pa Chin served as the honorary Chairman of the Chinese Writers' Association. He was undoubtedly pleased that in the post-Mao era Chinese writers could once again struggle with the tension between nationalism and cosmopolitanism. In 2001 Pa Chin was nominated for the Nobel Prize in literature.

教養的國際主義者之雙重身份。巴金因為愛國而支持共產黨，但無政府主義的人道思想又與此背道而馳。巴金終身厭惡權力架構，期望中國人民團結和諧，而不是同室干戈的暴力階級鬥爭，因此不時與黨內頑固的教條派發生齟齬。

一九六六年文化大革命爆發。文革期間，巴金因無政府及人道主義傾向，加上其他「乖離」，遭受虐打攻擊。他的著作不見容於書店及圖書館，上海的住宅被侵佔洗劫，還被迫在群眾大會跪碎玻璃「認罪」。受盡凌辱的巴金遭軟禁近十年之久。

一九七零年代末期，毛澤東去世，江青及極左派被捕，改革政策推行，巴金始獲准重新公開露面。不久，巴金的著作也重新刊行。一九八零年代初期，可讀的書刊不多，《寒夜》和不少民國時期的小說重新面世，頗受讀者歡迎。一九八四年，北京電影製片廠更把《寒夜》搬上銀幕（導演：闕文）。可惜電影拍得實在太糟，未能帶出原著的精華所在；希望巴金沒有浪費時間去看這齣電影。

一九九九年春，巴金因柏金遜病及其他頑疾住進上海華東醫院長期療養。自一九八零年代初，巴金就擔任中國作家協會榮譽主席。在毛澤東去世後的二十多年，中國作家能夠再次在植根本土及放眼世界兩股力量之間摸索平衡，巴金無疑會老懷大慰。二零零一年巴金獲提名競逐諾貝爾文學獎。

Japanese Invasion of China
日本侵華地圖

寒夜

Cold Nights

I

THE emergency air-raid siren had sounded nearly half an hour ago; the faint drone of enemy airplanes could still be heard in the sky; the streets were quiet without a trace of light. Rising from the stone steps in front of a bank's iron gate, he walked down to the pavement and stared blankly at the ashen sky. It was like a piece of faded black cloth. Apart from the dark shadows of some tall buildings opposite, he could see nothing. Dully he looked up for a while, not really paying attention to anything in particular, but simply to pass the time. Yet time deliberately seemed to thwart him; it passed slowly ... unbearably slow ... he felt as though it had stopped moving. The chilly night air, penetrating his thinly-lined gown, made him shiver slightly. Then he lowered his head, sighed painfully, and murmured to himself, "I cannot go on like this any more! "

"Then what are you going to do? Do you have the courage to change? You're a 'Softy'!" a voice rebuffed him. Startled, he turned his head and searched for the voice, but realized instantly that he had been talking to himself. Greatly irritated, he asked himself, "Why shouldn't I have enough courage? Must I always be a 'Softy'? "

He couldn't help looking around, but found no one near him — no one to rebuke him. He saw a flashlight gleam in the distance, like a twinkle in the eye of an old friend. It brought to him a feeling of warmth but the

一

緊急警報發出後快半點鐘了，天空裏隱隱約約地響着飛機的聲音，街上很靜，也沒有一線光亮。他從銀行鐵門前石級上站起來，走下到人行道上，舉起頭看天空。天色灰黑，像一塊褪色的黑布，除了對面高聳的大樓濃影外，他甚麼也看不見。他呆呆地把頭抬了好一會兒，他並沒有專心聽甚麼，也沒有專心看甚麼，他這樣做，好像只是為了消磨時間。時間彷彿故意同他作對，走得特別慢，不僅慢，他甚至覺得它已經停止進行了。夜的寒氣卻漸漸地透過他那件單薄的夾袍，他的身子微微抖了一下。這時他才埋下他的頭。他痛苦地吐了一口氣。低聲對自己說：「我不能這樣做！」

「那麼你要怎樣呢？你有膽量嗎？你有膽量嗎？你這個老好人！」馬上就有一個聲音在他耳邊反問道。他吃了一驚掉頭往左右一看，但他立刻就知道這是他自己在講話。他氣惱地再說：

「為甚麼沒有膽量呢。難道我就永遠是個老好人嗎？」

他不由自主地向四周看了一看，並沒有人在他身邊，不會有誰反駁他。遠遠地閃起一股手電的白光，像一個熟朋友眼睛的一瞬，他忽然感到一點暖意，但馬上光就滅了。在他周圍仍然是那並不十

light immediately went out. He was again enveloped in hazy darkness, the chilly air tingling his spine. He shuddered. Rubbing his hands together for warmth, he took two steps, then a few more. A shadow slipped past him. He took no notice. When he suddenly became aware that something had gone by, he looked back but was greeted by the same hazy darkness. He did not know what he was looking for. A light came on again, this time much closer to him; it flashed on and off a few times, coming closer and closer, and finally it passed him by. The passerby, wearing a gray overcoat, was of medium build, a man one could meet anywhere. He did not look at the man's face, and even if he had wanted to, he could not have seen it clearly anyway. But his eyes stubbornly followed the figure. What was he searching for? He did not know himself, and suddenly he stood still.

The sound of the airplanes had stopped some time ago, but at this moment he thought he heard their hum. He listened intently, then wondered if there had been any sound of planes at all. "I must have been dreaming," he thought aloud. "I can go home now." Still lost in thought, he headed for home. He continued walking slowly to the end of the street, his thoughts entangled in a confused web.

"The only business I had today," said a hoarse voice at a street corner, "was to sell five pieces of snow-flake pastry and a couple of cakes." He turned his head toward the corner and saw a shrinking shadow.

"I haven't had any customers at all tonight," replied a younger disheartened voice. "Business has never been worse. Many air-raid shelters won't let us inside. In the old days, I could get into any of them."

"We've no idea where the Japanese were bombing tonight. Was it Chengtu again? Why hasn't the warning been lifted after so many

分濃的黑暗。寒氣不住地刺他的背脊，他打了一個寒噤。他搓着手在人行道上走了兩步，又走了幾步。一個黑影在他身邊溜過去，他沒有主意，過後他忽然警覺地回頭去看，仍舊只看到那不很濃密的黑暗。他也不知道他的眼光在找尋甚麼。手電筒光又亮了，這次離他比較近，而且接連亮了幾次，愈來愈近，終於走過他身邊不見了。那個人穿着灰色大衣，身材不高，是一個極平常的人，他在大街上隨處都可以見到的。這時他的眼光更不會去注意那張臉，何況又看不清楚。但是他的眼睛仍然朝着那個人流失的方向望。他在望甚麼呢？他自己還是不知道。但他忽然站定了。

飛機聲不知在甚麼時候消失了。他直到這一刻才想起先前聽到過那種聲音的事，他注意地聽了聽，但他接着又想，也許今晚根本上就沒有響過飛機的聲音。「我在做夢吧。」他想道，他不僅想並且順口說了出來，「那麼我現在可以回去了。」他馬上接下去想道，他這樣想的時候，他的腳已經朝着回家的路上動了。他不知不覺地走出這一條街。他繼續慢慢地走着。他的思想被一張理不清的網裏纏住了。

「我賣掉五封雪片糕、兩個蛋糕，就是這點兒生意！」一個沙嗄的聲音從牆角發出來。他側過臉去，看見一團黑影縮在那兒。

「我今晚上還沒有開張。如今真不比往年間，好些洞子都不讓我們進去了。在早我哪個洞子不去？」另一個比較年青的聲音接着說，聲音裏含了一點失望。

「今晚上不曉得炸哪兒，是不是又炸成都，這們(麼)久還不解除

hours?" said the one with the hoarse voice, slowly as if talking to himself, hearing but not really paying attention to his companion's words.

"Last night, it wasn't lifted until the third watch.* Tonight it might even be later," answered the other.

The commonplace words of the hawkers jolted him out of his reverie. Why should he be reminded of last night's third watch by a mere street-vendor, a stranger?

Last night, the third watch? What had happened? The air-raid warning had been lifted, and along with many others, he walked home from an air-raid shelter.

But he was not alone last night. His 34-year-old wife, his 13-year-old son, and his 53-year-old mother were with him. They were laughing and talking while returning home from the shelter. At least they looked as if they were enjoying themselves.

But what happened later? he asked himself.

Once home, his son immediately went to sleep, while he himself chatted casually with his wife about a letter she had received at dinner that evening. He had hoped to slowly draw out the truth from her, but she became annoyed as soon as he brought the subject up. (It seemed that his wife knew his temperament very well, and most times she would deliberately pretend not to let on.) She began quarreling, and the mounting excitement made him stutter and his speech became less and less coherent. He knew he could not win the argument, yet he was unwilling to yield. At least he did not want it to look as

---

* A night is divided into five watches. The third watch is approximately between 11 and 1 in the morning.

警報？」前一個似乎沒有聽明白他同伴的話，卻自語似地慢慢說，好像他一邊說一邊在思索似的。

「昨天三更才解除，今晚上怕要更晏些。」另一個接腔道。

這是兩個小販的極不重要的談話。可是他忽然吃了一驚。昨天晚上……打三更……為甚麼那個不認識的人要來提醒他！

昨天晚上，打三更……究竟發生了甚麼事情？解除警報！他跟着眾人離開防空洞走回家去！

昨天那個時候，他不只是一個人，他三十四歲的妻子，他十三歲的小孩，他五十三歲的母親同他在一起。他們有說有笑地走回家，至少在表面上他們是有說有笑的。

可是以後呢？他問他自己。

回到家裏，兒子剛睡下來。他和妻談着閒話，他為了下午吃晚飯時，有人給妻送來一封信，問了她幾句話。他裝着無心的樣子向她發問。他想慢慢引出她的真實的回答。可是他一開口，就惹怒了她（也許她是過於知道他的脾氣，而平日故意裝作不知道的樣子。）她同他吵起來。他發急了，嘴更不聽指揮，話說得更笨拙，他吵不過她，但是他不願意讓步，至少在表面上。他們夫

though he had lost. They quarreled in the large room, while his mother and his son were in the adjoining bedroom; the door to his mother's room was tightly shut, and not a sound came through. The quarrel had gone on for no more than a quarter of an hour before his wife dashed out of the apartment in a rage. At first he thought she would soon return, and so paid no attention to her departure, but later he went downstairs to look for her in the street. Walking for two or three blocks, he saw no trace of his wife or any other woman. Though it was the business district of the wartime capital, there were only a few pedestrians in the street; everything was closed except for a few brightly-lit eating places with about half of their tables occupied. Where would he find her? He might walk this huge city in the mountains all night and not find her. She could be on any street or, perhaps, not outside at all. Where could he find her?

Indeed, where could he find her? He had been asking himself this question ever since last night. Why did he go on asking it? After all, a messenger had delivered a brief letter from her this very morning. It contained a few curt words, saying that she was staying with a friend, and that she would like a few of her things to be sent by the messenger. He had obeyed her instructions and written an even colder reply, not mentioning that he had searched for her, or that he wanted her home. His mother watched him write the reply, but said nothing at the time. Early that same morning, at breakfast, she commiserated with him by asking a few questions about his wife's "walking out on him," and then said no more about it. (Yes, "walking out on him" was the phrase he dwelt upon in his own mind.) She simply knitted her eyebrows together, and gently shook her head.

This 53-year-old woman was always full of worries; her health was not good, and her hair was mostly gray. She loved her son, she loved her grandson, but she definitely did not love her daughter-in-law. As for her daughter-in-law's desertion, she felt sorry for her son, but was

婦在一間較大的屋子裏吵，他母親帶着他兒子睡在另一間較小的屋裏。他們爭吵的時候他母親房門緊閉着，從那裏面始終沒有發出來甚麼聲音。其實他們吵的時間也很短，最多不過一刻鐘，他妻子就衝出房去了。他以為她會回來。起初他賭氣不理睬，後來又跑下樓去找她，他不僅走出了大門，並且還走了兩三條街，可是他連一個女人也沒有看見，更不用說她。雖說是在戰時首都的中心區，到這時候街上也只有寥寥幾個行人，街兩旁的商店都已關上舖門，兩三家小吃店裏電燈倒燃得雪亮，並且有四五成的顧客。他在甚麼地方去找她呢？這麼大的山城他走一晚都走不完！每條街上都可以有她，每條街上都可以沒有的。那末他究竟在哪裏可以找到她呢？

不錯，他究竟在哪裏可以找到她呢？他昨晚上這樣問過他自己，今晚上，就在現在也這樣問着。為甚麼還問着呢？她今天不是派人送來一封信嗎？可是那信上只有短短的幾句話，措辭冷淡，並且只告訴他，她現在住在朋友家裏，她要他把她隨身用的東西交給送信人帶去。他照樣做了。他回了她一封更冷淡的信。他沒有提到他跑出去追她的事，也不說請她回家的話。他母親站在他身邊看他寫信，她始終不曾提說甚麼。關於他妻子「出走」的事(他在思想裏用了「出走」兩字)，他母親除了在吃早飯時用着憐惜的語調問過幾句外，就沒有再說話，她只是皺着雙眉，輕輕搖着頭。這個五十三歲的女人，平素多憂慮，身體不太好，頭髮已經灰白了。她愛兒子，愛孫兒，卻不喜歡媳婦。因此她對她的媳婦的「出走」，雖說替她兒

secretly a little pleased. The son knew nothing of her thoughts and was waiting for her to suggest something. If she had given him the slightest encouragement, he would have written a passionate letter begging his wife to come home. He really wanted to write such a letter, but instead he wrote an indifferent one expressing no interest in her return. The letter, as well as his wife's suitcase, had gone with the messenger, and the misunderstanding between them had grown still greater. Since he could not find her, unless he went to her place of work and apologized, the possibility of a reconciliation between them would become even more remote. He had been thinking about a reconciliation and was considering it even now, but so far he had not found a way that satisfied him.

"Maybe our son, Hsiao Hsüan, could help," he mused, momentarily relieved by the thought. But, after a short time, he muttered to himself, "Useless. She doesn't care for him, nor he for her. They don't seem to have any affection for each other." In fact, Hsiao Hsüan had left for school early that morning without even asking about his mother, behaving as if he knew what had happened the previous night. He should have asked about her when he said goodbye to his father. But he had not.

Here he was now, pacing the streets alone. In utter despair, unable to restrain himself any longer, he cried inwardly, "What kind of family is this? Who cares about me? Everyone looks out for himeslf, and no one is willing to yield an inch!" Cries welled up from his heart, audible only to himself. Yet he thought he had awakened the whole neighborhood. Hastily he turned his head this way and that, looking all around. The area was completely dark and very quiet. The two street-vendors seemed to have vanished.

"Why am I standing here?" he asked himself in a rather loud voice. So much had his thoughts centered on himself that his own voice

子難過，可是她暗下也有一點高興。兒子還不知道母親的這種心理，他等着她給他出主意，只要她説一句話，他就會另外寫一封熱情的信，懇切地求他妻子回來。他很想寫那樣的一封信，可是他並沒有寫。他很想求他妻子回家，可是他卻在信裏表示他妻子回來不回來，他並不關心，信和箱子都被人帶走了。可是他同他妻子中間的隔閡也增加了一層。這以後，如果他不改變態度寫信到他妻子服務的地方去(他不願意到那裏去找她)，他們兩人就更難和解了。所以他到這時候還是問着那一句老問話，還是找不到一個滿意的答覆。

「説不定小宣會給我幫忙，」他忽然想道，他感到寬慰了。但是只有一分鐘。過後他又對自己説：「沒有用，她不關心小宣，小宣也不關心她。他們中間好像沒有多大的感情似的。」的確小宣一清早就回到學校去了。這孩子臨走並沒有問起媽，好像知道昨夜發生的事情似的。無論如何向父親告別時，小宣至少應該問一句關於媽的話，可是小宣並沒有！

他在失望中，忍不住怨憤地叫道：「我這是一個怎樣的家呵！沒有誰真正關心到我！各人只顧自己。誰都不肯讓步！」這只是他心裏的叫聲。只有他一個人聽見。但他自己並沒有留意到這一點，他忽然以為他嚷出了甚麼了，連忙掉頭向四周看。四周黑黑的，靜靜的，那兩個小販不知走到那裏去了。

「我站在這裏幹甚麼？」這次他説出來了，聲音也不低。這時他的思想完全集中在「自己」這兩個字上面，所以他會問。這問話把他

startled him. He mused to himself, "Wasn't I in the shelter? Yes ... I was in it.... I feel cold ... I'm taking a walk.... I'm thinking about my quarrel with Shu-sheng. I want her home, but will she come home? I can't even find her, so how can I get her to come home?"

Of course, no one answered him. He continued his musing, "Mother said Shu-sheng would return home; she said Shu-sheng would most certainly come back, and seemed rather cool, as if she didn't care. How could she know that Shu-sheng would return? Why didn't she encourage me to go find Shu-sheng? ... I wonder where Mother is now. Would she have gone to Shu-sheng's place of work while I was away? Maybe she and Shu-sheng are together in the same shelter. That would solve all my problems. All I'd have to do would be to walk home slowly when the warning is over. Maybe I shall see them laughing, talking, and waiting for me. In that case, what shall I say to Shu-sheng?" He hesitated for a moment. "First, I shall say anything to please her; then the words would flow."

Thinking of such a reunion he smiled broadly. He felt the burden had been lifted from his heart and, much relieved, his steps quickened. He walked to the street corner and then turned back.

"Look, only two red lanterns.* The warning will soon be over," said one of the hawkers. They had been conversing all along, but he had long ago stopped paying attention even though he had walked past them several times. The hawker's last few words caught his attention, however, and he looked in the direction of the emergency post on top of the bank across the street. There were two red lanterns hanging on a pole. The stillness was broken by the faint but gradually increasing volume of noise made by the people slowly starting to fill the streets.

* Air-raid signals.

自己驚醒了。他接着就在想像中回答道：「我不是在躲警報嗎？——是的，我是在躲警報。——我冷，我在散步。——我在想我同樹生吵架的事。——我想找她回來——」他馬上又問（仍在思想中）：「她會回來嗎？我們連面都碰不到，我怎麼能夠叫她回家呢？」

沒有人答話。他自己又在想像中回答：「媽説她自己會回來的。媽説她一定會回來的。」接着：「媽顯得很鎮靜，好像一點也不關心她。媽怎麼知道她一定會回來呢？為甚麼不鼓勵我去找她呢？」接着：「媽現在在甚麼地方？是不是媽趁着我出去的時候到那裏去了呢？説不定現在她們兩個在一塊兒躲警報。那麼甚麼問題都解決了。我只要在警報解除後慢慢走回家去，就可以看見她們在家裏有説有笑地等着我。——我對她先講甚麼話呢？」他躊躇着。「隨便講兩句她高興聽的話，過後話就會多起來了。」

他想到這裏，臉上浮出了笑容。他覺得心上的重壓一下子就完全去掉了。他感到一陣輕鬆。他的腳步也就加快了一些。他走到街口，又轉回來。

「看，兩個紅球了！快解除了吧！」這不是他的聲音，講話的是旁邊兩個小販中的一個，他們的談話一直沒有中斷，可是他早已不去注意他們，雖然他幾次走過他們身邊。他依着這話的指引，抬起頭去看斜對面銀行頂樓上的警報台，兩個燈籠紅亮亮的掛在球竿上。在他周圍沉靜的空氣被一陣隱隱約約的人聲攪動了。

"I ought to be home when they get there; then I could welcome them at the door," he said to himself excitedly. He looked at the lantern pole a second time. "I must go home immediately; the warning will be lifted almost any moment." No longer hesitating, he started walking briskly toward home.

The streets were beginning to come to life; even his inattentive eyes noticed the increased activity. Though the dark mesh of night still covered the streets, many lights had already pierced through. At one street corner, tiny acetylene lamps were ignited at a food stall specializing in spicy chicken from exotic Chia-ting. Two helpers were busy cleaning tables and making a fire, and a few people were standing by the tables, as if they were attracted there by the light. Inclining his head slightly, he glanced casually at the stall. He had no idea why he had looked in that direction, and went on walking.

When he was halfway down the street, a blaze of light suddenly flashed before his eyes as all the street lamps were turned on. Children clapped their hands in glee. He felt somewhat refreshed. "A dream, a nightmare! Now it is all over," he thought confidently and quickened his steps.

Soon he reached home. The front door was open and the roundish red door-light glowed dimly. Mr. Fang, a second-floor tenant and a store manager, was talking with his pregnant wife outside; cooks and maids walked in and out through the swinging door. After greeting him, Mr. Fang said, "The Japanese must have bombed Chengtu again tonight," to which he made some offhand response, and hurriedly went into the apartment complex. He passed through a long narrow corridor and ran up the stairs, reaching the third floor in one breath. By the dim corridor light he could tell that his own door was still locked. "Too early," he thought. He was the only one in the third floor corridor as he said to himself, "They haven't come home yet." He stood

「我應該比她們先回去，我應該在大門口接她們！」他忽然興奮地對他自己說。他又看了球竿一眼。「我現在就回去，警報馬上就會解除的。」他不再遲疑，就拔步往回家的路上走了。

街道開始醒轉來，連他那不注意的眼睛也看得見牠的活動。雖然那一片墨黑的夜網仍然罩在街上，可是許多支電光已經突破了這張大網。於是在一個街角，人點燃了電石燈，那是一個賣「嘉定怪味雞」的攤子，兩個夥計正忙着收拾桌面同發火，桌子前聚集了一些人，似乎都是被明亮的燈光招引來的。他側過頭朝那裏看了兩眼。他也不知道自己為甚麼要看那個地方。他又往前走了。

他大約又走了半條街光景。眼前突然一亮，兩旁的電燈重燃了。幾個小孩拍手歡叫着。他覺得心裏一陣暢快。「一個夢！一場噩夢！現在過去了！」他放心地想着。他加快他的腳步。

不久他到了家，大門開着。圓圓的門燈發射着暗紅光。住在二樓的某商店的方經理站在門前同他那大肚皮的妻子講話。廚子同老媽子不斷地穿過彈簧門，進進出出。「今晚上一定又是炸成都。」方經理跟他打了招呼以後，應酬地說了這一句。他勉強應了一聲，就匆匆地走進裏面，經過狹長的過道，上了樓，他一口氣奔到三樓。藉着廊上昏黃的電燈光，他看見他的房門仍然鎖着。「還早！」他想道，三樓的廊上只有他一個人。「他們都沒有回來。」他在房門前站

outside his door for a while before someone came upstairs. It was Mr. Chang, a civil servant who lived next door to him. Carrying a sleeping 2-year-old in his arms, Chang smiled mildly and asked, "Is your mother home yet?" Not wanting to say much, he replied, "I came back first." Chang asked no more questions and walked to his own apartment, immediately followed by his wife, wearing an old-fashioned black woolen overcoat which was faded and worn. Her thin face was always gentle. She had a pale complexion, wrinkles on her forehead, and dry, colorless lips. This 26- or 27-year-old woman had regular features, and was still not at all bad looking. Breathing hard from climbing the stairs, she greeted him and walked directly to her husband, with whom she spoke softly while she bent down to unlock the door. Once the door was opened, the two of them walked inside in an affectionate manner. Wang's eyes followed their every move with envy.

He looked at his door and at the staircase, but saw no one. "Not home yet?" he wondered, and became fidgety. Actually he had forgotten that since his mother's health was not good, she had to walk slowly. When he left for the shelter, she would usually hurry, but on returning, she took her time. Once home, she invariably slumped into the rattan chair in his room and rested for ten minutes or more. Usually she was either with his wife or with him, but now?

He decided to meet his mother downstairs; he was eager to see her. And he also hoped to see his wife returning with his mother.

So he ran downstairs to the front door and looked carefully up and down the street. He could not tell if his mother was among the pedestrians. Two women were approaching him. In fact they were not very far away and had already passed the tavern. The taller of the two, wearing a dark woolen overcoat, certainly looked like his wife; the shorter one, wearing a dark woolen padded robe, resembled his mother. It must be them! Smiling, he started walking in their direction. His heart was beating fast.

了一會。有人上來了。這是住在他隔壁的那個公務員張先生，手裏抱着兩歲的男孩，孩子已經睡着了，那個人溫和地對他笑了笑，問了一句：「老太太還沒有回來？」他不想詳細回答，他只說了一句：「我先回來。」那人也不再發問，就走到自己房門口去。接着妻子也上來了。她穿的那件褪色的黑大衣，不但樣式舊，並且呢子也磨光了。永遠是那張溫順的瘦臉，蒼白色，額上還有幾條皺紋，嘴唇乾而泛白。五官很端正，這一個二十六七歲的女人，現在看起來，還是並不難看。她一路喘着氣，看見他站在那兒，打個招呼，就一直走到她丈夫身邊。她俯下頭去開鎖，她小聲同她丈夫說話。門開了，兩個人親密地走進去了。他目送着他們。他用羨慕的眼光看他們。

過後他收回眼光，看看自己的房門，看看樓梯口。他並沒有看出甚麼來。「怎麼還不回來？」他想，他着急起來了。其實他忘記了他母親往常出去躲警報，總是比別人回家晚一點，她身體不太好，走路慢，出去時匆匆忙忙，回來時從從容容，並且回到家裏照例要倒在他房間裏那把籐椅上面休息十來分鐘。他妻子有時同他母親在一塊兒。有時卻同他在一塊兒。可是現在呢？……

他決定下樓到外面去迎接他母親，他渴望能早見到她，不，他還希望妻子同他母親一塊兒回來。

他轉身速下樓去。他一直跑到門口，他朝街的兩端一望。他看不清楚他母親是不是夾雜在那些行人中間。有兩個女人遠遠地走過來，其實並不遠，就在那家冷酒館前面。高的像他妻子，也是穿着青呢大衣。矮的像他母親，穿一件黑色棉袍。一定是她們！他露出笑臉，向着她們走去，他的心跳得很厲害。

When they were close, he discovered to his consternation that they were a man and a woman. The one he thought had been his mother was actually an old man. How could he have mistaken him for a middle-aged woman? How could his eyes have made such a ridiculous error?

"I shouldn't have made a mistake like that," he scolded himself in dismay. "There was very little resemblance."

"I'm too upset. This is terrible. When I see them, will I say the wrong things again? Maybe I won't be able to speak at all. After all, I haven't wronged my wife in any way; still I'm afraid that I may become too elated and get flustered. Why do I behave this way? I'm really useless."

He had said all this inwardly, arguing with himself. But he could come to no conclusion. He again returned to the front door, and there he heard someone calling "Hsüan." He looked and saw his mother standing in front of him.

"Mother!" he shouted in happy surprise. But the joyful look on his face soon disappeared. He said, "Why are you alone?" He swallowed his other unspoken words.

"You still think she will come back?" asked his mother in a low voice, shaking her head. Then she stared at him sympathetically.

"Then she hasn't returned at all?"

"She? Returned? I think it will be best if she doesn't." She glanced at him scornfully. "Why don't you go look for her?" As soon as she said this, she saw his anguish and her heart softened. She changed her tone, "She'll return. Don't worry. There is nothing serious about a quarrel between husband and wife. You'd better come up to your room."

He followed her. They both lowered their heads and walked

但是快要挨近時，他才發覺那兩人是一男一女，被他誤認作母親的人卻是一個老頭兒。不知道怎樣，他竟然會把那男人看作一個中年婦人，他的眼睛會錯得這樣可笑！

「我不應該這樣看錯的。」他停住腳失望地責備自己道。「並沒有一點相像的地方？」

「我太激動了，這不好，等會兒看見她們會不會又把話講錯——不，我恐怕講不出話來。不，我也許不至於在她面前講不出話。我並沒有對不起她的地方。不，我怕我會高興得發慌。——為甚麼要發慌？我真沒有用！」

他這樣地在自己心裏說了許多話。他同自己爭論，還是得不出一個結論。他又回到大門口。他聽見有人在叫他，叫他的名字：「宣。」他抬起頭。他母親正站在他面前。

「媽！」他禁不住驚喜的叫了一聲。但是他的喜色很快地便消失了。接着他又說：「怎麼你一個人——」以後的話他嚥在肚裏去了。

「你還以為她會回來嗎？」他母親搖搖頭低聲答，她用一種憐憫的眼光看他。

「那末她沒有回來過？」他驚疑問她。

「她回來？我看她還是不回來的好。」她瞅了他一眼，含了一點輕蔑的意味說。「你為甚麼自己不去找她？」她剛說了這一句責備的話，立刻就注意到他臉上痛苦的表情，她的心軟了，她便換了語調添加說：「她會回來的，你不要着急，夫妻間吵架沒有甚麼大不了的事。還是回房裏去吧。」

他跟着她走進裏面去。他們都低着頭，不作聲。他讓她提着那

silently. He let her carry the rather heavy cloth satchel she had brought to the air-raid shelter by herself, but when they reached the staircase, he took it from her.

They opened the door and entered the apartment. Its two rooms seemed somewhat larger and disorderly; the electric lights seemed particularly yellowish. The chill air rushed to his face, bringing with it a stuffy, coal smell. He coughed and dropped the cloth bag on the square table. There he stood, staring blankly at the chalk-white wall, his thoughts floating aimlessly like willow catkins in a breeze. Meanwhile his mother had gone into the adjoining room. She spoke to him, but he did not seem to hear her.

Later, coming out from her room, she asked him, "Why don't you take a rest? You must be very tired today." She walked to his side.

"No, I'm not tired," he replied as if waking from a dream, and glanced at her vacantly.

"You're not going to sleep? Tomorrow morning you have to go to work," she said with concern.

"Yes, I have to go to work," he answered dully.

"Then you should go to bed now."

"You go to bed first, Mother. I'll go too," he promised, knitting his brows.

She watched him quietly without moving. Her lips quivering, she wanted to say something, but decided not to. He remained motionless. She stood there for a few more minutes, then sighed softly, and returned to her room.

He continued to stand by the square table, not seeming to know that his mother had gone. He was trying to think, but his disorga-

個相當沉重的布袋，直走到樓梯口，他才從她手裏接過來。

他們開了鎖，進了房間，屋子裏這晚上顯得比往日空闊，凌亂。電燈光也比往常更帶昏黃色。一股寒氣撲上他的臉來，寒氣中還夾雜着煤氣和別的窒息人的臭氣。他忍不住咳嗽了兩三聲。他把布袋放到小方桌上去。他母親走進她的房裏去了。他一個人站在方桌前，茫然望着白粉壁，他甚麼也看不見，他的思想像飛絮似地到處飄。他母親在房內喚他，對他講話，他也沒有聽見。她後來又出來看他。

「怎麼你還不休息？」她詫異地問道。「你今天也夠累了。」她走到他身邊來。

「哦，……我不累。」他說，好像從夢裏醒過來似的。他用茫然的眼光看了她一眼。

「你不睡？你明天早晨還要去辦公，」她關心地說。

「是，我要去辦公。」他呆呆地慢聲說。

「那麼你應該睡了。」她又說。

「媽，你先睡吧，我就會睡的。」他說，可是他皺着眉頭。

他母親站在原處，默默地望了他一會，她想說話，動了動嘴卻又沒有說出甚麼來，他還是不動。她又站了幾分鐘，忽然低聲嘆了兩口氣，就回到自己房裏去了。

他還是站在方桌前面。他好像不知道他母親已經去了似的。他

nized thoughts were racing helter-skelter. Then they all came together and got knotted up. The more he tried to untie the knots, the more tangled they became. Next he felt as if a stone had become lodged in his head and, unable to bear the pain, staggered to his bed and dropped into it. Exhausted, he fell asleep immediately without turning off the light or covering himself with the quilt.

It was not a sound sleep, but a tense and restless one.

II

HE slept on, dreaming. Of course, he did not know he was dreaming.

He and his wife lived in a small but quiet city. They were not happy. They had many differences and quarreled over trifles. Although they cared for each other, they lacked mutual understanding. She had a bad temper, and he was often testy. In his dream, they were quarreling again. It was about his mother, and his wife was especially short-tempered. Angrily she overturned the dining table, breaking all the dishes. His mother was not at home, and their little son hid in a corner crying. His wife's behavior made him so angry that he became tongue-tied. He could only pound his head and curse himself.

Suddenly a deafening noise like a clap of thunder was heard. The jolt made the building shake violently.

"What's the matter?" he dreamed on, once the immediate shock had passed.

His wife stood by the door speechless; the child's crying had stopped.

在想，在想。他的思想跑得快。他的思想很亂，然後它們全聚在一個地方，糾纏在一起，解不開，他越是努力要解，越是解不開。他覺得腦子裏要被塞進了一塊石頭。他支持不住了。他踉蹌地走到床前，力竭地倒下去。他沒有關電燈，也沒有蓋被，就沉沉地睡去了。

這不是酣睡。

二

他做着連續的夢。他自然不知道自己是在夢中。

他和妻住在一個平靜的小城裏，他們生活得並不快樂，還是常常為着一些小事情爭吵。他們夫婦間的感情並不壞，可是總不能互相了解。她愛發脾氣，他也常感到煩躁。這天他們又為着一件小事在吵架。他記得是為着他母親的事情，這天妻的脾氣特別大。他們還在吃着飯。妻忽然把飯桌往上一推，飯桌翻倒在地上，碗碟全打碎了，母親不在家。孩子躲在屋角哭。他氣得說不出一句話，只是用含糊的聲音咒罵自己，用力打自己的頭。

正在這時候，他忽然聽見一聲霹靂似的巨響。這聲音不知道在甚麼地方發出，可是他們的屋子因此搖動了兩下，震動相當厲害。

「甚麼事？」他吃驚地説，他的頭腦比較清醒了。

妻默默地站在房門口，孩子的哭聲停止了。

"I'd better go out and take a look," he said, walking toward the staircase landing.

"Don't, unless we all go," she said. No longer angry, she prevented him from leaving.

He obeyed and stood still in the doorway, staring miserably at the shattered dishes and the food scattered over the floor, waiting for her to break the silence.

She said nothing, and he continued to wait. Suddenly he heard the sound of two cannon explosions, and then again everything was still. Almost simultaneously, his son began crying again and his wife was shrieking.

"The enemy is here," he told himself in alarm, and shouting, "Mother!" he dashed along the covered corridor toward the staircase.

"Hsüan, where are you going?" his wife called after him.

"To find my mother," he replied without turning, dashing down the stairs in one breath.

Dragging her son downstairs with her, his wife sobbed hysterically, "You can't abandon us. If we have to die, let's die together."

"I'm just going to look for my mother; we can't abandon her. If anything happens, what would she do?" While saying this, he opened the door to the street.

Noises and people. He saw thousands of people frantically running toward the city's outskirts. Some carried children in their arms; others carried small bundles or assisted the elderly. Children were crying; women were screaming for relatives; and men were instructing others not to waste any time.

Thick smoke rose in vast billows and covered the southern sky.

「我出去看看。」他說着，就往門外走，打算到樓下去。

「你不要去，要去我們一塊兒也好些。」妻不再生氣了，卻改變了態度，關切地阻止他出去。

他聽從她的話，就在門前廊上站住了。可是他也不說甚麼，他望着樓板上的碎碗剩菜，帶了一點懊悔，等着她講話。

她不作聲，他仍舊在等待。忽然他聽見了大炮聲(他想，這應該是大炮聲)。一聲，兩聲。又靜下去了。孩子又哭起來。妻發出一聲尖叫。

「敵人打來了！」他驚惶地自語道。接着他叫了一聲：「媽！」他就沿着走廊跑到樓梯口去。

「宣！」妻在後面喚他：「你到那裏去？」

「我找媽去！」他頭也不回地答她一句，就一口氣跑下了樓。

妻拖着孩子也跑下樓來。「你不能一個人走，你不能丟開我們母子。就是死，我們也要跟着你。」她歇斯特里地哭叫着。

「我要去找媽。我們不能丟開她。萬一有事情，她一個人怎麼辦！」他一面說，一面去打開大門。

門外人聲嘈雜。馬路上全是人，他只見萬頭攢動。大家瘋狂地背向着城奔跑。他們有的抱着小孩，有的拿着包袱，有的攙扶着老年人。小孩在哭，女人在喚她們的親人，男人在催促他們的同伴。

南面的天空被濃煙蓋滿了。這煙還不斷地一股一股朝上捲騰，

Explosion followed upon explosion, each more thunderous and frightening than the one before. He knew danger was at hand, and his first concern was his mother. He ran down the stone steps toward the street. He wanted to go into the city to find her.

"Where are you going? You can't leave us!" It was the voice of his wife, who had grabbed his arm. "You can't run away without us."

"I am not; I am only going to find my mother — she is still inside the city," he stopped to argue.

"Why?" she sneered. "Doesn't she have legs and eyes? Doesn't she know how to walk?"

"Please get a few things we'll need. As soon as I find her, we'll all leave together," he insisted, breaking loose from her grip. "Even if we leave, we must have our personal belongings."

"Isn't your mother over there?" She pointed at some shrubbery by a dry ditch across the street. He saw his mother standing by the trunk of an old tree covered with creeping vines. Her hair was disheveled, her complexion ashen, and she had what must have been bloodstains on her forehead. She was looking around, apparently searching for him. Frantically he shouted and waved his arms to attract her attention, but it was useless. He must force his way through the crowd; this he tried to do, but the crowd was so dense that even water would have had difficulty getting through it. He got to the edge of the road and tried to press forward, but he was pushed back each time. He thought he heard his mother calling him and he was calling back to her. All of a sudden his left arm was seized by his wife; in her other hand she carried a small leather suitcase and was followed by their son.

"Let's go. Forget her!" his wife ordered.

Angrily, he roared, "No, I can't do that!"

爆炸聲接連地響着，一聲高過一聲，一聲比一聲可怕。他知道危險就在面前了，他的第一個念頭是「媽！」他立刻跑下石階，他要跨過門前草地到馬路上去。他要進城找他母親。

「你要到那裏去！你不能夠丟開我們！」他妻子從後面拖住他一隻膀子，帶着哭聲嚷起來。「要逃難，你不能一個人逃，不顧我們母子死活！」

「我不是逃難！我去接媽回來，她還在城裏。」他站住分辯道。

「你還想在城裏找到她！」妻子冷笑地說。「難道她沒有腳沒有眼睛，自己不會走路。」

「你快進去收拾東西。等我去接媽回來，大家一塊兒走。就說逃難，也得隨身帶點東西。」他着急地掙脫她的手。

「你媽不是在那邊！」她指着馬路旁乾了的溝邊一叢牽牛籐說。他順着她的手指望過去。她母親就站在牽牛籐下面（這牽牛籐是沿着一棵老樹幹爬上去的），頭髮蓬亂，臉色慘白，額上好像有一點血跡。她正張大眼睛向四處看。顯然她是在找尋他。他抬起頭大聲叫：「媽！」他揮着手。可是沒有用。他想跑過去，然而他得穿過面前這條人擠得水洩不通的馬路。他剛跑到馬路邊。人們不給他留一個縫，他用力擠，人們總是把他推開。他似乎聽見他母親的叫聲。他也在叫，可是一隻手拉住他的左膀。那是他的妻子，她手裏提着一個小皮箱，孩子跟在她後面。

「我們走吧，不要管她！」她命令地說。

「不成，我要過去接媽回來。」他生氣地答道。

"I think you are crazy. Even now you still insist on getting her. Let me ask you one question: Do you want to go on living? I can't wait for you," she shouted sternly.

"Let me go, I must get her. She is right over there and I can't abandon her," he said, trying to free his arm from his wife's grip.

"Okay, you go get your darling mother. I'll take Hsiao Hsüan and we'll go on our way, but don't blame me later," she cried out furiously. Her enraged eyes glared as though they would pierce right through him. He had never seen anything like it and shuddered.

They left him. Leading her son away, she left him a look of defiance.

He hoped that she would return to him. Maybe he could catch up with her later on. But in a flash she had vanished. He felt people crowding in on him from all directions, pushing and jostling; his body was tossed to and fro like a ship in a tumultuous sea. Dazed and feverish, he pushed forward frantically with all his strength.

Then he woke up and his hands were shaking.

It was only a nightmare, the first of many weird ones he was to have that night.

III

IT was long after dawn when he opened his eyes. There was not a sound in the room though his mother's door was open. His heart was beating fast even though he appeared to be lying peacefully in bed. Terrifying images danced before him, and he was oppressed with a

「這時候還要去接她？我看你發昏了，我問你性命要不要。我可不能等你。」他妻子板起臉厲聲說。

「你讓我去，我一定要去接她。他就在我面前，我不能丟開她，只顧自己逃命。」他說，一面抽出他的左膀。

「那麼好，你去接你那寶貝母親，我帶着小宣走我們的路。以後你不要怪我！」她賭氣地說，他覺得她在豎起眼睛看他。並且她的眼睛豎得那麼直，他從沒有見過一個人的眼睛生得這樣！他不由自主地打了一個寒顫。

這女人果然轉過身牽着孩子走了。她沒有露一點悲痛的表情，不，她還用她那高傲的眼光看他。

但是他還想她會回來，回到他身邊來；或者他以後可以追上她。然而一轉眼她的影子就看不見了。人們好像正從四方八面向他擠來，彷彿有無數隻手在推他，他只覺得身子搖來幌去，似乎立在一隻受着大浪顛簸的船上一樣。他頭腦發熱、發昏。他也用力推別人，用力擠上去。

於是他醒了。醒的時候，他的手還在動。

這不過是他的一個夢。他這一晚卻做了好幾個跟這類似的荒唐的夢。

三

他睜開眼睛，天已經亮了。屋子裏沒有聲音。他母親的房門開着。他平安地躺在床上，心撲通撲通地在跳。眼前隱隱約約地現着那些可怕的影子。一種疲乏的、昏沉的感覺壓着他。他沒有動，也

weary and leaden feeling. He lay still, thinking about nothing. Gradually he moved his eyes and tried hard to open them wide. But he could not focus, nor could he separate reality from his world of dreams. He could not figure out what had happened to him except that he knew something was wrong. He had a slight headache; nonetheless, it was a headache. He felt that he was involved in a conflict, but without any idea of what it was about. Thus he spent some moments in a daze.

Suddenly, he felt a sharp pain in his head. Instantly he slipped out of bed and stood in the middle of the room (it must have been the middle for there was no furniture near him), staring all about in alarm. Scratching his head, he murmured in despair, "What should I do now?" For he remembered what had happened yesterday and the day before.

"It's all my fault. Yesterday I should have apologized to her in person; after all, I started the quarrel," he mused. "No wonder she is angry. Why did I write her that stupid letter? Why didn't I tell her the truth? Why don't I search for her? Why...? I must look for her." He made up his mind.

Just then his mother returned carrying a shopping basket in her hand. Seeing him still in the room, she asked in surprise, "It's nine-thirty. Why haven't you gone to work?"

Nine-thirty already! He should have been at work a long time ago. But he had forgotten all about it. He was already late by more than half an hour. What should he do?

"Have you washed your face? You don't look well. Are you all right? Maybe you should stay home today. Write a note and I'll take it to the office," said his mother without a pause, full of concern.

"No, no. I'm fine," He was apprehensive now. "I'll leave for work immediately."

沒有想。他緩慢地移動他的眼光。他努力睜大他的眼睛。可是他並沒有看清楚甚麼。他不知道現在同以前，哪一種是夢，哪一種是真。他也不知道自己現在處在甚麼樣的情形裏面。他只覺得有甚麼事情不對。但是他頭痛。痛得不厲害。但是他頭痛，他在掙扎，他也弄不清楚他在同甚麼掙扎。他這樣迷迷糊糊地過了一會兒。

忽然甚麼東西刺了他腦子一下。他一跳就下了床。他站在屋子中央吧(因為他不靠近一樣傢具)，驚愕地向四處望。過後他用力搔自己頭髮，絕望地自語道：「我應該怎麼辦呢？」他記起昨天的事情了，記起前天的事情了。

「這是我的錯。我昨天應該親自去找她解釋，向她道歉。事情是我鬧出來的，難怪她生氣。」他又說。

「為甚麼我昨天要寫那封信？為甚麼我不對她講老實話？為甚麼我不自己去找她。為甚麼？……」想到這裏他下了決心：「我現在就去。」

他母親回來了，手裏提着菜籃。她看見他還在房裏，便驚訝地問：「九點半鐘了，你怎麼還不去上班？」

九點半鐘！他應該去上班！可是他忘記了。他已經遲了半點多鐘了。怎麼辦呢？

「你還沒有洗臉？你臉色不好看。你有甚麼不舒服嗎？要不，請一天假也好。你寫個字條我給你送去。」他母親關心地接連說。

他吃了一驚，慌張地說：「我很好，我就去。」

Trying to avoid her, he picked up the basin to fetch some cold water from the container in the corridor. As soon as he had put the basin down on the table, she said, "Why are you washing with cold water? No, no. Go get some hot water. There's still some left in the pot. I'll get it for you."

"I've finished washing," he answered quickly; the cold water had refreshed him. He wrung the towel out and hung it on the back of a chair. Without emptying the water or brushing his teeth or donning his old felt hat, he walked out of the apartment in a great hurry, seemingly to avoid her.

"What a weakling! Just because he quarreled with his wife, he acts like a lost soul," she scoffed. He did not hear her.

Down the stairs and into the street. Many pedestrians and much dust. An unusually fine day for this hilly city, neither hot nor cold.

"Where shall I go first?" he wondered, standing on the sidewalk.

"To find her first," was his answer. He started walking toward her office. After taking a few steps, he thought it over and changed his mind.

"No, I must go to work. They'll deduct my salary even for a two-hour absence. That damn place!"

He arrived at his office, the headquarters of a combined book and stationery company supported by government and private funds. His desk was in a corner on the second floor. For the first time in three and a half years, he was late for work, too late to sign the daily roll. Quietly he climbed the stairs and passed the desk of his supervisor, Mr. Chou, the Chief Editor and the Managing Director. Chou looked up at him inquiringly but said nothing and then looked down again. He did not notice the look Chou gave him, for he was completely preoccupied with only one person — his wife.

他不願意再聽她講話。他拿着臉盆在走廊上水缸裏去舀了一盆冷水。他捧着臉盆進屋，剛把它放在方桌上，他母親又說：「你洗冷水？這怎麼要得？快點去換熱水。鍋裏頭還給你留得有熱水。我給你去倒。」她說着就伸手來拿臉盆。

「媽，我已經洗好了。」他連忙說，他的臉給冷水一浸，腦子倒清醒多了。他把臉帕絞乾往椅背上一搭，也不倒掉盆裏的水，就匆匆走出房裏去。他沒有刷牙，他忘記戴上他那頂舊呢帽。他走得這樣急，顯然他想避免同他母親談話。

「真沒有出息！跟自己老婆吵了架，就像失掉了魂魄一樣！」母親在屋裏這樣批評他。可是他已經聽不見了。

他走下樓。他走到街上，街上有那麼多的人，那麼多的塵土。這一天是這山城裏少有的不冷不熱的好天。

「我先到哪兒去？」他站在人行道上問自己。

「先去找她！」這是第一個回答。他順從這個意見，朝她辦公地方所在的方向走去。他走了幾步，他站住，想了一下。他又朝前走幾步。

「不對，我應該先去辦公。我那個鬼地方連請兩點鐘假，也要扣薪水的。」他最後這樣決定了。他又掉轉身子。

不久他到了他服務的地方。那是一個半官半商的圖書文具公司的總管理處。他的辦公桌在二樓的一個角落裏。樓下的簽到簿已經收起來了，這是他三年半來的第一次遲到。他默默地走上樓去。他走過編輯部主任兼代經理的周ＸＸ的寫字檯前，周主任略微抬起頭用驚詫的眼光看了看他，也不說甚麼，仍舊埋下頭去。他並沒有注意到這個。他的整個心思都放在一個人身上。那是她，仍然是她！

He began his monotonous and tedious proofreading job. When he came in he noticed that the galleys were already on his desk. Actually the pile was not as thick as yesterday's and the unintelligible text printed with a smelly ink was not any more distasteful than other piles of galleys. He had no interest in his work at all as his eyes, hands, and pen moved mechanically, checking for typographical errors. Though he never lifted his head from his work, he did not remember a single word on the galleys. But he did hear the old-fashioned wall-clock strike the hours of ten, eleven, and twelve, particularly when it struck twelve clearly and forcefully. For that was the signal for lunch.

The others having already gone downstairs, he got up automatically, put away his unfinished work and looked absent-mindedly out the window. The windows faced the street, but they were shut and the glass was dirty. He did not know what he expected to see there; he was simply thinking. But all his thoughts were centered on one person, on "her."

The lunch bell rang a long time ago; he did not notice it. His co-workers seemed to have forgotten him as well, and no one bothered to call him to lunch or even appeared to remember that he had been left behind.

At last his mind cleared. He went downstairs.

The dining room. Noise. People busy eating.

"Were you upstairs?" asked a co-worker in surprise, looking at him sympathetically.

He said something non-committal in reply and walked out of the building.

He imagined the sneer of his co-workers was following him. "They must know about my trouble," he thought, his ears burning with shame.

他的工作開始了，還是那單調沉悶的工作。他桌上一堆校樣(他進來時就看見牠們躺在那兒)並不比昨天那堆高。那些半清晰半模糊的字跡，那些似乎還帶着油墨氣味的字跡，今天並不比往常更叫人厭倦。他機械地移動眼光，移動手，移動筆。他在校樣上寫下好些字……而且他始終埋着他的頭。他們的辦公室有一個舊式大掛鐘。他聽見鐘敲了十點……十一點……十二點。他沒有記住校樣上面的一個字。可是鐘聲他卻聽得很清楚。特別是這堅決的十二下。他懂得牠們的意義。下班了！

他站起來，簡直可以說是不知不覺地就站了起來。但是別人比他更快，他們都已離開辦公桌了。他把沒有看完的校樣和原稿摺疊起來，放在一邊。他站在桌子前面，眼光遲鈍地望着那幾扇臨街的玻璃窗。窗戶關閉着，玻璃上積了不少塵土。他也沒有想過要看甚麼。他是在思索。不，他也不能說是在思索。他的思想停滯在一點，停滯在一個字上面——就是「她」！

鈴聲早已響過了。但他沒有聽見，而且他根本就沒有想到這時候他應該下樓去吃飯。別人好像也忘記了他的存在。沒有人上樓來叫他，他們更沒有想到他還留在樓上。

但是他的腦子終於活動起來。他醒了，他離開辦公桌，走下樓去。

飯廳裏碗碟狼藉的桌上還有人在吃飯。

「怎麼？你在上面！」一個同事驚訝地說，同時用了近似憐憫的眼光看了看他。

他含糊地答應了一句，就走出門去。

同事們的輕蔑的笑聲從後面追上來。

「一定是他們都知道我的事情。」他這樣想道，他覺得臉燒到耳根了。

He was not hungry, for he had completely forgotten about food. His only thought was of his wife.

After a few steps, he wondered whether his co-workers were following him. He hesitated and slowed down, but did not actually stop or look back. Instead, he visualized meeting her, the expression on her face, and what she would say to him.

Twice he told himself, "She'll forgive me." He smiled tenderly and imagined he was smiling at her. His courage returned.

Soon he arrived at her place of work.

IV

SHE was a clerk in a commercial bank located in the middle section of a long street. Just as he turned the corner, he saw her coming out of the bank with a thirtyish man. They were walking toward him. She wore her usual woolen overcoat but had had a permanent. Her companion, presumably a colleague, had a rather pleasant-looking face. Hatless, he had a head of smoothly-combed hair. Half a head taller than she, he wore a brand-new autumn coat, probably smuggled into China from Calcutta.

The man was talking boisterously and she was listening attentively; they did not see him. His heart sank and he wanted to avoid them. They were crossing the street. Instantly he changed his mind and followed them. Walking close together, the man deliberately moved his arm once so as to brush it against her body. She seemed to be avoiding the contact. At first he did not dare follow them too closely, afraid

他不餓，他也沒有想到「餓」同「飽」的事情。他只有一個念頭：去找她！

可是走了不到十步，他忽然想：他們會跟在我後面嗎？「他們」指的是他的同事們。這個念頭使他放慢腳步，他感到一點躊躇了。不過他並沒有把腳步停止，或者轉回身來，他開始在想像他要同她見面的情景：她會用怎樣的面孔，怎樣的話對待他？

「她會原諒我的。」他對自己說了兩遍。他溫柔地微微一笑。他覺得他是在對着她笑。他的勇氣又增加了。

他不知不覺中就到了她辦事的地方。

四

她是一家商業銀行的行員。銀行位置在一條大街的中段。他剛剛走到街角，就看見她從銀行裏出來。她不是一個人，她和一個三十左右的年青男子在一塊兒。他們正朝着他走來。的確是她。還是那件薄薄的藏青呢大衣。不同的是，她頭髮燙過了，而且前面梳得高高的。男人似乎是銀行裏的同事，有一張不算難看的面孔，沒有戴帽子，頭髮梳得光光。身材比她高半個頭。身上一件嶄新的秋大衣，一看就知道是剛從加爾各答帶來的。

男人帶笑地高談闊論，她注意地在聽着。他們並沒有看見他。他覺得心裏發冷。他不敢迎着他們走去。他正想躲開，卻看見他們走下人行道穿過馬路到對面去了。他改變了主意，他跟着他們走到對面去。他們腳步下得慢，而且身子挨得很近。他看得出來，男的故意把手膀靠近女人的身體，女的有意無意地在躲閃。他起初不敢

that she might discover him. But his courage grew. And as he came closer to them, he heard her suddenly burst into laughter at something the man said. Her laughter was familiar to him and it hurt him deeply. His face changed color; he stopped walking, and stared dully at her back. Her well-developed body looked more enticing than ever, adding to his pain. Then his view was blocked by a pedestrian. He ran after them. His heart pounding fast, he wanted to grab her or loudly call her, but, in fact, he did nothing. In the meantime, she and the man entered an exclusive café that had recently opened.

Indecisively he stood outside the café. Should he go in and try to talk to her? No, it might make matters worse. Should he return to work and seek an opportunity to speak to her later? No, he could not do that, either. Should he seek a reconciliation with her today or wait for them to come out of the café? No, that would embarrass her. And what if she should ignore him? Or if the man should speak up and give him a hard time? If he got into a quarrel, he really had no legal right to restrict her activities. Never legally married, he was only her common-law husband. He had objected to a formal marriage ceremony because he considered it unnecessary. (He still had no idea that his mother despised his wife because of this.) But now he regretted that he had so foolishly and so casually thrown away what might have been his rights to control her actions. Legally, she was completely free to do whatever she chose. When he realized the few options, if any, he had, he decided dejectedly to return to work.

On the way back to the office, he kept thinking of his wife chatting intimately with her beau; occasionally he would hear her carefree laughter. He was so preoccupied by his thoughts that he was almost hit by a rickshaw.

He walked into the office. Two co-workers on the ground floor were reading newspapers.

走近他們，怕她覺察出來他是在跟她。這時他忽然有了勇氣。他跟在他們後面。那個男人不知說了一句甚麼話，她聲音清脆地笑起來。這熟悉的笑聲刺痛着他的心。他臉色變了。他的腳也停住了。他呆呆地望着她的背影。她豐滿的身子顯得比甚麼都引誘人，這更傷了他的心。他望着，別人的身子遮了他的視線。他忽然向前跑去。他一張臉通紅，心跳得厲害，他想伸手去抓她，或者大聲喚住她。但是他甚麼也沒有做，她同那男人走進前面一家新開的漂亮咖啡店去了。

他站在門口，不知道應該怎樣做。他想：進去同她講話吧？——不好。說不定會把事情弄糟的。那麼回書店去，等着另一個機會，再找她談話吧。——不好，他放不下心。他應該爭取時間，早點同她和解。那麼就站在門口等候他們出來吧。——不好。這會傷她的面子。並且要是她不理他呢？要是另一個人幫忙她對付他呢？萬一爭吵起來，他沒有甚麼權利來約束她。他們中間只有同居關係，他們不曾正式結過婚。當初他反對舉行結婚儀式(他直到現在還不知道他母親就因為這個緣故，看不起他妻子)，現在他卻後悔她就那麼輕易地丟開了他可以使用的唯一武器。她始終有着完全的自由。這樣一想，他只有垂頭掃興地走回辦公地方去了。

一路上盡是妻同那個年青人親密講話的影子，偶爾還聽見她的笑聲，他差一點被一輛人力車撞倒了。

他走進公司，兩個同事坐在樓下辦公桌前看報。

"Wang,* what's the matter with you? You don't look well today. You didn't even have lunch. Are you worried about something?" asked P'an, hoping to learn some gossip. He thought that Little P'an† must know his troubles at home.

"It's nothing; I have a stomachache," he lied, smiling awkwardly.

"If you have an upset stomach, you should take some medicine. Go home for the rest of the afternoon," suggested his colleague Chung. Chung was about fifty, plump and completely bald. His sagging cheeks accentuated his oblong face and his unusually large nose was distinguished by its red tip. Always smiling, always funny, he enjoyed a cordial relationship with all his colleagues. He loved drinking and good conversation. Though a bachelor and without any relatives, he was known as "Uncle Chung."‡ All envied his life style.

"No, I'm fine," Wang answered perfunctorily, preparing to go upstairs.

"Wang, stay awhile," Little P'an urged him with a smile. "It is not yet time for work," he continued. "Why go up now?"

"You've lost weight lately. You must rest more. To sacrifice yourself this way for a meager salary is hardly worthwhile," Uncle Chung advised while looking at Wang with genuine concern.

Wang sat down again on one of the empty stools and sighed deeply.

"What's the matter? What's the matter?" asked Chung. Patting

---

* His full name is Wang Wen-hsüan. It is customary to address a colleague or a friend by his surname.

† He is called "Little P'an" because of his youth or his small size.

‡ A proper way to address elderly people.

「怎麼啦，老汪？你今天氣色不好，連飯也不吃，有甚麼心事嗎？」那個姓潘的年青人帶着諷刺的調子説。這人一定知道了他的事情，他想道。

「沒有事。我肚子不大好，」他連忙做出笑容，臨時編出一句假話來。

「肚子不好，吃點藥罷。今天下午不要辦公了。就請半天假吧，」另一個姓鍾的同事説，這人年紀在五十左右，身子肥壯，頭頂全禿了，兩腮的肉重重地垂下來，使他的臉成了方形。鼻子特別大，鼻頭發紅色。這是一個有趣的人，臉上常帶笑容，和同事們處得不錯。愛喝酒，愛説話，他在這裏沒有家室，也沒有一個親人。可是這裏的同事們都稱他做「鍾老」並且讚他「會生活」，「會享樂」，「會安排生活」。

「不要緊，我精神很好，」他(現在我應該寫出他的完全的姓名了：汪文宣)敷衍地答了一句，預備上樓去。

「老汪，在下面坐一會兒吧，現在還不到辦公時間，你何必就上樓去？」姓潘的笑着挽留道。

「你近來瘦了，應該多休息。為這點薪水賣命，也太值不得，」鍾老關心地看他一眼，勸道。

他在一個空櫈子上坐下來，忍不住低聲嘆了一口氣。

「甚麼事？甚麼事？」鍾老驚問道，接着就在他肩頭拍一下：「你

him on the shoulder, Chung went on, "You young people shouldn't take things so seriously. Who can be happy nowadays? The most important thing is to take care of your health."

"With this salary, one can't even properly feed his wife, let alone take care of his health," replied Wang sullenly.

"I know what you mean. You must have had a disagreement with your wife," said Uncle Chung.

"No, no," Wang denied quickly, but his face showed that he was lying.

"My dear friend, don't deny it," Chung said with a smile. "Husbands and wives quarrel all the time. If a quarrel develops, give in a little, and your honorable wife* will accept you. Why worry about such things?"

Wang did not respond. Lost in his own thoughts, he merely nodded.

"I disagree with Uncle Chung's view," laughed Little P'an, adding, "If husbands keep giving in to their wives, won't they become henpecked? In family quarrels, the husband must be firm. What can women do but cry and curse? Can they physically beat us?"

"You have no right to talk. Everyone knows you are the most henpecked husband of all," said Uncle Chung, waving his hands good-naturedly. "Why don't you tell the truth? You are among friends here."

Little P'an blushed, and kept quiet. Wang Wen-hsüan looked at P'an, his mouth quivering as if he wanted to say something. Then he closed his mouth tight.

---

* When a reference is made to a friend's wife or husband, the word "honorable" usually precedes it .

們年青人，看開點吧。不要太認真啊！這個年頭誰又真正高興啊！要緊的還是保養自己的身體。」

「靠這點錢連自己的老婆也養不活！哪裏說得上保養身體！」他汪文宣沮喪地答道。

「我懂囉，你是跟你太太又鬧過架了。」鍾老省悟地說。

「不是，不是，」他連忙搖頭分辯道，但看他的臉色，人便知道他是在掩飾。

「老兄，你不必否認，」鍾老微笑道。「夫妻吵架也是平常的事。要是真的吵起來，你讓她一點，尊夫人也就會體貼你的。這種事何必放在心上！」

他沒有做聲，心裏思索着，卻不由自主地點了點頭。

「鍾老這種說法，我不贊成。一味讓步豈不成了『懼內懦夫』嗎？」小潘笑着說，「夫妻吵架，男人不應該讓步。女人有甚麼本事，除了哭，除了罵，難道她們還打得過我們？」

「不要講了。誰不知道你是怕太太的！」鍾老揮着手笑道，「這裏又沒有外人。」

小潘一張臉通紅，掉開頭不作聲了。他汪文宣抬起頭看了小潘一眼，嘴一動，似乎要講話，卻又把嘴立刻閉緊了。

"My dear friend," continued Uncle Chung, "there is a popular saying: 'To heed advice is to succeed by fifty percent.'* Everyone is suffering in wartime, so what is there to bicker about? Since a woman can't be as philosophical as a man, she will sometimes complain a little. That's quite normal. Just let her say her piece, ignore her, and nothing will happen. Silence is the best weapon in dealing with wives."

"Uncle Chung, it sounds like you're talking from experience!" remarked Little P'an boisterously. Wang Wen-hsüan seemed to be only half-heartedly interested in Uncle Chung's advice, for he suddenly stood up, muttering to himself, "I must go out again and find her." He walked out.

"Wang, where are you going?" Little P'an called after him.

"I'll be back soon," Wang answered, without turning his head.

"Why did he leave like that?" Little P'an asked Chung curiously.

Chung shook his head but said nothing. A moment later he let out a gentle sigh.

V

WANG soon arrived at a certain bank. The afternoon office hours had not yet begun, and the front door was locked. He did not have the courage to enter the bank through its side door. What if she had not

---

* To listen and to accept good advice is the most important step in solving any problem.

「老兄，這裏有句俗話：聽人勸，得一半。這個年頭，大家都在吃苦，還有甚麼好吵的。女人不及男人會吃苦，有時候悶不過，發點牢騷，也是人情之常，你就讓她講幾句，不去理她，甚麼事都不會有了。對付太太的最好武器便是沉默。」

「鍾老這是經驗之談啊！」小潘大聲笑着說。他汪文宣吃了一驚。他似乎聽懂了這番話，似乎又沒有聽進去。他忽然站起來，低聲自語了一句：「我再去找她」。他就往外面走。

「老汪，走哪裏去？」小潘在後面問道。

「我就回來，」他匆匆答道，頭也不回地走出去了。

「他去幹甚麼？」小潘好奇地問道。

鍾老默默地搖着頭，過了片刻才輕輕地嘆了一口氣。

五

他到了ＸＸ銀行。沒有到辦公時間，大門還關着。他又沒有膽量從側門進去。要是她還沒有回來？要是她拒絕見他，或者見到他

returned from lunch? What if she refused to see him? What if she gave him the cold shoulder? What would he do? Could his awkward tongue adequately express his feelings? Could he make her understand him from his point of view? Could he persuade her to return home with him? Diffident and hesitant, he stood at the side door for several minutes, and then he turned away dejectedly.

The sharp click of high heels made him look up after he had walked a short distance. And there she was, standing before him in the same outfit. Obviously she had seen him and stopped. She looked at him in surprise, her lips quivering, and then she turned to walk away.

Summoning up all his courage he called, "Shu-sheng," and waited for her reaction. His heart was beating rapidly.

She stared at him in silence. He called her again in a trembling voice. And this time she walked toward him.

"What's the matter?" she asked coldly after eyeing him.

"Can you spare fifteen minutes? I must talk to you," he said, shaking all over, with his head bowed.

"I have to go to work," she answered simply.

"I have something important to say to you," he insisted, blushing like a child who has been scolded by his parents.

"Meet me here at five," she whispered softly, after a pause.

"Fine," he replied gratefully, almost moved to tears.

After giving him another quick glance, she walked away, disappearing through the bank's side door.

He had been separated from her for only a little more than a day. But why was she so cool toward him? Doubts suddenly arose in his

不給他一個笑臉，不回答他一句溫和的話，他怎麼辦呢？他的笨拙的口舌能夠表達他的感情麼？他能夠使她了解他的苦衷、明白他的胸懷麼？他能夠說服她，感動她，使她滿意地跟着他回家去麼？……他想着，他的決心動搖了，勇氣喪失了。他遲疑着，不知道應該把腳朝前放或者向後移好。他在側門前立了兩三分鐘，終於垂着頭轉身走開了。

一陣高跟皮鞋的響聲使他抬起頭來，他已經走了十多步了。她就立在他面前，還是先前那一身裝束。她迎面走來，認出了他，便停了步。她驚訝地看他，她動下一嘴，好像要說話，但忽然又把臉轉開，默默地走了。

「樹生，」他鼓起勇氣叫了一聲，他覺得自己心跳得厲害。他等待着她的表示。

她轉過頭來，帶着詫異的眼光看他，不作聲，他聲音顫抖地再叫一聲。她向他走來。

「甚麼事？」她冷冷地問了一句，連她的眼光也是冷峻的。

「你可不可以給我一刻鐘的時間？我有話跟你談。」他低着頭說，聲音還有點顫。

「我要上辦公去，」她簡單地答道。

「我有點要緊事跟你談談，」他紅着臉，像一個挨了罵後的小孩似地說。

她的表情軟化了，停了片刻，她低聲說：「那麼你五點鐘到行裏來找我。」

「好的，」他差不多要流淚地感激說。

她略略打量他一眼便走了。他望着她的背影在銀行側門中消失。

他同她不過分別了一天多，怎麼就顯得這樣生疏了？——他忽

mind. He was waiting for someone to give him an answer. He was waiting for the answer. As if some object had been deposited within his head, his head felt heavy. Suddenly, someone's arm accidentally bumped against him. Staggering, he nearly fell down on the sidewalk. He seemed as if he had just awakened from a deep dream. "Oh," he murmured. Quickly steadying himself, he saw pedestrians walking in the street, cars and rickshaws racing in the dust. He remembered that he had to return to work and started walking.

On the way he kept thinking about his troubles. Just before he reached his office, he said to himself, "It's all my fault. I must apologize to her this afternoon."

He returned to his desk. Mr. Chou was not in. Wang's two senior co-workers, Wu and Li, were smoking and chatting leisurely. They were laughing and watching him from the corners of their eyes. Suspicious, he was certain they must be gossiping about him and his wife. He felt his face reddening. Avoiding their eyes, he buried his head in his work.

He was proofreading a well-known writer's translation of a novel, but it read too much like an exotic Buddhist sutra.* The more he heard the carefree laughter of his co-workers, the harder it was for him to understand the translation. The louder the noise became, the deeper he buried his head in the galleys. The familiar stench of ink seemed particularly offensive. Nonetheless, he continued patiently with his work.

Mr. Chou returned to the office. For some reason he was very irritable and scolded a servant without any provocation. A man talked to him about a pay raise, pointing out that it was difficult for low-income staff members to make ends meet.

* Known for its incomprehensibility.

然有了這個疑問！他等着誰來給一個回答。他等待着。他腦子變得十分沉重，好像是一塊堅硬的東西放在那裏。一隻手膀迎面撞過來，他的身子搖幌了兩下，他差一點跌倒在人行道上。他彷彿從深夢中醒了過來一般。「哦，」他低低叫出一聲。他連忙站定身子。人們在他眼前來來去去，汽車和人力車帶着塵土狂奔。他想道：「我也應該去辦公。」他跨着大步走了。

他一路上還在想那個問題。走到公司前，他忽然自語道：「都是我不好。今天下午我應該向她道歉。」

他回到樓上辦公桌前。周主任不在。另外兩個高級同事吳股長和李秘書抽着香煙在談閒話。他們低聲在笑，眼睛斜視着他。他們一定在談他和他妻子的事情，他暗暗斷定道。他覺得臉在發燒，便把頭埋在校樣上面，不敢看他們一眼。

他校的是一位名家的譯文。原作是小説，譯文卻像佛經，不少古怪字眼，他抓不到一個明白的語句，他只是機械地一個字一個字校對着。同事的笑聲愈來愈高，他的頭越埋越低，油墨的氣味強烈地刺戟他的鼻子，這聞慣了的氣味今天卻使他發惡心。但是他只有忍耐着。

周主任來了，不知道為了甚麼事，他非常不高興，剛坐下就罵起聽差來。一個同事過來談起加薪的問題，說，目前這點薪金實在不夠維持生活，尤其是低級職員，苦得很。

Chou replied coldly, "This is government policy. What can I do? If they don't want to work here, they can go elsewhere!"

Wang thought bitterly, "Wouldn't it please you if you didn't pay at all? Your own annual bonus amounts to hundreds of thousands of *yüan*.* You don't care if we live or die. If you weren't so miserly and harsh, would my wife be quarreling with me?" He had carefully kept his grumblings to himself. In fact, he had even suppressed his breathing lest Chou might detect his discontent.

He did not dare leave early. His patience wore thin waiting for five o'clock. When the bell rang at five, he quickly put his work in a desk drawer and dashed downstairs. He did not hear Uncle Chung calling after him.

He walked to the bank where Shu-sheng worked. The front door was locked, but the side door was open. He saw her entering the lane from the side door with a faint smile on her face. She gave him a pleasant nod. What he saw was enough to make the drab surroundings instantly bright and spring-like. Smiling happily, he walked toward her.

Quietly she suggested, "Let's go to the International."

"Fine," he answered in a grateful tone. Little did he know that it was the same place where she went with her beau a few hours before. He felt carefree as though someone had lifted a millstone from his heart.

---

* During this period of rampant inflation, the denomination of the currency was extremely large. The official rate of exchange at this time was twenty *yüan* to one U.S. dollar, but in the open market, the *yüan* was much less. For details, see Chou Shun-hsin, *The Chinese Inflation 1937–1949* (New York: Columbia University Press, 1963), p. 157, for the *yüan* equivalent of the U.S. dollar.

「公家的事，這有甚麼辦法？他們不在我這兒做事，也得吃飯啊！」主任冷冷地答道。

「那麼你就一個錢也不給，不是更好嗎？」他汪文宣在旁邊暗暗罵道。你年終一分紅，就是十幾二十萬，你哪管我們死活！要不是你這樣刻薄，樹生怎麼會同我吵架？」可是他連鼻息也極力忍住，不敢發出一點聲音，怕周主任會注意到他心裏的不平。

好容易忍耐到五點鐘。他不敢早退，他聽到打鈴，才站起來，把校樣鎖在抽屜裏，急急地走下樓去。鍾老在後面喚他，要跟他講話，他沒有聽見。

他走到ＸＸ銀行門口，大門已經關上，側門還開着。他剛走進側門，就看見她從辦公室轉到巷子裏來。她看見他，臉上露出一絲笑意，她略略點一個頭。他的勇氣增加了，周圍突然明亮起來，彷彿春天即刻到了似的。他堆着一臉笑向她走過去。

「我們到國際去坐坐，」她低聲提議道。

「好的，」他感激地答道，他沒有想到國際就是幾個鐘點以前她同另一個男子進去的那個咖啡店。他覺得心裏很輕鬆，好像誰把這兩天來壓在他心上的石頭拿走了似的。

Walking on his right, she kept her distance from him. Except for coughing two or three times, she was silent.

So silent, in fact, that he finally asked, "Are you well?" When he looked at her face, however, he could see no sign of ill health.

"Yes, I am well," she said tersely. And again she closed her lips.

He lost his nerve and asked no more questions during the short walk. Soon they entered the International.

To him this café — with its tasteful decor, blue drapes, soft lights, new furniture and sophisticated patronage — was a strange place. They took the only vacant table facing the street.

"This is the first time I've been here," he remarked, not able to think of anything else to say.

"With your income you couldn't afford to come here often," she replied, pitying him with a smile.

He felt a stab of pain and murmured, with his head bowed, "I used to go to cafés, too."

"Yes, but that was eight or nine years ago. Things were quite different then. We've all changed a lot in the last two years." She sighed, and was going to say something more, but a waiter interrupted her. She ordered two coffees.

"That's true. Who knows when these terrible days will end? When we were in Shanghai, we never dreamed that we'd be so poor. We had ideals, we thought of our academic careers and wanted to establish a rural school of our own," he said with a dreamy smile. But immediately he frowned and continued, rather resentfully, "It's very strange, though, that our feelings toward each other should have changed so much. I don't know how or when the change began."

她在他右手邊走着，和他離得並不太近。她一路上閉緊嘴，一共只輕輕咳了三聲嗽。

「你不舒服嗎？」他實在不能忍耐了，關切地問道。他又看她的臉，她臉上沒有病容。

「沒有甚麼，」她略一搖頭，短短地答道。她的嘴又緊緊閉上了。

他發問的勇氣也就消失了。他一直沉默着。不久他們就進了國際的廳子。

國際對他是很陌生的。他覺得廳子佈置得十分好看，尤其是天青色的窗帷使他眼睛裏充滿了柔和的光。傢具全是新的，狹長的廳子裏坐滿了客人，可是談話聲並不嘈雜。只有靠裏一張臨街的桌子還空着，他跟着她走去坐下了。

「這個地方我還是頭一回來，」他說不出別的話，就這樣說了。

她臉上現出憐惜的哂笑，她低聲說：「拿你那一點薪水，那裏能常到咖啡店啊！」

他覺得一根針往心上刺，他低下頭來，自語似地說：「從前我也常坐咖啡店的。」

「那是八九年前的事。從前我們都不是這樣過日子的。這兩年大家都變了，」她也自語似地說，她小聲嘆了一口氣，她也許還有話說，可是茶房過來把她的話打斷了。她向茶房要了兩杯咖啡。

「以後不曉得還要苦到怎樣。從前在上海的時候我們做夢也想不到會過今天這樣的生活。那個時候我們腦子裏滿是理想，我們的教育事業，我們的鄉村化、家庭化的學堂。」他做夢似的微微一笑，但馬上又皺起眉頭來，接下去：「奇怪的是，不只是生活，我覺得連我們的心也變了，我也說不出是怎樣變起來的，」他帶了點怨憤的口氣說。

The coffee arrived. He took the lid off the sugar bowl and helped her to some sugar. She looked at him gently. "Yes, the past is like a dream. We had goals, courage, ambition.... Why don't we live like we did before?" she remarked slowly and earnestly. These words seemed to come straight from her heart. He was so moved by them that his heart beat faster. The gulf between them had narrowed. Quickly he seized the opportunity.

"Why don't you come home with me today?" he suggested, with trepidation.

She gave him no immediate answer, but she looked surprised and pleased. He noticed that her eyes had brightened, even if only for a moment. She turned her head away to look out the window for a minute and then turned back with a sigh, "Haven't you had enough misery?" He noticed for the first time that her eyes were red-rimmed.

"No, it's all my fault," he apologized. "I don't know why I've become so temperamental."

"It's not your fault," she interrupted impatiently. "Who can hold their temper nowadays? I too have a quick temper."

"I think we'll have better days in the future," he said with renewed courage.

"Let's not talk about a future which is filled with uncertainties. Life has no meaning any more. It is a disgrace that even with a degree in education I have to work as a junior clerk in a bank."

"What about me? I spend every day proofreading those awful texts. Shu-sheng, please don't talk like that. Forgive me this time and come home. I promise never to quarrel with you again," he said desperately, having lost his self-control.

茶房端上兩杯咖啡來，他揭開盛糖的玻璃缸，用茶匙把白糖放進她面前的咖啡杯裏。她帶着溫情看了他一眼。

「從前的事真好像是一場夢。我們有理想，也有為理想工作的勇氣。現在……其實為甚麼我們不能夠再像從前那樣過日子呢？」她說。餘音相當長，顯然這話是從她心裏吐出來的。他很受感動，心也跳得很厲害。他覺得她和他中間的距離縮短了。他的勇氣突然間又大大地增加了。他說，仍然帶着顫音：

「那麼你今天跟我回家去吧。」

她馬上並不答話，她注意地望着他，眼裏有一點驚訝的表情，又帶一點喜悅。他看出她的眼睛在放光，但過了片刻，光又滅了。她把頭掉開去看窗外，只一分鐘，她又回過頭，嘆息地說：「你還沒有過夠這種日子嗎？」她的眼圈紅了。

「過去都是我不好，」他埋下頭負罪似地說，「我不知道為甚麼我的脾氣變得這樣……」

「這不怪你，」她不能忍耐地打岔說。「在這個年頭誰還有好脾氣啊？這又不是你一個人的錯，我脾氣也不好。」

「我想我們以後總可以過點好日子，」他鼓起勇氣說。

「以後，那更渺茫了。我覺得活着真沒有意思，我一個學教育的人到銀行裏去做個小職員，也夠可憐了，」她說。

「那麼我又怎樣說呢，我整天校對那些似通非通的文章。樹生，你不要講這些話，你原諒我這一次，今天就跟我回家去，我以後決不再會跟你吵架，」他失去控制自己的力量，哀求地說了。

"Don't get so nervous. People are staring at us," she cautioned him, leisurely sipping her coffee.

He felt as if a ladle of cold water had been spilled on his head, chilling his heart as well. Tasting his coffee, he savored its bitterness and said to himself, "The more bitter, the better," downing the cupful in one gulp.

"Don't feel so sorry for yourself," Shu-sheng went on. "It's not that I can't go home with you, but just think of what would happen. Your mother dislikes me, and I can't take her abuse of me. Our fights will continue, and you'll always be trapped in the middle. With living costs so high, think of the extra burden it will mean to continue supporting me. At least this way, we can still be friends."

"But Hsiao Hsüan?" he uttered his son's name painfully.

"Hsiao Hsüan has his grandmother and his father. He has spent much more time with you than with me. He is older now and doesn't need a mother like me," she said, clearly enunciating every word.

"But I need you," he implored.

"Your mother needs you more, and I can't throw her out. As long as she stays, I'll never return," she said firmly.

"What can I do? I might as well be dead." Mournfully he buried his head in his hands.

"It is time to go. You should go home to dinner." She put some money on the table, called the waiter, pushed her chair back, stood up and walked out. He followed her meekly, having forgotten that he should play the part of the host.

They walked out into the chilly night air. He shivered.

Ready to go her own way, she said gently, "Goodbye, then."

「你鎮靜點，人家在看我們啊！」她把頭朝着他伸來，小心警告說。她拿起杯子放在嘴邊，慢慢地喝着咖啡。

他覺得一瓢冷水潑到他頭上，立刻連心裏也冰涼了。他也端起杯子喝着，今天的咖啡特別苦。「很好，越苦越好，」他暗暗地對自己說。他把滿杯咖啡喝光了。

「你不要難過，我並不是不可以跟你回去。不過你想想，我回去以後又是怎樣的情形。你母親看不慣我這樣的人，我也受不了她的氣，還不是照樣吵着過日子，只有使你更苦。而且生活這樣高，有我在，反而增加你的負擔。你也該想明白點，像這樣分開我們還可做個朋友……」她心平氣和地說，可是聲音裏還洩露出來一點壓抑住的酸苦。

「可是小宣——」他痛苦地說出這四個字。

「小宣跟他祖母合得來，他有祖母喜歡，有父親愛護也是一樣。反正他跟我在一起的時間並不多，現在年紀也不小了，用不着我這樣的母親了，」他一字一字十分清晰地說。

「但是我需要你。——」他還在要求。

「你母親更需要你。我也不能趕走她。有她在，我決不回去，」她堅決地說。

「那麼我怎麼辦？我還不如不活着好！」她兩手捧着頭悲苦地說。

「我們還是走吧，你也該回去吃飯了，」她說，便提高聲音叫茶房來收錢，一面把鈔票放在桌上，自己先站起來，推開椅子走了一步。他也只得默默地站起來跟她走了。他並沒有想到搶着付錢的事。

他們走出咖啡店，夜已經來了。寒氣迎面襲來，他打了一個冷噤。

「那麼，再見吧，」她溫和地說。她掉轉身子預備走了。

"No," he cried, unable to control himself. And when she turned back, he revealed the suspicion which had been gnawing at him for a whole day: "Please be honest with me. Is there another man?"

Her face and her demeanor underwent no change; his question did not anger her; it only heightened her concern for him. She understood him completely and gave him a melancholy smile.

"Yes, there is another man, but don't be concerned. I am not a girl but a 34-year-old woman. I know how to take care of myself," and without another word, she walked away resolutely.

Dazed, he watched her recede in the distance and visualized her handsome beau chatting with her in his smart overcoat, both of them walking ahead of him, forever ahead of him.

"A complete waste of time. So much said and so little accomplished. I still don't know what she is thinking. What shall I do? What can I do?" He felt darkness before his eyes.

"Go home," an inner voice told him. Obeying, he moved on listlessly.

"Home, what kind of home do I have?" he repeated, over and over.

VI

HE returned home. The partial blackout in the area made the main entrance of the apartment building look like a dark cave. No kind-hearted person had lit a paper lantern there this time; he had to grope his way through the pitch-dark corridor and up the winding staircase to the third floor.

「不，」他不能自主地吐出這個字。他看見她回轉身來，抑制不住，終於吐出了這天一直在他腦際縈繞的疑問：

「請你坦白告訴我，是不是還有第三個人，我不是說我母親。」

她的臉色和態度似乎都沒有改變。他的問話並不會觸怒她，卻只引起她的憐憫。她明白他的意思，她憂鬱地笑了笑。

「第三個人有是有的。不過你放心。我又不是小姑娘，我今年三十四歲了，我曉得管住我自己。」她點了點頭，便撇下他，毅然朝另一個方向走了。

他呆呆地站在原地方望着她的背影。其實他甚麼也看不見，他眼裏只有一個景象：她同那個穿漂亮大衣的年青男子在前面走着，永遠在前面走着。

「失敗了，談了許多話，一點結果也沒有。我真不曉得她究竟是甚麼心思。我應該怎麼辦呢？」他這樣想道，他覺得眼前只是一片黑。

「回家吧，」另一個聲音在他耳邊說。他順從着這聲音的指示，沒精打采地拔步走了。

「家，我有的是一個怎樣的家啊！」他一路上不斷地唸着這一句話。

六

他回到家。大門裏像是一個黑洞，今天又輪着這一區停電。也沒有一個好心人在門口點一盞油燈。他摸索着走完漆黑的過道，轉上樓梯。他上了二樓，又走上三樓。

A patch of light showed from beneath the door of his apartment. On hearing the sound at the door, his mother, eating her meal at the square table, said, "You're back. I waited for you such a long time ... I thought you might not return for dinner."

"I wasn't able to get back earlier," he replied weakly, joining her at the table. She stood up and filled a bowl of rice for him.

"Hurry and eat while the food is still warm," she said, sitting down, and continued, "This afternoon Mr. Fang from the second floor shared a catty* of pork with me, and I made your favorite dish —red-cooked pork.† You'll enjoy it. I kept it warm in the cooker." His mother hastily finished eating her bowl of rice.

While quietly listening to her, he noticed a few scattered grains of rice in her bowl. Somehow what he saw deeply touched him and brought him close to tears. Patiently he answered her endless questions; despite his lack of appetite, he swallowed his rice mouthful by mouthful and his pork bit by bit. He still acted like an obedient child before his mother.

"Aren't you feeling well today?" she asked. His listlessness and silence made her uneasy.

"I am fine," he replied, and continued to sit with his head bowed, not even looking at her.

After watching him for some time, she couldn't bear it any longer and asked, "Was the food too cold?"

"No," he answered mechanically, unable to lift his head.

His mother was disheartened by his apathy. She had waited all

* An Asian unit of weight generally equivalent to $1^1/3$ pounds avoirdupois.

† Pork steamed in thick soy sauce.

他的房門開了一個縫，漏出一點光來。他推門進去。母親坐在方桌前垂着頭吃飯，聽見門響，抬起臉，説聲：「你回來啦！」她的聲音和臉色都含得有欣慰。「快來吃飯。我等你到現在，我還以為你不回來了，」她絮絮地説。

「我有點事情，所以回來遲一點；」他有氣無力地説，他走到飯桌前，在母親對面的一個方櫈上坐下。母親站起來給他盛了一碗飯放到他面前。

「快吃吧，趁現在飯還熱，」她坐下愛憐地説。「我下午在二樓方經理那裏分到一斤肉，煮了一碗紅燒肉，這是你愛吃的，我放在飯鍋子裏，剛才拿出來，還是熱的，你嘗嘗看，這是你愛吃的菜。」她匆忙地把自己碗裏的飯幾口吃好了。

他靜靜地聽着母親的慈愛的話語，眼光在菜上盤桓了一會，他看到黏在碗邊的零星的飯粒，他覺得一陣心酸，他只想倒在床上痛哭。可是他仍然低着頭用唯唯的答應口吻敷衍他母親，並且不管自己有沒有口味，他還是一口一口地嚥着飯，一筷子一筷子地挾着紅燒肉。他在這樣的母親面前還是一個溫順的孩子。

「你今天不大舒服，是不是？」母親注意到他這種忍受性的沉默。她感到不安了，她便關切地問道。

「沒有，」他搖搖頭答道，接着添加一句：「我很好，」他又低頭不出聲了。

他母親關心地望着他，她希望他對她多講幾句話，但是他連看也不看她一眼。她忍不住又説：「菜沒有冷吧。」

「沒有，」他機械地答道，也不抬頭來。

她感到失望，等了他這一天，他回來卻這樣冷淡地對待她！她

day for his return, and now that he was here, he treated her so coldly. She was sure she knew why he acted in such a way. It was due to that woman who had bewitched him; she watched him even more closely. He put down his chopsticks and got up.

"Have you had enough to eat?" she asked, trying hard to control herself.

"Yes," he replied, and started to clean off the table.

"You only had one bowl of rice."

"Oh, I just had coffee with Shu-sheng," he said inadvertently.

Coffee with that woman! Her again! After taking great pains to prepare a nice meal for him, he still went out with that woman! They certainly knew how to enjoy themselves. He went to look for her! To fawn on that shameless whore! Oh, this was too much for her!

"You went to look for her? How could she face you?" she shrieked.

"I wanted her to come home with me," he answered quietly.

"How could she? Doesn't she have any sense of shame?" she said, glaring.

"So far she has refused to come back. But she might change her mind in a few days," he said sheepishly.

"You still think she might? You must be dreaming. If I were you, I'd put an announcement in the paper officially severing all ties with her. Water, once spilled, can never be gathered again," she observed furiously, her face beet-red. "At eighteen, I married into your Wang family. In over thirty years of married life, I've never seen the likes of her." Furious and at her wits'end, she realized that her son would not listen and that he still could not forget his wife. Even now she could

明白了，一定是那個女人在他心上作怪。她更留心地看他。他放下碗筷，默默地站起來。

「吃飽啦？」她壓住剛剛升上的怒氣，溫和地問道。

「是，」他答道，他動手收拾飯桌。

「你才吃一碗嘛，」她又說。

「我剛才同樹生喝了咖啡，」他大意地老實說出來。

她的怒火立刻冒上來了。又是那個女人！她在家裏燒好飯菜等他回來同吃，他卻同那個女人去喝咖啡。他們倒會享福。她這個沒出息的兒子。他居然跑去找那個女人，向那個不要臉的女人低頭。這太過分了，不是她所能忍受的。

「怎麼你還會去找她！她還有臉見你？」她大聲說。

「我要她跟我回家，」他低聲答道。

「哼！她還好意思回來！」她冷笑道。

「她不肯回來。我想，過幾天她會回心轉意的，」他膽怯地說。

「她還會回來？你真是在做夢！我如果是你，我就登報跟他離婚，橫豎潑出去的水是收不回來的，」她漲紅臉生氣說，「我十八歲嫁到你汪家來，三十幾年了，就沒有見過一個像她這樣的女人！」她氣得沒辦法，知道兒子不會聽她的話，又知道他仍然忘不了那個女

not get rid of that woman; he still spoke the name of "Shu-sheng" in a most affectionate tone of voice.

"I think she has her own problems. Perhaps she doesn't care to disclose them," he said without expression. His words were really meant to be heard only by himself. Nonetheless she butted in.

"You're still defending her? You're a weakling. She has a boy friend and she writes love letters openly. What problems could she possibly have?" Her saliva sprayed his face as she sputtered on excitedly, pointing her right forefinger at his nose.

"Maybe they're not love letters," he protested.

"If they weren't love letters, why was she afraid to show them to you? Why did she run away?" she paused after having said that. She stood in front of him, glaring at him with bulging eyes.

"Mother ... " Bursting out in tears, he could not say any more.

She would have liked to continue, but when she saw his tears, she stopped. Her rage dissipated as soon as she was confronted with her son behaving like a child who had been wronged and was entreating her. After a short while she said in a mild tone, "Tell Mama ... "

"You really don't understand Shu-sheng. She didn't run away. She is just staying with a friend for a few days and will come back soon," he said, deeply anguished.

"What do you mean I don't understand her?" Again she was displeased. "To tell the truth, I know her better than you do. I know she's not your type. She'll never be happy with you. Only I, your mother, will stay with you whether you be rich or poor. I don't understand her, indeed! Who told you that? Did she say that?"

"No, she didn't say anything of the kind." He shook his head; he

人，甚至在這個時候她還是壓不倒那個女人，樹生這個名字在他口裏唸着還十分親熱。

「我看她也有她的苦衷，不過她不肯講出來，——」兒子似乎並沒有在聽母親講話，他只顧想自己的事，說出的話也是給自己聽的，可是話說了一半，就被母親打斷了。

「你現在還替她辯護，真不中用。她背着你交男朋友，寫情書，還有甚麼苦衷可說！」母親也站起來責備地把右手食指指他的鼻端，說話時口沫也飛濺出來了。

「那不見得就是情書啊，」他解釋道。

「不是情書，為甚麼害怕拿給你看？為甚麼要私奔——」說到「私奔」兩個字，做母親的人也講不下去了，她瞪着兩眼立在他面前。

「媽，」他哀求地喚一聲，眼裏已裝滿了淚水。他半晌接不下去。

「你說嘛，」過了片刻，她和藹地說。他的眼淚贏得她的同情，她的恨消去了。她愛憐地望着他，彷彿他還是從前那個小孩子，在外面受了委屈，回家來向母親哭訴似的。

「媽，你太不了解樹生，她並不是私奔，她不過到朋友家裏住幾天，她會回來的，」他痛苦地說。

「哼，我不了解她，」她冷笑道。「老實對你說，我比你更了解她。她不會永久跟着你吃苦的。她不是那種女人，我早就看出來了，到現在你該明白了吧。只有你母親才不會離開你，不管你苦也吧，闊也吧。我不了解她！是不是她對你那樣說的？」

他看見母親又動氣了，對她的最後一句問話，他便不肯老實地

could not afford to be honest this time. She stared at him, then sighed and said, "Very well, go to bed. I'll wash the dishes. You must be tired."

Though he was near exhaustion, he said lethargically, "No, it is all right. I am not tired," He helped her wash the dishes and put them away in the cupboard.

Putting the earthen candlestick on the table, she said, "I'll do some sewing here. Since you have nothing to do, why don't you go to bed?" She went to her room to fetch her grandson's coat, then began to mend it, sitting by the table near the candlelight. Even with her glasses on, she leaned her head closer and closer to the mending. The candle was flickering, and before long the room became darker; she had to bend her head more and more toward her work.

He went to his bed, thinking he would rest awhile, but after sitting on its edge for a few seconds he decided to go back to the table. He looked at his mother's hair, gray as if it had been sprinkled with salt. He realized how much she had aged and how the color of her hair had changed. Unaware of him standing there, she took off her glasses, rubbed her eyes, and said to herself, "Poor Hsiao Hsüan. He has worn this coat for three winters, and it will be too small for him next year. He needs a new one, but where will the money come from? His father has his hands full just sending him to school. How can he afford it when a lousy candle like this costs thirty *yüan*? And me, old and useless. It takes me so long to do so little. My poor grandson! His mother doesn't care for him. What bad luck for him to have been born into this household!"

"Mother, please don't do any more work. It's late and your eyes are getting worse. You must take care of your health," he said emphatically, deeply moved by the scene.

"I am just about finished with my work," she replied. Smiling up

回答，他只是搖着頭說：「不是，她沒有說甚麼。」

母親瞪了他一眼，過了片刻，才長長嘆一口氣，她說：「你去休息吧，等我來收拾。你一天也夠累了。」

「不要緊，我不累，」他沒精打采地說。他的確很倦，但他終於支持着，幫忙他母親把碗筷洗乾淨了放進碗櫥裏去。

母親把瓦燭台放在屋中央方桌上，吩咐他說：「我在這兒縫點東西。你沒有事，還是躺一忽兒吧。」她進旁邊小屋去拿了一件男孩的大衣出來，坐在方桌前，將就着燭光，開始補綴着。她的頭埋得低。眼鏡也戴上了。燭光搖幌得厲害，過不多久，光線又暗淡了，她的頭似乎也埋得更低了。

他本來走到了床前，也想躺下睡一會。可是他只在床沿上坐了一下，又站起來，走回到方桌前，默默地立在那裏。他的眼光定在她母親的頭上，她頭上像撒了一堆鹽似的。他才注意到她竟然這樣衰老了，頭髮全變了顏色。她忽然取下眼鏡，用力揉了幾下眼，又把眼鏡戴上，繼續工作，「小宣也可憐，這件大衣穿了三個冬了。就是不壞，明年也穿不上身了。論理今年該給他做件新的。不過他爸爸這樣苦，能夠給他上學讀書已經不容易了。……唉，蠟燭越來越壞了，三十塊錢一支還是這樣的，一點也不亮，又傷眼睛。我究竟老了，人簡直不中用了。也只有這幾針，花了我這麼多的功夫。他媽又不管他，也是他命苦，才投生到我家裏來，」她嘮嘮叨叨地在自言自語，她似乎沒有覺察到他立在她旁邊看她。

「媽，你晚上不要做啦，你眼睛近來更壞了，你要好好保養啊，」他感動地、痛苦地大聲說。

「我快完啦，沒有幾針了，」她抬起頭看了看他，微笑答道。「晚

at her son, she said, "I must do this kind of work at night. I have no other time. During the day, I have to wash and cook. Besides I have little use for my eyes, so why should I treasure them so much?" She continued to sew; her hands were unsteady. "You see I am not like the child's mother. She always looks like a fresh flower. She can't do this and she can't do that. She can only make herself beautiful; she doesn't even have time for her son. What a joke it is that she's a university graduate and holds a responsible job in a bank! But I haven't seen her bring home any money yet."

"Mother, she pays for Hsiao Hsüan's tuition, which comes to more than twenty-thousand *yüan*, close to thirty, for this semester alone."

"She asked for it. Why did she insist that he go to that exclusive school? All his schoolmates are from well-to-do families, but he is poor and is always looked down upon by the others. She even refuses to give the poor boy extra pocket money. No wonder he complains."

He couldn't listen to her any longer. He was too tired and too upset. He could neither sleep nor work at peace, nor even watch his mother sew, for there was no peace in his soul. The room was cold and dark, and his heart seemed to be drifting away in space searching for some haven. Still, he felt that he had not yet been punished enough. He wanted to scream, to cry bitterly, to be beaten cruelly. Anything, except to remain quietly at home by his mother's side.

He walked to the door, opened it and went out, his mother calling after him. In the darkness, his right shoulder collided forcefully with something and began to swell, though he felt no pain at the moment of impact. His only thought was: "I've wronged everyone, and I need to be punished."

上不做，白天又要買菜煮飯，哪兒有功夫做啊！我這雙眼睛也沒有別的用處，還要保養牠做甚麼？」她右手拿着穿了線的針打顫地在那件舊大衣上面動着。「比不得他媽，像鮮花一樣，這也不能做，那也不能做。只顧自己打扮得漂亮，連兒子也不管。說是大學畢業生，受過高等教育，在銀行機關做體面事情，可是就沒有看見她拿過幾個錢回家用。」

「媽，小宣的學費還是靠她啊，這學期就花了兩萬多，快三萬了，」他插嘴說。

「那還不是她自己招來的，她一定要把他送到那種貴族學堂去，他同學都是闊人子弟，只有他是窮家小孩，處處比不過別人。她又不肯多給他錢花。難怪小宣常常叫苦，」她說。

他實在聽不下去。不管他怎樣倦，他心裏煩得厲害。他不能安靜睡去，也不能安靜做事，他甚至不能安靜地看他母親工作。屋子裏這樣冷，這樣暗。他的心似乎飄浮在空虛，找不到一個停留處。他覺得自己痛得不夠，苦得不夠，他需要叫一聲，哭一場，或者大大地痛一陣，挨一次毒打。但是他不能安靜地站在母親身邊。

他大步走向前，他拉開門出去了。「宣，宣，」他聽見母親在屋子裏喚他，他應都不應一聲，就匆匆走下樓去。他在黑暗中把右眉碰腫了，可是他並沒有感到痛楚。他只有一個思想：「我對不起每一個人，我應受罰！」

VII

OPPOSITE the building's main entrance he noticed the flickering lights from the acetylene lamps on the fruit and noodle stalls. Shivering in the dark, he asked himself, "Where shall I go?" He had no answer. In long strides, he quickly reached the middle of the block. Walking aimlessly, he was almost hit by a rickshaw speeding down the hill. The rickshaw-puller cursed him, but he didn't pay any attention, feeling quite detached from everything. His heart seemed to have been emptied of all feeling.

Still not knowing where to go, he walked along another street. But as he turned a corner, he saw numerous neon lights flashing in the distance, in sharp contrast to the dark streets he had just left. It looked like two different worlds. He walked toward the lights.

Approaching another street corner, he was astonished to hear someone calling him by name and saw a man beckoning from a wine shop. It was a middle-aged man in a Western-style suit who was sitting at a table near the door. The man stood up.

"Wang, you came at the right time. Sit down and have a drink," the man said in a loud voice.

Wang recognized the man as a high school classmate whom he had not seen for more than half a year. Ordinarily he would have exchanged a few pleasant words and left, but tonight he accepted the invitation.

"Bring some *hung-tsao*,"* the man ordered a waiter sitting behind

---

* A type of Chinese wine, also known as *ta-ch'ü*.

七

他走到大門口。對面人行道上水果攤和麵擔子旁邊幾盞電石燈星子似地在黑暗街道中閃光。他感到冷意，把肩頭聳了一下。「到哪裏去呢？」他問自己，他找不到回答。他大步走下街心。

他無目的地走過三條街，差一點被一輛飛跑下坡的人力車撞倒。車夫罵了他兩句，他也沒有聽進耳裏，彷彿他周圍的一切都和他隔得很遠似的。他心裏空虛得很。

他又走了一條街，他還是不知道應該走到哪裏去。但是越過路口，對面是燈光輝煌，不知燃了多少盞電燈。兩條街卻成了兩個世界！他朝着燈光走去。

他剛走到街角，忽然一個聲音在喚着他的名字：「汪文宣。」他吃驚地側頭一看。他發覺自己站在一家冷酒館門前。就在靠門一張方桌旁邊，一個穿西裝的中年人立起來招呼他。

「你來的正好，坐下來吃杯酒吧，」那個人大聲說。他認出這是他的一個中學同學。他們半年光景沒有見面，那個人卻蒼老了許多，若在平時，他至多站着談三四句話就走了。今晚他卻默默地走到方桌旁，拉開板櫈，在那同學的對面坐下來。

「拿杯紅糟來！」那個同學掉轉臉向着櫃台大聲吩咐道。

the counter. He drained his cup with his face reddening and smelling of liquor, and impatiently waited for another cup.

"Pai-ch'ing, you never drank before. When did you begin?" Wang asked innocently.

"Oh, I don't know. I simply want to drink and need to drink," Pai-ch'ing answered loudly, shaking his head. "But first, you have some. Bottoms up."

At first, Wang was a little bewildered, but quietly gulped down a mouthful. Immediately he felt a sensation rising within his throat. Unable to repress it, he belched.

"Drink it all, all of it. You didn't finish your cup; that won't do!" Pai-ch'ing urged drunkenly.

"I will, I will." Wang became agitated; with another gulp he finished the wine. His heart was beating fast, and his face seemed to be burning.

Offering Wang a piece of dried beancake* and some peanuts from the small dishes on the table, the other shouted, banging on the table, "Have another cup."

"I can't drink any more." Wang stopped his friend.

"My dear pal, what are you afraid of? It is much better to be drunk than sober." Another cup of wine was put before him.

With a sad smile on his face, Wang answered in all seriousness, "Yes, but who can remain intoxicated forever? Everyone must sober up sometime." Looking at his friend's face, he thought that this 30-year-old man had aged at least ten years within the last six months.

---

* Appetizer.

櫃台那面有人答應着，於是一杯香噴噴的大粬酒端上來了。

「給我再來一杯，」那同學一口把杯裏殘酒喝乾了，紅着臉拍着桌子叫道。

他説話了：「柏青，我記得你從前不會喝酒，你幾時學會的？」

「我沒有學過，我沒有學過。我想喝，我非喝不可，」那同學搖擺着頭大聲説，「你先乾一杯。」

他望着那同學，並不答話，過了片刻，他拿起酒杯，默默地喝了一大口。放下杯子，他長嘆了一聲，一股熱氣直往喉管冒，他壓不下去，他打了一個噎。

「乾一杯，乾一杯，你沒有乾，不行，」同學做着手勢接連地催促。

「我乾，我乾，」他激動地説，他真的一口把剩餘的酒喝乾了。他覺得心跳得厲害，臉也燒起來。

「再來一杯，」同學拍着桌子叫道，一面從桌子中央幾個瓦碟子裏拿了一塊豆腐乾，又抓了一把花生放在他面前説：「你吃。」

「我不能喝了，」他連忙搖手攔阻道。

「老兄，怕甚麼！吃醉了有甚麼要緊！我覺得醉了還比醒着好些，」同學説。酒已經送到他面前了。

「可是人不能一輩子喝醉啊，總有醒的時候，」他寂寞地苦笑道，他望着同學的臉孔，他發覺這個三十歲的人在半年中間至少老

He noticed the wrinkles, the sunken cheeks, the thick and bushy eyebrows, the lusterless eyes. Feeling sorry for his friend, he asked, "Isn't it more painful when one finally sobers up?"

His classmate said nothing. He just quietly swallowed a mouthful of wine, looked at Wang for a while, took another sip, and muttered, "I feel rotten."

"Why do you come here to drink then? Wouldn't it be better to return to your dormitory? I'll take you there," Wang volunteered.

"If I don't get drunk, what is there to do? The worst that can happen is that I'll get sick and then die. As for death, I am not afraid of it." With a pained look on his face, he added, "I'm finished — completely finished."

"I don't understand. Your situation is far better than mine, and even I go on living. Why can't you ?" Looking at his friend's thin face, Wang was somehow reminded of his own situation, trying hard to keep the tears from his eyes. Changing the subject, he asked, "How is your wife? Does she still live in the country?" He remembered his friend's child-like bride, having attended their wedding with Shu-sheng a year ago. The reception was at the Longevity Restaurant, and later he visited them in the country. Most of all, he remembered the bride's sweet and innocent smile, which Shu-sheng had praised so highly. Thinking of Shu-sheng, he was reminded yet again of his own troubles.

His friend looked away and answered, "She's no longer with us."

"What did you say? No longer with us? What did she die of?" Wang was stunned.

"Nothing." His friend shook his head.

"Then she ...," Wang paused, afraid of saying the wrong thing. He

了十年，額上現着好幾條皺紋，兩頰深陷進去，眉毛聚在一起，眼光完全失了光彩，兩顆眼珠呆呆地望着他，他心裏一陣難過，又加上一句：「醒來豈不是更苦嗎？」

那個人不作聲了，埋下頭喝了一口酒，又抬起臉看他一眼，然後又喝一口酒。「我心裏真不好過，」搖擺着頭自語似地說了。

「不好過為甚麼還到這裏來喝酒？早點回宿舍不好嗎？我送你回去，」他關心地說。

「不吃酒又幹甚麼？吃多了至多也不過病——死，我不怕。死了也好，」那人帶着痛苦的表情說。「我完了，我甚麼都完了。」

「你不明白，你的處境總比我好。我都能忍下去，你還不能嗎？」他同情地說，他望着那張瘦臉，覺得自己的傷痕被觸動了，心裏一陣痛，他差一點掉下淚來。「你太太好嗎？是不是還住在鄉下？」他換過話題說。他想到那個孩子面孔的女人，他們一年前在百齡餐廳結婚時，他同樹生還去參加了那個簡單的婚禮。他後來也到他們鄉下家中去作過客。那個年青太太笑起來多麼甜，樹生對她也保持着一個好印象。他想到自己的痛苦，就想到樹生，於是聯想到那位太太身上來。

「她過去了，」同學低聲說，掉開臉不看他。

「她不在了？甚麼病？」他吃驚地說，他彷彿坐到針尖上一樣，差一點要跳起來了。

「她沒有病，」同學搖搖頭冷冷地說，臉色卻十分難看。他難猜出這是甚麼意思。

「那麼她——」說到「她」字他連忙住了口，他自己也害怕聽下面

wondered whether it was suicide or an accidental death.

While Wang and his friend were talking about the young bride's death, desolation and unhappiness seemed to pervade the whole wineshop. Some patrons were complaining to one another about the hard times; others were arguing. For no apparent reason, one middle-aged customer arose abruptly and left. A waiter later told a pale-faced customer that the man who had just left was taciturn and came at the same hour every evening; he ususally ordered two pieces of beancake with his wine, and that was all he knew about him, since the man never divulged any information about himself or his occupation.

Bored with what he had heard, Wang Wen-hsüan raised his head and sighed bitterly, "There is sorrow everywhere."

Tearfully the friend said, "Today is the seventh day since my wife died. Ten days ago she was in the country, healthy and expecting to deliver our first baby very soon. The doctor said it would come a fortnight later. I'd been having trouble in my office because of my section chief, and my request for leave was not approved, so I had to leave her and return to work. Her labor began two days later and it was a normal delivery, but the intern was careless in cutting the umbilical cord and infection set in. She cried for me all night long, and her pitiful cries were even heard by the people on the floor below. She wanted to see me one last time; she wanted me to demand justice. But I was here in the city, far away from her. By the time they telephoned me and I rushed to her side, she was already stiff and cold. Her stomach was so swollen that it was difficult to close the coffin lid. The baby kept crying until it also died two days later. I am reduced to what I had been before — companionless. After the funeral I quit my job. I am haunted by her shrieks everywhere I go, at home or in the street. Only when I'm drunk, I don't hear her. Living is too painful for me. What's there to do but get drunk?" Covering his face with his right

的話：自殺？慘死？好像一根錐子在鑽他的心。

同學不作聲，他也不作聲。這沉默太叫人難堪了。在他們兩人的旁邊，別的桌上的酒客們似乎都不快樂，有的人嘮嘮叨叨地在訴苦，有的在和同伴爭論一件事情，右邊角落裏桌子旁邊一個中年酒客，低着頭，孤寂地喝着悶酒，忽然站起來付了酒錢走了。這人出門後，堂倌告訴一個白臉客人說，這是一個每晚必到的老主顧，不愛講話，喝酒也不過量，兩塊豆腐乾便是他的下酒菜。他按時來準時去，誰也不知道他是一個怎樣的人，有着甚麼樣的職業。

他汪文宣聽得厭煩了，昂起頭長嘆一聲，酸苦地說：「無處不是苦惱！」

那同學吃驚地望着他，眼淚一滴一滴地掉下來。「今天是她的頭七。」歇了一下又說：「十天前她還是很好的，一點病也沒有。她懷着小孩月份已經夠了，我陪她去醫院檢查，醫生說她還不到月份，最早也要在半個月以後，我不能夠在鄉下多住半個月，我那個機關科長跟我合不來，他故意搗亂，不准我的假，我進城來了，第三天我女人就發作了，同住太太送她進醫院去，檢查的時候，說是順產，一切都沒有問題。到半夜孩子果然平平穩穩地下來了。大人也很好。可是接生的是一個年青實習醫生，她剪臍帶時不當心，出了毛病，產婦血往上行。我女人一晚上不斷地叫着我的名字，她叫了一兩百聲才死去。據說她叫得很慘，她聲音連樓下的人也聽見。她只想在死去以前跟我見一面，要我給她伸冤。可是我住在城裏哪裏知道。我得到電話，立刻趕去，她已經冷硬了，肚皮脹大得很怕人，幾乎連棺材也蓋不上。孩子只是哭，過兩天也死了。我還是跟沒有結婚以前一樣，一個人。我葬了我女人，進城來第一件事就是請長假。我一天甚麼事都不能做，我只聽見我女人的聲音在叫我的名字。不管我在家裏，在街上，我都聽見那個聲音。你聽她在叫：柏青！柏青！」話說的人用兩根手指敲着右邊太陽角。「是，的確是她的聲音，她叫得多慘！……所以我只想吃酒，我只想醉，頂好醉得不省人事，那時候我才聽不見她的聲音。活着，活着，真不容易啊。以後除了酒，我還有甚麼伴侶呢？」用右手蒙着臉，這個人低低

hand, he sobbed like a child. Then he seemed to become completely dazed.

Wang felt cold shivers up and down his spine; his heart seemed to have been wrung tightly by a huge hand. He felt indescribably bitter and was on the verge of losing his self control. "You can't go on like this!" he said. "You have a master's degree. Don't you remember your plans to be a writer? Why don't you resume writing?"

"In order to live I've sold all my books. Writing is not for the likes of me," Pai-ch'ing answered, removing his hand from his tear-ridden face and exposing his dull-looking eyes. "What do you think I should do? Get married again? Have children? Bring suffering to another? No, I wouldn't do that; I'd rather suffer alone. This world is not for us. We are law-abiding and suffer, while others get rich and become high government officials at our expense."

"Therefore, we must drink more," shouted Wang Wen-hsüan suddenly, joining his friend. Losing all self-restraint, he was like the water bursting out of a broken dam. He wanted to forget everything in his exasperation, and a drunken stupor seemed the only way. "Bring me wine, bring me wine," he clamored. The waiter brought him another cup. He looked at the white fragrant-smelling liquid, thinking how crazy the world was. He put the cup to his mouth and forced a big swallow. As the sensation surged upwards into his nostrils, he hiccupped. "This seems to be too strong for me," he apologized, thinking: "I'm really useless. I can't even drink wine. No wonder everyone takes advantage of me." Determined, however, he forced himself to finish his drink.

"Your face is as red as Kuan Kung's.* Are you drunk?"

---

* Kuan Kung, a famous hero during the period of the Three Kingdoms (220–265), known for his red complexion.

抽泣了幾聲，然後像睡去了似地寂然了。

他汪文宣聽完了這個人的故事，他覺得彷彿有一隻大手把他的心緊緊捏住似的，他嘗到一種難熬的苦味，背脊上一陣一陣地發冷，他的自持的力量快要崩潰了。「你這樣不行啊！」他為了抵抗那越來越重的壓迫，說出這句話來。他心裏更難過，他又添加說：「你是個文學碩士，你還記得你那些著作的計劃嗎？為甚麼不拿起筆來？」

「我的書全賣光了，我得生活啊，著作不是我們的事，」同學突然取下蒙臉的手，臉上還有淚痕，兩眼卻閃着逼人的光。「你說我應該怎樣辦呢？是不是我再去結婚，再養孩子，再害死人？我不幹這種事。我寧願犧牲自己。這個世界不是我們這種人的。我們奉公守法，別人陞官發財……」

「所以我們還是拼命喝酒，」他汪文宣大聲接嘴說，他完全崩潰了，他用不着再抑制自己，堤決了一個口，水只有向一個地方流去。他悲憤到了極點，他需要忘記一切。醉自然成了他唯一的出路。「拿酒來，拿酒來！」他喝着。堂倌又送來一杯酒。他望着杯裏香噴噴的白色液體，心裏想：這是怎樣的一個世界啊！他端起杯子，喝了一大口，咬着牙吞下去，立刻一股熱氣衝上來，他受不住了打了一個噎。「我喝不了酒，」他抱歉地說，他想：我真不中用，連酒也不會喝，就該永遠受人欺負。於是他反抗似地把餘酒接連幾口就喝光了。

「你臉紅得跟關公一樣，你吃醉沒有？」同學關切地問道。

"No, not at all," he answered with an effort. His head felt heavy. And whenever he made an effort to speak, his head throbbed with pain. His face was burning and he seemed to be floating in the air. He tried to stand up but was so unsteady that he had to sit down again.

"What's the matter? You'd better be careful," his friend cautioned him.

"I'm not drunk, not drunk at all," he said, wanting to smile but unable to do even that. All his resentment against life surfaced, and he wished he could cry. Dizzy and unsteady, he saw his friend's eyes multiplying into many pairs of eyes, all dancing before him. By staring steadily he finally located his friend's thin weary face, but soon it was replaced by more pairs of eyes and revolving neon lights. After several attempts, he managed to get up. "I am drunk," he admitted, and nodding to his friend, he staggered out of the wineshop.

After lurching along for one block and half of another, he decided to go home. This idea was like a flash of light which illuminated everything around and even sobered him up a little, at least enough to ask himself, "How did I get to be like this?" He persuaded his body to turn in the direction of home. However, he had walked no more than two or three steps when what looked like a gigantic shadow collided with him face to face. The impact was so strong that he nearly fell down.

The man's curses followed him as he continued walking toward home. As much as he would have liked to hurry, his stomach would not cooperate. Finally he opened his mouth, and his dinner shot out like a cataract.

He thought everything in his stomach had come up. Without wiping his mouth, he walked on, disgusted by the offensive stench of the vomit. He wanted to get home and go to sleep. But the more he thought of home, the more his steps slackened. Soon he threw up again, and

「沒有，沒有！」他用力回答道，他覺得腦子凝成了一塊重重的硬東西，他一用力説話，腦子就痛。臉燒得厲害，身子輕飄飄的。他想站起來，沒有立穩，又頹然坐下。

「怎麼！當心啊！」同學大聲說。

「我一點也沒有醉，」他說着，想笑一笑，可是他連笑也不會了。他只想哭。他覺得一切可悲的事都湧到了他的心頭。他也分不清楚是甚麼事情。他頭暈得厲害，心裏也很難過。他熬不住。他覺得那同學的眼睛變成了許多對，在他面前打轉，他用力一看，還是那張憂鬱的瘦臉孔。但過了片刻，他又看見許多對眼睛了，連電燈光也在旋轉。他掙扎着，終於支住桌子站起來。「我醉了，」他認輸地說。他只對着同學點一個頭，就踉蹌地走出了冷酒館。

他東歪西倒地在人行道上走了一條多街，忽然想起了家。好像看見一道光，照亮自己的身子，他有點清醒了。「我怎麼會這樣啊，」他懊惱地想道。他掉轉身朝着回家的方向走去。剛走了兩步，一個龐大的黑影迎面撞來，撞得他腦子發響聲，大半個臉發巨痛又發燒，他身子搖幌兩下，差一點跌倒下去。

那個人兇狠地罵了兩三聲，他沒有聽進耳去，仍舊歪歪斜斜地走了。他想走得快，可是他心裏很難過，似乎有一肚皮的東西在向前翻騰。他還想忍耐，但他終於張開口，噴泉似地吐出了他先前在家裏吃的晚飯。

他覺得吐夠了，也不揩乾淨嘴，便又往前走。那酒臭連他自己也厭惡。他只想回家靜靜地睡一覺。他恨不得兩步就走到家。可是他心越急，腳越是走不快。走了大半條街他又吐了。這次吐得不暢

again. Some of the food seemed to have stuck in his windpipe and he could not dislodge it. His strange behavior drew the attention of several bystanders, but he paid no attention to them. In fact, he would not have cared, perhaps not even noticed, if someone had dropped dead next to him.

Two women walked out of a brightly-lit Lower-Yangtze style restaurant.* By chance, his eyes fell on their heavily made-up faces. Shocked at what he saw, he quickly turned away. Too late. His movements were rather slow, and the older of the two women had spotted him and called him by name.

Ignoring her, he headed toward the darkness. But his stomach was uncooperative. He threw up again along the sidewalk. The amount was minimal, but the effort pained him from his stomach to his palate. Only gradually could he straighten up. To catch his breath, he had to lean against an electric light pole.

Again someone was calling his name, this time softly. A woman's profile came into view. His eyes blurred with tears, he saw only a shadow against the light. But that was enough for him to recognize Shu-sheng.

"What's the matter with you?" she asked.

Breathing hard and staring at her, he did not know where to begin his long story. He was speechless.

"Are you sick?" she asked again.

His breathing improved but now he was overcome by emotion. Tears rolled down his cheeks and he shook his head in denial. They were tears mixed with gratitude and sorrow, different from those which had accompanied his vomiting earlier.

---

* This type of restaurant offers food other than the local Szechwan variety.

快了，彷彿未吐盡的飯菜都塞在他的喉管裏，他心裏又燒得難過。他用力掙一下，才吐出一口來，他一路走，一路嘔。過路人中有幾個好奇地看着他。那些眼光並不曾引起他的反感。周圍的一切都跟他不相干了。這時候就是有人死在他旁邊，他也不會掉頭去看一眼。

可是就在這時候兩個女人從一家燈光耀眼的下江飯館裏談着話走出來。他的眼光無意地觸到他們的粉臉上，他吃了一驚，連忙別開頭。他的動作十分不靈活，兩個女人中年紀較大的一個已經把他看清楚了。她叫了一聲：「宣。」

他不答應她，卻大步走向黑暗的地方去。但是走了不多遠，整個身體已經不由他控制了，他就站在人行道的邊沿上彎着腰吐起來。他大聲嘔着，吐出來的東西不多，可是心卻像被煎熬似地難過，滿口都是苦味。他慢慢地伸直身子，靠着旁邊一根電線桿喘氣。

「宣，」他聽見這一聲柔和的呼喚，他不自覺地掉過臉去，他眼裏淚水模糊，她又背了光立着，他匆促的一瞥，只看見她一個輪廓，但他自己認出樹生來。「你怎麼哪？」她驚問。

他喘氣，望望她，覺得有滿肚皮的話，不知道怎樣說起，實在也說不出一句話來。

「你生病嗎？」她關心地說。

他搖搖頭，覺得氣順了，但他很傷感，眼淚又流了出來，先前的淚水是嘔吐時掙出來的，現在流的卻是感激與悲傷的眼淚。

"Why aren't you home? Look at the way you vomited," she commented sternly.

"I am drunk," he admitted in a regretful tone.

"Why did you get drunk? You never drank before. Hurry up and go home before you become really sick," she said anxiously.

"I was very moody and depressed. A classmate invited me to drink with him. That's why I got drunk," he explained apologetically. "You'd better go on your way; I'm going home now." Staggering, he left the pole and walked across the street.

"Be careful, don't fall down. I'll walk you home." She went up to him and grasped his left arm.

"Really?" he said diffidently, hardly looking at her.

"If I don't, you'll probably go drinking again," she replied, smiling. He felt warm and comforted.

"I'll never drink again," he promised her, very much like a child promising his mother to be good. He allowed her to support him as she accompanied him home.

VIII

WHEN they reached the dark cave-like entrance of the apartment building, he knitted his eyebrows together, reluctant to enter.

"You can't see too well," she said. "Be careful, walk slowly." But instead of leaving, she clung a little closer to him, still supporting him under the arm.

「你怎麼不回家去？看你吐得這樣難過！」她又說。

「我喝醉了，」他悔恨地答道。

「你怎麼跑去吃酒？你本來不會吃的。快回家去躺躺，看真的鬧出病來，」她着急地說。

「我心裏煩，碰到一個同學拉我喝酒，就醉了，」他抱歉似地解釋道。「你也回去吧，我走囉。」他覺得好了些，便離開電燈桿走下街心去。身子仍然在搖搖幌幌。

「當心，看跌倒的，」她在後面大聲叮囑道，馬上又跟着他走下去，她走到他身邊，說聲：「我送你回去，」便挽着他左膀往前走了。

「你真的送我回去？」他聲音發顫地問道。但膽怯地看看她。

「我不送你，我怕你又會跑去吃酒，」她含笑地說。他感到一絲暖意，心裏也舒服多。

「我再也不喝酒了，」他孩子似地說，便讓她扶着他走回家去。

八

走到大門口，看見那個大黑洞，他就皺起眉頭，躊躇着不進去。

「你看不清楚，當心，慢慢走啊，」她並不離開他，反而偎得更緊，她關心地囑咐他，一面用力抬他的膀子。

"How about you? Won't you come in?" he asked eagerly.

"I'll walk you upstairs," she whispered.

"You're very kind," he said gratefully, wishing to embrace her and tell her his troubles. But taking one look at her, he lost his nerve and wordlessly climbed the familiar stairs. "Be careful," she reminded him again, supporting him with all her strength and making him walk very slowly. Secretly pleased at her concern, he assured her he would be careful.

As they stepped off the last step onto the third floor landing, they saw a neighbor, the one married to the civil servant, coming out of her room with a lit candle in her hand.

"Mrs. Wang, you're back!" the pale woman greeted Shu-sheng with a pleasant smile.

Moving somewhat away from her husband, Shu-sheng nodded to the friendly neighbor and asked, "Mrs. Chang, are you going out?"

Mrs. Chang asked in turn, "Is Mr. Wang ill?"

"No, he had a bit too much to drink, nothing serious," Shu-sheng answered, while her husband remained silent at her side.

"My Mr. Chang is a little high, too. I'm going out to buy a few tangerines. Mrs. Wang, you'd better accompany Mr. Wang inside; he should be all right after a nap," said the little woman with a sincere smile. Whenever she smiled, the wrinkles on her forehead became more visible and her eyebrows came together. Every time Shu-sheng saw her, she felt sorry that life had so unfairly burdened this little woman. Before the dim candlelight disappeared completely, Wang and his wife reached their own apartment.

He pushed open the unbolted door. The room was still damp and

「你勒？你不進去？」他耽心地問。

「我陪你上樓去，」她在他耳邊小聲回答。

「你真好，」他感激地說了一句，他想摟着她高興地哭一場。可是他只看了她一眼，就默默地低下頭，移動腳步，走進大門，踏下他極熟悉的台階。「當心啊，」她不斷地在他旁邊說，她還用了全力支持他。可是她的扶持只有使他走得更慢。「上樓啊，」她又在叮囑，他暗暗高興地又答應了一聲。

他們終於走上了三樓，剛踏完最上一級樓梯，就看見隔壁那位公務員太太拿着一支蠟燭從房裏走出來。

「汪太太，你回來哪！」那個蒼白臉的女人含笑招呼道。臉上露了一點驚訝的表情，不過人可以看出來這是帶善意的。

她把身子略為離開他一點，她對這溫順的女人點頭笑了笑，然後應酬說：「張太太，你下樓去？」

張太太一面應着，一面驚奇地看了他一眼，溫和地問道：「汪先生有甚麼不舒服嗎？」

他垂着頭站在妻子身旁，答不出話來。她代他答道：「不是，他吃了酒。」

「我們張先生也吃醉啦，我出去給他買幾個廣柑。汪太太，你快陪汪先生進去吧，讓他睡一會兒就好的，」小女人親切地微笑道，她的笑容並不是虛假的，不過就在笑的時候，她額上幾條憂鬱的皺紋還是十分顯露，雙眉也沒有完全開展。「這個小女人，生活把她壓得太苦了！」汪太太每次看見她，就要起這憐憫的念頭。小女人走着慢步子下樓去了。他們夫婦藉着她那燭光，走到房門口。

門並沒有上閂，他一推，門就大開了。屋裏還是那樣陰暗，蠟

dark, the candle still on the table, and his spectacled mother was still sitting by it, mending clothes. She looked so old, and her back so hunched. She was completely quiet, as if she had stopped breathing. Though the candlewick needed trimming, she had not bothered to trim it. It looked as though she had not stirred for quite some time.

"Hsüan, where have you been? Why didn't you tell me where you were going? Did you go to look for that woman? You are too much.... I told you to forget her. Women nowadays can't take suffering." Not looking up from her work, she assumed that her son had returned alone. "Hsüan, don't feel sorry for yourself. It's quite all right that she has left you. When the war is over and when you become rich, you won't have to worry about getting a woman!" Her son failed to respond. Raising her head in the darkness, she felt that her eyes were very dry. So she stopped her sewing, took off her glasses, and lightly rubbed her eyes.

When he heard his mother calling Shu-sheng "that woman," he grimaced. He tightly clasped his wife's hand, fearful that a quarrel might erupt between the two women. But his wife remained unruffled. At last he burst out in a pleading and sorrowful voice, "Mother."

"What's the matter?" responded his mother. This time she had a good view of "that woman" standing next to him.

"I walked him home," Shu-sheng said in a deliberately calm manner.

"Fine," his mother said scornfully to him. "You are really something. You even had the nerve to invite her here." She began to sew again. Shu-sheng smiled disdainfully, saying, "He didn't invite me. I don't know where and how he got drunk, but I saw him vomiting all over the streets and making a fool of himself. So I walked him home." She used these words intentionally to hurt his mother.

燭仍然點在方桌上，母親仍舊坐在方桌旁，戴着眼鏡，補衣服。她顯得那樣衰老，背彎得那樣深，而且一點聲息也不出。燭芯結了小小的燭花，她也不把它剪去。她好像這許久都沒有移動過似的。

「宣，你那裏去了？也不先對我講一聲。是不是又去找那個女人？你也是……我勸你還是死了心吧。現在的新派女人，那裏會長遠跟着你過這種苦日子啊？」母親一面說話，一面動針，她並沒有抬起頭來。她還以為她兒子是一個人回來的。「宣，不要難過，那個女人走了也好。將來抗戰勝利，有一天你發了財，還怕討不到女人！」她沒有聽見兒子回應，便關心地抬頭一看，她滿眼金光，甚麼也看不出來，眼睛乾得十分難過。她放下針線取下眼鏡，用手在眼皮上揉了幾揉。

他在他母親說到「那個女人」時，便痛苦地皺了皺眉，一面伸手去緊緊捏住他妻子的一隻手，他害怕他妻子會同他母親吵起來。可是他妻子始終不作聲。到這時他不能再忍耐了，便叫了一聲：「媽！」聲音裏含着懇求與悲痛。

「甚麼事？」母親驚問道。她把手從眼睛上拿下來。這次她看見了，在他的身旁就站着那個女人！

「我陪他回來的，」樹生故意裝出安靜的樣子說。

「好，你本領大，你居然把她請回來了，」母親冷笑道，她又埋下頭動起針線來。

樹生帶着輕蔑的微笑看了母親一會，她略略歪着嘴，最後她說：「並不是他去請我回來的，他不曉得在哪裏吃了酒，在街上到處亂吐，我看見，才送他回來的。他走路都走不穩了。」她故意用這樣的話來折磨那個母親。

"Hsüan, why didn't you say something before you left? Why go out drinking?" his mother roared. She was so furious that she walked up to him and glared at him. "You never drank before, so why start now? Don't you remember that your father died an alcoholic? You were never allowed to touch a drop since childhood. Why did you do it?" she screamed hysterically.

"He doesn't feel well, so why don't you let him go to sleep?" Shu-sheng cut in.

"I wasn't talking to you ," she snapped back.

Shu-sheng sneered, pouting, but she remained quiet.

"Hsüan, tell me how you became intoxicated, tell me," she said, speaking as if to a child who had always been doted on and from whom she intended to coax the truth.

Exhausted and weary, he said nothing.

"Go ahead and tell me! What's bothering you? Tell me and I won't blame you," she continued to urge him.

"I didn't feel well, so I thought I'd take a little drink," he answered honestly.

"How did you meet her?" she pressed him for an answer. Her bias toward Shu-sheng made her oblivious to her son's painful situation.

"Why don't you let him go to sleep?" Shu-sheng spoke again, this time more sharply.

Ignoring the young woman, the mother continued to demand a full explanation from her son.

"I... I...," he stuttered, searching for words. In his nauseous state

「宣，你怎麼不給我講一聲就偷偷跑出去吃酒？」母親差不多驚得跳起來，她把衣服針線全丟在桌上，走到兒子面前，她仔細地看他。「你不會吃酒嘛，怎麼忽然跑出去吃酒？你不記得你父親就是醉死的！我從小就不讓你沾一口酒。怎麼你還要去吃！」她歇斯特里地大聲說。

「他心裏難過，你讓他睡覺吧，」樹生打岔道。

「我沒有跟你講話！」母親掉過臉帶怒地搶白道。

樹生冷笑一聲，賭氣地不響了。

「宣，你告訴我你怎麼吃酒的，」母親像對一個被溺愛慣了的小孩講話似地柔聲說。

他疲倦地垂着頭不答話。

「你說訝！你心裏有甚麼事，你說呀！」母親催促道。「你儘管直說，我不怪你。」

「我心裏難過，我覺得還是醉了好些，」他被逼得失了主意，老老實實地答道。

「那麼你甚麼時候碰到她的？」母親還不放鬆地追問，另一種情感使她忘了她兒子的痛苦。

「你讓他睡吧，」樹生忍不住又插嘴說了一句。

母親不理睬，還是要兒子回答。

「我——我——」他費力吐出了這兩個字，心上一陣翻騰，一股

he lost his control and threw up again, spattering his mother and himself with food remains.

Forgetting her questions, his mother said, alarmed, "Quick, sit down!"

His wife patted him on the back and his mother gave him a stool to sit on. He finally spat out the rest. Then he sat panting, his hands on his lap.

"Why on earth all this suffering?" Shu-sheng said in pity.

Relenting, her mother-in-law said to her, "You put him to bed, and I'll get some ashes to sweep the floor."

Shu-sheng helped him to bed, quietly removing his shoes, socks, and clothes, something she had not done for him in years. He was as submissive as an obedient child. She covered him with a quilt, and when she turned around, he stretched out one arm from inside the quilt and held her right hand tightly.

"Sleep well," she comforted him.

"Don't leave me; whatever I did was because of you," he entreated, gazing at her with wide-open eyes.

She did not answer him but stood by the bedside for a long time, lost in thought.

Gradually he fell asleep, but he did not let go of her hand for a long while. She stayed for the night. His immediate problem was thus solved without his even being aware of it.

He had a restful night. When he awoke the following morning, much to his surprise and joy, he found his wife dressing in front of the little table by the window.

"Shu-sheng!" he called out, utterly happy in his surprise. She turned to him, smiling broadly, and asked softly, "Are you getting up?"

力量從胃裏直衝出來，他一用力鎮壓，反而失了控制力量，張開嘴哇哇地吐起來。他自己身上和母親身上都濺到了他吐的髒東西。

「你快坐下來，」母親慌張地説，她把她那些問題全拋在腦後了。

他仍舊立在原處彎着腰嘔吐，他妻子給他捶背，母親為他拿了櫈子來。他吐出的東西不多，可是鼻涕眼淚全掙出來了。他坐在櫈子上喘氣，兩手壓在兩個膝頭上。

「真是何苦來，」他妻子立在他背後憐惜地説。

「你照料他去睡吧，」母親終於心軟了，讓步地對她兒媳説，「我去弄點灰來掃地。」

母親出去後，妻子便扶着丈夫到床前，她默默地給他脱去鞋襪和外衣。她好些年沒有享過這樣的福了。他像孩子似地順從着。最後他上了床，她給他蓋好被。她正要轉身走開，他忽然從被裏伸出手來將她的右手握住，並且握得緊緊的。

「你好好睡吧，」她安慰他道。

「你不要走啊……我都是為了你……」他睜大眼睛哀求地説。

她不答話。她在思索。她在他旁邊站了好一陣子。他慢慢地睡去了。可是他的手始終沒有放鬆。

這晚上她就留了下來。他的一個難題就這樣簡單地解決了，他自己還不知道。

這一夜他睡得好，直到天已大亮他才醒過來。那時他妻子正坐在窗前小書桌前化粧。

「樹生，」他驚喜地喚道。她回過頭看他，臉上綻出燦爛的微笑。她柔聲問他：

「你起來嗎？」

Nodding, he stretched and said, "Yes."

She continued her toilet. Her hair was curled at the back; to him, this newest style of coiffure was most remarkable. Very lightly she coughed once or twice.

She had come home. It was not a dream. It was a fact.

IX

THEIR life was characterized by domestic tranquility for a little more than ten days. During that time, they went to work each morning and came home about the same time. There was no more talk of leaving home; one day Shu-sheng brought home her suitcase. That same evening, he took her to see an American movie at the Cathay Theater. But because of an air-raid warning, the movie was canceled after only one third of it had been shown.

Avoiding both her son and daughter-in-law, the mother kept to herself in her own room. When she ran into Shu-sheng, she was cordial but had little to say.

When Hsiao Hsüan came home from the boarding school one Sunday morning, the old woman ecstatically helped him into his coat, the one she had mended with so much care and affection. On this occasion Shu-sheng and she even exchanged a few kind words.

A constant drizzle kept the sky dark and gloomy, the streets and the sidewalks wet, muddy, and slippery. Half a month quickly went by. One day Wang fell at an intersection, bruised his left knee, and

他點點頭，伸一個懶腰，滿意地答道：「起來。」

她又轉過頭去繼續化粧。她腦後燙得捲起的頭髮在他眼裏顯得新鮮而好看。他輕輕咳了一聲嗽。

她回來了。這並不是夢。這是真實的事。

九

這一對夫婦過了十多天平靜的生活。兩個人都是按時上班，按時回家。妻子也不再提起離開的話，連那個箱子也從友人家拿了回來。就在拿回箱子的晚上，丈夫陪了妻子在國泰戲院看過一次美國電影，可是剛看到三分之一，就因警報台上掛出一個紅球而停演了。

母親常常躲在她那個小房間裏。她似乎故意避開她的兒媳，不過兩人遇在一處時，她也並不對樹生板面孔，説諷刺話。她只是少講話罷了。

星期日早晨小宣回家，下午搭最後一班汽車回學校去。祖母見到孫兒，特別高興。她自然把她親手補好的大衣給小宣試穿了。為了這件大衣，她的兒媳也對她含笑説過幾句話。

天永遠是陰的，時而下小雨，時而雨停，可是馬路始終沒有全乾過。有時路上佈滿泥漿，非常滑腳，人走在上面，很不容易站穩。人行道上也是泥濘的。半個月很快地過去了，他汪文宣某一天上午去公司辦公，剛走到十字路口就跌了一跤，把左邊膝頭皮擦破

limped all the way to work. He was early, but Uncle Chung was already there, sitting at his desk and watching the passers-by in the street. When Chung saw him he asked, "What's the matter? Did you fall?"

He nodded. Without saying a word, he signed his name on the roll sheet and headed for the stairs.

Concerned, Uncle Chung asked him, "Why don't you take a day off? Don't overwork and make yourself sick."

Wang, who by then had reached the staircase, turned around and replied softly with a forced smile, "You know I don't make enough to be able to take any cuts."

"In times like this, why do you still worry about such things? Don't you know that there aren't many working days left?" Chung grumbled, slightly agitated.

"What can we do? They only pay us a pittance," he replied with a weary smile.

"But our jobs aren't permanent," Chung replied.

"What do you mean?" He moved closer to Chung's desk, startled. "What have you heard?"

"The Japanese have occupied Kweilin and Liuchow. If they take Kweichow province, the Managing Director of the Company has indicated that he will move the whole operation to Lanchow. In fact, he has already wired Lanchow about space for a possible relocation. If that happens, we'll all be dismissed," Chung gloomily predicted.

Darkness enveloped his vision; Wang was dumfounded. In disbelief, he responded, "No, that wouldn't happen! It couldn't."

一塊，他忍住痛，一歪一拐地走到公司門口。還沒有到辦公時間。鍾老坐在辦公桌前，兩眼望着街上行人。看見他進來，便問：「你怎麼啦？跌了跤嗎？」

他點點頭，不答話，簽到後就往樓梯口走。

「你請天假吧，不要把身子累壞了啊！」鍾老關心地說。

他在樓梯口站住了。回過頭無可奈何地笑了笑，輕輕地答道：「你曉得的，我有多少薪水好扣啊！」

「這個時代，你還耽心扣薪水！你還要替店裏拼死命！你知道我們還能夠在店裏吃多少天飯！」鍾老埋怨地說，帶了點激動。

「有甚麼辦法！我們既然吃店裏的飯，」他疲倦地答道。他想笑，卻笑不出聲來。

「店裏的飯？我們這個不是鐵飯碗啊，」鍾老冷笑道。

他吃了一驚。連忙走近鍾老的辦公桌，小聲問道：「你聽到甚麼消息嗎？」

「日本人打下了桂林、柳州，來勢很兇啊。聽說總經理有過表示，要是敵人進了貴州，就把公司搬到蘭州去，他已經打電報到蘭州去找房子了。要是真的搬到蘭州的話，甚麼事都完了。我們這般人還不是只好滾蛋！」鍾老發牢騷地說。

會有這樣的事！他發呆了。他眼前一片黑暗。他疲憊地搖着頭說：「不會吧，不會吧。」

"It's hard to say. With employers like that, anything is possible. For instance, there are the laggards who do little or no work and draw large salaries. On the other hand, hardworking people, like yourself, receive practically nothing." Noticing the approach of Chief Editor Chou, Chung lowered his voice to whisper, "Why is he coming to work so early today? You'd better go upstairs."

He did. As he passed the Section Chief's desk, he noticed Wu examining him from head to toe with an icy stare that made him shiver through and through. Apprehensively, he walked to his desk, full of self-pity for himself and because of his un-ending work. "How useless I am! These people never graduated from college; they write rubbish, and yet I am intimidated by them!"

His aching knee made it difficult for him to concentrate. He thought of home, his job, his conversation with Uncle Chung, and the war. From time to time his family troubles loomed so large and complex that he hadn't had time to read the newspaper. In fact, even when he learned about the army's setbacks — the fighting in the northern part of Hunan, the fierce battle for Hengyang, the fall of Changsha and of Ch'üan-chou — he did not become alarmed. His own problems were so burdensome that for years he had not had a chance to think about other matters. Many people told him the future would be better, but his experience proved otherwise.

The lunch bell startled him and woke him from his tangled thoughts. Looking up, he saw a co-worker standing by him asking him to contribute to a birthday party for Chief Editor Chou. Though his other co-workers had each signed for a thousand *yüan*, he knew the sum was beyond his means. When he hesitated, his co-worker, unsympathetic and impatient, cleared his throat contemptuously. He quickly and timidly signed for a thousand *yüan*. Satisfied, the co-worker left. When he stood up, his knee, his bones and muscles all began to ache.

「也說不定。不過他們那種人甚麼事都做得出來。就拿店裏來說：一些人一事不做，拿大薪水；像你整天拼命賣氣力，卻只拿那麼一點錢，真少得可以！」鍾老還沒有把話講完，看見周主任大步走進來，便收了話頭，低聲對他說：「他今天怎麼來得這樣早！……你上樓去辦公吧。」

他沒精打采地上了樓。他走過吳股長辦公桌前，吳股長忽然抬起頭把他打量了一下，看得他毛骨悚然。他膽戰心驚地走到自己位子前坐下，攤開那部永遠校不完的長譯稿，想把自己的腦子硬塞到那一堆黑字中間去。「真沒有出息啊，他們連大學都沒有畢業。文章都做不通，我還要怕他們！」他暗暗責備自己，可是他仍然小心翼翼地做他的工作。

腿不斷地痛着，他的思想不能夠集中，他不知道自己一上午幹了些甚麼事。他想到家，想到這裏的工作情形，想到剛才鍾老的話。他好些天沒有看報了。他個人的痛苦佔有了他全個心，別的身外事情再也引不起他的注意。過去，湘北戰事爆發，長沙淪陷，衡陽苦戰，全州失守，都不曾給他增添一點苦惱。生活的擔子重重地壓着他，那幾年他一直沒有暢快地吐過一口氣。周圍的一切跟他有甚麼關係呢？人人都在對他說，世界大局一天一天在好轉，可是他的日子卻一天比一天地更艱難了。

開飯的鈴聲驚醒了他，把他從那些思想的糾纏中打救出來。他仰頭吐了一口氣，一個同事馬上走到他面前，說聲：「你簽個字吧，」就攤開一張信箋在他桌上。他吃驚地一看，原來是同事們發起的給周主任做壽的公啟，每人名下攤派一千元。一千元，這是一個不小的數目，他躊躇一下，但那個同事輕蔑地在旁邊咳嗽了。他惶恐地立刻拿起筆簽上自己的名字。那同事笑了笑走開了。他站起來，覺得不僅左膝還在發痛，連週身骨頭都酸痛了。他勉強支持着下樓去吃中飯。

In the lunch room, others were busy discussing the latest war situation and the enemy's intentions. Uninterested in their conversation, he wolfed down his lunch and got up. Shivering all over, he suspected he had malaria. His friend, Chung, noticing his paleness and strange behavior, suggested he take the afternoon off, go home, and rest.

He acknowledged he was not feeling well, and asked his friend to request a half-day's leave for him. Just as he stepped out of the office building, a rickshaw approached. Chung suggested that he take the rickshaw.

"No, I am all right," he replied. "It's not far; I can walk slowly." He summoned up all his energy and crossed the street.

He walked slowly. His head drooped low, as if a millstone were tied around his neck; his injured knee made each step an effort. All his physical ailments attacked him simultaneously. Bearing his discomfort in his head and knee, he walked to the vicinity of the International Café. By coincidence, his wife was admiring the cafe's display window and talking to the young man in the handsome overcoat. Without any idea that he was nearby, she followed the young man into the café.

His wife's back, more attractive than ever, made him acutely aware of her voluptuousness, her youthful-looking body. Although they were the same age, he was thin, weak, fatigued, and unsteady in his movements. They seemed to belong to two different generations, and he, clearly, was not a fit mate for her.

The very idea was agonizing. And the young muscular man standing by his wife's side only sharpened the contrast. The young man seemed so much more suitable than he for his wife, the young man having a great deal in common with her. And when the young man and his wife stood together, they looked like an ideal couple. The

在飯桌上同事們激動地談論着桂柳的失陷，和敵人的動向。他低着頭吃飯，不參加討論，也不傾聽他們談論。他覺得渾身發冷，疑心是「擺子」發作了。他放下碗離開飯桌，鍾老望見他，便走過來說：「你不舒服吧？臉色很難看，下半天不要辦公了。回家去睡個午覺也好。」

他感激地點一個頭，回答道：「那麼就請你替我請半天假吧；我自己也覺得精神不大好。」他便走出門去。一輛黃包車正拉到門前，車夫無意地看了他一眼。鍾老在門外勸道：「你坐車回去吧。」

「不要緊，路很近，我可以慢慢走，」他回過頭答道，便打起精神走下馬路，到對面人行道上去。

他走得很慢。身子有點飄飄然，頭變得特別重，不時要往頸上縮。走路時左膝的傷處仍在痛，但他咬緊牙關，三步一停地埋着頭走，終於走了一大段路。前面就是國際了。他忽然聽見一個女人的聲音。那明明是他的妻子在說話。他吃驚地抬起頭。果然是她，她正同那個穿漂亮大衣的年青男子站在玻璃櫥窗前，看裏面陳列的物品。但她馬上跟着那個人進裏面去了。她沒有看見他，也不會想到他離她就只有三四步的光景。

他看到她的背影，今天她的身子似乎比任何時候都動人，她豐腴並且顯得年青而富於生命力。雖然她和他同歲，可是他看看自己單薄瘦弱的身子和一顛一簸的走路姿勢，還有他那疲憊的精神，他覺得她同他相差的地方太多，他們不像是同一個時代的人。

這樣一想，他感到一種鋒利的痛苦了。那個身材魁梧的年青男人使他苦惱。她和那個人倒似乎更接近，距離更短，她站在那個人旁邊，倒使看見的人起一種和諧的感覺。他的心不安靜了。他本來

sharp contrast between him and his wife's companion distressed him to no end. Having already passed the café, he returned to it to admire the expensive items adorning its display window: luscious birthday cakes, American coffee, chewing gum, and chocolates. Most impressive! And the English words "Happy Birthday" inscribed on the flowery decoration of a large creamy cake reminded him of his wife's birthday in two weeks. He would like to buy her a cake. Had she and her companion looked at the display window with the same thought in mind? He wondered. Yet he could not afford the cake. The price tag was prohibitive: sixteen hundred *yüan* for a mere four-pound cake. He counted his money and realized that all he had was a little over eleven hundred *yüan*, nor did he forget the amount he had to contribute to Chou's party the next day. He cast aside the dream of the birthday cake, resenting that he could not afford even a pound of it while his rival could easily buy the whole cake. He entered the café and lingered by the candy counter, pretending to look at the different varieties of sweets and other refreshments. He found his wife and her companion, she sipping coffee leisurely, smiling pleasantly and responding warmly to her escort's comments. Disgusted and despondent, he walked out.

On his way home, he struggled to maintain his balance on the slippery road, with his head aching and his mind in torment. Finally he got home.

His mother, in her apron, her sleeves rolled up, was washing clothes by the square table. As usual, she asked, "Did you eat?"

"Yes, I did," he answered without much spirit. He forced himself to join her for a while.

"Why are you home so early? You look terrible. Are you sick?" she

已經走過了那個咖啡店，現在又轉回來，也站在櫥窗前，看看裏面放着些甚麼東西。大蛋糕、美國咖啡、口香糖、巧克力糖，真是五光十色。他們在看甚麼呢？——他想。Happy Birthday，蛋糕的奶油面上紅花綠葉中間現出這兩個紅色的英文字。他忽然記起來還有半個多月便是她的生日。他們剛才在看的，是不是這生日蛋糕呢：那個年青男人是在準備送她的生日禮物嗎？可是他自己呢？他又有甚麼禮物送給她？他不自覺地把手伸進衣袋裏去了。他掏出一把鈔票來。他低下頭數了一數，一千一百幾十元！這是他的全部財產。他明晚還得拿出公宴主任的份子錢一千元。他再看蛋糕，他看見旁邊一張白紙條，上面寫着：「四磅奶油大蛋糕法幣一千六百元。」他嘆了一口氣。他連一磅也買不起，多寒傖！他躲避似地掉開了頭。他剛把身子轉開，忽然想到：「他一定買得起的。」這個「他」指的是裏面那個年青人。這思想傷害了他。他已經走過了咖啡店，又回轉來，走進大門，站到玻璃貨櫃前，假裝着在看裏面陳列的糖果點心，卻偷偷側過頭朝咖啡廳看去。樹生正拿起杯子放到唇邊小口地呷着，她臉上帶着笑容。妒忌使他心裏難過。他又害怕她會看到他。他不敢再停留，便急急地走出大門。

一路上他只覺得心在翻騰，頭在燃燒，他耽心自己會倒在這傾斜不平的泥濘路上。他總算支持着到了家。

母親穿了圍裙，立在方桌前挽着袖子洗衣服，抬起頭驚訝地問他一句：「你吃過飯沒有？」

「吃過了，」他疲倦地答道。他勉強地在母親旁邊站了片刻。

「你今天怎麼回來得這樣早？臉色又這樣難看！你不舒服嗎？」

worried aloud. Taking her hands out of the tub, she dried them on her apron, insisting, "Go to bed, take a nap, hurry up." Supporting him, she practically forced him to his bed.

"I am not sick," he persisted, though he was unable to stand once he reached the bed. Without taking off his shoes, he fell into it.

"Take off your shoes. You will feel more comfortable," she said, standing by the bed.

He struggled to get up, but couldn't. He groaned.

"Go to sleep. I will take your shoes off." She bent down to untie his shoelaces and removed his shoes. With his eyes closed he lay in bed. Then she straightened up and looked at him. "Let me cover you with a blanket." She did so before he could even answer.

"I am afraid I have chills and a fever," His face and lips were as pale as a sheet of white paper.

"Go to sleep. In a little while, I will give you some quinine," she consoled him. Despite his discomfort, he noticed that she had a few extra wrinkles on her face and that her hair was completely gray. She had changed so much since she came to Szechwan. Now all she did was cook and wash, never complaining, never abandoning him. "She really is good," he thought gratefully.

Later, she gave him three quinine tablets and put the remaining half glass of hot water on the table.

"Mother," he called after her in an appreciative tone, tears welling up in his eyes. He looked at her and couldn't speak for some time.

"What's the matter?" she asked affectionately.

"You are too kind... too good to me... ," he said haltingly.

母親吃驚地說，她把兩手從盆裏拿出來，在圍裙上揩乾了。「快去睡下來，快去睡下來！」她半扶半推地把他送到床前。

「我沒有病，」他還在解釋，但到了床前他再也支持不住，連鞋子也不脱去，便倒下來。

「你把鞋子脱掉，舒服點，」母親站在床前說。

他掙扎着剛要坐起來，馬上又力盡似地倒下去了，同時他發出一聲痛苦的呻吟。

「你好好睡，我給你脱，」母親說着，她真的彎下身子去解他的鞋帶。他閉着眼睛躺在床上。母親把兩隻皮鞋都脱掉了。她伸直身子帶着痛苦的關切望他的臉。「我給你蓋床毯子吧，」她又說，便把那幅疊好放在床腳的毛毯整來打開，蓋在他的身上。

他睜開眼睛望着她，有氣沒力地說了一句：「我恐怕在打擺子。」他的臉色白得像一張紙，連嘴唇也是灰白的。

「你睡吧，你只管睡你的，等一會兒我給你吃奎寧，」母親安慰他說。她臉上的皺紋顯得更多了。頭髮也好像沒有一根是黑色的了。她剛回到四川來的時候完全不是這個樣子。現在她自己燒飯，自己洗衣服，這些年她也苦夠了。完全是他使她受苦的。可是她始終關心他，不離開他。「她真是好母親啊，」他暗暗地讚道。

後來母親拿三粒奎寧丸給他吞下了。她把剩下的半杯白開水放到方桌上去。

「媽，」他感激地喚了一聲，淚水已充滿眼眶了。他無力地望着他母親，半晌說不出話來。

「甚麼事？」母親又走到床前俯下頭親切地問道。

「你真好……你對我太好了……」他斷斷續續地說。

"Go to sleep. Say these things when you are well," she comforted him.

"Mother, I am really all right. I asked for a half-day's leave today, but tomorrow I must go to Mr. Chou's birthday party."

"Only half a day! You must take several days off. Don't worry about money."

"No matter what, I must go to the party tomorrow; otherwise my co-workers will belittle me for not keeping my word."

"So what? Why should you care what they think? Who is Chou anyway?" she replied, seething with anger. A moment later, she asked abruptly, "Have you seen Shu-sheng?"

"Yes, I just saw her," he said without thinking.

"Why didn't she come home with you? She could have taken a day off. Since she is as pretty as a flower-vase,* she doesn't have to worry about her salary being deducted." Her jealously and hatred of the young woman boiled up again, without knowing how each word was like a knife piercing his heart.

He looked at her dully for some time and then smiled painfully. As if speaking to himself, he remarked sadly, "She's too much of an angel; I don't deserve someone like her."

"You don't deserve her?" his mother responded sharply. "She doesn't deserve you! If she really works in a bank, why does she dress up like a socialite every day? Why? Who knows what she really does?"

His only reply to his mother's outburst was a deep, sad sigh.

---

* A derogatory reference to someone who loves to dress up at the expense of everything else.

「你睡吧，這些話等你好起來再說，」母親和藹地安慰他。

「我不要緊，」他搖搖頭無力地說。他看見母親並不注意聽他的話，又解釋道：「我只請半天假。明天他們公宴周主任，給他做生日，我還要去參加。」

「你只請半天假？」母親不以為然地說。「其實你可以多休息一天，不必去耽心扣不扣薪水。」

「我明天一定要去，不然他們會看不起我，說我太『狗』，想賴掉份子錢，」他用力說，臉都掙紅了。

「狗不狗是你自己的事，跟他們有甚麼相干？周主任又不是甚麼了不起的人！」母親氣憤地說，過後忽然又問一句：「你看見樹生嗎？」

「我剛才還看見的，」他不加思索地回答。

「那麼她不陪你回家？她很可以請假來看護你，她們當花瓶的，不必怕扣薪水，」她的妒忌和嫌恨又被引起來了，她只顧發洩自己的怒氣，卻沒有想到她的話怎樣傷了他的心。

他呆呆地望着母親，過了一會才露出一個微笑（多痛苦的微笑！），他自語似地低聲說：

「她，她是天使啊。我不配她！」

母親只聽清楚他後一句話，她氣惱地接嘴說：

「你不配她？明明是她不配你啊？說是在銀行辦公，卻一天打扮得妖形怪狀，又不是去做女招待，哪個知道她一天辦些甚麼公？」

他不答話，只是痛苦地嘆了一口氣。

X

HE slept fitfully all afternoon. Toward seven in the evening he awoke in discomfort, covered with cold sweat. He wanted to change his underwear, but the slightest movement brought a severe pain to his limbs, as if all his joints were about to come apart. He moaned.

"Are you awake? Do you feel better?" his mother asked.

That evening the electricity was on, and in its pale yellow light his mother's face looked ill, drawn, and fragile.

"Not bad," he answered. "Where is she?" His tired eyes widened, searched the room.

"She? Shu-sheng?" she replied scornfully. "She hasn't been back since morning."

"She should be home by now," he sighed after a while.

"Yes. Shouldn't she?" When she saw her son remained silent, she changed the subject. "Would you like something to eat?"

"No, I'm not hungry."

"Wouldn't you like some porridge? I made it specially for you. We have some preserved beancake which should go well with it."

"Maybe I could eat one bowl," he said gratefully, forcing a smile.

She happily fetched a bowl from the cupboard and filled it with porridge from an earthen pot simmering on a small clay-stove near the door.

He told himself once again that he had a very good mother. His

十

他昏昏沉沉地睡了一個下午，將近七點鐘他才醒過來，躺在床上，沒有一點氣力，汗背心濕透了，冷冰冰的貼着背上的肉。他知道自己淌了不少的汗，便動了一下身子，想把汗背心從肉上拉開，又想起床找一件汗背心來換過。可是他剛把身子一動，就覺得渾身酸痛，好像骨頭全脫了節似的，他不由得發出一聲呻吟。

母親走到床前，問他：「你醒來了？不舒服嗎？」

這一晚沒有停電，黃黃的電燈光塗在母親的臉上，她的臉也帶着病容。並且她顯得多麼孤寂，多麼衰弱！

「還好，」他答道。他睜大疲乏的眼睛，在屋子裏各處找尋。「她不在？」他失望地問道。

「她？你在說樹生嗎？」母親輕蔑地說，「早晨出去到現在還沒有回過來。」

「她也該回來了，」過了片刻，他才嘆息道。

「是啊，她哪天不該早回來？」母親氣惱地接嘴道。她看見他不做聲，便改了口問他：「你要不要吃點東西？」

「我不想吃，我不餓，」他說。

「吃點稀飯好不好，我給你煮的。家裏還有腐乳，可以拿來下稀飯，」母親說。

「吃一碗也好，」他感激地說，勉強笑了笑。

母親滿意地轉身到碗櫥前，拿了一個碗，又從門邊小泥爐上瓦罐裏舀了稀飯。

「究竟是自己母親好，」他小聲對自己說。他的心不像先前那樣

mind felt less troubled than before. He tried to get out of bed when his mother brought in the porridge and the beancake.

"Don't get up, you can eat in bed. I'll hold the plate for you," she said.

He sat up and took the bowl and chopsticks from her. As he ate, she held the plate with the beancake for him.

He had no appetite. To please her, he finished the bowl of porridge. She then gave him a moist towel to wipe his face, and again told him to rest.

He lay down, still with his clothes on. He wanted to stay up for his wife; he felt she should be home shortly.

A few minutes later, someone knocked on the door. "Is Mr. Wang home? Here's a letter from Miss Tseng."* Wang became nervous. "Where did the letter come from?" asked his mother. But the messenger left without answering her.

He saw his mother with the letter in her hand. She was standing stock-still like a block of wood, not knowing what to do. He called her and she came to him, murmuring with a feigned casualness, "She sent you a letter. I don't know what's up." Then she mumbled, "Miss Tseng? Her son is already thirteen years old. How shameless to call herself Miss Tseng!"

"Let me see what she wrote," he said, reaching for the letter. She had no choice but to give it to him.

He opened the letter, which was in Shu-sheng's handwriting. It read: "Hsüan, Friends have invited me to a dancing party at the

---

* Shu-sheng's maiden name.

空虛了。他正要拿出勇氣抬起身子下床去，母親已經把稀飯和腐乳端過來了。他說：「你不要起來，就坐在床上吃吧。我給你拿着碟子。」她等他坐了起來，就把飯碗和筷子遞給他，自己在旁邊端了碟子守着他吃。

他並沒有胃口，但為了母親的緣故，也勉強吃了一碗稀飯。他吃完飯，母親又拿了臉帕來讓他揩了臉，說：「你還是睡下吧，今天不要起來了。」

他聽從了母親的話，又躺下去，但他不肯脫去衣服，他還想醒在床上等候樹生回來，他覺得她馬上就會回家了。

有人在敲門，離他躺下的時間不過四五分鐘。母親把門拉開。一個男人的影子閃進來，粗聲說：「汪先生在家嗎？曾小姐有封信給他。」他驚了一跳。他聽見母親在問：「哪裏送來的？」可是沒有人回答，送信人已經退出去了。

他看見母親把信拿在手裏，呆呆地立在房中，彷彿不知道應該做甚麼似的，他忍不住，叫了一聲「媽」。母親立刻走過來，用一種不在意的口氣對他說：「她送了封信來，不曉得又有甚麼事情。」她並不把信交給他，只顧自己咕嚕道：「曾小姐？兒子都有十三歲了，還好意思叫曾小姐，真不害羞！」

「讓我看看她寫些甚麼話，」他說聲，便伸出手去拿信，母親只好把信遞到他手裏。

他接過信，戰戰兢兢地拆開來讀。是樹生的親筆，寫着：

宣：

朋友約我參加今晚勝利大廈的舞會，我恐怕會回來很晚，對不

Victory Building. I will be home late. Sorry. Please don't stay up for me and don't bolt the door. Don't tell Mother, so I don't have to listen to her moralizing tomorrow. Shu-sheng."

He read the letter and said nothing. Clutching it in his hand, he gazed at the ceiling as if lost in thought.

"What does she say?" his mother inquired impatiently.

"She's having dinner at a classmate's. She has some business to take care of and will be home late," he answered in a monotone.

"What business if it isn't going to the theater, playing mah-jong or dancing? What serious business could she have? When I was a daughter-in-law, did I ever dare go carousing like she does? Her own son is nearly an adult, and she is even an education major." *

"She does not play mah-jong," he defended his wife. Little did he know he was irritating his mother all the more.

"All right, can you deny that she plays cards? You are sick, but where is she? She doesn't even come home to look after you."

"She doesn't know I am sick. If she did, she'd have come home early," he replied, continuing his defense of his wife. He imagined he saw his wife's beaming face in front of him.

"You are too soft. She's mean to you, yet you protect her. Do you know why she has a bad temper? It is because you have spoiled her. If I were you, I'd teach her a lesson when she comes home tonight," she shouted, one of her fingers pointing at his forehead.

---

* According to a traditional way of thinking, anyone who majors in education is supposed to be a moral person, at least more moral than those who major in other subjects.

起，請你不要等我，也不要閂上門。不必對母親說我去跳舞，省得明天聽她發一番陳腐議論。

樹生　即晚

他看完信，一聲不響，信紙還捏在手裏，他望着天花板像在思索甚麼事情。

「她信上怎麼說？」母親不能忍耐地問道。

「她在一個同學家吃飯，說是有點事情，回來要晚一點，」他聲調平平地答道。

「甚麼事？還不是看戲、打牌、跳舞！你想她還有甚麼正經事情！我做媳婦的時候哪裏敢像她這樣！兒子都快成人了，還要在外面胡鬧，虧她還是大學畢業，學教育的！」母親咕嚕地抱怨道。

「她倒並不打牌，」他不知道母親這時候的心情，卻只顧自語似地替他妻子辯護，他並沒有想到他的辯護反而增加母親對樹生的惡感。

「不打牌？她不是打外國紙牌嗎？你生病她也不趕回家來看一下，做太太的規矩也沒有！」母親又說。

「她不曉得。如果曉得，一定早回來了。其實我這並不算生病，」他繼續替他妻子解釋，他眼前彷彿幌動着樹生的帶笑的臉孔。

「你這個人心太軟。他對你那樣不好，你還是要替她講話。我說，她那些脾氣都是你養成的。我要是你啊，她今晚上回來，我一定要教訓她一頓，」母親指着他的前額大聲說。

"It won't do any good to have unnecessary quarrels between husband and wife. Many times minor squabbles lead to big problems."

"What are you afraid of? She keeps boyfriends, and she certainly doesn't act like a married woman," she replied sharply.

Unable to convince her of his viewpoint, he groaned in frustration. His discomfort softened her and she began to wonder how ill he really was.

In one last effort to win her over, he shook his head. A little while later, he said emphatically, "Mother, Shu-sheng is not a bad woman."

The old woman quickly understood the implication. In a resentful tone she replied, "If she's not a bad woman, then I must be one. Is that it?"

"You misunderstood me, Mother," he said, beseeching her for sympathy. "I'm not protecting her."

"Who said you were!" said she, with a faint smile on her face, her anger gradually subsiding. "As far as I can see, she has completely bewitched you."

"No, it's not that. Both of you are good, and I'm the worthless one, because I make both of you suffer. No one knew that we would be so poor. You cook, you wash clothes.... " He stopped, choked with tears.

"I don't hold you responsible for our poverty. If it weren't for the war, we wouldn't be like this!" she said, averting her eyes from him whose sunken cheeks and sickly complexion were so different from what they had been. "I heard that we'll win the war next year. That will be good, for otherwise... ," she commented randomly, hoping to cheer him.

He interrupted, "Mother, did you say victory? The enemy is getting closer, and we may even have to flee from here."

「夫妻間吵架多了，也不大好。常常為了點小事會鬧出大問題來的，」他小聲答道。

「你怕甚麼，這又不是你錯。明明是她沒理，她不守婦道，交男朋友——」

他忍不住痛苦的呻吟一聲，母親吃了一驚連忙把下面的話嚥在肚裏了。她俯下頭看他，關切地問：「你怎麼啦？」

他搖了搖頭，過了半晌，才無力地吐出一句：「媽，她不是一個壞女人。」

母親聽着這意外的答話，起初有點不懂他的意思，但馬上就明白過來了，她略帶惱怒地說：「她不是壞人，那麼我是壞人吧。」

「媽，你不明白我的意思，」他着急地央求道。「我並不是在袒護她。」

「那個說你袒護她！」母親臉上微微露出笑意來，她的怒氣漸漸地消失。「我看，她把你迷住了。」

「不是這樣說，」他認真地解釋道，「你們都是好人，其實倒是我不好，我沒有用，我使你們吃苦。想不到我們現在會過着這種日子，你自己燒飯……洗衣服……」他覺得一陣鼻酸，眼淚迸出來了。他哽咽着，再也接不下去。

「不要講了，你好好睡吧。這不怪你，不打仗，我們哪裏會窮到這樣，」母親溫和地說，她心裏也難過。她不敢多看他：他臉色那麼難看，兩邊臉頰都陷進去了，他們初到這裏來時，他完全不是這樣。她記得很清楚：他臉頰很豐滿，有血色。「聽說戰事明年可以勝利了。這倒好，不然大家都——」這句話是隨便講的，她這樣說，只是為了安慰他。可是他不等她說完，便打岔道：

「媽，你說勝利？看着敵人就要打過來了，說不定我們馬上就要逃難……」他說到這裏又忽然耽心起來。

"Who told you that?" she asked, surprised but not really alarmed. "I heard that the Japanese were only interested in pillaging a few places in Hunan and Kwangsi, and that they would retreat after achieving these short-range goals."

Since he had no solid information on the subject, he was inclined to believe her. Though what she said sounded plausible enough, nonetheless, he answered, "I'm not sure about that. Someone in the office said that our whole Company might move to Lanchow if the military situation worsened."

"Lanchow? That desolate place? Who would go there? Isn't that like going into exile? The rich have no guts; they are more easily frightened than rats. The Japanese haven't bombed here for two years. I don't see how they can get here." She rattled on and on, as if searching for a subject through which she could release her pent-up wrath against her hedonistic daughter-in-law.

"I thought so too, but it's hard to tell." Looking fixedly at her as if he had found in her face some support in his loneliness and doubts, he added, "Mother, you'd better rest a while. You are tired."

"No, I am not." Sitting on the edge of the bed, she exchanged a few pleasantries with him. At last she said, "We have survived the last few years, but who knows what the future brings. I am so concerned about Shu-sheng.... " She had actually whispered the last few words, but he heard them clearly enough. The problem of his wife truly worried him. After a long while, he sighed and pressed his lips tightly together.

His mother sat by him until she assumed that he was asleep. She left him and then returned to put a chair against the back of the unbolted door. After switching off the light, she retired to her own room.

「你聽見哪個說的？」母親吃驚地問，但她並不懼怕。「沒有這樣嚴重吧。他們都說日本人這次打湖南、廣西，不過搶點東西。他們自己會退的。」

「那就好，」他帶點疲倦地回答，母親的話又使他心安了。他並沒有自己的明確的看法。他覺得她的話也很中聽。他又說：「我也弄不清楚，不過公司裏有人在講，時局不好，公司方面有搬到蘭州去的意思。」

「蘭州，那樣遠的地方！又不是充軍，哪個願意去！住得好好的要搬家，那些有錢人膽子比耗子還小。日本人這兩年炸都不敢來炸，哪還有本事打過來！」母親只顧在咕嚕，彷彿要把她對媳婦的不滿(因為兒子的緣故，她忍了一半在心裏)另外換一個對象盡量發洩出來。

「我也是這樣想，不過這些事也難說，」他答道，他的眼光定在母親的臉上，彷彿在寂寞徬徨中找到了一個支持。他感激地又說：「媽，你歇一忽兒吧。你太辛苦了。」

「我不累，」母親又換了語調，溫和地答道，她在他床沿上坐下來。

「你現在舒服了吧？」她問他。

「好多了，」他答道，可是他覺得非常疲乏，但又沒有一點睡意。人不能說是舒服。

「這幾年總算是熬過去了，以後不知道還要過些甚麼日子。我耽心的就是樹生——」她低着頭一個人自言自語，說到樹生這名字，她的聲音立刻低到除了她自己以外，再沒有人聽得清楚。但「樹生」這兩個字他一定聽見了的。他半響不開口，忽然小聲嘆了一口氣，又把嘴閉上了。

母親在床沿上坐了一會，又站起來，望了他一兩分鐘，見他閉上眼不出聲息，以為他睡熟了，便輕手輕腳地走出去。過了一陣她又進來，掩住門，不上閂，卻端了一把椅子抵住門，關了電燈，然後回到她的小屋子去。

Restless images of his wife appeared before him. He was not asleep but merely kept his eyes closed so his mother would leave him alone. His wife seemed to be smiling and crying; she was either angry or morose. Aching all over and drenched in sweat, he was very tired, but his ears kept listening for his wife's footsteps.

The room was dark. A streak of light from his mother's room enabled him to see the chair by the door. As the minutes passed, he wondered why his wife wasn't home and why his mother was still awake and coughing periodically. He felt sorry for his hard-working mother, while bemoaning how late the evening was.

It was the second watch. He heard a watchman's rattle* striking twice. She would surely be home soon. He strained to catch every sound both from within and outside the room. He heard the rats running outside in the corridor and inside the room. One stopped by the foot of his bed. What could it be doing? Was it biting his shoes? His five-month-old shoes had holes like those in a broken sieve, for the rats had twice attacked them. If they were attacked once more, he would not be able to wear them. Every night before he went to bed, he put his shoes on top of an old trunk, but ill as he was tonight, he had forgotten to take that precaution. He sat up, reached for his shoes, and saved them from a premature end, for the rats fled in an instant like a puff of smoke.

Lying down again he told himself that he must go to sleep. As he closed his eyes, he thought he heard the sound of high heels on the upstairs. But listening more attentively, he realized it had been his imagination. "Why isn't she home?" he kept wondering.

Many restless moments went by. He dozed on and off, his sleep

---

* An instrument used to sound the watch.

他其實並不曾睡熟。他閉上眼睛，只是為了使他母親可以放心地回她的小屋去休息。他不能睡，他的思想活動得厲害，他前前後後想了許多事情，在那許多事情中間總有一個女人的臉龐在搖幌。她時而笑，時而哭，時而發怒，時而憂愁。他累極了，頭痛起來，出了一身汗。他的耳朵始終在等着一個人的腳步聲。

房間暗而不黑，從母親房裏透出一線微光。他的眼睛看得清楚房門口的椅子。「她」為甚麼不回來？母親在咳嗽，她還不睡！她老人家太辛苦了。時候應該不早了吧。

是的，街中二更的梆子響了。「她」快回來了吧。他注意地傾聽着門外的聲音。有聲音了。老鼠在走廊上跑着。並且房裏也有老鼠了。牠似乎跑到他的床腳就停住了。牠在做甚麼？牠在咬他的皮鞋嗎？他那雙穿了五個多月的皮鞋已經遭過兩次難，鞋口被咬成像一隻破碗的缺口似的。牠再來光顧一次，他就無法穿它們上街了。每天晚上他臨睡時，總得把皮鞋放到床下一口舊皮箱上面。今天他忘了做這件事，現在他不能靜靜地躺着不管。他連忙抬起身子伸手去拿皮鞋。老鼠一溜煙跑掉了。他不知道皮鞋究竟被咬着沒有，但是他仍舊小心地放它們在皮箱上。

他又躺下來。他對自己說：我應該睡了。可是剛閉上眼睛，他就覺得他聽見了高跟鞋走上樓梯的聲音。他急急地睜開眼睛傾聽。甚麼也沒有。「她」為甚麼還不回來呢？

他終於睡去了，不過並不是熟睡，他迷迷糊糊地過了十幾分

accompanied by unpleasant dreams in the midst of which he started to cry and woke up. Finally, he could not even doze any more. There was no light now in his mother's room and the street was quiet. A little later he heard the sad and lonely voice of an old man hawking hot water* and fried rice-cakes. He knew the voice well. The old man unfailingly solicited customers in his shrill voice every night regardless of the weather. But tonight that shrill voice seemed to send a gust of cold wind under his warm covers. He shivered.

And then came the patter of high heels with which he was so familiar. She had come home at last.

Softly humming the tune of a popular Western song, she quietly pushed open the door and switched on the light.

Blinded by the electric light, he opened his eyes just enough to squint stealthily at his wife. She wore an excited smile, her lips were red, her face soft and tender, and her eyebrows well-defined. Her head tilting slightly upwards, she stood in the center of the room, reminiscing about the good time she had had. As she turned to look at him, he quickly closed his eyes.

She walked over to him, and he could smell her heavily scented body. When she saw that he was partly outside of the covers, she tried to adjust the quilt and noticed he was fully dressed.

"You went to bed without taking your clothes off. Were you waiting for me?" she asked gently with a smile.

He merely nodded, for he did not know what to say.

---

* The Chinese often drink warm water which has been sterilized by boiling. In many parts of China in the past there used to be shops which sold the drink.

鐘，醒了。沒有女人的腳步聲。他又睡了，不久又醒了。他做着不愉快的夢。有一次他低聲哭醒來，就再睡不着了。那時他母親房裏已經熄了燈，他也無法知道時候的早遲。街上相當靜。一個老年人用淒涼的聲音叫賣着：「炒米糖開水」。這聲音是他聽慣了的。那個老人常常叫賣一個整夜，不管天氣怎樣冷。這一次他打了一個寒慄，好像那衰老的聲音把冷風帶進了被窩裏似的。

就在這個時候他聽見熟悉的高跟鞋走路的聲音了。「她」到底回來了。

她輕輕推開門，走進屋子來，口裏哼着西洋曲子，打開了電燈。

這時的電燈光非常強。他的眼睛被刺痛了，但是他還微微睜開它們偷看她。她的臉上帶着興奮的微笑。嘴還是那樣地紅，眉毛還是那樣地細，臉還是那樣地白嫩。他在屋子中間站了片刻，抬着頭不知在想甚麼，過後忽然掉過眼光來看他。他連忙閉上眼睛裝睡了。

她卻緩緩地走過來，走到他床前。他聞到脂粉香氣。她俯下頭看他，她替他蓋好被。她發覺他沒有脱外面衣服，便輕聲喚他。他只好睜開眼睛，裝着從睡夢中醒來的樣子。

「你不脱衣服就睡了，你是在等我嗎？」她親切地含笑問。

他不知道應該怎樣回答她，卻默默地點了點頭。

"I told you not to stay up for me. Why didn't you listen to me?" she said, smiling.

"I've had some sleep already," he explained awkwardly. There was such a lot he wanted to say but he simply did not know how.

"Did you show my letter to Mother?" she asked in a very low voice.

He shook his head.

"Did she say anything?"

"No, since she didn't know. Did you have a good time?"

"It couldn't have been better," she said with obvious pleasure. "I haven't been dancing for such a long time, so it was lots of fun. I changed clothes at a friend's house; there wasn't time to come home." She swung herself around once to give him a demonstration of her dancing skill.

"How many people did you dance with?" he asked, smiling reluctantly.

"First with some American officers, but mostly with Department Chief Ch'en."

"Oh," he exclaimed unhappily, envying her youthful body. Department Chief Ch'en, he thought, must be the young man with whom she had had coffee at the café.

"You undress and go to sleep. You're really too good to me," she said, smiling at him tenderly. Then she sat down at the desk to brush her hair in front of the mirror.

In the deep recesses of his mind, he reasoned: "Shu-sheng has not had a change of heart. She has done nothing wrong; she should

「我說過叫你不要等，你怎麼還等呢？」她說，不過她露了一種感激的表情。

「我也睡了一覺，」他笨拙地答道。他心裏有許多話，卻沒有勇氣說出來。

「你沒有把我的信給媽看？」她又問，聲音更低。

「沒有，」他搖搖頭回答。

「她沒有說甚麼？」

「她不知道，」他答道，卻問了她一句：「你今晚上跳得痛快吧？」

「痛快極了，」她得意地說，「我好久不跳了，所以興趣特別好。我還是在朋友家裏換過衣服去的，來不及回家了。」她昂起頭，輕快地把身子旋轉了一下。

「你同哪幾個人跳？」他問道，勉強裝出笑容來。

「我也跟美國軍官跳過，不過還是跟陳主任跳的次數多，」她並不告訴他，陳主任是誰。

「啊，」他答了一聲，他想：陳主任大概是那位同她在國際喝咖啡的年青人吧，他苦痛地望着她那充滿着活力的身體。

「你好好脱了衣服睡吧，你對我太好了，」她溫柔地對他一笑，安慰他說，過後便走到書桌前坐下來，對着鏡子弄她的頭髮。

「她對我還是很好，她沒有錯。她應該有娛樂。這幾年她跟着我

have some fun. She has also been suffering a great deal during the last few years." At this, he turned to the wall and shed tears of shame.

XI

HE rose earlier than his wife the next morning. Despite his mother's objections, he was determined to attend the birthday dinner for Chief Editor Chou. For one thing, his job could depend on his attendance; for another, his co-workers would call him a cheapskate. And above all, he must keep his word. After breakfasting with his mother on a bowl of yesterday's porridge, he left the apartment with her, for she was going to market. Shu-sheng had arisen and was putting on her make-up.

Once in the street, his mother looked at him so closely that it aroused his suspicions. When they were about to separate, she said hesitatingly, "You can't go on living like this; you're sacrificing yourself for the family."

He frowned, and after a few moments said mildly, "What alternative do I have? Don't you sacrifice yourself just as much?"

"But she has such a happy life! Every morning when she goes to work, she dresses herself as though going to a wedding party," she exploded.

He remained silent.

"Hsüan, let me say something. She is not your type. Sooner or later, she will leave you."

過得太苦了。」他這樣想着，便翻一個身把臉轉向牆壁，落下了幾滴慚愧的眼淚。

十一

第二天上午他起身比他妻子早。母親要他在家多躺一天。他不肯。他說他精神很好，而且今天得去參加給周主任祝壽的公宴，他不去，同事們會以為他窮或者吝嗇，會更加看輕他。母親也放棄了她的主張。他陪着母親吃了一碗昨夜剩下來的稀飯。母親上街去買菜，他同她一塊兒出去。那時樹生，他妻子，還坐在書桌前化粧。

走出大門，母親關切地看了他一眼，他不知道母親懷着甚麼心思。兩人走了一段路，快要分手了，母親忽然聲音顫抖地喚着他說：「宣，你這樣下去是不行的，你要為家庭犧牲你自己了。」

他皺了皺眉，過了一兩分鐘才低聲說：「不這樣又有甚麼辦法？你還不是一樣吃苦？」

「可是她，她過得快活啊，上辦公還要打扮得那樣摩登，像去吃喜酒一樣，」她忍不住爆發地說。

他低下頭不出聲。

「宣，我給你說，她跟我們母子不是一路人，她遲早會走她自己的路，」她又說。

Some time later he replied, "But we've been married for fourteen years already."

"Yes, but what kind of marriage has it been?" she said contemptuously.

Annoyed by her scornful remarks, he left her at the intersection and went to work.

Uncle Chung greeted him at the office, saying, "You came back too soon! You should have stayed home for another day!" Uncle Chung rubbed his chubby hand over his shiny bald head.

"I am fine," he answered pleasantly with a smile, sensing his friend's concern for him. Old Chung had shown a genuine concern without making him feel inferior.

As usual, as soon as he was upstairs, he began to work on the unintelligible translations: exotic words and phrases, line after line, page after page, none of which made any sense to him. He had no right to change any of that; he was hired to check for typographical errors only. After an hour on the job, he started to feel chills running up and down his spine while his head began to burn with fever. Since there was nothing he could do, he kept murmuring to himself over and over, "I must work; I need the money." He continued working until noon.

For lunch he had a bowl of rice. I have to eat, he told himself. Ordinarily the hulled rice* sold at the official rate was not too distasteful, but on this day it was especially hard for him to swallow. Once he had a bowl of rice, he walked to the building's entrance and stood there for a while. The street held little interest for him.

---

* Low quality; cheap rice.

他停了半晌才回答一句：「她跟我結婚也已經十四年了。」

「你們那種結婚算甚麼結婚呢！」母親輕蔑地說。

他覺得這句話有點刺耳，心裏不高興，就閉緊嘴不再做聲了。

母親也不再說甚麼，他們分道走了。

他到了公司。還是鍾老帶着笑臉跟他打招呼。「怎麼不多休息一天？今天又來得這樣早！」鍾老說着，一面用肥大的手摸自己的發光的禿頭頂。

「我沒有甚麼病，我很好，」他笑答道，他在鍾老的眼光和態度中看出了憐憫，那老人在可憐他，他並不覺得受侮辱。他說了兩句閒話，便走上樓去。

單調的工作又開始了。永遠是那些似通非通的譯文，那些用法奇特的字句。他沒有權修改它們，他必須逐字校讀。他坐下不過一點多鐘，他就覺得背上發冷，頭發燒，他不去管它。「就為了幾個錢啊！」他不時痛苦地暗暗唸着。他勉強工作到十二點鐘。

他沒有胃口，可是他對自己說：「我至少應該吃一碗飯，我沒有生病啊。」他便走下樓去，在飯桌旁坐下，他果然吃完了一碗飯。碾過的平價米在平日吃起來倒不怎樣難吃，今天卻有點難下嚥了。放下碗，他立在門前看街景，站了一會，他覺得毫無趣味，便回到樓上辦公桌前去。

He returned to his desk. Shortly after he resumed his task, a servant handed him a letter. With pleasure he noted it was from his son; eagerly he read the letter: "The school announced some time ago that, due to inflation, every pupil must pay an extra three thousand two hundred *yüan* to cover rising costs. I knew you had no money so I didn't ask you for it, but the school just announced that deliquent pupils would not be allowed to sit for the final examinations. I must have the money. Please send it in three days."

The joy of reading his son's letter was gone as his eyes looked at his son's unevenly written script. "We have paid more than twenty thousand already and they still want more. Where is the money going to come from?" he moaned. No one noticed him.

"A school is not a store," he cursed. "Profits should not be the only goal. China has allowed people like this to run schools, and this is the result." The letter lay in front of him, requiring a response.

"I must talk to Shu-sheng and see what she can do about it," he mused. "I'd better go and find her."

"No," he thought, changing his mind. "It's best to leave it till this evening. She may not be in her office now, and I'm very tired and don't want to move."

He carefully put the letter in his pocket and resumed his work.

The translation he was working on read like bundles of hempen cord in his tangled mind. Extremely tired, he wanted to shut his eyes and forget all about it, or lay his head down and take a nap, but he did not dare to leave his work. Chief Editor Chou and Section Chief Wu were looking at him sternly all the time (or at least he thought so), and he dared not raise his head.

"Oh, Lord! How did I become so worthless! I take everything, I

他坐在自己位子上隨意翻了翻文件，又把看過的校樣整理好。工友送了一封信來。他看信封上的字，便知道是小宣從學校裏寄來的。他好像得了一點安慰似的，輕輕吐了一口氣。他把信拆開了：

……先生説：物價高漲，我們這期收的圖書費伙食費都不夠。每個人還應該補繳三千二百元，説是多了以後還可以退回來。很多同學都繳了。我知道爸爸很苦，沒有多的錢，不敢向爸爸要。不過先生又來催了，催得很厲害，説是不繳錢，今年不准參加學期考試。我只好向爸爸媽媽要求，請爸爸媽媽三天內把這筆錢寄到學校裏來……

僅有的一點安慰也消失了。他的眼光定在那幾行稚嫩的字跡上。「已經繳過兩萬多了，還要補繳，那裏來的錢！」他低聲抱怨道。沒有人注意他。

「學堂又不是商店，只曉得要錢怎麼成！中國就靠那班人辦教育，所以有這種結果！」他憤怒地小聲罵道。信紙冷冷的躺在他面前，不回答他。

「同樹生商量，看她有沒有辦法，」他想道；「那麼現在去。」

「現在不好，還是晚上吧，」他又想說，「她也許不在行裏，我也累，不想多動。」

最後他把信紙摺好放回在信封內，又鄭重地把信封揣在衣袋裏面。下半天的工作又開始了。

還是那些疙裏疙瘩的譯文，他不知道是哪一個世界的文字。它們像一堆麻繩在他腦筋裏糾纏不清。他疲乏極了。可是他不能丟開它們。他覺得渾身不舒服起來。他很想閉上眼睛，忘掉這一切，或者就伏在桌子上睡一覺。但周主任和吳股長的嚴厲的眼光老是定在他的臉上（他這樣覺得），使他不敢偷懶片刻。後來他連頭也不敢抬起了。

「天啊，我怎麼會變成這樣一個人啊，我甚麼都忍受，甚麼人都

endure everything, everyone thinks he has the right to bully me. Shall my life be forever spent on this kind of trash? Money, it's money that has made me so despicable!" he protested to himself silently.

But what was the use of protesting? He had said similar things to himself thousands of times, but no one was aware of his resentment. To his face as well as behind his back, he was known as a "Softy," a man with an easy-going nature who never "made waves," and for years he had been nothing more than that.

"I wasn't like this before," he thought to himself. "Shu-sheng, Mother, Hsiao Hsüan, and I didn't live like this before. I'm finished. Contentment, pleasure, the very meaning of my life have been robbed by the war; and those beautiful slogans, proclamations, and lofty words are no substitute. If the Japanese are defeated soon enough, perhaps I can still salvage something of my life. But how is this possible? They have even entered Kwangsi ... and now they are threatening Kweichow."

He dared not think further. In fact, he could not. His head ached too much. When he felt his forehead with his left hand, he knew that he was again stricken with the intermittent fever he had become used to getting in the afternoon. Lately he had stopped worrying about it. He was not going to die soon in any event, and he did not have the time to worry about his illness. What galled him was his superiors. Their stern, ruthless attitude made him feel scorned and unwanted. Why should they bully him like that? He was not inferior to any of them. Yet they could fire him if they wanted to without seeming to act inhumanely. But what could he do? In this hilly city he did not have a single influential relative or friend. Before he was recommended for this job by a good man from his home province, he had been unemployed for five months, during which period he was completely dependent upon his wife for financial support. But his benefactor had gone to some other place, and with him had gone his only chance for getting ahead.

欺負我。難道我的生命就該被這些糾纏不清的文字銷磨光嗎？就為了那一點錢，我居然墮落到這個地步！」他心裏發出了這無聲的抗議。

然而沒有用，這種抗議他已經發過千百回了。但誰也沒有聽見，誰也不知道他起過不平的念頭。當面也好，背後也好，大家喜歡稱他做「老好人」，他自己也以老好人自居。這樣的情形也已經繼續了好幾年。

「就是最近這幾年的事。我以前並不是這樣的。以前，我和樹生，和我母親，和小宣，我們不是這樣地過活的。完了，我一生的幸福都給戰爭，給生活，給那冠冕堂皇的門面話，還有街上到處貼的告示標語拿走了。」他的眼光不停地在校樣上面移動，他的心，他的思想卻在另一個地方。

「要是勝利早一點到來，我應該有辦法改善我們的生活情形。……但是日本人已經深入廣西……他們還說要攻取貴州——」

他不敢再往下想。事實上他也不能往下想了。他頭痛得厲害。他拿左手按住他的前額。他還在發燒。發燒，沒有關係。近年來他常常在下午發燒，他已經習慣了。反正他不會這麼早死去。並且他也沒有考慮死活問題的餘裕。那兩對嚴厲的眼睛老是這麼兇惡地望着他。「為甚麼要這樣欺負我？至多我不吃你們這碗飯就是了，我哪一點不及你們！」他曾經這樣想過。但是他離開這個吃飯地方，又到哪裏去呢？他在這山城裏沒有一個居高位或有勢力的親戚朋友，這個小小位置還是靠了一個同鄉的大力得來的。那是在他失業五個月，靠着妻的薪金過活的時候。那個對他有好感的同鄉已經到別的省份去了。他的唯一的希望也失去了。

"I must accept whatever happens just to survive." How often had he used these same words to console himself, and although they never solved his problem, they were again the words that came to him now.

He arrived at the Canton Restaurant shortly after five. Chief Editor Chou, a Cantonese, was partial to his native food. His co-workers, including the guest of honor, had arrived earlier. Unlike most of them, who were sitting in the brightly-lit parlor in a jovial and festive mood, he hid in a corner, ill at ease, occasionally sipping tea.

The Managing Director of the Company, for whom they had been waiting for more than half an hour, arrived in a motorcar and was warmly greeted by everyone. Nervously, Wang joined the reception. The dignified-looking executive, as thin as a monkey, sported a cane in one hand. As a matter of formality, he apologized over and over, "Sorry, I'm late."

"Not at all! Not at all! We just got here ourselves," all replied in unison, except for Wang. He had no intention of saying anything to the "Big Man" who had not even noticed his presence. In time, his co-workers seemed to have forgotten him and left him sitting by himself in a corner.

There were two dinner tables reserved for the party, and when the time came to be seated he could not decide where to sit, as all the others had comfortably sat down already. Uncle Chung, however, had reserved a seat for him and thus spared him from any embarrassment.

Many of his co-workers, following the customary practice, went over to the other table to drink to the health of Mr. Chou, and of the Managing Director, but Wang did not join them. With the exception of Uncle Chung, no one cared to speak to him. Even Little P'an appeared unwilling to associate with him. He despised their obsequious attitude, and he longed for quiet, for solitude amidst all the toasts and cheerful

「為了生活，我只有忍受，」他常常拿這句話來答覆他心裏的抗議，現在他又拿這句話來對付他的解決不了的問題。

好容易熬到了五點鐘。他停止辦公，倒在靠背椅上養養神，準備到廣州大酒家去參加宴會。周主任是廣東人，所以同事們今天揀了一家廣東菜館。他到那地方時，周主任和別的同事都到了，還沒有入座，說是在等候總經理。大家在燈光明亮的廳子裏興高采烈地談笑。只有兩個人不講話。他自然是其中的一個。他躲在一個角落裏，縮在一把椅子上，用茫然的眼光望着眾人，偶爾端起杯子喝一兩口茶。

等了半點多鐘，總經理坐着汽車來了。他一年中見不到這位瘦得像猴子般的大人物幾面。大人物點着一根手杖莊嚴地走進來，眾人一窩蜂地擁上去迎接着，他多少帶點惶恐地跟在後面。總經理帶笑道歉說：「對不起，我來遲了。」

「不遲，不遲，我們也是才來，」許多聲音一齊說。他沒有作聲，他不想跟那個大人物講話，那個人連看也不看他一眼，別的同事們也好像忘了他的存在似的，仍舊把他拋在角落裏。

擺好了兩桌酒席。就座的時候，大家客氣地讓座，他默默地遠遠站着，那幾個地位跟他的差不多的同事都有說有笑地坐定了。還是鍾老招呼他過去，鍾老給他保留了一個座位。

別人喝酒吃菜，興致非常好。總經理和周主任坐在另外一席。他這一桌的同事們都過去敬了酒，就只有他一個人不曾去。除了鍾老，誰都不理他，連小潘今天也不肯跟他講一句話。他看不慣大家對總經理和周主任巴結的樣子，那些卑下的奉承話使他發嘔。這個

banter. Actually no one had forced him to come, and he now deeply regretted that he had decided to come. He longed to leave the restaurant, but he did not stir from his seat.

Instead, he kept on drinking and responding incoherently to Uncle Chung's small talk. As a wartime measure, wine at banquets was prohibited. But it was an open secret that in restaurants a brown-colored liquor was poured out of teapots. The situation was such that despite the problems it would bring, Wang wanted to get drunk, to have his mind befuddled. He drank as much wine as he would normally drink tea, but he stayed sober throughout the evening. Mr. Chou, the Chief Editor, was drunk, giggling foolishly, and constantly saying things beneath his dignity. When some people started noisily discussing the various forms of after-dinner entertainment, Wang sneaked away.

After leaving the restaurant, he found himself in a quiet street, and though he felt somewhat cold, he also felt he could breathe more easily. With head raised high, he took long strides, inexplicably in high spirits.

Soon he reached home. "I thought I would be sick," he said to himself, "but I'm all right."

"You're home!" his mother said. She raised her head from sewing some underwear for him and smiled.

"Yes, Mother," he answered, his eyes searching for someone else.

"Were you well today? I worried about you all day. You didn't look well this morning," she said, putting the things in her hand on the table, taking off her glasses and rubbing her eyes.

"I'm fine. Why don't you rest a little? You are working at night again," he said.

環境跟他太不相宜了，尤其是在這個時候，他多麼需要安靜。他們並不需要他，他也不需要他們。也沒有誰強迫他到這裏來。可是他卻把參加這個宴會看作自己的義務。他自動地來了，而來了以後他卻沒有一秒鐘不後悔。他想走開，但他連動也不曾動一下。

他一直是埋着頭默默地喝酒。鍾老偶爾對他講兩三句話，他也只是唯唯地應着。説是為了禁酒的緣故，茶房把黃酒斟在茶杯裏冒充茶，免得警察來找麻煩。他現在真的把酒當作茶來喝了，沒有人向他勸酒，可是他自己喝了好幾杯。他知道自己酒量差，他想喝醉，他想使腦筋糊塗，但一直到席終他還是十分清醒。周主任卻醉得只會傻笑，接連講着一些不合身份的話。他趁着眾人吵鬧地糾纏在一起似乎在準備一些游藝節目時，一個人偷偷地溜走了。

他走出菜館，到了冷靜的街上，覺得有點冷，但呼吸卻舒暢多了。他昂起頭大步走着。他的精神似乎很好。

他急急走到了家，他寬慰地對自己説：「我還以為今天會生病，現在倒沒有事了。」他上了樓。他的房門微微開着，母親坐在方桌前做衣服，只有她一個人在等候他。房裏沒有樹生的影子。

「你回來了？」母親問道，她抬起頭親切地對他笑了笑。

「是，媽，」他答道。眼光還在找尋另外一個人。

「你今天不舒服吧。我倒耽心了一天，我看你早晨出去時候臉色不大好，」母親説着，就把手裏的東西放在桌上，又把眼鏡取下來，揉了揉眼睛。

「我很好，你不休息一下？晚上又要做東西？」他說。

She showed him what was on the table. "I am making you some underwear. I found a piece of inexpensive white cloth in the trunk today. Your underwear is so worn I thought I had better make you two suits while I can still sew."

"Mother, you mustn't work so hard. As for new underwear, I have no immediate need for any," he said, touched by her love for him. "The two changes of underwear I have should last me for another three to five months. We can buy new ones later."

"Buy new ones? How can we afford to buy any on your miserable salary? In the last two or three years, you haven't bought even a new pair of socks. You're too good-natured. If I weren't a burden to you, maybe your life wouldn't be so hard. You never think of your own good. In the last few years, you have lost so much weight. You look like you're over forty, and you're getting gray," she remarked, her eyes filling with tears.

"You shouldn't think about such things. Nowadays who doesn't live from hand to mouth? Simply being able to survive is already a blessing," he sighed. "Has she come back yet? " he asked suddenly, changing the subject.

"She? Are you asking about Shu-sheng? She came back, but then left again, saying that she had some business at the bank and that she would be back by ten o'clock." Immediately her tone of voice hardened. "As you see, she's the only one who has a good time. She doesn't care about anything at home, only about being entertained every day." She looked at him closely and asked, with much concern, "Were you drinking today? Not much, I hope? Your health is not good, and you shouldn't drink too much."

"No, I didn't drink much." But while saying this he realized that he had become increasingly uncomfortable and dizzy. His mouth and

她拿起剛才放在桌上的東西給他看：「我在給你做件汗衣。今天理箱子，找出一段平價白布來。我看你汗衣短褲破得實在不像話了，趁着我還能夠動針線的時候給你做兩套換一下。」

「媽，你也不能太累啊。這些東西緩點做也沒有關係，」他感動地說；「我那兩身舊的總還可以穿三五個月，以後我還可以買新的。」

「買新的？可憐你那幾個錢薪水，哪裏買得了？這兩三年你連襪子也沒有買過一雙。你脾氣也不太好了。要是沒有我累着你，你或許不會苦到這樣。你從不想到你自己。這幾年來你瘦得多了，看起來你好像過了四十歲的人，白頭髮也有了好多根了，」母親說着，眼圈也紅了。

「媽，」你不要老想這些事，在這個年頭誰不是過一天算一天，能夠活下去就算好的了，」他嘆了一口氣說。「她沒有回來過？」他忽然問一句。

「她，你說樹生嗎？她回來過，又出去了，說是行裏有甚麼事，十點鐘一定回來，」母親答道，但馬上又改變了語調加添道：「你看就是她一個人舒服。家裏事她甚麼都不管。一天就在外面交際。」她忽然望着他，關切地說：「你今天又吃了酒了，吃得不多吧？你身體差，不宜多吃酒啊。」

「我喝得不多，」他答道，又嘆了一口氣。這時他覺得人不舒服了，頭暈，口和喉嚨都像被甚麼東西在搔着一般。他打算去倒一杯

throat felt as if they were being scratched by a sharp object. He wanted to pour a glass of water for himself, but as soon as he got up and took a step, his body swayed to the right, as though he were about to fall down. He quickly steadied himself.

"What's the matter with you?" she asked in surprise, getting up.

"I had two cups of wine," he admitted reluctantly with a smile. She walked to his side, intending to support him. He shook his head and said, "It's all right; it's all right. I'm not drunk."

"Then go to bed early."

"No, I don't want to go to sleep, I want to wait up for her," he said, sitting down on the rattan chair in front of the desk.

"You want to wait up for her? How do you know when she'll get home?"

"Didn't she say that she would be back by ten?" he rebuked her.

"You can never take what she says seriously. You'd better go to sleep."

"All right, I'll get in bed. It will be good for me to lie down for a while," he said, getting up from the chair.

Dong-Dong-Dong-Dong-Dong-Dong — The siren of an early air-raid warning rang.

"Another air-raid warning. Mother, you'd better leave for the shelter. I don't care to go today," he said, sitting on the edge of the bed.

"If you won't go, I won't either. You'd better lie down. There isn't going to be an air-raid anyway," she replied calmly.

The usually quiet apartment building suddenly came to life. Footsteps reverberated and one could hear the sound of doors being locked.

開水來喝，剛走一步，身子就向右邊歪了一下，彷彿要倒下去似的。他連忙站定，但身子又接連搖幌了兩下。

「你怎麼啦？」母親驚問道，便站起來。

「我喝了兩杯酒，」他勉強笑了笑。母親走到他身邊要扶他。他搖着頭讓開身子接連說：「不要緊不要緊。我沒有醉。」

「那麼你早點睡吧，」母親說。

「不，我不想睡，我要等她回來。」他說着在書桌前那把籐椅上坐下了。

「你要等她？你曉得她甚麼時候回來？」

「你不是說她十點鐘回來嗎？」他反問。

「她的話相信不得。你還是睡吧，」母親催促道。

「好，我睡，我先躺一會兒也好，」他說着就站起來。

噹——噹，——噹——噹，噹——噹。預行警報的鐘聲響了。

「警報囉。媽，你躲一下吧，我今天不想走，」他說，走到床沿上坐了下來。

「你不走，我也不走。你還是躺一下吧，橫豎還沒有『空襲』，」母親鎮靜地說。

本來相當安靜的房屋突然活動起來了。到處都是人聲腳步聲，

In the street, some people were running, others talking or shouting.

"Hey, aren't you coming?" a neighbor shouted.

"No, I am not leaving. The enemy airplanes aren't coming. Why bother?" another answered.

"In the last two days, the enemy has been approaching Kweichow," replied the first. "A big air-raid here is almost certain. At the very least the enemy will try to panic the people. I heard from someone working in a bank that Kweiyang was heavily bombed yesterday. The damage was so severe that the press didn't dare report it. I advise you to go to the shelter."

"All right. We'll go together then."

This exchange was followed by the sound of doors being locked and people walking. Even though the two men were separated from the Wangs by a long corridor, their conversation could be clearly heard by mother and son through the thin walls.

"Mother, you'd better go," he pleaded with her.

"It's all right. It's still just the preliminary warning," she said slowly.

A few minutes later, the sirens became shriller, indicating a greater likelihood that enemy airplanes would bomb the city.

"Mother, it's time for you to leave," he urged her again.

"I'm going to wait for the last warning," she replied. She remained seated.

"If you leave too late, you won't be able to get into any shelter," he warned her anxiously. Getting no response, he suggested that they both go.

"The enemy airplanes may not come. It's so tiring to run to a shelter. If we are bombed to death, it won't make much difference to anyone.

還有關門的聲音。街上有人在跑，還有更多的人在呼喚，在講話。

「××，你不走啊？」隔壁有人在大聲問。

「我不走，敵機不會來，何必多此一舉，」另一個人答道。

「這兩天快打到貴州來了。說不定他們會來一次大轟炸，至少可以擾亂人心。我得着銀行界的消息，昨天貴陽炸得厲害，連報上都不敢登。我勸你還是去躲一下吧。」

「那麼出去走走也好，我們就一路走。」

接着是關門和走路的聲音。雖然中間還隔着一段走廊，但是薄薄的木板牆很容易傳聲。他們的談話全被這母子兩人聽見了。

「媽，你還是走吧，」他懇求道。

「不要緊，現在才是預行，」母親慢慢地回答。

過了幾分鐘空襲警報的汽笛聲突然尖鋭地響了起來。

「媽，走得了，」他催促道。

「我等着放『緊急』再走，」母親答道，她仍舊安靜地坐着。

「我看還是早點走好，遲了怕來不及進洞了，」他略略着急說。母親不曾回答。他忽然站起來，又說：「那麼我們一塊兒走吧。」

「敵機不見得會來，走一趟太吃力，我看還是等着放『緊急』再走好，」母親固執地說。他不作聲了。母親又說：「就是炸死了，也沒

It is sometimes better to be dead than alive," she urged pessimistically.

"Please don't talk like that. We haven't robbed or stolen from anyone or committed any crime. Why shouldn't we continue to live?"

At that moment Shu-sheng came in. She expressed surprise that they had not left for a shelter.

Equally surprised, he asked Shu-sheng why she had come home at such a time.

"I came back to give you the shelter pass. I didn't realize that I had it in my purse until just now."

He took the pass from her and put it into his pocket, from which he took out his son's letter. And then he said, "As a matter of fact, I hadn't thought about the pass. If the last warning hasn't sounded, maybe we won't have to go at all."

Pleasantly, Shu-sheng said to her mother-in-law, "Let's go now. It is best to leave early."

"No, I'm not going. I don't believe that I'll be killed by a bomb," the old woman answered crossly.

Though hurt and embarrassed, Shu-sheng tried to smile and turned to her husband. "What about you, Hsüan? Aren't you afraid of death either?"

"No, I am very tired. I don't care to go," he answered.

"Then I guess I'll have to go alone," Shu-sheng said, feigning cheerfulness.

"Shu-sheng, here is a letter from Hsiao Hsüan about an increase in his tuition fee. The school is asking for an additional three thousand two hundred *yüan*. Won't you please read it?" He gave her the letter.

關係。我們像這樣過日子，還不如炸死好。」

「媽，你不要這樣說，我們沒有搶過人，偷過人，害過人，為甚麼我們不該活呢？」他悲憤地說，他又在床沿上坐了下來。

門被推開，一個女人走進來。「你們還沒有走！」樹生驚喜地說。

「你不躲警報，怎麼跑回來？」他站起來迎着她問道。

「我回來給你送防空證的。我不知道甚麼時候把你的防空證也放到我皮包裏面去了，剛剛發覺了，特地趕回來送給你，」她含笑說道，一面打開手提包，拿出一張卡片來遞到他的手裏。

他感激地對她笑了笑，接過防空證攜在衣袋裏，又從那裏面拿出一封信來。他說：「其實我還沒有想到防空證上面去。要是不發緊急警報，我們就不躲了。」

「現在走吧，」樹生含笑催促他，「早點進防空洞好些。」她又望着母親說。

「我不走，我不信就會炸死，」母親板起臉賭氣似地說。

樹生碰了釘子，怔了一下，但馬上又裝出笑臉對他說：「你呢，你也不怕死嗎？」

「我很累，我不想走，」他疲倦地答道。

「那麼我一個人走了，」她仍然裝出笑臉說，她掉轉了身子。

「樹生，」他想起手裏捏的一封信喚了一聲。

她回轉頭來，他把捏信的手伸向她，一面說：「小宣來的信，他們學堂又要他補繳三千兩百塊錢。你看吧。」

"I'll send him the money tomorrow," she promised briskly. Then she put the letter in her purse and turned to go.

"Can you get the money?" he asked.

"I think so. I may have to borrow it from the bank. I'm better able to do it than you," she replied casually. "You're really not going to the shelter?" Without waiting for a reply she hurried out.

"See how arrogant she is. Only you could put up with her airs," his mother complained. The clickety-clack of Shu-sheng's high-heeled shoes could still be heard on the stairs.

"Yes, but let's not forget that Hsiao Hsüan's tuition depends on her. Without her, he'd have had to stop his schooling long ago. I'm a worthless father," he sighed.

"I'd rather have him stop his schooling than have to put up with her," she replied angrily.

Before he could answer, he felt something stuck in his throat. In an effort to dislodge it, he coughed hard.

His mother went to get some warm water for him, and while she was gone, he spat out some phlegm tinged with blood. Shaken by what he saw, he wiped the phlegm from his arm and from the floor, not wanting his mother to see it .

"It's good that you spat it out," his mother said, giving him a glass of water.

He took a few swallows. "I'm better now. I want to rest a while."

"Then don't undress. It'll be more convenient in case the last warning sounds," she instructed him.

He murmured something in reply and stretched out in the bed.

她走回來，接過信封，取出信箋來看了一遍。她用輕快的聲音說：「好的，我明天給他寄三千五百塊錢去。」他把信放了在手提包裏，又往外面走。

「你不為難嗎？」他問了一句。

「不要緊，我可以向行裏借。我總比你有辦法，」她不在乎地答道，又問他一次：「你不去躲嗎？」但並不等他回答，就匆匆走出去了。

「你看，她好神氣，也是你才受得了！」母親氣憤地說。這時高跟鞋的聲音還在走廊上響。

「不過小宣的學費也虧她。不是靠她，小宣早就停學了。我這個爸爸真不中用，」他嘆息地說。

「要是我，我寧肯讓小宣停學，」母親咬着牙說。

他覺得有一口痰貼在他的喉管上，他用力咳嗽，想把痰咳出來。

「我給你倒杯開水，你忍住一下，」母親說。等她把開水端來時，他已經把痰吐在地上了，不僅地上，他的左手背上也濺了些。他看見痰裏的血絲，心中一冷，同時連忙把手背在衣服上擦，又用腳把地板上的痰也擦去了。

「好囉，咳出來就好了，」母親安慰他說，一面把杯子遞給他。

他接過杯子，大口地喝了幾口，然後勉強裝出笑容，回答道：「是，我現在好多了。」他把杯子放到方桌上去，又說：「我累得很，我想睡一會兒。」

「那麼你不要脱衣服。萬一放『緊急』，跑起來也方便些，」母親關切地叮囑道。

他含糊應着，已經走到床前和衣睡倒下來。就在這一刻，他的

Both his spirit and his physical strength seemed to have been sapped in a single moment. He felt his mother cover him with a quilt.

XII

FROM his dear ones he concealed the fact that he had spat up blood; the next morning he returned to work as usual. Restless from the lack of sleep, he felt lousy, yet he had to face the same boring job, the same unintelligible translations, the hostile looks of Chou and Wu and his co-workers' stony stares. He took every situation in his stride. His heart not in his work, he had no idea of how many errors he found. When he heard the lunch bell, he dropped his pen, sighing as if he were a newly released ex-convict. His appetite was poor, so he ate little and said nothing at the lunch table, suspecting that the others were contemptuous of him. As quickly as possible he left the table. He looked at no one; no one spoke to him.

When he returned to his desk upstairs, it was too early for work. His vision blurred and his brain sluggish, he closed his eyes. He fell asleep at his desk until the noise of his returning co-workers woke him up. He vaguely remembered a few grotesque images and a far-fetched romance he had dreamed, and was annoyed by the interruption.

Chou and Wu were not in, so his co-workers chatted freely. First they cracked jokes; then they talked about the war situation, saying that the Japanese were moving steadily on, meeting little resistance, rapidly approaching I-shan.

精神和體力似乎完全失掉了。迷糊中他覺得母親來給他蓋上了棉被。

十二

他不肯讓母親和妻子知道他吐血的事。第二天他居然有力量到公司去辦公。晚上睡得不好，精神相當差，仍舊是那單調的工作，和糾纏不清的譯文，周主任和吳股長的敵視的眼光和同事們的沒有表情的面孔。他忍受着。他捱着時刻。他的心並不在紙上。他也弄不明白自己究竟校出多少錯字來。聽見開飯的鈴聲，他放下筆，輕輕嘆一口氣，他彷彿就是一個遇赦的犯人，他胃口還是不好，他吃得少，也不講話，他覺得全桌子的眼光都帶着憐憫在看他，他不安起來。好容易放下碗，他又像得救似地噓一口氣，離開飯桌，他不敢看旁人，也沒有誰理他。

他回到樓上，又在辦公桌前坐下。他並不看校樣，還沒有到辦公時間，他用不着多耗費他有限的精力。他的眼光茫然朝四處看。除了白茫茫的一片外，他似乎甚麼也看不見。身體相當倦，腦筋也較往日遲鈍，眼皮漸漸往下垂，頭越來越重。他沉沉地睡去了。

同事們的笑聲驚醒了他。他連忙坐正。頭腦裏還裝了些古怪的影子。他從悲歡離合的夢中醒來了。還有一種悵惘的感覺。

辦公時間近了。周主任和吳股長都不在，同事們高興地講着笑話。忽然一個同事提到戰局，另一個同事跟着報告昨晚得到的消息，空氣立刻緊張起來。日本人不停地向內地前進着，沒有誰來擋住他們。據説敵人已經到了宜山。

"It's not in the papers. How could they advance so rapidly?" Wang argued to himself. He could not and did not want to believe the truth of such shocking news.

"Are you sure? Where did you get the news? The newspapers report that our army is doing quite well at the front," Little P'an questioned skeptically.

"You believe in the papers? Don't you know that news is censored?" the well-informed co-worker commented in a sarcastic tone.

"Yes, I do. A relative who has lived in Kweiyang for four years now says he wants to move here," added another.

"That's nothing. I have a friend whose whole family is going to Lanchow," said still another. "Evacuation is all right if it is done properly."

"That's why our Company is planning to move to Lanchow. I suppose it makes sense from their point of view," the well-informed one said.

"Are you going?" asked Little P'an.

"Me? The Company is not going to take people like us. Do you still have such high hopes?" the colleague replied, even though he was not one of the minor staff and his basic pay was much higher than Wang's.

"Who wants to go anyway? But the Company should give us three months' severance pay," said Little P'an.

"Three months' severance? No. The maximum they'd give is two months' and what can you do with so little money? The Company is a semi-civil organization, so what can we do about it?" replied the well-informed co-worker. As he was about to continue his complaints,

「報上都沒有說，你知道！不會有這樣快！」他汪文宣暗暗地駁斥道。但他只敢在心裏說。今天他不願意聽到任何不好的消息。

「不見得吧。怎麼你的消息倒這樣靈通？報上還說這兩天前方戰況很好呢！」小潘插嘴說。

「你相信報紙？你曉得報上每天有多少檢扣掉的新聞？」那個消息靈通的同事反駁道。

「是啊，這兩天情形的確不妙，我有個親戚在貴陽住家四年了，現在也要把全家搬過來，」另一個同事說。

「這算甚麼。我有個朋友已經定了飛機票就要搬家到蘭州去。要逃索性徹底一點，」又一個同事說。

「所以我們公司要搬蘭州，這就是徹底啊，」消息靈通的同事說。

「你去嗎？」小潘問。

「我去？恐怕公司不會要我們這班小職員去吧。你還存着這個希望嗎？」消息靈通的同事說，其實這同事不能算是小職員，他是出版股的，進公司時間較久，底薪也比較他汪文宣的高得多。

「不要我們，總得發一筆遣散費。多支三個月薪水也好，」小潘滿不在乎地說。

「三個月？我看至多也不過兩個月。拿到那一點錢有甚麼用？逃難不夠用；不逃難更不夠用。況且這種半官半商、亦官亦商的機關——」消息靈通的同事說到這裏，聽見樓梯上的腳步聲，連忙

he heard footsteps on the stairs and quickly shut up after making a face.

Chief Editor Chou returned to the office, officially starting the work for the afternoon. Little P'an returned sheepishly to his desk downstairs.

Wang Wen-hsüan slowly digested what he had heard. The very idea of having to flee or the talk of severance pay meant that he would lose his job, signaling the end of his family and everything he held dear. He remembered what he had heard about the many domestic tragedies which occurred during the Hunan-Kwangsi evacuation, and he was such a helpless, almost useless, person. Was it going to happen to him one day... ? It made his blood run cold just to think about it, but he could not stop worrying. The more he tried to sort out his thoughts, the more confused he became. His work, the hostile stares from Chou, none of these meant anything any more. It seemed as though a familiar voice were whispering to him: Catastrophe! In his fantasy, he had been sentenced to death and he did not even want to appeal.

This horrid daydreaming lasted for about half an hour. His head burned and the fever did not abate for another hour. "It must be tuberculosis since I coughed up some blood last night," he said to himself. "But it won't matter. After all, isn't everyone mortal?" This truism comforted him somewhat and made him less afraid of death; instead, he was overcome by a feeling of sadness.

"I'll die alone. How lonely it is to die!" He wished he could go home and shed his bitter tears in the arms of his mother, his wife, and his son.

By closing time his spirits had become somewhat brighter, and he walked home slowly. At dinner his mother complained as usual about his wife. His reply, also as usual, was noncommittal. Though he knew

嚥下以後的話，同時做出一個可笑的怪相。

周主任來了。整個樓面立刻靜下來。小潘也悄悄地回到樓下去。下半天的工作開始了。

他汪文宣不出聲息地坐在辦公桌前，也不抬起頭。他覺得自己還是在夢中。他的眼睛看不見面前攤開的校樣。同事們的談話佔據了他整個腦子。逃難⋯⋯遣散⋯⋯這是他的毀滅，還有他的家庭⋯⋯湘桂撤退的慘劇，他從別人口中聽到的一切⋯⋯他又是一個這樣不中用的人⋯⋯要是真的到了那一天⋯⋯他覺得一身發冷。他不敢再往下想，卻又不能制止自己。他越想，心越亂。他翻過了兩張校樣，卻沒有把一個字裝進腦子裏去。工作，他已經不關心了。周主任的眼光，他也不再關心了。他彷彿聽見一個熟悉的聲音在他耳邊說：毀滅！他被人宣告了死刑。他沒有上訴的心思。

他昏昏沉沉地過了半點鐘光景。他覺得周身不舒服，頭忽然發燒起來。他用手一摸，是低熱。頭有點暈，幾分鐘，十幾分鐘，半點鐘，一點鐘以後，熱度還沒有退。「一定是肺病，我昨晚還吐過血！」他斷定道。「沒有關係，我反正要死。」他安慰自己。心稍稍安定了。他不再像先前那樣地懼怕。他卻另有一種淒涼的感覺。

「我死，我一個人死，多寂寞啊，」他想着，他恨不得馬上跑回家中，抱着母親，抱着妻，抱着小宣痛哭一場。

到下班的時候，他已經不發燒了。他覺得精神稍微好一點。他慢慢走回家去。

母親在家裏煮好飯等待他。她用慈愛的調子同他談話，問他這一天的工作情形。吃飯的時候，母親談起樹生，又發了一通牢騷。

his mother was not always reasonable, he also knew that Shu-sheng was not completely in the right.

"Since she doesn't eat dinner at the bank, she should come home. You know this yourself. But how many days in the month does she come home? What else could she be doing if she isn't seeing a lover!" his mother burst out as she removed the dishes from the table.

He remained silent. Her words had cut him to the quick. "Why always accusations and enmity! Can't you let me alone? Why can't you love my wife, since you know how much I need her?" he thought, but kept his thoughts to himself. He could not live without his wife, and this dependancy on her made him feel both lonely and uneasy. He got up without a word; pacing the room, he bit his lip lightly.

"Wouldn't you like to see a movie this evening? We are, after all, educated people, and need some entertainment," his mother suggested to him, after she had finished her domestic chores.

"I am tired," he replied. Later he added with a bitter smile. "Intellectuals are a lower class now. Only drug-dealers and smugglers can afford to go to the movies."

The door suddenly was pushed open — Shu-sheng had come home.

As always, he was delighted to see her; routinely he asked if she had had eaten her supper.

"Yes, I have," she answered. "I planned to come home for supper, but a girlfriend insisted on inviting me to eat with her. A funny thing happened at the bank today. I will tell you about it later."

"How radiantly she smiles, and how pleasantly she talks!" he observed to himself. His mother muttered something and went to her small room.

他唯唯地應着，他覺得母親的話有道理，又覺得樹生並沒有錯。

「晚飯她既然不在行裏吃，就應該回家來。你親眼看見的，她一個月有幾天在家？不是去找情人還有甚麼事！」母親收拾飯碗的時候，終於忍不住這樣地直說了。

他不作聲。他不相信母親的話。但是母親的話使他痛苦。永遠是這樣的控訴，仇視。「為甚麼不讓我安靜？既然你愛我，為甚麼也不愛她呢？你知道我多麼離不開她！」他想道。但是他不敢把這答語説出來。「離不開她」四個字傷了他自己，使他感到寂寞。寂寞中又夾雜了一點焦急不安。他默默地站起來，輕輕咬着嘴唇在屋子裏走了幾步。

「你沒有事，要不要去看看電影？我們究竟是讀書人，再窮也該有娛樂啊，」母親做完事情，過來對他説。

「我累得很，不想出去了，」他懶懶地答道。過了半晌，他又帶着苦笑加上兩句：「現在讀書人是下等人。看電影看戲，只有那班做黑貨白貨生意的人才花得起錢。」

樹生推門進來。

「你吃過飯嗎？」他驚喜地問道。

「吃過囉，」她含笑地答道：「我本來想趕回家吃飯的，可是一個女同事一定要請客，不放我回來。今天行裏出了一件很有趣的事，等一會兒告訴你。」

「她笑得多燦爛，聲音多清脆！」他想道。可是母親只含糊地應一聲，就走進小屋去了。

As Shu-sheng was changing her clothes, the electric lights went out. Quickly he looked for matches and the candles.

In the dark, she grumbled, "This town is really disgusting; there are always blackouts."

After he lit the candle and they were surrounded by the shadows it projected, she murmured to herself, "I hate darkness, quietness, and loneliness."

After a few minutes, she said to him, "Hsüan, why don't you talk to me?"

"I thought you might be tired. You had better rest," he replied, forcing a smile.

"No, I am not tired at all. My work at the bank isn't much, and I can do what I like, more or less. The boss has been rather nice to me." Then, frowning slightly, she continued in a different tone, "But when I come home, I always feel cold, lonely, and empty. Lately you haven't talked much to me."

"No, I am always afraid that you might not be in a good mood," he replied, unwilling to tell her the whole truth. In fact, he was afraid of displeasing her by saying too much. During the day, of course, they did not often see each other or have much opportunity to converse.

"You're really a good fellow. You don't feel well, and yet you think of me all the time. You're the type that neglects his own welfare," she laughed, reproaching him lightly.

"Not exactly. I do think of myself," he argued awkwardly.

No noise could be heard from his mother's room. The candle flickered even more, the shadows in the corners darkened, and a child on the second floor coughed and cried. Outside it was drizzling.

她換衣服和鞋子的時候，電燈忽然滅了。他慌忙地找尋火柴點蠟燭。

「這個地方真討厭，總是停電，」她在黑暗中抱怨道。

蠟燭點燃後只發出搖曳的微光。滿屋子都是黑影。他還立在方桌前。她走過來，靠着方桌的一面坐下。她自語般地說：「我就怕黑暗，怕冷靜，怕寂寞。」

他默默地側過頭埋下眼光看她。過了幾分鐘。她忽然抬起頭看着他，說：「宣，你為甚麼不跟我講話？」

「我怕你累，你休息一會兒吧，」他勉強做出笑容回答道。

她搖搖頭：「我不累，行裏工作不重，我們又比較自由，主任近來對我很好。同事們都不錯，就是——」她停頓一下，忽然改變了語調，輕輕皺一下眉頭。「回到家裏來，我總覺得冷，覺得寂寞，覺得心裏空虛。你近來也不肯跟我多講話。」

「不是，我怕你精神不好，」他惶恐地分辯道，這不是真話，事實是：他害怕講多了會使她不高興，並且一天他和她見面的時候並不多。

「你真是『老好人』！」她帶笑地責備道。「我一天精神好得很。比你好得多，你還耽心我！你就是這樣一個人，常常想到別人卻忘了你自己。」

「不，我也想到自己，」他笨拙地辯道。

母親的房裏沒有聲息。燭光搖幌得厲害，屋角的黑影比先前更濃。從二樓送來一個小孩的咳嗽聲和哭聲。窗外索索地下起小雨來。

"Let's play bridge," she suggested excitedly, suddenly rising from her seat at the square table.

He was tired and did not want to play. Nevertheless, he immediately brought out the cards and they began.

He could see that she soon lost interest in the game, and he had had none from the beginning. In a short while, bored, she quit.

He quietly put the cards away. He heaved a sigh. The wick of the candle had been blown to one side, and the table was being stained with candle drippings. So taking out a pair of scissors, he cut the wick shorter.

"Hsüan, I envy you. You can take anything and everything," she philosophized, in an agitated voice.

"Well, I hardly have any other choice."

"But how long can you go on like this?"

He answered that he did not truthfully know.

"I'm worried. When will we be able to stop living like this? When will we have a better life?" she asked, complainingly.

"When the Japanese are defeated we'll have a better life," he responded.

"Don't talk about victory. When that day arrives, I'll be too old to enjoy it, maybe even dead and gone. My only hope is to enjoy myself while I'm alive." Having said this in a resentful tone, she started pacing to and fro.

"It's all my fault," he apologized.

"What's the use of blaming you? I made the wrong choice," she said unkindly. Her every word stung like a sharp needle digging into his heart. In desperation, he frantically scratched his head.

「我們打兩盤 Bridge 吧，」她忽然站起來，興奮地提議道。

他很倦，他不想玩「橋牌」。可是他立刻答應了，並且去把紙牌拿來，放到方桌上，他坐下來洗牌發牌。

他看得出來她的興致愈來愈差，他自己對玩牌更少興趣。剛玩了兩副，她忽然厭倦地站起來說：「不打了，沒有趣味。看不清楚。」

他默默地把紙牌放進盒子裏去，低聲嘆了一口氣。他注意到燭芯偏垂在一邊，燭油流了一大灘在方桌上。他找着剪刀，把燭芯剪短了。

「宣，我真佩服你，」她站在方桌前看他做着這一切，忽然用激動的聲音說。他驚訝地抬頭望着他，不明白她的意思。「你真能忍耐，甚麼你都受得了，」她帶了抱怨的調子繼續說。

「不忍受又有甚麼辦法，這個年頭，」他帶着淒涼的微笑答道。

「那麼你預備忍到甚麼時候？」

「我不知道。」

「我煩得很。宣，你說我們要等到甚麼時候，才可以不過這種生活？到甚麼時候才可以過得好一點？」

「我想，總有一天，等到抗戰勝利的時候——」

她不等他說完，便煩躁地擺手打斷了他的話頭：「我不要再聽抗戰勝利的話。要等到抗戰勝利恐怕我已經老了，死了。我沒有別的理想，我活着的時候我只想活得痛快一點，過得舒服一點。」她激動地甚至帶點忿懣地說。她在屋子裏走來走去。

過了半晌他才吐出一句話：「這要怪我沒有出息。」還是用痛苦和抱歉的調子說出來的。

「怪你有甚麼用？這只怪我當初瞎了眼睛，」她冷冷地說。每個字像一根針似地刺進他的心。他捧着頭，默默地用他十根手指抓他的頭髮。

XIII

HE continued to lead a dull, monotonous, and agonizing existence. He had no idea what sustained him; in fact his health became steadily worse. He had a fever every afternoon and sweated a little every night. In addition, he coughed up blood twice more, a secret he carefully guarded. From time to time his mother commented on his poor complexion, and he would repeat the routine reply that he was all right. In pain she looked at him, but, unaware of his real situation, remained silent. One day, overhearing a conversation between mother and son, Shu-sheng remarked rather unsympathetically that he had not looked well for several years. What she said was certainly true, but, except for some concern and compassion, she offered him nothing helpful. Like his mother, Shu-sheng also did not fully understand him. And even though his mother expressed concern and was much more willing to sacrifice herself for him, she could not make him feel any better, either.

"Is it better to live or to die?" he frequently asked himself, sensing that death was around the corner. This premonition was strengthened by his frustrations at work and at home. In the office, his supervisors, Chou and Wu, whip in hand hounded him to death. At home his mother constantly complained about the hard times, and his wife, on the other hand, inevitably dazzled him with her vitality and youthful appearance. Afraid to look at his mother's aged face and equally unwilling to be reminded of his wife's radiance, he kept more and more to himself and became ever more reticent. A world of difference separated him from them. Whenever they spoke to him or looked at him with concern, he would say to himself, "You don't understand me."

十三

他繼續過着這樣的平凡、單調而痛苦的日子。是甚麼一種力量支持着他那帶病的身體，連他自己也不知道。他每天下午發着低熱，晚上流着冷汗，汗出得並不太多。他對吐痰的事很留心，痰裏帶血，還有過兩次。他把家裏人瞞過了。母親只注意他的臉色，她常說：「你今天臉色又不好看了。」他照例回答她：「我覺得倒還好。」母親痛苦地看他一眼，他不再說甚麼。她不會知道他的心。有一次妻在旁邊聽見母親關於他臉色的話，妻冷冷地插嘴說：「這幾年來他臉色哪一天好看過！」妻說的是真話。但是妻也不知道他的心。關切，憐憫——她們能夠給他的就只有這一點。母親似乎比妻更關心他，母親似乎更少想到她自己。但是連母親也減少不了他內心的痛苦。

「活着好，還是死好？」他常常偷偷地想着，尤其是在辦公的時候。他覺得「死」就在前面等他。周主任和吳股長的眼光似乎在鞭策他走向着「死」。回到家中，母親的關切和妻的憐憫並不曾給他多大的安慰。母親喜歡訴苦，妻老是向他誇耀豐盛的生命力，和她的還未失去的青春。他現在開始害怕看母親的憔悴的愁容，也怕看妻的容光煥發的臉龐。他變得愈不愛講話了。他跟他們中間彷彿還隔着一個世界。當她們關心地望着他或者溫和地跟他談話時，他總要在心裏說：「你們不了解。」她們的確不了解。她們也許覺得他有時會

They noticed that occasionally he had a curious glint in his eyes, though they were not particularly worried about it. He feared that his mother might discover the true condition of his health by her constant and relentless probing. When his wife seriously suggested that he go for a medical examination, he answered evasively, "It's very expensive to see a doctor or to receive medical treatment. We are fortunate enough that we are not starving like those poor refugees who died by the thousands on the road between Hunan and Kweilin."

His mother sighed resentfully. Shu-sheng replied, "Maybe one day we will be like those refugees. But as long as we are living, we must find a way to do the best we can." Briefly, a worried look surfaced on her face, but it disappeared quickly.

"Find a way to do the best we can?" protested his mother. "There isn't anything better for us and won't be until we die; we are living worse this year than last and the year before that."

"Well, that's because our man is too 'good'," said Shu-sheng in a mocking tone.

His mother's face changed color. "I would rather starve than compromise my moral principles. Hsüan has done nothing wrong."

Shu-sheng sniggered. After two or three minutes she mumbled to herself, "All I mean is, don't take life or morals too seriously. Why should one suffer needlessly?"

"I'm willing to be poor. Even to be a servant is better than being a flower-vase!" retorted his mother sharply.

"Mother, please don't say any more. Shu-sheng agrees with you." He tried to intervene between the two women, tired of listening to their quarrel.

"No, you're wrong. We have completely different views," said Shu-sheng, her face glaring angrily. "It is out-of-date to call a working girl a flower-vase."

用一種奇異的眼光看她們，但她們並沒有特別耽心。母親或許耽心，可是她的叮囑和詢問(叮囑他小心身體，問他是不是有病)反而增加他的畏懼和痛苦。「她就要看出來了，」他對自己說，他更加小心起來。有一次母親談起他的身體，妻立刻接口說：「讓他到醫院去檢查一下。」過後妻又掉過眼睛來看他，這次是真誠的要求：你去一趟吧。「我很好，我很好，」他慌張地防禦自己。「去檢查一次究竟穩當些，」妻說。他不直接回答她，停了片刻，他才有氣無力地自言自語：「現在看病吃藥住醫院都要花錢。像我們這種人只要有飯吃，就算是有福氣了。他們說湘桂路上不曉得餓死多少人。」

母親憤憤不平地嘆了一口氣。妻想了想，才說：「說不定有一天我們也會像他們那樣。不過我們活着的時候，總得想辦法。」她皺着眉頭，臉上掠過一個陰影。但陰影立刻散去了。她臉上已不留一點憂鬱的表情。

「想辦法？我看拖到死都不會有辦法，前年說到去年就好，去年說到今年就好，今年又怎麼說呢？只有一年不如一年！」母親終於在旁邊發起牢騷來。

「這要怪我們這位先生人太好囉，」妻帶了點嘲笑的調子說。

母親變了臉色，接着說：「我寧肯餓死，覺得做人還是不要苟且。宣沒有一點兒錯。」

妻冷笑了兩聲，過了兩三分鐘又自語似地說：「我看做人倒不必這樣認真。何必自討苦吃！」

「這是我甘心情願。無論如何，做一個老媽子，總比做一個花瓶好，」母親氣沖沖地說。

「媽，不要說了，樹生的意思其實跟你的並沒有不同，」他連忙插進來勸解道。他害怕再聽她們的爭吵。

「不同，完全不同！」妻掙紅臉用勁說。「現在罵人做花瓶，已經過時了。……」

"Shu-sheng, please don't say any more. It's all my fault, making you suffer with me. Don't blame Mother," he pleaded. "She's old and can't see things your way. Please give in a little."

"It is not she; it is you who can't see things properly," Shu-sheng replied, before sitting down on the edge of the bed.

"Surely, people today are very thick-skinned; they don't care about morals or anything," his mother added.

As he was about to comfort his mother, he saw the pale face of a woman standing by the door about to greet him and his wife. It was Mrs. Chang, their next-door neighbor. He invited her to come in.

"Mr. Wang, do you think we're safe here? If we have to flee, those of us who don't come from this area don't know what to do," Mrs. Chang said, fright showing clearly in her eyes.

Since he remained silent, Shu-sheng replied, "The situation is not that bad. There are many rumors circulating; don't listen to them."

"Rumors? What rumors?" he asked Shu-sheng, his heart pounding.

"People in the office told me that the Japanese have arrived at Nantan and are approaching Kweichow," answered Shu-sheng calmly.

"The last I heard is that the Japanese have taken Kweichow," said Mrs. Chang, almost in a panic. "My husband's department is planning to evacuate to somewhere else very soon, but he is a junior member and won't be included in the evacuation. What are we going to do?"

Bitterly amused, he thought to himself, "She's asking me for help, and I can't even help myself. How ironic!" Nevertheless, he tried to comfort his distraught neighbor and told her he would do his best to help.

「樹生，你不要多說。都是我不好，連累大家受苦，也怪不得媽，」他着急地向妻央求，拉開她，又低聲對她說：「媽上了年紀，想不通，你讓她一點吧。」

「哪裏是她想不通，明明是你想不通！」妻氣惱地罵他，但聲音不大，而且她坐到床沿上不再作聲了。

「當然啊，現在人臉皮厚了，甚麼都不在乎，」母親還在一邊嘲罵道。

他正要過去安慰母親，忽然聽見人在喚「汪先生，汪太太，」他吃驚地向房門那邊看去。隔壁的張太太蒼白着臉立在門前。

「張太太，請進來坐，」他連忙招呼道，妻和母親也跟着向那女人打招呼。

「汪先生，你看這裏不要緊罷？我真害怕，要是逃起難來，我們外省人簡直沒有辦法，」張太太剛剛坐定便驚恐地睜大兩隻眼睛說。

他沒有答話，倒是妻先說了：「我看不要緊。外面謠言很多，我就不去理它。」

「謠言？你聽到甚麼謠言？」他驚問道，他的心突然跳得很厲害了。

「說是日本人已經到了南丹，逼近貴州了。行裏同事都是這麼說，」妻相當鎮靜地回答。

「我聽說已經進了貴州啊。我們張先生的機關在準備搬家了。不過我們小職員是跟不去的。以後怎麼辦呢？汪先生，你是本地人，你要照料我們啊。」張太太用了焦急的聲調央求他。

他心裏想：你還找我，我自己都沒有辦法！可是他卻答道：「好，我一定幫忙。」

"We were planning to escape to the countryside. But wherever you go, my husband and I will follow," said Mrs. Chang.

"Planning to flee now? Isn't that a little premature? Mrs. Chang, don't be scared. We'll find some way out when the time comes," Shu-sheng said kindly to their pale, panic-stricken neighbor.

"I am worried about the future, for what if we do have to flee ... Mr. Wang, Mrs. Wang, and Mama Wang, thank you all. I'll tell my husband the good news. He'll breathe a little easier. Thank you. I must go now." She left with a smile.

After Mrs. Chang's departure, his mother asked him, "Do we really have to flee?"

His heart throbbed with pain; he did not dare answer.

"No, it won't come to that," Shu-sheng answered for him, smiling calmly.

The following day Shu-sheng came home and sadly reported additional news from the war front, "The Japanese are threatening Tu-shan, and there have been air-raids every day in Kweiyang."

Alarmed, his mother asked, "What shall we do?"

"Nothing," he answered, smiling nonchalantly. "Wait until they get here." Having become indifferent to living, suffering, or death, he was no longer afraid of the future, only unsure of its outcome. He knew he could not prevent what was going to happen, and he had therefore adopted a relaxed attitude toward the inevitable.

His mother, however, did not share his spirit of resignation. "We can't just wait for death to come," she said.

"Oh, it won't be that bad," said Shu-sheng. "When the time comes, we'll all leave. Just today a colleague invited me to spend some time

「我們想到鄉下去躲一下，最好你們去哪裏，我們也一起去，」張太太又説。

「現在就去躲？還早吧。張太太，你不要怕。到那時總可以想辦法，」妻微笑地安慰那個帶病容的年青女人。

「我就是説將來，萬一要逃難……汪太太，汪先生，老太太，謝謝你們啊，謝謝你們啊。我去告訴我們張先生去。他聽見也就放心了，」張太太站起來説着感激的話，臉上露了一絲笑容。

「多坐一會兒吧，」妻挽留道。

「不坐啦，不坐啦，」張太太一面説一面往房門外走。

客人走後，房裏三個人沉默了兩三分鐘，母親忽然發問：「宣，真的要逃難嗎？」

他的心在悸動，他不敢回答。

「不會的，不會壞到這樣，」妻接嘴説，她臉上浮現出一個平靜的笑容。

但是第二天妻下班回來，就皺着眉頭對他説：「今天消息的確不大好，説是連獨山也靠不住了。又説貴陽天天有警報。」

「那麼我們怎麼辦？」母親張皇地插嘴問道。

「除了等着他們打過來，也沒有別的辦法，」他斷念似地説，又淒涼地笑了笑。他沒有懼怕，他只有一種疑惑不定的感覺。死，活，災難對他並沒有甚麼區別。要來的事反正會來，他沒有力量擋住它。不來的，更用不着害怕它。

「我們不能等死啊，」母親焦急地説。

妻憐憫地笑了：「不會到這樣地步。該走時大家都會走開。今天

in the countryside, to avoid the bombing of the city, but I turned down the invitation."

"Of course, you've much more influence than we do," said her mother-in-law mockingly.

"Perhaps I do. I guess I can leave whenever I please," Shu-sheng said spitefully and somewhat conceitedly.

"But what about Hsiao Hsüan? You may not think it necessary to take care of your husband or me, but what about your son? You surely don't intend to abandon him?" her mother-in-law shouted angrily.

He looked at each of the women in turn, thinking. "I'm near death, and yet you continue to quarrel." But he did not say anything aloud for the women to hear.

"The school will take care of him. You don't have to worry about that," replied Shu-sheng coldly.

"Then I suppose you are free to go with your boyfriend. I've never seen a mother like you," said her mother-in-law, clenching her teeth.

"I'm sorry I'm not like you, and I also don't plan to live as long as you have," Shu-sheng shouted back.

"Shu-sheng, why don't you give in to Mother a little? We are all one family. Who knows, maybe one day, if disaster strikes, we will all ..." He started to speak up for he could bear the quarrel no longer, his head aching badly.

"I didn't intend to quarrel. Your mother did. Talk to her!" Shu-sheng turned aside defiantly.

"I don't want to hear any more of your fancy speeches," her mother-in-law scolded, pointing at Shu-sheng.

"Go on quarreling; go on," he mumbled to himself. The women's

還有個同事約我到鄉下去暫避一下，說是怕敵人來個大轟炸。我也沒有答應。」

「你自然比我們有辦法！」母親生氣地嘲諷道。

「也許吧，我高興走的時候，我總走得了，」妻故意做出得意的神情答道。

「可是小宣呢？可是小宣呢？我跟宣兩人你可以不管；小宣是你親生的兒子，你不能丟開他啊！」母親掙紅臉，大聲說。

他的眼光輪流地望着兩個女人的臉孔。他想說：「我都要死了，你們還在吵！」可是他不敢說出來。

「小宣有學校照顧他，用不着你們耽心，」妻冷冷地說。

「好的，這樣你可以跟着男朋友到處跑了。我從沒有見過像你這樣的母親！」母親咬牙切齒地罵道。

「對不起，我不是你那樣的人，我也不想活到那樣的年紀，」妻開始變臉色，大聲回答。

「樹生，你就讓媽多說兩句吧，都是一家人，何必這樣！說不定過兩天大難一來，大家都會——」他忍耐不住，終於苦痛地高聲說了。他覺得頭痛得厲害，便住了嘴咬緊牙齒。

「我並不要吵，是你母親吵起來的，你倒應該勸勸她，」妻把頭偏向一邊，昂然說。

「我不要聽你那些花言巧語，」母親指着妻罵道。

「你們吵吧，你們吵吧，」他氣惱地在心裏說。她們的聲音在他

voices jarred in his head until he felt it was about to burst open. Unable to bear it any longer, he silently walked to the door. The women paid no attention to his movements, and in one breath he ran down the stairs.

He walked along the sidewalk, highly agitated. The chill night air bathed his face, calmed him, and helped him clear his head.

"Where shall I go?" he asked himself, expecting no answer. Aimlessly he wandered toward the wine shop.

"Do what you must to forget the whole thing," a voice seemed to whisper in his ear. He looked into the little shop and saw that all the seats were occupied except one across a table from a long-haired, thin-faced lone patron wearing a worn-out cotton gown. He decided to share the table with the stranger.

"A cup of *hung-tsao*," he ordered loudly. After one swallow of the wine, the burning feeling in his stomach made him belch.

Raising his head, the patron across the table recognized Wang and called him by name.

Wang looked as though dazed at the sickly, dark, thin face which he could not place.

"Don't you recognize me? Are you drunk? How could you forget an old classmate?" The man laughed bitterly.

Recognition came quickly, and Wang said, "Pai-ch'ing, you look awful," completely shocked by his friend's heavy beard, husky voice, sunken cheeks, and blood-shot eyes. "What have you done to yourself? It isn't even a month since I saw you last."

"I'm finished, I'm as good as dead," the man answered hoarsely, with a sick smile that showed his yellowish teeth.

腦子裏撞擊，他覺得他的頭快炸開了，他再不能忍耐下去。他默默地走向房門。她們不理他。他走出門，一口氣跑下樓去。

他走在人行道上，腦子裏還是亂烘烘的。夜的寒氣開始洗着他的臉，他的頭腦漸漸地清醒了。

「到哪裏去呢？」他問自己，沒有回答。他無目的走着。又到了那個冷酒館門前。

「你應該使自己忘記一切，」一個聲音在他耳邊説。他朝那個小店裏面望。桌子都被客人佔據了。只有靠裏那張方桌比較空，那裏只坐了一個客人，穿一件破舊棉袍，頭髮長，臉黑瘦。那個人埋着頭喝酒，不理睬旁人。「我去拼個位子，」他低聲自語道，就走進去，在那人的對面拉開板櫈坐下來。

「一杯紅糟，」他大聲説，堂倌送來一杯酒。他馬上拿起杯子，大大地喝了一口。酒進到肚裏，一股熱氣冒上來，他受不住，打了一個嗝。

「文宣，」對面那個客人忽然抬起頭來看他，喚着他的名字。他呆呆地望着那張帶病容的黑瘦臉，一時認不出是誰來。

「你不認得我？你吃醉了嗎？連老同學——」那個人痛苦地笑了笑。

「柏青！你怎麼變成了這個樣子！」他睜大眼睛，吃驚地説，打斷了那人的話。相貌全變了，聲音也啞了，兩頰陷進那麼深，眼裏佈滿了血絲。圍着嘴生了一大圈短短的黑鬍子。

「你做了甚麼？還不到一個月！」他問着，他有點毛骨聳然了。

「我完了，我已經死了，」那人嘶聲回答，還勉強做出一個笑容，可是他笑得像在抽筋似的，牙齒黃得可怕。

"Don't talk like that. Have you been ill?"

"The illness is here," replied his friend, pointing at his forehead.

"Then you should stop drinking and go home."

"No, I can't. Drinking gives me pleasure," the man responded grimly, looking at his cup which was more than half full.

"Finish what's left and go home," he urged his friend.

"Home? I have no home. Where do you want me to go?"

"I'll take you to the place where you live."

"I have no place to live. Nothing, I have nothing," his friend snapped back angrily. Emptying his cup, he exclaimed, "Good! Good! I never thought that having been a student all my life, I'd end up like this. You know where I sleep? In flophouses, in the street, once even outside your house."

"You're drunk; don't talk any more; let's go," he said and paid the waiter. He took hold of his friend's arm and said hurriedly, "Let's go! Let's go!"

"No, I'm not drunk, I'm not. Really, I'm not," the friend insisted.

"Then let's find a teahouse," he suggested.

"Fine," said his friend getting up and then immediately sitting down again. "You go ahead; I have to sit here for a bit."

"Come home with me for a while. Shu-sheng often mentions your wife," he said, realizing too late that he had touched upon a delicate subject.

"In my condition how could I go to your home?" his friend groaned. His cheeks moved slightly but Wang could not tell whether he was

「不要這樣說，柏青，你是不是生過病？」他關心地問，他忘記了自己的苦惱。

「病在這裏，在這裏！」那人用手指敲着前額說。

「那麼，你不要喝酒了，快回家去休息，」他着急地勸道。

「我要吃，吃了酒才舒服啊，」那人獰笑答道，卻並不去動面前的酒杯，那裏面還有大半杯酒。

「那麼你快喝乾，好回家去，」他催促道。

「家！我那裏還有家？你要我到那裏去？」那人冷笑說。

「你住的地方，陪你回去，」他說。

「我沒有住的地方，我沒有，我甚麼也沒有，」那人生氣地答道，突然端起杯子，把酒一口喝光了。「痛快！痛快！」大聲說。「我白讀了一輩子書，弄成這種樣子，真想不到！你知道我住在那裏？有時候我睡小客棧，有時候我就睡馬路，我還在你們大門口睡過……」

「你喝醉了，不要多說，我們走吧，」他截斷了那人的話，一面站起來叫堂倌來把兩個人的酒錢收了。他拉着那人的膀子，接連說：「走，走。」

「我沒有醉，我沒有醉，」那人不停地搖頭說，不肯站起來。

「那麼我們找個地方喝茶去，」他說。

「好吧，」那人站起來，身子搖幌一下，又坐下了。「你先走吧，我多坐一會兒，」那人痛苦地看了他一眼，有氣無力地說。

「那麼到我家去坐坐，樹生還一直記掛你的太太，」他溫和地說，剛說出「太太」兩個字，他馬上明白自己說錯了話，便閉了嘴不作聲了。

「你看我這樣子怎麼能到你家裏去！」那人說着兩腮略略動了一下，人不知道他究竟在笑，還是在哭。他埋頭看看自己的胸膛，右

crying or laughing. "Such clothes," he muttered, "such a face. No, I can't go to your place. I'm already dead. Your old friend T'ang Pai-ch'ing is gone forever. What do I care what I wear, where I live, what kind of friends I have? My old friends avoid me. But who cares? I'm dead, already dead." Smiling wryly, he continued: "You just go home; don't mind me. Even you remember my wife, since you just mentioned her. And how can I ever forget her?"

Wang Wen-hsüan looked around and saw many pairs of eyes staring at them. He blushed and said, "Let's go. Everyone is watching you."

"Let them watch. Everyone here is in the same boat, all equally miserable. No happy soul ever sets foot in here, and that includes you." Wang shuddered, hearing these sad true words. But he continued to urge his friend to stop grumbling and leave.

But his friend was adamant. "Snobbishness, snobbishness," he said. "There isn't anyone who isn't snobbish. I can see through people's façade to their real nature. Even those old friends who attended my wedding pretend they don't recognize me when we meet in the street now. Money, just money." He smiled contemptuously and went on. "There is no one who doesn't love money; no one who doesn't worship money. And I, a poor tramp, might as well be dead. What's there for me to live for?" Finally, he stood up and said, "All right, I'll go with you to see your wife. When my wife was alive, she always said that she'd like to visit her. But now ... " He began to sob.

They left the wine-shop, but after a few steps his classmate suddenly stopped and said, "I'd better not go after all."

"Then where would you go?"

"I don't know. Just leave me alone," his drunken friend replied resolutely.

手五根手指在舊棉袍的油膩的前胸上敲了兩下：「我穿這樣的衣服；」摸摸下巴：「我這樣的臉貌。」搖搖頭：「不，我不去。我已經死了，你的老同學唐柏青已經死了。我為甚麼還要管這些？穿甚麼衣服，住甚麼地方，跟朋友有甚麼關係呢？朋友們都不理我，也好，橫豎我已經死了，死了。」他勉強笑了笑。「你回去，不要理我。啊，剛才你還說，你們都記掛我內人。你們都記得她，我怎麼能夠忘記她！」

他汪文宣轉頭看了看四周，幾張桌子上客人的眼光全向着他的同學。他臉紅了。

「快走吧，那些人都在看你，」他低聲催促道。

「看我？等他們看吧，我們都是一樣，」那人抬起頭望着他，兩眼射出一種近似瘋狂的光，「到冷酒館來吃酒的就沒有一個快活的人。你也一樣。」他汪文宣聽見這句話，忽然打了一個寒噤。他仍舊低聲在催促：「不要說了，我們走吧。」

「勢利，勢利，沒有一個人不勢利！」那人只顧自己地說下去。「我把人看透了。我那些老朋友，一年前我結婚，他們還來吃過喜酒的，現在街上碰見，都不理我了。哼，錢，錢！」勉強做出一個輕蔑的笑容。「沒有人不愛錢，不崇拜錢。我這個窮光蛋！你死吧，最好早點死，我活着有甚麼意思！好，」忽然站起來：「我跟你去看看大嫂。我內人活着的時候就說過要到府上拜望大嫂的，現在……」說不下去開始抽泣了。

他汪文宣拉着那人的膀子走出了酒館。兩個人在人行道上走了幾步，那同學忽然站住，說：「我不去了。」

「那麼你到哪裏去呢？」他問。

「我也不知道。你不要管我，」那人堅決地說。

"Pai-ch'ing, no. Stay at my place tonight," he said with concern.

"No, no. I can't do that."

"Pai-ch'ing, you can't go on like this; remember your previous ambitions. Why don't you try to be your old self?"

As they approached Wang's street, Pai-ch'ing once again insisted that he be left alone. He freed himself from Wang's grasp and ran away.

"Pai-ch'ing, Pai-ch'ing," Wang called after him in vain. Suddenly he heard the noise of a horrendous crash and a piercing scream. His vision blurred, he had the impression that an enormous truck was speeding by.

People scrambled quickly to the scene of the accident; a crowd gathered at the intersection. He merely followed the others, unable to see anything; he felt as though something horrible had happened.

"What a terrible sight! The head has been smashed beyond recognition," one bystander said to Wang.

"Trucks shouldn't be allowed on these streets. Several people have already lost their lives in accidents like this. A young housewife was killed just the day before yesterday at a minor intersection, and the driver hit and injured a policeman while trying to drive away," said another.

Finally, after what seemed like a long interval, he came out of his trance. He screamed in horror until his voice became hoarse. Tears streaked his face. He felt shattered.

Noiselessly he drew away from the crowd and went home. No one paid him any attention, but a familiar voice haunted him, shouting, "I'm finished; I'm finished."

When he reached home, his wife was reading at the desk. She lifted

「柏青，這樣不行，你到我家裏去住一晚吧，」他同情地勸道，又把那人的膀子拉住。

「不！不！」那人搖頭說。

「柏青，你不能這樣，你該記得你從前的抱負，你振作起來吧，」他痛苦地大聲說。他只想哭。

他們又往前走了幾步，剛要轉進他住的那條街，那個人忽然固執地大聲說：「不，我要走。」又說：「你放我！」掙脫了他的手，那人就跑下馬路朝對面跑去。

「柏青！柏青！」他失望地喚着。他預備跑過去追那人。他聽見一陣隆隆的聲音，接着一聲可怖的尖叫。他眼睛模糊了，他彷彿看見一輛大得無比的大卡車在他身邊飛跑過。

人們瘋狂地跑着，全擠在一個地方。就在這十字街口馬上圍聚了一大群人。他呆呆地走過去，站在人背後，甚麼也看不見。但是他覺得一個可怖的黑影罩在他的頭上。

「好怕人！整個頭都成了肉泥，看得我心都緊了，」一個聲音在他耳邊說。

「我說像這樣的地方，根本就不應該行駛卡車。這個月輾死好幾個人了。前天在小十字輾死一位年青太太，那才慘！車子也是逃掉了，還跌傷一個警察，」另一個聲音說。

他醒了過來。他明白了。他恐怖地，痛苦地叫了一聲。但是他喉嚨啞了。眼淚止不住地流了他一臉。他心裏難過得很厲害。他渾身發冷。

他悄悄地離開人群走回家去。沒有人注意他。只有一個聲音伴送他到家。那個熟悉的聲音不斷地嚷着：「我完了，我完了。」

他推開房門。電燈相當亮。妻一個人坐在書桌前看書。她放下

her eyes from the book and was surprised at seeing him. Her expression was affectionate. "You've been to the shop again, haven't you?" she asked.

He nodded; then he told her that he had had a dream, a most horrifying dream. His mother came out from her room saying. "Hsüan, you're home!"

"What dream? What happened to you?" asked Shu-sheng kindly.

He would have liked to tell her the whole story, but he was haunted by the memory of his friend and his friend's last words. Emotionally drained and physically exhausted, he was at the point of collapse. As he opened his mouth to tell the story, blood-tinged phlegm spurted from his mouth.

His wife and his mother, who had been anxiously waiting for him to speak, were shocked to see the blood in his phlegm.

"Blood! You spat out blood!" they cried in unison, and together they put him to bed.

"I, too, am finished; I, too, am finished," he muttered, borrowing Pai-ch'ing's words. Tears cascaded down his cheeks. He had no energy to struggle any more and he quietly closed his eyes.

XIV

THAT night he had a series of frightening dreams, one after another. The next morning he awoke exhausted, feverish, and fretful.

The two women, no longer quarreling with each other, waited on

書抬起頭看他，臉上現出驚喜的表情，親切地問了一句：「你又到冷酒館去了？」

他點點頭，過了一會兒，才費力地吐出一句：「我做了一個夢，一個可怕的夢。」

母親從屋裏跑出來大聲說：「宣，你回來了！」

「甚麼夢？你怎麼了？休息一會兒吧，」妻溫和地說。

他想答話。可是那聲可怖的尖叫還在他腦子裏震響。他的精力竭盡了，他似乎隨時都會倒下來。他努力支持着。兩對急切、關懷、愛憐的眼睛望着他，等待他的話語。他一着急，嘴動了，痰比話語先出來，他的心在燃燒。

「血！血！你吐血！」兩個女人齊聲驚呼。她們把他攙到床前，讓他躺下來。

「我完了，我完了，」他迷迷糊糊地唸着那句可怕的話，腦裏還響着那聲尖叫，眼淚像水似地流下來，他覺得他再沒有力量掙扎了。他順從地閉上眼睛。

十四

他一晚上不停地做着可怕的夢。早晨醒來他疲倦，發燒，四肢無力，心神不安。

母親和妻不再爭吵了，她們一樣親切地看護着他。下午醫生來

him with patience and concern. In the afternoon a physician who practiced Chinese herb-medicine visited him. Shu-sheng had wanted to call a Western-trained doctor who was also the Health Consultant to staff members of the bank, but she yielded graciously to her mother-in-law's insistence on consulting a Chinese-trained doctor. Before she went to ask the doctor to make the house call, she had obtained a day's leave for herself from her bank as well as sick-leave for her husband from his office. The physician, Mr. Chang Po-ch'ing, had a reasonably good reputation and was remotely related to Wang's mother; he would not charge a consultation fee except for a small sum to cover his fare. For economy's sake alone, Wang preferred him to a high-priced Western-trained doctor.

An amiable old man, the doctor carefully examined Wang and diagnosed his case as one of extreme exhaustion — in addition to the strong influence of the element of fire emitted from his liver — and not of tuberculosis. He prophesied that the patient would be well in a few days.

Despite Shu-sheng's doubts, Wang's mother professed great faith in Chinese medicine. As for Wang, he was not sure. Nonetheless, the physician's optimistic diagnosis made every one breathe a little easier and restored Wang's faith in Chinese medicine. He reasoned that since the Chinese had completely relied upon that type of medical practice for centuries, it would be difficult to deny its validity. Thus reassured, he had a glimpse of hope and the dark shadow of death receded into the background.

His wife bought and his mother cooked the herbs prescribed for him. But that night he was again restless and experienced some breathing difficulties.

In the evening he ran a high fever, which again plunged him into a nightmarish web of dreams. A variety of monstrous shadows flashed

給他診病。是一位中醫，妻子去請來的。妻相信西醫，主張請她銀行裏的醫藥顧問。可是母親堅持着請中醫。妻居然相當爽快地讓了步。她到他服務的公司去替他請了病假，又到銀行去為自己請一天假，然後去請醫生。醫生張伯情是他母親的一位遠親，在這城裏行醫三四年，也還有一點名氣，每次到他家裏來診病，除了車費外，並不另收診費。他自己單單為了這原因，也贊成請中醫診病。「西醫多貴！只要少花錢就好！我哪裏來那些錢呢？」他這樣想着。

醫生是一個和善的老人，仔細地把着脈，問着病情，又用溫和的調子安慰病人和家屬，說這是肝火旺，又加上疲勞，並不是肺病，養息幾天就會好起來。

妻不大相信醫生的話，母親卻很相信。他則是將信將疑。但無論如何醫生使他們三個人都心安了。他漸漸覺得中醫也有道理。「幾千年來我們的人都這樣地看病吃藥，怎麼能說沒有一點道理呢？」他安慰自己地想着，他又看見了一線的希望，死的黑影也淡了一點。

妻出去買藥。母親拿來煮給他吃了。吃過藥，他睡了一覺。他睡得不好，老是覺得透不過氣來。

傍晚時候，他的熱度加高，他又落進了可怕的夢網裏。龐大的

before his eyes, including that of T'ang Pai-ch'ing's dark, thin face with its blood-shot eyes. He kept hearing T'ang's last words: "I'm finished, I'm finished." Frightened, he started to run in his dream and was unable to stop even though he was dead tired. He ran into a dark forest, frantically searching for light. Some light came from trees that were in flames. The blaze was getting hotter as it got closer to him, finally scorching his clothes. In extreme desperation, he repeatedly yelled, "Help, help!"

He awoke in a cold sweat, partly covered by the quilt. He groaned mournfully.

"Hsüan, how are you?" Shu-sheng asked, worried by the frightful noises he was making. "How do you feel?"

Sighing, he replied evasively, "How long have you been home from work?"

"Don't you know that I didn't go to work today?"

"Oh, I forgot about that. I am confused," he admitted. "I dreamed that an old classmate was killed in an auto accident," mistaking reality for fantasy.

"Old classmate? Which one?" She felt his moist head. His fever had subsided.

"T'ang Pai-ch'ing. We attended his wedding party at the Longevity Restaurant. Don't you remember? His wife died in childbirth. Didn't I tell you about that a few days ago?"

"Yes, you did. But don't talk or think about the problems others have. Rest a little more," his wife consoled him affectionately.

"I'm afraid of dreaming again," he complained like a child.

"I'll sit by you, then you won't dream any more," she said with a smile.

黑影一直在他眼前幌動，唐柏青的黑瘦臉，紅眼睛，同樣的有無數個，牠們包圍着他，每張嘴都在說：「完了，完了。」他害怕，他逃避。他走，他跑。多麼疲倦！但是他不能夠停住腳。忽然他走進了荒山。他看不見人影。他也不知道要去甚麼地方。天黑了。他在黑暗中摸索。好累人的旅行啊！忽然他看見了光亮，忽然四周的樹木燃燒起來。到處是火。火燃得很旺，火越逼越近。他的衣服烤焦了。他不能忍受，他嘶聲大叫：「救命！」

他醒了。他躺在床上，蓋着棉被。一身都是汗。口裏發出痛苦的呻吟。

「宣，你怎麼啦？」妻坐着床沿上，埋下頭喚他。「你心裏難過嗎？」她溫柔地問。

他嘆了一口氣，望着她，過了一會才低聲問她：「你下班多久了？」

「我今天請了一天假，不是跟你說過嗎？」妻驚訝地說。

「我忘記了，」他答應道，接着加上一句解釋：「夢把我弄昏了。」停了片刻他再說：「我夢見，……好像是……我那個老同學給汽車壓死了。」

他騙了自己，把真實當作夢境了。

「老同學？你說哪個？」妻驚問道，她慢慢地伸過手去摸他的前額。前額潤濕，熱已退了。

「唐柏青，我們在百齡餐廳吃過他喜酒的，他太太生小孩死了，我前不幾天才跟你講過，」他吃力地說。

「是，你跟我講過，我記得。你不要多講話，不要想別人的事情。你精神差，先前還在發熱。你再睡一會兒吧，」妻溫柔地安慰他。

「我怕睡着了，又會做怪夢，」他像小孩似地訴苦道。

「不會的，你甚麼也不要想，你安心地睡。我在旁邊陪着你，你不會做怪夢，」妻含笑地對他說。

"Where's Mother?"

"She's cooking. You'd better go to sleep. Soon it will be time for the medicine," she said, turning her head away.

After a while he said, "Please get me some tea." He was not thirsty but wanted to talk to her.

She brought him half a cup of hot tea and held the cup in her hand so he could drink from it. After he had a few mouthfuls, she put the cup down and again urged him to sleep.

He opened and closed his eyes several times, and finally said ominously, "Shu-sheng, I don't think I will ever get well again."

"What nonsense! You're being silly. Didn't the doctor say you would be well after a few days' rest and one or two more doses?" she chided him mildly.

"But you don't believe in Chinese medicine," he said, after a short pause.

"Isn't the physician related to your family? He wouldn't lie to you."

"Who isn't lying these days?" he asked rhetorically, with a bitter smile. "I don't think I'll last until the end of the war, which is probably just as well. I'm not much help to you anyway. I only burden you." First he had seemed to be murmuring to himself rather than talking aloud to her, but suddenly his tone changed and he stopped abruptly. Noticing that he had become quite emotional, Shu-sheng tried to soothe him.

"Mother is old and irritable, and she fusses over trivial things. I hope you'll not be critical of her. She means well," he said slowly, somewhat pacified.

"I know," she said, holding one of his hands in her left hand. She was on the verge of tears.

「媽呢？」他又問。

「媽在煮飯。你睡吧。等會兒又要吃藥了，」她說，把頭掉開不再看他。

過了半晌他忽然說：「請你給我倒一點茶。」他並不真想喝茶，不過想同妻多談話。

妻倒了大半杯熱茶來，他抬起頭就在她的手裏喝了三口，說一句「謝謝你」，又把頭放下去。

「你可以再睡一會兒，」妻說着站起來，去放了茶杯在方桌上。

他剛閉上眼，又睜開。他偷偷地望着妻，不讓她覺察出來。但是過了十多分鐘，他忍不住了，又喊着妻的名字，又對她說話。

「樹生，我看我的病不會好了，」他說。

「你又在亂想了，」她柔聲責備他，臉上露出好意的微笑，「醫生不是說吃兩付藥，靜養幾天就會好嗎？」

他停了片刻才說：「可是你並不相信中醫。」

妻一時答不出話，後來便說：「他是你們親戚，不會對你說假話的。」

「這個年頭哪個不說假話啊，」他苦笑說。「我知道我的病。我這個身子拖不到抗戰勝利。也好，我活着不但不能給你們幫忙，我只會累你們。」他好像在自言自語，最後聲音變了，他突然閉了嘴。妻注意到他在淌眼淚，她心裏也不好過。她只說了一句：「你不要這樣說，」便用力咬自己的下嘴唇。

「還有媽年紀大了，脾氣不大好，有時候多發幾句牢騷，希望你能夠原諒她，她的心是好的，」他又說，他吐字慢，不像剛才那樣激動。

「我知道，」她說了三個字，低着頭，伸過左手去捏住他一隻手。她也想哭。

"Thank you. I'll go to sleep now."

The yellowish electric light made the room seem particularly lifeless and accentuated his sallowness and thinness. Overcome by sympathy for him, Shu-sheng held his hand with mixed emotions.

A current of resentment surged upwards from her heart. She asked herself, "Why do we have to live like this?"

Clasping his weak, cold hand, she remonstrated against the unfairness of life, "This may be his reward for being honest and patient, but what about me? I don't and won't accept the same fate."

She looked at him again. He was sleeping soundly. Gently she let go of his hand and felt his forehead.

In the background she heard people chatting next door, motorhorns in the street, and the sounds of rats. The cold night air came through the planks in the walls and encircled her. Shivering, she wrapped her coat a little tighter around herself and directed her bitterness at the room's single electric bulb hanging from the ceiling, for the faint glow from the bulb's filament offered little warmth.

"The bulb seems to symbolize our life," she murmured. "It has never been full of light; it never burns out completely; it simply goes on and on. Two or three years ago we still had a goal; we were still able to go on, but now ... " She frowned at the realization that that possibility had steadily diminished. Bored, confused, distressed, she paced back and forth. But before long she stopped, for she was afraid that the noise might disturb him.

The old woman came into the room with dinner.

"She has also suffered," Shu-sheng thought to herself, knowing how her mother-in-law labored the whole day long.

「謝謝你。我現在睡了，」他似乎寬慰地說。

電燈光孤寂地照着這個屋子。光線暗得很。比蠟燭光強不了多少。那種病態的黃色增加了屋子的淒涼。他閉着眼，半張開嘴，一張瘦臉像塗上一層蠟，顯得十分可憐。

她仍舊捏住那隻手不放鬆，仍舊坐在床沿上，用寂寞的眼光看屋子的各處。同情和愛憐苦惱着她。但是另一種說不出的感情在搔她的心。

「為甚麼我們應該過這種日子？」一個不平的聲音在她心裏說。

她覺得左手裏捏的那隻手非常軟弱無力，並且指頭發冷。她想抗議：「這就是他忍受的報酬！我不能——」

她吃驚地看他一眼。他輕微地吐着氣。現在他似乎舒服多了。似乎並沒有噩夢驚擾他的睡眠。她輕輕地放開他那隻手。她又伸手去摸他的額角。她站起來，伸一個懶腰。

隔壁傳來一陣沙沙的語聲。從街中又傳來幾聲單調的汽車喇叭。老鼠一會兒吱吱地叫。一會兒又在啃樓板。牠們的活動似乎一直沒有停過。這更攪亂她的心。她覺得夜的寒氣透過木板從四面八方襲來，她打了一個冷噤。她把大衣在她身上裹得更緊一點。她無目的地望着電燈泡。燈泡的顏色慘澹的紅絲暖不了她的心。

「這就是我們的生活，永遠亮不起來，永還死不下去，就是這樣拖，前兩三年還有點理想，還有點希望，還可以拖下去，現在……」她說，這次她皺起了眉頭。她心裏更煩，不知道怎樣安放她這顆心。她在屋裏踱起來。但踱了幾步，她又停止了，她害怕腳步聲會驚醒他。

半掩的房門突然大開了。母親捧了飯鍋子進來。

「她也在吃苦啊，」她看見母親那種吃力的樣子，禁不住這樣想道。

"Is he sleeping?" her mother-in-law quietly asked with a faint smile.

"He seems to be sleeping quite well this time."

"Then leave him alone and we'll eat without him."

Shu-sheng ate just a bowl of rice, and her mother-in-law also had little appetite. The two chatted a little.

Watching her mother-in-law taking everything in stride, Shu-sheng was a little ashamed for not being able to do the same. But she could not dispel her feeling of quiet despair.

Finally she told herself, "Let the Japanese come. At least that would be the end of everyone." This thought made her more fretful and she castigated herself still more.

The evening passed uneventfully.

Wang appeared to be a little better the next day. Shu-sheng went back to work but suspended all her social activities. For a few days she returned home immediately after work and helped her mother-in-law with the cooking; she helped her husband take his medicine and served him breakfast and supper; and she talked to him in the evenings when he was awake. With the exception of current events, her conversation ranged from her work to other topics.

The medicine seemed to have a positive effect on Wang, much to the delight of his mother, who became more convinced of the efficacy of Chinese medicine. Shu-sheng only smiled. But actually it was Shu-sheng's change of attitude toward him that was the real cure.

"Where are the Japanese now?" he wondered. He did not want to ask Shu-sheng because he was afraid to hear any bad news. Sometimes he would study her face, secretly searching for a clue to the war situation, but she was always smiling. And when he caught her deep

「他睡了？」母親的憔悴的面容上露出一絲笑容，她把臉向着床低聲問道。

她點點頭，低聲回答：「這回好像睡得還好。」

「那麼讓他多睡一會兒，等他醒來再吃藥吧，」母親說，「我們先吃飯。」

她和母親對面坐着吃了一碗飯。母親沒有胃口，她覺得寂寞，覺得沒趣，在飯桌上勉強和母親講了幾句話。

「她都受得了，她似乎就安於這種生活，為甚麼我就不可以呢？」她暗暗地責備自己，可是這並沒有減輕她的寂寞之感。

「好吧，日本人早點打來也好，大家都毀滅……」她更煩躁，她第二次在心裏責備自己。

但是這一晚終於平靜地過去了。

第二天他的病勢稍微減輕一點。她仍舊去銀行辦公，不過上午去得較晚，午後下了班便回到家裏來。她把同事朋友間的交際應酬全斷絕了。她幫忙母親燒飯。有時候照料他吃藥和吃早飯、晚飯。晚飯後他不想睡覺時，她還陪他談些閒話。她談着她那個銀行裏外的事，她甚麼都談，就只不談時局。

中藥似乎很有功效。他的身體一天一天地好起來。母親當着妻的面稱讚中醫高明，妻並沒有反駁，只是微微一笑。其實有效的藥倒是妻的態度的改變。他需要的正是休息和安慰。

「究竟日本軍隊打到了甚麼地方？」他覺得病漸漸好起來，精神可以集中時，就常常想着這個問題。但是他不敢問她，他害怕聽到一個令人心驚的回答。有時候他也注意地看她的臉色，他想從她的表情上猜出戰局的好壞，但是這沒有用。在這些天裏她常常給他看

in thought, she would quickly cover her thoughts with a smile. Furthermore, she had made peace with his mother, with whom she would voluntarily talk from time to time. To Wang, who was a witness to this when he was not asleep, it all seemed too good to be true. His illness, he felt, had brought the two women closer together.

One day Shu-sheng came home and announced in great excitement, "Good news! The bombing of Kweiyang was only a rumor. Tu-shan still belongs to us. The Japanese never occupied Kweichow."

Her smile was sunny and brought him great enjoyment.

"Really?" he answered, looking at his wife gratefully. "Tomorrow I should get up and go out."

"No, no. You've rested only four days, and you need at least ten days to two weeks," she said. "Please just take care of your health and think of nothing else."

"What about money?" he asked.

"Don't worry about it. I know how to get it."

"But I hate to use your money. You have a lot of expenses, and Hsiao Hsüan is also spending your money," he said apologetically.

"Isn't he my son too? Between us, what's yours or mine? Isn't mine yours too?" she reproved him with a smile.

Her logic was such that he could not argue with her.

"Some time ago the bank planned to revise its pay scale. This was interrupted because of the uncertainty of the Hunan-Kwangsi campaign. Now they say that the new scale will be adopted as soon as confirmation is received that the situation is better. Once it becomes official, I will earn a third more. Therefore it's quite all right to spend some money," she explained, noticing her husband's continued pensiveness.

到她的溫和而愉快的表情。偶爾他看見她在沉思，但她馬上就用笑容掩飾了一切。她不再跟母親爭吵了。他覺得，有時也恍惚地看見(當他閉着眼或半閉着眼睛假寐時)她們兩人常常在一處交談。「只希望她們從此和好起來，那麼我這次吐血也值得，」他也曾寬慰地這樣想過。

一天妻下班回來，很興奮地對他說：

「我告訴你一個好消息，貴陽大轟炸全是謠言，獨山失守也是謠言，日本人根本就沒有進貴州。」

她燦爛地笑了，他喜歡看她這樣的笑容。

「真的？」他欣慰地嘆一口氣，用感謝的眼光看着她。「明天我倒想出去看看，」他慢聲說。

「你才只睡了四天。至少你要睡上十天半月才好，」妻勸他道。「你只管養病好了，別的事情你一概不用管。」

「錢呢？」他微笑地問道。

「我有辦法，你不必管它，」妻回答。

「不過多用你的錢也不好。你自己花錢的地方很多。小宣也在花你的錢，」他抱歉地說。

「小宣不是我的兒子嗎？我們兩個人還要分甚麼彼此！我的錢跟你的錢不是一樣的？」她笑着責備他道。

他不作聲，他找不出話來駁她。

「前些天我們行裏在鬧着調整待遇，後來給湘桂戰事擱下來了。現在又在說，戰事好轉後就可以實行。調整後我的收入可以增加三分之一。所以多花點錢也不要緊，」她看見他閉着嘴在沉思，便又含笑解釋道。

"But still a man of my age ought to be able to support himself."

"Why are you so old-fashioned? Why can't you see things another way? Once you get well, once the Japanese are defeated, you'll find a good job. Do you think I enjoy my work at the bank? I simply have no choice. When the war is over, maybe I'll join you in an educational program to help the people."

"Yes, once the Japanese are defeated ...," he muttered in disbelief.

His mother came in with dinner.

"Mother, let me help you," Shu-sheng volunteered.

"You'd better go and check his porridge. Don't let it be overcooked. I can handle the work here." Although she heard her, Shu-sheng still picked up an old newspaper and put it on the table to enable her mother-in-law to place the hot pan on it.

After Shu-sheng had left to look after the porridge, Wang thought with self-satisfaction: "She's still very nice to me, no matter how unworthy I am. This good woman! But using her money embarrasses me so. One of these days she'll despise me for it. I must do something." Then he remembered what she had said: "Once the Japanese are defeated ... I will go back to education."

"What is it. Hsüan?" His mother thought he had spoken to her.

"Nothing, I didn't say anything," he said, shaking his head. His mother's question awoke him from his daydreaming, which offered him everything that the chilly room could not.

"How do you feel now?" his mother asked softly, after having felt his forehead.

"Fine. I feel that the medicine has been helpful."

"We'll ask the doctor to look at you again tomorrow," she said.

「不過這總不大好，我過意不去。想不到我活到這樣大，連自己也養不活，」他沉吟地說，態度十分認真。

「你怎麼這樣迂！連這點事也想不通，你病好了，時局好了，日本人打退了，你就有辦法了。你以為我就高興在銀行裏做事嗎？現在也是沒有辦法。將來我還是要跟你一道做理想的工作，幫忙你辦教育，」她溫和地安慰他。

「是啊，日本人打退了，我就有辦法了，」他喃喃地自語道。

母親端着飯鍋子進來了。

「媽，讓我來，」她走着輕快的步子去迎母親，想從母親手裏接過鍋子來。

「你快去看看宣的稀飯，不要燒焦了。這個我自己會弄，」母親搖搖頭說，但是她仍然檢了一張舊報放在方桌上給母親墊鍋子。

他望着妻的背影在門外消失了，他感激地暗暗對自己說：「她仍然對我好。不管我多麼不中用，她仍然對我好。這個好心的女人！只是我不好意思用她的錢，她會看輕我的，她有一天會看輕我的。我應該振作起來。」他想了一會兒，忍不住出聲唸着她剛才說過的話：「時局好了，日本人打退了，就有辦法了。我將來還是回到教育界去。」

「你要甚麼，宣？」母親以為他在跟她講話，便過來問道。

「我沒有講話，」他搖頭說，他好像剛剛走進一個夢境，就突然被他母親喚醒了。這個陰暗寒冷的房間能夠給他甚麼希望呢？

母親還立在床前，她伸手摸了一下他的前額，過後又柔聲問：「你現在覺得怎樣？」

「很好，」他答道。「我覺得藥很有效。」

「明天再請醫生來一趟，」她說。

Shu-sheng brought in the porridge. At that moment the lights went out. "No electricity again?" he grumbled aloud. "They never let you have enough light."

"Light? Do you want light, too?" Shu-sheng asked. He did not know whether she was being sarcastic or not.

His mother lit a candle; then she left the room. The unsteady candlelight and its yellowish flicker colored every object in the room with a melancholy hue. Inside the room, two rats were now running around; outside, a woman's tragic voice wailed so that her offspring might be restored to health.

"Light! How dare I hope for it?" he sighed resignedly.

"Don't be too pessimistic. Concentrate on taking care of your health. I'll get the medicine for you before you fall asleep," said Shu-sheng.

"No, go ahead and eat. Actually I don't think it matters very much whether I take the medicine or not. I know you don't believe in this kind of drug. I'd appreciate it though, if you gave it to me after you eat. It may be effective after all, for I do feel better this evening. I hate the bitter taste, but then it has always been said the more bitter the medicine tastes, the more effective it is. Mother believes in it. She lives in her own world, which includes only two people besides herself: me and Hsiao Hsüan. But I am so hopelessly useless." He paused. "Where is she now? Is she still cooking supper? Or is she preparing my medicine? Please see what she is doing.... I feel quite happy this evening. Since the war situation is improving, we won't have to flee. Otherwise I would be a great burden to you."

Shu-sheng walked out of the room. His listless eyes looked at the dark shadows caused by the flickering candlelight. He could see hardly anything. He sighed painfully.

「不必了，我已經好了，」他說。心裏卻想道：「我哪裏有錢看病吃藥呢？你真要我靠樹生過日子嗎？」

妻進屋來照料他吃了稀飯。電燈突然熄了。「怎麼今晚上又停電？」他掃興地說。「他們總不給你看見光明，」他訴苦地又加了一句。

「光明？你現在也要光明了？」妻說。他不知道妻是在讚美他，還是在諷刺他。

母親點燃了蠟燭，又走出去了。屋子裏亮起來，但搖幌不定的慘黃色的燭光，給每一件東西都抹上一層憂鬱的顏色。兩隻老鼠穿過屋子賽跑。樓下有一個女人用淒涼的聲音在給小孩叫魂。

「光明。我哪裏敢有這個妄想啊？」他嘆口氣斷念地說。

「你不要悲觀，你好好養病吧。你還有一道藥要吃。我去跟你弄來，你吃了好早點睡覺，」妻柔聲勸慰道。

「不，你自己先吃了飯再說。其實吃不吃藥都沒有關係，我知道你並不相信這種藥。你吃過飯再給我吃藥也好，也許這種藥很有用處，我覺得今晚人好多了。我有點怕吃這種藥，真苦啊。不過也有人說藥越苦越靈驗。我吃了藥也放心些，媽相信這種藥。她的世界裏就只有我同小宣兩個人，偏偏我又不中用。」他勉強笑了笑。「你快去吃飯。媽怎麼不進來？她還在弄菜嗎？她一定是在給我弄藥。她真是太好了。你快去看看她，你們快點吃飯吧。不要管我的事。我可以閉着眼睛睡一會兒。」他又笑了笑。「你快去！我今天很高興，戰局好轉，也免得大家逃難，不然我這個身體會累壞你們。」

妻走出了房門。他的眼光無力地向屋子四周移動。燭光搖幌得厲害。屋裏到處都是陰影，他甚麼也看不透。他痛苦地嘆了一口氣。

The next day Shu-sheng returned home early. Her eyebrows knitted together, she dejectedly slipped into the room. With a forced smile she said hello to her mother-in-law and to her husband, and then sat down quietly by the desk.

"Why are you home so early?" asked her mother-in-law in surprise.

"There wasn't much to do. I didn't feel good, so I left early."

"Will you be going out tonight?" her mother-in-law asked, almost without meaning to.

"No. The war news is bad, and no one wants to work," Shu-sheng said, shaking her head in a hesitant manner.

"What have you heard? What's happened?" her mother-in-law asked in alarm.

"The Japanese have taken Tu-shan, and they are approaching Tu-yün."

"What shall we do? Hsüan is still sick. Will the Japanese get to Szechwan?"

"Probably not. If they do, we'd have to flee. I'd be evacuated with the bank personnel; the problem is Hsüan."

"Of course, you'd have no problem, but what would we do? How could we go anywhere empty-handed? With Hsao Hsüan away at school and Hsüan sick, what would we do?" asked her mother-in-law.

"Mother, I'm almost well. I can move around, so don't worry about me. Maybe my Company has made some arrangements for the employees," Wang interjected, well aware that he was lying.

"Your Company? Aren't you expecting too much? I have my doubts

第二天妻回來得很早。她鎖住眉頭，疲倦地走進屋來，招呼了他和母親，勉強一笑，就默默地在書桌前坐下。

「怎麼你今天回來得這樣早，還不到下辦公時間？」母親問道。

「行裏沒有事，坐着心煩得很。所以我早退了，」妻沒精打采地答道。

「你今天沒有甚麼應酬吧？」母親無意地問了一句。

「沒有，」妻搖搖頭，過了片刻，又說：「今天消息不大好，大家都沒有心情辦公。」

「究竟怎麼啦？」母親變了臉色問道。

「聽說獨山已經失守了。又說日本人已經過了獨山，就要到都勻了。」

「那麼我們怎麼辦？宣又在害病！」母親慌張地說。「你看日本人會不會打到四川來？」

「我想也許不會。不過打來了，我們也只有逃難。我可以跟着銀行走，就是宣的問題——」妻皺着眉頭沉吟地說，但母親打斷了她的話。

「你自然有辦法。不過我跟宣，還有小宣，我們往哪裏去好？我們赤手空拳怎麼好逃難？偏偏小宣兩個星期都沒有進城，說是功課忙。宣又在害病，真急死人！」母親只顧訴苦地說下去，她帶着一種徬徨無助的可憐樣子。

「媽，我的病差不多全好了，我可以走動的，你不要耽心。我們公司一定也有辦法安置我們，」他忍不住提高聲音插嘴說，關於公司的話，是他說來安慰母親的，那只是他的妄想，話一說出，他馬上看見了周主任的冷冰冰的臉孔和嚴厲的眼光，他的心就冷了半截。

「你們公司有辦法？你太老好了！你對公司還有甚麼指望？我看

about that boss of yours; with his thievish eyes, he wouldn't be any help," Shu-sheng said. "If I had anything to do about it, I wouldn't let you work for him."

He knew she was telling the truth, but he resented her saying it so bluntly before his mother. He protested, "Why shouldn't I work for him? I earn an honest living, don't I?"

"Certainly. But did he ever give you enough to live on? What kind of living do you have? He doesn't make it worth your while to take all his nonsense," Shu-sheng replied heatedly.

"Why remember all the unpleasantness? What's past is past," he sighed.

"But you still have a future ...," Shu-sheng answered with tear-filled eyes.

Her gentle tone of voice made him look at her gratefully.

"Mr. Wang! Mr. Wang!" called Mrs. Chang suddenly, standing just outside the room.

"Please come in, please come in," Wang's mother said warmly.

Mrs. Chang stepped into the room. Surprised at seeing Shu-sheng, she said to her, "You are off work early." Then turning to Wang, she asked, "Mr. Wang, are you feeling better today?" And finally, to the old woman, she said, "You must have had your hands full in the last few days." Then she spoke to all of them: "Mr. Wang! Mrs. Wang! Mama Wang! You must help us. When you flee, please take us with you. My husband, my two-year-old baby, and I are strangers in this area. We have no relatives here, no money, and no means of transportation. My husband's office may close down at any time, and he probably won't be evacuated with the rest of the staff. If the Japanese come, you must help us. Wherever you local folks go, either into

那個周主任就不是個好人，他那對賊一樣的眼睛真討厭！」妻帶了點氣憤地說。「要是我有辦法，我一定不讓你在他手下做事。」

他知道她說的是真話。但是當着母親的面說出來，這真話傷了他的心，引起他的反感。「為甚麼我不能在他手下做事？我是靠我的勞力吃飯的，」他分辯道。

「你的話不錯，可是他給你吃飽沒有？你應該記着他叫你過的甚麼日子，叫你受他欺負，太不值得！」妻說。

「記着有甚麼用？過去的橫順已經過去了，」他嘆口氣說。

「可是你還有將來啊。你不應該灰心，」妻又說，她的聲音突然變得非常柔和，眼睛裏湧現了淚水。

她的聲音使他吃驚，他感激地望着她的眼睛。

「汪先生，汪先生，」隔壁張太太的聲音在門外響起來，把他的眼光喚到房門口去。

「請進來，請進來，」母親連忙大聲招呼。

張太太推開掩着的門進來。「汪太太，你今天下班早！」她沒有想到會看見樹生在房裏。「汪先生，今天身體好些了吧。」然後她又向着他母親：「老太太，你這兩天夠辛苦啊！」再後：「汪太太，汪先生，老太太，一定要請你們幫忙。要逃難時讓我們跟你們一道。我跟我們張先生，帶個兩歲小孩，又是外省人，無親無戚，逃難，沒有錢，又沒有車。他們的機關說不定隨時都會撤銷，不會帶我們走的。萬一日本人打來，你們做做好事救救我們吧。你們本省人，到鄉下去，也可以，到別的縣份去也可以，總之我們跟着你們走，好

the countryside or to another district, please let us go with you."

Though Wang knew little about the current war situation, he said, seeking to calm his hysterical neighbor, "The situation is probably not as bad as you think."

"I heard that Tu-yün is lost. The Japanese are only several dozen miles away from Kweiyang.... Some say that they can get here without even going through Kweiyang. Mr. Wang, Mrs. Wang, you must help us."

"Mrs. Chang, don't be frightened," interrupted Shu-sheng. "Things may not have deteriorated that much."

"Everyone has been frightened in the last four days," she replied. "With little else to do, my husband drinks all the time. That is worrisome enough. Well, just let me thank you all in advance. I must get back before the child wakes up from his nap. If anything happens, I'll come again." The faint smile on her face could not hide her worries or brighten her wrinkled face.

"Shu-sheng, your news is now verified," he said to his wife. His voice was calm, as if he were talking about something of no concern to him.

"I am not sure what to do. My boss, Department Chief Ch'en, has advised me to leave here," she replied with equanimity, although her thoughts were in a whirl.

"Where would you go?" he asked, very softly.

"Mr. Ch'en has been promoted to a manager's post in Lanchow, and he wants me to go with him," she replied in an equally low voice, turning her face away from him.

"Are you going?" He raised his voice, agitated.

不好？」她帶着一種孤苦無助的神情哀求道。

「事情還不會壞到這樣吧，」他安慰她說，為了表示鎮靜，他勉強露出一個笑容。

「聽說都勻已經完了。日本人離貴陽只有幾十里了，」張太太好像害怕人聽見似地，做出嚴肅的樣子放低聲音說。「有人說還有一條路可以不經過貴陽就到四川來。汪先生，汪太太，實在要找你們幫忙啊。」

「張太太，你不要怕，都是謠言，事情不會壞到這樣，」樹生溫和地說。

「這兩天外面人心惶惶，我們張先生沒有辦法，就只顧吃酒，你們看怎麼不叫人着急！好的，謝謝你們啊，我回去囉，小孩恐怕要醒了，有事情我再過來。謝謝你們啊，」張太太的蒼白臉上現出一個微笑。但這微笑並沒有使她的雙眉開展，額上的皺紋平順。她輕腳輕手地走出去了。

「樹生，那麼你的消息證實了，」他低聲對妻說，話語裏不帶感情，好像還是一件與他毫無關係的事一樣。

「我也不清楚，不過陳主任勸我準備走，」妻冷冷地答道，好像這事情也跟她不相干似的，可是實際上它正攪亂着她的心。

「走，走哪裏去呢？」他極力壓低聲音問道。

「他運動升調蘭州，今天發表了，他做經理，要調我去，」妻也極力壓低聲音說，她故意掉開眼睛不看他。

「那麼你去不去？」他又問，聲音提高許多，他無法掩飾他的慌張了。

"I don't want to. If I could stay here, I'd rather stay," she answered thoughtfully.

"If he insists that you go, can you refuse him?"

"Certainly I can, though it is generous of him to offer me the opportunity," she answered loudly.

Impatiently her mother-in-law asked, "If you leave, what about your son and your husband?"

"Please stop worrying. I haven't agreed to go," she said calmly, not letting her mother-in-law's query irritate her.

"But you haven't refused him either," her mother-in-law probed further.

"No, I just haven't made a decision. Who knows whether or not the entire bank will evacuate to Lanchow? Everything is up in the air." Her voice was unpleasant, but she spoke with composure.

"I know you want to abandon us. Don't think I can't see through you!" said her mother-in-law emotionally.

Shu-sheng made no direct reply but walked over to her husband's bed and sat down by him. When she saw the tears running down his cheeks, she clasped his hand and promised that she would not leave him.

"I know, I know," he said, deeply grateful. Then as an afterthought, he added, "But you should go. What's the good of your staying here? My life is finished."

"Don't talk like that; don't blame yourself. You've suffered greatly all these years. You must take care of your health first."

"Well, who else is there to blame? Why do others do so well?" He

「我不想去，我能夠不去就不去，」她沉吟地答道。

「行裏調你去，你不去可以嗎？」他繼續問。

「當然可以，我還有這自由，至多也不過辭職，不過陳主任也是一番好意，」她也提高聲音回答。

「你一個人走了，那麼小宣怎麼辦？宣怎麼辦？」母親忽然板起臉問道。

「我還沒有答應去，」妻坦然回答，母親的話並沒有激怒她。

「那麼你也沒有回絕他，」母親不肯放鬆地說。

「不過我並沒有答應去。況且會不會調，還不知道。現在只是一句話。」妻的聲音裏帶了一點不愉快，但她還能夠保持安靜。

「我看你很想拋下我們，一個人走。你的心我還不知道！」母親仍然在追逼。

妻不回答，她走到床前，在床沿上坐下，略略埋下頭看他。她看出了他的眼淚。她默默地抓住他一隻手，過了好一會兒，她才掙出一句話：「我不會走的。」

「我知道，」他點着頭感動地說。「謝謝你啊！」過了半晌，他又低聲說：「其實你應該走，你跟我一輩子有甚麼好處？我這一輩子算是完結了。」

「你不要這樣說，這是境遇，不能怪你，這兩年你也苦夠了。你先養好身體再說，」妻感激地勸慰他。

「不怪我，又怪誰呢？為甚麼別的人又有辦法？」他說。聽見她

held himself responsible for his family's poverty.

"Because you are too good," his wife said, smiling and giving him a loving and compassionate look.

"Too good!" Those accursed words had been making him sick for some time already, and here they were hurting him once again. Shu-sheng had not intended to be sarcastic, but just hearing them was enough to depress him. He thought: "I don't want to be 'too good.' But how can I not be 'too good'? It's my nature to act that way." He became reconciled with himself. He sighed lightly.

"You're unhappy again?" asked Shu-sheng, somewhat surprised.

He shook his head. Only then did he realize that his mother had retired to her own room.

Shu-sheng suggested he rest for a while, saying. "I'll stay with you. Don't worry."

Nodding, he replied in a low voice. "I know, I know."

Shu-sheng stood up, went to the window and looked out aimlessly. The window on the right-hand side overlooked a small lane and a street, and their building was taller than any of the surrounding ones. The main street came down from a hillside, and she saw rickshaws racing down the hill, the feet of the rickshaw-pullers flying in the air. She felt dazed.

"How busy they are," she commented to herself casually, without thinking. Her mind might have been filled with many thoughts, but it could have just as well been empty. Looking down at the dusty street below, she felt time streaming past her like water in a creek, slowly but steadily, as her blood also flowed.

"Am I going to live like this for the rest of my life?" she sighed, unable to find an answer.

這樣勸慰的話，他更不能抑制下責備自己的念頭。

「這是因為你太老好，」妻微笑說，她的眼光裏含着愛和憐憫。

老好！這兩個字使他的心隱隱地發痛。又是這個他聽厭了的評語！雖然她並沒有一點譏諷的意思。他不再作聲了。他想那個他永遠解決不了的問題。「我不要做老好人！」「可是怎樣才能夠不做老好人呢？」「沒辦法。我本性是這樣。」這三句話把他的一切不平和反抗的念頭完全消耗盡了。他這幾年的光陰也就浪費在這問答上面。……於是他輕輕嘆了一口氣。

「怎樣你又不快活了？」妻吃驚地問。

「沒有，」他搖搖頭說，他這時才注意到母親已回到小屋去了。

「那麼，你再睡一會兒。我就在家裏陪你。我不會一個人走的，你不要耽心，」妻柔聲安慰他。

「我知道，我知道，」他小聲答應着，一面微微地點頭。

她站起來，慢慢地走到一扇窗前，無目的地看望下面的街景。窗戶開在這建築的右面磚牆上。下面是一條小小的橫街(其實只是小巷)。這建築比它四近的房屋都高，並沒有牆壁和屋頂遮住窗內的視線。她也可以看見大街。大街是從山坡開闢出來的。迎着她眼光的正是高的一段。因此她能夠看見幾輛人力車銜接地從坡上跑下來，車夫的幾乎不挨地懸空般跑着的雙腳使她眼花繚亂。

「他們都忙啊，」她自語道，這是她隨口說出來的，聲音低，只有她自己聽得見。她說這話好像並沒有用意，但又像有很多意思。她心裏彷彿裝了不少的東西，但又好像空無一物。她並不想看甚麼，卻一直站在窗前望着塵土瀰漫的馬路。她覺得「時間」像溪水一樣地在她身邊流過，緩緩地，但是從不停止。她的血似乎也跟着在流。

「難道我就應該這樣過完一輩子？」這是她心裏的聲音。她不能回答。她嘆一口氣。

Shortly afterwards a bank messenger knocked on the door and walked in.

"Miss Tseng, Mr. Ch'en has a letter for you," he said and handed it to her.

She read the brief note, an invitation to dinner at the Victory Building, and then she tore it up.

To the messenger she said, "I know all about it. You can go back."

The messenger left, closing the door behind him. Holding the torn pieces of the letter in her hand she stood in front of the window. The light in the room was fading fast and the night, like a painter's brush moving from here to there, darkened every corner. Her husband was breathing hard, and no one knew what he was dreaming; her mother-in-law was in the adjoining room, and the stillness accentuated her loneliness. She felt the blood coursing through her veins and wondered about her future. "Am I to die like a dry stump?" she asked, pacing the room and not knowing what to do.

Her mother-in-law entered the room and switched on the pale, yellowish light. Tauntingly she asked. "Ah, haven't you left yet?"

Without hesitation, Shu-sheng replied. "I am leaving now." Looking at the hands that had just torn up the invitation, she turned toward her mother-in-law with a vindictive smile.

"Have you been invited to supper?"

"Yes, someone from the office just invited me."

"What for? To bid you farewell?"

A blush spread over the young woman's face. Infuriated, she almost exploded, but regaining control of herself, she nodded, smiled,

忽然門上起了兩下叩聲。她吃驚地掉轉身子。銀行裏的工友推開掩着的門進來。

「曾小姐，陳主任有封信給你，」工友把信遞給她。

她拆開信，看了信上寥寥幾句話。他約她到勝利大廈吃晚飯。她默默地把信箋撕了。

工友站在她面前。等候她說話。「知道了，你回去吧，」她吩咐道。

「是，」工友唯唯應着，掩上門走出去了。

她捏着撕碎了的信箋，背靠着窗站了一會。屋子漸漸地在褪色，但是夜像一管畫筆，在屋角胡亂塗抹。病人的臉開始模糊了。他在床上發出急促的呼吸。不知道他在做着怎樣的夢。母親在小屋內沒有一點聲息。他們把寂寞留給她一個人，她覺得血在流走，不停地流走。她漸漸地感到不安了。「難道我就這樣地枯死麼？」她忽然起了這一個疑問。她在屋子裏走了幾步。她不知道自己應該做些甚麼。

母親從小屋走出來，扭燃了這屋子的電燈，又是那使人心煩的灰黃色，「啊，你還沒有走？」母親故意對她發出這句問話。

「我就走，」她不加思索地回答。她看了看那隻捏着撕碎的信箋的手。她露出一個報復的微笑。她本來還沒有考慮去和不去的問題，現在她決定了。

「今天又有人請吃飯？」母親逼着再問一句。

「行裏的同事，」她簡單地答道。

「是給你們餞行吧？」

母親這句話刺傷了她。她臉一紅，眉毛一豎，她準備和這個老婦人爭吵。但是話還未出口，她立刻把怒氣壓止了，她故意做出一

and said, "Yes."

She changed her clothes, put on some make-up, and left without waking her husband. Her mother-in-law murmured something as she disappeared down the stairs.

She thought angrily how she would have loved to tell her mother-in-law that she had left not because she wanted to, but simply to show that she was free and independent.

XV

SHE took a rickshaw to the Victory Building. Ch'en was waiting for her at the door and escorted her upstairs, where a table had been reserved in the dining room. He helped her take off her coat and be seated, smiling at her so happily that it was embarrassing. She asked, "Did you get your airplane ticket?"

"Yes, I have. I'll leave in three days," he said with a serious look.

"That's good. Then 'bon voyage.' Will you come back next year?" she asked with a smile.

Her smile puzzled and encouraged him. With an earnest expression, he whispered, "Shu-sheng." This was the first time he had called her by her first name; she was surprised and blushed a little. He continued, "I've just received some reliable news. The Japanese have occupied Tu-yün, and there are rumors that Kweiyang is in danger."

"So soon?" she said surprised, trying hard to conceal her fear.

個滿不在乎的微笑。她點頭説:「是。」

她換了一件衣服,再略略化粧一下。她想跟他講幾句話。可是他還在睡夢中。她看了他一眼,然後裝出得意的神氣走出了房門。她還聽見母親在她後面嘰咕,便急急地走下樓去。

「你越説,我越要做給你看,本來我不一定去的,」她撅起嘴氣惱地自語道。

十五

她坐人力車到了勝利大廈。陳主任在門口等候她。他陪她上樓。他已經在餐室裏定了座位。他幫忙她脱去大衣,讓她坐下來。他坐在她的對面。他含笑地望着她,看得她有點不好意思。她便開口先説:

「飛機票弄好嗎?」

「弄好了,大後天走,」他換了一個比較緊張的表情回答。

「很好,那麼再見了。明年還回來吧,」她笑着説。

她這笑容使他不知道她的真意是甚麼,但是這鼓舞着他。他做出懇切的表情,低聲説:「樹生,」他喚她的名字,這是第一次,以前他都稱她為「Miss曾。」她聽見這稱呼,稍吃一驚,臉微紅一下。他接下去説:「我剛才得着可靠的消息,敵人已經打進了都勻,看這情形是擋不住的了,還有謠言説貴陽已經靠不住了。」

「不會這樣快吧?」她搖搖頭説,極力掩飾她的心裏的恐懼。

"Yes, sooner than anyone expected," he said. He was saved from showing his own fear by the arrival of a waiter carrying the soup. After he tasted it, he asked her, "What are your plans?"

"Mine? What plans could I have but to stay here?"

"What if the Japanese come here?"

"Well, if there's time, we might flee to a safer place; otherwise we'd hide in the countryside," she said, seemingly unconcerned. Bending her head, she continued to eat her soup.

"No, that won't work. When the Japanese come, they'll be looking for women in the countryside. There is no problem at the bank. I can arrange a black-market air ticket for you, and you can leave with me in three days."

"That's too soon. I couldn't manage it." She raised her eyes to glance at him; then she looked down.

"But the Japanese might come here even sooner. This is a rare opportunity for you. What I have said is true. The situation is really bad and you must make a decision."

She remained quiet, thinking of her husband's anemic face, her mother-in-law's sulky, jealous looks, their dreary lifeless rooms, the enemy's atrocities, and of the horrors of the Hunan-Kwangsi Road described by the refugees. Confused and worried about the future, she put down her spoon and admitted her apprehension. "But can I leave now?" she asked.

"Why can't you? Remember this is your last chance. Isn't your family situation rather simple? What makes it so difficult?" Although he knew she had an ailing husband and a disagreeable mother-in-law, he did not know she had a 13-year-old son and a husband whose sickness was so serious she could not leave.

「快得很，簡直叫你想不到！」他差一點要把舌頭伸出來了。這時茶房端上湯來，他連忙把嘴閉上，低下頭拿起湯匙喝了兩口湯。「你打算怎麼辦？」

「我嗎？我往哪裏去呢？我還不是留在這個地方！」她故意笑着回答。

「那麼日本人打來怎麼辦？」他又問。

「等他們打來再說。來得及就逃，來不及就躲到鄉下去，」她故意裝出不在乎的神情回答。她埋下頭喝湯。

「這樣不行，日本人來，會到鄉下找花姑娘的。你還是早走的好，行裏的事沒有問題。我有辦法給你弄張黑市飛機票，你大後天跟我走，」他做出嚴肅的表情說。

「大後天太快了，我來不及，」她說，抬起眼睛看他，又略略埋下頭去。

「你還嫌快？日本人來得更快啊！」他着急地說。「這是一個機會，錯過了就不容易找了。我說的全是真話，現在局勢的確很嚴重，請你早點打定主意。」

半晌不作聲。她開始在思索。丈夫的沒有血色的病臉，母親的嫌恨與妒忌的眼光，永遠陰暗的房間。……還有湘桂路上逃難的故事，敵人的暴行……這一切全擠到她的腦子裏來。她的心亂得很，她無法打定主意。她不能再裝假了。她放下湯匙，抬起頭嘆息地說：「我目前怎麼走得了？」

「走不了？你記着這是逃難的時候啊。你家庭不是很簡單嗎？你還有甚麼丟不下的！」他說，他知道她有一個丈夫和丈夫的母親，他也知道她丈夫多病，她又跟那母親合不來，他也知道她不大喜歡她這個家。他卻不知道她還有一個十三歲的男孩。他也不知道她「丟不下的」還是那個多病的丈夫。

"I can't decide right now. Please give me time to think," she replied. She hoped he would not press her; she did not like to make grave decisions on the spur of the moment.

"Fine. I'll give you until tomorrow. It will be nearly impossible to get airplane tickets after that."

"Let me think," she answered. Then suddenly changing her mind, she shook her head and said. "I think it would be better if I gave you an answer now. I can't leave with you."

Her answer took him by surprise. "But why? This will be your last chance. Don't give it up. Don't sacrifice yourself for others. They don't care for you. Why should you care for them?"

She remained silent. They were now having fish, the main course.

"Shu-sheng, think hard. You must not sacrifice yourself like this. You'd better leave with me," he said beseechingly.

"But what about them?" she spoke softly as if talking to herself.

"They can take care of themselves. Your staying here wouldn't help them anyhow."

"But he ... " She stopped on the verge of revealing her true situation to Ch'en, a man three years younger than she. It was the sallow face of her sickly husband that prevented her from doing so. It would expose her to ridicule.

"Even at this late date, you are still thinking about others? Don't. You're too kind," he continued. "What good is a kind heart? You'll only sacrifice yourself needlessly. It's not worth it."

Displeased by his remarks, she said crossly, "Staying here won't mean instant death, will it?"

「太快了，讓我多想想，」她搖頭說，她不希望他再拿這樣的話逼她。她不願意馬上就決定這個大問題。

「那麼我明天早晨聽回信，過了明天就難弄到飛機票了，」他說。

「等我想想，」她沉吟地答道，但是接着她又搖一下頭。「我看還是現在回答你吧，我不去了，」她含笑說。

「這是一個最後的機會，你不能放過啊，」他稍為變了臉色說。「你不應該為你家裏人犧牲，他們都不關心你，你何必還耽心他們的事。」

湯盆早已收去，現在換上了魚來。她低着頭，不做聲。

「樹生，你多想一想。你不能這樣白白犧牲你自己啊。你還是跟我一起走吧，」他懇求道。

「但是他們怎麼辦？」她像在對自己說話似地說。

「他們會照顧自己，你不走對他們恐怕也沒有好處。」

「可是他——」她原想說「他在生病」，但是剛說出「他」字，她忽然住了嘴。應該說是那張黃瘦的病臉堵住了她的嘴。她不願意在這個年紀比她小三歲的男人面前提到她的丈夫，那太寒傖了。

「在這種時候，你還想到別人，你的心腸太好了，」他連忙接下去說。「可是心腸好，又有甚麼用？你只有白白犧牲你自己，太不值得。」

他這幾句話她聽起來不大入耳，她略略皺着眉，冷冷地說一句：「不走也不見得就會死吧。」

"Shu-sheng, you've no idea how serious the situation is. I'm not joking with you."

"I'm not joking either," she said with a faint smile. Then she added, "There are thousands and thousands of people here. Why are you so concerned about me?"

"Because I ... " he started to explain, stammering. However, she was afraid to hear what he was going to say. So she blushed and interrupted him, understanding full well what he had in mind.

While they were drinking coffee, they overheard a patron speaking to another. "I've decided to move my whole family to the country. What about you? Have you made up your mind yet?"

"I just got here. I'm completely exhausted," answered the other patron. "I am, in fact, quite prepared to die here if necessary. Where else can we go? We're the people from the Down-under region,* and we've nowhere to go even if we wanted to flee again."

Seizing the opportunity, Ch'en said to Shu-sheng, "Did you hear that? That's the real situation, and you must leave with me."

"Even if I were to say yes, it's not so simple. I'd have so many things to do," she said, confused and frightened.

"Why should you worry about anything at this critical time? Don't argue any more. Just get ready," he urged her excitedly.

"You sound as though you're forcing me to run away with you," she said smiling, deliberately trying to conceal her uncertainty.

"Of course it sounds that way, because I care about you," he said tremulously, reaching for her hand.

---

* People in Szechwan used to refer to those who came from the Lower-Yangtze regions in this way.

「樹生，你不知道，戰局多嚴重。我並不是在跟你開玩笑，」他着急地說。

「我並沒有說你在開玩笑，」她說，微微一笑，接着又加添說：「不過這個地方有千萬的人，你為甚麼就關心我一個？」

「因為我——」他答道，但是她害怕聽他說出下面的話，她已經明白他的意思，她臉一紅，連忙用別的話打岔了。

到最後喝着咖啡的時候，他們忽然聽見鄰座一個人說：「我決定全家搬回鄉下去。你呢？不可不早打主意啊。」

「我才逃到這裏來，已經精疲力盡了。還有甚麼辦法呢！我只好準備死在這裏。」另一個聲音回答：「我們『腳底下人』，要逃都沒有去處。」

「你聽他們的話！」陳主任低聲提醒她說。「可見時局的確嚴重，你非跟我走不可。」

「要走也沒有這樣容易，我有許多未了的事啊，」她順口答道，她有點害怕，她的心思更不定了。

「這個時候還管那些事情！你不必多講了。你準備大後天走吧，」他激動地說。

「聽你這口氣，你好像要強迫我跟你走，」她微笑說，故意掩飾她的不定心。

「當然，因為我關心你，」他用了顫抖的聲音。他伸過手為拿着她的一隻手。

Slowly she withdrew her hand from his, stood up, and said softly, "I want to go home."

"Wait a few minutes. I'll take you home," he said, blushing. She sat down again.

As they left the Victory Building, they saw several cars stopping, nicely-groomed ladies and handsome foreign military officers queuing up to get into a dance hall.

"Well, this certainly doesn't look like wartime. I think all the so-called bad news are rumors," commented Shu-sheng.

"Rumors? Don't you believe me?" he said peevishly, disagreeing with her. "I guarantee you that within a week all of these people will have left here." In his mind, he vividly saw scenes of the impending destruction of the city.

"But there are only a few, a very few, who will be able to escape," she said, feeling sorry for her husband.

"Well, those who can will certainly flee."

As they slowly walked past the waiting cars and into a small lane, Ch'en suggested that they take a walk.

"I'd rather go home," she said, meaning to discourage his ardor.

"If you were a little bit late, just half an hour, surely it wouldn't make too much difference. I suspect that you must be rather lonely at home."

His last sentence touched her to the quick. She wanted vehemently to deny that she was lonely at home, but she could not with any honesty. She was truly lonely. Biting her lip, she obediently followed him.

It was not very late, but the streets looked desolate: only a number

她低着頭不作聲，慢慢地把手縮回，過了兩分鐘她忽然站起來，低聲說：「我要回去了。」

「等兩分鐘，我送你回去，」他紅着臉說。她又默默地坐下來。

陳主任付了帳，陪着她走下樓。她們站在大廈門前。幾輛汽車叫吼着一齊開到前面空地上來。人聲嘈雜。盛裝的淑女貴婦和魁梧的外國軍官從車中走出，魚貫地往旁邊跳舞廳走去。

「不像就要逃難的樣子。我看那些話都是謠言，」她疑惑地說。

「謠言？你還不相信我的話？」他不以為然地說。「我敢說不到一個星期，這班人都會溜光的！」在他的腦中這個城市的前途是一片漆黑，除了毀滅，他再也看不見甚麼。

「可是走不了的人也很多，能走的究竟是少數，」她感慨地說，她又覺得她的丈夫很可憐。

「不管怎樣，有辦法走的人總得走啊，」他說。

他們慢步穿過汽車群中，慢步走出了巷子。

「現在回家未免太早。我們散散步好不好？」陳主任提議說。

「我想早點回去，」她低聲回答。

「稍為遲一點也沒有關係，你遲半點鐘回家，不會有甚麼不方便。我想你在家裏一定很寂寞吧，」他說。

她覺得末一句話搔着了她的癢處，她想拒絕他的提議，她想分辯說她在家裏並不寂寞，可是她的心反抗。她咬緊嘴唇，甚麼話也不說。但她的腳卻順從地隨着他的腳步走去。

夜並不晚，可是顯得十分淒涼。街燈昏暗，店舖大半已經關了

of dim and scattered streetlights and a few restaurants open for business. The street was not what it used to be. The cars and the pedestrians all moved hastily in the cold wind.

In a tone that presaged some future menace, he said, "You see everything has changed. In a few days, this place will be even more desolate."

She had no answer; she just followed him, envying the well-dressed ladies whom she had seen earlier in the evening. "They are much luckier," she thought.

They walked past her street and her apartment, but she did not even notice the building. They walked on the road leading to the river. The road sloped downward, and they walked until they stopped by a railing to admire the lights across the dark river. The lights decorating the river flashed like innumerable pairs of eyes, or like stars exchanging secrets. Twenty paces away was a pair of lovers, confiding in each other.

"I've had enough of this damned place; I must leave," he spoke, more or less, to himself.

"While we're here, we are discontented; but if we move on to another place, we don't know how we'll feel there either," she said.

"Anything is better than this damned place. Lanchow, by the way, is famous for its nice weather," he answered.

"If I go to Lanchow, will I have my job?"

"Absolutely no problem. I can arrange everything," he assured her enthusiastically. "Have you then made a decision?"

"I am still against going," she said after a pause. He did not know whether she was teasing him or not.

門。只有幾家小食店還在營業，雖不冷靜，但看起來總沒有往日那樣熱鬧。寒風暗暗地吹着。路上的行人和車輛都帶着怕冷的樣子匆匆地逃走了。

「你看，一切都變了，」他帶點恐嚇的調子在她耳邊說。「過兩天還要變得更荒涼哩！」

她不講話，只顧低頭跟着他的腳步走。她的眼前還幌動着勝利大廈門前淑女貴婦們的面影。「她們都比我幸福，」她不平地想道。

他們走過她住的那條街口，她甚至忘了抬頭看一眼她的家所在的那個建築。他們走向江邊。他們沿着那條通到江邊去的馬路走着。馬路蜿蜒地向下彎。他們轉下坡去。在中途，在可以望到對岸的地方站住了。他們靠着石欄杆，眺望對岸的星子似的燈火。江面昏黑，燈火高低明滅，像無數隻眼睛在閃動，像許多星子在私語。

就在這一段馬路上，離他們有二十步光景，有一對戀人似的青年男女，也靠着石欄杆。那兩個人咕嚕地一直講個不停。

「我在這個鬼地方住夠了，也應該走了，」他自語似地說。

「住在這裏，覺得這裏不好。到了別處去，又不知道怎樣，」過了半晌她也自語似地說。

「無論如何總比這個鬼地方好。蘭州天氣好，是出名的，」他接嘴說。

「我要是去蘭州，我的工作不會成問題嗎？」她忽然問道。

「不成問題。包在我身上！」他興奮地說。「那麼你決定了。」

「我還是決定不去，」過了一會她才回答了一句話。他不知道她是在說真話，還是開玩笑。

"Let's talk about Lanchow tomorrow," he suggested. "How tranquil the night is! I'd love to write a poem."

Incredulous, she asked, "My Department Chief, do you really write poetry?" She had some difficulty suppressing her laughter.

"Yes, I do, but it's not very good. I enjoy reading both classical and contemporary poetry," he said with mixed feelings of uneasiness and pride.

"I never suspected that Department Chief Ch'en was a poet; I look forward to reading some of your poems."

"Please don't call me 'Department Chief,' call me by my name: Feng-kuang."

"No, I am used to calling you Department Chief Ch'en and it is not a habit that can be easily changed. So I'll continue to call you Department Chief Ch'en, if I may." She was for some reason becoming excited by her own words. She also felt that she was imagining things, but she could not clearly define what they were.

"You'll have to call me something else anyway," he said after a pause, pleased with his choice of ambiguous words. "In Lanchow, my official title will be 'Manager'."

"That's fine. In the future, if we come to Lanchow, poor and hungry, please don't reject us."

"In the future? Aren't you leaving with me?" he said, half-jokingly.

Suddenly, she could feel his breath on her cheek. Evading him, she said, "I haven't decided yet.... I cannot leave them and go alone"

"You shouldn't give up your airplane ticket. And you shouldn't sacrifice yourself. If you leave now, they can always come later, and ... " Becoming excited, he suddenly put his hand lightly around her waist.

「我們明天再談去蘭州的事，今晚上不要再提這種事情，」他連忙岔開說。「你看夜多麼靜，我真想寫首詩。」

最後一句話差一點惹她笑出聲來，但她竭力忍住了。她故意放低聲音問道：「陳主任還寫詩嗎？」

「我新詩舊詩都愛讀。也偷偷寫過幾首，寫得不好，怕你見笑，」他帶點慌張也帶點得意地答道。

「沒有想到陳主任還是詩人，我倒想拜讀陳主任的詩，」她說。

「你不要再叫陳主任，你就叫我名字，叫我奉光吧，」他央求道。

「我們叫陳主任叫慣了，改不過口來。還是叫陳主任順口些，」她帶笑回答說。她有點興奮。她起了一點幻想，連自己也弄不清楚的幻想。

「橫順以後要改的，」他想出這句雙關話，他自己也很得意，故意停了一刻，才補上一句：「在蘭州我是經理了。」他笑了笑。

「我們將來逃到蘭州來，沒有辦法時，向你要碗飯吃，你不要板起面孔拒絕啊，」她也故意笑着說。

「將來？你不預備大後天走嗎？」他半開玩笑地說。

她的身子微微顫了一下。她覺得他的熱氣噴到她的臉頰上來了。她便把身子移開一點。「我還沒有決定啊。」接着又添加說：「我不能夠丟開他們一個人走。」

「你不能放棄這張飛機票。而且你不應該為別人犧牲你自己。而且你先走，他們可以隨後跟來，而且……」他着急地說，他把一隻手突然伸出去輕輕摟着她的腰。她想避開，但已經來不及了。她覺得

It was too late for her to resist him and it had happened too suddenly for her to analyze her own feelings. She felt her heart beating rapidly, and she blushed. She tried to divert his attention. "Look at the shore across the river, the river and its surroundings, so tranquil and peaceful. Why should we be alarmed about anything? As for you, you have a job and a career in Lanchow, but what reason do I have to go there?"

"Because ... because I love you," he whispered in her ear, summoning up all his courage.

Though not completely surprised at this declaration, she was nevertheless startled. Her whole body tingled and her heart beat more quickly; she could not describe her feelings. Not knowing what to say, she lowered her head and kept looking at the dark surface of the water.

"Now you know how I feel about you. Won't you leave with me?" he continued, whispering in her ear.

Pictures of her tear-ridden husband, her mother-in-law's sour face, her son's serious expression, so out of keeping with his age, flashed through her mind. In anguish, she whispered, "No, no, no." She did not, in fact, know what she meant by this denial.

"Why not? Don't you trust me?" he asked. He wanted to look at her face, but she kept her head lowered.

"I'm very confused, and I'd like you to take me home," she said at last. She stood with her head bowed, full of uncertainty, as if she were at an intersection unable to decide which road to take.

"But you haven't given me an answer," he pleaded with her in a low voice.

She remained silent. A thin white smog now covered the river,

自己臉紅，心也跳得厲害。她沒有功夫分析她這時的心理。她極力約束自己。她打斷他的話：「你看對岸，看江上，看我們周圍，多寧靜，多和平。大家都很安靜，我們何必自相驚擾。你有任務當然應該走。可是我趕去做甚麼呢？」

「因為——因為我愛你啊，」他鼓起勇氣激動地在她耳邊說。

這話對她並不全是意外。但是她仍然吃了一驚。她渾身發熱。心跳得更急。她有一種形容不出的異樣的感覺。她不知道怎樣回答他才好。她把頭埋得更低，眼睛望着黑暗的水面。

「你現在知道我的心了。你還不跟我走麼？」他還在她耳邊絮絮地說。

她看見丈夫的帶哭似的病臉，他母親的帶着憎惡的怒容，還有小宣的帶着嚴肅表情(和他的小孩臉龐不相稱)的蒼白臉，她搖着頭痛苦地說：「不！不！不！」他以為她在表示她不願跟他走。可是她自己都不知道這三個「不」字裏含着甚麼意思。

「為甚麼還說『不』呢？難道你不相信我？」他溫柔地問道，一隻手還放在她腰間。他想看出她臉上的表情，可是她始終不抬起頭。

「我心亂得很。你送我回去啊，」最後她說了，仍舊埋着頭。她這時有的只是一種惶惑的感覺，她彷彿站在十字路口，打不定主意要往甚麼地方去。

「可是你還沒有回答我啊，」他低聲催促道。

她不作聲。江面上橫着一片白蒙蒙的霧，她也沒有注意到霧是

and she had no idea when it had appeared. She could actually smell it. The smog reached the shore and now encompassed them. The smell was stifling, as if it were set on destroying one's lungs. No one else was in sight; the lovers had disappeared in the smog. Remembering a familiar voice saying: "I can only burden you two," she shivered in the cold, her earlier romantic sentiments having dissipated. She asked him again to take her home.

"It's still early. Shall we go somewhere else?"

"No, I want to go home," she insisted. "I'll see you at the Kuan-sheng Yüan Restaurant tomorrow morning at eight."

"You must then give me an answer."

She nodded and put her arm through his. They walked toward the center of the street, now filled with the thick white vapor.

"Is there anything wrong with your family? You look so sad," he asked with concern.

"No," she said, walking through the smog, a little frightened and a little vexed. Wishing to hold on to something, she clung to his arm.

"If I leave you in Chungking, I'll worry about you; I doubt you'll have a good time here either."

His words made her unhappy and bitter about her life. These feelings crept upon her suddenly and she wanted to cry but managed to control herself. Instead of a warm and comfortable home, she had quarrels, enmity, loneliness, and poverty. What happened to her youth? It had been buried in the war. Where were the many attempts to find happiness? Her efforts dwindled away each time. And her future? More of the same, perhaps even worse times. What Ch'en said was obviously true, and how could she deny it? She was young and

甚麼時候加濃的。現在卻嗅到霧的氣味了，那種窒息人的、爛人肺腑似的氣味。夜在發白，霧瀰漫到岸上來了。霧包圍着她。她除了他外，看不見一個人。那一對青年男女已經被霧吞食了。她有點膽怯。她彷彿聽見一個熟悉的聲音輕輕說着：「我只會累你們。」她打了一個冷噤。她再說一句：「我們還是回去吧。」先前被引動起來的那一點浪漫的情感早已消失了。

「時候還早呢！我們再找個地方坐坐好不好？」他說。

「我想早點回去，」她短短地說。「明早晨八點鐘我在冠生園等你。」

「那麼你明天一定要回答我啊，」他鄭重地叮囑道。他很高興，可是他又覺得在這樣情形中他也沒有別的辦法。

「明天，好的，」她點頭答道。她把左手插在他的右腋下，挽着他的右膀，走下人行道，向濃霧掩罩的街心走去。

他們默默地走了一會兒。他忽然關心地問她：「你家裏有甚麼事情吧？你今天好像不大高興。」

「沒有，」她搖搖頭說，她仍舊挽住他的膀子在霧中走着。她有一種茫然的感覺。有一點怕，又有一點煩，她只想抓住一件東西，所以她更挽緊他的膀子。

「這樣離開你。我實在不放心，」他又說。「你在這裏不會過得好。」

他的話使她想到別的事情。她覺得心酸，她又起了一種不平的感覺。這是突然襲來的，她無法抵抗。她想哭，卻竭力忍住。沒有溫暖的家，爭吵和仇視，寂寞和貧窮，在戰爭中消失了的青春，自己追求幸福的白費的努力，灰色的前途……這一切像潮似地湧上她的心頭。他說了真話：她怎麼能說過得好呢？……她才三十四歲，

still attractive; she felt entitled to her share of happiness. It was not she who was in the wrong. She would rebel. Finally she said to the only man who could offer her an alternative, "I might as well leave here. I can't take this place any more." Her voice was very low, as if she were murmuring to herself.

"Then you've decided to accept the airplane ticket. Once we're in Lanchow, all the problems will be solved," he promised her, feeling irrepressibly happy.

"No," she said. "I'll give you my answer tomorrow." Once again she had changed her mind.

"Tomorrow? What a long night this is going to be!"

"I must think about it more thoroughly. This time I will make up my mind for sure," she said to him in a business-like manner, trying not to feel the joy of loving or being loved.

"Then you won't say 'NO' tomorrow." He had still not lost hope. "See you at the restaurant."

"Tomorrow I might decide to leave.... I can't stand the smog here. For two years it has rotted my heart. I have had enough." She could see the thin white smog enveloping her, but she had no definite vision of the future.

XVI

WHEN she got home, she entered a different world. Everything was familiar, but nothing pleased her. It was as if she had been reluctantly dragged into the room by a mysterious hand.

還有着旺盛的活力，她為甚麼不應該過得好？她沒有錯。她有權利追求幸福。她應該反抗。終於她說了：「走了也好，這種局面橫豎不能維持長久的。」聲音很低，她像是在對自己的心說話。

「那麼就決定搭這班飛機吧。到了蘭州一切問題都容易解決，」他的聲音裏露出來被壓抑的喜悅。

「不！」她驚醒般地說。但過後她又添加一句：「我明天回答你。」

「明天？這一晚上的時間多長啊，」他失望地嘆息道。

「我得回去好好想一想，這回我要打定主意了，」她說，她並沒有感到愛與被愛的幸福。她一直在歧途中徬徨，想決定一條路。可是她一直決定不了。

「那麼你明天不會拒絕吧，」他結束地說，希望還未完全消失。「明天八點鐘冠生園，我等你答覆。」

「明天也許我會決定走，」她說，「這裏的霧我實在受不了，好像你的心都會給它爛掉似的。這兩年我也受夠了。」她心煩，她想反抗。可是她眼前只有白茫茫的一片霧。她看不見任何遠景。

十六

她又回到了家。進了大門，好像進了另一個世界。一切都是那麼熟悉，可是她不由得皺起眉頭來。她似乎被一隻手拖着進了自己的房間。

A streak of light could be seen under the door of her mother-in-law's room but not a sound could be heard; her husband was lying quietly awake in bed. Without complaining he said tenderly, "You're back." His gentleness shamed her, so she asked, needlessly, "Are you still awake?"

"I have been waiting up for you."

"Your health is so important. Why do you think only of me?"

"I sleep a great deal during the day, so I have difficulty falling asleep at night," he answered softly. "Mrs. Chang was here and said that the refugees are pouring in from Kweiyang and that their luggage is piling up outside the main entrance. She advised us to leave as soon as possible. What do you think?"

"When I came in, I didn't notice any luggage. The situation is probably not all that bad," she said indifferently.

"Perhaps not. In reality there is no reason for us to flee since we have neither money nor power. If we die, our death will make little difference, because being alive, to us, isn't any better than being dead. I'm not worried." Lowering his voice, he continued. "I have been wanting to speak to you. Since Mother and I never agree on anything, I don't like to consult her very often. You have a better grasp of things and you understand the situation more clearly. Therefore I have been anxious for you to return so that I could have a serious talk with you."

"What do you have in mind? Is it about getting away from here?"

"Yes, indeed," he said earnestly. "Most probably this place is unsafe, and I'm too sick to go anywhere. As far as I'm concerned, I have nothing to fear, but I fear for you; you don't have to stay here. If you could take Hsiao Hsüan with you and find a safe place for Mother, I would feel most relieved." Although his voice trembled a little, it was not sentimental.

母親房裏有燈光，卻沒有聲息。丈夫靜靜地躺在床上。他沒有睡，看見她進來，他說：「你回來了。」聲音是那麼親切，他沒有抱怨，這倒使她覺得慚愧，她走到床前，溫柔地對他說：「你還不睡？」

「我等你回來。」他答道。

「你自己身體要緊啊，為甚麼還只想到我？」她感動地說。

「我白天睡得多，所以晚上睡不着。」他柔聲回答。「今晚上張太太又來過，她說我們這裏大門口堆了很多行李，說是有一些從貴陽逃來的難民。張太太聽人說連貴陽都保不住了。她勸我們早走，你看怎麼樣？」

「我好像沒有看見甚麼。大門口冷清清的。情形不會壞到這樣吧。」她心不在焉地說。

「我也是這樣想，不會這樣快，其實我們這種人無錢無勢，也用不着逃難。就是遇到不幸，也不過輕如鴻毛，活着不見得比死好。這樣想我的心倒也定了。我一直等着你回來，想跟你談談。」他小心地放低聲音：「我跟媽常談不攏，我也不敢多跟她商量。你比她懂得多，更明白，所以我盼望你回來，我好跟你商量。」

「甚麼事？你說逃難嗎？」她隨口問道。

「是，就是逃難的事。」他用懇切的眼光望着她，答道。「我看這回十分之八九有問題。我是逃不動的了，我也不怕甚麼。不過你應該早作準備。你不必陪我守在這裏。你能把小宣帶走，也給媽找個安身地方，那我就心安了。」他的聲音略帶顫抖，卻沒有感傷的調子。

Tersely she answered, "I'm not leaving." His unexpected generosity upset her and made her remorseful over her own selfishness. The other man had begged her to leave; now her husband was making the same plea. She began to feel pricks of conscience.

"When it is time to leave, you must. Don't worry about me. I can always evacuate with my Company," he lied, unconvincingly. "Men can always find something to do. Didn't you say that your bank wants to transfer you to Lanchow? Just now ..., " he paused, then went on: "I've thought about this for a long time, and you'd better leave with them. It's a rare opportunity."

Turning her head away, she repeated what she had said earlier, "I don't want to go."

He called her name softly. "Shu-sheng, I've come to this decision reluctantly after careful consideration. I know I'm not wrong."

"Did your mother have anything to say to you about me?" she asked suddenly.

From the adjoining room the old woman shouted, "I never say things behind anyone's back."

Shu-sheng became so angry that she bit her lip but did not say a word in reply. Her husband came to her defense, "Mother, Shu-sheng didn't mean that you had said anything disparaging about her."

His mother continued, "I know. I know everything. She won't stay with us anyway. It's better that she goes soon."

"I'll not leave. See what you can do to make me!" Shu-sheng said harshly, her temper rising. But her voice was so low that her mother-in-law could not have heard her.

"You know how she is. Let her say what she wants," he pleaded with Shu-sheng.

「我不走。」她簡短地說，他這番話是她沒有料到的，他在這時候顯得十分大量使她感到良心的責備。她暗想：「他要我走，你居然也讓我走！」她反而覺得心裏不痛快。

「到那時候你不走是不行的。你不要只顧想着我，我臨時可以跟着我們公司走。」他着急地開導她。「我們男人的辦法多一點。你不是說行裏有意思調你去蘭州嗎？剛才⋯⋯」他停了一下，又接着說：「我想了半天我覺得你還是答應去的好。這是一個難得的機會。」

「我不想去。」她仍舊簡短地回答他，她坐在床沿上，他那種誠摯的表情，使她心裏更不舒服，她掉開頭不看他。

「樹生。」他顫聲喚她，她不得不回過頭來。「我這個意思不會錯，我是平心靜氣想過的——」

「是不是媽跟你講過甚麼話？」她打斷他的話頭，突然問道。

「我沒有講過！我才不在背後講人壞話！」母親意外地在小屋裏大聲分辯道。

樹生不做聲，卻氣得用力咬嘴唇。他卻提高聲音回答：「媽，並不是說你講過樹生的壞話，請你不要多心。」

「我知道，我甚麼都知道。」母親繼續說，「她橫豎是留不住的，讓她早點走了也好。」

「我偏不走，看你有甚麼辦法！」樹生賭氣地說，但聲音低，母親並沒有聽清楚。

「媽就是這個脾氣，你不要認真，就讓她說兩句吧。」他低聲安慰她。

"I've had enough of her. You've seen for years how she treats me," she said in an even lower voice.

"Leave by yourself then. If you can take Hsiao Hsüan with you, take him; otherwise go alone. You shouldn't torment yourself," he said, picking up the thread of their previous conversation. His words were clear and gentle, though spoken so softly that they could hardly be heard.

"Is this your decision?" she asked unemotionally, trying not to reveal her own feelings.

"It would be the best decision," he replied seriously and frankly. "It would be good for all concerned."

"Are you throwing me out? Why do you insist that I leave?"

"No, I am not throwing you out, far from it. It is only because the war has deteriorated to a point where you have to think of saving yourself. If you've a chance, why should you give it up? I'll find some way to leave here, and we can meet later. You go while you have the chance and we'll follow you as soon as we can."

"What if you can't follow me?" she said, still self-composed.

He waited for a while, then replied, "At least you'll be saved."

Moved to tears, she was overcome by sadness and sentiment. "You must go to sleep now. Why don't you think of yourself?" she sighed, standing up.

"I'll be all right, I'll be all right," he repeated.

"I can't do it," she murmured to herself. Pacing the room, as if in the grip of an extremely strong sentiment, she added aloud, "I won't go, I won't go without all of you." However, it was doubtful whether this decision brought her any satisfaction.

「我這幾年也受夠了，你親眼看見的。」她低聲答道。

「那麼你一個人先走吧，能帶小宣就帶小宣去，不能帶，你自己先走。你不要太委屈了你自己。」他溫和地，清清楚楚地說，聲音低，故意不讓他母親聽見。

「你真的是這樣決定嗎？」她冷冷地問道，她極力不洩露出自己的感情。

「這是最好的辦法。」他懇切、直率地回答：「對大家都好。」

「你是不是要趕我走？為甚麼要我一個人先去？」她又發問。

「不，不，我沒有這心思。」他着急地分辯。「不過時局壞到這樣，你應該先救你自己啊，既然你有機會，為甚麼要放棄？我也會有辦法走，我們很快地就可以見面。你聽我的話先走一步，我們慢慢會跟上來。」

「跟上來？萬一你們走不了呢？」她仍舊不動感情地問。

他停了片刻，才低聲回答她：「至少你是救出來了。」他終於吐出了真話。

她的眼裏浮出了淚水。她心裏難過得很，她想大哭一場，然後決定一條路，就不再躊躇。

「你睡吧，為甚麼你總是不想到自己啊？」她站起來嘆息地說。

「我是不要緊的，我是不要緊的。」他接連地說。

「可是我不能這樣做。」她自語似地說。她在房裏來回走了幾轉。一股強烈的感情抓住了她。「我不走，要走大家一齊走。」她說，她決定了，雖然這決定並沒有給她帶來快樂。

The next morning at the Kuan-sheng Yüan Restaurant, her answer to Ch'en was a clear and unequivocal "No."

Disappointed, he paled. Pretending to smile, he asked, "Have you then finally decided?"

"I have decided to stay," she said, pretending to be unruffled.

"I am not trying to scare you, but our branch office in Kweiyang has closed its operations. The situation is growing ever more tense. You must think of yourself."

"I have already done so."

"Think it over. The news today is worse than it was yesterday. Fewer people are breakfasting here, and how nervous they all look. Catastrophe is close at hand. There are only a few days left before it strikes."

She changed the subject and asked, "Did you get your plane ticket?"

"Not yet. I have to inquire again this afternoon."

"You'd better go to the airline office early. Aren't you worried that someone else might get your ticket?"

"Well, if that happens, so be it. For myself, leaving or staying makes little difference," he said in distress, glancing sideways at her. When a bowl of Cantonese-style porridge was brought to him, he ate it quickly.

With nothing more to say, she sipped her tea and gazed at him, believing him sincere and feeling sorry for him. At the same time she wondered if she had made the right decision. As she pondered about what a future with him might be like, her attitude toward him gradually softened. She became increasingly indecisive. The more she indulged in her speculations, the more she felt she should say

第二天早晨她帶給陳主任的答覆就是這三個字：我不走。

陳主任立刻變了臉色。過了一會他才勉強做出笑容問一句：「你真的這樣決定了？」

「我仔細地想過了，我決定留下來。」她故意做出冷靜的樣子。

他臉色發青。過了幾分鐘他帶着嚴肅的表情低聲對她說：「我不是故意恐嚇你，我告訴你一個消息：銀行裏昨晚得到貴陽分行的電報，說在辦結束了，你得打定主意啊。」

「我已經打定主意了。」她冷淡地說。

「你多考慮一下。今天情形更不對了。你看在這裏吃早點的人比往天少得多，而且都是慌慌張張的。大難近在目前，就是拖只有幾天的功夫好拖。」他說。

「你的飛機票拿到了嗎？」她打岔地問，她不願意聽他講那些話。

「還沒有，今天下午再去問。」他無精打采地答道。

「你要早點去啊，你不怕票子給別人搶去嗎？」她故意催促。

「票子給別人搶去也好，我一個人走不走也沒有關係。」他自語般地說，他用愁苦的眼光看了她一眼。這時茶房送來他要的一碗廣東粥，他就埋下頭去，用湯匙舀起粥來喝着。

她覺得無話可說，就端起杯子在嘴邊，呷着茶。她看了他兩眼，她相信他不是在裝腔作勢，她相信他的痛苦和失望是真的。她開始同情他。她開始懷疑自己的決定是否合理。她想：我答應跟他

something conciliatory to him. And so she said, "You go to Lanchow first; may be I'll follow you later."

But this brought him no consolation, only bitterness. "Later? There may be no 'later'," he replied, glaring at her accusingly. "Why don't you wake up to reality?" he added.

His answer, his facial expression, and his tone of voice all offended her, and she answered bluntly, "No 'later'? If that is so, you can arrange for my burial once everything is over."

"I'm telling you I'm not leaving," he said sternly.

"You're not leaving? Isn't this new position what you've always wanted? You've even bought an airplane ticket."

"At first I thought you had agreed to come with me, but apparently you've changed your mind."

She blushed; she understood him only too well. She did not want to hear what else he had to say because she was afraid she might change her mind again. Finding his silence too icy and his burning eyes too demanding, she told him that she would like to leave the restaurant. But she made no attempt to get up, nor did he seem to have heard her. Finally she said, "If the bank really wants to transfer me, I'll go." She had made a major concession and yielded to his stronger will, but both of them seemed to have missed the importance of what she said.

After leaving the restaurant, he walked with her to the bank where they parted. She thought he would go to the airline office, but he went to the International Café instead to while away his time.

As she passed the many office desks, the innumerable abacuses, the accounting books, and the people's heads that never seemed to change inside a bank, she felt alone and wanted very much to call him back. But she did not turn toward the main entrance, nor did she know

去，會有怎樣的結果？她的決心動搖了。

「你先去吧，說不定我將來會跟着來的。」她並不存心要說這樣的話，現在只是為了安慰他才順口說了出來。

「將來？我看等不到將來了！」他着急地說。他睜大兩眼望着她，好像在責備她：你怎麼還不覺悟啊？這激起她一點反感。她賭氣般地冷冷答道：

「那麼你將來回來替我們收屍吧。」

「我給你說，我不去了。」他板起面孔說。

「你不去？這不是你自己想了好久的位置嗎？」她驚訝地問道。「你連飛機票也弄好了。」

「我原先準備好你也去的。」他只回答一句。她立刻臉紅起來。他的意思她完全了解。她不願意聽他說這樣的話，可是她又有意無意地逼着他說出這類話來。這時她不敢再答話了。她的決心本來就並不怎樣堅定，她害怕讓他來攪擾它。他也不再說話。他默默地望着她。這注視，這沉默，使她難堪。她覺得那對一對火似的眼光在燒她的臉，她受不住。她低聲說：「我們走吧。」她自己卻坐着不動。他似乎沒有聽見她的話。過了一會兒，她再說：「要是行裏一定要調我去，我也會去的。」她已經讓步了，可是他並不曾感覺到，而且連她自己也不覺得。

他們從冠生園出來，他送她到銀行門口，就走開了。她以為他去航空公司。他自己卻不知道應該去甚麼地方，最後他決定到國際咖啡店去消磨時間。

她進了銀行，看見那許多辦公桌，那些玻璃板、算盤、帳簿，那些人頭（這一切似乎永遠不會改變！），她突然感到寂寞。她想跑出去喚他進來，但是她並不曾向大門走一步，她自己也不知道要他

why she needed him. Quietly she went back to her own desk.

The new chief of the Accounting Department had already arrived. About fifty, he seemed to be a conservative type. He looked curiously at Shu-sheng for a while, and then shook his head silently.

She felt devoid of any feeling. No one was in the mood for work; people were coming in and out freely, chatting with one another. There were even two empty desks. Some time later, a regular customer of the bank dropped in to say that Kweiyang had been lost to the Japanese. The news alarmed quite a few of her colleagues, since Kweiyang was only two days away from Chungking by car. Some started to cry, but she thought it was just another rumor.

The young man in charge of the savings accounts was frightened and said, "What shall we do?"

Calmly the middle-aged customer replied, "You're a native here. What are you afraid of? I am not going to flee myself. To run is to die and to stay is also to die. So what's the difference?"

"I've decided to send my family away tomorrow," said the man in charge of remittances.

"It'll be too late to go anywhere if the Japanese are advancing with such speed," commented the man in the Savings Department.

Shu-sheng dismissed all the so-called news as rumor, but the stories kept on spreading the entire morning. Though the manager and department heads had placed phone calls to many places, they could not get any reliable information, only conflicting reports, all discouraging. No one had any heart for work, and the slightest noise seemed to be an emergency air-raid warning.

She could not concentrate on her work in this atmosphere, thinking instead of her home, husband, and son. To her son, she immediately

來做甚麼。她默默地走到她自己座位上去。

新會計主任已經到了，是一個五十光景的老先生，為人似乎有點古板。他帶着奇怪的眼光看了她兩眼，微微擺了一下頭。

她坐在辦公桌前，覺得心裏很空虛。辦公時間早到了，可是往日那種認真嚴肅的空氣已經消失。同事們自由地進出，交頭接耳地談話，也不遵守辦公時刻。她忽然發覺兩張桌子空了，辦事人不知道去了甚麼地方。忽然一個平日跟這銀行有着不少來往的客人跑來報告：「貴陽已經失守了。」貴陽到此地只有兩天的汽車路程。有些同事失聲叫起來，「謠言！」她在心裏說。

「那我們怎麼辦？」一個管儲戶的年青男同事惶恐地問。

「你是本地人還怕甚麼？我決定不逃，逃也光，不逃也光，還不如不逃省事。」那個中年客人鎮靜地說，他昂着頭，似乎沒有一點懼怕。

「我打算明天就把家眷送走。」另一個管匯兑同事說。

「要是敵人真的來得這樣快，那麼逃都來不及囉。」管儲戶的同事接嘴道。

「謠言！」她在心裏駁斥道。

但是這樣的謠言被人們反覆不停地散佈着，銀行裏整個上午的時間都被它佔去了。經理和主任往各處打電話探詢消息。他們得到的消息雖然互相衝突，不一定可信，但其中卻沒有一件不是叫人耽心的。誰都沒心情辦公。聽見甚麼響聲，大家就記起警報來。

她受不了這種空氣。她忽然想起家，想起丈夫和兒子。她立刻

wrote a note asking him to come home as soon as possible. Once she had finished writing the note and sent an office boy to mail it for her, she became increasingly fretful and felt unable to stay in the office. So she left early, there being no one in the bank to stop her.

She walked on as if in a dream, wondering why she was going home and what she would do when she got there. "What am I doing? Why should I go home? Where is my home? Why am I hurrying so?" she questioned herself. "Have I really made up my mind? Why can't I make my decision and stick to it? What shall I do?"

Before she could answer any of these questions, she was home.

As she reached the front door to the apartment building, she heard people gossiping about the war and saw porters carrying luggage out on their shoulders. People were leaving the city. The exodus had begun. She hurried upstairs.

On the third floor it was unusually quiet. Mrs. Chang, the self-styled helpless neighbor, had locked her door and left earlier in the day. Her own door, usually half-open, was shut. Noticing her husband was not in bed, Shu-sheng asked, "Where is he?"

"He went to work," her mother-in-law replied dully.

"But he is not well. Why did you let him go?"

"He wanted to go. What could I do?"

"You shouldn't have let him. He can get worse any time," Shu-sheng replied sharply, her spirits now completely dampened.

Already distressed about her failure to keep her son from leaving, the old woman became even more upset by Shu-sheng's curt manner. Whatever she had done, she felt her daughter-in-law had no right to speak to her so disrespectfully. After all, what had this young woman

寫了一封信給小宣，要他向學校當局請假回家走一趟。她寫好信把它交給工友拿去寄發，過後她覺得心裏更煩，她實在坐不住，就自動提早下班。也沒有人來干涉她。

走在街上，她覺得一切都跟往日不同，她好像在夢中，對自己的過去和現在都很模糊。「我在做甚麼？我為甚麼要回家去？我的家究竟在甚麼地方？我這樣匆忙奔走究竟為着甚麼？」她這樣問她自己。「我決定了沒有？我為甚麼不能夠決定？我應該怎樣辦？」

她在這麼短的時間裏找不到一個答覆。她已經到了家。

大門口站着一堆人在談論時局。挑夫們正抬着大皮箱從過道裏走出來。有人在搬家，或者離開這個城市。她有點着急，便用快步子走上樓去。

三樓相當靜，她自己說沒有辦法的張太太一家人大清早搬走了，不知道去了甚麼地方，但房門還鎖着。汪家的房門平日總是掩着的，今天卻緊緊關上了，她推不開門，便用手叩了幾下。

自然是母親來開門。她進屋後第一眼便發覺他不在房間裏，他的床空着。

「媽，他到哪兒去了？」她吃驚地問道。

「他上班去囉。」母親平平淡淡地答。

「他的病還沒有全好，怎麼今天就去上班？」她不以為然地說。

「他自己要去，我有甚麼辦法？」母親板起臉答道。

她好像挨了一下悶棍，過了半晌，才自語似地吐出話來：「其實不應該讓他去，他的病隨時都會加重的。」她懷着滿腔熱情回家來，現在心完全冷了。她臉上的表情和說話的聲調都會使那母親感到不痛快。

母親沒有能留住兒子，正為這事情懊惱着。現在聽見媳婦的這種類似責備的話，不由得不動氣，心想：我就是做錯了事，也沒有

ever done for her son? Or for her grandson? Was she not planning to elope with her boyfriend? And now she had the impudence to blame her for something she could not help.

"Why didn't you come home early enough to prevent his leaving? And now that you have returned, you talk such nonsense! Why did you leave so early this morning? What for?" she fumed, pointing two fingers at Shu-sheng.

"I went to meet my boyfriend. To be blunt about it, it's none of your business," Shu-sheng shouted back, her face reddened with anger.

"It is my business. You're my daughter-in-law. It is my business. It is!"

Thus the two women began another quarrel.

XVII

ALL this time Wang was at his office and had no idea of what was happening at home.

When he woke up that morning, his wife had already left. He got up and told his mother after breakfast that he was going back to work. She could not dissuade him.

"I am all right," he insisted. "I must not have too many sick leaves; otherwise my job will be jeopardized. What's more, we can't forever rely on Shu-sheng for money. In the last few days, she has paid for all my medical expenses."

His mother could not deny what he said, even though she would

由你來責怪的道理。何況你從來就不關心他，只顧自己在外面交男朋友。你這個連家也不要，打算跟男朋友私奔的人，還有臉對我講話！

「那麼你為甚麼不早回來拉住他？現在倒要説漂亮話！我問你：今天你走得那樣早，究竟為了甚麼事情？」母親掙紅臉，伸着右手兩根手指威嚇地對她説。

「我去會男朋友，我明白地給你説，你管得着嗎？」她也掙紅臉大聲回答。

「我管得着，你是我的媳婦，我管得着！我偏要管！」母親罵道。

兩個女人就這樣地吵起來。

十七

這時候他汪文宣在公司裏辦公。他不會知道家裏發生的事。

他離家上班時是這樣的情形：妻已出門了，他才起床，他吃過早點後，忽然説要去辦公。母親阻止不了他。

「不要緊，我已經好了。」

「我不能請假太多。再不去辦公，連飯碗都會成問題。」

「我們不能把全家人都交給樹生一個人養活啊，我這幾天吃藥治病都是她花的錢。」

他拿這些話來回答母親。

母親找不到反駁的話了，雖然她心裏想着：我寧願挨餓，寧願

rather starve and bear any type of hardship than have her daughter-in-law support her. At last, she said, "Let me go out and find a job as a maid." She looked at him with red-rimmed eyes.

"How can you say that? You're an educated person. How can you think about doing that kind of work?" he replied, without looking at her.

"I regret that I ever had an education, and I shouldn't have sent you to school either. Frankly, I don't think I qualify as a maid."

"Nowadays everyone is doing all right except the educated," he commented. "My job can't even be compared to that of an office boy in a bank, and yours not even to a maid." He raised his head, sighed resentfully and hurried off. His mother shouted after him, urging him to come back, but he didn't even look back.

When he reached the office, it was too late to sign the roll. The ground floor was very quiet; Chung greeted him with a smile. When he got to his floor, he noticed several empty seats. Chou, after completing a telephone call, asked him. "Are you well now?"

He answered, "Yes, thank you."

"I don't think you're in good health. You need an extended rest," the Chief Editor said in an impersonal tone, while Section Chief Wu coughed quietly in the background.

He replied "yes" noncommittally and escaped to his desk and chair.

A worker brought him a stack of galley proofs, bluntly informing him that Mr. Wu expected him to complete the work that day because of its urgent nature. He wondered why he had to work twice as hard on a day when everyone else was talking about the war. Who would have done his work had he stayed at home? It was not fair! Yet he promised the worker that he would.

忍受一切痛苦；她不願意讓樹生來養活她。

「還是讓我出去做事吧，我當個大娘，當個老媽子也可以。」母親最後吐出了這樣的話。她充滿愛憐地望着她這個獨子，她的眼圈紅了。

「媽，你怎麼這樣說，你是讀書人啊，哪能做那種事！」他痛苦地說，掉開眼光不敢看她。

「我只後悔當初不該讀書，更不該讓你也讀書，我害了你一輩子，也害了我自己，老實說，我連做老媽子的資格也沒有！」母親痛苦地說。

「在這個時代，甚麼人都有辦法。就是我們讀書人吃苦。我連一個銀行工友都不如，你也比不上一個老媽子。」他憤慨地說，最後他抬起頭嘆了一口長氣，就走出了房門。母親追出去喚他，要他留下，他卻連頭也不回地走下樓出去了。

他到了公司，樓下辦公室似乎比平日冷靜些。簽到簿已經收起了，鍾老帶笑地對他點一個頭，他上了樓。二樓辦公室裏也有幾個空位，周主任剛打完電話，不高興地瞪了他一眼，淡淡地問一句：「你病好了？」

「謝謝你，好了。」他低聲答道。

「我看你身體太差，應該長期休養。」周主任冷冷說。他不知道周主任懷着甚麼心思，卻聽見旁邊吳股長咳了一聲嗽。

他含糊地答應了一個「是」，連忙到自己的位上坐了。

他剛坐下，工友就送了一疊初校稿樣到他面前。「吳股長說，這個校樣很要緊，當天就要的。」工友不客氣地說。他心想：時局這樣緊張，同事中今天也有幾位沒有來辦公的，大家都是忙忙慌慌，為甚麼單單逼我一個人加倍工作？要是我今天不上班呢？你們就只會欺負我！這太不公道了。可是他哼都不哼一聲，只溫和地點點頭。

"Section Chief Wu said that the work must be finished today," the worker reiterated.

Again he answered "yes" and the worker left.

He proofread the original, a book about Party ideology with several forewords written by important Party elders and printed in big characters. He read the forewords first, and then the text. He continued his proofreading despite his dizziness and lack of energy. Moreover, his heart was not in the job.

Meanwhile the Chief Editor and the Section Chief had left the office. Wang's co-workers immediately began discussing and exchanging the news of the war. All of them looked worried; no one wanted to work. The only person working was Wang, who remembered the worker's warning. Resentful of his workload, he said to himself, "Don't push me too hard. The most you can get from me is my life."

The bell for lunch at twelve o'clock was most welcome. He promptly left his desk. As usual his appetite was poor and he sensed that the others at the lunch table were still contemptuous of him. Some frightened him with a few additional rumors, one commenting sarcastically: "Wang, the way you work, you deserve a bonus at the end of the year." He did not reply and quickly fled upstairs. Since he did not smoke and had no desire to read, he fell asleep at his desk.

Some time later a worker woke him and handed him a note. "A person brought this for you and asked you to go right away," the worker said with a contemptuous smile. It was from Shusheng asking him to meet her at the International Café immediately. What could the note mean, he wondered as he went downstairs.

「吳股長說，當天就要的。」工友站在旁邊看着他，像在折磨他似地又說一遍。

他抬起頭，但是他連憤怒的表情也沒有，他溫和地答了一聲「好」。工友走開了。

他默默地翻開校樣和原稿，他不覺皺起眉來。這是一本關於黨義的書，前面還有好幾位黨國要人的序言，是用四號字排的。他埋下頭低聲唸這些序文，又唸正文。他的心不知跑到哪裏去了。他覺得頭昏，四肢乏力。但他還勉強支持着繼續把校樣看下去。

在這之間，周主任走了。吳股長又走了。同事們大聲交談起來。他們在交換戰事的消息。每個人都帶着憂慮的表情講話，並不熱心工作。只有他仍舊把頭埋在校樣上面。「當天要的。」一個粗魯的聲音不斷地在他的耳邊說。最後他忍不住在心裏答覆了：「不要逼我，至多我把命賠給你就是了。」

到了十二點鐘，開飯的鈴聲響了。他好像遇着救星似的離開了辦公室。他的胃口仍然不好。他勉強吃了一碗飯，他覺得同事們都帶了輕蔑和憐憫的眼光在看他，並且故意發一些關於戰事的「危言」恐嚇他，「老汪，你不久要加薪了，在這種時候你居然還能夠埋頭工作，年底真該得獎金啊。」一個同事這樣譏笑他。他不回答，卻又躲到樓上辦公桌前面去。他不抽煙，又沒有精神看書。他無聊地坐在位子上，對着玻璃窗打起瞌睡來。

不知道過了多少時候，他忽然聽見有人在叫「汪先生」，他吃驚地睜開眼睛，挺直身子。那個工友又立在他面前，皮笑肉不笑地望着他說：「有人給你送了一個字條來，要你立刻去。」

字條躺在桌上，是樹生的筆跡，上面寫着：

宣：

有事情同你談，請即刻到國際一晤。

樹生　即日

他吃了一驚。「有甚麼事情呢？」他想道，連忙站起來，匆匆走下樓去。

"Wang, where are you going?" asked Uncle Chung.

He made an unintelligible reply to Chung and walked hurriedly out into the street. He imagined a roar of laughter trailing after him. "They must have read her note," he thought, blushing. He entered the International and saw only a few customers. Shu-sheng was sitting alone at a round table, staring at the entrance, her face beet red with anger. As soon as she saw him, she got up but immediately sat down again, waiting for him to approach her. "I came as soon as I got your message. What's up?" He sat opposite her, smiling.

Glaring at him in anger and curling her upper lip, she said abruptly, "I want to divorce you."

He was stunned. He knew that something must have happened, but he did not dare to question her. He just bowed his head, his mind in turmoil.

"I can't tolerate your mother anymore. Today I made up my mind and you'll have to choose: it's either her or me. I have put up with her long enough, and I'm sick of her. I'm fed up."

He breathed a little easier. It was the same old problem. He had always been able to explain to her, apologize for his mother, and she would eventually be pacified.

"What's the matter? Tell me," he asked, almost perfunctorily. "You know her temper. She's old-fashioned and can't think clearly. Sometimes she is difficult to live with, but she's basically a good woman."

"What's the matter? It was all because of you. I went home, but you weren't there. I felt she should have kept you home. When I questioned her, she exploded ...," she tried to explain, highly agitated.

「老汪，到哪裏去？」鍾老問道。

他含糊地答應了一聲，就走到人行道上去了。他好像聽見一陣輕薄的笑聲，「他們一定看見了她的字條。」他對自己說，臉有些發紅了。

他走進國際，顧客很少，桌子大半空着。樹生坐在靠裏的一張圓桌旁，眼睛正向着門口，她的臉相當紅，帶着憤怒的樣子。看見了他，她忽然站起來，但馬上又坐下，望着他，等候他走過去。

「我接到字條馬上就來了。」他陪笑地說，在她對面坐下。「甚麼事？」

「我要和你離婚！」她圓睜眼睛，撅起嘴，沒頭沒腦地說了一句。

他幾乎不相信自己的耳朵了。但是她的表情他卻看得十分清楚。他知道一定發生了甚麼事情。然而他不敢再問她，他默默地埋下頭，心裏很難過。

「我受不了你母親的氣，我今天下了決心了。有我就沒有她，有她就沒有我。這一個星期我全忍着，快蹩死我了！」

他吐了一口氣，抬起頭來，他覺得事情不十分嚴重；還是那個老問題。他可以向她解釋，他甚至可以代母親向她陪罪，她的怒氣會慢慢地平靜下來的。

「甚麼事呀？你得先跟我講明白。」他鼓起勇氣陪笑道，「我媽的脾氣你是知道的，她腦筋舊，思想不清楚，有點嚕嗦，不過人倒是頂好的。」

「甚麼事，還不是為了你。我下了班回家去看你，知道你走了，我覺得她不應該放你走，多說了幾句話，她就吵起來⋯⋯」她紅着臉激動地說。

Without letting her finish her sentence, he interrupted, "It's all my fault. She didn't want me to go to work, but I persisted. You know how mean Chou is. I've no freedom as long as I work for him."

"But you're not well. You coughed up blood. Can't you ask for a leave of absence? He hasn't bought your life, has he?"

"But he's not running a charity institution," he laughed bitterly. "Chou even hinted today that I should resign because of my poor health."

"Okay. Resign. I can support you." She was pouting.

"But ..., " he stammered, his facial muscles twitching.

"Yes, I know. Your mother doesn't want you to quit. She not only doesn't respect me; she hates me."

"She has nothing to do with my job. And she does not hate you."

"She hates me and she doesn't respect me. She told me so herself. She said that I am your mistress, worse than a prostitute. I pity her ignorance but I don't care to quarrel with her any more. I am quite serious in what I said. If you don't find a separate place for her to live, I'm divorcing you." She was so angry that her face was scarlet and her eyes fiery with rage.

"Be patient, Shu-sheng," he said. "Once victory comes, she'll go to Kunming."

"Victory? When will that be?" she sneered. "You're dreaming. The enemy are nearing Kweiyang, and you're talking about victory."

"Then why should we quarrel with each other? Wouldn't it be better if you were more patient?" He tried to smile.

「這是我不好，媽本來不放我走，我一定要走，我怕請假多了，公司方面不滿意，你也知道我們那位周主任是刻薄成性的，我吃了他的飯就沒有自由了。」他不等她說完，便插嘴說。

「可是你在吐血生病啊，難道生病也不能請假嗎？他又沒有買了你的命！」她答道。

「公司不是慈善機關，哪裏管得了這些。」他苦笑道，「聽周主任今天的口氣，好像他嫌我身體不好，倒希望我辭職。」

「辭職，就辭職！你不做事我也可以養活你！」她賭氣地說。

他臉上肌肉搐動了一下，他略略低下頭喃喃說：「不過……」

「是，我知道，又是你母親，她不願意。」她氣憤地說。「她看不起我，她恨我。」

「不，你誤會了，她不恨你，這跟她不相干。」他連忙打岔道。

「她恨我，她看不起我，她剛才還對我講過，我沒有跟你正式結過婚，我不是你的妻子，我不過是你的姘頭。她罵我不要臉，她罵我比娼妓還不如，我可憐她沒有知識，我不屑於跟她吵。我不是在跟你開玩笑，我跟你說明白，如果你不另外找個地方安頓她，我就跟你離婚！」她愈往下說愈激動，也愈生氣，一張臉掙得通紅，兩隻眼睛裏燃着怒火。

「樹生，你稍微忍耐一下。」他惶恐地說，「等到抗戰勝利了，她要到昆明——」

「等到抗戰勝利！」她冷笑了一聲，「你真是在做夢！日本人已經打到貴陽了，你還在等待勝利？」

「那麼大家何苦還要吵架？彼此忍耐一點不好嗎？」他說時臉上勉強做出笑容，可是他心裏很難過。

"Be patient! Be patient! How much patience do you expect me to have?"

"If only we were a little better off financially, we could live amiably together like human beings."

"I've been listening to your pep talks for years, and we're worse off than ever before. I'm married to you, so I don't mind suffering with you. But I can't tolerate your mother...."

"For my sake, please forgive her. She has suffered enough in the last two or three years," he implored her, his face ashen.

"To have raised a darling son like you she deserves every bit of it," with which denunciation she threw three one-hundred *yüan* bills down on the table and left the café in a huff.

He remained sitting in his chair. Several minutes passed before he realized what had happened.

Where should he go to find her? He thought that she might have returned to work. Feverish and perspiring, he ran after her. After racing down more than half the length of the street, he caught a glimpse of her back in the crowd. He ran even faster, calling her again and again. She stopped and waited until he caught up with her. Holding her arm, he beseeched her, "Shu-sheng, whatever I did was for you." He was breathing hard; beads of perspiration were on his forehead and his face was flushed with excitement.

Pitying him, she said, "Why do you do this? Why don't you go home and rest? You're not well. Why did you go to work?"

"To tell you the truth," he said excitedly, "I went because I wanted to borrow money from the office."

「忍耐！忍耐！你總是説忍耐的話，我問你，你要我忍耐到幾時？」她煩躁地問。

「只要環境好一點，大家就可以相安的。」他帶着希望地答道。

「等環境好一點，這樣的話我聽你說了幾年了。環境只有一天天壞下去。跟你吃苦，我並不怕，是我自己要跟你結婚的。可是還要我受你母親的氣，那不行。」她又生起氣來，臉又掙紅了。

「那麼你看在我的份上，原諒她吧，她這兩三年也吃夠苦了。」他臉色慘白地央求道。

「那是她活該，生出你這種寶貝孩子來！」她忽然變了臉色罵道，從手提包裏掏出三張百元鈔票丟在桌面上，也不再説甚麼就站起來，氣沖沖地走出去了。

他呆呆地坐在椅子上。過了幾分鐘慌忙地跑出去追她。

他滿眼都是人，他應該到哪裏去找她呢？他掉頭四望，他看不見她的背影。「她一定是去銀行。」他想，他便朝那個方向走去，他大步走着，全身發熱，出汗。

他走過大半條街，終於見到她的背影了，他興奮地喚了一聲：「樹生！」她似乎沒有聽見，他鼓起勇氣向前跑去。他離她愈來愈近了。他第二次喚她的名字，她停下來，回頭看他，他連忙跑上去，抓住她的膀子。他睜大兩隻眼睛瞪着她，半晌才氣咻咻地吐出一句話：

「樹生，我都是為了你。」他的額上冒着汗。臉病態地發紅，嘴邊無力地張着在喘氣，臉上帶着一種求恕的表情。

「你何苦來？」她憐憫地看着他說，「為甚麼不回家躺躺：你病還沒有好，怎麼能辦公啊？」

「我應該向你説真話。」他仍舊很激動地説，「我去辦公，我不過想借支一點錢。」

"Didn't I tell you to get the money from me? There was no need to go to work," she interrupted.

"I wanted to buy something for your birthday, just a little present. Maybe a birthday cake," he said with embarrassment.

Surprised at his answer and grateful for his thoughtfulness, she relented and said gently, "Was that what you planned to do?"

He nodded. "But I didn't have the money."

"Why didn't you tell me?"

"If I had told you, you wouldn't let me." The tension dissipating, he started to smile.

"I've forgotten about my birthday, but you haven't," she said gratefully.

"Then you're no longer mad at me?"

"I was never angry with you," she replied frankly.

"Then you won't leave us," he asked, his voice quivering slightly.

Seeing how relieved he was, she pointed out gently, "I never intended to leave you, but your mother ... " After a pause, she continued, "You'd better go home now. Don't go back to work."

"I have to finish a few chores in the office, then I'll go home," he promised her. Shu-sheng nodded, and the two said goodbye to each other at an intersection.

He returned to his office, and although refreshed, he still felt tired. He sat down and resumed his work, burdened by his workload. He wanted to go home, but when he thought of Mr. Wu's instructions, he knew he had to continue.

「我原先就說過，你要用錢，我可以拿給你，用不着你去辦公，」她打岔地說。

「我想買點東西……後天是你生日，……我想送你一點禮物……至少也要買一個蛋糕……」他斷斷續續地說，帶了一點羞慚的表情，略略低下頭。

她顯然吃了一驚。他的話是她沒有料想到的。她臉上的表情漸漸在變化：憐憫被感激和柔愛代替了。「你是這樣的打算？」她感動地低聲問。

他點點頭，過後卻添加一句：「可是我還沒有拿到錢。」

「你為甚麼不早說？」她微笑說，溫柔地望着他。

「我說了，你一定不讓我做。」他答道，他的緊張的心鬆弛了，他的臉上也露了笑容。

「你倒還記得我的生日，我自己倒忘記了。」她感激地微笑說。

「那麼你不再生我的氣了？」他也懷着感激地說。

「我本來沒有跟你生氣。」她坦白地回答。

「那麼你不離開我們？」他又問，聲音略帶戰抖。

「我本來就沒有離開你的意思。」她答道。她看見了他臉上現出了寬慰的表情，便柔聲勸他：「你放心，我沒有別的意思。不過你母親——」她突然住了嘴，改口說：「你還是早點回家去休息罷。不要再去公司了。」

「我去一趟，我把東西收拾一下，就回去。」他說。妻點點頭，兩個人就在這十字路口分別了。

他回到公司，已經是辦公時間了。他的精神比較爽快，可是身體還是很疲乏。他坐下來，立刻開始工作。他覺得很吃力，有點透不過氣來。他打算回家休息，但是他想到「當天要」三個字，他連動也不敢動了。

Page after page of the same boring, meaningless words. His heart was beating unevenly, and a hard lump seemed to have lodged itself in his head. The words were blurred as though a screen of mist were in front of his eyes. In the background he felt Chou's vicious eyes watching him. To Chou he cried, but only in his heart: "Why don't you ease up the pressure on me? You're really nothing, only a little wealthier and a little more powerful than I am."

Suddenly he coughed, then again. In slightly over ten minutes, he had gone to the corner spittoon twice, each trip bringing forth a murmur of displeasure or a low growl from Chou. He wanted so much not to go to the spittoon and his very effort to suppress the cough made him cough again. This time he managed to swallow his phlegm. He barely managed to finish the last batch of proofs.

Three or four minutes later, his throat started itching again. This time the phlegm exploded within his throat and fell haplessly onto the last proof sheet. The phlegm was tinged with fresh blood and he could smell its stench. On seeing it, he lost his powers of resistance, and patience.

Pronouncing his own verdict, he said, "I'm a hopeless incurable." At the same time, sensing a pair of hostile eyes watching him, he heard Editor Chou's light cough. With a piece of waste paper he wiped the phlegm off the proof sheet, but immediately he started coughing again. He staggered to the spittoon and spat out a large amount of phlegm. He was left with a foul dryness in his mouth. He would have liked some tea, or at least some sympathy, but no one offered him either. Standing by the spittoon and putting his hand on his chest, he tried to catch his breath.

"Mister Wang, you'd better go home. I don't think you're in very good health," Chou said unemotionally. His glance at Wang was as sharp as the cutting edge of a blade.

校樣一頁一頁地翻過了。他弄不清楚自己看的是甚麼文章。他的心在猛跳，他的腦子似乎變成了一塊堅硬的東西。眼前起了一層霧，紙上的黑字模糊起來，他隱隱約約地看見周主任的那對兇惡的眼睛（周主任剛從外面回來）。「這時候還不放鬆我？你不過比我有錢有勢！」他憤慨地想道。

也不知道是怎麼起來的，他忽然咳一聲嗽，接着又咳了兩聲。他想吐痰，便走到屋角放痰盂處去。在十幾分鐘裏面，他去了兩次。周主任不高興地咳嗽一聲，不，周主任只是哼了一聲。他便不敢去第三次。偏偏他又咳出痰來，他只好嚥在肚裏。他居然忍耐住把剩下的十多頁校樣看完了。

過了三四分鐘，他覺得喉嚨又在發癢，他想忍住不咳出聲來，可是他心裏發慌，最後，一聲咳嗽爆發出來了。一口痰不由他管束地吐在校樣上。是紅色的，是鮮紅的血，他彷彿聞到了腥氣。他呆呆地望着牠。他所有的自持、掙扎、忍耐的力量一下子完全失去了。

「那麼到了無可挽救的時候了。」他痛苦地想着。忽然聽見周主任一聲輕咳，他彷彿又看到了那一對眼睛，他吃了一驚，連忙俯下身在字紙簍裏拾起一片廢紙把血痰揩去。剛揩好痰，他又發出接連的咳聲。他走到痰盂前彎下身子吐了幾口痰。嘴裏乾得厲害。他想喝一杯茶，卻沒有人理他，他按着胸膛在喘氣。

周主任講話了：「Mister汪，你今天不要辦公了，還是早點回家休息吧，我看你身體太差……」聲音裏不含絲毫的溫情，眼光像刀似的割着他的臉。

Resentfully, he thought, "You still bully me, even now ..., " but said calmly, "I'm all right. I can go on." His actions belied his words, however, for he was swaying as though his limbs could hardly support him. He felt dizzy.

"Mister Wang, you need a lot of rest. When and if you become really sick, the medical expense will be quite staggering," Chou added.

"Well, give me a half-day's absence," he said, covering his mouth with his handkerchief. He bitterly resented Chou's pressing him so relentlessly.

"You'll need more than half a day. Why don't you just go home first?" Chou said slowly.

Wouldn't he love to quit that damned place forever, immediately? However, he said to Chou in a pleading tone, "I'd like to have a month's salary in advance, if I may. I hope ... "

Obviously annoyed, Chou waved his hand to stop him from completing the sentence and said, "You can have half a month's, if you like. Go to the cashier's office for the money."

He pocketed his three-thousand five-hundred *yüan*, an insignificant amount at the time. What he wanted to do with the money, he had no idea. He handed over the corrected proofs and left. No one spoke to him, although sympathetic as well as contemptuous looks followed him as he went away. Shaking his head, Chou murmured something like, "Why so much trouble to ...," but Wang did not hear the remark. Listlessly, he walked downstairs, hoping for a few words of sympathy from Uncle Chung. Chilled through and through, he badly needed some warmth. But Uncle Chung was out.

「到這時候你還要逼我；」他憤憤地想道。但他還竭力裝出平靜的聲音回答一句：「不要緊，我還可以支持。」然而他的身體卻不想支持下去。他頭昏眼花，四肢無力，身子忽然搖幌起來。

「Mister汪，身體不好，趁早休息。不然病倒了，醫藥費是一筆大數目啊。」周主任又說。

「回去就回去，不吃你這碗飯，難道就會餓死！」他氣惱地想道，口裏卻用溫和的調子說，「那麼我就請半天假吧。」他連忙用手帕掩了嘴咳起來。

「半天恐怕不行吧……。也好，你先回家再說。」周主任帶了點嘲笑的表情慢吞吞說。

他不想再說甚麼，恨不得馬上離開這個可怕的地方。可是他不得不硬着頭皮向那個人要求：「我想借支一個月薪水，請主任……」

周主任不等他說明理由，立刻截斷他的話，厭煩地揮手說：「支半個月吧，你去會計科拿錢。」

他沒有第二句話說，只好忍着羞到會計科去支了三千五百元。他想：這點點錢能夠做甚麼用呢？他帶着苦笑地把鈔票揣了在懷裏。

他把看完的校樣交出後，便走下樓。沒有人理會他，卻有些憐憫和輕蔑的眼光跟隨他。「何苦啊，」周主任搖搖頭低聲說了這三個字。他沒有聽見。

他希望在樓下看見鍾老，他盼望着聽到一句安慰的話。他的心太冷了，需要一點溫暖。但樓下沒有鍾老的影子。

The sky was gray and overcast, threatening rain. Like a stranger in an alien world, he felt that his familiar homeward journey was long and hazardous. Unlike the other pedestrians sparkling with life, he hunched his back and dragged his feet very slowly toward death.

XVIII

AT last he reached home. He pushed open the half shut door and saw his mother standing in front of the square table washing clothes. With one look he knew that his lined gown was soaking in the old enamel wash-basin.

"Hsüan, you are home," said his mother, pleasantly surprised.

"I am very tired," he said, breathing hard. "Mother, why are you still washing my clothes? Didn't I tell you to give the wash to the laundry woman?" He moved a rattan chair and sat down by the desk.

"It'd be too expensive," she answered. "It'd cost eight hundred *yüan* a month. Unlike Shu-sheng, I don't have much to do at home. She can go out and earn money."

"Has she returned?" he asked.

Her facial expression changed, she answered him in a displeased tone, "Yes, she threw a temper tantrum before she left. With each passing day she's becoming more ludicrous. You should control her. As for me, I can't put up with her any more. Once you get better, I plan to return to Kunming for a while." Changing her tone and sighing, she

天還是灰色，好像隨時都會落下雨點似的。走慣了的回家的路突然變得很長，而且崎嶇難走。周圍是一個陌生的世界，人們全有着那麼旺盛的精力。他們和他中間沒有一點關聯，他彎着腰，拖着腳步，緩慢地走向死亡。

十八

他到了家。房門半掩着，他推開門進去。母親立在方桌前洗衣服。他一看便知道舊洋磁臉盆裏泡着的正是他的罩袍。

「宣，你回來了！」母親驚喜地說。

「我累得很。」他喘息地答道。接着他苦笑地對她說：「媽，你還在給我洗衣服，我不是說過給外面洗衣服的大娘洗嗎？」他把書桌前的籐椅掉轉方向在那上面坐下來。

「包月洗要八百元一個月，太貴了！橫順我在家裏沒有事做。我不比樹生，她可以到外面去掙錢。」母親發牢騷地說。

「樹生回家來過嗎？」他忍不住發問道。

母親馬上變了臉色，不高興地回答：「她沒頭沒腦地發了一通脾氣又走了。我看她越來越不像話。你也得管管她。像她這種脾氣，我實在侍候不了。我想等你身體好一點，我要回昆明去一個時候。唉……」(她改了語調嘆一口氣)「我離開雲南二十多年了。我二哥他

went on, "I left Yünnan province more than twenty years ago and I don't even know how aged my second brother has become." Her eyes glistened with tears.

Her tears deeply touched him. Feeling sorry for her, he said, "Don't be so sad. I won't side with her. After all, I am your son."

Immediately she interrupted, "That's right. She's no more than your mistress. Whenever there is a fuss, she always threatens to leave. I say, let her. Once she leaves, I will get you a better woman."

Her reply provoked him, though he dared not argue with her. In a miserable tone of voice, he said, "How could I get married again? I can't even support the wife I have. How could I think of taking another?" He smiled wryly.

"So what if you can't afford it? What decent man makes a good living today? No matter what happens, we must live and raise the family. We can't give up simply because we're poor," she replied, stirred with indignation.

"But I can't leave Shu-sheng. I've been married to her for fourteen years; we have some understanding of each other," he responded. Feeling dizzy, he turned his chair around and rested his head on the desk. For some time he made no sound.

Pitying him, she walked over. Fondling his head lovingly, she said, "You're a complete silly ass!" Shaking her head she did not say anything else. Later she asked him to rest in bed, assuring him that Shu-sheng would come back.

"It's not that," he replied weakly. "I know she will return. As a matter of fact, I saw her earlier today."

"You've seen her?" she shouted. "Did she go look for you in your office? I guess she's shameless enough to go complaining to you!" To

們不曉得老到甚麼樣子。」她的眼睛裏開始閃耀着淚光。

看見母親的眼淚，他覺得心裏一陣難過，他自己也就想哭了。他連忙安慰說：「媽，你不要傷心。我不會偏袒她，我是你的兒子——」

不等他說完她便插嘴說：「是啊，她不過是你的姘頭，她動不動就說走，其實她走了倒好。她走了，我另外給你接一個更好的來。」

母親的這句話激起他的反感，他不敢反駁，卻用不安的聲調說：「我們這樣人家，還有甚麼錢來結婚？連有的都養不活，還敢妄想再接新的？」他苦笑了。

「養不活，怕甚麼，這個年頭哪一個有良心的人能夠活得好？拖也好，捱也好，我們總要活下去。我們不能因為沒有錢，就連妻子、兒女都不要了！」母親憤慨地說。

「不過樹生我實在離不開她，結婚十四年了，我們彼此還相當了解……」他痛苦地說，話還未說完，他覺得一陣頭暈，就把籐椅拉過去將頭壓在書桌上，像睡着了一般，他半天都不出聲息。

母親走到他身旁，她那充滿慈愛和憐憫的眼光撫着他的頭。「你真是不到黃河心不死。」她低聲說，無可奈何地搖搖頭。過後她喚道：「宣。」他應了一聲，卻不抬起頭來。

「你到床上去躺躺吧。」她柔聲說：「她會回來的，你何苦這樣難過。」

「我不是為了她的事情。」他有氣無力地搖搖頭說：「她會回來，我知道，我先前還看見她。」

「你看見她？她去公司找過你嗎？真不要臉！還好意思向你告

herself she said angrily, "I wonder what trick that woman's trying to play on us now."

"She didn't say much except something about the deteriorating war situation," he replied, scowling.

"Why should it bother her? If she wants to leave, let her. Why should she hurt others?"

"Mother!" he screamed. "She promised not to leave and she'll be back soon." It was too much. He wondered how his mother could hate Shu-sheng so much and why the two women could not tolerate each other.

"She's coming back? How can she face me?" she said.

"I asked her to come back," he admitted timidly.

"You want her back? You don't know what you're doing! You don't know!" Pacing the room, she finally sat down on his bed, covering her face with her hands as if weeping. Then she uncovered her face and stood up, mumbling, "I can take everything except her. I'd rather die. I don't want to see her again. If she returns, I'll leave immediately." She was gnashing her teeth as though she were biting into Shu-sheng's flesh, and after this outburst, taking no heed of him, she returned to her room.

A jumble of noises reverberated in his head. He dully stared after his mother, as if in a dream. When the turmoil had subsided, he finally understood what she had said. He got up and went into her room.

She was lying sideways on the bed, facing the wall, crying.

"Mother," he called loudly.

With tears rolling down from the wrinkled corners of her eyes, she

狀？」母親氣紅臉，離開他走一步，大聲說。她惱怒地想：這個女人究竟在玩甚麼花樣？

他痛苦地看了她一眼，皺着眉頭說：「她沒有講甚麼，她……她不過說時局不……大好。」

「時局好不好，跟她有甚麼相干！」母親氣憤地說，「她要走，一個人走就是咯。做甚麼還要來害人！」

「媽。」他不能忍耐地叫起來，這太過份了！為甚麼她要這樣恨樹生？為甚麼女人還不能原諒女人？「她不走，她說過，她不走，她就要回來。」

「她回來？她還有臉見我？」母親又驚奇又憤恨地說。

「是我要她回來的。」他畏怯地說。

「你還要她回來？你不知道，你不知道！」她在房裏走了兩步，忽然走到床前，在床沿上坐下，兩手蒙着臉，好像在哭。過後她又放下手，站起來，自語似地說：「我甚麼苦都受得了，就是受不了她的氣。我寧願死，我不要再看見她！她回來，我立刻就走！」她咬牙切齒地說，彷彿就在咬那個女人的肉似的。她說完並不理他，馬上走進她的小屋去了。

他的腦子裏雜亂地響着聲音。他呆呆地望着她，彷彿在做夢。聲音漸漸地靜下來。他忽然明白了，立刻站起來，走進母親的屋子裏去。

母親側着身子躺在床上，臉向着牆壁，低聲在哭。

「媽！」他大聲喚道。她應着，翻身坐起來，淚珠從她的皺起的眼角落下。

said hoarsely, "What else do you have to say?"

"Please don't be like this. I won't let her come back," he gently promised her, standing by her bed.

"Are you serious?" She wiped her tears with a handkerchief, pleased.

"Yes, I am," he answered, without thinking.

"Then you have made a promise to me?" she pressed him.

"Yes, I promise you," he said impulsively. Looking at her weary face, he forgot himself, his illness, his past, and his future.

"If you promise that I won't have to see that woman again, I can take poverty and any hardship that comes along," she said triumphantly. "Indeed, how could she come back? I think she's flying to Lanchow with that department chief of hers." In the belief that she had won a major concession from her son, she, no longer angry, calmly walked out of the room and plunged her coarse hands into the icy water of the wash-basin.

He followed her out of the room and silently watched her wringing and rinsing the clothes. All of a sudden, he felt dizzy, his vision became blurred, and his heart pained him. Almost collapsing on the floor, he leaned against the wall to support himself and closed his eyes to rest for a moment.

Her head lowered, she was unaware of her son's condition, saying, "At home, things would be much simpler without that woman.... Hsiao Hsüan should be home this week. The poor boy! His mother has never really cared for him.... There have been so many rumors today, and people are all nervous as if disaster is imminent. As for myself, what do I have to fear? I've weathered all types of storms in the past, and things can't get any worse. Have you heard from your Company?"

「你還有甚麼話？」她嗄聲問道。

「媽，你不要難過，我不讓她回來就是咯。」他立在床前，溫和地說。

她用手帕揩了眼淚，臉上稍微露了一點喜色。「你這是真話？」她問道。

「媽，是真話。」他不加考慮地回答。

「那麼你答應我了？」她不放心地再問一句。

「我答應你，你放心吧。」他望着他母親的受苦的面顏，他感情衝動地回答。他忘了自己，忘了病，也忘了他的過去和將來。

「只要你肯答應我，只要我不再看見那個女人，我甚麼苦都可以吃，甚麼日子我都過得了。」她帶着欣慰的口氣說，她站起來。「其實她那裏會回來啊？我看她一定會跟着她的甚麼主任飛蘭州的。」她露了一點得意的口氣說，她覺得自己得到勝利了。她的憤怒消失了。她的痛苦也消失了。她心平氣和地走出她的小屋，回到洋磁臉盆前面，把她一雙變成了粗糙的手伸進冰冷的水中去。

他帶着苦笑跟在她後面，默默地望着她搓洗衣服，忽然他覺得頭發暈，眼睛發黑，心裏難受得很，他差一點跌倒在地上。他連忙倚着牆壁，閉上眼睛養神。

母親埋着頭，看不見他這情形。她還在對他講話。她說：「家裏少了這個女人，甚麼事都簡單多了。……小宣這個星期一定要回來的。這個孩子很可憐，他媽就從來不管他。……今天外面謠言更多，人心惶惶，好像大禍就要臨頭。她卻不管，這些年頭甚麼日子我沒有過過！未必還有更苦的在後頭！……你公司裏有甚麼消息嗎？」

"Ah," he said, aroused, as if from a sleep. "No."

"Any chance of a transfer to Lanchow?" she asked again.

"Maybe, maybe not. I am not sure," he said, coughing.

"You're coughing again, go lie down." For the first time she turned around to look at him. "You'd better go to bed quickly. You look terrible. You must be having a relapse," she added, alarmed.

Hearing her talk this way, the little strength he had, which had sustained him so far, disappeared completely. Without saying a word, he staggered to the bed and dropped into it. He gave a sigh, which expressed as much desperation as it did relief.

"What's happened to you? What's happened?" she asked.

"I want to sleep a little, I want to sleep," he mumbled.

"Hsüan, you must be careful. The war situation is bad, and you're sick again. What shall I do?" she said sobbing, all aflutter.

"I'm not sick, not at all," he tried to lie, speaking weakly. His cough sounded hollow and frightening.

Tears rolled down her cheeks. She said desperately, "You still insist that you're not sick and that you don't want to rest. If you suddenly collapse, what will you do?"

"Don't worry, Mother. I won't die. Death doesn't come so easily to the likes of me," he argued emotionally, though the terrifying thought of death had always made him morose.

"Don't speak any more. Go to sleep." She covered him with the quilt, hiding her own grief.

"Actually, wouldn't it be a blessing to die? There's no place for us here," he muttered.

「啊。」他好像夢醒了似的應道，「沒有。」他搖搖頭。

「那麼不會搬蘭州……」她又說。

「好像要搬，又好像不搬，我不大清楚。」他答道，接連咳了幾聲嗽。

「怎麼你又在咳嗽？你快躺下去歇歇吧？」她關心地說，她抬起頭來看他。「你快去睡！你臉色這樣難看！你的病剛剛好一點，現在怕又要發作了。」她驚惶地說。

他一直咬着嘴唇在支持着。但自他聽見母親這幾句話後，他的精神力馬上崩潰了。他並不回答她，卻搖搖幌幌地走到床前，倒在床上。他發出一聲像是斷念又像是放心的呻吟。

「你怎麼啦？你怎麼啦？」她驚問道，急忙走到床前來。

「我睡一下，我睡一下。」他喃喃地說。

「宣，你要當心啊，時局這樣壞，你又病倒，叫我怎樣辦？」她有點張惶失措的樣子，帶着哭聲說。

「我不是病，我不是病。」他有氣無力地說，接着他又咳了幾聲嗽，他的咳聲空虛無力，很可怕。

「你還要說不是病！還不肯休息！要是真的再倒下來，你怎麼受得住？」母親着急地責備道，她的淚水沿着臉頰直流。

「媽，你放心，我不會死。我們這種賤骨頭不會死得這麼容易。」他吃力地、感傷地說，而其實他所想的正是一個「死」字。「死」使他悲觀，使他難過。

「你不要說話，你先睡一會兒吧。」她忍住悲痛說，她給他蓋上了棉被。

「其實死了也好，這個世界沒有我們生活的地方。」他自語似地說。

"Don't talk like that. We've never stolen, robbed, killed, or done anything unjust to others. Why shouldn't we live?"

At that moment the door was opened and Shu-sheng came in. "Hsüan, why are you in bed again?" she asked casually in a crisp, clear voice.

"I was tired from walking; I'm just resting a little," he said, supporting himself in a sitting position. His mother's reaction was a mixture of surprise, shame, and anger.

"Go to sleep. I've some good news. Tu-shan has been recaptured from the Japanese," Shu-sheng said cheerfully before handing him the evening paper.

"Well, that means we won't have to flee," he said after reading the paper. He wanted to get up but fell back as soon as he put his legs on the floor. He sighed resignedly.

Without saying a word, his mother retreated to her own room. He called after her, but she made no response.

"Leave her alone, let her go," Shu-sheng whispered to her husband and gestured with her hands.

He shook his head earnestly. "No, that won't do. For my sake, please make up with her."

"She doesn't respect me. How could she make up with me?" Shu-sheng answered, still in a happy mood.

"But I can't leave either of you. Whenever you two squabble, I'm always in the middle. How can I go on like this?" he pleaded.

"Then if one leaves, the problem will be solved. Whoever wants to leave, leave. Isn't that fair?" Shu-sheng suggested, almost flippantly.

「你不要這樣想。我們沒有偷人、搶人、殺人、害人，為甚麼我們不該活？」母親憤憤不平地說。

就在這時房門突然大開，樹生回來了。

「怎麼，宣，你又躺下來了？」她順口問了一句，聲音還是那麼清脆，臉上帶着笑容。

「我走累了，現在躺一會兒。」他連忙撐起半個身子答道。

母親看見樹生進來，大吃一驚。她一張臉漲得通紅，半晌說不出話。羞和憤壓倒了她。

「你睡你的，不要起來，我給你帶來好消息：獨山克服了。」樹生望着他高興地大聲說，「這是晚報。」她把手裏捏着的一張晚報遞給他。

「我們可以不逃難了。」他讀完那條消息寬慰地說，他想下床，可是他剛剛移動他的腿，身子就力竭地倒了下去。他嘆了一口長氣。

母親甚麼話也不說，她板起臉孔躲進小屋去了。「媽。」他在床上喚她，可是她連頭也不回過來。

「讓她去，讓她去。」樹生低聲對他說，一面還做了一個手勢。

他搖搖頭懇切地說：「這樣不好，你看我的面上對媽客氣點。你們和解吧。」

「她看不起我，怎麼肯同我和解？」樹生說，她仍然保持着愉快的心情。

「可是你們兩個人我都離不開，你同媽總是這樣吵吵鬧鬧，把我夾在中間，我怎麼受得了？」他開始發牢騷。

「那麼我們兩個中間走開一個就成咯，哪個高興哪個就走，這不很公平嗎？」樹生半生氣半開玩笑地說。

"To you it might be fair, but what about me?" he replied, irritated.

"It's quite fair to all concerned. If you keep us both, you must pay the price," said Shu-sheng frankly.

"But I'm willing to," he expostulated, while a cough louder than his voice exploded from his itching throat.

The cough immediately drew both women to his side. Tearfully he looked at them, coughing and breathing with difficulty. In the confusion Shu-sheng suggested that he have some tea, and his mother went to bring it. Shu-sheng only stared at her, saying nothing.

Eventually, globs of phlegm came up. Temporarily relieved and resting with the cup in his hand, he declared, "I'll die soon."

"What nonsense! You'll be well in two days," replied Shu-sheng.

"I don't really care," he said, shaking his head. "I know I'll never get well. My mouth reeks of death, and I've been spitting out blood continuously."

Shu-sheng looked into the spittoon and shuddered at what she saw. Nonetheless, she comforted him: "Well, it may not be that bad. Didn't you get well last time?"

Looking gratefully at his wife, he said, "How can my illness be cured by a few doses of herb medicine? You don't believe in Chinese medicine yourself."

While his mother was wiping her tears, Shu-sheng, still calm, said softly, "Even if you've tuberculosis, it can be cured."

"Cured? Where would I get the money? It's always the poor, never the rich, who are afflicted with such illnesses. You say 'rest.' It would take at least three to five years to get well. Where would the money come

「對你這自然公平，可是對我你怎麼說呢？」他煩躁地說。

「對你也並沒有甚麼不公平，你要把兩個人都拉住，這只有苦了你自己。」樹生坦然答道。

「可是我寧願自己吃苦啊。」他痛苦地說，終於忍耐不住，爆發了一陣咳嗽，咳聲比他們談話聲高得多。

妻連忙走到床前，母親立刻從小屋裏跑出來。兩個女人都站在他身邊，齊聲問着：「怎麼又咳嗽啦？」

他側起身子，咳着，喘着氣，喉嚨癢，心裏難過。他眼淚汪汪地望着她們。

「你喝點茶吧？」妻說，他點點頭，母親卻搶着去端了一杯茶。妻瞪了母親一眼，也不說甚麼。

他咳出了三口痰，緩了一口氣，接過了茶杯，喘吁吁地說：「我要死了。」

「哪裏的話？你不要怕，過兩天就會好的。」妻柔聲安慰道。

「我不怕。」他搖搖頭說。「不過我知道我不會好了。我滿嘴腥氣，我又在吐血。」

妻不由自主地朝床前痰盂裏看了一眼，她打了一個寒慄。過後她勸慰道：「吐血也沒有多大關係。你上次吐血，不是吃幾付藥就好了嗎？」

他感激地看了妻一眼，他說：「你自己就不相信中醫，我這個病哪裏是隨便幾付藥就可以醫好的？」

母親不說話，低着頭在揩眼淚，妻似乎還保持着鎮靜，她繼續溫和地勸他：「就是肺病吧，也可以養得好。」

他苦痛地笑了笑，眼裏還包着一腔淚水。「養？我哪裏有錢來養病？偏偏我們窮人生這種富貴病。要養吧，一睡就是三五年，哪裏

from? We are all suffering now and I have such needless expenses."

"I will get the money if you will accept the treatment," she said, intending to raise the money, though she had no idea what a colossal amount she would need.

"I can't burden you any further. I know your income is not much and your expenses are great. Even if you could borrow the money, how would I ever pay it back? I simply can't let you incur such debts for me."

"Your health is much more important than any of that. You can't go on untreated. When you get well, you will find a way to pay it back."

"But what if I die after all the expenses? It would be a waste of money. It wouldn't have done anything for me," he insisted stubbornly.

"But life is much more precious than money. The rich treat their sick pets. You are a human being."

"You should know by now that human lives are cheap, especially the literati's. And I may be the most useless one among them. It is much better to die!" He kept on coughing. Though it was not a heavy cough, it hurt.

"Don't talk to him any more. Can't you see how hard he is coughing? Don't you feel sorry for him?" said his mother to Shu-sheng in a stern voice.

"I am trying to help him, and what business is this of yours?" Shu-sheng snapped, visibly furious. She walked toward the window.

"He is coughing so hard and yet you won't give him a moment of peace. What do you intend to do anyway?" His mother stared at Shu-sheng's back.

來的錢？現在我們大家都在吃苦，我還要亂花錢。」

「我可以設法，只要你肯安心養病，錢總有辦法。」妻聲音緩慢地說，顯然她一面說話，一面在思索。的確她在打算怎樣籌這筆款。可是她並沒有想到這應該是一個怎樣大的數目。

「我不能再增加你的負擔，」他搖頭地說，「我知道你收入也不會太多，花處卻不少。就說你能找到錢，我將來拿甚麼來還，我不能給你們留一筆債啊。」

「你的身體比錢要緊。不能為了錢就連病也不醫的。」妻勸道。「等你病好了，我們可以慢慢還出這筆錢。」

「萬一我再花你許多錢，仍舊活不了，這筆錢豈不等於白花！實際上有甚麼好處？」他固執地說。

「可是生命究竟比錢重要啊！有的人家連狗啊、貓啊生病都要醫治的。你是人啊！」妻痛苦地說。

「你應該看明白了：這個年頭，人是最不值錢的，尤其是我們讀書人，我自然是這裏面最不中用的。有時想想，倒不如死了好。」他說着，又咳起嗽來。咳得不太厲害，但很痛苦。

「你不要再跟他講話，你看他咳得這樣，心裏不難過嗎？」母親忽然抬起頭，板着臉責備妻子說。

妻氣紅了臉，呆了半晌才答道：「我這是好意，我難不難過，跟你並不相干！」她把身子掉開，走到右面窗前去了。

「他咳得這樣，還不讓他休息，你這是甚麼居心？」母親氣憤地說，帶着憎厭的目光瞪了妻一眼。

The old woman's voice was low, but Shu-sheng heard every word. Standing before the window, she turned around and almost snarled. "I plan to marry someone else. That's my intention. Are you satisfied?"

"I know your type. I knew you couldn't take it," said the old woman, obviously satisfied, thinking she had exposed her daughter-in-law's true nature.

"My type is not any cheaper than your type," Shu-sheng responded with mounting fury.

"How dare you compare yourself to me? You are a mistress at best, and I was formally carried to the wedding in a bridal sedan-chair," said her mother-in-law with pride, knowing that she could deeply wound her rival with these words.

Shu-sheng's expression changed and she nearly lost all of her self-restraint, trying to think of a most effective way to fight back. At this moment, Wang, the son and the husband, intervened.

Why should they fight all the time? Such a small family, such simple relationships! Why can't they live together in harmony? Why do these two women, both of whom he loved and who loved him, continually go at each other like eternal enemies? These questions had plagued him more than once. Their noises jarred on his ears, and their shrieks hurt his head. Now his head was aching and swelling; his mind was in turmoil. Where were the words of concern and love? They were glaring at each other with hostile and contemptuous looks, oblivious to his existence. When would their squabbles stop so that he could be left alone?

He begged them, "Mother, Shu-sheng, both of you stop this nonsense. We are one family. Compromise and let's have no more fights." He wanted them to show him at least a little consideration.

她的聲音不大，可是仍然被妻聽見了。

妻從窗前掉轉頭來冷笑道：「我好另外嫁人——這樣你該高興了！」

「我早就知道你熬不過的——你這種女人！」母親高傲地說。她想：你的原形到底露出了。

「我這種女人也並不比你下賤。」妻仍舊冷笑說。

「哼，你配比我！你不過是我兒子的姘頭，我是拿花轎接來的。」母親得意地說，她覺得自己用那兩個可怕的字傷了對方的心。

妻變了臉色，她差一點失掉了控制自己的力量，她在考慮用甚麼武器來還擊。但是他，做着兒子和丈夫的他插嘴講話了。

她們究竟為着甚麼老是不停地爭吵呢？為甚麼這麼簡單的家庭，這麼單純的關係中間都不能有着和諧的合作呢？為甚麼這兩個他所愛而又愛他的女人必須像仇敵似地永遠互相攻擊呢？……這些老問題又來折磨他。她們的聲音吵鬧地在他的腦子裏響着，不，她們的尖聲在敲擊他的頭。他的頭發痛、發脹。他心裏更痛。那些關切和愛的話語到甚麼地方去了？現在兩對仇恨和輕蔑的眼光對望着，他的存在被忘記了。這爭吵要繼續到甚麼時候？甚麼時候他才能夠得到休息？

「媽，樹生，你們都不要說了。都是一家人，彼此多少讓點步，就沒有事了，」他痛苦哀求道。他心裏想說：「你們可憐我，讓我休息吧。」

"Your mother started it. I didn't say anything to provoke her. What right does she have to call me a mistress? I demand an apology from her." Obviously Shu-sheng's pride had been deeply wounded.

"Everyone knows you are his mistress. May I ask, on what date you married him? Who was the matchmaker?"

Hopelessly, he buried his head in the quilt.

"That is no one's business but mine," Shu-sheng answered defiantly.

"You're my daughter-in-law, therefore it is my business. I have every right to interfere, and I intend to ..., " said her mother-in-law sharply.

"Let me put you straight. This is the thirty-third year of the Republic of China,* not the reign of the Emperor Kuang-hsü or Hsüan-t'ung,"† sneered Shu-sheng. "As for me, I never had the privilege of having my feet bound."

"Are you mocking my bound feet? Who cares? No matter what, I am Hsüan's mother and your elder. Don't you have any respect for age? Get out!" the old woman said, gnashing her teeth.

He could not take it any longer. He felt his body was about to explode, his heart splinter into pieces. Those last words, "Get out," hit him like a fatal blow on his chest. He was so aggravated that he threw off his covers and madly pounded his forehead with his fists, screaming, "Let me die."

---

* 1944.

† The last two Manchu emperors before the founding of the Republic of China in 1912.

「是你母親先吵起來的，我今天好好的，又沒有得罪她，她憑甚麼罵我是你的姘頭？我要她說個明白！」妻把臉掙得通紅，她的心的確被刺傷了，她需要着補償。

「你是他的姘頭，哪個不曉得！我問你：你哪天跟他結的婚？哪個做的媒人？」

他絕望地用棉被蒙住了頭。

「你管不着，那是我自己的事。」妻昂然回答。

「你是我的媳婦，我就有權管你。我偏要管你。」母親厲聲說。

「我老實告訴你：現在是民國三十三年，不是光緒宣統的時代了。」妻冷笑道。「我就不曾有過纏腳的福氣。」

「你挖苦我纏過腳？我纏過腳又怎樣？無論如何我總是宣的母親，我總是你的長輩。我看不慣你這種女人，你給我滾！」母親咬牙切齒地說。

他實在忍受不下去了。他覺得頭要爆炸，心要碎裂。一個「滾」字像一下結實的拳頭重重打在他的胸上。他痛苦地叫了一聲，立刻掀開被頭，瘋狂地用自己兩個拳頭打他的前額，口裏接連嚷：「我死了好了！」

"What's the matter? What's the matter?" Shu-sheng cried out, dashing to him.

"Hsüan, are you all right?" his mother asked in alarm.

"Don't, don't fight with each other. That's all I ask," he said simply, sobbing.

"We won't any more," his mother pledged.

"But you will, you will!" he cried.

Shu-sheng was silent, biting her lip. A while later she said, "Truly, Hsüan, there won't be any more quarrels."

Uncovering his face and looking at the two women, he said, "I am afraid I won't live long. Please let me have a few peaceful days."

"Hsüan, you won't die ... just rest," said his mother.

"Please don't worry," added Shu-sheng.

"If you two didn't fight all the time, I might even get well," he said almost smiling.

After he fell asleep, his mother went to fetch the doctor; his wife stood by the window staring at the street scenes below. Beset by doubts, this 34-year-old woman suddenly felt that something was preventing her from thinking clearly. She felt extremely uneasy. Doubts whirled about in her head: "What have I gotten from this life? Have I had any satisfaction?" Having struggled for so long to decide whether she should free herself from this relationship, she finally realized that she gained neither spiritual nor temporal satisfaction living with him. She asked herself, "What's the price of my sacrifice? What will my life, my future be like if the situation stays like this?" She shook her head, her mind full of the memories of bitter family quarrels and of abject poverty. She could still hear his cries

「甚麼事？甚麼事？」妻驚恐地叫着，就跑到他的床前，俯下頭看他。

「宣，你怎樣？」母親驚惶地問道。

「你們不要吵……」他抽泣地說，他只說了這五個字就蒙着臉低聲哭起來。

「你不要難過，……我們以後再也……不吵了。」過了片刻母親悲聲說。

「你們會吵的，你們會吵的……」他病態地哭着說。

妻默默地望了他一會，她咬着下嘴唇在想甚麼。她憐憫地說：「真的，宣，以後不會再吵架了。」

他取下蒙臉的手，一雙淚眼看看母親，又看看妻。他說：「我恐怕活不到多久了，你們讓我過點安靜日子吧。」

「宣，你不會的，你安心養病吧。」母親說。

「好的，你只管放心。」妻說。

「你們只要不吵架，我的病也好的快些。」他欣慰地說，他差不多破涕為笑了。

可是等着他沈沈睡去，母親出去請醫生，妻一個人立在右邊窗前看着街景時，這個三十四歲的女人忽然感覺到像被甚麼東西搔着她的心似的不舒服。一個疑問在她的腦子裏響着：

「這種生活究竟給了我甚麼呢？我得到甚麼滿足麼？」

她想找出一個明確的答覆，可是她的思想好像被困在一叢荊棘中間，掙扎許久，才找着一條出路：

「沒有，不論是精神上、物質上我沒有得着一點滿足。」

「那麼我犧牲了我的理想，換到甚麼代價呢？」

「那麼以後呢？以後，還能有甚麼希望麼？」她問自己。

她不由自主地搖搖頭，她的腦中裝滿了近幾年生活中的艱辛與不和諧。她的耳邊隱隱約約地響着他的疲乏的、悲嘆的聲音，和他

of agony and hopelessness, her mother-in-law's merciless tongue, her looks of hate, her scorn and contempt, all crowned by the ultimatum: "Get out!"

She looked at him again — the pallor of his face, the deeply sunken cheeks, the shallow breathing — all signs of a dying man. What a horrible thought! She again looked out the window. "Why fight to keep him? Ch'en was right. I must plan for my own life right now. It's still not too late. 'Get out!' All right, I will 'get out.' I'll go my own way and it will be none of your business. Why do I hesitate? I mustn't be so weak! I must decide now, this very moment. For myself, for my future happiness. I need it, I deserve it."

Suddenly the image of a boy, a child's face wearing an adult expression, flashed in front of her eyes. She was about to call: "Hsiao Hsüan" — and then she thought, "He doesn't care for me either. Without me, he'll live just as well. I can always help him, but I must not let him prevent me from going my own way. Even Hsüan can't do that."

She looked at her husband again. He was sound asleep, totally unaware of her mental anguish. Could she really leave him? If not, could she remove his mother's jealousy so that she might live peacefully with them? No, it was impossible. She must save herself and salvage what was left of her life. A Chinese fighter plane flew overhead, and the noise momentarily disrupted her thoughts.

She must find Ch'en to arrange her escape, and immediately. Without losing any time, she picked up her purse and left the room. Out in the corridor she remembered that her husband was all alone. She went back to check if he was still asleep.

的母親的仇恨的冷潮、熱罵，這樣漸漸地她的思想又走進一條極窄的巷子裏去了。在那裏她聽見一個聲音：「滾。」就只有這一個字。

她輕輕咳了一聲嗽。她回頭向床上看了一眼。他的臉帶一種不潔的淡黃色，兩頰陷入很深，呼吸聲重而促。在他身上看不到一點力量和生命的痕跡，「一個垂死的人！」她恐怖地想道。她連忙把臉又掉回窗外。

「為甚麼還要守着他？為甚麼還要跟那個女人搶奪他？『滾！讓你拿去！我才不要他！』陳主任說得好，我應該早點打定主意。……現在還來得及，不會太遲！」她想道。她的心跳得厲害。她的臉開始發紅。

「我怎樣辦？……『滾！你說得好！我走我的路！你管不着！』為甚麼還要遲疑？我不應該太軟弱，我不能再猶豫不決，我應該硬起心腸，為了自己，為了幸福。」

「我還能有幸福麼？為甚麼不能？而且我需要幸福，我應該得着幸福。……」

她的眼前忽然閃過一個孩子的臉，一個帶着成人表情的孩子臉。「小宣！」她快要叫出聲來。

「為了小宣」——她想。

「他沒有我，也可以活得很好。他對我好像並沒有多大的感情，我以後仍舊可以幫助他，他不能夠阻止我走我自己的路。連宣也不能夠。」

她又掉轉頭去看床上睡着的人。他仍舊睡得昏昏沈沈，他不會知道她這種種的思想，這個可憐的人！

「我真的必須離開他嗎？——那麼我應該犧牲自己的幸福來陪伴他嗎？——他已經完結了。我能夠救他，能夠使他母親不恨我，同他母親一塊兒和睦地過日子嗎？」

她想了一會，她低聲說出來：「不能。」接着她想：沒有用，我必須救出自己。……飛機聲打岔了她，聲音相當大，一架中國戰鬥機飛過去。

她得到結論了；找陳主任去。他可以幫忙她離開這個地方。

她興奮地把頭一昂，她覺得渾身發熱，心也跳得很急。但她充滿着勇氣，她不再躊躇了。她從抽屜裏拿出手提包，走出門去。她已經走到門外廊上了，忽然想起他母親不在家，他一個人睡在床上，她覺得不放心，便又推開門，回到房裏去，看看他是不是睡得很好。

When she entered the room, she heard him calling her name in his sleep. Astonished, she asked softly, "What's the matter? Is there anything wrong?"

Turning over he reached for her hand and held it tightly. After groaning for three or four minutes, he opened his eyes and gazed at her. In a weak but happy voice he asked, "You're still home? You haven't left?"

"Where to?" She was puzzled.

"To Lanchow. I dreamed that you had left me to go to Lanchow, and that I was abandoned in a hospital, very lonely and very terrified.... "

She shuddered at his strange dream, but said nothing.

"Fortunately it was only a dream. You won't leave me, will you?" he asked. "Frankly, we don't have many days together. I'm beyond cure." His voice and even his tears were begging her.

"I won't leave you," she promised, grateful and disheartened, abandoning her earlier decision.

"I know you won't, but Mother always insists that you will. Old people are strange at times."

The word "mother" slapped her mercilessly. A strong force urged her to retract the promise she had just made and she was resisting it. She frowned, her face twitching. She did not know how to respond to him.

In the meantime, he thanked her again. "I won't burden you for too long now. As for our son, I only regret that I haven't fulfilled my obligations to him."

"Please don't say any more," she interrupted, withdrawing her hand from his. His words seemed to have been uttered deliberately to torment her, and she could hardly bear them. She wished she could

她剛走到他的床前，忽然他在夢中發出了一聲哭叫。他喚着她的名字。她吃了一驚，連忙問：「甚麼事？甚麼事？」她俯下頭去。

他略略向外一翻身，伸出一隻手來抓她的手，她把右手送過去，他抓到她的手便緊緊捏着，他低聲呻吟着，再過三四分鐘，他睜開眼來。他的眼光挨到她的臉，就停住不動了。

「你在這兒！」他驚喜地說，聲音軟弱無力。「你沒有走？」

「走哪裏去？」她問。

「蘭州去，我夢見你離開我到蘭州去了。」他答道，「把我一個人丟在醫院裏，多寂寞。多害怕！」

她打了一個冷噤，說不出一句話來。

「幸而這是夢。」他無力地噓了一口氣，「你不會丟了我走開吧？」他的聲音顫得厲害。「其實我們相處的日子也不會多了，我看我這個病是不會好的了。」不僅聲音，連他的眼淚也在哀求。

「我不會走，你放心吧。」她感激地說。她的心冷了。剛才那個決定在這一瞬間完全瓦解了。

「我知道你不會走的。」他感激地說，「媽總說你要走，請你原諒她，上了年紀的人總有點怪脾氣。」

這個「媽」字像一記巴掌打在她臉上，她驚呆了，她皺着眉，臉部肌肉微微在搐動，似乎有一個力量逼迫她收回她那句話，她在抗拒。

「謝謝你，謝謝你啊。」他很興奮地說。「我不會久拖累你的。還有小宣，說起來我實在不好意思，我並沒有好好盡過做父親的責任。」

「你不要再說了。」她抽回她的手，略帶粗聲地打斷了他的話，他那些話似乎是故意說來折磨她的，她再也不能忍受下去了。她想

go to a quiet place and unburden herself of all that was in her mind, all her suffering. But she remained sitting on the edge of the bed.

"Shu-sheng," he called. "I think it's best you leave Chungking. I'm deeply indebted to you for having suffered so much, but there is no future for you here. Why should I be a stumbling block to your happiness? I am hopelessly ill ... my health ... You're young and you can still get away," he choked.

"You'd better rest. What's the use of thinking so much?" She heaved a sigh and stood up.

He had another uncontrollable coughing spell. Something stuck in his windpipe that he could not spit out despite his most desperate efforts. His face grew redder and redder.

She rubbed his back and gave him some water. After a few sips, he coughed again. This time he spat out a glob of phlegm tainted with blood, but he managed not to let her see it.

To comfort him, she said casually, "The doctor will be here soon."

"There is no need for a doctor. It is a waste of time, energy, and money," he sighed. "I see him just to please Mother."

"Why don't you think of yourself for a change? Your kindness is your ultimate undoing. This world is not made for the likes of you. Don't you realize that in sacrificing yourself, you also sacrifice others?" she asked.

The sound of footsteps interrupted her thoughts. Thinking that her mother-in-law must have returned with the doctor, she walked to the stool by the table and sat down.

The door was pushed open and her mother-in-law entered the room accompanied by the physician, Chang Po-ch'ing, still the usual friendly,

找個安靜地方暢快地哭一場，她彷彿受了不知若干的委屈。結果她還是坐在床沿上。

他半晌不作聲，後來忽然嘆了一口氣，柔聲喚道：「樹生。」她側過頭看他。「其實你還是走的好。我仔細想想，你在我家裏過着這樣的日子，我真對不起你。以後的日子……我不敢想……我何必再耽誤你……我是沒有辦法……我這樣的身體……你還能夠飛啊……」他的喉嚨被堵塞住，他的聲音啞了。

她站起來，短短地嘆一口氣，說：「你還是睡一會兒吧。現在多想這些事又有甚麼用？……」

他突然又爆發了一陣咳嗽。他接連咳着，好像有痰黏在他喉管上，他在用力要咳出它來，可是他把臉都掙紅了，卻始終咳不出來甚麼。

她過去替他輕輕地捶背，又給他端來一杯白開水。他喝了兩口，又咳起來，這一次他咳出痰來了。痰裏帶了點血絲，不過她沒有看見，(他也不讓她有機會看清楚)。

「醫生快來了吧。」她為了想安慰他，順口說道。

「其實何必再看醫生，白淘神，還要花錢。」他嘆息說。「我是為了媽，我是為她的緣故。」

「你到這種時候，還只想到別人，你太老好了。」她感動地說，但感動中還夾雜了一點點埋怨。「你為甚麼不多想到你自己。你吃了一輩子老好的虧。」她短短嘆一口氣。「這個世界並不是為你這種人造的，你害了你自己，也害了別人。……」

一陣腳步聲打岔了她，她知道母親回來了，一定是跟醫生一塊兒來的。她便走到方桌前在一個櫈子上坐下了。

於是門被推開，母親伴着張伯情醫生走進來，醫生向她和他打

clever face and the usual superficial diagnosis.

"He's just helping him drag on and delay the inevitable. He can't cure him!" Shu-sheng thought to herself, frowning.

"Don't worry, don't worry! A few more doses will do the trick," the physician said confidently.

"Do I have tuberculosis?" the patient asked nervously.

"No, no," answered the physician, shaking his head. "You've a mild indisposition, though the element of fire in your liver is still powerful. Take the medicine, have plenty of rest, and you'll get well." The old man smiled pleasantly.

His mother walked the doctor to the door and thanked him repeatedly. Shu-sheng remained silent.

"I don't want you to fill the prescription," Wang said to his mother, who was carefully deciphering what was written on the paper.

"Why not?" she asked, startled.

"Because the result will be the same whether I take it or not. His medicine can't cure me," he said.

Disagreeing with him completely, she ignored his request and prepared to go to a drugstore.

"Do you have money?" he asked.

"I've some here," Shu-sheng said immediately.

"I've the money," said his mother more or less to herself, without looking at Shu-sheng. Shu-sheng flushed, and without saying a word went to the window, her eyebrows arched together in a frown.

"Take a thousand from this. I was advanced this amount by my

招呼，仍舊是那張和善而又通世故的臉，仍舊是那樣近於敷衍的診斷。

「他不過在拖着他捱日子啊，他那裏能治好他的病？」她想着。她略略皺着眉頭，心裏很難過。

「不要緊，不要緊。多吃兩付藥就會好的。」醫生很有把握似地說。

「我看這是肺病吧。」他膽怯地說。

「不是，不是。」醫生搖頭道。「是肺病還了得，肝火旺。吃兩付藥，少走動，包你好。」這個老人和藹地笑了笑。

「謝謝你啊。」送走這醫生時，母親還接連感謝道。妻一句話也沒有說。

「媽，我看用不着去檢藥了。」他忽然說。

母親正拿着藥方在看，聽見這話便驚問道：

「我看吃不吃藥都是一樣，我這種病不是藥醫得好的。」他斷續地答道。

「哪有藥醫不好病的道理？」母親不以為然地說，她摺好藥方。「我去給你檢藥。」她拿着手提包，預備走出房門。

「你身邊錢不夠吧？」他問道。

「我這裏還有錢。」妻馬上接嘴說。

「我有。」母親望着他說，並不看妻一眼，好像沒有聽見她說話似的。妻紅了臉，眉毛一豎，但哼都不多哼一聲，就走到窗前去了。

「你拿一千元去吧，我今天借支了薪水。」他說，一面伸手在自

office," he said, taking some money out of his pocket. "If you use the money budgeted for food, you will need money later anyway. Just now you used some food money for the physician."

"Don't worry. I've money, I've some extra money," said his mother.

"Where did you get it? I know.... You sold your ring," he said.

"I'm an old woman, and I don't need it, " she explained.

"But that was my father's gift to you. You should have kept it."

"I'll be seeing your father soon. The ring makes no difference to me," she said, pretending to smile.

"That's the only valuable thing you had. I'm a worthless son, worthless!"

"What's the use of crying over spilt milk? As long as you get well, I'll be happy," she said. She hurriedly left the room.

Shu-sheng stood pensively by the window. In the background was the sound of rats chewing on the wood in the room.

While he was tossing and turning in bed, his restless mind made him speak aloud, "My mother has had a hard time, too. For me, she has sold her only piece of jewelry." He had meant the remark for Shu-sheng's ears, but she stood by the window without turning her head.

XIX

THE following evening, Ch'en sent a letter via a personal carrier. It said, "due to unexpected difficulties with my ticket, my departure

己衣袋裏掏錢。「你把伙食錢扯了，還是要填補的。剛才請醫生已經扯過錢了。」

「你放心，我有錢，我另外找了點錢。」母親說。

「你在哪裏找的錢？……我知道，你一定把你那個戒指賣掉了！」他說。

「我是老太婆，不必戴戒指，放着它也沒有用處。」母親解釋地說。

「那是父親送你的紀念品，你不能因為我的緣故賣掉啊。」他痛苦地說。

「橫豎我跟你父親見面的日子近了，有沒有它都是一樣。」母親裝出笑容回答道。

「不過你就只有這一件貴重的東西。現在連這個也光了。這是我沒有出息，我對不起你啊！」他帶着悔恨地說。

「事情既然做過了，還說它做甚麼？你好好地養病吧，只要你身體好，我就高興了。」母親說罷，不等他講話就匆匆走了出去。

妻仍舊立在窗前，沈浸在自己的思想中。屋子裏只有老鼠啃木頭的聲音。

他反來覆去地想着，他的腦子不肯休息。他睡不着，他感動地說：「媽也很苦啊，她為了我連最後一件寶貝也犧牲掉了。」他這話是對妻說的。可是妻靜靜地立在窗前，連頭也不掉過來。

十九

第二天傍晚，陳主任差人送來一封信，信裏有這樣的幾句話：

……我的飛機票發生問題，要延遲一個星期。但下星期三一

has been delayed for a week, but I can definitely leave on next Wednesday.... Everything has been arranged for you. You'll receive your formal letter of transfer within the week. Meet me at the Kuan-shang Yüan Restaurant tomorrow at eight."

When Shu-sheng lifted her eyes from the letter, they met her mother-in-law's. She could sense the old woman's mockery and contempt as if the latter were saying, "I know your tricks, all of them." Coughing lightly, Shu-sheng mused, "You have no right to control me." Her mother-in-law finished eating before she did.

Lying in bed, Wang coughed from time to time. The two women had become accustomed to his coughing spells. He often massaged his chest to ease the pain and help his breathing. Often he felt an urge to cough, but no phlegm came out. When he tried to cough up the phlegm, he felt a sharp pain in his chest. He suffered as best as he could; his groans were so faint that they could hardly be heard, for he didn't want them to know his true condition. He attentively watched their every move and intently listened to their conversation.

"Was there a letter from the bank? Anything important?" he asked Shu-sheng in a low voice, stopping his cough.

His wife did not hear him. Apparently his mother did not hear the question either, for she asked, "Hsüan, what do you want?"

"Nothing." Two or three minutes later, he said, "I asked if there was anything important in Shu-sheng's letter." This time he spoke loud enough to be heard by Shu-sheng.

"A note from a colleague, nothing important," Shu-sheng answered dully. His mother quickly gave the young woman an accusing look, clearly implying, "You're deceiving him, I know."

A moment later he said again, "I heard the messenger say the letter was from Ch'en."

定可以走。……你的事已經講妥了。

這星期內調職通知書就會下來。……明早八點鐘前仍在冠生園等候……

樹生看完信抬起頭，她的眼光無意間同母親的眼光碰到了。她看出了憎恨和譏笑。「我都知道，你那些鬼把戲！」母親的眼光似乎在這樣說。

「你管不着我！」她心裏想，她輕輕咳了一聲。這時她同母親兩人正在吃晚飯，母親比她先放下碗。

他在床上斷續地乾咳，這咳聲在她們兩人的耳裏漸漸變成熟悉的了，他時常用手在胸膛上輕輕擦揉，他內部有甚麼東西出了毛病，在發痛，而且使他呼吸不暢快。這樣的擦揉倒可以給他一點舒適，他時時覺得喉管發癢，他忍不住要咳嗽，卻又咳不出痰來。有時他必須用力咳。但是一用力，他又覺得胸部疼痛不堪。這痛苦他一直忍耐着，他竭力發出一聲響亮的（甚至別人可以聽見的）呻吟。他盡可能不讓她們知道他的真情形，然而他卻仔細地注意她們的動作，傾聽她們的談話。

「行裏送信來，有要緊事嗎？」他停止了咳嗽，關心地問，聲音不高。

妻沒有聽見，母親掉過臉來看他，顯然她也沒有聽清楚他的話，因為她在問：「宣，你要甚麼？」

「沒有甚麼。」他搖搖頭答道，但是停了兩三分鐘他又說：「我問樹生信裏是不是有甚麼要緊事情？」這次聲音較高，被妻聽見了。

「一個同事寫來的，沒有甚麼要緊事。」妻淡淡地回答。母親馬上掉過頭看了她一眼，那神情彷彿在說：「你在騙他，我知道。」

「我聽見說是陳主任送來的。」他想了想又說。

Listlessly Shu-sheng replied, "Yes, it was from him."

"Wasn't he supposed to have left for Lanchow? Is he still here?"

"At first he was to leave tomorrow, but some problem has come up. He has postponed his departure for a week or two."

While his wife removed dishes from the table and his mother went to bring in the kettle of hot water, he remarked, "I remember you once said something about being transferred to Lanchow, but I haven't heard you mention it lately."

She turned to him, with a surprised look on her face. Calmly she said, "Nothing of the kind. It was only a joke my friends made up."

Bringing a kettle of hot water into the room, his mother heard Shu-sheng's answer. Immediately she "humphed" and darted a look which implied that Shu-sheng was lying.

Her lips quivering, Shu-sheng blushed. But she said nothing and turned her eyes away.

"What if the bank insists that you accept the transfer?" he asked.

"I'm not sure whether I'd go," she answered briefly, visibly annoyed by his persistence.

"If they transfer you, I'm afraid you'll have to go," he went on, not knowing what was in her mind.

"Then I'll resign," she answered, though she had never thought about this possibility.

"Resign? No! With me ill and Hsiao Hsüan in school, what would we live on?"

「是他。」妻淡淡地回答。

「他不是要飛蘭州嗎？怎麼還沒有走。」他又想了一下，再問。

「本來說明天飛的，現在又說飛機票有問題，要延遲一兩個星期。」妻仍舊用淡漠的調子回答。

過了幾分鐘，妻站起來，收拾飯桌上的碗碟，母親到外面去提開水壺。他忽然又問：

「我記得你說過行裏要調你到蘭州去，怎麼這兩天又不見提起了？」

妻掉過頭，用詫異的眼光看了他一眼，她竭力做出平淡的聲調回答：

「那不過是同事間開玩笑，沒有這回事。」

恰恰在這時母親提了開水壺進來，她聽見樹生的話，低低哼了一聲，她又看樹生一眼，彷彿說：「你撒謊！」

妻臉上微微發紅，嘴動了一下，但她並沒有說甚麼，就把眼睛掉開了。

「萬一行裏真的調你去，你去不去呢？」他還在追問，妻不知道他存着甚麼樣的心思。

「我不一定去。」她短短地答道，他這種近似審問的問話使她心煩。

「既然調你去，不去恐怕不行吧？」他不知道她的心情，只顧絮絮地講下去。

「不行，就辭職。」她答得很乾脆，而其實她並沒有考慮這個問題。

「辭職，怎麼行？我又病在床上，小宣又要上學。我們還有甚麼辦法活下去。」他自語似地說。

"Sell things or borrow money. We wouldn't starve," Shu-sheng said, parodying her mother-in-law's earlier statement. She had suffered so much at the old woman's hands that she welcomed the chance to be sarcastic.

"Is there anything of value left to sell? We've consumed everything in recent years. And borrow from whom? You still have a few rich friends left, perhaps ... "

"Please stop, stop," she impatiently interrupted him. "You shouldn't talk so much. You should rest."

"No, I can't. Whenever I close my eyes, it's like I am seeing a movie. My mind won't rest," he moaned.

"You worry too much. It would be better if you rested quietly." Shu-shengs's tone was mild and comforting.

"How can I stop worrying? I'm only thirty-four, and I'm so ill. I don't know if I can be cured," he cried.

"Hsüan, don't worry. You'll be all right. Chang Po-ch'ing said maybe it would take only half a month and a few more doses ..., " interrupted his mother.

"I think you'd better go to a hospital for a thorough medical examination. An X-ray will be necessary. I have doubts about Chinese medicine," Shu-sheng said very slowly, expressing her opinion at last. She was immediately interrupted by him.

"What if I'm in the terminal stage of tuberculosis?" he asked.

"Then you should receive proper treatment," Shu-sheng answered unhesitatingly.

"It's an illness only the rich can afford," he replied. "Apart from the medical fees, the convalescent expenses would be staggering."

「那麼賣東西，借債。總不會餓死吧。」妻接嘴說，她故意說給母親聽。她覺得今天受那個女人的氣太多了，她總想找個機會刺那女人一下。

他苦笑了。「你看，我們還有值錢的東西嗎？這兩年甚麼都吃光了。借錢向哪個借？只有你還有幾個闊朋友……」

「不要說了，不要說了。」她帶點厭煩地打斷了他的話，「你有病不能多講話，你好好地睡吧。」她掉開臉不看他。

「我睡不着，一閉上眼，就像在演電影。腦子簡直不能夠休息。」他訴苦般地說。

「你思慮太多，你不要多想，還是安安靜靜地睡吧。」妻同情地看他一眼溫和地安慰他說。

「我怎麼能不想呢？才三十四歲就害了這種病，不知道能不能好啊！」他痛苦地說。

「宣，你不要着急，你一定會好的，張伯情說吃幾付藥，養半個月，一定會好。」母親插嘴說。

「我主張你去醫院檢查一下，最好透視一下，這樣靠得住一點。我對中醫……」妻沈吟半晌終於正色說道。但是話未說完，就被他打岔了。

「萬一檢查出來是第三期肺病，又怎麼辦？」他問。

「那麼就照治肺病的辦法醫治。」妻毫不猶豫地回答。

「那是富貴病啊，不說醫，就是養，也要一筆大錢。」他苦笑道。

"But should the poor then go untreated?" Shu-sheng asked. "In any case, we're not dirt poor."

"It's no use! No use! Don't say any more," he said, shaking his head. Something heavy was pressing on his chest, threatening to choke him at any moment. He groaned and breathed heavily, his face red from coughing.

"Let him rest," said his mother, glaring at Shu-sheng. To him, she said softly, "Stop talking. Too much talk is harmful. Close your eyes." He answered "yes," sighed softly, and closed his eyes.

Rebuffed, Shu-sheng was resentful. She blushed and was about to explode, but asked herself what would be the point of another quarrel. It would achieve nothing. Despite the endless barrage of meaningless words, the exchange of hostile looks, there would never be either a complete rift or a reconciliation. Wang could not bring her and her mother-in-law together or choose between the two; he could only delay the ultimate confrontation and no more. What could he give her? Comfort? Support? He had sighed before; now it was her turn to sigh. Having wasted her youth in this dark and chilly room, she was being rewarded with hostility. She had reached the limit of her endurance. In her heart she said to her arch rival, "You know how to please him. Fine. I'll let you. I don't care for him in the least bit." Smiling scornfully, she walked to the window to watch the street scenes below.

The chilly night air cooled her face. She saw a few isolated lights amidst a background of darkness, for the surrounding areas were scheduled for a blackout that night. She shuddered, shrugged her shoulders, and complained about the shortage of electricity. No one in the house paid any attention to her. Frightened by loneliness, she looked at the electric bulb, which, like her husband's eyes, gave her little warmth. She turned to look at her failing husband. He was breathing heavily, his eyes closed. In pity, she rearranged the quilt for him.

「那麼窮人生病就該死嗎？」她憤慨地說。「而且我們也並不太窮。」

「沒有用，沒有用，你這些空話都沒有用。」他搖頭說，他的胸部像被甚麼東西壓住了似的，氣緊得很，彷彿隨時都會閉塞住。他接連沙沙地咻着。呼吸聲也很粗重，臉也掙紅了。

「請你讓他休息一會兒吧。」母親瞪妻一眼，氣惱地說。她馬上又走到他的床前，改用憐憫的眼光望着他，柔聲說：「你不要多說話，說話傷神，會加病的，你閉上眼睛。」

他答了一個「是」字，過後輕輕嘆了一口氣，真的把眼睛閉上了。

妻碰了一個釘子頗不甘心，她臉一紅，很想即刻發作。但她又想：這樣單調的爭吵有甚麼用處呢？永遠得不着結果，不管怎樣把那些沒有意義的話語反覆重說，不管怎樣用仇恨的眼光互相注視。沒有和解，也沒有決裂。他沒有辦法把母親和妻拉在一起，也沒有毅力在兩人中間選取一個。永遠是敷衍和拖。除了這，他似乎再不能做別的事情。現在他病在床上，他還能夠給她甚麼呢？安慰？支持？……他在那邊嘆氣。現在應該她嘆氣了。她把她的青春犧牲在這間陰暗、寒冷的屋子裏，卻換來仇視和敷衍。她覺得自己的忍耐快達到極限了。

「你會討好他。好吧，我就讓你，我並不希罕他。」她在心裏罵道，她輕輕冷笑一聲，就慢步走到右側窗前，隔着玻璃窗去看街景。

夜相當冷。寒氣涼涼地摸她的臉，下面是一片黑。只有寥寥幾盞燈光。原來她這所樓房是一個界線，樓房外算是另一區域，那一區今天停電。她打了一個冷噤，又聳了聳肩，「為甚麼總是停電？」她煩躁地低聲自語。沒有人理她。在這個屋子裏她是不被人重視的！她的孤獨使她自己害怕。她又轉過身來迎着電燈光。電燈光就跟病人的眼睛一樣，它也不能給她的心添一點溫暖。她把眼光移向病床，他閉着眼睛張着嘴重重地在吐氣。他似乎一點鐘一點鐘地瘦

He awoke with a strange expression on his face, as if he did not know her. Her heart seemed to miss a beat, but she regained her composure at once and explained mildly, "Your quilt almost fell to the floor, so I pulled it up for you."

"Thank you," he said. "Is Mother sleeping now? You're still up?"

"It is still early," she said. "Go back to sleep."

"I just complained that I couldn't fall asleep, but I suppose I did," he said with a smile. "I've something to tell you.... Tomorrow is your birthday."

"I had forgotten it myself. Why bring it up?"

"Here is sixteen hundred *yüan*. Would you please order a four-pound birthday cake for tomorrow? I don't dare trouble Mother, and so I have to ask you." Unsteadily from under the covers he stretched out his hand and gave her a roll of old bills.

"I don't have the spirit to celebrate my birthday. I don't want the cake," she said, visibly moved by his generosity and love.

"You must order one.... You must order one for me.... I can't go out myself, so I must trouble you.... Take the money."

Someone was knocking on the door. "Can it be a messenger from Ch'en?" she wondered.

To her surprise, a bald middle-aged man walked in. It was Uncle Chung. Hurriedly she thanked her husband and put the money away.

"Wang, what's the matter? Are you sleeping already? Greetings to you, Mrs. Wang."

"Sit down please," said Shu-sheng.

"Uncle Chung, what brings you here? I'll be well soon. It was very

下去。「他也實在可憐。」她想道，母親已經出去了。她走到病床前把棉被輕輕拉了一下，他忽然睜開眼睛來看她，他定睛望着她，好像不認識她似的。她的心猛然跳了一下。但是她接着就鎮定了。她溫和地解釋說：「你的鋪蓋快掉下地了，我給你拉上來。」

「是嗎。」他說，接着問：「媽睡了？你不休息？」

「還早啦。」她應道。「你好好睡吧。」

「我正說不睡，怎麼又睡着了。」他微笑說，「我有話對你說，明天是你生日……」

「連我自己都忘了，你還提它做甚麼？」她溫柔地插嘴說。

「這是一千六百元，請你替我去定一個四磅重的蛋糕，明天要的，我不敢麻煩媽，只請你自己去定，很對不起你。……」他顫抖地伸出手來，手中有一卷舊鈔票。

「我沒有心情過生日，你不要買吧。」她感動地說，差一點流下淚來。

「你要去定啊……一定要替我定啊……我自己不敢出去，只好麻煩你……你把錢拿着；……」他斷斷續續地說。

有人在叩門。她想：「難道又是他差人送信來？」這個「他」是指陳主任。她隨口說了一句：「請進來。」

出乎她的意外，進來的是一個禿的半老頭兒，他公司裏的同事鍾老。「好，謝謝你。」她小聲說，就把鈔票收下了。

「老汪，怎麼啦？現在就睡了嗎？」鍾老一進門就大聲說，又向着她說；「大嫂好。」

「鍾先生，請坐。」她連忙招呼道。

「鍾老，怎麼你跑來了？我的病不要緊，就會好的，對不起你跑

nice of you to come all the way to see me. I was planning to return to work this morning, but I felt dizzy and so I stayed home," said Wang. He managed to sit up in bed.

"Please don't sit up. I'll be leaving shortly," said Chung.

"It's all right. I want to sit up anyway. You see I haven't undressed."

"Be careful not to catch cold. You'd better lie down. We can talk just as well," Uncle Chung said kindly.

"Mr. Chung, please sit down. Have some tea," Shu-sheng said, pouring a cup of tea for him and placing it on the square table.

"Thank you, Mrs. Wang," said Chung courteously, sitting down on a stool.

"I just read in the evening paper that Liu-chai has been recaptured from the enemy. This is good news," said Chung, sipping his tea.

"Yes," said Wang, coughing four or five times. "Maybe our Company won't have to move elsewhere."

"Of course not. Evacuating to Lanchow was never anything more than idle rumor."

"Then would you please ask for an additional day of leave for me? I'd like to go back to work the day after tomorrow so they won't deduct too much from my salary."

"You must not go back so soon. Rest a few more days at home. The work in the office is too hard on you, and your health comes first," Chung advised his friend.

"But you know Chou's temper. If one works for him, one must put up with him," said Wang, knitting his brows. Before Uncle Chung could interrupt, he asked worriedly, "By the way, did he say anything about me after I left yesterday?"

一趟，我今天早晨剛起來，正預備去上班，忽然頭暈得很，便又睡下了，一直睡到現在。」他抱歉地說，就勉強坐起來。

「你睡，你睡，我坐坐就走的。」鍾老走到床前，一面說話，一面做着要他睡下的手勢。

「不要緊，我就在床上坐坐，我不想睡，你看我衣服都沒有脫。」他坐在床上說。

「看受涼啊，你還是躺下吧，你躺下我們談，也是一樣。」鍾老和藹地說。

「鍾先生，請坐吧，請吃茶啊。」她倒了一杯茶放在方桌上，一面對鍾老說。

「謝謝，大嫂。」鍾老客氣地帶笑說，就在一個櫈子上坐下了。

「剛才看見晚報，六寨也克服了。這倒是個好消息啊。」鍾老端起茶杯呷了一口。

「是。」他說，乾咳了四五聲，「那麼公司不會搬家了？」他略微感到一點寬慰地說。

「當然不會搬了。搬蘭州不過是一句話，現在用不着逃難了。」鍾老說。

「那麼請你明天替我請一天假，我想再休息一天就上班，免得他們多扣薪水。」他說。

「你用不着後天就去，你可以在家裏多休息幾天，公司裏校對的工作對你身體不大好。還是身體要緊。」鍾老勸他道。

「不過我們周主任的脾氣你是知道的，要吃他這碗飯，就只好忍點氣。」他說着，皺了兩次眉頭。鍾老還要開口，他忽然關心地問：「昨天我走後你沒有聽見他說起我甚麼事吧？」

"At the time I was downstairs, so I couldn't have heard anything if he did. However ... " Chung took out a roll of bills and put it by Wang's pillow. "Here is your salary for a month and a half. Chou wanted you to have it."

"A month and a half's salary. Why?" Wang was stunned. After a few seconds, he cried out, "Is he dismissing me?"

"He said ... he said ..., " Chung stammered.

"But what have I done wrong? He can't dismiss me without cause," Wang roared with rage, his blood pressure rising, the pain in his left chest increasing, and gasping for breath. "I've always behaved properly. I never complained. I was fed up, yet ... I took all types of insults ... I was like ... "

"Wang, don't be angry. He didn't mean to dismiss you.... He said your health is not good ... you might have tuberculosis and he thinks you ought to rest for half a year," explained Chung, after mustering up some courage. "This of course is his decision. Personally I don't think you have TB. You are simply undernourished and overworked. I think you'll be well after a few days' rest. But Chou thinks differently. He wants you to have an extended rest. He said he was ready to give you two months' salary, but you already had half a month's advance. Here's a month and a half's pay. It's not so bad; with this money you can rest longer. When you get well, maybe you can get another job."

Wang remained silent.

"This is ridiculous!" Shu-sheng interrupted, "Hsüan has slaved for Chou like a horse for two years. Yet once he is sick, he immediately gets thrown out." Speaking to her husband, she continued, "Mr. Chung is right. When you get well, look for a different job."

Lifting his head, Wang moaned, "It is so difficult to get a job."

「我在樓下辦公，怎麼聽得見呢？」鍾老答道。「不過——」鍾老從懷裏掏出一卷鈔票，又站起來，走到床前，把鈔票放在病人枕頭旁邊。「這裏是九千五百塊，是你一個半月的薪水，周主任要我給你送來。」

「一個半月的薪水，他要你給我送來？為甚麼？」他驚問道。停了片刻。他忽然大聲說：「是不是他要裁掉我？」

「他說……他說。」鍾老結結巴巴地說着，他紅着臉講不下去。

「我做了甚麼錯事呢？他不能無緣無故地就趕走我。」他憤慨地說。他覺得自己的血往上直沖，整個頭都在發燒。左胸一股一股地發痛，他開始喘氣。「我在公司裏一向規規矩矩辦公，一句話也不敢說。我已經忍無可忍了，我甚麼氣都受下了，我簡直——」

「老汪，你不要生氣，他不是趕你走……他說……你身體不好……恐怕有TB，他要我勸你休息半年再說。」鍾老鼓起勇氣說了出來：「這自然是他的武斷，據我看你不見得就有肺病。你不過營養差一點，平日人也太累，休息幾天就會好的。不過周主任，他不這樣想，他要你多休息。他說送你兩個月薪水，你支了半個月，所以這裏只有一個半月的錢，也好，你索性多休息幾天，身體養好了，另外找個事，反倒痛快些。」

他埋下頭不作聲。

「真豈有此理！給他們做了兩年牛馬，病倒了就一腳踢開。」妻氣憤地插嘴說。「鍾先生的話不錯，等你病好了，另外找個比較痛快的事。」

「現在找事也不容易。」他抬起頭說。

"I'll ask someone to help you. I am sure you could find one at least as good as the one you had," said Shu-sheng.

"You're right, Mrs. Wang. Actually our Company, being semi-civil in nature, offers no future to anyone. It is not such a big deal that Mr. Wang lost the job," Chung philosophized.

"He's so very kind; people often take advantage of him. If you hadn't helped him during the last two years, he'd have lost his job a long time ago," Shu-sheng said to Chung.

"You're too kind, Mrs. Wang. I haven't done anything for him." Chung answered politely but also somewhat apologetically. "But he is always pleasant to talk to, and I admire his character. Everyone knows about our friendship, and that's why I was sent here."

"I know. I know. Since Chou has made his decision known, I suppose Wen-hsüan had better resign," said Shu-sheng with a reluctant smile. Immediately she turned to ask her husband, "Don't you think so, Hsüan?"

"Yes, yes," Wang responded vaguely.

"You're right, Mrs. Wang," Chung praised Shu-sheng. "There is no future with the Company; it's no big deal to lose the job. Wang, you'd better take care of your health. When you get well, it won't be too difficult to get another job." Chung chatted with the Wangs a little longer; then he said, "I don't want to take any more of your time. I'll drop in to see you again soon. Wang, take care of yourself. A person's health is most important nowadays."

"Uncle Chung, stay a while. We've nothing to do," Wang said. Shu-sheng also felt that a guest would add some variety, some warmth, some liveliness to the room.

"No, no. I have to go. I'll come back some other day," Chung

「我可以托人設法，我不信連一個像你現在這樣的事也找不到，」妻說，他不再說話。

「大嫂意思不錯，其實我們公司，那種官而商商而官的組織是弄不好的。汪兄丟了這裏的事並不可惜。」鍾老接嘴說。

「他人太老好，在外面做事容易吃虧，這一兩年要不是靠着鍾先生關照，恐怕早就站不住了。」妻說。

「大嫂太客氣了，我哪裏說得上關照，一點忙也沒有幫到，實在對不起汪兄。」鍾老帶笑地說，臉上微露出歉意來。「不過我和汪兄平日還談得攏，我很敬佩汪兄的為人，公司裏都知道我跟汪兄熟，所以周主任要我來辦這個差事。」鍾老接着又解釋道。

「我知道，我們明白鍾先生的意思，既然周主任有這樣表示，文宣就遵命辭職吧。」妻也帶笑說（她的笑容看得出是很勉強的）她馬上又向着她的丈夫問道：「是不是這樣，宣？」

「是，是。」他含含糊糊地應道。

「大嫂這個意思很不錯。」鍾老稱讚道，「公司既然沒有前途，也值不得留戀，汪兄好好保養身體，身體好了，另外找事也不難。……」他又談了幾句閒話，忽然立起來客客氣氣地說：「我不打擾你們了，我改天再來。汪兄，你好好養病吧，在這時代還是身體寶貴啊。」

「鍾老，再坐一會，我們很閒。」他挽留說，妻覺得他替她說了話。來一個客人，至少給這屋子添一點變化，一點熱，一點生氣。

「不坐了，改天再來暢談。」鍾老帶笑地告辭道，「我還有別的

insisted. "I have a few chores to attend to."

"I'm sorry that I can't see you to the door," Wang said, disappointed.

"There's no need. I'll come back often," Uncle Chung replied courteously, heading for the door.

"I'll walk Mr. Chung to the door," Shu-sheng offered.

"Mrs. Wang, please don't," said Chung. He was already at the door.

"It's quite dark outside. Please allow me to accompany you downstairs," insisted Shu-sheng. Using a flashlight, she walked Chung to the staircase. As Chung proceeded downstairs, she cautioned him to walk carefully.

"I can see quite well, Mrs. Wang. Please go back," Chung said when he reached the bottom of the staircase. As Shu-sheng was returning to the apartment, she overheard Chung speaking to someone below.

"Mother is back," thought Shu-sheng, overcome by a feeling of unpleasantness. She hurried back to the room.

Wang asked her, "Is he gone?" The question was as unnecessary as was an answer. Already lying down in bed again, he had asked it out of boredom.

"Yes, he's left," she replied listlessly. The sickly yellowish electric light, the few pieces of worn-out furniture, and her husband's sallow face intensified her feeling of gloom. She could not take it any more. A person of flesh and blood, she wanted to be with another living person.

"Would you please put the money away for me?" he asked. "This money is for selling my life."

He spoke the last sentence so softly that she did not hear it. On her

事。」他加上這句解釋。

「那麼，我不送你了，走好啊。」他失望地說。

「不要送，我以後會常來的。」鍾老客氣地回答。一面朝房門走去。

「我送鍾先生。」她說。

「大嫂，不敢當，請留步吧。」鍾老說，他已經走到房門口了。

「外面黑得很，我送鍾先生出去。」她說，她打着手電筒把客人送到樓梯口，就站在那裏用手電光照着鍾老走下樓去，她一面叮囑：「走好啊，走好啊。」

「看得見，大嫂，請回去吧。」鍾老在下面客客氣氣地說着。她懶洋洋地轉過身打算回屋去。忽然聽見鍾老的聲音在跟人講話。

「她回來了。」她想道，這個「她」自然是指他的母親。她馬上起了一種不愉快的感覺，便急急走回房去。

「他走啦？」他問道。「這是不必問也不必回答的問話，他顯然是為了排遣寂寞才說的。他已經走下去了。

「走了。」她沒精打采地答道。屋子裏沒有一點熱氣，永遠是那種病態的黃色的電燈光，和那幾樣破舊的傢具。他永遠帶着不死不活的樣子。她受不了！她覺得自己還是個活人，她渴望看見一個活人。

「這筆錢你替我收起來。」他慢聲說。「這是我賣命的錢啊。」

她應了一聲。後一句話聲音更低，沒有被她聽見。她似乎要走

way to his bed, suddenly she retreated, full of loathing, and snapped, "You'd better give it to your mother, so she won't say anything."

He sighed and said nothing. Soon his mother's steps were heard in the corridor.

"Mother, where have you been?" he asked affectionately when she came in. His voice sounded lonely in the dim, cold room.

"To see Dr. Chang because I am worried about your illness. He told me again that you do not have TB and that you should be well after a few more doses of the medicine."

"Why did you go? It must be quite cold outside. Your day is exhausting enough, and you slave like a servant. I am most unworthy of you." He burst into tears.

"You'd better rest, and please don't worry about such trifles. I'm used to working like a maid. I don't have Shu-sheng's good fortune," she said, deriving some pleasure from her sarcastic reference to Shu-sheng. She cast an unconscious glance at her daughter-in-law.

Standing by the table, Shu-sheng overheard every word. It was like being unexpectedly slapped in the face again. She returned her mother-in-law's glance, but the latter paid no attention to her. Then she heard her mother-in-law say to her husband. "Dr. Chang suggested that the smoggy winter climate here is unsuitable for your health and that we should move to a different area."

"We should move? Where to? Where is the money coming from?" he sighed.

Always the same insulting insinuations, frittering life away piece by piece and drop by drop. Shu-sheng had reached the ultimate limit of her patience. Why should she be punished, when she had wronged

到床前去，但她忽然又憎厭地退後一步，她說：「你交給媽吧，免得她講話。」

他輕輕嘆一口氣，也不說甚麼。在外面廊上已經響着母親的腳步聲，接着那個老婦人走進來了。

「媽，你到哪兒去了？」他親切地問道。他的聲音在這陰暗寒冷的屋子裏寂寞地顫抖着。

「我到張伯情那兒去了一趟。我不放心，我問他究竟你的病怎樣，他說不要緊，並不是肺癆。吃幾付藥，就會好的。」母親溫和地說，但她的聲音裏卻露了一點焦慮。

「是，不要緊，我也知道不要緊。」他感激地答道；「你何必還出去，外面一定很冷。你一天也夠累了，你簡直是在做我們的老媽子，我真對不起你啊。」他的眼淚流出來了。

「你好好養病吧，不要管這些閒事。我這些年已經做慣老媽子了。我沒有樹生那樣的好命。」母親答道。說了最後一句，她感到一陣痛快，她不自覺地瞥了樹生一眼。

樹生正立在方桌前聽他們母子談話。她彷彿又挨了一記意外的嘴巴，她在心裏叫了一聲：「哎呀！」她回看了他母親一眼。但是母親已經丟開她，走到病人床前去了，現在還在說：「不過張伯情說這個地方冬天的霧對你的身體實在不相宜，他勸我們搬個地方。」

「搬地方……我們朝哪裏搬？我們哪裏還有錢搬家？」他嘆息道。

永遠是這一類刺耳的話，生命就這樣平平淡淡一點一滴地消耗。她樹生的忍耐力到了最高限度了。她並沒有犯罪，為甚麼應該

no one? Was this place supposed to be a prison in which to waste life away? She should fly away, she must fly away, while she still had the wings. Why shouldn't she leave? She had nothing in common with them. She shouldn't sacrifice herself for them. She must save herself.

Her mother-in-law was still talking to her husband. Each word was like an arrow, shooting at her heart. "Shoot them at me. I'm not afraid of them or you. I just don't care to squabble with you," she reflected with surging pride. Her heart suddenly warmed up.

XX

ON Saturday afternoon Shu-sheng came home with the bank's formal letter of transfer. Excitedly she dashed upstairs and pushed the door open. She found her son reading in the rattan chair by the desk, her mother-in-law on a stool by the table, and her husband in bed. They had been talking. Standing up, Hsiao Hsüan greeted her rather indifferently.

She asked her son, "Did you get my letter?"

"Yes, I did, but I had a lot of school work. Some classmates could not even keep up with the work," he answered, unsmiling. That was his reason for not coming home recently.

After making some vague response she looked at him, an anemic, adult-like stoical boy who had never been a child. Though only thirteen, he looked much older. To avoid looking at him, she knitted her eyebrows, quickly turned to her husband and asked, "Are you better today?"

受罰？這裏不就是使生命憔悴的監牢？她應該飛，她必須飛，趁她還有着翅膀的時候。為甚麼她不應該走呢？她和他們中間並沒有共同點。她不能陪着他們犧牲，她要救出她自己。

母親還在那裏講話，聲音像箭似地朝着樹生的心射過來。「你射來吧，我不怕，我不屑於跟你爭……」她昂起頭，自負地想道。她的心突然暖和起來了。

二十

星期六下午樹生拿着調職通知書回家，她興奮地上了樓，推開自己的房門，小宣坐在書桌前籐椅上看書，母親坐在方桌旁一張櫈子上，他仍然躺在病床上。他們正在談論甚麼事。小宣看見她進房，便立起來，喚了一聲「媽」。聲音冷冷的，並不親熱。

她應了一聲，接着就問「我的信收到了嗎？」

「收到了，學堂功課太嚴，我們好些同學都趕不上。」小宣像板起臉孔似地説，這算是他好些天不曾回家的理由。

她含糊地答應一句。她注意地看了她這個兒子，貧血、老成、冷靜，在他身上似乎永遠不曾有過青春。他是一個十三歲的孩子，但他已經衰老了！她皺了一下眉頭，逃避似地掉開了眼睛。她走到床前，問病人：「今天好些吧？」

"A little," her husband answered, nodding.

Despite his unchanging condition, this question-and-answer ritual went on. Everyday she would ask the same question and he would give the same answer.

She heard him cough and saw him spit into a mug by his pillow. His cheeks had become more sunken. His big eyes kept staring at her.

"Have you taken your medicine?" she asked in compassion.

He nodded, seemingly in pain.

"I think you'd better have a physical examination at the hospital," she said, repeating what she had said so many times before.

"Let's wait a few more days," he said, weakly shaking his head.

"Why don't you go now? You'll only get worse," she gently reminded him.

"I can go on. I've nothing but a cough," he answered slowly.

"Coughing is a form of illness. Also, you've a fever every day," she said. "I am afraid that ... " She did not finish the sentence.

"Are you afraid that I have TB?" he asked.

She dared not answer his question. She looked embarrassed, regretting that she had said so much to him.

"Even without an examination I know I've TB," he said. "What's the use of getting further proof? If I do, it'd be like a prisoner hearing a judge pronounce his death sentence." He felt very dejected, unwilling to say any more.

She quietly looked at him, thinking, "He knows everything, including the unbearable truth." What could her advice do for him?

「好些了。」病人點頭回答。

這樣的問答成了「例行公事」。她每天照樣地問，他每天照樣地答，雖然他的病一點兒也不見好。

她聽見他在咳嗽，看見他拿着枕畔漱口杯(臨時作了吐痰杯)吐痰，又慢慢把漱口杯放下，他的兩頰陷得更深了，兩隻大大的眼睛帶着一種可怕的眼神望着她。

「藥吃過了？」她憐憫地再問一句。

他點點頭，看他那神情好像是相當痛苦。

「我看，還是到醫院去檢查一下吧。」她忍不住又說了那句不知說過若干次的話。

「過幾天再說吧。」他力竭似地搖頭說。

「為甚麼不早去？不要把病耽誤了啊。」她低聲提醒他。

「我現在還可以支持，除了咳嗽也沒有甚麼病。」他慢聲答道。

「咳嗽就是病啊，並且你每天發燒。」她說，「我耽心——」她嚥下了後面的話。

「你是說我害肺病嗎？」他問。

她不敢回答。她現出窘迫的樣子。她有點後悔不該對他多講話。

「其實不用檢查我也知道我這是肺病。」他說，「可是知道了又有甚麼用；我去檢查，等於犯人聽死刑宣告。」話說出來，他覺得心裏很難過，自己也不想再說下去了。

她默默地望着他，她想：他甚麼都知道，甚至那個殘酷的真實。她的勸告對他有甚麼用處呢？他躺在床上，不過在捱日子。不

Sooner or later he would die. What could she do to save herself? Nothing. She could wait for a miracle to happen or she could leave and save herself. Torn by internal conflicts, she secretly wept and hoped that he would recover. Meanwhile she comforted him, "Even TB can be cured."

"To be cured a patient needs money and a cheerful frame of mind. Living the way I do, how can I ever be cheerful?" he said.

"Don't talk any more; sleep a little. Soon it will be time for medicine," his mother impatiently interrupted.

After staring at her mother-in-law for a moment, Shu-sheng sat down by the table, not knowing what to do. Her son was busy reading, and her mother-in-law was talking to her husband. No one paid her any attention. Completely fed up, she did not even know in which direction to look.

Dully she sat still for some moments. Must she wait for her mother-in-law to serve supper? It would be lifeless during supper and cheerless afterwards. The yellowish electric light (or the blackout, which occurred very often), the insipid conversation, and the sickly complexion of her husband made up her whole life. She could not bear it any longer; she'd not allow the last moments of her youth to be wasted; and she could not save the others. But at least she must do what she could for herself; otherwise, she'd die in this place, in this room.

She stood up suddenly. She had made up her mind and there would be no more hesitation. She had the letter in her purse. Why should she pass up the opportunity?

Excitedly she walked over to her son, saying, "Please come for a walk with me."

"Shouldn't we wait for supper?" said Hsiao Hsüan lethargically,

論是快，或慢，他總之是在走向死亡。她還有甚麼辦法拯救他？……沒有。她只有等待着奇跡。或者……或者她先救出自己。她的腦裏有着矛盾的思想。所以她一邊偷偷流淚，一邊又暗暗地抱着希望。

「不見得，肺病也養得好。」她隨便說了一句安慰他的話。

「養病就不說要花錢，也應當有好心境，這你是知道的。像我這樣生活，那裏會有好心境啊！」他又說。

「你不要再講話，睡一會兒吧，又快要吃藥了。」母親不耐煩地插嘴說。

妻暗暗地瞪母親一眼。她走到方桌前坐下來。她坐在那裏不知道應該做甚麼事好，小宣埋頭在書桌上翻看一本書。母親在同他談話，沒有人理睬她，連小宣也不過來跟她講話。她感到厭倦，現在連眼光也似乎無處可放了。

她覺得無聊地枯坐了一會。她想難道必須坐在這裏等着母親煮好飯送上來嗎？連吃飯的時候也是冷冷清清沒有生氣的。飯後更不會有溫暖。永遠是灰黃的燈光(不然就是停電的漆黑，那樣的時刻也不少)，單調而無生氣的閒談，帶病的面容。這樣的生活她實在受不了。她不能讓她的青春最後的時刻這樣白白耗盡，她不能救助別人，至少先得救出她自己。不然她會死在這個地方，死在這間屋子裏。

她突然站起來，她又一次下了決心，她用不着再遲疑了。她的手提包裏還藏着調職通知書。她為甚麼要放棄這個機會呢？

她興奮地走到小宣身旁。「小宣，你跟我出去走走。」她說。

「不等吃飯啊？」小宣抬起頭看她，有氣無力地問道，這孩子講

lifting his head from his reading. He spoke like an adult, very much like his father.

"We can eat in a restaurant," she answered.

"Then shouldn't we ask grandmother to come along?" The boy raised his voice.

"All right, we won't go," she said, abruptly changing her mind, disturbed and angered by her son's reply.

Giving her an astonished look, he asked, "Mother, aren't you going yourself?"

"No," she said, shaking her head, further distressed by this unnecessary question.

Hsiao Hsüan gave her a blank stare, stopped talking, and resumed his reading at the desk.

"He doesn't resemble me the least bit," she thought, standing behind him and looking at him for some time, unbeknown to Hsiao Hsüan. He was reading a modern play. As the sunlight was fast fading and the electric light was none too bright, his head sank deeper and deeper into the book. "He's probably ruining his eyes," she thought. At last she said to him, "Hsiao Hsüan, stop reading for a while; don't work so hard."

Again lifting his head and looking at her with surprise, Hsiao Hsüan answered, "Yes." His eyes were blinking as if they were bothering him. He closed his book and slowly got up.

"Why doesn't he ever smile? He moves so slowly, and doesn't act at all like a child. He's too much like his father," she mused.

Quietly Hsiao Hsüan walked over to his father's bed. As she

話像大人，尤其是像父親。

「我們到外面去吃飯。」她短短地答道。

「那麼不約婆婆一道去？」小宣又問，聲音提高了些。

「不去也罷。」她突然改變了主意，她覺得心煩，不知怎樣，這孩子的話激怒了她。

小宣詫異地看了她一眼，他還問一句：「媽，你也不出去？」

「不出去。」她搖搖頭說，心想這孩子怎麼這樣多嘴！

小宣淡淡地看她一眼，也不再說話，又把頭埋到書桌上去了。

「他好像不是我的兒子。」她想道，她還立在小宣身後，她禁不住看了他好幾次。小宣一點也不覺得。他在讀一個新生的劇本。白日光線漸漸消失，剛剛亮起來的電燈光又不大明亮。所以他把頭埋得很深。「他是在弄壞自己的眼睛啊！」她又想。她忍不住憐憫地說：「小宣，你歇一會兒吧，你不要太用功啦。」

小宣又抬起頭，驚異地看她一眼，他回答一聲：「是。」他的眼睛不住地閃着，好像它們不大舒適似的。隨後他闔上書，懶洋洋地站起來。

「怎麼，他笑都不笑一聲，動作這樣慢，他完全不像一個小孩，他就像他父親。」她又想。

小宣靜靜地走到床前去看父親。「他對我一點也不親熱，好像我

watched him, she thought unhappily, "Hsiao Hsüan's so aloof toward me. He treats me like his stepmother." She sat down in the rattan chair where her son sat a moment ago.

Sitting on the edge of the bed, the old woman was talking to her son; her grandson stood by the bed listening to them; the three seemed to be in a private conversation.

"She didn't want me to talk to him; then why doesn't she leave him alone? A really selfish old woman!" Shu-sheng thought in anger. "She hates me; I'm her enemy. She has made Hsiao Hsüan cool toward me. Hsüan loves her more than he loves me." The more she thought, the more agitated she became. She could not bear being so lonely and neglected; she needed some diversion. She picked up and looked at her son's book. It was Ts'ao Yü's play, *The Prairie*.* She had seen its stage production years ago, and later learned that for some reason it had been banned by the government. What a coincidence that the play should be about a vicious mother hating her daughter-in-law, with the husband caught in the middle. The end was tragic. She would not allow it to be the same for herself. She was not that kind of woman. She was not needed here and she could get away. The letter of transfer was in her purse. Why should she give up the opportunity? No, she had already made up her mind. Unless she resigned, the bank would not send another person to Lanchow in her place. Of course, she wouldn't resign, for if she did, it would take some time before she could find another job. Furthermore the bank had advanced her some salary.

---

* A famous modern Chinese playwright (real name Wan Chia-pao), born in 1905. His play, *The Prairie* (*Yüan yeh*, 1937) concentrates on the old country gentry, the decaying conservative force in the country life; the hatred of a desperate villager is vented on the descendants of the despotic landowner.

是他後母一樣。」她痛苦地想。她就在孩子剛離開的籐椅上坐下。

母親還坐在床沿上同宣講話，小宣立在床前靜聽着，他們似乎談得很親熱。

「她不要我跟他講話，怎麼她又不讓他休息呢？這個自私的老太婆！」她憤憤地想道。她無意間伸手在書桌上拿起小宣剛才看的那本書來。「她就恨我！我是她的仇人！小宣對我冷淡，一定是她教出來的，宣也在敷衍她！不，他其實更愛她。」她繼續想道，心更加煩起來，她受不住這寂寞，這冷淡。她需要找一件分心的事情，她把眼光放到拿在手裏的書上去，她首先看到兩個字：《原野》。是曹禺寫的那個劇本。她看過它的上演。可是又聽説後來被禁止了，不知道為甚麼，偏偏是這個戲，多麼巧！戲裏也有一個母親毒恨着自己的兒媳婦。那個丈夫永遠被夾在中間，兩種愛的中間受苦。結果呢？那結果太可怕了！她不會弄出那樣的結果，她不是那樣的女人！她在這裏是多餘的。她有機會走開，調職通知書還在她的手提包裏。她為甚麼要放過機會呢？不，那是已經決定的事情了。行裏不會改派另一個人，除非她辭職。自然她不會辭職的。離開那個銀行，她一時也找不到別的職業。而且她還借支了薪金。

"Fly away, fly away!" a voice kept telling her, cheering her and bolstering her courage. The transfer letter seemed to loom larger and larger before her eyes; Lan-chow, these two magic words were transformed into a big airplane flying in the recesses of her mind. Slowly she felt happy again and gained new courage. She gave her mother-in-law a contemptuous look, thinking, "All of you may be united against me, but I am not afraid. I've my route to freedom and I will fly away."

XXI

IN the deep recesses of an eerie dream his wife eloped with someone and his mother died somewhere. When he woke up, he was in tears, his heart pounding. He listened to the drumbeat of his heart; with his mouth open, he explored the darkness with his eyes. He had the feeling that his head and his body were covered by a huge piece of dark cloth. Breathing hard and experiencing a slight pain in his chest, he started to reenact the nightmare as soon as he closed his eyes. He manfully tried to keep his eyes open.

"Where am I? Am I alive or dead?" he wondered. There was no human sound around him except a tiny bothersome noise. "I am all alone," he said in utter loneliness. He felt bitter and cried. "Is it really true that the dead are dead and the living gone away?" he painfully asked himself as he tossed and turned in his bed. "Still no sound? Am I dreaming?" He felt teardrops on his cheeks. His throat began to itch and he coughed.

Throwing off the coverlet, he got up and switched on the light,

「飛啊，飛啊！」好像有一個聲音反覆地在她的耳邊輕輕地鼓舞她，調職通知書漸漸在她的眼前擴大。蘭州！這兩個大字變成一架飛機在她腦子裏飛動，她漸漸地又高興起來，她覺得自己又有了勇氣了。她甚至用輕蔑的眼光看那母親。她心想：「你們聯在一起對付我，我也不怕，我有我的路，我要飛！」

二十一

他做了一個可怕的夢：她丟開他跟另一個男人走了；母親也好像死在甚麼地方了。他從夢中哭醒，他的眼睛還是濕的，心跳得厲害，他傾聽着這敲鼓似的聲音。他張着嘴，睜大眼想在黑暗中看出甚麼來。但是屋子很黑，就好像有一張黑幕蓋在他的頭上和全身一樣。他覺得氣緊，呼吸似乎不十分暢快，胸部還在隱隱發痛，他疲乏地閉上眼睛，但他即刻又睜開，因為那個可怕的夢境在他的眼前重現了。

「究竟我在甚麼地方？」他疑惑地想，「是死還是活？」四周沒有人聲，但並不是完全的靜寂，因為屋子裏充滿了細小的聲音。「我一個人。」他寂寞地說了出來，忽然一陣心酸，他又落下了眼淚。

「果真是走的走、死的死了嗎？」他痛苦地問自己。沒有回答，他翻了一個身，又一個身。「怎麼一點動靜也沒有？」他不能忍耐地想，「我在做夢嗎？」他的手摸着自己頰上的淚痕。他的喉嚨發癢，他咳起嗽來。

他突然揭開被，跳下床。他扭燃了電燈，屋子亮起來，燈光白

which momentarily blinded his eyes. He threw on his clothing and stood in front of the square table. The first object that came into view was his wife. Half of her face was covered by the quilt; her long black eyelashes gave the impression that her eyes were open when she was asleep; she had no wrinkles on her forehead; and her face was just as youthful looking as ten years ago. When he thought of himself, he realized the painful contrast between her and him. His silk robe had faded in color and his long blue padded gown had become a sickly gray. With his aching bones and gobs of phlegm threatening to choke him, he hardly seemed to be her contemporary. He had changed. This was not a recent discovery, a fact he had known for some time. But at the moment this knowledge hit him like a heavy blow on the chest.

He staggered, grabbed the table securely and stood there for a moment, shivering in the chill. The room was still as bright as it ever got; the rats were chewing on the wooden floor, and a hawker was selling hot water and fried rice-cakes downstairs below the window.

He sighed helplessly, shifted his eyes to his mother's door and detected his son's snoring. It was not loud, barely discernible, in fact. He listened to it again, and it remained the same. Sorry for both his mother and his son who had suffered so much, he, nonetheless, took comfort in the fact that they were safe, at least for the time being.

He coughed twice; he felt he must spit out the phlegm in his throat. Afraid to awaken the others, he softly coughed, feeling pain in his chest. Covering his mouth with a hankerchief, he walked to the desk and stumbled into the rattan chair. He coughed a few more times, finally expelling the phlegm which became immediately stuck to his lips. In desperation he lamented that he had become so weak that he did not even have enough strength to spit out the phlegm.

His throat was dry, and when he went to get some tea a black

得像雪似的，使他的眼睛差一點睜不開，他披着衣服站在方桌前。他第一眼便看他那個睡在床上的妻。謝謝天，妻睡得很好，棉被頭蓋着她下半個臉，黑黑的長睫毛使她睡着的時候也像睜開眼睛，她的前額上沒有一條皺紋，她還是像十年前那樣地年青。他看看自己，絲棉袍的綢面已經褪了色，藍布罩衫也在泛白了。他全身骨頭一齊發酸發痛，痰似的東西直往喉管上冒。他同她不像是一個時代的人。他變了！這並不是一個新發現。但這一次卻像有一個拳頭在他胸膛上猛擊一下。他的身子幌了幌，他連忙扶着方桌站定了。

他在方桌前癡立了一會，他忽然打了一個寒噤，他不自覺地把頭一縮。屋子裏依然很亮。老鼠又在啃地板。外面街上有一個人的腳步聲，那人走得慢，而且用一種衰老而淒涼的聲音叫着：「炒米糖開水。」他無可奈何地嘆了一口氣。

他把眼光掉向母親的房門，門關着，裏面傳出來一個人的鼾聲，是小宣的，並不太高，不過他聽得出，他們睡得很好，他傾耳再聽，那還是小宣的鼾聲，「這孩子也可憐，偏偏生在我們家裏。」他想。「媽也是，老來受苦。」他又嘆一口氣。「不過幸好他們都還是很平安的。」另一個念頭倒給他一點安慰。

接着他咳了兩聲嗽，他覺得痰貼在喉管上，他必須咳它出來。他不敢大聲咳，他害怕驚醒妻和母親。他慢慢地咳着，他的胸部接連發痛，他摸出手帕掩着嘴。他走到書桌前，跌坐在籐椅上。

他咳了好幾聲，居然把痰咳出來，他要吐它在地上，可是痰貼在他的舌尖唇邊，不肯下地。「我連這點點氣力也沒有了。」他痛苦地，灰心地想道。

他吐出痰後，覺得喉嚨乾，他想喝兩口茶，他便站起來。他無意間把書桌上一件黑黑的東西碰落在地上，他即刻彎下身去拾那件東西。那是樹生的手提包，他拾起來時，手提包打開了，落下幾張

object accidentally fell from the desk onto the floor. It was Shu-sheng's purse, from which a letter, some pieces of paper, and a lipstick tube fell out. He picked up the items and noticed the letter of transfer.

Sitting in the rattan chair, he read the letter again and again. Meanwhile his body chilled as if he had stumbled into a deep freeze. "She has concealed her plans from me," he muttered. "Why did she do it? I'd never have stopped her." Feeling betrayed, he quietly bit his lower lip. The pain in his chest returned again. Lightly rubbing his chest with his left hand, he said to himself, "Let the germs eat my lungs; let them have a feast."

"Is she really going to leave me?" he wondered. The letter left no doubt that she would. "It's better that she leave. She should find a new world. Keeping her here would only ruin her," he reasoned. He turned to look at her. She had turned on her side. He saw her head of beautiful dark hair. "She is sleeping soundly." Resting his head on the chair, he fell asleep, still clutching the letter.

He soon awoke. The room was still bright, but quiet and cold. He again looked at his wife, whose plump right arm looked so lovely, bared and unprotected as it was, in the chilly night air. "She'll catch cold," he thought. He slowly walked to the bed and put her arm inside the quilt. Though he was very quiet, she woke up.

"Are you still awake?" she asked with a smile. But suddenly startled, she asked, "What are you doing out of bed?"

"I saw your arm outside the quilt. I was afraid that you might catch cold," he explained, still holding the letter in his hand.

She gave him another smile before spotting the letter in his hand. "Where did you get the letter?" She sat up, fastening the collar of her pyjamas.

紙和一支唇膏。他再俯下身去拾它們，他看見了那張調職通知書。

他把通知書拿在手裏，又坐回到籐椅上，他仔細讀着，雖然那上面不過寥寥幾行字，他卻反覆不厭地唸了幾遍。他好像跌在冰窖裏一樣，他全身都冷了。

「她瞞着我。」他低聲自語。接着他又想；她為甚麼要瞞我呢？我不會妨礙她的。他感到一種被人出賣了似的痛苦和憤慨。他想不通，他默默地咬着自己的下嘴唇。胸部還是隱隱在發痛。他用左手輕輕擦揉着胸膛。「病菌在吃我的肺，好，就讓牠吃個痛快吧。」他想着。

「她真的要走嗎？」他問自己，他又埋頭看手裏那張調職書。他用不着再問了，那張紙告訴他，她會走的。

「走了也好，她應該為自己找一個新天地，我讓她住在這裏只有把她白白糟蹋。」他安慰自己地想。他又把頭掉過去看她，她已經向裏翻了過身，他只看見她一頭黑髮。「她睡得很好。」他低聲說。他把頭放在靠背上，閉着眼睛。休息一會，通知書仍然捏在他的手裏。

他忽然又驚醒似地睜開眼睛，屋子裏多麼亮，多麼靜，多麼冷！他又掉過頭去看她，她還睡在床上，但又已翻過身，面向着他，並且把右膀伸了到被外來，是一隻白而多肉的手膀。「她會受涼的。」他想着，就站起來，走到床前，伸手去把她的手膀放回到被裏，他輕輕地拿着她的手，慢慢地動着，但仍然把她驚醒了。

她起先哼了一聲，慢慢地睜開眼睛。「你還不睡？」她微笑說。但接着她又吃驚地說：「怎麼你下床來了？」

「我看見你一隻膀子露在外面，怕你着涼。」他低聲解釋道，通知書還在他手裏。

她感激地對他一笑，過後慢慢地把眼光移到別處去，她看見了那張通知書。

「怎麼在你手裏？」她驚問道，就坐起來，把睡衣的領口拉緊一點。「你從哪裏找到的？」

"I saw it when it fell out of your purse," he explained, embarrassed.

"I just received it today. I still don't know what to do," she said apologetically, remembering that she had carelessly left her purse on the desk. Shivering, she hastily covered herself with the quilt.

"You can go. There is no problem with me," he said in a low voice.

"I know." She nodded. With him staring at her, she felt sad, sensing that he had much to say but was unable to express himself. "I don't want to go, but how are we going to live?"

"I know ...," he stammered, interrupting her.

"Department Chief Ch'en has obtained an airplane ticket for next Wednesday," she said.

"Yes," he said mechanically.

"Luckily I don't have much luggage to take with me. In the Northwest fur goods are cheap, and I can make clothes there," she continued.

"Yes, the fur goods are cheap there," he agreed apathetically.

"I'm to receive a traveling allowance and I'll also borrow some money from the bank. I plan to leave fifty thousand *yüan* at home."

"Fine," he replied curtly, for he felt his heart was being pounded by a wooden pestle.

"Just take care of your health. Since I've been promoted a grade, I'll make more money and I can send you more. I'd like to see you get well soon." The more she said, the more enthusiastic she became about her future. She smiled happily.

Unable to stand on his feet any longer, he said, "I'd better go back to sleep." Without even enough strength to put the letter back in her purse, he staggered to the bed and collapsed. He covered his head

「我看見了。」他低下頭答道，他的臉立刻發紅。他連忙加上一句解釋：「你的皮包從桌上掉下來打開了。」

「我今天才拿到，我還不知道應該怎樣辦。」她抱歉似地說，她記起來是自己大意把手提包忘了在書桌上。她打了一個冷噤，連忙用棉被裹住自己的身子。

「你去吧，我沒有問題。」他低聲說。

「我知道。」她點點頭。她看見他望着自己好像有多少話要說，卻又說不出來，她心裏也有點難過。「我本來不想去，不過不去我們這一家人怎麼生活——」

「我知道。」他結結巴巴地說，他打斷了她的話。

「陳主任幫我定了飛機票，下星期三可以走。」她說。

「是。」他機械似地答道。

「橫豎我也沒有多少行李，西北皮貨便宜，我可以在那邊製衣服。」她接下去說。

「是，那邊皮貨便宜。」他沒精打采地應道。

「我可以在行裏領路費，還可以借支一筆錢，我想留五萬在家裏。」

「好的。」他短短地回答，他的心像被木棒搗着似的發痛。

「你好好養病，我到那邊升了一級，可以多拿薪水，也可以多寄錢回家。你只管養病。」她愈說愈有精神，臉上又浮起了微笑。

他實在支持不下去，便說：「我睡咯。」他想走到書桌那邊，把通知書放回她的手提包裏去。可是他走了兩步又回到床前，他頹然

with the cotton quilt and wept. Not wanting her to hear him cry, he crumbled the letter into a ball and stuffed it into his mouth, biting and chewing on it until he gagged. He thought he heard her calling him.

XXII

BEGINNING that night, his stock of nightly "adventures" grew into a veritable realm of terror. His dreams tortured him. One followed another; in each he bade farewell to his wife, who was either leaving for Lanchow or somewhere else. Occasionally she would leave full of resentment, following a quarrel with his mother. When he woke up, he was usually soaked in a cold sweat. He sighed helplessly, realizing he was deteriorating.

At night, his wife slept beside him, but because of his illness they were not intimate. And although they were together, they were far apart in spirit. She went to work every morning and came home late, spending her evenings attending farewell parties given in her honor. Every evening his mother kept him company until Shu-sheng returned. When she entered the door, his mother would go to her own room. Then she would sit on the edge of his bed or the stool in front of the square table and tell him what she had done that day. She spoke much more now, and he much less; he was also more pensive, wondering whether he would ever see her again once she left.

When he was not asleep, he counted over and over the days and hours left for them to be together. As her departure date drew nearer, the conflict within himself became more acute. Should he allow her to go or try to detain her? Should he give her freedom or try to keep her with him?

倒下去，用棉被蒙着頭，低聲哭起來，為了不要她聽見他的哭聲，他把通知書揉成一團塞進他的口裏去，他嚼着那團紙，直到他發出嗆咳，他彷彿聽見妻在喚他。

二十二

從這一晚起，他又多了做夢的資料。夢折磨着他。每晚他都得不到安寧。一個夢接連着另一個。在夢中他不斷地和她分別，她去蘭州或者去別的地方，有時甚至和他母親吵架後負氣出走。醒來，他常常淌一身冷汗。他無可奈何地嘆一口長氣，他知道自己的病勢已經很深了。

晚上妻睡在他的旁邊。他為了自己的病，常常避免把臉向着她。他們睡在一處，心卻隔得很遠。妻白天出門，晚上回家也不太早。她有應酬，同事們爭着替她餞行。她每晚回家，總看見母親在房裏陪伴他，但等她跨進了門，母親就回到小屋去了。然後她坐在床沿上或者方桌前櫈子上絮絮地講説她這一天的見聞。現在她比平日講話多，他卻較從前沉靜寡言。他常常呆呆望着她，心想分別後還能不能有重見的機會。

不做夢時他喜歡數着他們以後相聚的日子和時刻。日子和時刻逐漸減少，而他的掙扎也愈加痛苦。讓她去，或者留住她？讓她幸福，或者拉住她同下深淵？

"Will you remember me after you leave?" He wanted to ask her this question but he never did.

The fifty thousand *yüan* came: twenty thousand in cash and a thirty-thousand-*yüan* bank deposit slip which would yield approximately seven percent interest to be drawn fortnightly, according to Shu-sheng. She always knew so much more than he. She also had her luggage ready. Then she told him that her departure had been postponed for a week. The change meant nothing to her, but to him it was good news. Since he could not keep her, he welcomed the chance to be with her for this extra week, just to look at her youthful and radiant face.

Being with her exacted a heavy toll from him. By now he could tell from the casual way she treated the separation that her heart had soared away from him. Smiling, she told him again and again. "I'll come to see you in three or four months. Department Chief Ch'en knows someone in the airline office, and he can always get a ticket for me. It's really very convenient." He agreed with her, but thought to himself, "When you return, where will I be?" Where would he be? He had no idea. He wanted to weep loudly, but the phlegm stuck in his windpipe and the pain in his chest prevented him from doing so. He could groan, but the groaning had become so commonplace to Shu-sheng that only occasionally did she give him a sympathetic look to say a few words of concern.

He could sit up and move freely about the room. Except for his cough, his sallow countenance, and a few awkward movements, he looked almost normal. He was still taking the Chinese medicine, though the number of doses had been reduced. His mother would periodically remind him to go for an X-ray examination, but each time she brought up the subject it met his gentle resistance. He preferred the inexpensive Chinese medicine, which brought him some slight

「你去後還會想得起我麼？」他常常想這樣問她，可是他始終不敢說出來。

五萬元交來了：兩萬元現款和一張銀行存單，妻告訴他，存「比期」，每半個月，辦一次手續，利息有七分光景。到底妻比他知道得多！妻的行裝也快準備好了。忽然她又帶回家一個好消息：飛機票還要再延遲一個星期。在她這消息無所謂好壞。可是再沒有比這更能安慰他的了。他無法留住她，卻只好希望多和她見面，多看見她那仍然充滿生命力的面顏。

但這樣的見面有時也會給他帶來痛苦，連他也看得出她的心一天一天地移向更遠的地方。和他分離，在她似乎並不是一件怎麼痛苦的事。她常常笑着對他說：「過三四個月我就要回來看你。陳主任認識航空公司的人，容易買到飛機票，來往也很方便。」他唯唯應着，心裏卻想：「等你回來，不曉得我還在不在這兒。」他要去甚麼地方呢？他想着，覺得要哭一場才痛快。可是痰貼在他的喉管裏，他用力咳時，左胸要發痛，他只好輕輕地咳着。這咳聲她也聽慣了。但偶爾還能夠得到她的憐憫的注視，或者關心的詢問。

他已經坐起來，並且在房裏自由地走動了。除了臉色、咳嗽和一些動作外，別人不會知道他在害病。中藥還在吃，不過吃得不勤。母親現在也提起去醫院檢查照X光一類的話。但他總是支吾過去。他願意吃中藥，因為花錢少，而且不管功效如何，繼續不斷地

comfort and fostered the faint hope that he would eventually be cured. When he was lonely, he read books. He could not sleep in the daytime since he had enough sleep during those long winter nights. During the day he liked to read, to move around the room and to talk, for this made him feel much better. But his mother often prevented him from exerting himself, reminding him that he needed plenty of rest.

Why couldn't he live like everyone else? Lying in bed during the day made him worry more, and consequently more fretful and distressed. Every day he would calculate how much money had been spent and how much was left. His total assets consisted of his dismissal pay, his wife's salary, and the insignificant fortnightly interest from the bank. With the amount of money, how long could he last? He saw money flowing out continuously day after day, and no way to prevent its flow. Without much income but with limitless expenses, he dreaded the bleak future. But what could he do other than frown?

One afternoon his mother bought a chicken, made broth, and brought him some in a bowl. For two days he had had no appetite.

"If you like the broth, I can make it for you regularly," she said.

"No, no. That'll be too extravagant. How can we afford it?" he answered with a worried look. Yet he took the bowl from her.

"I bought this chicken cheap, for a little over a thousand *yüan*. It's very nourishing," she gently said, somewhat disheartened.

"But we don't have much money," he said obstinately. "I'm unemployed and sick. Sitting at home will consume all our resources. What are we going to do?"

"Don't worry. As long as we still have some money, we have to get you well," she said, wearing a reluctant smile.

吃着藥，總可以給自己一點安慰和希望。

有時他也看書，因為他寂寞，而且冬天的夜太長，他睡盡了夜，不能再在白天閉眼。他也喜歡看書、走動、說話，這使他覺得自己的病勢不重，甚至忘掉自己是一個病人。但母親不讓他多講話，多看書，多走動，母親卻時時提醒他：他在生病，他不能像常人那樣地活着。

可是他怎麼能不像常人那樣活着呢？白天躺在床上不做任何事情，這只有使他多思索，多焦慮，這只有使他心煩。他計算着，幾乎每天都在計算，他花去若干錢，還剩餘若干。錢本來就只有那麼一點點，他的遣散費，和他妻子留下的安家費再加上每月那一點利息，湊在一起又能夠用多久呢？他彷彿看着錢一天一天不停地流出去。他束着手無法攔住牠。他沒有絲毫的收入，只有無限期的花費……那太可怕了，他一想起，就皺着眉頭。

有一次母親為他買了一隻雞回來，高興地煮好雞湯用菜碗盛着端給他吃。那是午飯後不久的事。這兩天他胃口不好。

「你要是喜歡吃，我可以常常煮給你吃，」母親帶點鼓舞的口氣說。

「媽，這太花費了，我們哪裏吃得起啊，」他卻帶着愁容回答，但他還是把碗接了過來。

「我買得很便宜，不過千多塊錢，吃了補補身體也好，」母親被他澆了涼水，但她仍舊溫和地安慰他。

「不過我們沒有多的錢啊，」他固執般地說，「我身體不好，偏偏又失了業。坐吃山空，怎麼得了！」

「不要緊，你不必耽心。橫豎目前還有點辦法，先把你身體弄好再說，」母親帶笑地勸道，她笑得多少有點勉強。

"Every day prices are going up and the money becomes less and less. We'll soon be using Shu-sheng's money even before she leaves," he said, holding the steaming soup-bowl in his hand.

Her smile vanished. She turned her head to hide her embarrassment. Annoyed and perturbed, she told him to drink the broth.

Feeling uneasy, he held the bowl to his mouth and slurped the soup down. She stood by his side, sighing with a bowed head, as if she had just seen the other woman's smile. The noise he made in eating the soup attracted her attention. He praised its excellent taste and greedily looked at the bowl. He held a chicken leg in his hand and nibbled on it slowly.

"Mother, you should have some, too," he said with a smile.

"No, I'm not hungry," she replied quietly, looking at him with sympathetic and sorrowful eyes.

"I'm not ill, just a little undernourished. I'll get well gradually," he said.

"Yes, you will," she agreed mechanically.

He concentrated on the meat with great intensity as if he had never before eaten anything like it. "If I had been better nourished, I wouldn't have become sick," he murmured. His mother stood up, watching him. One moment she would smile; the next she would rub her eyes.

"He's probably recovering. Look how good his appetite is," she thought.

"Mother, you have some, too. It is delicious, very delicious. Human beings need nutrition," he said happily, still holding the bowl in his greasy hand after devouring the chicken meat.

「東西天天貴，錢天天減少，樹生還沒有走，我們恐怕就要動用到她那筆錢了，」他皺着眉頭說。雞湯還在他的手裏冒熱氣。

母親立刻收斂了笑容。她掉開頭想找個地方停留她的眼光，但是沒有找到。她又回過臉來，痛苦而且煩躁地說了一句：「你快些吃罷。」

他捧着碗喝湯，他不用湯匙，不用筷子，還帶了一點慌張不安的樣子。母親在旁邊低聲嘆了一口氣。她彷彿看見那個女人的得意的笑容。她覺得自己的臉在發燒。她埋下頭。但是他的喝湯的響聲吸引了她的注意。「很好，很好，」他接連稱讚道，他的愁容消失了。他用貪婪的眼光注視着湯碗。他用手拿起一隻雞腿在嘴邊啃着。

「媽，你也吃一點吧，」他忽然抬起頭看看母親，帶笑地說。

「我不餓，」母親輕輕地答道。她用愛憐的眼光看他。她心裏有點難受。

「我不是病，我就是營養不良啊，我身體以後會慢慢好起來的，」他解釋般地說。

「是啊，你身體會慢慢好起來的，」母親機械地答道。

他又專心去吃碗裏的雞肉，他彷彿從來沒有吃過好飲食似的。他忽然自言自語：「要是平日吃得好一點，我也不會得這種病。」他一面吃，一面說話。母親仍然站在旁邊看他，她一會露出笑容，一會又伸手去揩眼睛。

「他身體大概漸漸好起來了。他能吃，這是好現象。」她想道。

「媽，你也吃一點。味道很好，很好。人是需要營養的，」他吃完雞肉，用油手拿着碗，帶着滿足的微笑對母親說。

"Yes, I will." In truth she felt there was not even enough for him. She took away the empty bowl, and when she returned, she found him asleep in the rattan chair. Tiptoeing to his side, she was planning to cover him with something. As she neared him, he caught her hand and called her Shu-sheng.

"What's the matter?" reacted his mother, dumfounded.

"Has Shu-sheng returned yet?" he asked, his eyes searching the room.

"No, not even her shadow," she replied angrily. He shouldn't think of Shu-sheng all the time. What good had Shu-sheng ever done him? She was always deceiving and tormenting him.

"I must have been dreaming again," he sighed.

"You'd better go to sleep," she said.

"No, I don't want to. I have slept so much that my bones ache." He stood up slowly.

"Shu-sheng's really too busy. She's about to leave, and still she can't spare one or two days for us," he mumbled, leaning on the desk. Then he pushed away the rattan chair and walked slowly to the half-shut window on his right.

"Be careful of the draft," she cautioned him. She was not happy, for she had heard him mention that woman's name again. She could hardly remain silent but she did; after all it was not her son she was angry with.

"It's too stifling inside. I want to breathe some fresh air," he said. But what he breathed was really polluted air, heavy with the smell of coal. At the same time, something seemed to sting his face. He felt the pain and it made him quite uncomfortable.

「好，我會吃，」母親不願叫他多講話，就含糊地答應了，其實她心想：「就只有這麼一隻瘦瘦的雞，給你一個人吃還嫌少呢。」她接過空碗，拿了它到外面去。等她走回來時，他靠在籐椅上睡着了。母親輕手輕腳地走過去，想給他蓋上點甚麼東西，可是剛走到他面前，他忽然睜開眼喚道：「樹生！」他抓住母親的手。

「甚麼事？」母親驚問道。

他把眼睛掉向四周看了一下。隨後他帶了點疑惑地問：「樹生沒有回來？」

「沒有。連她的影子也看不見，」她帶着失望的口氣回答。他不應該時常想着樹生。樹生對他哪點好？她(樹生)簡直是在折磨他，欺騙他！

他無可奈何地嘆了一口氣，露出一個苦笑。「我又在做夢了，」他說。

「你還是到床上去睡吧，」母親說。

「我睡得太多了，一身骨頭都睡痛了。我不想再睡，」他說，慢慢地站起來。

「樹生也真是太忙了。她要走了，也不能回家跟我們團聚一兩天，」他扶着書桌，自語道。他轉過身推開籐椅，慢步走到右面窗前，打開掩着的窗戶。

「你當心，不要吹風啊，」母親聽見他又提到那個女人的名字，她忍住心裏的不痛快，不講話。但是現在她不能沉默了，她不是在跟他賭氣啊。

「太氣悶了，我想聞一點新鮮空氣，」他說。可是他嗅到的，冷氣中夾雜了一股一股的煤臭。同時甚麼東西在刮着他的臉，他感到痛和不舒服。

The sky always wore a sad look, and the air was forever stifling. The streets were perennially gray; the pedestrians came and went with heads bowed and necks tucked deep into their collars.

"It's best you sleep for a while. I see you're bored," she advised.

He closed the window. Turning around he looked at his bed apprehensively, unsure whether to approach it. At last he sighed, "The days go so slowly."

Finally he walked to the bed and lay down on it without taking off his clothes. His eyes remained open.

His mother, with her eyes closed, was resting in the rattan chair. She heard him toss restlessly in the bed and knew what troubled him. Resentful at the thoughts her son was cherishing, she said, "Hsüan, please stop thinking about it. Go to sleep."

"I haven't been thinking about anything," he whispered.

"I know. You can't fool me. You're thinking about Shu-sheng," she said.

"I'm the one who advised her to leave. At first she didn't want to," he argued. "A change of environment will do wonders for her. She is tired of living here. With her promotion, the job at Lanchow will give her a bigger salary."

"I know, I know," she said emphatically. "Why do you think of her? Why not of yourself? Why do you worry about somebody else?"

"Of myself?" he asked in astonishment. "Am I not well?" Immediately he realized how ridiculous this must sound. "I'm almost well, and she can give me more help in Lanchow."

"She? You still believe in her?" Ridiculing his complete naiveté, she snickered, "She is like a wild bird. Once you set her free, she'll never return."

天永遠帶着愁容。空氣永遠是那樣地悶。馬路是一片黯淡的灰色。人們埋着頭走過來，縮着頸走過去。

「你還是睡一會兒，我看你閒着也無聊，」母親又在勸他。

他關上窗門，轉過身來，對着母親點了點頭說：「好的。」他望着他的床，他想走過去，又害怕走過去。他終於無可奈何地嘆了一口氣。「日子過得真慢，」他自語道。

後來他終於走到床前，和衣倒在床上。但是他仍舊睜着兩隻眼睛。

母親坐在籐椅上閉着眼養神。她聽見他在床上連連地翻身，她知道是甚麼思想攪擾他。她有一種類似悲憤之感。後來她實在忍耐不住，便掉過頭來看他，一面安慰他說：「宣，你不要多想那些事。你安心睡罷。」

「我沒有想甚麼，」他低聲回答。

「我知道的，你瞞不過我，還是樹生的事情，」母親說。

「那是我勸她去的，她本來並不一定要去，」他分辯。「換個環境對她也許好一點。她在這個地方也住厭了。去蘭州待遇高一點，算是升了一級。」

「我知道，我知道，」母親加重語氣地說。「不過你光是替她着想，你為甚麼不想到你自己，你為甚麼只管想到別人？」

「我自己？」他驚訝地說，「我自己不是很好嗎！」他說了「很好」兩個字，連他自己也覺得話太不真實了，他便補上一句：「我的病差不多全好了，她在蘭州更可以給我幫忙。」

「她？你相信她！」母親冷笑一聲，接着輕蔑地說，「她是一隻野鳥，你放出去休想收她回來。」

"Mother, you're nice to everyone except Shu-sheng. She's not that kind of woman. It's only for the good of all of us that she agrees to go to Lanchow," he said, agitated and sitting up in bed.

She gazed at him. Then she nodded reluctantly, saying. "You win. I believe you.... Now go to sleep. Too much talking exhausts you, and you'll get worse."

Lost in thought, he said no more. His defense of Shu-sheng made his mother protest inwardly, "Why can't he wise up?" But in a loving voice, she said, "Hsüan, you'd better lie down. Sitting up like that, you'll catch cold."

He looked at her, grateful for her love. Then he got out of bed, announcing hurriedly, "Mother, I want to go out for a while." He bent down to tie his shoelaces.

"Why are you going out? What for?" she asked in surprise.

"I've some business to attend to," he replied.

"What business do you have? You've been dismissed. It's cold outside, and you're weak," she remonstrated, bordering on panic.

His face flushed, he said, "Mother, it's all right. Let me go this once." Having said that, he went to fetch his long blue padded gown hanging on a nail in the wall.

"Let me do it," she quickly volunteered. She helped him put on the gown. "Don't go, you can't go," she implored while she wrapped an old black-and-white scarf around his neck. "Don't go. If you've some business, write a note and I'll deliver it."

"Don't worry. I'll be back soon. It is not far ...," he said, walking out of the door. She looked at him, dreamily.

"What's he doing? I don't understand him at all," she murmured

「媽，你對甚麼人都好，就是對樹生太苛刻，她並不是那樣的女人。而且她還是為了我們一家人的緣故才答應去蘭州的，」他興奮地從床上坐起來說。

母親呆呆望着他，忽然改變了臉色，她忍受似地點着頭說：「就依你，我相信你的話。……那麼你放心睡覺吧。你話講多了太傷神，病又會厲害起來的。」

他不作聲了。他低頭好像在想甚麼事情似的。母親用憐憫的眼光望着他，心裏埋怨道：你怎麼這樣執迷不悟啊。可是她仍然用慈愛的聲音對他說：「宣，你還是睡下去吧，這樣坐着看招涼啊。」

他抬起頭用類似感激的眼光看了母親一眼，停了一會，他忽然下床來。「媽，我要出去一趟，」他匆匆地說，一面彎着身子繫皮鞋帶。

「你出去？你出去做甚麼？」母親驚問道。

「我有點事，」他答道。

「你還有甚麼事？公司已經回了你了。外面冷得很，你身體又不好，」母親着急地說。

他站起來。臉上略現出興奮的紅色。「媽，不要緊，讓我去一趟，」他說，便去取下那件掛在牆上洋釘上的藍布罩袍來穿着。

「等我來，」母親不放心地急急說，她走去幫忙他把罩袍穿上。「你不要走，走不得啊！」她一面說一面卻把一條黑白條紋的舊圍巾取下替他纏在頸項上。「你不要去，有事情，你寫個字條，我給你送去，」她又說。

「不要緊，我就會回來，地方很近，」他說着，就朝外走。她望着他，突然覺得自己像是在夢中一樣。

「他這是做甚麼？我簡直不明白，」她孤寂地自語道。她站在原

desolately. After standing in the same place for a while, she went to make his bed.

Because of its proximity to the street, dust filled the room whenever a truck passed by. That day the dust and the dirt were particularly offensive to her; she frowned, then took a broom from the corridor outside the door to sweep the dusty floor, spotted in several places with remains of half-dried phlegm. She also dusted the desk and the table.

Resting in the rattan chair, she thought how nice it would be if she had someone to massage her back, but realized how useless it was to indulge in such fancies: "What a vain hope! I myself have become a servant and have been one for a long time." She closed her eyes; the image of her deceased husband appeared before her. At first it was blurred; then it became clear and vivid. She prayed to him in a low voice. "I don't care about myself. I know I'll have a miserable life, but why can't you protect him?" You can't let him live like this." And she wept.

Soon Wang returned home and found his mother sitting in the chair wiping her tears.

"Mother, what's the matter? Why were you crying?" he asked in a weary but startled voice.

"I was sweeping the floor, and a speck of dust got into my eye. It just came out," she lied.

"Mother, you've also made my bed," he said gratefully and walked over to her.

"I had nothing to do, I was bored," she replied. "Where have you been?"

He was panting and coughing. Turning to her he said, "I went to see Uncle Chung."

處思索了片刻。過後她走到他的床前，彎下身子去整理床鋪。

她鋪好床，看看屋子，地板上塵土很多，還有幾處半乾的痰跡。她皺了皺眉，便到門外廊上去拿了掃帚來把地板打掃乾淨了。桌上已經墊了一層土。這房間一面臨馬路，每逢大卡車經過，就會揚起大股的灰塵進屋來。這一刻她似乎特別忍受不了骯髒，她又用抹布把方桌和書桌連櫈子也都抹乾淨了。

做完這個，她便坐在籐椅上休息。她覺得腰痛，她用手在腰間擦揉了一會。「要是有人來給我搥背多好啊，」她忽然想道。但馬上她就明白自己是處在甚麼樣的境地了，她責備自己：「你早已做了老媽子，還敢妄想嗎！」她絕望地嘆一口氣。她把頭放在靠背上。她的眼前現出一個人影，先是模糊，後來面顏十分清楚了。「我又想起了他，」她哂笑自己。但接着她低聲說了出來：「我是不在乎，我知道我命不好。不過你為甚麼不保佑他？你不能讓他就過這種日子啊！」她一陣傷心，掉下幾滴眼淚。

不久他推開門進來，看見母親坐在籐椅上揩眼睛。

「媽，你甚麼事？怎麼在哭？」他驚問，聲音裏帶着疲倦。

「我掃地，灰塵進了我的眼睛，剛剛才弄出來。」她對他撒了謊。

「媽，你把我的床也理好了，」他感動地說，他走到母親身邊。

「我沒有事，閒着也悶得很，」她答道，接着又問：「你剛才到哪裏去了來？」

他喘了兩口氣，又咳了兩三聲嗽，然後掉開臉說：「我去看了鍾老來。」

"What for? Have you been to your Company?" she asked.

"I asked him to get me a job," he answered in a whisper.

"To get you a job? Why are you in such a hurry? Your health is more important," she said, disapprovingly.

"Most Chinese are rather weak and sickly. Sometimes minor illnesses drag on for most of their lives. I feel better, and Uncle Chung admitted that I look better than I did before. He promised to help me find a job." It took him some effort to say these words, for he was still quite weak. He went over and sat down on the edge of the bed.

"Why are you in such a hurry? We won't starve right away," she said.

"I just can't lie around and watch you slave all day. No man should be idle," he argued.

"You're my only son. If you don't attend to your health, whom can I depend on in the future ...? " She sat down in the rattan chair, choked with emotion.

Lifting his left hand in his mouth, he bit down hard on his left thumb. But he was unaware of any pain, for none could compete with the piercing pain in his left lung. After a while, he put down his hand without looking at the mark his teeth had made on his thumb. He looked at his mother, who sat there silently. He thought, "Your dreams and hopes about the future will all come to nothing." For him, his future was like a monster with two rows of terrifying white teeth.

Neither one spoke or moved. The silence was oppressive and tormenting. The street noises outside did nothing to relieve the oppressive air of lifelessness inside. Mother and son were immersed in their own thoughts, thoughts that traveled in different directions but still arrived at the same inevitable conclusion: his death.

「你找他甚麼事？你到公司去過嗎？」她驚奇地問道，便站了起來。

「我托他給我找事，」他低聲說。

「找事？你病還沒有全好，何必這樣着急。自己的身體比甚麼都要緊啊，」母親不以為然地說。

「我們中國人身體大半是這樣，說有病，拖起來拖幾十年也沒有問題。我覺得我現在好多了，鍾老也說我比前些天好多了。他答應替我找事。」他的臉上仍舊帶着病容和倦容，話似乎說得很勉強。他走到床前在床沿上坐下。

「唉，你何必這樣急啊！」母親說。「我們一時還不會餓飯。」

「可是我不能夠整天睡着看你一個人做事情。我是個男人總不能袖手吃閒飯啊，」他痛苦地分辯。

「你是我的兒子，我就只有你一個，你還不肯保養身體，我將來靠哪——」她說不下去，悲痛堵塞了她的咽喉。她又坐倒在籐椅上。

他把左手放到嘴邊，他的牙緊緊咬着大姆指。他不知道痛，因為他的左胸痛得厲害。過了一回，他放下手，也不去看指上深的齒印。他看他母親。她默默地坐在那裏。他用憐憫的眼光看她，他想：「你的夢、你的希望都落空了。」他認識「將來」，「將來」像一張兇惡的歪臉，有着兩排可怕的白牙。

兩個人不再說話，不再動。這靜寂是可怕的，折磨人的。屋子裏沒有絲毫生命的氣象，街中的人聲車聲都不能打破這靜寂。但是母親和兒子各人沉在自己的思想中，並沒有走着同一條路，卻在一個地方碰了頭而且互相了解了：那是一個大字：死。

He walked to his mother, speaking gently, "Mother, don't grieve too much. You can still depend on Hsiao Hsüan. He'll be much more of a man than I am."

Now his mother understood what he implied and felt even more sorrowful. She sighed, "Hsiao Hsüan is just like you when you were little. The resemblance is too great." She was unwilling to let him see her anguish.

Yet, he understood her well. If Hsiao Hsüan were a replica of himself, how could his mother possibly depend on his son for the future? On whom then could she depend? He had had some hope for his son, but now he knew that little could be placed in that hope.

"He is still young, and he will grow up. I am sorry that I've been such a poor father," he said in an effort to comfort her.

"To tell the truth, it's not your fault. You never had a chance to enjoy the fruits of life, only its hardships," she responded. Deeply upset, she stood up and escaped from the room.

He quietly walked to the windows, opened one and looked out at the street. He shivered; the dreary sky, overcast with clouds, resembled closely-knitted eyebrows. A gust of cold air and a few drops of rain blew in at the open window. "It's going to rain," he listlessly commented to himself.

"Hsüan, I am leaving tomorrow," he suddenly heard footsteps and an excited voice say. Shu-sheng had entered the room.

"Tomorrow? Why so soon? Didn't you say next week?" he asked in a startled tone.

"There is a special flight tomorrow. Friends helped me get a ticket on it. It's a shame that I've a dinner engagement tonight," she said in the same excited tone.

兒子走到母親的身後。「媽，你不要難過，」他溫和地說，「你還可以靠小宣，他將來一定比我有出息。」

母親知道他的意思，她心裏更加難過。「小宣跟你小時候一模一樣，這孩子太像你了，」她嘆息似地說。她不願意把她的痛苦露給他看，可是這句話使他更深透地看見了她寂寞的一生。她說得不錯。小宣太像他，也就是說小宣跟他一樣地沒有出息。那麼她究竟有甚麼依靠呢？他自己有時也在小宣的身上寄托着希望，現在他明白那是很渺茫的了。

「他年紀還小，慢慢會好起來。說起來我也真對不起他，我始終沒有好好教養過他，」他說，他想安慰母親。

「其實也怪不得你，你一輩子就沒有休息過，你自己甚麼苦都吃……」她說到這裏，又動了感情，再也說不下去，她忽然站起來，逃避似地走到門外去了。

他默默地走到右面窗前，打開一面窗，天像一張慘白臉對着他。灰黑的雲像皺緊的眉。他立刻打了一個冷噤。他覺得有甚麼東西冷冷地挨着他的臉頰。「下雨咯，」他沒精打采地自語道。

他背後起了腳步聲，妻進房來了。不等他掉轉身子，她先說，而且是用了興奮的調子：「宣，我明天走。」

「明天？怎麼這樣快？不是說下禮拜嗎？」他大吃一驚，問道。

「明天有架加班機，靠朋友幫忙，票子已經買好了。真糟，晚上還有人請吃飯，」她仍舊用興奮的調子說。

"You're really leaving tomorrow?" he asked disappointedly.

"Yes, I must be at the airport before six, which means I have to get up before dawn," she said.

"You must book a car tonight; otherwise you may be late," he suggested.

Hurriedly she said, "Don't worry. Department Chief Ch'en will have a car ready for me. I must do some packing. I am not packed." Bending down, she pulled a suitcase from under the bed.

"Let me help you," he said, walking to her side.

Squatting on the floor, she opened the suitcase and began to pack her clothes. From time to time she stood up to fetch something — a dress or some cosmetics — and then she'd put it in the suitcase.

"Do you want to take this? How about that?" Excited, he brought things to her for her decision.

"Thank you very much. You shouldn't move about, let me ... " was Shu-sheng's repeated reply.

His mother appeared at the door, coldly eyeing them. She was silent but full of resentment. As soon as he noticed her presence, he told her loudly, "Mother, Shu-sheng is to fly off tomorrow."

She responded coolly, "She can fly her merry way. It has nothing to do with me."

Standing up, Shu-sheng had intended to say a few nice words to her mother-in-law, but when she saw her contemptuous attitude, she quietly squatted down again.

Her face red, the old woman angrily returned to her own room. Closing the suitcase, Shu-sheng stood up, half of her anger having disappeared. He kept looking at her, pleadingly.

「那麼明天真走了？」他失望地再問。

「明早晨六點鐘以前趕到飛機場。天不亮就得起來，」她說。

「那麼今晚上先僱好車子，不然怕來不及，」他說。

「不要緊，陳主任會借部汽車來接我。我現在還要整理行李，我箱子也沒有理好，」她忙忙慌慌地說。她彎下身在床下去拿。

「我來給你幫忙，」他說着也走到床前去。

她已經把箱子拖了出來，就蹲着打開蓋子，開始清理箱內的衣服。她時而站起，去拿一兩件東西來放在箱子裏面，她拿來的，有衣服，有化妝品和別的東西。

「這個要帶去嗎？」「這個要嗎？」他時不時拿了一兩件她的東西來給她，一面問道。他也現出興奮的樣子。

「謝謝你。你不要動，我自己來，」她總是這樣回答。

母親從外面進來，站在門口冷眼看他們的動作。她不發出絲毫聲息，可是她的心裏充滿了怨憤。他忽然注意到她，便大聲報告：「媽，樹生明早晨要飛了。」

「她飛她的，跟我有甚麼相干！」母親冷冷地說。

樹生本來已經站直了，要去招呼母親，並且說幾句帶好意的話。可是聽見母親的冷言冷語，她又默默地蹲下去。她的臉漲得通紅，但她只是輕輕地哼了一聲。

母親生氣地走進自己的小屋去了。樹生關上箱蓋，立起來，怒氣已經消去一半，他望着她，不敢說一句話。但他的眼光在向她哀求甚麼。

"Can't you see how she hates me? She just hates me," Shu-sheng said to her husband.

"It's all a misunderstanding," he whispered. "She will understand one day; please don't blame her."

"For your sake, I won't hate her," she replied gently.

Slowly raising his head, he thanked her. "Tomorrow I will see you off at the airport." His words were barely audible.

"Please don't. You are not well enough," she quickly said. "In any case, Department Chief Ch'en will take care of me."

Her last sentence was like a spike driven into his heart. Tears glistening in his eyes, he said, "Then we say goodbye in this room."

"Don't be like that. I am not leaving you this very minute. Tonight I will be home a little early; then we can talk." Her heart softened and, full of understanding, she wanted to comfort him.

He nodded. He wanted to tell her he would stay up for her, but he only managed to mutter some unintelligible sounds.

"You'd better lie down. It's too exhausting for you standing up: You're not completely well. I can sit on your bed for a while," she said.

He obeyed her and she covered him with half of the quilt. Then sitting on the edge of the bed, she thought, "I don't know what will be happening to me at this time tomorrow." But she said to him, "I don't really want to go. If you don't want me to, perhaps I won't go."

"You must go. If you've made up your mind, it must be right," he replied gently, forgetting his own anguish.

"I really don't know if it is the right decision and if it brings happiness or misery. If only you were not ill, I'd have someone to discuss this with."

「你看，都是她在跟我過不去，她實在恨我，」樹生輕輕地對他說。

「都是誤會，媽慢慢會明白的。你不要怪她，」他低着頭小聲回答。

「我不會恨她，我看在你的面上，」她溫和地說。

「謝謝你，」他說，慢慢抬起頭來。「我明早晨送你上飛機，」他用更低的聲音說。

「你不要去！你的身體受不了，」她急急地說：「橫豎有陳主任照料我。」

末一句話刺着他的心。「那末我們就在這屋裏分別？」他痛苦地說，他眼裏含着淚光。

「不要難過，我現在還不走勒。我今晚上早點回來，還可以陪你多談談，」她的心腸軟了，便用同情的聲調安慰他。

他點了點頭，想說一句「我等你」，卻又說不出來，只是含糊地發出一個聲音。

「你睡下吧，站起太累，你的病還沒有完全好啊！我可以在你床上坐一會兒，」她又說。

他依了她的勸告去躺下了。她給他蓋上半幅棉被，然後坐在床沿上，「明天這個時候我不曉得是怎樣的情形，」她自語道。「其實我也不一定想走。你要是把我拉住，我也許就不走了，」這是她對他說的話。

「你放心去好了。你既然決定了，不會錯的，」他溫和地回答，他忘了自己的痛苦。

「其實我自己也不曉得這次去蘭州是禍是福，我連一個可以商量的人也沒有，你又一直在生病，」她望着他，略略皺眉說。

The words echoed in his ears: "If only you were not ill." She, as well as others, would never let him forget his illness; they treated him as a patient all the time. He heaved a sigh. As if having fallen from a great height, he gave up his last thread of hope. Looking at her enviously, he only said, perfunctorily, "Yes, yes."

"You don't look too good, you must have plenty of rest," she said in a concerned tone of voice. "Money problems can always be solved. You just take care of yourself. I will send you money every month."

"I know," he replied.

"I wrote to Hsiao Hsüan," she went on. Suddenly there was the honking of a car's horn outside. "I asked him to come home on Sunday," she completed her sentence. The honking grew more insistent. "I must go. My friends are waiting." She brushed her dress lightly, opened her purse and took out her lipstick, compact, and a little mirror. While putting make-up on her face, she urged him not to get up. But he did. "I am going. I will be back early tonight." She nodded to him and walked out smiling.

In the cold air of the room the scent of her perfume lingered. But she took with her the smiles and her pleasant voice. All alone, he stood before the table, gazing at the door, its paint peeling, through which she disappeared. "Don't leave, don't leave!" He seemed to hear himself calling after her in the innermost recesses of his heart. But the sound of her footsteps had been gone for some time.

His mother reappeared from her room, looking at him sympathetically. She said to him, "Hsüan, give up your hopes. You and Shusheng will be separated sooner or later. You are a poor, simple, honest man. How can you expect to keep her?" Feelings of love for her son and hatred for her daughter-in-law intermingled, one with the other; she needed an outlet for them.

「病」字敲擊着他的頭。她們永遠不讓他忘記他的病！她們永遠把他看作一個病人！他嘆了一口氣，彷彿從一個跟她同等的高度跌落下來，他最後一線游絲似的希望也破滅了。

「是啊，是啊，」他敷衍地連連說。他帶了羨忌的眼光仰視她。

「你氣色還是不好，你要多休息，」她換了關切的調子說：「經濟問題總可以設法。你只管放心養病。我會按月寄錢給你。」

「我知道，」他說，把眼光掉開。

「小宣那裏我今天去過信，」她又說。但是沒有讓她把話說完，汽車的喇叭聲突然在樓下正街旁響起來了。她略微驚訝地掉過臉來，朝那方向望了望，又說下去：「我要他禮拜天進城來。」喇叭似乎不耐煩地接連叫着。她站起來，忙忙慌慌地說：「我要走了，他們開車來接我了。」她整理一下衣服，又拿起手提包打開它，取出了小鏡子和粉盒、唇膏。

他坐起來。「你不要起來，你睡你的，」她一面說，一面專心地對鏡撲粉塗口紅。但是他仍舊下了床。

「我走咯，晚上我早一點回來，」她說着，掉過臉，含笑地對他點一個頭，然後匆匆地走出門去。

屋子裏寒冷的空氣中還留着她的脂粉香，可是她帶走了笑和清脆的語聲。他孤寂地站在方桌前面，出神地望着她的身影消去的地方，那扇白粉脫落了的房門。「你留下吧，你留下吧！」他彷彿聽見了自己的內心的聲音。但是橐橐的輕快的腳步聲早已消失了。

母親走出小屋，帶着憐惜的眼光看他。「宣，你死了心吧，你們遲早要分開的。你一個窮讀書人哪裏留得住她！」母親說，她心裏裝滿了愛和恨，她需要發洩。

He looked down at his body, then held his right hand up to his eyes. It was thin and yellowish, resembling a chicken's claw more than a human hand and shaking weakly. Pulling up his sleeve a little, he looked at his wrist. It, too, was very thin and fleshless. He felt a chill encompassing his whole body. Dully he kept staring at his frightening hand. He was like a convict who had just received his death sentence, his ears ringing with his mother's words to "give up" his hopes.

Indeed, he had been sentenced to death. What right, what reason could he possibly have to beg her to stay with him? The problem was with him, not with her. Now he thoroughly understood.

His mother switched on the light, adding a little brightness to the room. He went up quietly to the desk and examined sentimentally the objects on it before collapsing into the rattan chair, overwrought with grief. He covered his head with both hands, but no tears came. He was unwilling to look at his surroundings, and he was prepared to be swept away by anything or anyone who cared to come and collect him.

"Hsüan, cheer up. There's plenty of women. You can find a better one when you recover," his mother comforted him in a soft voice.

He uttered a low cry of anguish. Looking vacantly at her, he felt like screaming. Why did she bring him back to life and let him, a man doomed to death, view the gaiety of the world again? Why did she dangle impossible dreams before him when he had learned to accept his fate? Greatly agitated, he was experiencing the torment of his troubled heart. Shu-sheng had taken love away with her and with it all that he had ever had — the dreams of his college years, the sweet days following his marriage, his grandiose pre-war plans to establish a school — all finished, all gone.

他埋下頭看看自己身上，然後他把右手放到眼前。多麼瘦！多麼黃！倒更像雞爪了。它在發抖，無力地顫抖着。他把袖子稍稍往上挽。多枯瘦的手腕！哪裏還有一點肉。他覺得全身發冷。他呆呆地望着這隻可怕的手。他好像是一個罪人，剛聽完了死刑的宣告。母親的話反覆地在他耳邊響着：「死了心吧，死了心吧。」的確他的心被判了死刑了。

他還有甚麼權利，甚麼理由要求她留下呢？問題在他，而不在她。這一次他徹底地明白了。

母親扭開電燈，屋子裏添了一點光亮。

他默默地走到書桌前，用告別一般的眼光看了看桌上的東西，然後崩潰似地坐倒在籐椅上。他用兩手蒙着臉。他並沒有眼淚。他只是不願意再看見他周圍的一切。他放棄了自己，準備交給要求拿走他的任憑甚麼人，或甚麼東西。

「宣，你不要難過，女人多得很。等你病全好了，可以另外找一個更好的，」母親走過去，用慈愛的聲音安慰他。

他發出一聲痛苦的低叫。他取下手來，茫然望着母親，他想號哭。為甚麼她要把他拉回來？讓他這個死刑囚再瞥見繁華世界？他已經安分地準備忍受他的命運，為甚麼還要拿於他無望的夢來誘惑他？他這時並不是在冷靜思索，從容判斷。他只是在體驗那絞心的痛苦。樹生帶走了愛，也帶走了他的一切；大學時代的夢，婚後的甜蜜日子，戰前的教育事業的計劃，……全光了，全完了！

"Go lie down. I don't think you look too good. Shall I get a doctor now? Even someone who practices Western medicine," his mother said in a trembling voice. She could not understand his thoughts, but she was clearly frightened by his looks.

"No, no doctor. It won't be long," he replied, pronouncing his doom. His voice was feeble, and he was gasping for breath from time to time. When he stood up, he reeled and swayed on his feet.

"What did you say? Let me help you." Alarmed, she supported his right elbow to keep him from falling.

"Mother, don't be frightened. I can walk by myself," he said, as if waking up from a dream. Wrestling himself free from her support, he left the rattan chair and walked to the table. Putting one hand on it, he looked around vaguely. The yellowish light, the simple and worn-out furniture, everything looked so chilly. Then suddenly, without warning, the light went out. Immediately all was dark, but after their eyes had adjusted to it, there was some hazy gray light.

"There was a blackout just yesterday, why again today?" his mother grumbled.

He sighed, "We are doing nothing anyway. Let it stay dark."

"Let's light a candle; otherwise it will be too dreary," she replied. She lit what remained of the candle they used yesterday. The light flickered, creating dark shadows everywhere. In the wind, the candle's wax was guttering in a flowing stream. The makeshift candlestick — a broken teacup turned upside down — stuck to the table, surrounded by piles of melted wax.

"Bring a pair of scissors quickly! Bring a pair of scissors quickly!" The words came to him automatically without any conscious effort. He had become accustomed to this manner of doing or saying things,

「你快去躺躺，我看你不大好過吧。要不要我現在就去請個醫生來，西醫也好，」母親仍舊不能了解他，但他的臉色使她驚恐，她着急起來，她聲音發顫地説。

「不，不要請醫生。媽，不會久的，」他絕望地説，聲音弱，而且不時喘氣。他搖搖地站起來。

「你説甚麼？等我來攙你，」母親驚駭地説，她連忙攙着他的右肘。

「媽，你不要怕，沒有甚麼事，我自己可以走，」他説，好像從夢裏醒過來一樣。他擺脱了母親的扶持，離開籐椅，走到方桌前，一隻手壓在桌面上，用茫然的眼光朝四周看。黃昏的燈光，簡陋的陳設，每件東西都射出冷氣。突然，不發出任何警告，電燈光滅了。眼前先是一下黑，然後從黑中泛出了捉摸不住的灰色光。

「昨天才停過電，怎麼今天又停了？」母親低聲埋怨。

他嘆了一口氣。「橫豎做不了事，就讓它黑着吧，」他説。

「點支蠟燭也好，不然顯得更淒涼了，」母親説。她便去找了昨天用剩的半截蠟燭點起來。燭光搖幌得厲害。屋子裏到處都是黑影。不知從哪裏進來的風震搖着燭火，燭芯偏向一邊，燭油水似地往下流。一個破茶杯倒立着，做了臨時燭台，現在也被大堆燭油焊在桌上了。

「快拿剪刀來，快拿剪刀來，」他並不想説這樣的話，話語卻自然地從他的口中漏出來。而且他現出着急的樣子。這樣的事情不斷地發生，他已經被訓練得了好些習性。他做着自己並不一定想做的

not necessarily those which he wanted to do or say.

The light became a little steadier after his mother had trimmed the wick. "Maybe you'd like to have supper now. Let me warm up the broth for you," she said.

"All right," he replied reluctantly. His interest and appetite of a few hours ago had completely disappeared. His reply was made merely to appease his mother. "Why does she still want me to eat? Have I not eaten enough?" While asking himself these questions, he gave his mother a strange glance. Holding a candle shorter than a thumb, she was about to get the food.

"Mother, you'd better take this long candle with you," he said. "I don't need it." To him neither broad daylight nor deep darkness made much difference.

"I am all right," she said, leaving the room with the short candle. A dim candlelight kept him company. "Another day gone by. I don't know how many more days are left," he muttered, sighing. No one answered him; his shadow on the wall wavered and trembled. He did not know whether to sit or stand, to sleep or stay awake, as he stood in front of the table. With the cold air penetrating his outer garment and the cotton-padded gown underneath, he shivered. He then left the table and took a few steps just to warm up a little.

"I am only thirty-four, and I haven't done anything at all," he mused. "But, I am finished," he sighed with regret. As swift as lightning, scenes of college life flashed before his eyes. The campus itself, many familiar faces, the words of an ambitious young man all came back to him momentarily. "How could I know ...

"Imagine how silly I was at that time. I was so keen to start an ideal secondary school." He smiled. In his mind he seemed to see the many smiling faces of his young pupils, who all looked active,

事，說着自己並不一定想說的話。

母親拿了剪刀來，把倒垂的燭芯剪去了。燭光稍稍穩定。「你現在吃飯好嗎？我去把雞熱來，」她說。

「好的，」他無可奈何地答道。幾小時前的那種興致與食慾現在完全消失了。他回答「好」，只是為了敷衍母親。「她為甚麼還要我吃？我不是已經飽了？」他疑惑地想道。他用一種奇異的眼光看他母親。母親正拿了一段還不及大姆指長的蠟燭點燃了預備出去。

「媽，你拿這段長的去，方便點，」他說。「我不要亮，」他又加添一句。他想：有亮沒有亮對我都是一樣。

「不要緊，我夠了，」母親說着，仍舊拿了較小的一段蠟燭出了房門。

一段殘燭陪伴他留在屋子裏。

「又算過了一天，我不知道還有多少天好活，」他自語道，嘆了一口氣。

沒有人答話。牆壁上顫搖着他自己的影子。他不知道自己應該坐下還是站着，應該睡去還是醒着。他甚至不知道自己要做甚麼動作。他仍舊立在方桌前，寒氣漸漸浸透了他的罩衫和棉袍。他的身子微微顫抖。他便離開方桌，走了幾步，只為了使身子暖和點。

「我才三十四歲，還沒有做出甚麼事情。」他不平地、痛苦地想道。「現在全完了，」他惋惜地自嘆。大學時代的抱負像電光般地在眼前亮了一下。花園般的背景，年青的面孔，自負的言語……全在他的腦裏重現。「那時候哪裏想得到有今天？」他追悔地說。

「那時候我多傻，我一直想着自己辦一個理想中學，」他又帶着苦笑地想。他眼前彷彿現出一些青年的臉孔，活潑、勇敢、帶着希

courageous, eager for learning and full of gratitude. Alarmed, he opened his eyes wide, only to see that snuff had again formed on the wick. Under the gradually dimming light in the room he felt even lonelier. "It was just a dream ...," he mused. Bitterly disappointed, he left the candle untrimmed. Then he heard his mother's footsteps approaching from the corridor.

"It is time to eat again. What sort of life is this to go on and on!" he commented to himself in sorrow, his eyebrows knitted together.

His mother came carrying a bowl of steaming hot chicken broth and rice. With a satisfied look she said, "I have made some soupy rice for you. Eat it while it's hot." The room seemed to have brightened somewhat with her smile.

"Fine, I will eat as much as I can," he said obediently. He sat down on a stool by the table as a gush of hot steam reached his face. Watching his mother trim the candle, he realized how much older she had become, how many more wrinkles she had and how her cheekbones had become more sharply defined.

"She too has suffered because of me," he said to himself, unable to shift his thoughts in another direction. He wanted to cry, gazing at the bowl.

"Hurry up, don't let it get cold," his mother urged him again.

XXIII

EVER since supper time he had been waiting for his wife, but she came home very late.

望……。他們對着他感激地笑。他吃驚地睜大眼睛。蠟燭結了燭花，光逐漸暗淡。房裏無限淒涼。「我又在做夢了，」他不去剪燭花，卻失望地自語道。他忽然聽見了廊上母親的腳步聲。

「又是吃！我這樣捱日子又有甚麼意思！」他痛苦地想。他皺起眉頭來。

母親捧了一菜碗熱氣騰騰的雞湯飯進來，她滿意地笑着說：「我給你煮成湯飯趁熱吃，受用些。」整個屋子似乎因她的笑容變得較光亮了。

「好！我就多吃一點，」他順從地說。母親把碗放在方桌上，他也到方桌前一個櫈子上坐下。一股熱氣立刻沖到他臉上來。母親俯着頭在剪燭花。他看着她。這些天她更老了。她竟然有那麼些條的皺紋。顴骨顯得高，兩頰的肉也失去了些。

「連母親也受了我的累，」他不能不這樣想。他很想哭，他對着湯碗出神了。

「快吃吧，看冷了啊，」母親還在旁邊催促。

二十三

他吃過晚飯後就盼望着妻，可是妻回來得相當遲。

Time passed ever so slowly. He either sat in the rattan chair or lay in bed with all his clothes on. Unwilling to spend the money to repair his old watch, which had stopped running for several days, he kept it by his pillow but repeatedly asked his mother for the time. Seven, eight, and nine o'clock went by; the tormenting slowness of time was matched by his patience.

At last it was ten o'clock. Putting away the mending and her spectacles, his mother rubbed her eyes, saying, "Hsüan, go to bed. Don't wait any more."

"Mother, I can't go to sleep yet. Why don't you go?"

"She's still not home. She has simply forgotten us. Since she's leaving tomorrow, she should be home tonight with her family," she groused.

"She has a lot of engagements and activities. It's not her fault," he gently defended his wife.

"What engagements? What activities? But to go dancing with that Ch'en fellow?" she sneered.

"No, no, she wouldn't do that." He shook his head.

"You always defend and cover for her. I don't want to be a wet blanket, but to tell you the truth, she and that Ch'en fellow ... " She paused. "You're too honest and trustful and can't even see the obvious."

"Mother, you don't know her side of the story. Keeping a job involves some social activities, and she is a person who loves to keep up a good appearance," he continued to defend his wife, "I don't believe she really likes Ch'en. I trust her."

"Then I must be a character assassin," she replied angrily.

He was amazed at her vehement reaction, and did not argue

時間過得極慢。他坐在籐椅上或者和衣躺在床上。他那隻舊錶已經壞了好些天了，他不願意拿出一筆不小的修理費，就讓它靜靜地躺在他的枕邊。他不斷地要求母親給他報告時刻。……七點……八點……九點……時間似乎故意跟他為難。這等待是很折磨人的。但他有着極大的忍耐力。

終於十點鐘又到了。母親放下手裏的活計，取下老光眼鏡，揉揉眼睛。「宣，你脱了衣服睡吧，不要等了，」她說。

「我睡不着。媽，你去睡，」他失望地說。

「她這樣遲還不回來，哪裏還把家裏人放在心上？明天一早就要走，也應該早回來跟家裏人團聚才是正理，」母親憤憤不平地說。

「她應酬忙，事情多，也難怪她，」他溫和地說，他還在替他的妻子辯解。

「應酬，你說她還有甚麼應酬？還不是又跟她那位陳主任去跳舞去了，」母親冷笑地辯道。

「不會的，不會的，」他搖頭說。

「你總是袒護她、縱容她。不是我故意跟你潑冷水，我先把話說在這裏擱起，她跟陳主任——」她突然噤住以後的話，改變了語調嘆息道：「你太忠厚了，你到現在還這樣相信她，你真是執迷不悟。」

「媽，你還不大了解她，她也有她的苦衷。在外面做事情，難免應酬多，她又愛面子，」他接口替妻辯護道：「她不見得就會喜歡那個陳主任，我相信得過她。」

「那麼我是在造謠中傷她！」母親勃然變色道。

他吃了一驚，偷偷看母親一眼，不敢做聲。停了一兩分鐘，母

further. In a minute or so her rage subsided as she said with regret. "Don't mind me. I'm getting old and don't know how to control my temper any more. What's the use of bickering? But I don't understand why she snubs me so; after all, I'm your mother."

Encouraged, he said, "You misunderstand her. She has never disparaged you." He thought that there might be a chance to iron out their mutual animosity.

But she sighed, her finger pointing at his face. "You're too kind-hearted. How could she tell you the truth? But I can see through her. I know her better than you. Just because she can support herself, she despises me for depending on you."

"Mother, you truly misunderstand her. She never meant that," he replied confidently.

"How do you know?" she argued. The short candle standing on the makeshift candlestick had accumulated a large quantity of snuff on its wick and was about to flicker out when the light came on. She blew out the dying flame and pursued the subject from a different angle. She asked, "It's ten-thirty, but where is she? Would you say she has us on her mind?"

He was silent. Slowly he sighed, and his face twitched. He felt pain again in his left side. He stole a glance at her, wanting to beg her to forgive him. Instead, he suggested unemotionally that she go to bed. She did.

He promised her that he would go to bed soon, and before she left she switched off the light at his request. But he had no intention of going to sleep. Sentimentally he looked at the door, the table, the rattan chair, and every object that Shu-sheng had used, knowing that everything would be different tomorrow and that there would be no trace of her left.

親的臉色緩和下來，那一陣憤怒過去了，她頗後悔自己說了那句話，她用憐惜的眼光看他，她和藹地說：「你不要難過，我人老了，脾氣更壞了。其實這樣吵來吵去有甚麼好處。——我也不明白為甚麼她那樣看不起我。不管怎樣我總是你母親啊！」

他又得到了鼓舞，他有了勇氣，他說：「媽，你不要誤會她，她從沒有講過你的壞話。她對你本來是很好的。」他覺得有了消解她們中間誤會的機會與希望了。

母親嘆了一口氣，她指着他的臉說：「你也太老好了。她哪裏肯對你講真話啊。我看得出來，我比你明白，她覺得她能夠賺錢養活自己，我卻靠着你們吃飯，所以她看不起我。」

「媽，你的確誤會了她，她沒有這個意思，」他帶着充分自信地說。

「你怎麼知道？」母親不以為然地反問。就在這時候電燈突然亮了。整個屋子大放光明。倒立的茶杯上那段只燃到三分之一的蠟燭戴上了一大朵黑燭花，現着隨時都會熄滅的樣子。母親即刻吹滅了燭，換過話題說：「十點半了，她還沒有回來！你說她是不是還把我們放在眼裏！」

他不作聲，慢慢地嘆了一口氣。他臉部起了痙攣。左胸又厲害地痛起來。他用乞憐的眼光偷偷看他母親，他甚至想說：你饒了我吧。可是他並沒有這樣說。他抑制了情感的爆發(他想痛哭一場)。他平平淡淡地對母親說；「媽，不必等她了。你去睡吧。」

「那麼你呢？」母親關心地問。

「我也要睡了。我瞌睡得很。」他故意裝出睜不開眼睛的樣子，並且打了一個呵欠。

「那麼你還不脱衣服？」母親又問。

「我等一會兒脱，讓我先睡一覺。媽，你把電燈給我關了吧，」他故意慢吞吞地說，他又打了一個呵欠。

「好的，你先睡一覺也好，不要忘記脱衣服啊，」母親叮囑道。她真的把電燈扭熄了。她輕手輕腳地拿了一個櫈子，放在掩着的門背後。於是她走進她那間小屋去了。她房裏的電燈還亮着。

他並無睡意。他的思潮翻騰得厲害。他睜着眼望那房門，望那方桌，望那籐椅，望一切她坐過、提過、用過的東西。他想：到明天早晨甚麼都會變樣了。這屋子裏不會再有她的影子了。

Softly he spoke his wife's name under the quilt. More than once he wished that a hand would pull back the cover and say, "Hsüan, I'm here."

His wish remained just that. Nothing happened.

In her small room, his mother coughed a few times, followed by quietness.

"Shu-sheng, are you really leaving me?" he asked again, hoping to hear in reply, "No, Hsüan, I will never leave you." But there was no answer; the only noise was the sad cry of the old hawker selling hot water and fried rice-cakes. It was a weak, hollow, lonely voice. Wang visualized himself as a poor man, neck drawn into his collar, his back hunched and his hands tucked into the sleeves of a torn, greasy cotton-padded gown, one so thin that it could not protect him from the howling wind. For an educated man how lonely and sickly he was and ever would be! He wept under the quilt.

Fortunately his mother did not hear him weep, and hence no one came to comfort him. Gradually he regained his composure. He heard footsteps in the corridor. Shu-sheng's footsteps. Excitedly he uncovered his tear-stained face, and when his wife came in he had turned to face the wall.

Assuming that he was asleep, Shu-sheng switched on the light and tiptoed to the desk. She sat down in the rattan chair, changed into her slippers, combed her hair with the help of a small mirror she had taken out of a drawer. She put some things from the drawer in one of the suitcases. Everything was done with a minimum of noise. Before she finished her packing, she suddenly remembered something else and went over to the bed where she watched him silently.

By the noises in the room, he was fully aware of her every move

「樹生！」他忽然用棉被蒙着頭帶了哭聲暗暗地喚她。他希望能有一隻手來揭開他的被，一個溫柔的聲音在他耳邊輕輕回答：「宣，我在這兒。」

但是甚麼事都不曾發生過。母親在小屋裏咳了兩聲嗽。隨後又寂然了。

「樹生，你真的就這樣離開我？」他再說。他盼望得着一聲回答：「不，我永不離開你。」沒有聲音。不，從街上送進來淒涼的聲音：「炒米糖開水。」聲音多麼衰弱，多麼空虛，多麼寂寞。這是一個孤零零的老人的叫賣聲！他彷彿看見了自己的影子，縮着頭，駝着背，兩手插在袖筒裏，破舊油膩的棉袍擋不住寒風。一個多麼寂寞病弱的讀書人。現在……將來？他想着，他在棉被下哭出聲來了。

幸好母親不曾聽見他的哭聲。不會有人來安慰他。他慢慢地止了淚。他聽見了廊上的腳步聲，是她的腳步聲！他興奮地揭開被露出臉來。他忘了淚痕還沒有揩乾。等到她在推門了，他才想到，連忙用手揉眼睛，並且着急地翻一個身，使她在扭開電燈後看不到他的臉。

她走進屋子，開了燈。她第一眼看床上，她以為他睡熟了。她先拿了拖鞋，輕輕地走到書桌前，在籐椅上坐下，換了鞋，又從抽屜裏取出一面鏡子，對鏡略略整理頭髮。然後她站起來，去打開了箱子，又把抽屜裏的一些東西放到箱裏去。她做這些事還竭力避免做出任何響聲。她不願驚醒他的夢。但正在整理箱子的中間，她忽然想到甚麼事，就暫時撇下這個工作，走到床前去。她靜靜地立在床前看他。

他並沒有睡去，從她那些細微的聲音裏他彷彿目睹了她的一舉

and knew that she was standing by him. He thought she would go away presently, but she stood still. Puzzled and unable to bear it any longer, he coughed. And when he heard her call him, he pretended he had just awakened, turned over, yawned, and opened his eyes.

"Hsüan," she called him again. "I am late. How long have you been sleeping?" she asked gently.

"I didn't want to sleep but then I fell asleep," he lied.

"I planned to come home very early," she explained, "but the dinner was late. Afterwards my friends dragged me to have coffee elsewhere. I very much wanted to be with you, but they wouldn't let me leave."

"I know," he interrupted. "Your colleagues must be unwilling to see you leave." This was meant to be a casual remark devoid of any sarcasm. But as soon as he spoke, he realized it had been misunderstood.

"Are you unhappy that I came home late?" she asked. "I thought about you all evening, and I'd have liked so much to be with you. I was afraid that ... " She looked toward her mother-in-law's small room.

"I know. I am not blaming you," he said. "Are you packed?" He changed the subject.

"Almost," she replied.

"Then finish packing," he hurried her. "It's almost midnight, and you must get up before dawn."

"Don't worry. Department Chief Ch'en will come to pick me up. He has borrowed a car," she responded.

"But you still have to get up early," he said with a reluctant smile.

一動。他知道她到了他的床前。他以為她即刻便會走開。她竟然立了好一陣。他不知道她在做甚麼。他不能再忍耐了。他咳了一聲嗽。過後他聽見她小聲喚他的名字，他便裝出睡醒起來的樣子翻一個身，伸一個懶腰，一面睜開眼來。

「宣，」她再喚他，一面俯下頭，「我回來遲了。你睡了多久？」她柔聲說。

「我本來不要睡，不曉得怎樣就睡着了，」他說了謊，同時還對她微笑。

「我本來早就要回來，誰知道飯吃得太遲，他們又拉着去喝咖啡，我說要回來，他們一定不放我走……」她解釋道。

「我知道，」他打斷了她的話。「你的同事們一定不願意跟你分別。」這是敷衍的話。可是話一說出，他卻覺得自己失言了。他絕沒有要譏諷她的意思。

「你是不是怨我不早回來？」她低聲下氣地說，「我不騙你，我雖然在外面吃飯，心裏卻一直想到你。我們要分別了，我也願意同你多聚一刻，我就是怕——」她說到這裏轉過臉朝母親的小屋望了望。——

「我知道。我並沒有怨你，」他接嘴說，「你行李全部弄好了嗎？」他改變了話題問。

「差不多了，」她答道。

「那麼你快點弄吧，」他催促道；「現在大概有十一二點了。你要早點睡啊，明天天不亮便就要起來。」

「不要緊，陳主任會開汽車來接我，他車子也借好了，」她順口說。

「不過你也得早起來，不然會來不及的，」他勉強裝出笑容說。

"Then you ... " She choked, obviously becoming emotional.

"I am quite sleepy," he lied again, pretending to yawn.

She thought for a little while. Then raising her head, she said, "Well, go to sleep. Don't get up tomorrow morning when I leave. You might catch cold. You know, you're not quite well yet."

"Yes, I know. Don't worry." Having said this, he made a rather unsuccessful attempt to smile pleasantly at her. And when she left his side to resume packing, he cried under the quilt.

She was busy packing for almost an hour, assuming he was asleep. The fact was he was awake all the time. His recollections included places and events of many years ago, transcending time and space and centering on his wife. She was still near him, but he did not dare breathe or cough lest she might be frightened away. Memories of marital bliss, of his younger days, and even of the family squabbles and torments all raced by. Facing him were the imminent departure of his wife, the lonely future, and his illness. The pain in his left lung was persistent, and he wondered if she'd ever return and, if she did, whether he'd still be alive. Facing the wall, he wept until he dozed off. And that was some time after she had quietly crept into the bed.

In the small hours of the night, he woke up, drenched in cold sweat, his undershirt soaked through and through. In the pitch darkness he felt dizzy, unable to see anything clearly. There was no sound except Shu-sheng's even breathing. He wondered what time it was, then remembered that Ch'en was coming to pick up his wife. Yes, Department Chief Ch'en, a man so superior to him in every respect. He felt stupefied for several minutes. Something was bursting and burning in his heart, and his face twitched violently.

Slowly he fell asleep again. Soon Shu-sheng woke up. She was late

「那麼你——」她開始感到留戀，她心裏有點難過，說了三個字，第四個字梗在咽喉，不肯出來。

「我很瞌睡，」他故意打了一個假呵欠。

她似乎沉思了一會兒，然後她抬起頭說：「好的，你好好睡。我走的時候你不要起來啊。太早了，你起來會着涼的。你的病剛剛才好一點，處處得小心，」她叮囑道。

「是，我知道，你放心吧。」他說，他努力做出一個滿意的微笑，雖然做得不大像。可是等她轉身去整理行裝時，他卻蒙着頭在被裏流眼淚。

她忙了將近一個鐘頭。她還以為他已經睡熟了。事實上他卻一直醒着。他的思想活動得厲害，它跑了許多地方，甚至許多年月。它超越了時間和空間的限制，但是它始終繞着一個人的面影。那是她。她現在還在他的近旁，可是他不敢吐一口氣，或者大聲咳一下嗽，他害怕驚動了她。幸福的回憶，年青的時日都去遠了。……甚至痛苦的爭執，互相的折磨也去遠了。現在留給他的只有分離(馬上就要來到的)和以後的孤寂。還有他這個病。他的左胸又在隱隱發痛。她會回來嗎？或者他能夠等到她回來的那一天嗎？……他不敢再往下想。他把臉朝着牆壁，默默地流眼淚。他後來也迷迷糊糊地睡了一些時候。但那是在她上床睡去的若干分鐘以後了。

他半夜驚醒，一身冷汗，汗背心已經濕透了。屋子裏漆黑，他翻身朝外看，他覺得有點頭暈，他辨不出一件東西。母親房裏沒有聲息。他側耳靜聽。妻發出均勻的呼吸聲。她睡得很安靜。「甚麼時候了？」他問自己。他答不出。「她不會睡過頭嗎？」他想。他自己回答：「還早吧，天這麼黑。她不會趕不上，陳主任會來接她。」想到「陳主任」，他彷彿挨了迎頭一悶棍，有幾分鐘光景他楞了。甚麼東西在他心裏燃燒，他覺得臉上又起了一陣痙攣。「他甚麼都比我強，」他妒忌地想。……

漸漸地、慢慢地他又睡去了。可是她突然醒來了。她跳下床，

and hurriedly began dressing. Outside the window a car was honking. "He's already here; I'd better hurry," she told herself. Looking at her sleeping husband, she decided not to wake him. Her mother-in-law's door was tightly shut too. She lifted up her two suitcases, but immediately put them back down and went over to the bed. He was snoring, and she stood there motionlessly until the horn sounded again. She said goodbye to him softly, and hoped that he was not dreaming of her leaving him. She felt like crying and bit her lower lip; she scribbled a short note and left it under the ink stand. Carrying one suitcase with her, she left the room.

While she was descending the stairs, he suddenly awoke from a terrible dream of her having abandoned him. He immediately looked for her. The door was open, the electric light blinding, and the one lone suitcase stood in the middle of the room. Hastily he put on his cotton-padded gown without properly buttoning it up and carried the suitcase downstairs.

It was heavy. There was no light on the landing and his gown restricted his movements. He managed to haul it down to the second floor, just as two shadows were coming up the stairs with a flashlight.

"Hsüan, you're up," a familiar female voice greeted him. The flashlight shone on his face. "Oh, you've even carried my suitcase down." She walked over to him and said, "Please give it to me."

He would not release the suitcase, for he wanted to carry it down for her, insisting that he could manage it.

"Allow me," a man volunteered in a young strong voice. Startled, Wang immediately looked at him. He realized that the stranger was young and muscular and felt that compared to him, he was coarse and shabby. Obediently, he yielded the suitcase. At the same time, he

穿起衣服，扭開電燈，看一下手錶。「啊呀！」她低聲驚叫，她連忙打扮自己。

突然在窗外響起了汽車的喇叭。「他來了，我得快。」她小聲催促自己。她匆匆打扮好了。她朝床上一看。他睡着不動。「我不要驚醒他，讓他好好睡吧，」她想道。她又看母親的小屋，房門緊閉，她得意地説句：「再會。」她去試提一下她的兩隻箱子，剛提起來，又即刻放下。她急急走到床前去看他。「他的後腦向着她，他在打鼾。她癡癡立了半晌。窗下汽車喇叭聲又響了。她用柔和的聲音輕輕説：「宣，我們再見了，希望你不要夢着我離開你啊。」她覺得鼻頭酸痛，便用力咬着自己的下嘴唇，她掉轉身子，離開了床，但馬上又回轉身來看他。她躊躇片刻，忽然走到書桌前，拿了一張紙，用自來水筆在上面匆匆寫下幾行字，用墨水瓶壓住它，於是提着一隻箱子往門外走了。

正當她從走廊轉下樓梯的時候，他突然從夢中發出一聲叫喚驚醒了。他叫着她的名字，聲音不大，卻相當悽慘。他夢着她拋開他走了。他正在喚她回來。

他立刻用眼光找尋她。門開着。電燈亮得可怕。沒有她的影子，一隻箱子立在屋子中央。他很快地就明白了真實情形。他一翻身坐起來，忙忙慌慌地穿起棉袍，連鈕子都沒有扣好，就提起那隻箱子大踏步走出房去。

他還沒有走到樓梯口，就覺得膀子發酸，腳沉重，但他竭力支持着下了樓梯。樓梯口沒有電燈，不曾扣好的棉袍的後襟又絆住他的腳，他不能走得快。他正走到二樓的轉角，兩個人急急地從下面上來。他看見射上來的手電光。為了避開光亮，他把眼睛略略埋下。

「宣，你起來了！」上來的人用熟悉的女音驚喜地叫道。手電光照在他的身上。「啊呀，你把我箱子也提下來了！」她連忙走到他身邊，伸手去拿箱子。「給我，」她感激地説。

他不放開手，仍舊要提着走下去，他説；「不要緊，我可以提下去。」

「給我提，」另一個男人的聲音説。這是年青而有力的聲音，他吃了一驚。他看了説話人一眼。恍惚間他覺得那個人身材魁梧，意態軒昂，比起來，自己太猥瑣了。他順從地把箱子交給那隻伸過來

heard Shu-sheng say to the stranger, "Department Chief Ch'en, would you please go first? I'll follow you shortly."

"Come quickly," the young voice responded. The muscular body disappeared, and so did his heavy footsteps. Shu-sheng switched off the flashlight.

The two stood in the midst of darkness and wintry chill, listening to each other's breathing.

The car kept honking. He was jolted back into reality as he heard her say, "Hsüan, you'd better go up. Let's say goodbye here, and please don't walk me to the door. I've left you a letter." She grasped his thin, hard hand, a hand so cold it barely seemed human. She shuddered, suppressed her emotions, and said again, "Goodbye," She was ready to leave him.

He caught her arm and cried in despair, "When shall I see you again? When will you come back?"

"I'm not sure, but I will definitely come back. Probably in a year, not longer." She was deeply moved.

"A year? So long? Can't you come sooner?" He was disappointed and was afraid that he could not wait that long.

"I will try to come back soon," she answered. The irritating horn sounded again. "Don't worry. I will write to you." As an afterthought, she added, "Please say a few words for me to Mother. I didn't dare disturb her." Thus she left him and, with the help of the flashlight, ran down the remaining steps. Tears streamed down her cheeks.

Dazed, he ran to the main door in the dark without stumbling. But it was too late; the car had already started. Hoarsely he called for her; indistinctly he caught a glimpse of her through one of the car windows. The car sped away, arrowlike, into the smog, as he ran hopelessly

的手。他還聽見她在說：「陳主任，請你先下去，我馬上就來。」

「你快來啊，」那個年青的聲音說，魁梧的身影消失了。「冬冬」的腳步聲響了片刻也寂然了。他默默地站在樓梯上，她也是。她的手電光亮了一陣，也突然滅了。

兩個人立在黑暗與寒冷的中間，聽得見彼此的呼吸聲。

汽車喇叭叫起來，叫了兩聲。他夢醒似地動了一下；她說話了：「宣，你上樓睡吧，你身體要當心啊……我們就在這裏分別吧，你不要送我，我給你留了一封信在屋裏，」她柔情地伸過手去，捏住他的手。她打了一個寒㾕。瘦而硬（雖然不怎麼冷）！她不像在握一隻人的手啊。她竭力抑制了感情聲音發顫地說：「再見。」她預備撇下他走了。

他忽然抓住她的膀子，又着急又悲痛地說：「我甚麼時候可以再見到你？你甚麼時候回來？」

「我說不定，不過我一定要回來的。我想至遲也不過一年吧，」她感動地說。

「一年？這樣久！你能不能提早呢？」他失望地低聲叫道。他害怕他等不到那個時候。

「我也說不定，不過我總會想法提早的，」她答道，討厭的喇叭聲又響了。她安慰他：「你不要着急，我到了那邊就寫信回來。」又說：「媽面前你替我講一聲，我沒有敢驚動她。」她終於決然地撇開他，打着手電筒急急忙忙跑下剩餘的那幾級樓梯。她覺得淚水從眼眶裏迸出來了。

他癡呆地立了一兩分鐘，突然沿着樓梯追下去。在黑暗中他沒有被甚麼東西絆倒。但是他趕到大門口，汽車剛剛開動。他叫一聲「樹生」，他的聲音嘶啞了。她似乎在玻璃窗中露了一下臉，但汽車

after it for a short distance. Despondently he walked back to the apartment building. The moon-shaped lamp at the entrance was shining on a section of the sidewalk. By the door were two 10-year-old children huddled together and sleeping soundly in their faded cotton jackets, unaware of the light and the cold. Their faces and jackets were dirty and greasy, and small knots of grayish cotton had already burst out of the jackets covering their bodies. But their dirty faces looked lovely in the soft light.

Looking at the children, he shivered. What a dreadful chilly night. Here were two children soundly asleep, and he the only person awake. He wanted to wake the children and invite them to his room, or at least to cover them with his gown. But he did neither and left, reminded of the fate of his classmate T'ang Pai-ch'ing, who had also slept in the open. Without losing any more time, he went indoors, avoiding the children as if they were a deadly pestilence.

He read the letter his wife had left him:

> Hsüan,
>
> I am leaving. You were sound asleep, so I didn't wake you. Don't be sad. I will write to you as soon as I get to Lanchow. Department Chief Ch'en will take good care of me, so you needn't worry. I will write to you frequently. Please say a few words to Mother for me. I don't bear any grudge against her. Ask her to forgive me.
>
> *Ch'i**

As he read the letter, he wept, but the word *"ch'i"* made him feel grateful.

Standing by the desk, he held the letter in his hand for a few

---

* "Ch'i" means wife. When a woman calls herself *"ch'i"* before her husband, it implies affection and intimacy.

仍然在朝前走。他叫着追上去。汽車卻像箭一般地飛進霧中去了。他趕不上，他站着喘氣。他絕望地走回家來。大門口一盞滿月似的門燈孤寂地照着門前一段人行道。門旁邊牆腳下睡着一個人堆。他仔細一看，原來是兩個十歲上下的小孩互相抱着縮成了一團。油黑的臉，油黑的破棉襖，滿身都是棉花疙瘩，連棉花也變成黑灰色了。他們睡得很熟，燈光溫柔地撫着他們的臉。

他看着他們，他渾身顫抖起來。周圍是這麼一個可怕的寒夜。就只有這兩個孩子睡着，他一個人醒着。他很想叫醒他們，讓他們到他屋子裏去，他又想脱下自己的棉衣蓋在他們的身上。但是他甚麼也沒有做。「唐柏青也這樣睡過的，」他忽然自語道，他想起了那個同學的話，便蒙着臉像逃避瘟疫似地走進了大門。

他回到自己屋子裏，在書桌上見到她留下的字條，他拿起它來，低聲唸道：

宣：

我走了。我看你睡得很好，不忍叫醒你。你不要難過。我到了那邊就給你來信。一切有陳主任照料，你可以放心。我會常常給你寫信。

媽面前請你替我講幾句話。我不會記仇的，請她原諒我。

妻

他一邊唸，一邊流淚。特別是最後一個「妻」字引起他的感激。

他拿着字條在書桌前立了幾分鐘。他覺得渾身發冷，特別是兩

minutes. His whole body was chilled, particularly his legs, which felt as though they were frozen. He could not stand up any longer. So he went to bed and put the letter securely by his pillow. After taking off his padded gown, he crawled under the warm quilt.

But he could not sleep, tossing and turning. No sooner did he close his eyes than he was tormented by nightmares and intense physical discomfort. He had a fever, a headache; his ears buzzed. At dawn he heard an airplane flying overhead, and he thought: "She's gone, far, far away. I will never see her again." Crying, he remembered what she had always said about him, "You are an honest and kind man, and you only know how to cry." Indeed, he was crying much more now.

XXIV

STARTING the second day after Shu-sheng's departure, he had to stay in bed again for a time. During that period he received two letters from Lanchow. The first read:

Hsüan,

I've arrived in Lanchow; everything looks strange. The air is fresh, chilly, but pleasant.

The building to be occupied by the bank is still being renovated and all the emloyees are housed in a hotel. Manager Ch'en (formerly Department Chief Ch'en) has been kind to me, so there's nothing for you to worry about. I'm still very much unsettled, and I'll write you a long letter tomorrow or the day after next.

Is Mother still having tantrums? When I was at home, she disapproved of me in so many ways. Now that I'm gone, I hope she doesn't hate me so much.

條腿，好像就要凍僵的樣子。他支持不住，便拿着字條走到床前，把它放在枕邊，然後脱去棉袍鑽進被窩裏去。

他一直沒有能睡熟，他不斷地翻身，有時他剛合上眼，立刻又驚醒了。可怖的夢魔在等候他。他不敢落進睡夢中去。他發燒，頭又暈，兩耳響得厲害。天剛大亮他聽見飛機聲。他想：她去了，去遠了，我永遠看不見她了。他把枕畔那張字條捏在手裏，低聲哭起來。

「你是個忠厚老好人，你只會哭！」他想起了妻罵過他的話，可是他反而哭得更傷心了。

二十四

妻走後第二天他又病倒了。在病中他接到妻兩封信。第一封信寫着：

宣：

我到了蘭州，一切都很陌生，只覺空氣好，天雖冷，卻也冷得痛快。

行裏房屋還在改修中，我們都住在旅館裏。陳經理對我很好，你可不必耽心。初到一個地方，定不下心來，過一兩天再給你寫長信。

母親還發脾氣嗎？我在家她事事看不順眼，分開了她也許不那麼恨我吧。

Take care of yourself. Eat more nourishing food, and don't be too thrifty. I'll send you money regularly.

Best wishes.

Ch'i

There was no return address, but he was pleased with the tone of the letter except for the reference to Manager Ch'en. He received the second letter several days later. Briefer than the first, it was rather disappointing. She wrote that she had been busy preparing for the grand opening of the bank and that she expected him to write to her frequently. She did enclose a return address but signed the letter "Shu-sheng," instead of the more affectionate "*ch'i*."

After reading it, he sighed. When his mother wanted to read it, he gave it to her without comment. After she read it, her reaction was predictably unfavorable. She resented Shu-sheng's arrogant tone. But then, she had not read the first letter.

Hiding his disappointment and mounting doubts, he defended Shu-sheng, "She's probably very busy. Their new office doesn't have a large staff, and since Department Chief Ch'en treats her well, she has to work hard."

"He's not a department chief any more but a manager," she corrected him. "Treating her well? You just watch, there'll be further developments to this story," she said indignantly.

"Mother, isn't it time for me to have the medicine?" he said, changing the subject.

"Yes, I'll go and boil it for you." Her thoughts immediately centered on her son's illness and she forgot about "that" woman. Affectionately she looked at his sallow face and was pleased to notice that his eyes were slightly brighter and his lips not quite so pale. Quickly she went off.

你的身體應該注意，多吃點營養東西和補品，不要省錢，我會按月寄給你。　祝福

你

妻　×月×日

沒有寫明回信地址，但這短信使他很滿意，只除了「陳經理」三個字。他等着第二封信，這並不要他久等。過了四天第二封信來了。這信卻給他帶來失望。這是一封更短的信。在這信內她只說她正為籌備銀行開幕的事忙着，一時沒有功夫寫長信，卻盼望他多去信，告訴她他的生活狀況。信末寫上了她的通信處，署名卻改用了「樹生」兩個字。

他讀完信，嘆一口氣，不說一句話。母親伸手來索信看，他默默地交給她。

「她好神氣，才去了幾天就拿出要人的派頭來了，」母親看完信，不滿意地說。她還不曾看到樹生的第一封信。

「她大概真忙，也難怪她，新開行人手少，陳主任對她好，她也得多幫忙，」他還在替妻辯護，他竭力掩飾了自己的失望與疑慮(的確他有一點點的疑慮)。

「還說陳主任，陳經理了！對她好，你看着吧，總有一天會鬧出花樣來的！」母親憤憤地說。

「媽，我該吃藥了吧，」他不願意母親再談這個問題(它使他心裏很難過)，便打岔道。

「是啊，我去給你煎藥，」母親接着說，想起他的病，她立刻忘了那個女人。她用慈愛的眼光看他。他還是那麼黃瘦。不過眼神好了些，嘴唇也有了點血色。她匆匆忙忙地走出房去了。

He sighed, facing the wall, then turned over and stared at the ceiling. Wherever he looked, he saw his wife's beaming, beautiful face, one fit for an actress on the stage. His own face was burning, his ears kept hearing monotonous sounds like that of a bell ringing, and his eyes were as dry as kindling sticks. He dozed for a while and had several brief and strange dreams; occasionally he groaned. Then he was awakened by his mother, who carried a bowl of some medicinal concoction. He was startled and soaked in sweat. He looked at her beseechingly.

"Hsüan, what has happened?" She was frightened and nearly spilled the bowl of medicine.

He did not seem to understand her. After a while, he heaved a deep breath. Recovering somewhat, he said, "I had many strange dreams. It's all right now."

She was puzzled, then said, "The medicine is ready. It isn't too scalding hot, so won't you drink it?"

"Yes, please give it to me," he said. He pushed off the warm coverlet and sat up.

"Put on your gown! You'll catch cold." She handed the bowl to him and then put his gown over his shoulders. "It's very cold today; it's snowing," she added.

"Is the snow heavy?" he asked, after he had taken a few swallows of the medicine.

"No, the snow isn't heavy, but it's cold. You must dress properly," she said.

When he handed the empty bowl back to her, he noticed her red and puffed hands, remarking in surprise, "How did you develop such horrible chilblains?"

他又嘆了一口氣，把眼睛掉向牆壁。過了兩三分鐘，他又把眼睛掉向外面，後來又掉向天花板。不管在哪裏他都看見那個女人的笑臉，她快樂地笑，臉打扮得像舞台上的美人臉。他整個臉熱烘烘的，耳朵邊響着單調的鈴子聲，眼睛乾燥得像要發火。他終於昏沉沉地睡着了。

他做着短而奇怪的夢，有時他還發出呻吟。直到母親端了藥進來，他才被喚醒。他大吃一驚，而且出了一身汗。他用了求救的眼光看着她。

「宣，你怎麼了？」母親驚駭地說。她差一點把碗裏的藥潑了出來。

他好像沒有聽懂她的話，過了半晌，他才長長地吐出一口氣來。他的表情改變了。他寬慰地說：「我做了好些怪夢，現在好了。」

母親不大明白地看了看他。「藥好了，不燙，現在正好吃。你要起來吃嗎？」她關切地說。

「好。你遞給我，」他說着就推開被坐起來。

「你快披上衣服，看受涼啊，」母親着急地說。她把藥碗遞給他後，便拿起他的棉袍替他披上。「今天很冷，外面在下雪，」她說。

「大不大？」他喝了兩大口藥，抬起頭問道。

「不大，墊不起來的。不過冷倒是冷，所以你起來一定要先穿好衣服，」她說。

他喝光了藥，把碗遞還給母親。忽然他拉着她的紅腫的手驚叫道：「媽，你怎麼今年生凍瘡了？」

Drawing her hand back she answered calmly, "I had them last year, too."

"But they were not as bad as they are now. Don't wash clothes in this cold weather. You'd better give the wash to the laundry woman."

"Do you have any idea of how much that would cost? One thousand four hundred *yüan* a month. The price has been doubled."

"So what! Your hands are more important. You suffered ... "

"Money is money. I'd rather save it for your medicine than give it to the laundry woman," she said.

"Didn't Shu-sheng say she'd send money? At present, we don't need to be so frugal." He took off his gown and lay down again.

She became silent, an expression of severe pain appearing on her face. She turned her head away so as not to let him see it.

"Mother, you should take care of yourself. Why should you suffer like this?"

"I'm not suffering," she said, unconsciously feeling her swollen hands.

"Don't try to fool me. I know you don't want to use Shu-sheng's money," he said.

"That's not true. Am I not using her money now?" Her voice became high-pitched, her color changed and tears came to her eyes. Biting her lip, she turned away again.

"Mother, I'm really worthless. You brought me up and educated me, and I can't even support you." A moment later he asked, "Do you still hate Shu-sheng?"

母親縮回了手，淡淡地說：「我去年也生過的。」

「去年哪有這樣厲害！我說冷天你不要自己洗衣服吧，還是包給外面大娘洗好些。」

「外面大娘洗，你知道要多少錢一個月！」她不等他回答，自己又接下去：「一千四百元，差不多又漲了一倍了。」

「漲一倍就漲一倍，不能為了省一千四，就讓你的手吃苦啊，」他痛心地說。「我太對不住你了，」他又添上一句。

「可是錢總是錢啊。我寧肯省下一千四給你醫病，也不情願送給那班洗衣服的大娘，」母親說。

「樹生不是說按月寄錢來嗎？目前也不在乎省這幾個錢，」他說，伸了個懶腰，拿掉棉袍，又倒下去。

母親不作聲了。她臉上現出不自然的表情，她立刻掉開頭，不給他看見她的臉。

「媽，」他溫和地喚道。她慢慢地回過頭來。「你也得保重身體啊，你何必一定要叫自己多吃苦。」

「我並不苦，」她說，勉強笑了笑。她不自覺地摸着手上發燙的腫痕。

「你不要騙我，我曉得你不願意用樹生的錢，」他說。

「沒有這回事，我不是已經在用她的錢嗎？」她說，聲音尖，又變了臉色，眼眶裏裝滿了淚水，她咬着嘴唇並且把身子掉開了。

「媽，我真對不起你，你把我養到這麼大，到今天我還不能養活你，」他答道，頭也不回。她真想跑進自己的房裏去暢快地哭一場。

「你現在還恨樹生嗎？」過了半晌他又問。

"No, I've never hated her," she replied, wishing she could leave the room.

"Shu-sheng said that she has nothing against you," he said.

"Then I've to thank her," she replied coldly.

"If she wrote to you, would you write back?" he asked timidly.

After some hesitation, she promised that she would. But she tried not to show her face to her son.

"Then everything will be fine," he said with obvious satisfaction.

"Would she write to me?" she asked realistically.

"I think she would." He was, however, not so sure that Shu-sheng would.

Though she knew this was all rather unrealistic, she was unwilling to crush his illusions. She was severely tempted to say, "You're dreaming," but she refrained. She even wished that his fantasies would, miraculously, become true. For her only son, she would forgo her pride, her desire for revenge, or anything else.

That night, after his mother had retired to her small room, he got up, went to the desk and wrote Shu-sheng a long letter telling her about himself and his conversation with his mother, expressing hope that Shu-sheng would write his mother a long, friendly letter, and adding that he himself would also welcome the promised long letter from her. When he finished the letter, he was so exhausted that he returned to bed and immediately fell asleep.

The following morning he asked his mother to send the letter registered airmail. She took the letter without a word, just shaking her head as she left the room. He did not have to guess at her reaction. His

「我不恨，我從沒有恨過她，」她說，她巴不得馬上離開這間屋子，她害怕他再談樹生。

「她說過她對你並沒有惡感，」他說。

「謝謝她，」她冷淡地插嘴說。

「那麼要是她寫信給你，你肯回信嗎？」他膽怯地問。

她想了片刻，才答道：「回信。」她仍然不讓他看見她的臉色。

「那就好，」他欣慰地說，吐了一口氣。

「不過她會寫信來嗎？」她忽然轉過身來，問道。

「我想她會的，」他帶了幾分確信地答道。

她微微地搖搖頭，她想說：「你在做夢！」可是她剛剛開了口立刻就閉上了。她不忍打破他的夢。同時她還存着一絲的希望。不管她的自尊心受了損害，復仇心落了空，她還盼望他這個夢會實現，即使是來得像奇跡似的。

這一天關於樹生的事他們就談到這裏為止。晚上等母親回到自己小屋睡去以後，他從床上起來，穿好衣服，伏在書桌上給樹生寫了回信。他報告了他的近況。他也說起他和母親間的那一段談話，他請她立刻給母親寫一封表示好感的長信來。他自己也等待着她允許過的長信。封好了信，他疲倦不堪地倒在床上昏沉地睡了。

第二天早晨，不管他發着熱，他還親自把信放到母親的手裏，叮囑她趁早到郵局作為航空掛號信寄出去。母親接過信沒有說甚麼，走出房門後卻暗暗地搖頭。他沒有功夫去猜測母親的心思。他

fever had returned and his cheeks were flushed, his eyes glistened with hope as if he were expecting a miracle.

He had to stay in bed for four days to regain his strength and energy after writing that one long letter. A week went by without the mailman calling at the door. But her letter came the following week, registered airmail as before. When he opened it, his heart was pounding violently; by the time he finished reading it, his face had sunk. It was a brief letter enclosing a postal money order. She said she was busy with the opening of the bank and had no time to write.

"What did she say in the letter?" his mother asked.

"She's fine but she's busy," he replied curtly. Giving the letter and the money order to her, he added, "You'd better keep them."

She took them with knitted eyebrows. She did not say anything.

"Mother, from now on please give the wash to the laundry woman. Don't be too frugal. Shu-sheng will send us money every month," he said.

Frowning, she replied, "The money we have is not going to last very long. It's only a little more than ten thousand *yüan*."

"But you've forgotten the money Shu-sheng left," he reminded her.

"We've used even a little of that. The rest is probably not enough to pay for Hsiao Hsüan's tuition. Last semester the tuition was over twenty thousand, and for the coming semester it'll be well over fifty thousand." Getting no response from her son, she went on, "I think we'd better send Hsiao Hsüan to a public school. He is a child of poor parents and he has no reason to go to that exclusive school."

"But it was his mother's idea, and I think it'd be best to leave him

的臉頰發紅(因為發熱)，兩眼射出希望的光輝，他好像在盼望着奇跡。

為了寫這一封信，他多睡了四天。可是一個星期白白地過去了，郵差就沒有叩過他的門。在第二個星期裏面她的信來了。同樣的航空掛號信。他拆信時，心顫抖得厲害。但是他讀完信，臉卻沉下來了。一張郵局匯票，一張信箋。信箋上只有寥寥幾行字。銀行開幕在即，她忙，仍然沒有功夫寫長信，家用款由郵局飛匯。

「她信裏怎樣說？」母親問道，她看見了他的表情。

「她很好，很忙，」他短短地答道。他把匯票和信封遞給他母親：「這個交給你吧。」

母親接了過來。她皺了皺眉，一句話也不說。

「媽，以後衣服給洗衣大娘去洗吧。今天說定了啊，」他說。「你也不必太省儉了，橫順樹生按月寄錢來。」

「不過這萬把塊錢也不經用啊，」母親蹙額說。

「媽，你忘了她留下的那筆安家費，」他提醒她道。

「我們不是已經動用了一點嗎？剩下的恐怕還不夠繳小宣的學食費，上次是兩萬多點。這學期說不定要五萬多了。」她看見他不答話，停了片刻又接下去說：「其實我倒想讓他換個學校。我們窮家子弟何必讀貴族學堂？進國立中學可以省許多錢。」

「這是他母親的意思，我看還是讓他讀下去吧。他上次考了個備

at the same school. At the entrance examination he only qualified as an alternate. His mother went through a lot of trouble getting him admitted." Regardless of their poverty, he was unwilling to oppose Shu-sheng's wishes.

"Then you should write to her, tell her that there isn't enough for tuition and that she should raise the money," she said.

He promised her that he would, even though he had not decided whether or not to mention the subject in his next letter.

"Maybe we should have Hsiao Hsüan live at home. At least he can keep us company." She changed the subject.

"No, in his letter he said he planned to stay with a classmate near the school during the vacation. They could review their school work together. Leave him alone. Why call him home?"

"But you're so lonely. If Hsiao Hsüan is home, he can liven up the place a little," she said sympathetically.

"But I'm afraid he may catch my disease. He's young, and his resistance is low," he whispered.

Though convinced by his arguments, she felt depressed. No sooner did she walk away to go to the window than she returned to him and said gently, "Relax. Don't think about your illness so much. You're still young and you shouldn't always torment yourself."

Raising his head slightly and looking at her, he nodded. "I know. Please don't worry."

She felt fate had been too cruel to him. In a burst of emotion, she said, "I can take this kind of life. I'm a useless old woman, but why do you have to live like this?"

"Mother, you'll be all right. If only we can last until the day of

取，他母親費了大力輾轉托人講情他才能夠進去，」他不以為然地說。他想：我不能夠違反她的意思。

「那麼你寫信提醒她，說學費還不夠，要她早想辦法，」她說。

「好，」他應了一聲。他還沒有決定要不要在信裏寫出那種話。

「我想還是叫小宣回家來住吧，他回來也多一個人跟你作伴，」母親換了話題說。

他想了想，才說，「他既然來信說，假期內到學堂附近同學家去住，溫習功課方便，就讓他去吧，何必又叫他回來？」

「我看你也實在太寂寞了，他回來，家裏也多點熱氣，」母親帶着憐惜地說。

「不過我怕他會染到我的病。他最好跟我隔開，他年紀太輕，容易傳染到的，」他用低沉的聲音說。

「好吧，就依你，」母親簡短地說，她心裏難過，臉上卻裝出平靜的樣子。她走開了，剛走到右面窗前，她又轉回到他身邊。她慈愛地看着他：「你寬心點，不要太想你的病。你究竟還年青，不要總苦你自己。」

他略略仰起頭看母親，然後點頭說：「我知道，你放心。」

「這種生活，我過得了。我是個不中用的老太婆了。對你，實在太殘酷，你不該過這種日子，」她過了一會，忽然抑制不住感情的奔騰，她說了以上的話，她無可奈何地嘆了一口氣。

「媽，不要緊，我想我們總可以拖下去，拖到抗戰勝利的一天你

victory, then all will be well," he said, having carefully chosen the pronoun "you" to reassure his mother. For he worried that he would not last that long.

"But I'm afraid that I won't live that long," she commented gloomily. "At best, that day seems quite far away. A man who lives on the second floor told me that victory would come about the end of the year, and this is only January. I don't know how we're going to win the war."

"Well, you think too much. Now that we have the Americans fighting for us all we have to do is to wait for victory. Maybe lazy people have lazy people's luck," he said with a wry smile.

"Yes, that's true. Not long ago, everyone was so frightened because the Japanese were nearing Kweiyang. Now the enemy has retreated and business goes on as usual. The rich continue their luxurious living; bureaucrats and businessmen are just as important and as prosperous as before."

"But they're also waiting," he said with a sad smile.

"Yes, when victory comes, they'll be the ones to reap the harvest."

"Of course, that goes without saying."

They looked at each other and remained silent, feeling that they had exhausted their observations and comments on life. The room appeared exceptionally large (though it was small), and chilly (though a faint sun light came in constantly). Time seemed to have stopped as they sat listlessly. He was in the rattan chair with his back against the desk and his hands tucked into his sleeves. His head was gradually drooping as was his body. She was sitting on a stool, using one hand to prop up her chin, an elbow on the square table, her eyes blinking idly. A big rat leisurely passed in front of them; they did not want to

就好了，」他反而用話去安慰母親，他説「你」，不用「我們」，只因為他耽心，他相信，自己多半拖不到那一天。

「我怕我等不到那一天了，看起來也很渺茫，」母親感慨地説。「我今天碰到二樓 位先生，他説今年就會勝利。固然今年才開頭，還有十二個月，不過我們拿甚麼來勝利，我實在不明白。」

「你老人家也想得太多了，現在橫順有美國人替我們打仗，我們自己倒用不着麻煩，我們都是在拖，説不定懶人有懶人的福氣，」他苦笑説。

「是啦，就是這樣。前些時日本人要打到貴陽來了，大家慌張得不得了。現在日本人退了，又沒有事了，那班有錢人還是有吃有穿，做官的、做大生意的還是照樣神氣，」母親又説。

「他們也是在拖啊，」他苦笑地説。

「那麼拖到勝利一定還是他們享福，」母親憤憤不平地説。

「當然咯，這還用得着説，」他答道。

母親不再説話，她默默地望着他，他也常常掉過眼光看她。兩個人都有一種把話説盡了似的感覺。屋子顯得特別大（其實這是一個不怎麼大的房間），特別冷（雖然有陽光射進來，但陽光卻是多麼的微弱），時間好像停滯了似的。兩個人沒精打采地坐着；他坐在籐椅上，背向了書桌，兩手插在袖筒裏，頭漸漸地變重，身子漸漸往下沉；母親一隻手支着臉頰，肘拐壓在方桌上，她覺得無聊地常常眨眼睛。一隻大老鼠悠然自得地在他們面前跑來跑去，他們也不想把牠趕開。

chase it away. The room gradually darkened, seemingly to share their darkening mood, and they felt a gust of cold air rising from the floor through the soles of their shoes.

Getting up slowly from her chair, she said, "I'd better go prepare supper."

"No, it's early yet. Why don't you wait a little longer?"

She sat down again, but was unable to think of a new topic. A little later, when it was almost completely dark, she got up to make supper. He also rose from his chair, offering to help her cook.

"No, don't move. I can do it myself," she said.

"I like to move a little," he replied. "I'm tired of sitting around."

Without much appetite, they had a simple supper. After washing the dishes, they returned to their seats and chatted about trifles for a while before surrendering themselves to total silence. Yet, it was still too early to go to bed for it was only seven (according to her watch). At last it was eight-thirty. She retired to her room. And he, to his bed.

The whole winter passed thus, except that, at times, there was a blackout. When they had electricity, she would mend clothes under the light, or else retell some of her old stories for the umpteenth time. Sometimes, Hsiao Hsüan would spend a night with them, providing them with a little warmth and companionship, but only a little because the child was so quiet, somber, and bookish by nature. Sometimes Wang would feel a little better and at other times a little worse.

"What else can I do other than eat, sleep, and feel ill?" he asked himself constantly. Forever failing to find an answer, he gave up thinking about it with a bitter laugh. Once he came perilously close to finding an answer. The word "death" sent cold shivers down his spine and made him shudder. He seemed to see his own body disintegrating

房間裏漸漸地陰暗，他們的心境也似乎變得更陰暗了。他們覺得寒氣從鞋底沿着腿慢慢地爬上來。

「我去煮飯，」母親說着，懶洋洋地站起來。

「還早，等一會兒，」他哀求般地說。

母親又坐下，默默地想不出甚麼話來說。過了一陣，房間快黑盡了。她又站起，說：「現在不早了，我去煮飯。」

他也站起來。「我去給你幫忙，」他說。

「你不要動，我一個人做得過來，」她阻止道。

「動一動也好一點，一個人坐着更難過，」他說，便跟着母親一起出去了。

他們弄好一頓簡單的晚飯，單調地吃着。兩個人都沒有胃口。吃過飯，收拾了碗筷以後，兩個人又坐在原處，沒有活氣地談幾句話，於是又起了說盡了話似的感覺。看看錶（母親的錶），七點鐘，似乎很早。他們捱着時刻，終於捱到了八點半鐘，母親回到自己的小屋，他上床睡覺。

這不是他某一天的生活，整個冬天他都是這樣地過日子。不同的是有時停電，他們睡得較早，有時母親在燈下補衣服，有時母親對他講一兩段已經講過幾十遍的老故事，有時小宣回家住一夜，給屋子添一點熱氣（那個不愛講話，不愛笑的「小書獃子」又能夠添多少熱氣呢！」），有時他身體較好，有時他精神很壞。

「我除了吃、睡、病，還能夠做甚麼？」他常常這樣問自己。永遠得不着一個回答。他帶着絕望的苦笑撇開了這個問題。有一次他似乎得到回答了，那一個可怕的字（死）使他脊樑上起了寒慄，使他

in the grave and worms crawling all over it. For many days thereafter he did not dare to think about it again.

His mother could not comfort him, nor could his wife. At least once a week Shu-sheng would write him a short letter. She was forever busy, forever asking about his health and sometimes about his mother, but she never wrote to his mother directly as he had requested her to do. From her "busyness" and the briefness of her letters, he realized that she had traveled a long way from him, a painful discovery that he could share with no one. Quietly, he would meditate upon the real distance that separated him from his wife.

XXV

THE chilly winter disappeared like a nightmare, giving way to a new season of hope. The spring breeze dissipated the thick smog which had hovered over the city and stirred the people sufficiently to make them speak optimistically about the war.

But to Wang Wen-hsüan, life changed little. Sometimes he felt better and other times worse. He took walks when he felt good, or lay in bed all day when he felt bad. In addition to preparing medication for him, his mother cooked, swept, and cleaned. Hsiao Hsüan came home once every two weeks to recount one or two stories about school. He was never talkative and rarely smiled. If there was a little excitement when he was home, then a death-like quietness prevailed when he was gone. Shu-sheng continued to write her weekly letters and to send money once a month. Each short letter used no more than two sheets of paper. She was forever busy and he remained patient. He wrote

渾身發抖，使他彷彿看見自己肉體腐爛，蛆蟲爬在全身。這以後，他好些天不敢胡思亂想。

母親不能夠安慰他，這是他的一個秘密。妻更不能給他安慰，雖然她照常寫短信來（一個星期至少一封）。她永遠是那樣地忙，她沒有一個時刻不為他的身體耽心，她每封信都問候他的母親，可是她從不曾照他的要求直接給母親寫一封信。從這一件事，從她的「忙」，從來信的「短」，他感覺到她和他離開得更遠了。他從不對母親說起妻的甚麼，可是他常常暗暗地計算他跟妻中間相距的路程。

二十五

寒冷的冬天像夢魔似地終於過去了。春天給人們帶來了希望。濃霧被春風吹散了。人們帶着笑談論戰事消息。

但是在他汪文宣的生活裏並沒有甚麼變化。他的身體仍舊是時好時壞。好時偶爾去外面走走，壞時整天躺在床上。母親照常煮飯，打掃屋子，他病時還給他煎藥。小宣兩個星期進城一次，住一個晚上，談一兩段學校的故事，話不會多，這個孩子更難得有笑容。小宣回來時，屋子裏聽不見笑聲，可是這孩子一走，屋子更顯得荒涼了。妻照樣來信、寄款，款子一月一匯，信一星期一封，她從沒有寫過兩張信箋以上。她始終是很忙。但他永遠有着耐心，他

long letters in which he fabricated lies about himself to hide his true condition. His letters to her were his only diversion and his only work.

The long spring days intensified Wang'struggle against the slow-passing hours. Once, after a cold, he almost lost his voice and could speak only hoarsely. He feared he was losing his voice permanently. As for his mother, the ageing process had sharpened its attacks on her, adding many more wrinkles to her already sorrow-laden face, and she, in turn, had less and less to say. Often mother and son would sit in the room for hours facing each other without saying a word. Often, too, he would not utter more than thirty sentences during an entire day.

Time dragged on like a sick old man pulling a rickshaw. It went so slowly that he felt it had almost come to a halt. But he was still alive, capable of feeling and thinking, despite the increasing pain in his left lung, the cold sweats at night, and the never-ending dry cough. Sometimes there was blood in his phlegm. Increasing pain took over his body, lighthearted laughter having vanished like a dream. Yet he did not groan nor did he complain. He consigned each gray day to the darkness of night but received an even grayer one the next morning. He spoke less and less, for he was afraid to further injure or even hear his hoarse voice. Sometimes out of boredom he sighed, but quietly, for he did not want his mother to hear him. Each day seemed longer than the last. It became more and more difficult for him to pass the time. Haunted by the thoughts of death, he had almost depleted his energy, and was unable to go on living.

But he was not allowed to give up the fight. His wife insisted that he wait for her return; Uncle Chung promised to get him a job; and his mother continued to bring home famous Chinese medications and Western drugs. He never knew whether these were good for him or not, but to please his mother he took them occasionally when she

常常寫長信寄去，甚至編造一些謊話。他不願意讓她知道他的實際生活情形。寫信成了他的唯一的消遣，也可以說是他唯一的工作。

春天裏日子變得更長，度日更成為一件苦事。他覺得自己快要喪失說話的能力了。他某一次受涼失了嗓音後，就一直用沙啞的聲音講話。母親更現老態，她的話也愈來愈少。常常母子兩人在屋中對坐，沒有一點聲音。有時他一天說不上三十句整句的話。

時光像一個帶病的老車夫拖着他們慢慢地在走，是那樣地慢，他有時會覺得車子已經停住了。

但是他仍然活着，仍然有感情，仍然有思想。他左胸時常隱隱發痛。他夜間帶出冷汗，他常常乾咳。偶爾他也暗暗地吐一兩口血——那只是痰裏帶血。痛苦繼續着並且不斷地增加，而歡樂的笑聲卻已成了遠去了的渺茫的夢。

他沒有呻吟，也沒有抱怨。他默默地送走一天灰色的日子，又默默地迎接一天更灰色的日子。他的話更少，因為他害怕聽見自己的沙啞聲音。有時氣悶得無辦法，他只好長嘆，但是他不願意讓母親聽到他的嘆聲，他總是背着人嘆息。

日子愈來愈長，也愈難捱。一個念頭折磨着他：他的精神力量快要竭盡，他不能再拖下去了。

但是沒有人允許他不拖下去。妻還是叮囑他安心等待她回來。鍾老答應設法替他找適當的工作。母親不斷地買藥給他吃。她拿回來的有中國的丹方，也有西洋的名藥。他不知道那些藥對他的身體

insisted. Once she persuaded him to go to a public hospital. He waited for three hours in an overcrowded waiting room which opened onto a chilly courtyard before he was casually examined by an impersonal doctor with a mustache. The doctor, after instructing him to unbutton his clothes, taking his pulse and tapping his body here and there, gave him a prescription for a bottle of medicine to be taken at home and advised him to come back the following week for a fluorescent examination. The doctor pointed out that an X-ray would be better, but that a fluorescent examination was cheaper. Wang inquired later at the office about the cost of this "cheaper" examination and found that even it was prohibitively expensive. He went back to the hospital once and received the same treatment and the same advice. After estimating the expense of that month and conjecturing about the usefulness of an examination, he said to himself, "Let what is to come, come; I don't care about anything." Thus he decided to save his money and to surrender his life to fate, which was about the only thing he could do.

One beautiful day after lunch he went out for a walk. The same dusty streets were still crowded with cars, the traffic conditions still chaotic, and the same unsightly garbage still piled on each street corner. Covering his nose, he walked along the streets. Unwittingly his feet took him to the International Café, where his eyes dwelt on several birthday cakes and all sorts of American candy in its display window. He was surprised that the display was about the same and that things in general had changed so little except that he no longer heard his wife's bewitching laughter or saw her alluring figure.

For purely sentimental reasons, he entered the café and sat at the same round table where he had sat with her. Two white uniformed waiters were busy moving among the many boisterous customers who were trying to outshout one another in giving their orders. Timidly he sat in a corner, waiting quietly.

有無益處，他只是順從地斷斷續續地吃着。他這樣做大半是為了敷衍母親。有一次母親還拉着他到公立醫院去看病。他掛着普通號，足足等候了三個鐘點。母親已經讓步到拉他去醫院了。他也只有忍耐地等待着他們的輪值，不管候診室裏怎樣擁擠，天井內怎樣冷（那還是春天到來以前的事）。一個八字鬚的醫生對他擺出一張冰凍了的面孔，醫生吩咐他解開衣服，聽了脈，又各處敲敲，然後皺着眉，搖搖頭，又叫他穿好衣服，開一個方，去藥劑室購了一瓶藥水。醫生似乎不願意多講話，只吩咐他下星期去「透視」。醫生說照X光最好，不過「透視」費低。他出來在詢問處問明了透視費的數目，他吐了吐舌頭，默默地走出了醫院。後來他又去過一次醫院，那個醫生仍舊吩咐他下星期去透視。他計算一下這一個月已經用去了若干錢，又猜想透視以後會有甚麼樣的結果，他不敢再到醫院去了。

「要來的終於要來，一切讓它去吧，」他對自己說。他頗想「聽命於天」了。事實上除了這裏他的心也沒有一個安放處。

有一天午飯後他出街散步。天氣很好，不過街上仍多塵土，車輛擁擠不堪，而且秩序壞，在一個路角堆了大堆垃圾，從那裏散佈出來一股一股的的霉臭。他掩着鼻走過了一條街。無意間側頭一看，他正立在國際咖啡廳的玻璃櫥窗前。櫥窗裏陳列着幾個生日大蛋糕，和好幾種美國糖果。一切都和幾個月前一樣。不同的是他再聽不見那一個人的笑聲，再看不見那一個亭亭的身影。

他進去了。廳子裏客人相當多，剛巧他從前坐過的那張小圓桌正空着，他便擠到裏面去坐下來。兩個茶房忙碌地端着盤子各處奔走。客人們正在競賽叫喚茶房的聲音的高低。他膽怯地坐在角落裏，默默地等待着。

A waiter finally came to take his order. "Two cups of coffee," he whispered.

"Eh?" the waiter queried rudely.

"Two cups of coffee," he repeated, raising his voice.

The waiter walked away abruptly and returned shortly with two cups, one of which he put before Wang and the other across from him. "Milk in your coffee?" the waiter asked, holding a can of milk. Wang shook his head no. Pointing at the other cup he added, "That cup takes it." The waiter glared at him, poured some milk into the cup, and left. Wang put a teaspoon of sugar into the cup opposite him, stirred it a bit, and then put some sugar in his own cup.

"Go ahead and drink," he said to the empty seat across from him, fantasizing that Shu-sheng was there. Remembering how much she enjoyed coffee with milk, he imagined he saw her smiling at him. He swallowed a mouthful of coffee with pleasure. But when he looked at the other cup again, he found it untouched and the seat empty. He took another sip, and the smile of a moment ago became sour. "Do you still remember me?" he whispered on the brink of tears. Stealthily he looked at the other patrons at the café who were talking excitedly in a mist of tobacco smoke, unaware of his presence.

A chubby fellow wearing a Sun Yat-sen-style suit* shouted exultantly, "I guarantee you that Germany will surrender in two months and Japan in less than a year. I predict we will celebrate the New Year in Nanking."

---

*A close-fitting jacket with buttons down the front and a pair of pockets on the chest, usually made of khaki in summer and flannel in winter. It was designed by Dr. Sun Yat-sen and during the wartime period this was commonly, though not exclusively, worn by government officials.

一個穿白制服的茶房終於走過來了。「兩杯咖啡，」他低聲說。

「嗯？」茶房不客氣地問。

「兩杯咖啡，」他提高聲音再說。

茶房不回答，猝然轉身走了。過了一會這茶房端了兩個杯子走回來，一杯咖啡，放在他面前，另一杯放在他對面。「要牛奶嗎？」茶房拿起牛奶罐頭問道。他搖搖頭說：「我不要。」又指着對面那個杯子說：「這杯要。」茶房瞪了他一眼，把牛奶注入杯中便拿着罐頭走開了。他拿起茶匙舀了糖先放進對面的杯裏，又用茶匙在杯裏攪了一下，然後才在自己杯中放糖。

「你喝吧」，他端起杯子對着空座位低聲說。在想像中樹生就坐在他的對面，她是喜歡喝牛奶咖啡的。他彷彿看見她對他微笑。他高興地喝了一大口。他微笑了。他睜大眼睛看對面。位子空着，滿滿的一杯咖啡不曾被人動過。他又喝了一口。他嘴上還留着剛才的微笑，但這笑容慢慢地在變化，現在是淒涼的微笑了。「你還會記着我麼？」他小聲說，他的心顫得厲害。他覺得鼻酸。他連忙掉開臉去看別人了。四座都是煙霧，人們在高談闊論，大抽香煙。沒有誰注意到他。

「我敢寫保票，不到兩個月德國就會投降。日本也熬不過一年。説不定我們會在南京過下一個新年！」旁邊一張桌上一個穿中山裝的大塊頭眉飛色舞地大聲說。

The news stunned him and he cast another glance at the man. The prediction produced a strange feeling in him: he was not elated, only a little envious of the speaker. Reluctantly bidding farewell to the empty seat with the full cup of coffee in front of it, he paid the check and went home.

His mother was coming out of the apartment with a pile of wet wash.

"Mother, why are you washing clothes again?" he asked in surprise.

"It's all right. I can wash," she replied, smiling.

"You mustn't try to save money. You mustn't overwork yourself," he said in disappointment.

"The laundry woman has raised her price again. With the little money that Shu-sheng sends, we can't afford to have her do the wash," she growled. "Prices have shot up, but not our income. What choice do I have?"

He had no answer. He watched her carry the laundry up to the sun terrace, and then sullenly stepped into the room. He did not want to sit, to lie down, or to read, so he paced around the room asking himself why his wife was always busy, why she had written him only brief notes and why she was so secretive about her life. He was puzzled and disturbed. There was no answer; perhaps there would never be an answer.

Someone was coming. Heavy footsteps. A mailman pushed the door open, speaking in a loud voice, "Wang Wen-hsüan, a letter for you. Stamp the receipt."

He took the letter from the mailman — a thick letter with lots of stamps on it. He recognized the handwriting as Shu-sheng's.

Happily he stamped his seal on the receipt and thanked the mailman profusely.

他吃了一驚。他看看說話的人。這預言給他帶來一種奇特的感覺。他沒有快樂，他卻感到了羨慕和妒忌。他又望了一下空座位和滿杯的咖啡，他無可奈何地嘆了一口氣，他站起來付了帳走出去了。

回到家，他正碰見母親捧着一堆濕衣服從房裏出來。

「媽，你怎麼又自己洗起衣服來？」他驚問道。

「不要緊，我可以洗，」母親笑答道。

「其實你不應該省這點錢，你也該少累點，」他失望地說。

「可是洗衣服大娘又漲價了，樹生只寄來那麼一點錢，不省怎麼夠用！」母親略帶煩躁地說。「從過年到現在物價不知漲了多少，收入卻不見增加。我有甚麼辦法！」

他找不到答話，只好埋頭進屋，讓母親到曬台上晾衣服去。

屋子裏只有他一個人。他不想坐，不想躺，也不想看書。他只好在屋子裏踱來踱去。

「為甚麼她永遠是那樣忙？為甚麼她總是寫一些短信？為甚麼她不肯讓我知道她的生活情形？」他疑惑地、煩躁地想道。

沒有回答。他永遠找不到回答。

但是有人來打岔了。他聽見粗重的腳步聲。於是一個郵差推開門進來，大聲叫道：「汪文宣收信！蓋圖章！」

他接過來，重甸甸的一封信，郵票在信封上貼滿了。他一眼就認出樹生的筆跡。

他在一陣歡喜中蓋好圖章，把郵件回執交了給郵差。「謝謝你」他感激地對郵差說。

The long letter finally came. This was the reply he needed. Gratefully he kissed the envelope again and again. He smiled; he read the address on the envelope again and again; he forgot his worries, even his own illness.

Then he opened the envelope and took out a thick stack of sheets.

"She wrote me a long letter! She wrote me a long letter!" he exclaimed several times. He read the first word. It was his name "Hsüan." Then he put the letter back into the envelope and walked excitedly around the room a few more times. Finally, he settled down in the rattan chair and took the letter out again, prepared to savor every word.

XXVI

THE handwriting was unmistakably Shu-sheng's and every character was neatly written, but the overall tone of the letter struck a different note than her previous ones had. No longer reiterating how busy she was or the activities of the bank, she loosened her heartstrings, revealing her emotional conflict. His hands shook as he breathlessly read every word, a record of his wife's thoughts, wondering why she now chose to tell him all this and fearing the worst. The letter continued:

> ... I always knew my temper would probably destroy me and bring a lot of anguish to those who cared for me; I also know that I've given you moments of grief and sorrow in the last two or three years. I admit that I haven't been a good wife and that I've failed you in many ways. My conscience often troubles me on this account. I really don't know how to say

長信終於來了，這正是他需要的回答，他感恩地接連吻着信封。他低聲笑，他反覆唸着封面地址。他忘了自己的煩愁，甚至忘了自己的病。

於是他拆開了信，拿出厚厚的一疊信箋來。

「她給我寫長信了！她給我寫長信了！」他自己帶笑地說了幾遍。他打開了信箋，可是他只看了稱呼的「宣」字後，馬上又把信摺起，拿着它，興奮地在屋子裏走了幾轉。

最後，他在籐椅上坐下來。他從容地打開那一疊信箋，開始讀着她的來信。

二十六

那一疊信箋上全是她的筆跡，字寫得相當工整，調子卻跟往常的不同，她不再說她的「忙」和銀行的種種事情。她談着她的內心，申訴她的痛苦。他的手跟着那些字顫抖起來，他屏住氣讀下去。那些話像一把鐵爪在抓他的心。但是他禁不住要想：「她為甚麼要說這些話呢？」他已經有一種預感了。

她繼續吐露她的胸懷：

……我知道我這種脾氣也許會毀掉我自己，會給對我好的人帶來痛苦，我也知道在這兩三年中間我給你增添了不少的煩惱，我也承認這些年我在你家裏沒有做到一個好妻子。是的，我承認我也有對不起你的地方。有時我也受到良心的責備。但是……我不知道怎樣說才

> this or how to make you understand. I have felt for some time that we could never be happy together, that there is something lacking between us. When I was unreasonable and angry, you always submitted to me, never saying one harsh word; you only looked entreatingly at me. I hate that look. Why were you so weak? How many times have I wished that you'd fight back, that you'd do something ungentlemanly and turn our world completely upside down! Had you done so, I'd have felt fulfilled; but you'd only beg, sigh, and cry. When a quarrel ended, I always wanted to apologize to you, and to promise that I'd be nice to you next time. I could only pity you, but I was never able to love you.

A knock at the door interrupted him. Someone was calling outside, "Lao Wang."* Startled, he at once slipped the letter inside his gown just before Uncle Chung walked in.

"Lao Wang, good to find you home. How have you been? You didn't go out today, did you?" Uncle Chung said with a big smile on his face.

"Please sit down, sit down," Wang said courteously, smiling reluctantly, his interest centered on the letter. "Have you been busy?" he asked Chung casually while fetching his friend some water to drink. His movements were very slow as the image of Shu-sheng dominated him.

"No tea, no tea. I just had some," Chung said politely.

"We have only water. Please have some," he said, feeling ashamed, while putting a glass of water before his guest.

"I like water, I like water," Uncle Chung said. "It's hygienic." He drank some, put the glass down and went on, "Your mother isn't home? Is she well?"

---

* "Lao Wang" means "Old Wang." It is customary to address a friend in this manner as a sign of familiarity.

好，我不知道怎樣才能夠使你明白我的意思……特別是近一兩年，我總覺得，我們在一起不會幸福，我們中間缺少一些東西，你不了解我。常常我發脾氣，你對我讓步。不用惡聲回答，你只用哀求的眼光看我。我就怕看你這種眼光。我就討厭你這種眼光。你為甚麼這麼軟弱！那些時候我多麼希望你跟我吵一架，甚而鬧得天翻地覆，我也會感到痛快。可是你只會哀求，只會嘆氣，只會哭。事後我總是後悔，我常常想向你道歉。我對自己說，以後應當對你好一點，可是我只能憐憫你，我不能愛你。……

突然一下叩門聲打岔了他。一個人在門外大聲叫：「老汪！」

他大吃一驚，連忙把信箋摺起往懷裏揣。鍾老已經走進來了。

「老汪，你在家，近來好嗎？沒有出街？」鍾老滿面笑容大聲說。

「請坐，請坐，」他客氣地說，他勉強地笑了笑，他的心還在信箋上。「近來很忙吧，」他隨口說，他一面倒開水敬客。他舉動遲緩，他的眼前還有一張女人的臉在搖跎，那是樹生的臉，臉上帶着嚴肅的表情。

「不喝茶，不喝茶，剛才喝了來的，」鍾老連忙點着頭，客氣地說。

「我們這裏只有開水，隨便用一杯吧，」他端了一杯白開水放在鍾老面前，略帶羞慚地埋頭說。

「我喝開水，我喝開水，」鍾老陪笑說，「喝開水衛生。」接過來喝了一口，放下杯子，又說：「伯母不在家，近來好吧？」朝四周看了看。

"She is fine. Thank you," he responded with a brief smile. His heart was still pounding, his thoughts still on the letter. "My mother just went out," he said, suddenly remembering Chung's question. He did not tell his friend that his mother was hanging the wash on the rooftop.

"I've some good news for you," Uncle Chung said pleasantly. "Chief Editor Chou has been transferred and the new Chief Editor is a nice man. Yesterday he talked to me about you, and he feels quite sympathetic toward you. He is willing to give you your old job. He asked me to talk to you first. You'd have no problem getting the job back."

"Yes, yes," he responded, smiling weakly, without showing much interest. His eyes wandered as though he were not listening.

"When can you come back to work?" Chung asked, a little disappointed at Wang's attitude. Chung thought that he would have been very pleased with the news but there was no sign of it.

"Maybe in a few days. Ah! Thank you for thinking of me," he said, raising his voice a little. He was about to put on a smile, but he changed his mind. His face was expressionless.

"How have you been? Are you well?" Chung said with some concern this time.

"I am all right. I can still manage," he answered darting a surprised look at his friend and shaking his head. He wondered, "Does Shu-sheng want to separate from me?" His face reddened with emotion, and its muscles twitched.

"Then, you'd better come to work as soon as possible. If you wait too long, the situation might change again. This is a rare opportunity," Chung reminded him after a pause.

"Yes, I will be there in a few days," he answered briefly, almost

「還好，謝謝你，」他也笑笑，但立刻又收斂了笑容，他的心還在咚咚地跳，他的思想始終在那一疊信箋上盤旋。「家母剛剛出去，」他忽然想起了對方的問話，便慌忙地加上一句。他沒有說出他母親在曬台上晾衣服。

「我有個好消息來報告你，」鍾老略現得意之態説，「公司裏周主任調走了。新主任人還不錯。昨天我跟他談起老兄的事，他很同情你，他想請老兄回去，仍舊擔任原來的職務，他要我來先同老兄談談，那麼老兄的工作沒有問題了。」

「是，是，」他答道，他只淡淡地笑了笑，他並沒有現出十分欣喜的表情。他的眼睛望着別處，他好像並不在聽對方講話兒的。

「那麼老兄甚麼時候去上班？」鍾老問道，他的反應使鍾老感到驚訝。鍾老原以為他會熱烈地歡迎他帶來的好消息，卻想不到他連一點興奮的表示也沒有。

「過兩天吧。啊，謝謝你關照，」他驚醒般地說，還提高了聲音。他剛要做一個笑容，卻在中途改變了主意，仍舊板起臉孔來。

「你身體怎樣？還有甚麼不舒服嗎？」鍾老又問，這次帶着關心的樣子。

「沒有甚麼，我還好，」他吃驚地看了對方一眼，搖頭回答。心裏在想：樹生寫這封信來有甚麼用意，難道她真要——他的臉突然發紅，臉上肌肉搐動了起來。

「那麼你早點來上班吧，日子久了，恐怕又要發生變化。這個機會也很難得，」鍾老停了片刻又叮囑道。

「是的，我過兩天一定來，」他短短地答道，又不作聲了。鍾老

hinting that he would like to be left alone.

Chung looked at him, puzzled. He knew that Wang must have some private worry on his mind, but thought it would be improper for him to enquire. He felt that carrying on a conversation would not interest his host very much, and therefore, after a few more words, this kindhearted old man said he had to go.

Wang did not ask his guest to stay any longer, but accompanied him to the staircase. Chung politely urged him to go no further, but he insisted on going down with Chung to the main entrance on the ground floor.

"My old friend, please come back to work as soon as possible," said Chung again.

"Yes, I will," he responded politely.

Then he rushed back upstairs, accidentally bumping into a maid who was carrying a pot of hot water, a few drops of which spilled on his feet. It was so scaldingly hot that he yelled in pain. The maid cursed him and he apologized to her for his carelessness. Bearing the pain he ran upstairs. His thoughts still concentrated on the letter, he had no interest in anything else. Even Uncle Chung's "good news" did not bring him any joy.

He returned to his room. His mother was not in, though she should have returned from hanging up the wash. Her absence gave him a perfect chance to read the letter. Sitting in the rattan chair, he took it out. Even before he read, his heart was beating very fast and his hands were trembling.

> ... I've told you the truth. Please believe me. We can't be happy together now or later. I don't say that you're completely responsible for this, or that I'm faultless. Together, however, we only make each other and

驚詫地看了他一眼，知道他一定有甚麼心事，卻又不便問他。多講話也引不起他的興趣。這個好心的老人再坐一會，又講了幾句話，覺得沒趣便告辭走了。

他也不留客，便陪着鍾老走出房來，到了樓梯口，鍾老客氣地要他留步，他卻堅持着把客人送到大門。

「老兄，請早點來上班啊，」鍾老在大門口和他分別時又叮囑了一次。

「一定來，」他恭敬地點頭答道。他轉過身急急走上樓去，在過道裏他撞在一個女傭人身上，那個女人提着一壺開水，開水濺了好幾滴到他的腳背上，燙得他叫出聲來。女傭人破口大罵，他連忙道了歉，忍住痛逃回樓上去了。他的心仍然被束縛在那一疊信箋上，任何別的事情都不能使他關心。甚至鍾老的「喜訊」也沒有給他帶來快樂。

他回到房裏，母親還是不在，照理她應該曬好衣服回房來了，她不在正好給他一個安心讀信的機會。他在籐椅上坐下，又把妻的信拿出來讀着。他還沒有開始，心就咚咚地大跳，兩隻手像發寒顫似地抖起來。

他在信箋上找到先前被打斷了的地方，從那裏繼續讀下去：

……我說的全是真話。請你相信我。像我們這樣地過日子，我覺得並沒有幸福，以後也不會有幸福。我不能說這全是你的錯，也不能說我自己就沒有錯。我們彼此痛苦，也使你母親痛苦，她也使你我痛

your mother miserable, and she makes me miserable, too. I don't understand why it should be like that. It's neither your fault nor mine. I don't believe it is fate, but only the result of an unfortunate set of circumstances. I'm not like you or your mother. Your mother is old, and you're weak and sickly. But I'm young and full of life, and I can't adapt to your monotonous life or spend the rest of my days amidst quarrels and family discord. I am gregarious by nature, and I want to live my life to the fullest. At home with you, I can only wither away like a cut flower in an old monastery. I won't tell you any lies. I really tried to be a good wife and mother; I never hated you. I really wanted to make you happy. But I've failed miserably. In truth I have tried my best in resisting many temptations. I once swore I'd be with you forever, loving you, comforting you, and staying by you in poverty. Every time I tried, I failed.

The kinder you are to me, the more your mother hates me. Toward her I have no ill feelings but only pity for her misfortunes. She may brag about her education and her moral character; the undeniable fact is that at her age she has to slave like a maid — cooking, washing, and cleaning the house, none of which she can do well. Probably she thinks of me as the mistress who enslaved her and that is why she hates me so much. I still remember the cruel and pleased smirk she had on her face when she denounced me as your mistress. Please forgive me for talking about her in such a way. I don't hate her. Why should I? She has already suffered much more than I have, and I won't be quarreling with her any more. You know she was technically right in stressing that we had never been formally married, and that, therefore, I was only your mistress. So now I want to make a formal announcement: I don't want to be your mistress any more. I want to leave you. Maybe I will marry someone else; maybe I will remain single. But what is certain is that from now on I want no part of your life nor to remain your mistress....

He cried in anguish. It was as if someone had dealt him a hard, painful blow. He heard the dull ringing of a gong in his ears and was on the verge of fainting. He was so dazed by the shock that only after some rest was he able to breathe normally again. The sheets of the letter were all over the floor.

苦。我想不出這是為了甚麼。並且我們也沒有方法免除或減輕這痛苦。這不是一個人的錯。我們誰也怨不得誰。不過我不相信這是命。至少這過錯應該由環境負責。我跟你和你母親都不同。你母親年紀大了，你又體弱多病。我還年青，我的生命力還很旺盛。我不能跟着你們過刻板似的單調日子，我不能在那種單調的吵架、寂寞的忍受中消磨我的生命。我愛動，愛熱鬧，我需要過熱情的生活。我不能在你那古廟似的家中枯死。我不會對你説假話：我的確想過，試過做一個好妻子，做一個賢妻良母。我對你始終沒有惡感，我的確願意竭力使你快樂。但是我沒有能夠做到，我做不到。我自己其實也費了不少的心血，我拒絕了種種的誘惑。我曾經發願終身不離開你、體貼你、安慰你，跟你一起度過這些貧苦日子。但是我試一次，失敗一次。你不了解我這番苦心，不管你怎樣對我好(你並沒有對不起我的地方。)你母親愈來愈恨我。她似乎把我恨入骨髓。其實我只有可憐她，人到老年，反而嘗到貧苦滋味。她雖然自誇學問如何，德行如何，可是到了五十高齡，卻還來做一個二等老媽，做飯、洗衣服、打掃房屋，哪一樣她做得出色！ 她好像把我看作在奴使她的主人，所以她那樣恨我。我至今還記着她罵我為你的「姘頭」時那種得意而殘忍的表情。

這些都是空話，請恕我在你面前談你母親。我並不恨她，她過的生活比我苦過若干倍，我何必恨她。而且以後我同她也不會再有衝突的機會。她説得不錯，我們沒有正式結婚，我只是你的「姘頭」。所以現在我正式對你説明，我以後不做你的「姘頭」了，我要離開你。我也許跟別人結婚，也許獨身一輩子，總之，我不願意再回到你的家，過「姘頭」的生活……

他痛苦地叫了一聲。彷彿誰在他的耳邊敲着大鑼。他整個頭都震昏了。過了半晌他才吐出一口氣來。信箋已經散落在地上了，他

Perspiring, he hurriedly picked them up and greedily read the rest:

> Hsüan, please forgive me. I am not joking with you, I'm dead serious. I've reached my decision only after long hours of soul searching. There'll be no happiness for either of us if we live together again, only mutual humiliation and suffering. We must be separated; we can be friends. Together, we will be enemies. Perhaps you will feel sad about losing me, but I am thirty-four and I can't afford to wait any longer in my battle against age and time. A woman's life is very short. I'm not selfish, I just want to live my life to the fullest. I need freedom. It's a pity I've never lived a life like that, and why shouldn't I? A person lives only once and if one misses the chance, it's gone. In the interest of my own future I must leave you. I want freedom. I know you will forgive me. I don't want to say I'm divorcing you because, according to your mother, we never married, so there's no legal action to be taken. I don't want any alimony or any kind of paper from you — I don't demand the custody of my child. I want nothing from you, and I will continue to help you get well. Only, from today on, I am no longer your wife, no longer Mrs. Wang. You may, someday, find someone who understands you, who loves you and has a sweet temper. I've failed you and my son, and I'm not worthy to be your wife or his mother. Perhaps you will take this separation hard, but time heals all wounds, and in one or two years you'll have forgotten me. There are many who are better than I am, and I hope you will find one that fits your mother's specifications — or, better yet, let her select one for you and have a formal wedding.

He groaned, tearing desperately at his hair. The pain in his left side became more pronounced and spread over his entire chest. Why should she wound him so? Every word stabbed him like a sharp knife, making his blood boil. What had he done to her that she should hate him so? Such deep hatred. If it were really her freedom she was looking for, she had no need to use those words against a defenseless man. He raised his head and heaved a long sigh. "Why should calamities fall on me alone? Why punish me? What have I done?" he wanted to say.

連忙拾起來，貪婪地讀下去。他額上冒汗。身上也有點潤濕。

> 宣，請你原諒我，我不是在跟你賭氣，也不是同你開玩笑。我說真話，而且我是經過長期考慮的。我們在一起生活，只是互相折磨，互相損害。我們必須分開。分開後我們或許還可以做朋友，在一起我們終有一天會變做路人。我知道在這時候離開你，也許使你難過，不過我已經三十四歲了，我不能再讓歲月蹉跎。我們女人的時間短得很。我並非自私，我只是想活，想活得痛快。我要自由。可憐我一輩子就沒有痛快地活過。
>
> 為甚麼不該痛快地好好活一次呢？人一生就只能活一次，一旦錯過了機會，甚麼都完了。所以為了我自己的前途，我必須離開你。我要自由。我知道你會原諒我、同情我。
>
> 我不向你提出「離婚」的字眼，因為據你母親說，我們根本就沒有結過婚。所以我們分開也用不着甚麼手續。我向你討贍養費，也不向你要甚麼字據。我更不要求把小宣帶走。我甚麼都不要，我還願意繼續幫忙你養病。從今天起我不是你的妻子，不再是汪太太了。你可以另外找一個能夠了解你，而且愛你，而且脾氣好的女人做你的太太。我對你沒有好處，我不是一個賢妻良母的典型。這些年來我的確有對不住你，對不住小宣的地方，我不配做你的妻子同他的母親。我不是一個好女人。可是我生就這種脾氣，我自己也沒有辦法。離開我，你也許會難過一些時候，但是至多也不會超過一兩年，以後你就會忘記我。比我好的女人多得很，我希望填我這個空位的女人會使你母親滿意。你最好讓她替你選擇，並且叫新人坐花轎行拜堂的大禮。……

他發出一聲呻吟，一隻手瘋狂似地抓自己的頭髮。他的左胸痛得厲害，現在好像不單是左胸，他整個胸部都在發痛。她為甚麼要這樣兇狠地傷害他？她應該知道每一個字像是一根鋒利的針刺，每根針都在渴望他的心血。他在甚麼事上得罪了她？她對他的恨竟然是這麼深！單是為了自由，她不會用這些針刺對待一個毫無抵抗的人！想到這裏，他抬起頭呼冤似地長嘆了一聲。他想說：「為甚麼一切的災禍全落在我的頭上？為甚麼單單要懲罰我一個人？我究竟做過了甚麼事？」

There was no reply. He could not find an impartial judge to preside over his case; nor could he find anyone to share his burden. In a daze he stared at the ceiling. What was he staring at? He did not know. Some time later, he remembered he had to finish reading the letter. Lowering his head, he read:

(Here two and a quarter lines had been inked out. He could not decipher them.) I don't know why I have written so much except I want freedom. Hsüan, please forgive me. You see, I too have changed a great deal. I don't want to talk about the ideals we once had; I have no right to talk about them living in an age and a life like mine! I am a woman and I have never hurt anyone, nor done anything wicked. But what else can I do? Hsüan, don't cry; let me go; let me go with a willing heart. Forget me; don't even think of me. I'm not worthy of you, but I'm not a bad woman; my only fault is that I treasure freedom and happiness.

I don't want to write to Hsiao Hsüan, so please explain everything to him for me, for I can't do it properly and, before long, I may even lose the right to be called his mother. Please understand that I am not leaving you to marry another, though someone has proposed to me. But if you won't let me go freely, if you won't forget me, then I will have to marry him to force you to let me go.

Please forgive me; don't think that I'm a bad woman. Say a few kind words to Mother for me. Now that I am no longer her mistressed-daughter-in-law, she can save her energy by not hating me. Please take care of your health. I will continue to send money monthly. Don't let Hsiao Hsüan stop his schooling, and please allow me to write you regularly. I wish you good health. If possible, let me have an early reply, even if it be but a few words.

Shu-sheng

This was the end of the letter and he thought it marked the end of his life as well. In utter despair he slumped in his chair in a death-like trance. When his mother called him, he was startled and unclenched his hands, dropping the many pages of the letter on the floor.

沒有回答。他找不到一個公正的裁判官。這時候他甚至找不到一個人來分擔他的痛苦。他呆呆地望着天花板，他在望甚麼呢？他自己也不知道。

過了一些時候，他忽然想起了未讀完的信，才埋下頭把眼光放在信箋上繼續讀着：

(這裏還有兩行又四分之一的字被塗掉了，他看不出是甚麼字。)我不知道為甚麼要寫了那許多話。我的本意其實就只有那一點。我要自由。宣，請你原諒我。你看，我也改變得多了。這樣的時代和這樣的生活，我一個女人，我又沒有害過人，做過壞事，我有甚麼辦法呢？不要跟我談過去那些理想，我們已經沒有資格談教育、談理想了。宣，不要難過，你讓我走吧，你好好地放走我吧。忘記我，不要再想我。我配不上你。但我並不是一個壞女人。我的錯處只有一個：我追求自由與幸福。

小宣那裏我不想去信，請你替我向他解釋。我自己說不明白。而且說不定在不久的將來我就要失去做他母親的權利。不過我希望你們不要誤會，我並不是為了要同別人結婚才離開你，雖然已經有人向我求婚，我至今還沒有答應。不過要是你不肯放走我，要是你還不肯忘記我，那麼我就只好同別人結婚，來使你斷念。

請原諒我，不要把我看作一個壞女人。在你母親面前也請替我說幾句好話。我現在不是她的『姘頭』媳婦了。她用不着再花費精神來恨我。望你千萬保重身體，安心養病。行裏的安家費仍舊按月寄上。不要使小宣學業中斷。並且請你允許我繼續同你通信。祝你健康。

倘使可能，盼早日給我回音，就是幾個字也好。

樹生　×月××日

信完了，他也完了。他頹然倒在椅背上。他閃着眼睛，死去似地過了好一會兒。忽然他被母親喚醒了。他吃驚地把胸部一挺，手一鬆，那一疊信箋又落在地上。

"Mother, you went to hang the wash. What took you so long?" he asked.

"I went out. Hsüan, why aren't you in bed?" she said. Upon seeing the sheets of paper on the floor, she asked,"Where did they come from?" and proceeded to pick them up.

"Mother, let me do it," he said, bending down. "It's a letter from Shu-sheng," he added, answering her question.

"Such a long letter. What did she say?" she asked.

"Nothing much," he answered evasively and proceeded to hide the letter in his pocket.

"Did she say anything derogatory about me? I'm not worried. Let her say whatever she wants about me," she said, noticing his strange behavior.

"She didn't mention you, just about her life in Lanchow and Manager Ch'en ..., " he loudly defended Shu-sheng. His voice becoming hoarse, he stopped in the middle of the sentence.

Guessing that the letter must be of a delicate nature, she changed the subject, "I just met Mr. Chung outside. He said you could have your old job back. I asked him to request the new Chief Editor, if he is kind and sympathetic, to allow you to stay home for another two months. If Chung speaks to him, there shouldn't be any problem."

"I want to go back to work tomorrow," he said with determination, his face expressionless.

"Why such a hurry? Wait until Chung brings a reply from the Chief Editor."

"Chung told me to come to work as soon as possible; he said the situation might change if I waited too long," he replied. Hiding his

「媽，你晾衣服，怎麼這樣久才回來？」他問道。

「我出去了。宣，你怎麼不到床上去睡？」母親說。她看見落在地上的信箋，便問道：「哪個寫來的信？」她走去想拾起信箋。

「媽，等我來，」他連忙俯下身子去檢信，一面解釋似地加上一句：「樹生的信。」

「寫得這樣長，她說些甚麼？」母親再問。

「她沒有說甚麼，」他慌張地回答，立刻把信揣在懷裏，顯然他在掩飾。母親想，一定是那媳婦在對丈夫說她的壞話。她忍不住又說：

「她一定在講我的壞話，我不怕，讓她講好了。」

「媽，她沒有講你，她在講別的事，講——她那邊的生活，陳經理對她……」他大聲替寫信人辯護道，可是他說到一半，他的聲音啞了，他只得中途閉了嘴。

母親注意到這情形，她不再談論那封信了。她想起另一件事，便換過話題說：

「剛才我碰見鍾先生，他說已經跟你講過，你的事情已經弄好了，你可以回公司做事。不過我說，如果新來的主任容易說話，最好讓你多休息兩個月再去上班，只要他幫忙先講好，就不會有問題了。」

「我想，明天就去，」他忽然說，他板着臉孔，沒有絲毫欣喜的表情。

「何必這樣急，等鍾先生來回話以後再去也不遲，」母親說。

「鍾老要我早點去，他說日子久了恐怕會發生變化，」他抑制了

emotions as best as he could, he tried to speak in a nonchalant tone, though he felt that the germs were not only eating his lungs but also his heart.

"But tomorrow is too soon. Maybe the day after tomorrow. I plan to prepare a dinner tomorrow for physician Chang Po-ch'ing, who has never been properly rewarded for treating you," she said in a seemingly jovial mood.

But he knew that she was just hiding something. "What have you sold or pawned this time?" he asked loudly. "Why are you getting rid of everything you have?"

With an even more unnatural smile on her face, she answered, "Don't worry about me. Please don't."

"Just think, if I die, what will you do? How are you going to support yourself?" he asked her, as if arguing with her.

"Don't worry about that. I'll die before you. If I don't, there is Hsiao Hsüan. He'll soon be an adult. And then there is Shu-sheng. After all, she is your wife and my daughter-in-law, isn't she?" She pretended to smile but her heart was in agony as if being squeezed in a powerful grip.

"Mother, how can you depend on them? Hsiao Hsüan is so young, and Shu-sheng ..." He stopped before he betrayed himself, but his emotions told a clear and eloquent tale of his sorrow. He got up and left the room.

He heard his mother call after him from the room; he did not reply. Taking big steps, he walked downstairs and out to the sidewalk. Standing on the pavement of the dusty street, he hesitated, for he did not know where to go. People were passing by him swiftly, like shadows, for they were all strangers to him. The broad street seemingly had no

感情的奔騰，竭力裝出淡漠的聲調說。可是他自己覺得有許多小蟲在吃他的肺，吃他的心。

「明天就去，未免太急了。或者你後天先去看看情形。明天不要去，明天我做好幾樣菜請你吃，我想把張伯情也請來。他給你看了好多次病，我們也沒有多少錢酬勞他，」母親裝出高興的樣子說。

他想了想，又看了看母親的臉，他痛苦地大聲說：「媽，你又當了賣了甚麼東西？你為了我把你那一點點值錢的東西全弄光了！」

「不要緊，你不要管，」母親答道，她的笑更顯得不自然了。

「不過你不想想，萬一我死了，你怎麼辦？你拿甚麼來過日子？」他爭吵似地指着母親說。

「你不要耽心，我會死在你前頭的。即使我不死，還有小宣，他一定長大成人了。並且還有樹生，她究竟是你的太太、我的媳婦啊，」母親裝出不在乎的樣子微微笑道，可是她的心卻像被鐵爪捏緊了似的發痛。

「媽，你怎麼能靠他！小宣太小，樹生——」下面的話已經滑到他的嘴邊，他連忙收住，但感情的流露卻是收不住的。淚水已迸出他的眼眶來了。他猝然站起來，甚麼話也不說，就走出房去。

他聽見母親在屋子裏喚他，他並不答應，卻邁着大步急急走下了樓。但是到了大門口，他又遲疑起來。對着這一條街的灰塵，他不知道應該到哪裏去。他站在門前人行道上，他的腳好像生了根似的，他朝東看看，又朝西看看。他眼前盡是些漠不相關的陌生人影。他覺得這茫茫天地間只有他一個渺小病弱的人找不到一個立足

room for a weak and sickly man. He was indescribably lonely, with tears in his eyes and his mind starkly empty. He saw three young women selecting colorful materials from the counter of a fabric shop, and the picture of a smiling waitress on a billboard inviting passers-by to patronize a newly-opened restaurant. They all seemed happy and contented. Why was he cursed with all the worries in the world?

Unconsciously he put his hand on his chest, for the pain was increasing. His mother caught up with him, panting and calling him. "Where are you going, Hsüan?"

"Just for a walk," he replied indifferently.

"You don't look well, I think you'd better come home and rest. You don't have much to do anyway," she urged him.

He did not answer. "You'd better come back," she repeated.

He paused for a while, and then said, "No, Mother, Let me go." He added in a low voice, "I am troubled."

She sighed. Then she said, "Don't go too far away and come back early."

"Very well," he agreed and walked off, leaving her behind.

She stood at the entrance to the building, watching him gradually disappear.

He walked on aimlessly: neither briskly nor strolling. He wanted to find a place where he could forget everything or destroy himself. The burden of misery had become too heavy for him to bear, nor could he endure any longer his endless torment.

He collided with other pedestrians and bumped against rickshaws; he was hurt by bricks and pebbles on the unevenly-paved road; and more than once he stumbled. He could hardly distinguish colors and differences in shades. All the world seemed the same grayish hue.

安身的地方。他寂寞，他自己也說不出是怎樣深的寂寞。他臉上的淚痕還不曾乾去。心裏似乎空無一物。

旁邊布店裏櫃臺上堆着各式各樣的布，生意似乎還好，三個少婦模樣的時髦女子(並不太時髦)有說有笑地在挑選布。另一邊一家新開的食店門前立着兩塊花花綠綠的廣告牌，牌上有一個年青女侍在對着行人微笑。

「他們都比我快樂，」他想道，但這所謂「他們」，究竟是誰，連他自己也沒有想過。可是他覺得胸部仍舊一陣一陣地在痛。他不自覺地把手按在胸上。

「宣，宣，」他聽見母親的聲音又在後面叫喚。他茫然轉過頭去，母親走得氣咻咻的，她剛走到他身邊，便問：「你到哪裏去？」

「我走走，」他做出淡漠的樣子回答。

「我看你臉色不大好，你還是改天上街吧。橫順你沒有甚麼事，」母親勸道。

他不作聲，母親又說：「你還是回屋去吧。」

他想了想，其實他並沒有用腦筋，他不過楞了一下，接着他就說：「不，媽，你讓我走走，」他又放低音聲加一句：「我心煩。」

母親嘆了一口氣，用疑慮的眼光看了看他，她低聲囑咐道：「那麼你快點回來，不要走遠啊。」

「是，」他應着就撇下母親拔步走了。母親卻立在門前，望着他的背影慢慢地消失。

他沒有目的地走着。他不是在「疾走」，也不是在「散步」。他懷着一個含糊的渴望，想找一個使他忘記一切的地方，或者乾脆就把自己毀滅。痛苦的擔子太重了，他的肩頭載不起，他受不了零碎的宰割、沒有終止的煎熬。他寧願來一個痛快的了結。

人碰到他的頭，洋車撞痛他的腿。他的腳在不平的人行道上被石子磚塊弄傷了，他幾次差一點要跌倒在街上。他的眼睛也似乎看不見顏色和光亮。他的眼前只有一片灰暗，他的世界裏就只有一片灰暗。

He sat down on a bench by a square table in the familiar wine shop. He was well acquainted with the table.

"A cup of *hung-tsao*?" a waiter asked him, approaching.

"Hurry up!" He did not know why he shouted this reply. He drank his wine in big swallows, belching after each one. He re-read Shu-sheng's letter, a few lines here and there, weeping all the while. He wanted to put it down and stop reading, but he could not help picking it up again and reading another passage, and yet another, and as he read he felt worse and worse. His tears flowed freely. He finally put the letter away and concentrated on his drink. The strong wine irritated his throat and his stomach. His head burning with fever, he had difficulty thinking, and his memory became hazy. But the letter tormented him like a whip lashing at his feelings until they gradually became numb.

In the shop there were only two other patrons. When he finished his cup, the waiter returned, asking if he would like another one. "No, no!" he said loudly, his reddened face shining brightly from the two ounces of white liquor he had already had. He re-read parts of the letter over and over again. He had stopped crying and only sighed and shook his head. The waiter standing close by looked at him in astonishment.

After he had sat there motionless for quite a while, the waiter approached him once again. This time he ordered another cup of *hung-tsao*. After a big swallow, he became very warm and dizzy. Gazing at the pages of the letter, he suddenly saw an image sitting opposite him drinking wine with a lowered head. The image quickly vanished. Rubbing his eyes, he said to himself, "It was T'ang Pai-ch'ing." As he lowered his head, he seemed to see T'ang smiling at him. "Now I'm his equal. How did I reach this condition?" he mused. Then he paid the bill and rushed off as if there were an air raid.

他的腳在一個小店門前停住，為甚麼？他自己也不知道。他走了進去，在一根板櫈上坐下。這家冷酒館於他並不陌生。連那張方桌也是他坐過了的。

堂倌走過來問一句：「一杯紅糟？」

「快，快，」他驚醒似地大聲說，他其實也沒有想到甚麼意思。

堂倌端上酒來。他糊裏糊塗地喝了一大口。一股熱氣直往喉管冒，他受不住，立刻打了一個嗝。他放下酒杯，又從懷裏摸出樹生的信來，先放在桌上，又拿起杯子喝了一口。又打一個嗝。他賭氣不喝酒了。他拿起信箋，隨意地翻着，低聲唸了幾句。他心裏很不好過。眼淚又流出來了。他想不再看信。可是他剛把信箋摺好，忍不住又打開來，重新翻看，又低聲唸出幾句，他心裏更難過。眼淚成股地流下來。他下了決心地端起酒杯，大口喝着。他感覺到一股熱流灌進肚子裏去。他的喉管裏，他的胃裏都不舒服。他整個頭發燒，思想停滯，記憶也漸漸模糊。只有信箋上的字句像一根鞭子在他那逐漸麻木的情感上面不停地抽。

酒館裏白天很清靜，除了他，另外還有兩個客人對酌談心。其餘的桌子全空着。沒有人注意他。堂倌看見他的酒杯空了，便走過來問一句：「再來杯紅糟？」

「不！不！」他含糊地搖頭說，他一張臉喝得通紅，他才只喝了一兩白酒。

堂倌站在旁邊用驚奇的眼光看他。他也沒有注意到。他反覆地翻看她的來信。他自己也不知道看了幾遍。他不再流淚了。他只是搖頭嘆息。

「再來杯紅糟？」過了一會堂倌看見他不動也不走，便又來問一句。

「好，好，」他短短地回答。酒送上來，他立刻喝了一大口。他放下杯子，全身發熱。頭又有點暈。他埋着頭，眼光在信箋上，心不知放在哪裏去了。他忽然覺得對面坐了一個人，也低着頭在喝酒。他便抬起頭睜大眼睛看，甚麼也沒有。「我想到唐柏青了，」他自語着，揉了揉眼睛。他又埋下頭去。他恍惚地看到唐柏青在對他苦笑。「怎麼我現在也落到他的境地來了？」他苦痛地想。他就像聽見警報似地立刻站起來，付了錢便往外面走。

On his way home he felt T'ang's shadow was following him. As soon as he got in, he sat down to answer Shu-sheng's letter. While writing, he vaguely heard his mother say something and murmured a reply without actually knowing what he had heard or said. He wrote:

> I've read your letter several times, and I apologize for having wasted your youth. It is my great offense against you. The only remedy is to set you free. You're right about everything, and I'll abide by your instructions. I only beg you to forgive me. The Company has reinstated me, and I return to work tomorrow. Please don't send any more money. Mother and I can survive on my income.
>
> Wen-hsüan

When he had completed the letter, although he seemed to have written it without much obvious effort, nevertheless he was exhausted. The building in which he lived seemed to have collapsed on him. He was finished, and so was his entire world.

Seeing her crestfallen son slouched in the rattan chair sobbing, the old woman asked what was troubling him. Like a child crying before his mother he gave her the letter to read. But instead of giving her Shu-sheng's letter, he gave her his reply. She understood the situation well. However, she felt more or less gratified that her predictions about her daughter-in-law had come true. "I said before that her marriage with you couldn't last long. Now you see I was absolutely right. I saw through her long ago," she said. She was angry, but she also felt pleased. She even saw the resolution of the matter as good news, and therefore did not think to sympathize with her son.

一路上唐柏青的影子追着他。他只有一個念頭：回家去。

到了家，他才稍稍心安。一進屋坐下來就給樹生寫信。母親同他講話，他含糊着，一句話也沒有聽進去。他在信上寫着：

> 收到來信讀了好幾遍，我除了向你道歉外無話可說。耽誤了你的青春，這是我的大不是。現在的補救方法，便是還你自由。你的話無一句不對。一切都照你所說辦理。
>
> 我只求你原諒我。
>
> 公司已允許我復職，我明日即去辦公，以後請停寄家用款。我們母子二人可靠你的薪津勉強過活。請你放心。祝福。
>
> 文宣

他一口氣寫了這些話，並不費力，可是剛把信寫好，他就覺得所有的氣力全用盡了。他覺得好像整個樓房全塌了下來，他完了，他的整個世界都崩潰了。他絕望地伏在書桌上低聲哭起來。

「宣，甚麼事？甚麼？」母親驚問道。她連忙到他身邊去。

他抬起頭來，讓她看見他滿臉的淚痕，他就小孩似的哭着說：「你看她的信。」但是他遞給她看的卻是他寫給樹生的信，並不是樹生寄來的信。

母親看了那封短信，不用聽他解釋，便明白了一切。她說：「我原說過，她不會跟你白頭偕老的。現在怎樣！我早就看透了她的心了。」

她氣憤，但是她覺得痛快，得意。她起初還把這看作好消息。她並沒有想到應該同情他的兒子——

XXVII

LIKE a pebble thrown into a pool of tranquil water, Shu-sheng's letter stirred up his otherwise monotonous life and created many ripples. Then the water surface calmed down while the pebble, having sunk to the bottom, remained there forever, immobile. She wrote once or twice a month, inquiring about him and their son, but said little about herself. Ignoring his objections, she continued to send money every month. He accepted the money, did not spend it, nor did he return it to her but deposited it in a bank, though his mother would rather that he return it to Shu-sheng. When he asked her to write more about herself, she wrote in reply that she was "fine" and "busy." Stoically he endured everything; he did not want to write a single line or do a single thing to hurt her.

He went back to work the day after receiving the long letter. He had work and an income, found the new Chief Editor to be a friendly middle-aged man who even occasionally comforted him. His co-workers became more cordial, and his work, the same as before, seemed less distasteful.

At home the only break in the monotony was the fortnightly visits of his son, who would eat one or two meals with them and spend a Saturday or Sunday night at home. Sometimes either his mother or he would go out, leaving the other to mind the apartment.

No entertainment, no diversion, time simply passed by. He lost interest in writing letters and in talking to his mother. Thus the joyless spring passed.

Summer made him feel even more miserable; he never felt well;

二十七

樹生的信像投了一個石子在他的生活裏，激起一陣水花，攪動了全個水面，然後又平靜下去了。但石子卻沉在水底，永遠留在那裏，不能拿開。她以後還有信來，不過一個月只有一兩次。信上話不多，不講自己的生活情形，只探詢他和小宣的健康與近況。她仍舊按月匯款。他母親要他把款子退回去，他沒有照辦。他收下款子，不用，也不退回，他把匯款領來全部存入銀行。他寫回信時有過請她不要再匯款的話。可是她好像沒有見到他的信似的，下次照常匯寄。他要她敘說她的近況，她卻一字不提，偶爾提到，也僅有「忙」和「好」兩個字。他只有默默地忍受一切，他不願寫一個字或做一件事傷她的心。

他有了工作和收入。他在接到她的長信的第二天，便到公司去上班了。新主任是一個和善的中年人，對他也很客氣，甚至向他說了一番安慰的話。同事們（除了鍾老）雖然沒有甚麼歡迎的表示，不過全對他點頭打招呼。他心裏高興，因此對那些奇怪的譯文或官場公式文章也就不覺得怎麼討厭了。

家中仍舊少有人聲。除了星期六或星期天（常常是兩個星期一次）小宣回來坐坐，吃一兩頓飯或住一個晚上外，就只有他和母親兩人，有時甚至只有他們中的一個在家。

日子仍舊單調地一天一天過去，無所謂快，也無所謂慢。他只有一種類似「捱」和「拖」的感覺。他沒有娛樂，也沒有消遣，他連寫信和談話的快樂也得不到。春天並沒有給他帶來喜悅。但是春天也終於捱過了。

夏天裏他更憔悴了。他的身體從來不曾好過，他的病一直在加

and his battle with life grew increasingly desperate. He did not know what sustained him or what kept him from a complete collapse. He had a fever every afternoon, cold sweats at night, shortness of breath, a dry cough, blood in his phlegm occasionally, and an acute pain in both his lungs. At first, he had to grit his teeth and struggle against his ailments, but in time he grew accustomed to them. "Killing time" was, after all, not so difficult for him since his life was already monotonously dark and gray. He abandoned all hopes or illusions, reacting with apathy to the news of Germany's surrender. Even the prediction of the forthcoming collapse of Japan did not bring him any pleasure. It seemed that any bright and beautiful prospects for the future had no relationship to him at all. Like an old cart-puller, he concentrated on dragging a full load step by step without knowing when he would arrive at his destination and could be relieved of the burden, nor even how much of the journey had already been covered. He would just plod on, one step at a time, pulling the cart until he became completely exhausted.

One night at supper his mother suddenly looked at him and said, "Hsüan, have you been well for the last few days? Why do you look so poorly?"

"I'm all right. I don't feel any particular discomfort," he said, trying to be jovial. But his throat would not cooperate. He began to cough and hurriedly covered his mouth. He was afraid that he would cough up some blood, as he had in the office earlier that day when some phlegm had stained the proofs. Even though he had wiped it off as best he could, the red stains on the paper remained visible.

"But you must be careful. You're still coughing. It has never stopped," his mother said worriedly, knitting her eyebrows together.

"No, it almost stopped for a while, though I never got rid of it

劇。他自己也不知道是一種甚麼力量在支持他使他不倒下去。他每天下午發熱，晚上出冷汗，多走路就氣喘，又不斷地乾咳，偶爾吐一口帶血痰。左胸有時痛得相當厲害，連右胸也扯起痛了。他起初咬着牙在掙扎，後來也漸漸習慣了，捱日子在他並不是一件難事。反正他的生活就只是一片暗灰色。他對一切都斷念了。他再不敢有甚麼妄想。甚至德國投降也不曾帶給他快樂和安慰。他聽見人說日本在一年內就要崩潰，他笑不出聲來，那些光明美麗的希望似乎都跟他斷絕了關係。他覺得自己就像一個衰老的車夫，吃力地推着一輛載重的車子，一步一步地往前面走，他早已不去想甚麼時候能達到目的地，卸下這一車重載，他也不再計算已經走了若干路程，他只一步一步緩慢地走着、推着，一直到他竭力的時候。

一天晚飯後母親忽然望着他說：「宣，你這兩天沒有甚麼不舒服吧。怎麼你臉色這樣難看？」

「我還好，沒有甚麼不舒服，」他裝出高興的樣子說。可是他的喉嚨不肯幫忙他掩飾，他接連乾咳幾聲，他急忙用手掩嘴。他害怕又像白天那樣咳出血痰來。白天在辦公時間裏他咳了一口血痰在校樣上面，雖然他已小心地揩去了血跡，但紙上的紅點卻隱約看得見。

「不過你得當心啊，你又在咳嗽。我看你的咳嗽，就一直沒有好過，」母親皺着眉說。

「不，也好過一陣子，不過總不能根斷。人一累，就要發，」他

completely. Whenever I'm tired, it comes back," he explained to her, lying. But he wanted to say those things, conscious of a desire to fool not only his mother but himself as well.

After a few moments of silence, she sighed, "Frankly, you shouldn't go to work. But what alternative do you have?"

He felt uncomfortable, but could say nothing. The more he wanted to suppress his cough, the harder he coughed. And the coughing would not stop, making him red in the face and forcing tears from his eyes. Panic-stricken, his mother ran to get him some water to drink and then massaged his back. Finally, as the coughing spell came to an end, he took from her a handkerchief to wipe his face.

"I'm all right now," he said with an effort, looking at her gratefully.

"You'd better lie down," she suggested in pity.

"It's all right. Let me sit a little longer," he answered in a hoarse voice.

"Hsüan, tomorrow I'll go to your office and ask them to give you one or two months' leave of absence. You should rest and not worry about money. If necessary, I'll go out and work as a servant,"she said with determination.

He shook his head, speaking weakly, "Mother, you're already old. How could you take the drudgery? Really, what's the use? We're not the only ones to suffer. We must hang on as long as possible even if we don't want to."

"I'd rather not live," she said indignantly.

"Nowadays, it's not so easy to die either," he said, feeling the pain in his chest. In his imagination, the bacteria were eating his lungs. Without much resistance left in his body, he would die soon whether he wanted to or not.

解釋地說，他自己也知道這不是真話。但是他願意這樣說，他不僅想騙過母親，同時也想騙他自己。

母親沉默半晌，才嘆了一口氣說：「其實你不應該去做事的，不過我們還有甚麼別的辦法！」

他心裏很不好過，他答不出話來，他越是想不要咳，越是咳得厲害，一咳就不可收拾，臉掙得通紅，淚水也咳出來了，急得他的母親在屋子裏亂跑，拿開水，又替他搥背。他終於緩過氣來，他從母親手裏接過臉帕揩了臉。

「不要緊了。」他吃力地說，用感激的眼光望着母親。

「你躺躺吧。」母親憐惜地說。

「不要緊，等我多坐一會兒。」他沙聲答道。

「宣，明天我就去公司替你請一兩個月的假，你應該休息，你不要愁生活。實在沒有辦法，我出去當老媽子。」母親下了決心似地說。

他搖搖頭，有氣沒力地說：「媽，你是個上了年紀的人，怎麼吃得消，這種辦法有甚麼用！受苦的並不只我們一兩個人，我們不拖也只好拖……」

「這樣我寧肯不活。」母親憤憤地說。

「這年頭死也死不下去啊！」他說了一句，他又感覺到胸部的隱痛。病菌在吃他的肺。他沒有一點抵抗的力量。他會死的，不管他願意不願意，他很快地就會死。

His mother looked at him dully, but he did not seem to notice it. He remembered what his co-workers said about people dying of TB and particularly Little P'an's comment on the death of a relative. "The death of TB patients is the most agonizing. If I were in the terminal stage of TB, I'd take my own life," so said Little P'an, looking directly at him. Apparently it had been said deliberately for him to hear.

"The most agonizing," he thought to himself, unable to chase away such thoughts. Despair and fear crept up on him, and he started shivering. (Despite the heat of summer, he felt cold. He felt he had fallen into an ice-cellar.)

"Why isn't there a special cure for TB? Why is science so behind?" he desperately asked himself.

"Hsüan, you'd better go to sleep early. We'll see if you should go to work tomorrow morning," said his mother. She saw that he did not have any energy, his sallow face looked terrible, and his motionless eyes were full of fear. Though full of anxiety, she dared not discuss the matter further and only wanted to comfort him.

He looked up alarmed, as if awakening from a horrible nightmare. He scanned his surroundings, as dusk was beginning to fall. From downstairs came human sounds, people shouting and cursing, the sound of gongs and drums accompanied by some opera singing.* Thirsty, he poured himself a glass of lukewarm water from a teapot.

"Yes, I'll go to sleep now," he said with a weak smile. "Mother, you should go to sleep, too. I see you're very lonely."

"I'm used to loneliness. After all, I'm nearing my grave. I don't mind loneliness," she sighed softly.

---

*Gongs and drums are the usual musical accompaniment for Chinese opera.

母親呆呆地望着，他似乎沒有注意到。他想到這天在公司裏聽見的同事們關於肺病的閒談。那是在吃飯的時候，小潘賣弄似地敘述一個親戚害肺病死去的情形。「只有害肺病的人死的時候最慘最痛苦。我要是得那種病到了第二期，我一定自殺。」小潘說，眼光射到他的臉上，話一定是故意說給他聽的。

「最慘最痛苦。」他想着，就再也不能把那個念頭驅逐開去，絕望和恐怖從遠處逼近。他不自覺地打了一個冷噤(雖然已經是夏天，他還感到冷，他真有一種整個身子落進冰窖裏去的感覺)。

為甚麼就沒有特效藥？為甚麼科學對這個病就沒有辦法？

他絕望地暗暗問他自己。

「宣，你早點睡吧，不要再想甚麼事情，請假的話明早晨再說。」母親看見他精神不好，臉色黃得可怕，眼光停滯而帶恐懼，她暗暗充滿了焦慮，不敢再跟他講話，便溫和地勸慰他道。

他吃了一驚。他好像從一個可怖的夢中醒過來。可是他看看四周，屋子裏白日光線才開始消去，樓下人聲嘈雜，打鑼鼓唱戲，罵街吵架，種種奇特的聲音打成一片。他覺得口乾，便去拿茶壺，倒了杯微溫的白開水來喝。

「好的，我就睡。」他帶着苦笑地說，「媽，你也睡吧，我看你也很寂寞。」

「我倒也過慣了，我橫順是個快進墳墓的人，我不怕寂寞。」母親微微嘆息道。

She went into her small room and shut the door. He crawled into his bed, feeling the pain in his lungs. Not just limited to his chest, the pain seemed to cover his entire body. All the while, he remained lucid. He could not sleep. The sound of drums and gongs and the opera singing continued in the street, while a specially invited shaman was performing rituals for the dead in the neighborhood. An actor impersonating a female role was singing with great gusto. Wang did not want to listen to him, yet the noises forced themselves into his ears, interrupting his thoughts. Tossing and turning in his bed, he became restless and fretful and began to sweat. But he was afraid to throw off the covers for fear of catching cold. He did not want to harm his body any further, even though he had decided a little earlier that it was being eaten away by bacteria and that his death was imminent.

A streak of light came from underneath his mother's door. She was not yet asleep, coughing once or twice. He wondered what she was doing, why she had to work all the time, and what she received as a reward. She lived only for him and for Hsiao Hsüan. What could he do to repay her? He went on thinking, scratching his head.

Then he thought of Shu-sheng. Her beautiful face seemed to be beaming at him. Was she ridiculing or pitying him? She had sent him a brief, impersonal letter with a bank draft the day before yesterday, inquiring about his health and about the family. He had put the money in the bank and written her a reply already, never mentioning that he had not touched any of her money. What was she after? She was already separated from him; he had agreed to the separation because he wanted to oblige her. Why was she still concerned about him? Why did she continue to send him letters and money? The more he thought about these questions, the more confused he became. And amidst all these thoughts he suddenly experienced a surge of desire.

母親進了小屋，關上門。他上了床，左胸又在痛，不只左胸，好像全身都痛。他的頭腦卻是十分清醒。他睡不着。街中的鑼鼓聲和唱戲聲仍然沒有停止，不知是那一家請巫師做法事，那個扮旦角的正唱得起勁，他不要聽那些戲詞，可是它們卻不客氣地闖入他的耳朵裏來，攪亂了他的思想。他在床上翻來覆去，越想越睡不着，越着急，出了一身大汗，他又不敢把那床薄被掀開。他害怕受涼，他不願意隨意損傷自己的健康，雖然他先前還在想他的內部快要被病菌吃光，他已逼近死亡。

母親房裏還有燈光，她不曾睡，她偶爾發出一兩聲咳嗽。她在做甚麼？她為甚麼整年不歇地工作？她換得了甚麼來呢？她的生存似乎完全是為着他，為着小宣。但是他拿甚麼來報答她呢？他想着，他接連抓自己的頭髮。

然後又是樹生，她的美麗的臉在對他微笑。她嘲笑他，還是憐憫他？她前天還來過一封短信，以朋友的口氣問起他的健康和他一家的生活情形。她又附寄了匯票來。自然他仍舊把款子存入銀行。他寫了回信，卻始終沒有告訴她他並未動用她寄來的款子。她究竟是甚麼意思呢？她已經跟他脱離了夫妻關係。這還是順從她的意思呢，那麼她為甚麼還不忘記他？為甚麼還要按月寄款通信？他越想越不明白，可是一種渴望被這思想引起來了。

Though he was a man nearing death, he still had a man's normal desires. His urges tortured him all the more because he knew that they could never be fulfilled. Yet he could not suppress them. He struggled with himself, his underwear becoming drenched in cold sweat and sticking to his feverish back.

Unable to control himself any longer, he cried out in his hoarse voice, "I want to live! I want to live!"

No one heard him; no one paid him any atttention. All kinds of noises reverberated outside his window. People were walking by; a few recently established noodle-stalls at the end of the street were busy serving their customers; a waiter was shouting boisterously and customers were talking to one another in rising tones; a new young voice had replaced that of the old hawker selling hot water and fried rice-cakes. Competing with the young voice were the shrill voices of several women, also in the business of selling hot water and fried rice-cakes. He was the only one lying quietly in bed. And though he was nearing death, no one came to look after him.

"I want to live!" he beseeched in a voice audible only to himself. But to whom was he pleading? He really did not know.

XXVIII

GRADUALLY he lost his voice, his body weakening.

Everyday returning from work, he breathed with difficulty and collapsed into his rattan chair, where he would stay for a long while before he could get up.

他一個垂死的病人卻有着一個健康人的渴望，這渴望折磨得他很苦，因為連他自己也明白他的渴望是不會得到滿足的，一絲一毫的滿足也得不到。但是他又不能抑制它、消滅它。他在掙扎，濕透了的汗衣冷冰冰的貼在他發熱的背上。

「我要活，我要活。」他控制不住自己地叫了出來，聲音不高，他的嗓子開始啞了。

沒有人聽見他的叫聲，再沒有人理睬他。在窗外響着各種各樣的聲音，那麼多的人來來去去，巷口新近擺起來的麵攤上正是生意興隆的時候，么師大聲叫喚，顧客們高談闊論。他也聽到「炒米糖開水」的叫賣聲。可是那是一個年青的聲音，而且有幾個清脆的女性的尖聲在叫「買開水」或「炒米糖開水，這兒。」現在連賣「炒米糖開水」的也換了別人，而且也正忙着。只有他一個靜靜躺在床上，哪怕他已經走近死亡，也沒有人來看顧他。

「我要活。」他還在叫，聲音只有自己聽得見。他究竟在向誰呼籲呢？他說不出。

二十八

他漸漸地失去他的聲音。他的體力也在逐漸消失。

他每天下班回家，走進門總要喘氣，並且要在籐椅上像死人似地坐了好一陣才能夠走動講話。

"Hsüan, please ask for a leave of absence; otherwise you'll be sick in bed again," his mother begged him. She knew he was gravely ill, but what could she do for him? Physician Chang Po-ch'ing and the hospital were both useless to her. What was left were her two bare hands.

"No, it's all right. I can continue," he said stoically, though his heart felt like it was being stabbed by a bundle of needles. He vividly remembered his coughing spells at work, his shortness of breath, and his co-worker's look of disgust at the lunch table. How long could he last? He dared not think about it, nor did he want anyone to talk about it.

His mother watched him in tearful silence, wondering about his stubbornness. Unable to keep quiet, she said, "You must take care of yourself." She saw him nod. Then she blamed herself for his illness, and ultimately shifted the blame to Shu-sheng, the thoughts of whom made her eyebrows stand on end.

Through the window came the sounds of firecrackers and a woman's loud wailing. "Who's crying?" he asked his mother in a frightened voice.

"A tailor, who lived across the street, was healthy and sound yesterday and he suddenly died of cholera," she explained.

"It's at least quick. Why cry?" he muttered to himself.

"You'd better be careful. Cholera is reaching epidemic proportions and your resistance is low," she reminded him.

"Yes, I know," he said casually, preoccupied with the thoughts of death. He wondered if his own spirit after death would recognize the ones he loved.

Who could give him a definite answer to this question? He knew

「宣，你請幾天假吧，再這樣你又要病倒了。」母親憐惜地勸道。她也知道他的病逐漸在加深。但是她有甚麼辦法救他呢？張伯情沒有用，醫院也沒有用。並且他們母子兩人就只有空空的兩雙手啊。

「不要緊，我還可以支持下去。」他裝出淡漠的聲音答道，他的心卻像被一大把針戳了一下似的。他清清楚楚地記得在公司裏一面看校樣一面咳嗽，看多了就要喘氣的情形，他還記得在吃飯時同事們的討厭的眼光。他還可以支持多久呢？他不敢想，他又不能叫自己不想。可是他不願意別人對他提起這事情。

母親默默地望着他。她悲痛地想：你為甚麼要這樣固執啊？「不過你總該小心保養身體。」母親忍不住又說了句。她看見他微微地搖頭，臉上現出一種無可奈何的表情，她忽然想起來：是我害了他，累了他。她想哭，卻極力忍住，「不，是那個女人害他的。」她反抗地想，她豎起眉毛來。

窗下馬路上傳來的哭聲和鞭炮聲，一個女人哭得很傷心。

「哪個在哭？」他忽然用驚懼的聲調問道。

「對面裁縫店裏死了人，害霍亂，昨天還是好好的，才一天的功夫就死了。」母親解釋道。

「這樣倒也痛快，何必哭。」他想了想，自語道。

「你這兩天在外面要當心啊，我知道你不會吃生冷，不過你身體差，總以小心為是。」母親關切地囑咐。

「我知道。」他順口答道。可是他心裏想的卻是另一件事：人死了是不是還有靈魂存在，是不是還認識生前的親人。

對這疑問誰能夠給他一個確定的答覆呢？他知道這是一個永遠

that it was one which could have no answer. Someone had asked him the same question a long time ago, and he only laughed. Now he was asking the same question. Must he bid farewell to his mother, Shu-sheng, and Hsiao Hsüan?

Involuntarily, he looked at his mother. What a gentle face she had. Unable to restrain himself, he called softly, "Mother."

"Eh," she turned to look at him. Since he did not say anything else, she asked, "What's the matter?"

"I was just looking at you," he said affectionately, then continued, "Hsiao Hsüan will be home the day after tomorrow. I wonder if he has lost any weight in the past two weeks."

"His constitution is much like yours, and he doesn't look too good. Vitamins are too expensive; otherwise it would be nice to buy him some," she said, eyeing him attentively. Then she bit her lip and turned her face away with two big teardrops in the corners of her eyes.

Hsiao Hsüan came home, adding a little life and sound to the family. At least there was one additional person to talk to. The old woman asked her grandson about his activities, school work, and diet during the last two weeks. His answers were brief. This quiet boy felt he was obligated to answer his grandmother's questions.

"Your father has been talking about you the last two days, and he's very anxious to see you. When he comes home, he'll be very pleased," the old woman said to her grandson.

"Yes," Hsiao Hsüan answered, without a trace of smile on his face.

"How could this boy have changed so much and have become so adult-like?" she wondered. With concern, she asked, "Have you been well?"

得不着回答的問題。以前有人拿這問題問過他，他還哂笑過那個人。現在他自己起了這同樣的疑問了。母親、樹生，還有小宣，是不是他們必須全向他永別？

他不覺又把眼光射在母親的臉上。多麼慈祥的臉，他禁不住柔聲喚道：「媽。」

「嗯？」母親也掉了眼光來看他，她看見他不說話，便問道：「甚麼事？」

「我看看你。」他親熱地說。他勉強笑了笑，接着他又說；「小宣後天要回家了，這兩個星期裏面不曉得他是不是又瘦了一點。」

「他的體子跟你差不多。他的臉色也不大好看，補藥又太貴，不然買點給他吃也好。」母親說。她注意地看他，忽然她咬着嘴唇皮把臉掉開，立刻有兩顆眼淚掛在她的眼角。

小宣回來給這寂寞的人家添了些語聲。至少多了一個人講話。做祖母關心地詢問孫兒半個月中的生活情形，功課飲食等全問到了。小宣答得簡單，這是個不喜歡開口的孩子，不過祖母的問話必須得到回答，這使寡言的人也得講一些話。

「你爹這兩天常常掛念你，他很想見你。等一陣他回來看見你一定很高興。」祖母對孫兒說。

「是。」小宣答得這麼短，也沒有笑。「這孩子怎麼變得更老成了！」祖母奇怪地想。她便關切地問：

「你是不是有甚麼不舒服？」

"Yes, I have been well," he gave her a short answer. Frowning, he added, "But I have trouble with my school work."

"Don't worry too much, you are still young," she consoled him.

"My teachers are all so demanding. I'm afraid that I may have to be kept in the same grade next year, and that I'll disappoint you," Hsiao Hsüan said in a complaining tone.

"But you're still young. Don't worry about repeating the grade; otherwise your health will suffer like your father's," she said compassionately.

Wang pushed the door and entered. Breathless, his pale face resembled a piece of dusty window-paper. He stumbled into the rattan chair by the desk. The chair wobbled somewhat as one of its legs had been damaged. Without saying a word he tightly closed his eyes as though he were already dead. He did not stir.

The old woman winked at her grandson to indicate that he should not disturb his father; her own eyes stared at her son full of concern and consternation.

A little while later, Wang opened his eyes and called, "Mother." He had almost completely lost his voice, his eyes moving from side to side searching for her.

She walked over to him and gently asked, "Hsüan, what's the matter?"

He stretched out a trembling hand to reach for her, and then he tightly held her hand. His eyes searched for his son but his head did not move. In his tremulous voice he called "Hsiao Hsüan!" though the latter was standing right behind him.

In near panic, the old woman said to Hsiao Hsüan in a shaken

「沒有。」小宣仍舊短短地回答，後來皺着眉頭加添一句：「功課總是趕不上。」

「趕不上，也不必着急，慢慢來，橫豎你年紀輕得很。」她溫和地安慰道。

「不過先生逼得很緊。我害怕不及格留級，對不起家裏。」小宣訴苦般地說。

「你這樣小，還管甚麼留級不留級，你身體要緊啊，不要又弄到你父親那樣子。」祖母痛惜地說。

他，做父親的他推開門進來了。口裏喘着氣臉色灰白，像一張塗滿塵垢的糊窗的窗皮紙。他一直走到書桌前跌倒似地坐在籐椅上，籐椅搖動幾下，他的一隻腳已經在向外偏斜了。他不說話，死人般地閉着眼動也不動一下。

祖母向孫兒丟了一個眼色，叫這孩子不要驚擾剛回家來的父親。她帶着恐懼的表情望着他。

過了一會兒，他忽然睜開眼叫了一聲：「媽。」聲音差不多全啞了。他轉動眼珠去找尋她。

她走過去，溫柔地問他：「宣，甚麼事？」

他伸起一隻顫抖的手去拉她的手。他的手抓到了她的手便緊緊捏住不放。「小宣呢？」他拖長聲音說，又用眼光去找尋他的兒子。小宣本來站在他的後邊，不過稍稍向後一點，可是他的眼光始終在他前面盤桓，沒有能力把小宣找到。

「你快過來，快來，你爹叫你。」她還以為他已經到了垂危的地

voice, "Come closer. Your father is calling for you." She thought his death was imminent and that he was bidding them farewell.

Wang held his son's hand and asked affectionately how he had been. Then he closed his eyes and tightly held the hands of his mother and his son.

His mother was crying, and his son stared at him. They both thought his end had come. "All finished," his mother thought, darkness enveloping her eyes. Her only hope was that his hands were not yet cold.

"Hsüan," she called in anguish, unable to restrain her sorrow. The boy followed suit and called, "Father."

Gradually he opened his eyes, his body stirring. A reluctant smile quivered on his face. "Don't worry," he said, "I am not dead yet."

His mother heaved a sigh of relief. Controlling her tears, she whispered, "How do you feel?"

He shook his head and said, "Nothing."

His son kept staring at him; his mother said in a soft voice, "Lie down. I will get a doctor for you."

He let go of their hands, shifted his body a little and said with effort, "Don't go, Mother. I am not ill."

"Hsüan, don't be stubborn. How can you say you are not ill? Illness is not to be feared, if a person seeks early treatment."

He shook his head and said, "I am not afraid." He searched in his pockets for a while before he found a folded letter. Without a word, he gave it to her.

She opened the letter and read it. It was dated and signed by six of her son's co-workers:

步，他在向家人告別，她的聲音抖得厲害，他的心抖得更厲害，她用了類似慘叫的聲音對小宣說。小宣即刻走到父親的膝前去。

他用另一隻手抓住兒子的手。他注意地看了這孩子一眼。「你好吧？」他說，他似乎想笑，但並沒有笑，卻把眼睛閉上了。兩手仍然緊緊捏着他母親和他兒子的手。

他母親流着眼淚，孩子望着他發楞，他們以為一樁慘痛的事就要發生了。「完了。」他母親這樣想，眼前開始發黑。唯一的希望是手始終不冷。

「宣。」他的母親忍不住悲聲喚他，他的兒子也跟着悲聲叫「爹」。

他睜開眼，勉強笑了笑，他的身子動了。「不要怕，我還不會死。」他說。

他的母親吐了一口氣，緊張的心略感到鬆弛。她忍住淚低聲問：「你心裏難過？」

他搖搖頭，說：「沒有甚麼。」

小宣一直不轉睛地望着他。母親柔聲說：「那麼你睡下吧，我去給你請醫生。」

他鬆開雙手，搖動一下身子。他用力地說：「不要去，媽，我不是病。」

「宣，你不要固執，你這樣怎麼能說不是病？」母親說：「有病不必怕，只要早點醫治。」

他又搖頭，說：「我不害怕。」他伸手在懷裏摸索了一會兒，掏出一張摺好了的信箋來，也不說明這是甚麼，就遞到母親的手裏去。

母親攤開信箋低聲讀出下面的話：

Wen-hsüan:

> We are a group of junior employees, undernourished and overworked, weak and frequently sick, and we have always expressed our sympathy with TB patients, but, sir, you are already in the terminal stage of TB, and you should be home, attending to your health. If you must work, you should have enough consideration for others not to eat with them, for fear of infecting them with your disease. For the welfare of all concerned, we beg you to withdraw from the lunch hour and eat at home. This is to be effective immediately; otherwise extreme measure will be taken against you.

"Did they give you the letter in person?" she asked abruptly.

"No, a servant brought it to me. It was drafted by Little P'an and signed by everyone eating at the same table, except for Uncle Chung." After a pause, he added, "What they say is true, but did they have to use that kind of language? I am human and I have feelings." He said no more and closed his lips.

"What nonsense! They don't even know how to write a letter, yet they are so arrogant. After one year working together, don't they have feelings for a colleague? " She was so incensed that she was red in the face; then she tore the letter to pieces.

"I say, Father, ignore them. See what they can do to you," said Hsiao Hsüan, sharing his grandmother's resentment.

"You are all colleagues. Why shouldn't you eat at the office? If TB is so contagious, why is it that we are not all dead? Only cowards are scared," she continued to fume, unable to suppress her anger.

Wang shook his head. After a while he uttered in a very hoarse voice, "It's all because I've contracted this incurable illness." His mother and his son both looked at him in astonishment. After a while, he went on, "You can't blame them; they are afraid of infection. What if they should catch my disease?"

文宣先生：

同人皆係靠薪津生活的小職員，平日營養不良，工作過度，身體虛弱，疾病叢生。對先生一類肺病患者，素表同情，未敢歧視。但先生肺病已經到第三期，理應告假療養；縱為生活所迫，不得不按時上班，也當潔身自愛，不與人同桌進食，同杯用茶，以免傳佈病菌，貽害他人。茲為顧全同仁福利起見，請先生退出伙食團，回家用膳。並請即日實行。否則同人當以非常手段對付，勿謂言之不預也。(後面還有六個人的簽名和日期)

「他們當面交給你的？」母親沒頭沒尾地問了一句。

「叫工友送來的，小潘起的稿，同桌七人就只鍾老沒有簽名。」他答道，歇了一下又說：「話自然也有道理，不過措辭不應該這樣，有話可以好說，我也是一個人啊……」他吐不出聲音來，就索性閉了口。

「真豈有此理！連信也寫不通的人，居然這樣神氣！大家同事一年，難道連一點感情也沒有！」母親氣得臉通紅，過了半晌才顫巍巍地講出這幾句話來，她幾下就把信撕得粉碎。

「我說爹不必理他們，看他們怎樣對付你！」小宣也居然變了臉色，氣憤地說。

「大家都是同事，為甚麼你不能在公司吃飯？要說害肺病就那麼容易傳染，怎麼這裏的人又未見死絕？哪個心虛，才害怕！」母親的怒氣不能平下去，她繼續罵着。

他搖搖頭，很吃力地吐出一句啞聲的話：「其實還是怪我生了不治的病。」他母親和他兒子都帶着驚疑的表情望着他。過了片刻他又說：「不能怪他們，他們也怕生這種病。真的他們染到了這種病又怎麼辦？……」

His mother interrupted him, "You are hopeless. At your stage, why do you worry about them? If it were I, I'd let them be infected. Let them suffer; let no one be spared." She was so angry that she spat on the floor.

"How would that help me?" he asked. His voice was so hoarse it made one think that his throat might be decaying. Unsteadily he got up from the rattan chair and muttered more or less to himself, "I want some tea."

Losing no time, his mother helped him stand and told her grandson, "Go and get your father a cup of tea."

Hsiao Hsüan brought in a cup of steaming hot water. "Only water?" Wang said, looking at the cup. Nonetheless, he gulped it down and gave the empty cup to his son, warning him, "Hsiao Hsüan, make sure you wash the cup thoroughly." He had made a considerable effort to make his meaning clear to his son.

"No need to be that cautions. I am not afraid of infection. Are we going to act like all the others, too?" his mother interrupted.

Looking at her and then at his son, he said, "But Hsiao Hsüan is young, and he is the only male child in the family." He walked slowly toward his bed, murmuring, "I am going to lie down for a while." He collapsed into his bed.

The next day he went back to work in his cheap, soiled gown. While signing the roll, he accidently tore his inner lapel. He heard snickering, but paid no attention to it. Perspiring and panting, he climbed the stairs, sat down at his desk, pulled his drawer open, and took out yesterday's unfinished galley proofs.

He had not even started working before a spell of weakness overcame him. He was sweating, felt light-headed, and did not know what

那母親氣得朝地上吐痰。她打斷了他的話：「你這人真沒有辦法，自己到了這個地步，還去管他們做甚麼？要是我，我就叫他們都染到這個病。要苦，大家一齊苦。不讓有一個人幸災樂禍。

「這對我又有甚麼好處呢？」他苦笑地說。他的沙啞聲使人想到他的喉嚨開始在潰爛了。他搖搖頭地站起來，自語道：「我吃杯茶。」

母親連忙扶着他，一面吩咐小宣：「你去給你爹倒杯茶來。」

小宣答應着，很快地就把杯子端了來，裏面還是冒熱氣。他接過杯子看了一眼，愁苦地說了兩個字「開水」，然後拿起來骨都骨都地喝光了。他把杯子交還給小宣，一面小心囑咐：「小宣，你記住好好用開水把這個杯子洗乾淨。」他費了大力才把這句話對小宣講清楚。

「用不着那樣洗，我不怕傳染，難道我們自己家裏人還要寫信逼你嗎？」母親痛苦地悲聲說。

他看看母親，又看看小宣，然後他說：「不過小宣究竟很年青啊。」接着他又加一句：「我們汪家就只有他一個男丁……」他慢慢地朝着床走去。「我躺一會兒。」他到了床前，低聲自語道，於是他跌下似地倒在床上了。

第二天他照常上班。他那件平價布的長衫前後表現出幾塊灰白色跡印。他簽到時不小心後襟被掛破了一塊。他聽見了笑聲。但他無心去注意，他又流汗，又喘氣地上了樓，走到自己的辦公桌前，坐下來，打開抽屜，拿出昨天未看完的校樣。

他還不曾開始工作，就覺得精神支持不住，汗不停地出。頭腦

he was doing. Gnashing his teeth, he calmed down and forced himself to carry on with his work.

He was proofreading, word for word, a document glorifying the recent progress made in China: how from her semi-colonial past she had evolved into one of the four great world powers; how the living conditions of her people had improved; what achievements were being made in furthering human rights; how the govermment cared for the people; and how the people showed their gratitude by enlisting in the military service and by paying their taxes. He dismissed these assertions as blatant lies. Nevertheless, he had to proofread each word carefully and correct all the words that had been miss-set.

The work was more than he could handle. Yet he must continue, although slowly. He could faint any minute, so he supported his chin with his left hand. He coughed often, but in so muted and soundless a manner that it ceased to be an irritant to his co-workers. Of course phlegm came up, mixed with blood. He spat out the phlegm on a piece of waste paper, rolled it into a ball and threw it into a basket. Once he coughed up some phlegm which accidently fell on one of the proof-sheets. In wiping it off with a piece of waste paper, he smeared the sheet with his blood-tinged phlegm. Exasperated, he wanted to tear all the sheets to shreds, for they told nothing but lies about improvements in the people's living conditions. But he did not dare. As for himself, he had given all his blood to try and make a living.

Suddenly, he heard people stirring downstairs, as if an accident had occurred. People dashed downstairs, and this was immediately followed by a commotion on his floor, for everyone was discussing what had happened. Sheepishly he stayed in his own chair, staring at the proof-sheets while his head was buzzing as if it were filled with crickets. Suddenly, he heard people repeatedly mention Uncle Chung's

空空的，不知道自己在做甚麼，他只咬緊牙關，定下心來，強迫着自己開始辦公。

面前攤開的是一本歌功頌德的大著的校樣，他一個字一個字地校對着。作者對他誇說中國近年來怎樣在進步、改革，怎樣從半殖民地的地位進到成為四強之一的現代國家。人民的生活又怎樣在改善，人民的權利又怎樣在提高；政府顧念到民間的疾苦，人民又如何感激而踴躍地服役、納稅、完糧⋯⋯「謊話！謊話！」他不斷地在心裏說，但是他不得不小心地看下去，改正誤植的字，拔去一些「釘子」。

這工作已經是他的體力所不能負擔的了。但他必須咬緊牙關支持着，慢慢地做下去。他隨時都有倒在地上的可能。可是他始終用左手托着腮在工作。他常常咳嗽，不過他已經用不着耽心他的咳聲會驚擾同事們了。他已經咳不出聲音來了，自然他會咳出痰來，痰裏也帶點血。他把痰吐在廢紙上，揉成一團，全丢在字紙簍中去。有一次他不小心濺了一點血在校樣上。他用一片廢紙拭去血跡，他輕輕揩了一下，不敢用力，害怕弄破紙質不好的校樣。他拿開廢紙，在那段歌頌人民生活如何改善的字句中間還留着他的血的顏色。「為了你這些謊話，我的血快要流盡了！」他憤怒地想，他幾乎要撕碎那張校樣，但是他不敢做。他凝視着那淡淡的血跡，他無可奈何地嘆了一口氣，他終於把這張校樣看完翻過去了。

忽然樓下人聲嘈雜，好像發生了甚麼意外事情。有人跑下樓去，接着樓上起了一陣小騷動，人們大聲在談論一件事，他卻退縮在自己的坐位裏，眼光定在校樣上，整個頭響着蟋蟀叫聲。他連動也沒有動一下。忽然他聽見「鍾老」兩個字，人們不只一次地講着「鍾

name. Lifting his head in astonishment, he saw the Chief Editor speaking to the Section Chief.

"What has happened to Uncle Chung?" he wondered. He wanted to get up but did not have the courage. He sat still, rooted to his seat.

Soon the Chief Editor and the Section Chief went downstairs. His inquisitive eyes followed them. Shortly, the Section Chief came back upstairs, and the noise below subsided.

"Gone. It must be cholera. Fortunately, we were able to borrow a car to take him to a hospital. It's more than twenty miles from here," he heard the Section Chief tell someone.

"Did anyone go with him?"

"Little P'an did. He'll return in the same car. We'll send someone to see him later," said the Section Chief.

"Little P'an?" Wang thought to himself. "Why isn't he afraid of infection now? He only knows how to bully me!" He felt a stab of pain in his chest.

At lunch-time he stayed at his desk. The Chief Editor, preparing to go downstairs, asked him why he did not go to lunch.

"I don't feel like eating," he lied, in embarrassment.

"Are you sick?"

"No," he said, shaking his head and standing up, thankful that the Chief Editor knew nothing of his co-workers' letter to him.

"Have you taken any shots against cholera?"

"No," he replied, shaking his head.

"You must get them. Chung had to be sent to the hospital. He must have caught cholera," the Chief Editor said with concern.

老」。他吃驚地抬頭看，主任帶着嚴肅的表情在同股長講話。

「鍾老甚麼事？」他想道，他要站起來，但他鼓不起勇氣。他仍舊坐着不動，像生根在椅子上一樣。

接着主任和股長也下樓去了。他用探詢的眼光送他們下樓。不久股長一個人走上來。樓下的鬧聲早已消失了。

「走了，一定是霍亂，幸好借到汽車送去，有二三十里路啊！」他聽見股長對人說。

「有人陪去吧？」

「小潘去，他原車回來。等會再派個工友去看看他。」股長說。

「小潘！」他驚奇地想道。「他現在怎麼又不怕傳染呢？他單單欺負我。」他覺得胸部一陣劇痛。

開午飯時，他沒有下去。主任最後下樓，看見他端坐不動，便問道：「你不下去吃飯？」

「我不想吃。」他帶窘相地答道。

「你不舒服嗎？」

「不。」他連忙站起來搖頭說。「他不知道。」他感激地想。

「你打過預防針沒有？」

「沒有。」他搖頭答道。

「你要打才成，鍾老已經送進醫院去了，一定是霍亂症」。主任關心地囑咐道。

"Yes, thank you," he replied, so grateful that he almost burst out in tears.

"Your voice has been hoarse for some time. Have you seen a doctor?"

"Yes, I have, but it doesn't seem to get better," he replied with his head lowered.

"You must be careful. Your health does not strike me as particularly good. You should take a few days off and rest," the Chief Editor advised him, knitting his eyebrows together.

"Yes," he answered, unable to raise his head.

The Chief Editor went downstairs while he remained upstairs alone. He wondered if his superior had implied that he should resign. If another such unexpected blow were to strike his weak and sickly body and knock him down, he was sure that he would never be able to get up again. With both hands supporting his chin, he looked dully at the proofs.

"No, he seems to be rather nice to me," he murmured. This conclusion somehow reduced both his pain and his suspicion, and he felt a little better.

No news from Little P'an. It was not until about an hour before closing time that the young man returned. He talked first to someone downstairs, and then came up.

"The car broke down on the way to the hospital, and we were delayed for nearly two hours," explained Little P'an.

"How is Chung? Is his illness serious?" the Chief Editor asked.

"The hospital is terrible. It's a makeshift clinic with two doctors, four nurses, and twenty beds, but there were more than thirty patients.

「是，謝謝你。」他答道，感激得快要流淚了。

「你嗓子啞了好幾天了，還沒有看醫生嗎？」

「看過，一直在吃藥，不過始終不見好。」他低着頭回答。

「你要當心啊。」主任皺皺眉頭說，「你身體不好，告一兩天假也不要緊。」

「是。」他應道。他抬不起頭來。

主任下樓去了。他一個人留在樓上。他忽然想：「主任是不是在暗示我要辭職？」他心裏很不好過。本已病弱的身體似乎又遭受到一個意外的打擊，他快要倒下去爬不起來了。他兩手托腮，一個人對着校樣納悶。

「不會的，他對我好像還客氣。」他忽然自語道。這個念頭減少了他的痛苦和疑慮，他的心稍稍舒暢一點。

小潘一直沒有消息，到下班前一個多鐘點光景那個年青人突然回來了，先在樓下講話，後來又上了樓來。

「去的時候汽車在路上拋錨，差不多就擱了兩個多鐘頭。」小潘說。

「鍾老的病怎樣？不要緊吧。」主任關心地問。

「那個醫院糟透了，是臨時改設的，一共只有兩個醫生，四個護士，二十張病床。現在收了三十幾個病人，有的就擺在過道上、地

Some of them had been left alone in the corridor, on the floor, and there wasn't even time to give them injections of alkaline salt solution. Excrement and urine were everywhere. The stench was nauseating. Being the only hospital treating epidemics, there was a constant flow of patients. No car could drive up to the main entrance and patients had to be carried on stretchers from a nearby road. Uncle Chung had to wait for more than one hour for an injection after it was diagnosed that he had cholera. The doctors and nurses were just too busy, too exhausted. We must send someone to look after Uncle Chung.... " Little P'an poured all this out excitedly in one breath.

"What did the doctor say about Chung? If it's cholera, the injection would help. There shouldn't be any danger to his life," the Chief Editor said.

"The doctor didn't say much. He just sighed and shook his head, as if to say that he was only a mortal and should not be held responsible for the lives of the people in the city," replied Little P'an.

"I think we should take the day off tomorrow and get this place thoroughly disinfected so no one else will catch the disease," the Chief Editor announced after some thought.

"Yes, that'll be good. It's safer that way," added the Section Chief, pleased with the decision.

While his co-workers continued talking about Chung, Wang quietly carried on with his own work. He did not dare to interrupt his co-workers. Instead, Uncle Chung' s kind and slightly comical face kept appearing to him, and he felt as if he were dreaming. He had not seen Uncle Chung that day. When he signed the roll in the morning, he had not seen Chung. Perhaps Chung was late to come to work and was beginning to feel sick about that time. Was Chung in real danger? No, Chung could not be. Chung had been so robust and healthy the

板上，連打鹽水針也來不及，大小便滿地都是，奇臭不堪。病人還是陸續送來。全城就只有這麼一個時疫醫院，而且汽車開不到門口，還要用滑竿抬上去。鍾老送到醫院，看了病，的確是霍亂，差不多還等了一點多鐘，才有人來給他打鹽水針。醫生護士們實在忙不過來，他們也累得很。看情形非派個工人去照料不可。……」小潘興奮地一口氣說了這許多話。

「醫生怎麼說？既然是霍亂，打了鹽水針，總不會有生命危險了。」主任說。

「醫生沒有說甚麼，他只是搖頭嘆氣。也好像在說，他不過是個平平常常的醫生，現在把全城的人的性命交給他一個人照料，他擔不起這個責任。」小潘說。

「好，這樣吧，這裏明天放一天假，好好打掃一番，也消消毒，免得再傳染人。」主任想了想又說。

「好的，這樣妥當一點。」股長滿意地附和道。

同事們繼續談論着鍾老的事。只有他一個人把頭埋在校樣上，不敢插一次嘴。但是鍾老的和善而略帶滑稽的面顏一直浮現在他的腦際。他有一種似在夢中的感覺。他這一天沒有看見鍾老，他簽到時鍾老還不曾來，大概鍾老是帶病上班的，所以這一天會遲到，而且突然發了病。鍾老的病會不會有危險呢，不會的吧，鍾老昨天還

day before, and Chung's case was completely different from his own. He himself was simply wasting away. But why then did Little P'an give such a horrible account? He kept on thinking about his only friend in the office, the one who had always befriended him and had courageously refused to join the others in signing the letter. He could not stop thinking about Chung.

When he returned home, he told his mother the bad news. She merely sighed and said a few words of sympathy for Chung, and then dropped the subject. He did not sleep well that night, disturbed by the mosquitoes, flies, and scurrying rats, as well as the noises of people quarreling, pleading, joking, and cursing that went on outside his window until midnight. He kept seeing Chung's smiling face, his shining bald head, and his red-tipped nose. Would Chung die? Would medical science save Chung? He was not unfamiliar with cholera. He had seen people die of it when he was eleven or twelve, though it was called "benumbedfoot plague" at that time.

Tossing all night long as if he carried an oppressive burden on his chest, he groaned from time to time. He dreamed that Chung had died, and that all the others who worked in the office had also died. Fortunately, his weeping was not loud enough to awaken his mother.

The next morning he felt dizzy and weak. Concerned, his mother asked, "Hsüan, why are your eyes so swollen? Did you sleep well last night?"

"No, not at all. I don't know how many times I woke up," he answered.

"Then you'd better not go out today. Since today is a holiday, you might as well rest," she said.

"I'd like to find out if Uncle Chung is feeling better," he replied thoughtfully.

是那麼健康，那麼結實。跟他一天天在瘦下去的情形完全不同。那麼為甚麼小潘又說得這樣可怕呢？他想着，鍾老是他在公司裏的唯一的友人，鍾老沒有在那封信上簽名，他不能不想着鍾老。

下了班回到家裏把這個不幸的消息告訴了母親，母親只嘆了兩口氣，說了兩三句同情的話，以後就不再提起鍾老的名字了。可是他一晚上都沒有睡好。有幾隻蚊子和蒼蠅來攪擾他，老鼠們把他的屋子當作競走場。窗下街中，人們吵嘴哭訴，講笑話罵街一直鬧到半夜。他不斷地看見鍾老的笑臉，發光的禿頂和發紅的鼻子。他一直想着鍾老的事。鍾老會死？不會死？科學能不能救活那個老人？霍亂對他並不是一個陌生的名詞，他十一二歲的時候就見到「麻腳瘟」的「威力」了。

這個夜晚他時睡時醒，老是覺得有一個可怕的重量壓在他的胸膛上，他不斷地低聲呻吟。他夢到鍾老死去，甚至全公司的人死去，他低聲哭叫。他的聲音只有他自己聽得見，所以沒有驚醒母親。

第二天早晨他起身後只覺頭暈，四肢無力。他母親關心地問他：「宣，你眼睛怎麼這樣紅？昨晚睡得怎樣？」

「不好，不曉得醒過多少回。」他答道。

「那麼你今天不要出街吧，既然放一天假，你也落得休息一天。」她說。

「我想去看看鍾老是不是好了一點。」他沉吟地說。

"Do you want to go to the hospital?" she asked in surprise.

"No, to the office. People there may know," he explained.

"Today is a holiday. Why would anyone be there with news?" she inquired of him.

He looked at her and remained silent. He obeyed and spent the whole day at home, sleeping. Yet he could not forget Chung. Would Chung be all right? He was so worried about his friend that he almost prayed for him, asking either the divine powers to spare his friend or medical science to save him. All through the day he was completely engrossed in thoughts of his friend and the night was spent in a restless sleep worrying about his friend.

Finally, morning came, and he patiently waited until office time and went to work. Everything was the same at the office except that Uncle Chung's seat was now vacant. After settling down upstairs in his seat, he took out the proof-sheets and began his work. Soon a staff servant brought a note from Section Chief Wu requesting him to write a blurb for the "famous work" he was proofreading.

The note was tantamount to an order, one which he must obey. After deliberating for a few moments, he took out a sheet of paper to write a draft statement of one to two hundred words. But he found it very difficult to go on after the first sentence. The sentences became entangled in his mind, and his thought processes stalled. Holding a writing brush in his hand, he continually dipped it in the ink. For a long time, he could not write a single word. Beads of sweat appeared on his forehead, and his whole body seemed on fire. Unable to write anything, he put away the paper and resumed proofreading.

Suddenly he heard the Section Chief cough and became anxious, thinking that the cough might be an indication of the Section Chief's dissatisfaction with his work. Quickly summoning his energy, he

「你去醫院？」母親驚問道。

「我到公司去，公司裏會有消息的。」他解釋道。

「今天放假，怎麼還會有消息？」母親不以為然地說。

他看了母親一眼，也不再說話了。這一天也一直在家裏睡覺，他完全照母親的意思辦。可是他心裏老是在想鍾老的事情。凶呢？吉呢？他幾乎要禱告了。留下「他」吧。用科學的力量救活「他」吧！他整天呼籲着。整夜希望着。

他的心一上一下，始終沒有安寧。好容易捱到另一天天明，捱到上班時間，他到了公司，一切如舊，只有鍾老的座位空着。上樓就坐後，他攤開前天未看完的校樣繼續校對下去。不久工友送來一張吳股長的字條，要他為這本他正在校對的「名著」寫一篋廣告詞。

這字條等於命令，他不能不服從。他想了想，抽出一張信箋，拿起筆預備試寫一兩百字。可是寫了一句，他就不知道應該寫些甚麼。字句混雜在一起成了一個整塊擱在他的腦子裏，他不能夠把它們一一分開，他的思想停滯了，他拿着筆，不住地在硯台中醮墨汁，許久寫不出一個字。他的額上滿是汗珠，全個臉像火燒似的發燙。沒有辦法，他拿開信箋，又繼續看校樣。

忽然他聽到一聲吳股長的咳嗽，他吃了一驚，吳股長是隨意咳出來的。他卻以為是對他不滿的表示。他連忙振作精神，又把那張

picked up the paper again and started writing. "It doesn't matter at all. It's a routine thing that I can do superficially and be done with it," he thought. In a short while he had an article of a little more than one hundred and fifty words. After reading it once, he realized it was all lies. He was ashamed of himself. He went to the Section Chief, stood respectfully before the latter's desk and handed it to him.

"Not very good. Too few complimentary words," said the Section Chief, frowning and shaking his head. "Such an important work needs proper publicity; otherwise the author will be highly displeased."

Since the author was a candidate for membership on the Central Executive Committee and a busy man in political circles, would he notice such a minor thing as a publicity article by a publishing company? Wang highly doubted it and said without thinking, "You think Mr. So-and-so will really see this article?"

"How can you tell? Important officials are very meticulous and they notice everything. Mr. So-and-so comes from cultural circles, and he's particularly interested in publishing activities. His interest in publishing is only second to his interest in politics. Moreover, he is a member of the Standing Committee of the Board of Trustees of this Company," said the Section Chief rather unpleasantly.

"I see, I see," Hsüan answered, with his head bowed.

Returning the article to him, the Section Chief said, "You'd better rewrite it."

He agreed. As he walked away, the Section Chief added, "Be very careful with the book you are proofreading now. It is imperative that not a single misprint be found. Mr. So-and-so also watches very closely for typographical errors, too."

Feeling disgusted and without raising his head, he said that he

信箋拿起來，放在面前，「沒有關係，隨便敷衍幾句吧。」他想道，就糊裏糊塗地寫了一百五六十個字。自己唸一遍。「謊話，完全說謊！」他罵自己。可是他卻拿起這廣告詞，走到吳股長的辦公桌前，恭敬地把它遞到吳股長的手裏。

「不大妥當，恭維的話太少。」吳股長皺皺眉搖搖頭說：「像這樣的名著非鄭重介紹不可，不然某先生看見會不高興。」

某先生就是這書的作者，是一位候補中委和政界的忙人，難道他連書店的廣告詞也要注意嗎？他汪文宣不大相信吳股長的話，他順口說了一句：

「某先生不見得會看得見吧。」

「你哪裏知道，他們做大官的對甚麼事情都注意，某先生是文化界出身的，他非常關切文化，對著作的興趣也不亞於從政，他又是我們公司的常務董事。」吳股長板起臉說。

「是，是。」他低下頭答道。

「你拿回去重寫過吧。」吳股長說，把廣告詞交還給他。

他唯唯應着，正要轉身走開，又聽見吳股長吩咐道：

「還有你校對那本書，要特別小心，最好不要有一個錯字，某先生對於書上的錯字平日也很注意。」

他厭惡地應了一聲，連頭也不抬地回到自己座位上去了。他憤

would be careful. He returned to his desk. Indignant, he said to himself, "All right, I'll give you what you want." As he heaped the most lavish praise on the book, he grumbled silently, "You see, I also know how to lie." Fortunately, no one heard him.

Suddenly he heard Little P'an run up breathlessly from downstairs and announce to the Chief Editor, "An aide just telephoned from the hospital. He said Uncle Chung died early this morning. He tried to call several times before, but he couldn't get through."

Wang felt he would black out from the shock. Bells kept ringing in his ears. Hurriedly he propped up his head with both hands.

XXIX

UNCLE Chung was his only friend in the office, and Chung's death severed his link with it; the office meant no more to him. After work that day he thoroughly cleaned out his desk. Going downstairs, he dreamily paused briefly before Uncle Chung's old desk, not sure what he intended to do. Once he stepped outside the building, he looked back at the door uncertainly, feeling that he was bidding a final goodbye to the place forever. But in reality, he returned to the office the next day, the third day, the fourth day, and right through the sixth day.

On the afternoon of the sixth day, he and a few of his co-workers took a long-distance bus to visit Chung's grave. Passengers were packed in the bus like sardines and it was stiflingly hot inside. It was not possible for him to stand properly, for his left foot was suspended in the air. The ride was so bumpy he almost vomited.

憤不平地對自己説：「好吧，我來大捧一場。」他拿起筆費力地在腦子裏找尋最高的讚頌詞句胡亂寫到紙上去。「你看，我也會撒謊的。」他痛苦地自語道。好在這些無聲的語言不怕被別人聽見。

忽然他聽見小潘的腳步聲。小潘氣急敗壞地跑上樓來，喘息地説：「×主任，張海雲剛剛打電話來説鍾老一早就死了。他連打幾個電話，都打不通。」

他眼前一陣黑，耳朵裏全是鈴子聲，他連忙用雙手捧住頭。

二十九

他在公司裏就只這鍾老這麼一個朋友。跟着鍾老的死，他失去了自己同公司中間的聯繫。公司同他現在可以説完全沒有關係了。下班時仔細地把自己的辦公桌收拾清楚。下樓出門時，他還在鍾老的座位前站了一會。他不知道自己要做甚麼。他好像在夢中似的。後來走出大門，他又用奇異的眼光看了看門前，他覺得自己就要同這個地方永別了。

事實上他第二天還來，第三天還來，第四天還來，一直到第六天他還來。

那天下午有幾個同事約好到鍾老的墓地去。他也參加。搭長途汽車去，也搭長途汽車回來。他們被人像裝沙丁魚似的塞在車子裏面。他幾乎連一個站的地方也找不到，他不得不把左腳懸在空中。一路上車子顛簸得厲害，車裏悶熱，空氣壞，他心裏很不好過，差一點要在車中嘔吐了。

Chung was buried on a small plot of land on a little slope near the Epidemic Hospital. The ground was dry and bare. On the grave lay a paper wreath of three different colors — red, white, and green — inscribed with the following words: "To the eternal repose of Mr. Chung Yu-an, from the Such-and-such Book Co." A standing wreath was from the Chief Editor of the Company. There was no headstone and these two scentless wreaths — one lying on the ground and the other standing up — were the sole companions for that kind, gentle, departed soul.

"It was too frugal a funeral. The Company didn't spend anything," commented one co-worker.

"It was good enough. If Chief Editor Chou were still in charge, he wouldn't even have had this kind of funeral," another interrupted.

"Truly, when a person dies, nothing matters. It is much more important to treat the living decently," mused a third.

"That's right. My feelings exactly. Since our Company doesn't treat the living decently, how can you expect it to do much for the dead?" added the second man.

No one spoke to Wang. They seemed to be avoiding him. Standing in a corner, he looked sheepishly at his friend's grave, fearful that his co-workers might chase him away.

His lungs, throat, and eyes all bothered him. Tears dimmed his vision and he rubbed his eyes hard, imagining he saw his own name "Wang Wen-hsüan" on the wreath. He steadied himself and looked again — it was his friend's name all right. No, no, he did not see it right. In his mind's eye, he saw an identical wreath clearly inscribed with his name. He would forever lie under a small mound of earth identical with this one: the same desolation, the same arid surroundings.

鍾老就葬在時疫醫院的附近，斜坡上的一塊小地方，墳上土已經乾了，還沒有長草，只放了一個紙花圈，是用紅白綠三色土花紙紮成的。上款寫「又安先生千古」，下款寫「×××書局輓」。另外還有一個花圈縛在一個木架子上，高高地立在墓前，上款仍是「又安先生千古」，下款卻是「弟×××敬輓」，這是主任送的，也是紙紮的花圈。來不及立碑，就讓這兩個沒有香味的花圈，一立一躺地默默陪伴着那個和善的老人。

「公司就這樣辦喪事，也太簡陋了，一共花不了幾個錢，」一個同事說。

「這已經不容易了，要是周主任在這兒，恐怕連這樣也辦不到，」另一個同事說。

「其實想得深一點，人死了，再怎樣，也沒有意思。還不如生前待得好一點，」第二個同事插嘴說。

「對，我就是這個意思，公司對我們活着的人也不過如是，何況死人，」第二個說話的人接口說。

沒有人跟汪文宣講話。他們好像都在避開他。他一個人站在一個角裏，畏怯地望着他那朋友的墳頭，就好像他真害怕他們隨時都會把他趕走似的。

淚水使他的眼睛模糊了。他肺痛、喉痛，現在眼睛又痛。他揉眼睛，用力擦眼睛。怎麼花圈上寫着他的名字：文宣！他定了定神。他看錯了，那裏明明是「又安」兩個字。不，不是他看錯。他想到了另一個同樣的紙花圈，白紙條的上款的確寫着他的名字。他也會躺在這同樣的土堆下面。陪伴他的也只有這同樣的荒涼而枯燥的環境。

Without telling him, his co-workers had left and returned to the city. He stood by the grave, looking around. He was not visiting a friend's grave but paying a preliminary visit to his simple future residence.

Thick clouds had gathered and darkened the surroundings. He realized a storm was coming and he could not stay any longer, so he headed toward the bus station. He did not run. But by the time he reached the station, he was breathless and perspiring profusely. After a thirty-minute wait at the station, he was pushed into a bus by other passengers. Since there was no empty seat available, he again had to stand, this time for an hour and a half, riding a distance that would normally take a little more than forty minutes. The rain had made the ride take much longer. When he reached home, he collapsed onto his bed.

He never went back to the office again but stayed in bed all day long, a little feverish, sweating and short of breath. When he talked, he made a funny noise. His chest and his throat were always sore. He groaned rarely, bearing his pain in silence. He refused to let his son come home, and talked much less with his mother. To make her a little happier, he sometimes forced a faint smile on his face.

Though he had lost hope of recovery, his mother had not. She brought in a Western-trained doctor who pronounced his case incurable. She then again sought the help of physician Chang Po-ch'ing, who had at one time brought a ray of hope to her, but this time he too felt most uncertain, even hopeless.

Wang finally lost his voice. And when he tried to speak, he could not hear himself. Upon discovering this new development he cried bitterly. Tears gushed from his eyes while he sobbed, and he felt slightly better afterwards. When his mother saw him cry, she came and asked why. He opened his mouth and pointed at his throat. She understood.

同事們都走了，他們回到城裏去了，他們臨走時並不喚他一聲。他一個人立在墓前不時左右觀望，他不是在拜望一位朋友，他現在是來看他的簡陋的新居。

天空裏黑雲愈積愈厚，四周景色逐漸陰暗，後來連他也覺察出來了。他不能再留下去。他便匆匆趕到長途汽車站去。他並沒有跑，但到了車站時，他已經滿頭大汗，氣喘得沒有辦法。他只等了半點多鐘就被人擠上了車子。在車上站了一點又二三十分鐘，才到了他住處的附近。本來汽車只走四十多分鐘，這次因為半途遇雨，雨太大，車子在中途停了若干時候。

他回到家就力竭地睡倒下來。從這時起他便沒有再去公司了。

他整天躺在床上，發着低熱，冒着汗，不停地哮喘，講話時喉嚨呼盧呼盧地響。他的胸部、喉嚨，都痛得厲害。但是他並不常發呻吟。他默默地忍受一切。他不讓小宣回家。在母親面前他的話更少了，看見母親對他流淚時，他常常苦笑。

他完全斷了念。可是母親卻不肯放棄這個絕望的戰鬥。母親請了西醫來給他診病，西醫搖搖頭，表示這個病不是藥力所能治療；她只得又向張伯情求助，張伯情曾帶給她一線希望。可是現在連張伯情也覺得沒有治愈的把握了。

他的聲音終於完全失去，現在他說話連自己也聽不見了。當他第一次發覺這情形時，他傷心地哭了一場。這所謂哭也不過是眼淚暢流，哭出來他倒覺得心裏較為暢快。母親看見他在哭，過來問他

After a momentary silence, she said, "Hsüan, don't feel sorry.... " You're a good man.... Heaven pity us!.... " Her voice had also, temporarily, become hoarse.

"Mother, I am all right. Since when have you started to believe in Heaven?" Those were the words that he would have liked to say to her, but he could not. He tried to mask his sorrow by shaking his head and forcing a smile.

"Don't be afraid. You won't die," she said.

"I am not afraid of death. We all die some time, but leaving you alone saddens me. And my son is too young," he said with effort. All his mother heard was a faint sound, without any idea of what he said. But his condition terrified and pained her.

Alarmed and grief-stricken by his suffering, she looked at him and interrupted, "Don't speak any more. You'd better rest." Her facial muscles were twitching and teardrops welled up in her eyes.

He uttered a long sigh and looked at her beseechingly.

It was hot and humid inside the room, so hot that the walls looked as though they might burst into flames at any moment. Lifting the cheap bed-sheet off himself, he exposed his hole-filled undershirt, revealing his yellowish chest, his skin, and his bones.

From that time on, his mother bought him a bell. When he needed her, he rang the bell; when he wanted anything, he used paper and pencil. Besides the occasional visits of the mailman and a doctor, the only person he saw was his mother. The mailman did not come frequently enough, for Hsiao Hsüan and Shu-sheng were not diligent letter writers. Shu-sheng still sent money every month, but it was quickly spent. At his mother's insistence the money Shu-sheng sent earlier had been withdrawn from the bank and used. For her son, his

為了甚麼。他答不出聲，只有張開嘴用手指指着喉嚨。她明白了他的痛苦。她沉默半晌，才憐愛地說：

「宣，你不要難過。……你是個好人……天應該有眼睛……」她的喉嚨暫時也啞了。

「媽，我不難過。你怎麼相信起天來了！」他想說卻說不出來，他只有竭力止了悲搖搖頭，裝出笑容來。

「你不要怕，你不會死的，」她說。

「我並不怕，人人都要死，不過留下你一個人受苦，我心裏很難過。小宣年紀又太小，……」他用力說，但母親只聽見一點聲音，她不知道他在說甚麼，可是那種掙扎的情形使她又害怕又痛苦。她望着他，一面打斷了他的話：

「你不要講話了，你好好休息吧。」她臉上肌肉在搐動，眼裏裝滿了略帶白色的淚水。

他長長地嘆一聲，睜大淚眼用了求助的目光看着母親。

屋子裏異常悶熱，板壁好像隨時會燃燒起來似的。他把蓋在身上的一幅平價布床單也揭開了，從破舊汗衣的洞口中他看見了自己那個只有皮和骨頭的黃色胸膛。

這以後母親為他買了一個鈴子。喚人時他用鈴子代他說話，請人做事時他求助於紙筆。這裏所謂人，其實就是母親一個，此外就難得有人到他的屋子裏來，除了醫生和郵差。但郵差也不常來，因為小宣和樹生的信寫得不勤。樹生仍舊按月寄款來。款子已經動用了。以前存在銀行裏的也由母親取了出來。還是母親開口向他要了

mother swallowed her pride and did everything except write to Shu-sheng directly. He still managed to write to Shu-sheng without asking his mother to write for him. In every letter he wrote words like, "I am fine; my health is improving and don't worry about me." As for the letters to Hsiao Hsüan, sometimes he wrote them and at other times his mother did. He instructed his son not to come home — Hsiao Hsüan was at a classmate's house during the vacation — but to study and work hard in his school work. His mother's letters to Hsiao Hsüan were a little more detailed, but she, too, was unwilling to divulge the true situation at home. She continued to hope for her son's recovery.

But reality crushed her hopes. Her son's condition steadily deteriorated. He felt that every part of his body was disintegrating, the pain in his chest and throat increasing. His mother realized that he was dying.

But she would not abandon hope easily. She administered drugs and fed him fresh milk and chicken bullion; she helped him change his clothes, to go to the toilet; in fact, she did things for him that a paid domestic would not do. Yet one day, he wrote on a piece of paper, "Mother, please give me some poison. Let me die quickly. I can't bear to see you suffer, and I'm suffering too much."

She wept when she read it. "I can't allow you to say that. You are my only son."

"Sooner or later I will die," he wrote again.

"When you die, I will die with you. For I won't care to live any longer." She cried openly now, no longer restraining her sorrow.

He dropped his pencil, his head slumped wearily on the pillow, and he bit his lip forcefully.

The heat increased his suffering; the noise irritated him all the more.

存單後去取的。現在為了兒子的生命，她甚麼事都肯做了，只除了先給樹生去信。所以寫給樹生的信都是他自己寫，他不要母親代筆。他在每封信上都寫着：「我還好，我的健康漸漸在恢復，你不要為我耽心，」一類的話。給小宣的信，有時他寫，有時母親寫，他只叫孩子不要回家(暑假中那個孩子住在同學家中)，好好唸書，溫習功課。母親的信裏話多一些，但她也不忍講出真實的情形，並且她還暗暗地抱着一線的希望。

然而跟她的希望相反，真實的情形卻逐漸壞下去。他自己清清楚楚地感覺到他的內部一天一天地在腐爛，他的肺和他的咽喉的痛苦一天一天地增加。母親也看得出他在用緩慢的腳步走向死亡。」

但是母親的心還是不能輕易放棄。她繼續給他吃藥，給他吃鮮牛奶和雞汁，她幫他穿衣，伺候他大小便，她為他做着一切連老媽子也不願意做的事。可是有一天他終於吃力地在紙上寫下了這樣的話：

「媽，你給我吃點毒藥，讓我快死。我不能看見你這樣受苦。我太痛苦。」

母親看這字條時，他淚汪汪地望着她。

「我不能，我就只有你一個兒子，」她哭着說。

他又寫：「我遲早還是要死。」

「你死，我跟你一起死，我也不要活了，」母親大聲哭着說，她制止不了自己的悲痛。

他放下筆，頭疲倦地倒在枕上。他用力咬自己的嘴唇。

炎熱增加他的痛苦。喧嘩更像在火上添油。霍亂為這城市帶走

Cholera had taken the lives of many and brought much loud mourning in the street. He lay in bed all day, occasionally changing his position — now on his back, then on his side or on his stomach. But he was never at peace with himself or had a moment of sound sleep.

He could not change his clothes by himself; he could not sit up easily. Every time he wrote to Shu-sheng it was a strain, and he had to bear severe pain before he could finish writing a few lines, such as: "I am still fine; my body can carry on." He used the same words over and over.

"Why are you doing all that? Let me write the letters for you," his mother begged him. All her pleading fell on deaf ears. He would not listen to her. If he did not write to Shu-sheng in his own hand, she would know that he was gravely ill.

"Why don't you let her know the truth?" his mother asked, unable to control herself.

He hesitated for a long time, and finally he wrote on a piece of paper, "I wish her happiness."

"Shu-sheng already belongs to someone else. Why don't you let her suffer a little? Why don't you let her conscience prick her a little?" she thought. "You silly ass!" she gently chided him. As she saw his shaky handwriting on the paper, her heart softened, thinking, "What happiness did he ever have in this world? He toiled all his life. I must let him have his last wish." After all, he was her flesh and blood. Gazing at his dark thin face, she ached as if her heart were being squeezed together. In frantic desperation she wished that there were a hole in the ground that would drop her straight down to hell, that a bomb would destroy her little world completely.

That afternoon a young man in the neighborhood died of cholera.

了不少人，這條街上常常有悽慘的哭聲。他躺着，成天地躺在床上，仰着，側着，伏着。他的心靜不下來，他從沒有能夠痛快地睡一刻鐘。

他不能夠自己穿衣服，也不能夠自由地坐起來。每次他給樹生寫信，總要懷着拼死的決心，忍受極大的痛苦，才能夠寫下四五行字。「我還好，我的身體可以支持下去，」他永遠這樣說。

「你何苦啊，我替你寫吧，」母親用了類似哀告的聲音說，也沒有用，在這件事上他不肯聽從母親的話。要是他不能親筆寫信，那麼她知道他一定是病重了。

「為甚麼不讓她知道呢？」

有一天母親忍不住吐出了這句話。

他遲疑了半天才寫出五個字的答語來：

「我願她幸福。」

母親想：「她已經是別人的人了，為甚麼不讓她難過一下，讓她受點良心的責備呢？」「你這傻子，」她溫和地責備他。可是她再看一眼紙上斜斜歪歪的字跡，她的心軟下來了。她又想，他活在世上究竟有過了甚麼幸福？他苦了一生，為甚麼連這樣一個小小的願望她也不肯幫忙實現？他到底是她的親骨血啊。她默默地望着他的沒有光澤的瘦臉，她的心像被甚麼東西絞着似地發痛。她想哭，她想叫。她願意地板上開一個洞讓她跌落進地獄裏去，她願意天上丟下一顆炸彈把她這個小小的世界整個毀滅。

這天下午隔壁人家的一個年青人害霍亂死了。兩個女人哭得很

His death was mourned by two women whose crying was so loud that Wang could hear them clearly. On a piece of paper he wrote, "Mother, please don't cry after my death."

"Why do you say things like that?" she asked.

"Because if you do, I won't be able to die in peace," he wrote.

"You won't die, you won't," she insisted, tears flowing.

The hottest days of summer went by. The air in the room was a little fresher, but his illness worsened and his pain increased. He tried his best to bear the pain; when it was too much he would groan. But even his groaning was almost noiseless.

One night his mother fed him chicken broth. After two mouthfuls, he pushed the spoon and her hand away. He shook his head.

"Eat a few more mouthfuls, you must," she pleaded.

Unsteadily, he scribbled that his throat was hurting him.

She shivered, the hand holding the soup bowl quaking. "Try two more mouthfuls even though it hurts. You can't go on without food," she said, putting the spoon back into his mouth. With his mouth wide open, his eyes rolling upwards and his hands clasping the thin quilt tightly, he swallowed a little more.

"Hsüan," she whispered. Looking at her tearfully, he slowly heaved a sigh.

She tried again with the spoon. He, in pain, swallowed two or three times; then unexpectedly he spat out a mouthful. Hurriedly she put the bowl down and rubbed his chest.

He slowly closed his eyes. He wanted to take a nap, but pain kept him awake. He could neither groan nor scream. Silently he wrestled

傷心。哭聲進了他的房間。他傾聽了一陣後忽然寫給他母親：

「媽，我死了，你不要哭啊。」

「你為甚麼說這種話？」母親痛苦地問。

「想到你哭我就死不下去，我心裏更苦，」他回答。

「你不會死，你不會死！」母親流着淚大聲說。

最熱的氣候過去了。屋子裏的空氣比較好受一點。可是他的病還是照常在進行，痛苦也不斷地在增加。他用了更大的忍耐來對付這個病。有時候忍不住了，他也呻吟，可是連這痛苦的呻吟也是無聲的。

一個晚上母親拿雞湯給他吃。她用湯匙餵他。他吞了兩口，忽然推開她的手，又微微搖着頭。

「你再吃幾口吧，你一天只吃那麼少的東西不行啊，」母親勸道。

他用顫抖的手拿起筆，費力地寫了兩個字「喉痛」。

母親打了一個冷噤。她那隻拿着湯匙的手也在打顫。她忍着心痛再勸道：「你忍住痛再吃兩口吧，不吃東西怎麼行！」她又把湯匙送到他的嘴邊。他顫動地張開了口，努力吞下那雞湯，一次兩次他的眼珠往上翻，手抓緊了薄被。

「宣，」母親低聲呼喚，他含淚地看她，緩緩地吐了一口氣。

母親咬緊牙關再把湯匙放進他嘴裏去。他照樣痛苦地把湯吞下了。以後又吞了兩次。再一次他把一匙的雞湯全噴了出來。他無聲地嗆咳了一陣。母親連忙放下碗揉擦他的胸膛。

他慢慢地閉上了眼睛。他想睡。可是痛苦使他清醒。他不能呻

with the pain, somewhat smoothed by his mother's massaging. He tried hard to focus his thoughts on her, hoping he could temporarily forget his pain.

Suddenly firecrackers exploded in the street, a sound rarely heard in the city during the last few years. At first, few people took any notice of it, but the noise went on unabated, from far and near, as if an important event were being celebrated. People were scrambling everywhere, many running, many singing, and others noisily chatting with one another.

He was about to ask what was going on when his mother started to speak up.

"The Japanese have surrendered! The Japanese have surrendered!" a boy's voice drowned her out, yelling the news in the street, a voice echoed by many other voices.

He was astounded. Forgetting everything, she asked him in a loud voice, "Hsüan, have you heard the news? The Japanese have surrendered."

He shook his head in disbelief, but the sounds of the firecrackers became increasingly louder and more frequent.

Like waves, crowds gathered in the streets.

"It must be true; otherwise they wouldn't be celebrating like this," she added excitedly.

He continued to shake his head. The news had come so suddenly!

"The Associated Press reported that the Japanese government has unconditionally surrendered to China, the United States, Great Britain, and the USSR," someone shouted in the street.

吟，不能叫喚。他默默地同痛苦戰鬥。母親的手使他感到一點安慰，他努力把思想集中在母親身上，他希望暫時忘卻他那個痛苦。

忽然街上響起了鞭炮聲。雖然在這城市裏幾年來很少聽到這樣的聲音，但是他們對它並不注意。出乎他們的意外，鞭炮聲接連地響着，遠遠近近都在放鞭炮，好像發生了甚麼大的喜慶事，人聲嘈雜，許多人在跑，有人大聲唱歌，有人笑着講話。

「甚麼事？」他想道，母親卻說了出來。

「日本投降啦！日本投降啦！」孩子的聲音在街中叫着，年青人的聲音響應了。

他吃了一驚。母親忘了一切地大聲問他：「宣，你聽見沒有？說是日本投降啦！」

他搖搖頭，他還不相信。可是外面鞭炮聲響得更密了。

人們像潮湧似地走過窗下街心。

「大概是真的，不然不會這樣！」母親興奮地說。

他還是在搖頭。這個消息來得太突然了！

「合眾社電報：日本政府向中美英蘇四國無條件投降！」有人在街中大聲報告。

"Did you hear that? The Japanese have surrendered! The War of Resistance is over. No more suffering for us," exclaimed his mother hysterically. She laughed, she cried, forgetting that she was in a dark room. One lone candle flickered violently, its wick leaning precariously toward one side and the wax leaking out through a small crack.

He stared at his mother, puzzled by her behavior, tears gushing out from his eyes. Momentarily he felt like laughing and crying, but he soon calmed down and sighed. His end was near, too, he thought.

"Extra! Extra! The Japanese have surrendered!" shouted a newspaper vendor, walking by the window.

His mother held his hand and said, "Hsüan, are you happy? Victory! Victory!"

"Now I can die without any regrets," he wrote on a piece of paper with his shaking hand.

She saw his unevenly written script. Forgetting everything, she said between laughter and tears, "Hsüan, you won't die! You won't! Victory is here. No one should die any more."

Her tears flowed freely now. She tightly clasped her son's hand, not knowing whether she was happy or sad.

XXX

HIS mother's wish was unfulfilled, and some nights later she sat at the side of his bed keeping vigil. The electric light was dim. On a wooden bench was a small bowl of chicken broth with a spoon in it.

「你聽，這還不是真的嗎？日本投降了！抗戰勝利了！我們不再吃苦了！」她歇斯特里地高聲叫道。她一邊笑，一邊流眼淚，她好像忘了自己是在一間黑暗的屋子裏，床前一根板櫈上放着一支蠟燭，燭光抖得厲害，燭芯偏垂在一邊，燭油從一個小缺口流下來。

他睜大眼睛呆呆地望着母親，彷彿不懂得母親的意思，突然他迸出了眼淚，他想笑，又想哭。但很快地他又冷靜下來，他吐了一口長氣。他想：你完了，我也完了。

「號外！號外！日本人投降！」報販大聲叫着跑過窗下。

母親拉着他的手，溫和地帶笑問他「宣，你高興嗎？勝利啦！勝利啦！」

他用發顫的手捏着筆吃力地在紙上寫着：

「我可以瞑目死去了。」

母親看見這些歪斜的字，她忘記了一切，又哭又笑地叫起來：「宣，你不會死！你不會死！勝利了，就不應該再有人死了！」

她的淚水暢快地流下來，她緊緊捏着兒子的手，不知心裏是喜是悲。

三十

那個母親的願望並沒有實現。在她說了那些話以後，某一天的夜晚，她坐在床沿上，守着她的兒子。電燈光還是半明半暗的，旁邊一根板櫈上放着滿滿一小飯碗雞湯，碗裏有一把湯匙。

"Hsüan, you eat some," she said.

He rolled his eyes upward, moved his body a little, hands gesturing in the air. He did not pick up his pen, nor did he answer her.

"Hsüan, you haven't eaten for two days. Bear the pain and have a little," she begged him in a loud voice.

Slowly he moved his head and opened his mouth. Then he stretched out his hand, put it by his mouth and tore his lower lip. Later he put his fingers in his mouth, acting as though he wanted to tear out his tongue.

"Hsüan, how do you feel? Be a little more patient," she said sadly, holding his other hand.

He nodded, took his hand out of his mouth and put it on his throat. Tears welling in his eyes, he stared at his mother.

"Don't, you won't die," she consoled him.

His five fingers were rubbing his throat continuously; his movements were awkward and his fingers stiff. His chest heaved upward.

"Hsüan, what do you want?" she asked.

He did not respond. After a while, his stiff fingers unleashed their fury as well as they could on his throat. His body was shaking and the wooden bed was squeaking.

"Hsüan, be patient," she said. Getting up, she took his hand away from his throat. But two or three minutes later it returned to his throat. With his mouth wide open, he scratched hard, while his eyes turned white. Scratching his throat madly, his five fingers, with their long nails, left several bloody stripes on his throat.

"Hsüan, be patient. You can't do this, you can't do this," his mother implored him in anguish.

「宣，你吃兩口吧，」她說。

他翻了翻白眼，微微動一動身子，手揮舞一下，也不去拿筆。他不回答。

「宣，你兩天不吃東西了，忍着痛吃一點吧，」她哀求地大聲說。

他慢慢地動一下頭，他張開嘴，又伸起手，很費力地移放到嘴邊，抓住下嘴唇，過後又鬆開，把手指伸進口裏去，像是要抓舌頭。

「宣，你難過嗎？你忍耐點吧，」她捏緊他的另一隻手悲聲說。

他點點頭，把手從嘴裏拿出來，就放在喉嚨上。他眼裏含着淚，用力望他母親。

「你不要難過，你不會死的，」她安慰道。

他那五根手指不停地在喉嚨上擦揉，動作仍是遲緩而手指僵硬。忽然他把胸膛向上挺了一下。

「宣，你要甚麼？」母親問。

他不回答。過了半晌，他那五根好像僵硬了的手指忽然狂亂地抓他的喉嚨。身子顫抖着，床板發出響聲。

「宣，你忍耐點，」母親說着，便站起來，把他那隻手從他的喉嚨上拉開。但是過了兩三分鐘他的手又放到那地方去了。他大大地張開嘴，用力地抓着，他的眼睛翻白。他的手指在喉嚨上亂搔。那五根手指都長着長指甲，它們在他的喉嚨上劃了幾條血痕。

「宣，你忍耐點，這樣是不行的，你不能這樣啊，」母親悲痛地

Gradually he shifted his gaze toward her face. His eyes seemed to say, "I'm in great pain." His body moved about in the bed, shaking and trembling.

She asked again, "Hsüan, is the pain very bad?"

He nodded and managed to free his hand from her grasp. Seeing his fingers gesturing wildly in the air, she did not know what he wanted.

"Hsüan, what do you want?" she asked.

His eyes slowly shifted to the pencil by the pillow.

"You have something to say? You want the pencil?" As she handed him the pencil, he grabbed it, but his fingers were shaking so violently that he nearly dropped it on the floor. She gave him a book. "You can write on the back of this book."

One hand holding the pencil, the other holding the book, he wrote one single word: "Pain." Though he had used all the strokes necessary for the word, they were written so shakily it scarcely resembled the original word.

Tears burst from his mother's eyes. "Hsüan, be patient," she said again. "Soon Hsiao Hsüan will come home with the doctor." As soon as she finished speaking, she began sobbing.

He was lucid and understood everything. He acutely felt the pain and realized how feeble he was; he knew that his organs were dying and that his condition was critical. But as the end approached, his love of life grew stronger than his fear of death. He saw the sorrow he brought to his mother; just now he saw her walking to the window and weeping. What could he do? If only he could say or write some last words. "What wrongs have I committed? I'm just an ordinary law-

求他。他的眼光慢慢地移到她的臉上。他的眼光説着話：我痛得厲害。他的身子在床上搖擺，顫抖。

「宣，你痛得厲害嗎？」她又問。

他點點頭。他把另一隻手從她的掌握中掙脱出來。手指頭在空中亂抓，她不知道他要甚麼。

「宣，你要甚麼？」她問。

他的眼光慢慢地移到枕旁那枝鉛筆上。

「你有話要説，要筆嗎？」她一面問，一面把鉛筆拿起來遞到他的手裏。他似乎要搶過筆來，可是他的手指顫得厲害，他接過筆時，差一點把它落在被上。

母親遞了一本書給他。「你就寫在書後面吧，」她説。

他一隻手拿筆，一隻手拿書，但費力地在書的封底上寫了一個「痛」字。其實只有七分像字，筆劃寫夠了，卻安排得不勻整。

母親看到這個字，眼淚又迸出來了。「宣，你忍耐點吧。等到小宣把張伯情請來就好了，」她雖然在安慰他，可是説完話就背過臉低聲哭起來。

他的神志很清醒，他明白這一切情形。他敏鋭地感到痛，感到自己的衰弱。他知道他的身體組織的各部分逐漸在死亡，而且就要到了最後的關頭。他到這時強烈地感到對於生命的依戀，對於死亡的恐懼。他也看見自己所帶給母親的痛苦。他看見母親哭着走到窗前去。他能夠做甚麼呢？哪怕就説一句話，留下幾句遺言也好。「我做過了甚麼錯事呢？我一個安份的老好人！為甚麼我該受這懲罰？

abiding citizen: why am I being punished? There is my mother. After my death, how is she to survive? How is Hsiao Hsüan to live? What bad deeds have they committed?" Full of grievances, he wanted to cry, to scream, but he could not produce a sound. No one could hear him. He demanded justice, but where could he find it? He could not even shout out his grievances; he must die in silence.

A couple was squabbling in the street: the woman screaming, the man striking her and cursing, a third person trying to mediate between the warring couple; and another man, passing by his window, was singing an aria from a Szechwan opera.

"Why should they be living? Why should I be dying? And dying so painfully?" he thought. "I want to live!" he cried soundlessly.

His mother turned to look at him. Her eyes were swollen and her face ashen; she looked as though she might collapse at any moment.

"She has had a hard life," he painfully reflected. And even as he moved his head slightly, he was attacked by a sharp pain. Simultaneously his throat and his lungs hurt him so intensely that his two hands clawed the air. He opened his mouth as much as he could. He tried his utmost to open his mouth, but no sound came out. He was sweating. He felt his hands were being tightly held, and he thought he heard his mother saying something.... The pain was so intense that he finally fainted.

His mother's weeping brought him back to consciousness. Lying in bed he was drenched in cold sweat, having also wet his pants. He held his mother's hand tightly, dully looking at her affectionate face. His pain eased. He wanted to smile at her, but tears came instead.

"Now that you've regained consciousness, nothing serious will

還有她，我母親，我死了，她一個人怎樣生活？拿甚麼生活？小宣又怎樣活下去？他們又做過甚麼壞事呢？」他裝滿了一肚皮的怨氣，他想叫，又想哭。但是他沒有聲音。沒有人聽得見他的話。他要求「公平」。他能夠在哪裏找到「公平」呢？他不能夠喊出他的悲憤。他必須沉默地死去。

街中有一對夫婦在吵架，女的在哭在叫，男的在打在罵，還有第三個人在勸解。另外有一個人唱着川戲走過窗下。

「為甚麼他們都應該活，而我必須死去，並且這麼痛苦地死去。」他又想。「我要活！」他無聲地叫道。

母親掉回臉來看他。她的眼睛紅腫，臉色慘白。她好像隨時都會病倒似的。

「她也太辛苦了，」他痛苦地想，他把頭一動。忽然一陣劇痛襲來。喉嚨和肺一齊痛，痛得他忍耐不住。他兩隻手亂抓。他張開嘴叫，沒有聲音，他拼命把嘴張大，還是叫不出聲音來。他滿頭是汗，他覺得兩手被人捏住，母親的聲音在說着甚麼。……但是他痛得暈過去了。

他又被母親的哭喚聲驚醒。他躺在床上滿身冷汗，褲子被小便打濕透了。他抓緊母親的手，呆呆地望着那張親愛的臉。痛苦稍微減輕了一些。他想對母親笑，但是眼淚不由他控制地流出來。

「你醒過來了，以後不要緊了，」母親噓了一口氣，親切地說，

happen to you," heaved his mother, her eyes and cheeks spotted with teardrops.

Disagreeing with her, he shook his head.

Hsiao Hsüan came in and said, "Grandma, Dr. Chang has malaria and he can't come."

The old woman immediately realized that her son's fate was sealed. It took her some time before she asked her grandson, "Why did it take you so long to come home?"

"The streets were crowded with people preparing to celebrate victory tomorrow. I lost my way in the crowd and I was also delayed for quite a while at Dr. Chang's residence," he answered. "By the way, there will be full-scale celebrations with lanterns and silk festoons tonight," he added.

"Are you hungry? You still have a little pocket money left. Why don't you go out and have two bowls of noodles? I didn't cook today, and I had some leftover rice. Please go and eat," she said.

Hsiao Hsüan agreed and left.

Wang Wen-hsüan overheard the whole conversation. "They're celebrating," he thought. He'd like to smile for them, but the pain deterred him. "Would victory bring relief to them? To Mother and Hsiao Hsüan?" he wondered. Meanwhile pain kept interrupting his thoughts and monopolizing his whole being. Pain was foremost, pain gradually increasing, continuously increasing and chasing away all other thoughts. Pain made him forget everything; he only remembered bearing or avoiding pain. He waged a desperate battle against it. He was defeated. Soundlessly he pleaded, "Let me die! I can't go on."

Yet his dear ones, his mother and his son could not understand his

她的眼角和兩頰都還有淚痕。

他不以為然地搖搖頭。

小宣從外面走進屋子。他一進門就說：「婆，張伯情打擺子不能來。」

母親楞了一下，完了！她心上挨了一下石子。過後她才問：「怎麼你去了這麼久？」

「大街上人多得很，明天慶祝勝利，到處都在準備，我走錯路，到張家又耽擱了好一陣，」小宣答道。他又加一句解釋：「今晚上很熱鬧，到處紮好了燈彩。」

「你肚子餓不餓？你身上還剩得有錢，你出去吃兩碗麵罷。我今天下午沒有煮飯，上午有點剩飯我炒來吃了。你快去吃吧，」她又說。

「好，」小宣應道。

這一番對話他汪文宣全聽進去了。「他們在慶祝，」他想道，他願意為他們笑一笑，可是痛苦阻止了他。「勝利會不會給他們帶來解救呢？」他又想，第二個「他們」指的是母親和小宣。可是痛苦又來阻止了他。他被痛苦佔有了。痛苦第一。痛苦逐漸增加，不停地增加，痛苦趕走了別的思想。痛苦使他忘記了一切。他只記得忍受痛，或者逃避痛。一場絕望的戰鬥又在進行。他失敗了。但是他不得不繼續作戰。他無聲地哀叫着：「讓我死吧，我受不了這種痛苦。」

然而他的親愛的人，他母親和他兒子不能了解這種無聲的語言。他們不會幫忙他解除這痛苦。

silent speech. They could not help him escape from his pain.

Pain continued and increased.

September 3 — Day of Victory and Day of Joy — did not bring any change to this room. In the streets smiling crowds welcomed the victory parades; airplanes performed many stunts and scattered celebration leaflets. Yet in Wang Wen-hsüan's room there were only pain and tears.

On that day he three times lost and regained consciousness. He felt that he had reached the pinnacle of man's capacity to endure; he wished that death would deliver him immediately, but he continued to live. His mother and his son maintained their vigil by his bed. Tearfully he gazed at them and begged them to help him die even a moment sooner.

His life was coming to an end minute by minute. Although he could not do much thinking, he was lucid. During those last moments, he was unwilling to take his eyes away from his dear ones whose faces gradually became blurred. He imagined he saw a third person's face by his bedside: that of Shu-sheng, whom he had not forgotten. But even the third person's face could not reduce the pain, which stayed with him until his last breath. His last breath lingered and he could not die for some time. His mother and his son each held one of his hands and watched him draw his last breath.

When he finally expired, his eyes were half closed, showing their whites, and his mouth wide open as if he were demanding justice from someone. It was eight o'clock in the evening, and the people in the city were busy celebrating victory amidst displays of fireworks and the sounds of countless firecrackers.

痛苦繼續着，而且不停地增加。

九月三日，勝利日，歡笑日，也沒有給這個房間帶來甚麼變化。在大街上人們帶着笑臉歡迎勝利遊行的行列。飛機在空中表演並且散佈慶祝的傳單。然而在他汪文宣的屋子裏卻只有痛苦和哭泣。

他這一天暈過去三次，而又醒了轉來。他覺得已經到了一個人所能忍受的痛苦的頂點了，他願意「死」馬上來帶走他。可是他仍舊活着。母親和小宣一直守在床前。他眼淚汪汪地望着他們。他只求他們幫助他早一刻死去。

他的生命一分鐘一分鐘地慢慢死去。他的頭腦一直是清醒的，雖然不能多用思想。在這些最後的時刻裏，他始終不肯把眼光從母親和小宣的臉上掉開。後來他們的面影漸漸地模糊起來，他彷彿又看見了第三個人的臉，那自然是樹生的，他並沒有忘記她。但是甚至這三個人的面顏也不能減輕他的痛苦。他一直痛到最後一刻。一口氣吊着，他許久死不下去。母親和小宣各人捏緊他的一隻手，望着他嚥氣。

最後他斷氣時，眼睛半睜着，眼珠往上翻，口張開，好像還在向誰要求「公平」。這是在夜晚八點鐘光景，街頭鑼鼓喧天，人們正在慶祝勝利，用花炮燒龍燈。

Epilogue

ONE night, more than a month later, there was a blackout throughout the hilly city: the generators were being overhauled. After rain in the morning, it suddenly grew chilly in the afternoon, with gusts of cold wind sweeping through the city and driving customers away from the street stalls. The stench of acetylene lamps was everywhere, their flickering lights also seemed to be shuddering.

A lone rickshaw, after trudging through the dark, chilly, and desolate streets, stopped in front of an apartment building and a well-dressed woman passenger got out. Clutching her purse under her arm and switching on her flashlight, she entered the swinging door, walked through the tunnel-like corridor and climbed to the second floor, and then to the third floor.

Stopping by the door of one apartment, she felt her heart beating faster than usual. Excitedly she knocked on the door.

No answer. She could see a light in the room and its unlocked door. Thinking that there must be someone inside or that the people might already be asleep, she knocked a little harder.

"Who is it?" a woman asked. The voice was familiar to her, though she could not identify it.

"Me," she answered casually.

The door was open; a weak light gleamed in the room. She saw a candle on the square table. A woman came to the door. With the woman's back against the light, she could not tell who she was.

尾聲

一個多月後的一個夜晚，在山城裏說是因為修理鍋爐全市停電。早晨下過一陣雨，下半天氣候驟然轉寒，冷風一陣一陣地吹過市空，趕走了攤頭的顧客。電石燈的臭味隨着風四處飄送，火光孤寂地打着寒顫。

一輛人力車經過陰暗、寒冷、荒涼的市街，到了一所大樓的門前。從車上走下來一個裝束入時的女人，她夾着手提包走進彈簧門去。她用手電光照路，走過了黑洞似的過道，上了二樓，又走上三樓。

在一間屋子的門前她站住了。她的心跳得厲害。她興奮地敲着房門。

沒有應聲。她看見房內有亮，門上沒有鎖，心想屋子裏不會沒有人，也許他們睡着了，她便用力再敲兩下。

「哪個？」屋子裏有一個女人的聲音問着。這聲音似乎是她熟悉的，但她又說不出是誰的聲音來。

「我，」她順口應了一個字。

開了，射出一道微光。她瞥見方桌上燃着一支蠟燭。開門的也是一個女人，臉背着光，她認不清楚是誰的臉孔。

"Whom do you want to see?" the woman asked in surprise.

"Don't the Wangs live here?" she asked, even more surprised.

"There are no Wangs here," answered the woman.

"Didn't they live here before? It's the same room and even the same furniture," she said, very much puzzled.

"Oh, you must be Mrs. Wang. Please come in. There's no electricity tonight, so I couldn't see you very well," the woman said with a smile. Stepping aside, she let Shu-sheng in.

"Mrs. Fang, didn't you live on the second floor before? When did you move upstairs?" Shu-sheng felt a little at ease when she recognized it was Mrs. Fang, who used to live on the second floor. The interior arrangement of the room had not changed except the walls had been repainted. The room looked more pleasing to the eye.

"Almost a month ago," Mrs. Fang answered. "Oh, Mrs. Wang, I really don't know how to address you. Weren't you in Lanchow? When did you come back?"

"Just today. Mrs. Fang, I'm still the same; I haven't married anyone else," Shu-sheng answered, blushing slightly. "Mrs. Fang, where are they? I mean Wen-hsüan and the others," she asked in a trembling voice.

"You mean Mr. Wang? Haven't you heard?" Mrs. Fang asked in astonishment.

"No, I haven't. I haven't received a letter from them in over a month. None of my recent letters has been answered," Shu-sheng said apprehensively.

"Mr. Wang passed away," Mrs. Fang whispered.

「找哪個？」開門人驚訝地問。

「請問汪家是不是住在這兒？」叩門人更驚訝地問。

「這兒沒有姓汪的，」開門人回答。

「以前不是汪家住在這兒嗎？明明是這一間屋，傢具也是，」叩門人説，她的驚奇更大了。

「啊，你是汪太太，請進來坐，今天停電，我沒有看清楚，」開門人笑着説，她閃開身子，把叩門人讓了進去。

「方太太，你們不是在二樓住嗎？幾時搬上來的？」叩門人想起開門人原來是住在二樓的方太太，畢竟遇到一個熟人，她稍稍心安一點。房間裏陳設沒有多大的改變，就是四壁白亮了許多，看起來順眼點。

「快一個多月了，」方太太回答。「汪太太，啊，我不曉得現在要怎樣叫你才好，你不是在蘭州嗎？幾時回來的？」

「今天剛到的，方太太，我還是那樣，並沒有另外結婚啊，」樹生略略紅了臉。接着她聲音發顫地問：「方太太，他們搬到哪兒去了？我説文宣他們。」

「你説汪先生嗎？你還不曉得？」方太太驚問。

「我的確不曉得。我一個多月沒有接到他們的信。我寫信去，總是沒有信息，」樹生不安地説。

「汪先生不在了，」方太太低聲説。

"Passed away? When did this happen?" Shu-sheng cried, tottering momentarily from the shock.

"Last month, about the time when people were celebrating the victory," Mrs. Fang said. A tremor went through Shu-sheng. "The old lady left and took her grandson with her. She let us have this apartment and the furniture for a small sum of money."

Shu-sheng's heart sank, as if someone had poured a bucket of cold water over her. Her face paled. Dumfounded for a while, she murmured, "Where did they move him to?" Tears gushed out. She quickly wiped her eyes and turned her face away.

"I don't know. I asked the old lady once, and she said she was going to move in with some relatives here or go back to Kunming. She even asked someone to get her steamer tickets," Mrs. Fang answered as well as she could in a blank tone of voice, seemingly quite certain of her answer.

"There was no need to get steamer tickets if they were going to Kunming, and they don't have any relatives here," Shu-sheng said. "Where would they have gone to? "

"That's what the old lady told me," Mrs. Fang continued. "Most likely they've moved away. Before they left, they sold all their belongings in a temporary stall in the street. Oh, excuse me. I've forgotten to bring you tea." Apologetically she rose and walked to a tea-table, on which were a thermos bottle, a teapot, and tea cups.

"Mrs. Fang, please don't bother. I'm not thirsty," Shu-sheng stopped her. "Let me ask you something else. Do you know what happened before Wen-hsüan died? Where is he buried?"

"Mrs. Wang, don't grieve too much. First, have some tea," Mrs. Fang said, gently putting a cup of tea in front of Shu-sheng.

「他不在了？甚麼時候？」樹生身子一動，幾乎要跳起來，她驚叫道。

「就在上個月慶祝勝利那一天，」方太太說。樹生的身子猛然顫抖了一下。「老太太帶小少爺走了。我們這間房子就是老太太讓給我們的，傢具也是她讓的，我們出了一點錢。」

樹生好像被人迎頭澆了一桶冷水似的，她全身發冷，臉色變成了慘白。她呆了半晌才吐出一句問話：「他們搬到哪兒去了？」她禁不住流出眼淚，她連忙伸手擦揉眼睛，一面把臉掉開。

「我不曉得。我問過老太太，她說搬到一個親戚家去住，又說要去昆明，又好像聽她說在托人買船票，」方太太一邊想一邊答道，她聲音平淡， 好像對自己的話並沒有確信似的。

「去昆明也用不着買船票，他們在這個地方並沒有甚麼親戚，」樹生懷疑地說。「不曉得他們到哪兒去？」

「老太太是這樣說的，」方太太說，「不過我想他們走的成份居多。他們搬走以前，差不多把東西都賣光了，就在這個門口擺地攤賣了的。啊，汪太太你坐了半天我還沒有倒茶，」她抱歉似地說着就站了起來，走向一個茶几，那裏放着熱水瓶茶壺和茶杯。

「方太太，你不要客氣，我不口渴，」樹生連忙欠身阻止道。「我請問你，你知道我們文宣臨死的情形嗎？他現在葬在哪裏？」

「汪太太，你不要難過，你歇歇先吃杯茶吧，」方太太溫和地說，端了一杯茶放在樹生面前。

"Thank you. Please tell me what happened before he died. In Lanchow, I thought he was improving. In every letter he claimed his health was all right. Please tell me. I'm not afraid. Tell me the truth."

"In fact, I don't know. I really don't know. But I did visit your mother-in-law once when Mr. Wang was ill. I know he was hoarse and died a month or so later. When I saw him, he was in bed and couldn't talk. He was very very thin," Mrs. Fang said in a melancholy tone.

"Where is he buried? I want to visit his grave," Shu-sheng interrupted. She felt a sharp pain stabbing her heart. She was sorry, wishing she could go to his grave immediately.

"I don't know. I heard that Mr. Wang did not leave any money, that his body remained in the room for two days before the old lady could find enough money to buy a coffin. I asked her where Mr. Wang was buried, but she'd not tell me. The poor old woman! She suffered greatly. She was much thinner and her hair was all gray," said Mrs. Fang, casting a sympathetic glance at Shu-sheng.

While listening, Shu-sheng bit her lip. Her nose ached, her heart pounded; she felt torn apart by feelings of regret, tears flowing freely from her eyes. She tried her utmost to control herself. "Maybe the neighbors next door know where he is buried. He can't be missing like that. Or maybe someone at the office knows; at least Chung should know, " she muttered, as if arguing with someone. She did not know Uncle Chung was no longer in the world.

"Nobody here has any idea. The coffin was taken out early one morning; no one attended the service; and the old lady didn't tell any of us. But someone at the office should know," Mrs. Fang said kindly. She was willing to help her guest, though she knew she could not be of much use.

「謝謝你，請你告訴我他臨死的情形。我在蘭州還以為他的病漸漸好起來了。他每封信都說他的身體不壞。請你告訴我，我不怕，你說真話吧。」

「其實我不曉得。我實在不曉得。汪先生生病的時候我只去看過老太太一次，我只曉得他聲音啞了，睡了一個多月就死了。我那次看見他睡在床上，說不出話，瘦得可憐——」方太太用了一種近似悒鬱的聲調說。

「他葬在哪兒？我要去看他！」樹生忘了一切地打岔道。她感到一陣劇烈的心痛，她後悔，她真想立刻就到他的墓地去。

「我不曉得。我聽說汪先生臨死身邊並沒有甚麼錢，屍首擱在房裏，甚麼東西都沒有預備。也虧得老太太，她跑了兩個整天才弄到一點錢買了棺材抬出去葬了。我不曉得汪先生葬在哪兒。我問過老太太，她也不說。老太太也真苦，這兩個多月她瘦得多，頭髮全白了。」方太太一面說一面用同情的眼光看她。

樹生一邊聽，一邊咬嘴唇，她的鼻頭有點酸痛，心跳得猛烈，悔恨的情感扭絞着她的心。眼淚又一股一股地流下來。她還竭力控制自己。「那麼隔壁鄰舍總有人知道他葬在哪兒吧？他不能夠就這樣失蹤的。公司裏一定有人知道，至少鍾先生總曉得，」她像同誰爭論般地說。她不知道鍾老已經不在這個世界上了。

「這兒的人都不曉得。棺材是大清早抬出去的。也沒有人跟去安葬。老太太也沒有通知我們。不過公司裏總有人曉得，」方太太好心地說，她很願意給這位客人幫忙，可是自己也知道沒有辦法。

"I'll find out at the office tomorrow," Shu-sheng said disappointedly. She lowered her head and wiped her tears with a handkerchief. "When did the old lady move out?" she asked again.

"More than a month ago. The first day after they moved out, we had the walls repainted and moved in on the fourth day. My husband uses our rooms downstairs for business. By the way, Mrs. Wang, I haven't asked you where you're staying," Mrs. Fang added with concern.

"At the moment with a friend. I must return to Lanchow in a few days," Shu-sheng said.

"Then are you going to look for them?"

A baby's cry came from the adjoining room. Without waiting for a reply Mrs. Fang got up and said quickly, "My daughter is awake. Please stay for a while." She hurriedly went inside.

This spared Shu-sheng from having to answer a difficult question. Sitting alone by the candle, she felt like dreaming. This was the house where she had once lived: the same old furniture, the square table, the desk, the bookshelf, the China cabinet, the bed. All were familiar to her. Although the broken items had been repaired, the dirty ones cleaned, and the walls repainted white, she, sitting there on the same stool she had sat on for so many years, felt like a stranger, a guest, unable to find any trace of herself in these objects. There also used to be a lit candle here in the past as there was now, but the present one was much brighter. Only a few months had passed, but everything had changed: her husband dead and her mother-in-law and her son gone. Where was he buried? And where had they gone? Why didn't they let her know? Could she still find out?

A different child was weeping in the room. How strange the voice! The young mother was walking the floor and singing a lullaby with

「我明天到公司去打聽明白，」樹生失望地說，她低下頭用手帕揩淚痕：她又問：「老太太他們哪天搬出去的？」

「一個多月了，她頭天搬走，我們第二天粉刷牆壁，第四天就搬進來。樓下那一間，我們先生拿來做會客辦公講生意用。啊，汪太太，還沒有問你住在哪兒？」方太太關心地問。

「我暫時住在……朋友家裏……我過幾天就要回去，」樹生囁嚅地說。

「那麼你還去不去找老太太他們？」方太太繼續問。

嬰孩的哭聲突然從小屋傳來。方太太不等客人回答馬上站起來，着急地說：「我女兒醒了，你請坐一下吧。」她忙忙慌慌地走進那裏面去了。

樹生免去了回答一個難題的痛苦。她仍舊坐着，一個人伴着一支蠟燭。她忽然起了一種在夢中似的感覺。這是她自己住過的屋子，自己用過的傢具：方桌、書桌、小書架、碗廚、床……一切都是她熟悉的，雖然破的修理好了，舊的弄乾淨了，牆壁刷得白白的。可是她坐在她坐了幾年的櫈子上，現在卻變成了一個陌生人，一個生客。甚至在那一切熟悉的東西上她也找不到過去的痕跡了。同樣的燃着一支蠟燭，可是現在卻比從前亮了許多。只有幾個月功夫，一切都改變了。他死了，母親和孩子走了。他葬在哪裏？他們去到哪裏？她不知道。為甚麼不讓她知道？她還有甚麼辦法知道？別人的孩子在她的屋子裏哭。多麼新奇的聲音。現在那個年青的母親在小屋裏抱着小孩走來走去，唱催眠曲。她從前也這樣做過的。

the baby in her arms. She had done the same thing years ago for her son, but where was Hsiao Hsüan now? The boy had never been close to her, and she had never loved him with the fullness she thought a mother should. She had ignored him, and now she would lose him forever. Mrs. Fang remained in the next room. Her baby cried sporadically, and Mrs. Fang patiently walked the floor with it and sang a lullaby, oblivious of herself and the presence of a guest in the other room. She could only sit alone and wait, tormented by memories of the past. She recalled her farewell to Hsüan on the stairs. They shook hands — in the darkness. She wondered why he had not told her about the true state of his health. When she stepped off the airplane that morning, she had decided that she would frankly say to him, "If it'll do you any good, I can come back. I haven't been unfaithful to you." But now it was all too late. It would be too painful to visualize his last moments. Too late, too late. For her own happiness, she had helped destroy his. The very thought made her get up quickly. Why did she remain here? Everything here, every piece of furniture in the room was telling her about her past with him and sharply stabbing her heart. She could not even bear to hear the young mother's lullaby any longer; it too stirred up buried memories, for she too had been a mother once. It was time for her to leave. She arose and shouted, "Mrs. Fang, I'm leaving, please don't come out." She picked up her purse and walked toward the door.

Rushing out of the small room with the baby in her arm, Mrs. Fang said sincerely, "Mrs. Wang, stay a while. It's early yet."

"Thank you, I must leave," said Shu-sheng, stopping and turning around.

"Goodbye, then," said Mrs. Fang softly. Then she added, "You'll come back?"

"No, thank you. I won't," said Shu-sheng, shaking her head. She

那是十幾年前的事了，為了小宣。可是現在她的小宣又在哪兒呢？那個孩子。他並不依戀她，她也沒有對他充份地表示過母愛。她忽略了他。現在她要永遠失掉他了。她就只有這麼個孩子啊。方太太還不走出來，小孩仍舊不時哭叫，方太太有耐性地繼續唱催眠曲，一面走一面拍拍孩子。那個女人似乎忘了她的存在，只顧着孩子，就忘記了客人，讓她冷清清的坐在外屋裏，被回憶來包圍折磨。她忽然想起了樓梯口的一幕。他們在黑暗中握手。「保重！」為甚麼病到那樣還不使她知道。「只要你好，我可以回來，我並沒有做過對不起你的事情，」她今天下飛機時，還這樣想過。她可以坦白地對他説這種話。然而現在太遲了。她不敢想像他臨死的情形。太遲了，太遲了。她為了自己的幸福，卻幫忙毀了另一個人的……她想着，想着，她突然站起來，她為甚麼還留在這兒？她再受不了這個房間和這些傢具，每件東西都在敘説他和她的故事，每件東西都在刺痛她。她甚至受不了那個年青母親的催眠歌。這歌聲使她想起她自己也曾做過母親，給她喚起她久已埋葬了的回憶。她應該走了。她大聲説：

「方太太，我走了，你不要出來。」她便拿起手提包朝房門外走。

方太太抱着小孩趕出來，誠懇地叫道：

「汪太太，你再坐一會啊。還早嘛！」樹生停了腳步回過頭來。

「我走了，謝謝你，」樹生説。

「慢走啊，」方太太柔聲説。接着又加一句：「你還要再來吧。」

「謝謝你，我不再來了，」樹生搖搖頭説，這次她不曾流淚，可

did not cry this time, because her anguish was too great to be washed away by tears.

"Then wait a second. Let me get a candle. It's quite dark outside," said Mrs. Fang. Holding her baby in one arm, Mrs. Fang carried a candlestick in the other.

"Please don't bother, Mrs. Fang. I have a flashlight, and I know my way around," Shu-sheng said politely. She walked to the corridor outside.

"Mrs. Wang, wait, wait. Let me walk you to the staircase," Mrs. Fang said loudly. "It's really disgusting that we still don't have electricity all the time. It's been more than two months since victory, and many services seem to have become worse," she complained.

Shu-sheng was already at the stairs. She turned around and signaled Mrs. Fang with her flashlight. "Mrs. Fang, please go back. I'm leaving now." Without waiting for an answer, she rushed downstairs. It was truly a place that she knew very well. It took no time for her to get downstairs.

Once outside the main door a gust of cold wind made her shiver. "Why is this October night so chilly?" she wondered, aware that her autumn coat was not warm enough. No rickshaws or cars in sight. Turning to look at the door and its dim doorlight, she softly sighed. She did not know where she should go, and she felt empty inside. She wished that she could go somewhere and cry to her heart's content behind closed doors. But there was no place. She walked slowly along the sidewalk.

"Miss, we're refugees from Kweilin and have lost everything." A shadow darted out from the dark and stood next to her, stretching out a thin hand in front of her. She was startled. Looking closely at the person, she saw it was an old woman.

是她覺得比流了淚還更痛苦。

「那麼你等等，我拿蠟燭來送你，外面很黑，」方太太殷勤地說，她一隻手抱小孩，一隻手拿起了燭台。

「方太太，你請留步，我有電筒，看得見，這個地方我住慣了的，」樹生客氣地說，就急急往門外廊上走去。

「汪太太，等等，等等啊，我送你到樓梯口，」方太太大聲喚道。接着她又在抱怨：「真討厭，現在還停電。勝利了兩個多月，甚麼事都沒有變好，有的反而更壞。」

樹生已經走到了樓梯口。她回過頭，朝着方太太打了一下手電，大聲說：「方太太，請回去，我走啦！」她也不等回答，就急急走下樓了。的確這是她走慣了的地方，走起來並不費力。

她剛走出大門，迎面一股寒風使她打了一個冷噤。「怎麼才陽曆十月夜裏就這樣冷！」她想道，她覺得身上那件秋大衣不夠暖了。門前連一輛車子也看不見。她回頭看了看大門，和那盞閉着眼睛似的門燈，她輕輕嘆了一口氣。她不知道現在到甚麼地方去好。她心裏空虛得很。她只想找個地方關上門大哭一場。但是沒有辦法。她只好緩緩地在人行道上走着。

「小姐，我們是從桂林逃難來的，東西都丟光了……」突然從黑暗裏閃出一個黑影，一下就跑到她的身邊，一隻枯瘦的手伸到她面前，使她大大地吃了一驚。她仔細一看，說話的原來是一個老太婆。

She opened her purse and put a bill into the dark hand.

"Miss, thank you, thank you," the old woman said, shrinking back into the darkness again.

She slightly shook her head and walked on. Then she saw some light.

"It's a bargain! It's a bargain! Five hundred *yüan*, three hundred *yüan*, two hundred *yüan* ... "

In the cold wind, the foul smell of acetylene lamps hit her nostrils. A wailing sound came from a woman's lips. A young woman was sitting on a short stool with a sleeping baby in her arms. Her dull gaze was fixed on a pile of items she could not sell.

She shivered again. "The night is really cold." She thought, "She's also a mother." She stood by the stall for a moment and sympathically looked at the woman and the baby with mixed feelings of sympathy and shame. "I must find Hsiao Hsüan," she told herself. Looking at the woman and the baby again, she was reminded of her mother-in-law and her son, who had had to set up a similar stall. As she continued to think about what she saw, she became very sad.

"When are you leaving?" a man was speaking to another.

"I can't leave. Common people can never get steamer tickets," said another.

"Try to find a way; be a stowaway."

"Now is the time for officials to reclaim their positions, not for common people to return home. One of my relatives couldn't get a ticket and became a stowaway. He was caught."

"You, your situation is not so bad. Even if you stay in Szechwan for a few months you don't have to worry about food. But if I don't

她打開手提包拿出一張鈔票遞到那隻黑手裏。

「小姐，謝謝你啊，」老太婆說着，又把身子縮進黑暗裏去了。

她微微地搖搖頭，又繼續往前面走。於是她看見了光亮。

「相因賣，相因賣，五百塊錢……三百塊錢……兩百塊錢……」

電石燈的臭味隨着寒風撲上她的鼻端。從那些帶笑的嘴唇裏發出哀叫似的聲音。一個年青女人坐在矮櫈上，懷裏抱着一個睡着的嬰孩，正用沉滯的目光望着面前一堆賣不出去的東西。

她又打一個冷噤，「夜真冷啊！」她想道：「人家也是母親啊，」她又想：她在那個地攤前站了片刻。她用同情的眼光看那個女人和懷裏的孩子，又用慚愧的眼光看他們。「我總得要找到小宣，」她在心裏說。她又看看他們，「他們也擺過這樣的地攤，」她再想，這個「他們」是指老太太和小宣，她心裏更加難過了。

「你哪天走？」她旁邊有人在講話。

「走不了。船票哪有我們老百姓的份！」另一個人說。

「想辦法吧，當黃魚總行！」

「現在是官復員，不是老百姓復員。我有親戚買不到票當黃魚，上了船給人抓下來了。白出了船錢。」

「你，還好走不了，在四川多住幾個月也不愁沒飯吃。我下個月

leave next month I'll starve. I've sold just about everything. At first I thought I could go home right after victory."

"Victory is for them, not for us. We haven't made any profit out of the country's misfortune, and it hasn't done us any good. I should have known there was no point in participating in that victory demonstration."

She shivered again. She felt chilled all over, as if she had been placed in an ice-cellar. Unconsciously, she hunched over and looked vacantly at her surroundings. All the things around her looked unreal. The evening before she had been dining in a restaurant in a different city, listening to the flattering words of her suitor, and now here she was standing in front of a makeshift stall eavesdropping on two strangers. Why did she come back to this city? What sort of feeling did she have when she left her old apartment? What should she do now? She could wait for the next day.

The dead was no more, the living gone. Even if she waited until the next day, even if she found her husband's grave, could she find her son? Could she change her present situation? What should she do? Continue her futile search? Or go back to Lanchow and accept another man?

She had two weeks of vacation, and she must decide within that time: twelve or thirteen days. But why stand in front of this stall and be battered by a chilly wind?

"I still have time to decide," she told herself, and walked away slowly and steadily. And suddenly while walking in the darkness of the night she was overcome by a curious feeling. She glanced from time to time at both sides of the street as if afraid the quivering acetylene lights at the stalls might be extinguished by the chilly wind. The night was so cold ... so cold.

再走不了，那就要餓飯了。東西快賣盡吃光了。原先以為一勝利就可以回家的。」

「勝利是他們勝利，不是我們勝利啊。我們沒有發過國難財，卻倒了勝利楣。早知道，那天真不該參加勝利遊行。……」

她又打了一個冷噤。她好像突然落進了冰窖裏似的，渾身發冷。她不自覺地縮起頸項來。她茫然四顧，她覺得眼前的一切都是假的。她好像在做夢。昨天這時她還在另一個城市熱鬧的酒樓上吃飯，聽一個男人的奉承話。今天她卻立在寒夜的地攤前，聽這些陌生人的訴苦。她為着甚麼回來？現在又懷着怎樣的心情走出那間屋子？……以後又該怎樣……她等待着明天。

死的死了，走的走了。就是到了明天，她至多不過找到一個人的墳墓。可是她能夠找回她的小宣嗎？她能夠改變眼前的一切嗎？她應該怎樣做呢？走遍天涯地角去作那明知無益的找尋嗎？還是回到蘭州答應另一個男人的要求呢？

她只有兩個星期的假期。她應該在這兩個星期中決定自己的事情。……至少她還有十二三天的功夫。為甚麼她必須站在這地攤前忍受寒風的吹打呢？

「我會有時間來決定的，」她終於這樣對自己說。她走開了。她走得慢，然而腳步並不搖幌。只是走在這陰暗的街上，她忽然起了一種奇異的感覺，她不時掉頭朝街的兩旁看，她耽心那些搖顫的電石燈光會被寒風吹滅。夜的確太冷了。

——完——

Appendix I

《寒夜》後記

一九四四年冬天桂林淪陷的時候，我住在重慶民國路文化生活社樓下一間小得不可再小的屋子裏，晚上常常得預備蠟燭來照亮書桌，午夜還得拿熱水瓶向叫賣「炒米糖開水」的老人買一點白開水解渴。我睡得遲，可是老鼠整夜不停地在那三合土的地下打洞，妨礙着我的睡眠。白天整個屋子都是叫賣聲、吵架聲、談話聲、戲院裏的鑼鼓聲。好像四面八方都有聲音傳來，甚至關在小屋子裏我也得不着安靜。那時候，我正在校對一部朋友翻譯的高爾基的長篇小說，有時也為着幾位從桂林逃難出來的朋友做一點小事情。有一天趙家璧兄突然來到文化生活社找我，他是空手來的。他在桂林創辦的事業已經被敵人的炮火打光了。他搶救出來的一小部分東西也已在金城江的大火中化為灰燼。那損失使他痛苦，但他並不灰心。他決意要在重慶建立一個新的據點，我答應給他幫忙。我了解他，因為我在桂林也有着同樣的損失。

於是在一個寒冷的冬夜裏我開始寫了長篇小說《寒夜》。我從來不是一個偉大的作家，我連做夢也不敢妄想寫史詩。誠如一個「從生活的洞口……」的批評家所說，我「不敢面對鮮血淋漓的現實」，所以我只寫了一些耳聞目睹的小事，我只寫了一個肺病患者的血痰，我只寫了一個渺小的讀書人的生與死，但是我並沒有撒謊。我親眼看見那些血痰，它們至今還深印在我的腦際，他們逼着我拿起筆替那些吐盡了血痰死去的人和那些還沒有吐盡血痰的人講話。這小說我時寫時輟，兩年後才能夠把它寫完，可是家璧兄服務的那個書店已經擱淺了(晨光出版公司是最近才成立的)。並且在這中間我還失去了一個好友和一個哥哥，他們都是吐盡血痰後寂寞地死去的；在這中間「勝利」給我們帶來希望，又把希望逐漸給我們拿走。我沒有在小說的最後照「批評家」的吩咐加一句「哎喲喲，黎明！」並不是害怕說了就會被人「捉來吊死」，唯一的原因是那些被不合理的制度摧毀、被生活拖死的人斷氣時已經沒有力量呼叫「黎明」了。

但有時我自己卻也會呼叫一兩聲的。譬如六年前我在桂林寫的一篇長夜裏，就說過「這是光明的呼聲，牠會把白晝給我們喚醒起來。漫漫的長夜逼近牠的終結了。」那文章的確是在寒冷的深夜寫的，我真實地寫下我當時的感覺和感想。在桂林冬天也常常看得見太陽，而且一出太陽，天氣就和暖，那個冬天我初到桂林住在郊外，衣服不夠，被褥不夠，晚上我常常點一盞植物油燈在書店宿舍的飯廳裏讀書，我受不了長夜的寒冷，聽見雞聲，便渴望早早天明。……這全是事實。

王魯彥兄(他後來也死於肺病)住在我的隔壁，他那時正在編輯《文藝雜誌》，便把我這篇短文拿去在創刊號上發表了。他把牠列在散文欄內，我也沒有不贊成的表示。不過當時不論他或者我，我們絕對沒有想到這篇文章在五六年後會成為我的罪證。

上面的話是我在一年前寫的。現在《寒夜》再版本要發印了，我不想為它另寫「後記」，因為要說的話太多，假使全寫出來，應該是另一部更長的《寒夜》。今天天氣的確冷得可怕，我左手邊攤着的一張《大公報》上就有着「全天在零度以下，兩天來收路屍數具」的標題。窗外冷呼呼地吹着，沒有關緊的門不時發出依呀的聲音，我那躲在皮鞋裏的兩隻腳已經快凍死了。一年前、兩年前都不曾有過這樣的「寒夜」。我還活着，我沒有患肺病死去，也沒有凍死，這是我的幸運。書銷去五千冊，並不是甚麼可以得意的事。我知道許多寫得更壞的書都有更暢的銷場。

初版本的後記原不只那麼一點點，我刪去了後面的兩頁。因為我的小說是為讀者寫的，不是為那些「敢面對鮮血淋漓的現實」的批評家寫的。他們找到了「鮮血淋漓的現實」自然會寫出「很痛快」的作品。目前我用不着去麻煩他們。

巴金　一九四八年一月下旬

Appendix II
Preface to the English Edition

Since the early 1970s interest in Chinese fiction in the West has been growing steadily and has resulted in the publication of English translations of several novels and short stories. Among them have been *Modern Chinese Stories*, edited by W. J. F. Jenner (London: Oxford University Press, 1970); C. T. Hsia and Joseph S. M. Lau's *Twentieth Century Chinese Stories* (New York: Columbia University Press, 1971); Lao She's *Cat Country*, translated by William A. Lyell, Jr. (Columbus: Ohio State University Press, 1972); Cyril Birch's *Anthology of Chinese Literature*, Vol. 2: *From the 14th Century to the Present Day* (New York: Grove Press, 1972); the first two volumes of Ts'ao Hsüeh-ch'in's *Story of the Stone*, translated by David Hawkes (Baltimore: Penguin Classics, 1974, 1977); Nathan Mao's rendering of Li Yü's *Twelve Towers* (Hong Kong: The Chinese University of Hong Kong, 1975); Joseph Lau and Timothy Ross's *Chinese Stories from Taiwan: 1960–1970* (New York: Columbia University Press, 1976); Anthony Yu's *Journey to the West*, Volume One (Chicago: The University of Chicago Press, 1977), and a number of titles published by the Foreign Languages Press of Peking. Important and encouraging as this may be, there is no doubt that many Chinese works of high quality are still unavailable in English, particularly works written during the twentieth century when China and her suffering people experienced, without respite, wars, natural catastrophes, and political upheavals.

One of the most popular writers of twentieth-century China is Pa Chin, a favorite of both students and the general public during the 1930s and 1940s. In a survey conducted among Chinese college and high school students in 1937, he was second only to Lu Hsün as the most popular writer.[1] Reports from Mainland China in 1972 showed that he was then once again a favorite writer of the people, and that many readers ranked his books with such classical Chinese novels as *The Water Margin* and *The Romance of the Three Kingdoms*.[2] In the West, there have been several critical studies of his works: O. Briere's article in 1942, Jean Monsterleet's in the 1940s and 1950s,[3] and Olga Lang's monumental work, *Pa Chin and His Writings*, in 1967. In 1975 he and Mao Tun were nominated for the Nobel Prize in Literature. The nominators, British and French writers, felt that Pa Chin and Mao Tun were the two authors who best reflected social and political life in China prior to the Communist victory in 1949.[4]

A number of Pa Chin's works have been translated into foreign languages: e.g., Joseph Kalmer's German translation of *Ch'i-yüan* entitled *Garten der Ruhe* (München: Hanser, 1954); an English translation of a collection of short stories entitled *Living amongst Heroes* (Peking: Foreign Languages Press, 1954); Sidney Shapiro's translation of *Chia* entitled *Family* (Peking: Foreign Languages Press, 1958, reprinted in 1972 by Doubleday Anchor Books); and Japanese and

1. Olga Lang, *Pa Chin and His Writings* (Cambridge: Harvard University Press, 1967), pp. 3, 275, 285, 363. See also A. Bonninger, *Etudiants chinois: Silhouettes et tendencies* (Paris, 1948), pp. 123–125.
2. *Chung-yang jih-pao* [Central Daily News] (Taipei, Taiwan), August 2, 1972.
3. See Donald A. Gibbs and Yun-chen Li, *A Bibliography of Studies and Translations of Modern Chinese Literature, 1918–1942* (Cambridge: East Asian Research Center, Harvard University, 1975), pp. 150–151.
4. *Ming-pao yüeh-k'an* [Ming Pao Monthly], Vol. 10, Number 11 (November 1975), pp. 10–11.

Russian translations of *Han-yeh* or *Cold Nights* (*Kan'ya.* Tokyo: Chikuma shobo, 1952; *Kholodnaia noch* tr. by E. Rozhdestvenskaia in *Pa Chin*: *Sochinenia* [Pa Chin: Works], Vol. 2. Moscow: Gosudarstvennoe izdatelstvo khudozhestvennoi literatury, 1959). There have also been translations of his works in both Italian and Polish.[5]

Among the works not translated previously into English, one that best represents Pa Chin's pre-Communist period is the novel *Cold Nights* (1947). Dealing with the weariness induced by the long Sino-Japanese War, the novel focuses on his personal experience in Chungking during the last year of the war.[6] He stresses at great length Chungking's runaway inflation, high unemployment, epidemics, starvation, indifference of the government toward her people, and the bankruptcy of the people's morale. It is a work of bitterness and hate — a harsh indict-

5. Lang, pp. 353–355.
6. In the novel's postscript Pa Chin writes: "In the winter of 1944, when Kweilin fell to the Japanese, I lived in a tiny room below the Culture and Life Publishing Company office on Ming-kuo Road in Chungking. At night I frequently had to use a candle for light and at midnight had to use my thermos jug to carry the hot water I bought to drink from an old hawker selling 'fried rice-cakes and hot water.' Usually I slept late, disturbed by the scurrying rats digging holes in the floor. During the day, street noises of various sorts ... deprived me, enclosed as I was in a tiny cell, of any quiet. At that time I was proofreading a novel by Gorki and sometimes I did a few favors for my refugee friends from Kweilin. One day Mr. Chao Chia-pi came to see me at the [Culture and Life] office. He was penniless. His career in Kweilin had been destroyed by the enemy.... Then one winter night I began to write my long novel *Cold Nights*. I was never a great writer, and I had never dared to write an epic. As one critic pointed out I 'dared not face the bloody realities of life,' so using tidbits of what I knew and had heard, I wrote about the blood-tinged phlegm of a tuberculosis victim, the life and death of an insignificant but educated man. I did not lie. I saw his blood-tinged phlegm.... The phlegm forced me to speak out for all those dead.... With frequent interruptions I completed the novel after two years.... In the interim, victory had come bringing us hope which soon dissipated into thin air."

ment of Chinese society and of the government. He demonstrates how an average man can be victimized by everyone, including himself. Technically, he maintains the feeling of doom through his use of the imagery of dark and lonely nights and the change of seasons; he conveys to the reader a feeling of participating in the action through his use of scene and other literary devices; and he enables the reader to live inside the minds of his characters. By involving the reader in the mental and emotional experiences of its characters, *Cold Nights*, as a psychological novel, adds a significant dimension to the art of Pa Chin's prose fiction. Herein lies the achievement of *Cold Nights*.

This is a complete translation of *Han-yeh*, based on the easily available but undated edition published by Wen-hua shu-tien of Hong Kong instead of the post-1949 version included in *Pa Chin wen-chi* [Collected Works of Pa Chin] (14 volumes. Hong Kong: Nan-kuo ch'u-pan she, 1970). Although there are only minor stylistic and political changes between the two versions, we feel that the pre-1949 version is more faithful to Pa Chin's original intent and that his later revised version reflects his attempt to adapt to the trends of Chinese politics in the 1950s and 1960s.

Because of the differences between Chinese and English, we have striven for fluency in English without sacrificing completely the Chinese flavor of the original. In a few instances where the original appears to be overly verbose, we have taken the liberty of deleting some redundancies and paraphrasing certain phrases and expressions. We have also in other instances re-arranged paragraph divisions in order to make the translation more readable to a Western audience. The Wade-Giles system of transliteration is used.

We wish to express our gratitude to Professor C. T. Hsia of Columbia University for his encouragement and advice, to Professor William Schultz of the University of Arizona and Miss Ludmilla Paskaya of the Australian National University and to Professor Mark A. Givler of Shippensburg State College for reading the entire manuscript and offering their valuable suggestions, and to our wives for their patience and understanding.

We also wish to express our deepest gratitude to Dr. Francis K. Pan, Mr. T. C. Lai, Father John Deeney, Mr. Stephen C. Soong, and others of The Chinese University Press for their editorial assistance and advice.

Chambersburg & Canberra NATHAN K. MAO
December 1977 LIU TS'UN-YAN

Appendix III
Introduction to the English Edition

ON the eve of Pa Chin's birth, the goddess of childbearing appeared to his mother in a dream. The goddess informed her that she had been chosen to give birth to a child that had been intended for her sister-in-law, because the gods were afraid that the sister-in-law might not take good care of the infant.[1] On the next day, November 25, 1904, Pa Chin, whose real name is Li Fei-kan, was born into a traditional upper-class family in Chengtu, Szechwan Province, in western China. Pa Chin's grandfather and great-grandfather had both been magistrates, and a few years after his birth, his father assumed a magistrate's position. The huge family, including Pa Chin's parents, uncles, aunts, brothers, sisters, cousins, nieces, and nephews as well as a large number of servants, lived in a traditional family compound under the rule of his grandfather. Of the first few years of Pa Chin's life little is known.

In the second half of 1907, Pa Chin's immediate family moved to Kuang-yüan in northern Szechwan, where his father served as the

---

1. *Pa Chin wen-chi* [Collected Works of Pa Chin] (14 volumes. Hong Kong: Nan-kuo ch'u-pan she, 1970), 10, *Yi* [Memoirs], p. 10. Since this is the most accessible edition in print, all references are made to this edition, unless otherwise noted. Hereafter, cited as *PCWC*.

local magistrate. Together with his parents, two elder sisters, and two elder brothers he lived in the *yamen*, an official walled compound. Life was pleasant for Pa Chin. Every day a mild-mannered tutor taught the basic classics to him and the other children in a special room. While classes were being held, an elderly gray-haired servant waited on the pupils. After class every afternoon, Pa Chin played in the courtyards with his elder brother and a 13-year-old bondservant. The courtyards were overgrown with tall grass and mulberry trees and filled with chickens. The children picked mulberries, gave names to the chickens, and played games.

Outside the Li family, changes were taking place quickly. In April 1911, the Manchu government's plan to nationalize all railways met stiff opposition from the business communities in Hunan, Kwangtung, and Hupei provinces. There were student strikes, business boycotts, and riots. In Szechwan Province, opposition to the plan was especially fierce. At one demonstration, the government arrested more than ten petitioners, and when more demonstrators protested, troops opened fire, killing more than forty people. The government's action led to increasing outcries against its policies and accelerated the revolutionary movement led by Dr. Sun Yat-sen. On October 10, 1911, the revolution began in earnest in Wuchang. Other provinces rapidly declared their independence from the Manchu government. With the abdication of the Manchu emperor on February 12, 1912, the Republic of China was established. Having anticipated the coming social and political storm, Pa Chin's father had resigned from the post as magistrate of Kuang-yüan early in 1911 and moved his family back to Chengtu.

Leaving the carefree days of Kuang-yüan behind, Pa Chin lived the life of an affluent 7-year-old in his grandfather's compound in Chengtu, totally unaware of the political changes taking place. Besides playing with his cousins and studying with a tutor, he spent much of his time with the servants, sometimes assisting them with their work. This close and warm contact with the servants continued throughout the time he was growing up, liberating him from his elders' rigid prejudices and making him appreciative of the virtues of the poor. Having been impressed by generous hearts among the poor and downtrodden during his childhood, he later became their passionate defender.

In the summer of 1914, Pa Chin's mother died after a three-week illness. The full significance of her death was not fully understood amidst the funeral preparations. His mother's death left a permanent scar on his psyche. In novel after novel, his fictional characters seem unable to shake off the memories of their mothers, probably a reflection of Pa Chin's psychological dependance on his mother. Even as late as 1929 he included these words in a sentimental essay entitled "Wo ti hsin" ["My Heart"]: "In this wide ocean of blood and tears, what does one person's heart amount to? What can it do? Mother, ... please take away my heart. I don't need it anymore. But my mother has been dead for many years."[2]

In 1917 his father died. The loss of both parents within three years was a hard blow. In *Yi* [Memoirs] he wrote: "The first blow in my life was my mother's death; then came my father's. At that time I was very young and I should have been a child sheltered and protected by my parents. One blow after another was too much for me to bear."[3] His father's death ended his childhood innocence and opened his eyes to the hatred and perfidy within his family, which had been well hidden by a facade of family unity and harmony.

Late in 1917 Pa Chin's grandfather allowed the boy to attend English

---

2. *PCWC*, 10, *Sheng chih ch'an-hui* [Confessions of a Life], p. 29.
3. *PCWC*, 10, *Memoirs*, p. 5.

classes at a YMCA school in the belief that a knowledge of English would help Pa Chin obtain a well-paying position in the postal service. However, during that one month at school, Pa Chin was sick three times. As a result, his grandfather insisted he resume taking private lessons at home. Following his father's death, his grandfather had been kind to him. Gradually he began to see his grandfather as less a stereotyped figure and more a person.

In 1915 Ch'en Tu-hsiu (1879–1942) founded a magazine called *Ch'ing-nien* [Youth], later renamed *Hsin Ch'ing-nien* [New Youth]. Ch'en advocated the abolition and repudiation of obsolete institutions and values and the adoption of new ideas. In 1916, Ch'en was the dean of the School of Letters at National Peking University, then under the leadership of President Ts'ai Yüan-p'ei. In 1917 and 1918 *New Youth* and other progressive magazines mushroomed, all advocating a critical examination of the old China and the adoption of Western ideas. These intellectual activities in Peking reached a peak in 1919 in the May Fourth Incident, leading to what was later known as the May Fourth Movement. The May Fourth Incident convinced intellectuals of the need to espouse new ideas to educate the people to oppose imperialism and to direct their literary activities so as to help build a new China. Within six months some four hundred new periodicals, written in the vernacular, appeared on the market.[4]

Meanwhile in Chengtu, Pa Chin and his brothers avidly read newspapers and periodicals from Shanghai and Peking. At the same time, Pa Chin also became interested in Kropotkin's "An Appeal to the Young" (1880), an eloquent exhortation to political activity. Partly in-

4. James E. Sheridan, *China in Disintegration* (New York: The Free Press, 1975), p. 121. Specifically, "May Fourth" refers to the student demonstrations in Peking in 1919. In a broad sense, "May Fourth" refers to a period of ten years, roughly from 1917–1927.

fluenced by Kropotkin, he became dissatisfied with merely reading and wanted to do something positive.

But no one gave him any guidance. He wrote to Ch'en Tu-hsiu, the editor of *New Youth*, but received no reply. He then obtained a copy of a Chinese translation of Leopold Kampf's *Yeh wei-yang* [On the Eve]. It opened his eyes to the tragedy of the youth of another country in their heroic struggle to win liberty and happiness for the people.[5] He then read works by the anarchist Emma Goldman. Her essays so overwhelmed him that he called her his "spiritual mother" and later corresponded with her. In his reading, Pa Chin was attracted to anarchism's total attack upon those institutions, attitudes, and theoretical positions which were based upon the acceptance of authority and to its belief in man's reason, goodness, and perfectibility.

His opportunity for action finally came. After reading an article in a local newspaper, *Pan yüeh* [Semi-monthly], he wrote to the editor and offered to join its *Shih she* (Equitable Society), an anarchist organization. He was immediately accepted as a member. Soon he and his new friends formed a new organization called the *Chün she* (Equity Society). Identifying himself as an anarchist, he wrote and published articles and books, communicated with other members of the Society, recruited new members, and distributed propaganda in the streets.

At home, Pa Chin became aware of the luxurious lifestyle of his family, all of whom lived in a spacious compound staffed by more than twenty male and female servants and maintained primarily by rents from land leased to farmers. He saw too the debased life of the servants who toiled and slaved for his family with little recognition or reward. He resented the social injustice upon which his family

5. *PCWC*, 10, *Tuan-chien I* [Short Notes I], p. 8.

depended for its standard of living and was disgusted by the constant bickering among his relatives and by their unproductive lives. He considered his grandfather's control of the family to be authoritarian, and he characterized his family as a "despotic kingdom" with outdated customs and rules which stifled individual growth and fostered hypocrisy and deception.[6] Moreover, he considered his eldest brother as a prime victim of the traditional family system. A bright young man, his eldest brother had married a woman of his father's choice, discontinued his studies, and taken charge of the household after the death of his father. Angry at the system and at himself, his eldest brother would take out his frustrations by breaking the glass windows of his sedan-chair late at night. Every time Pa Chin saw his eldest brother commit this wanton act of frustration, his heart writhed in sympathetic anguish.

On Chinese New Year's Eve in 1919, Pa Chin's grandfather died. After his grandfather's death, Pa Chin's third uncle ruled the family. Pa Chin felt that the family had gone from bad to worse, but, in fact, he had more freedom to do as he pleased.

In the summer of 1920, he and his elder brother enrolled in a foreign language institute in Chengtu. He studied there for two and a half years but did not receive a diploma because he did not have the necessary middle school credentials. This kind of treatment prompted his stepmother to send both him and his elder brother to study in Shanghai.

Near the end of spring in 1923, Pa Chin and his elder brother arrived in Shanghai. Six months later, they went to Nanking to attend a middle school affiliated with Tung-nan University. After graduating from middle school in Nanking in 1925, Pa Chin intended to take the

---

6. *PCWC*, 10, *Memoirs*, p. 66.

entrance examination for the National Peking University, but illness and the May Thirtieth Incident derailed his plan.

On January 15, 1927, Pa Chin left Shanghai for Marseilles. From Marseilles he went to Paris, where he rented a small and poorly-ventilated room on the fifth floor of a dilapidated hotel. His life was cheerless. Reading and boredom gnawed away at his youth. To combat his loneliness he began to write the novel *Mieh-wang* [Destruction] and to translate Kropotkin's *Ethics*. He returned to China in December 1928, and published his first novel, *Destruction*, using the pen name "Pa Chin" to indicate the influence of Bakunin and Kropotkin on his writing career.[7] During his two years in France he did not obtain a diploma or a degree. Later he wrote: "I learned nothing, not even French. I just read a bunch of books haphazardly, and wrote a novel called *Destruction*."[8] In fact, he had become a writer and had acquired an extensive knowledge of radical literature.

China in 1928 was as chaotic as it had been in late 1926. Chiang Kai-shek's Northern Expedition did not achieve its objectives. Warlords controlled more of China than did Chiang's Nanking government. Meanwhile, labor unrest continued; in 1928 alone there had been one hundred and forty strikes in Shanghai. In the countryside peasants continued to suffer at the hands of landlords and from the capricious whims of cruel nature.

Under such circumstances, Lu Hsün (1881–1936), China's best known and most respected writer and critic, rallied young men and women to the use of writing as a weapon to effect social change. After

7. Olga Lang, p. 7. "'Pa' stands for the first syllable of the name Bakunin, and 'Chin' for the last syllable of the name Kropotkin (Pa-k'u-ning and K'o-lu-p'ao-t'e-chin respectively in Chinese transcription)."
8. *PCWC*, 14, *T'an tzu-chi ti ch'uang-tso* [Discussion of My Creative Work], p. 5. Hereafter, *Discussion*.

the serial publication of *Destruction* in *Hsiao-shuo yüeh-pao* [Fiction Monthly] from January through April, 1929, Pa Chin responded to Lu Hsün's call. He used his writing to express his personal views and to propagate anarchist ideas.

In 1930 Pa Chin completed *Ssu-ch'ü ti t'ai-yang* [The Setting Sun] and a volume of short stories entitled *Fu-ch'ou* [Revenge]. Driven by an internal fire, he wrote ceaselessly. Under intense personal anguish (his eldest brother committed suicide in 1931), he completed *Chia* [Family], the first in his *Chi-liu* [Turbulent Stream] trilogy, *Hsin-sheng* [New Life], *Wu* [Fog], and a volume of short stories, *Kuang-ming* [Light]. In the winter of 1931 he spent a week in a coal mine, the experience of which became the basis for a novelette originally called *Meng-ya* [Germs] but later retitled *Hsüeh* [Snow] and published in 1934.[9] In 1932 he wrote *Ch'un-t'ien li ti ch'iu-t'ien* [Autumn in Spring], a romantic tale, and *Sha-ting* [The Antimony Miners], a proletarian novelette.[10]

Pa Chin worked compulsively day and night but had doubts about the effectiveness of his work as a weapon to bring about social change.[11] In 1933 he declared that his writing had little impact on the masses and only wasted his energy and life.[12] In a short story called "Kuang-ming" ["Light"], a writer, presumably Pa Chin himself, wonders aloud: "Writing books — what's the use? It can only bring sorrow to mankind."[13] Frequently, in a mood of self-pity, he said that his work had "extracted"

---

9. Lang, p. 249. Lang compares *Snow* to Zola's *Germinal* and regards both works fascinating.
10. *PCWC*, 2, *Sha-ting* [The Antimony Miners], pp. 3–4.
11. *PCWC*, 7, "Hsieh-tso sheng-huo ti hui-ku" ["Recollections of a Writer's Life"], p. 8.
12. *PCWC*, 10, *Memoirs*, p. 104.
13. *PCWC*, 7, *Kuang-ming* [Light], p. 10.

too much of his flesh and blood.[14] But in calmer moments he acknowledged that he did achieve "satisfaction" from his writing and considered his work therapeutic for his mental health.[15]

Despite his widespread fame as a writer, Pa Chin continued to be harassed by government censors, who considered many of his works subversive. Resenting the stifling political climate in China and seeking greater freedom and a better perspective on life, he went to Japan and stayed there from November 1934 through July 1935. His Japanese sojourn was disappointing. In his essay "Fan-hsing" ["Galaxy of Stars"], written in January 1935, a fictional character presumably speaking for Pa Chin asks: "Why did I come here [to Japan]? The freedom I craved is non-existent here. I have left a 'crooked road' for a little temporary peace and quiet in a strange land and spent my time on useless books. Isn't this a life of indulgence?"[16] Like his fictional character, Pa Chin experienced even greater political oppression in Japan than he had in China. Because of the impending visit to Tokyo of Henry P'u-yi, the Emperor of Manchukuo, Pa Chin was arrested by the Japanese police and detained for a day in a police station, an experience which later became the basis of his short story "Jen" ["Man"]. In short, during his most productive period, Pa Chin was deeply disturbed by inner discord and a search for his true self. He was haunted by his call for action by others, while he himself remained inactive, and by his gradual awareness of his own inability to change things.

In a less than happy mood, Pa Chin returned to China in July 1935 to become editor of the Wen-hua sheng-huo [Culture and Life] Publishing Company in Shanghai. He edited and published many Chinese and foreign classics as well as works by young Chinese writers. He also

---

14. *PCWC*, 10, *Memoirs*, p. 104.

15. *PCWC*, 10, *Confessions of a Life*, p. 37. See also *PCWC*, 10, *Tien-ti* [Drops], p. 23.

16. *PCWC*, 10, *Drops*, p. 26.

translated a number of Turgenev's works into Chinese from Russian and wrote *Ch'un* [Spring] and *Ch'iu* [Autumn], sequels to the novel *Family*. Among his prose works of the period were *K'ung-su* [J' Accuse], *Yi* [Memoirs], *Tien-ti* [Drops], and *Tuan-chien* [Short Notes].

After the outbreak of the Sino-Japanese War in 1937, Pa Chin wrote war poems, essays, and letters to condemn the wanton Japanese bombings and to praise the heroic efforts of the Chinese.[17] When the Chinese troops withdrew from Shanghai following a valiant defense of the city, Pa Chin moved to the French Concession. In sorrow he heard of the fall of Nanking (December 13, 1937) and of the atrocities committed there by the Japanese, and of the fall of other major Chinese cities including Tsingtao and Hangchow.

In 1937 and 1938, besides his work at the Culture and Life Publishing Company, he served on the editorial boards of *Feng-huo* [Beacon] and *Nahan* [Outcry] magazines and resumed his writing of *Spring*. In April 1938, after he saw the galley proofs of *Spring*, he left Shanghai for Canton, where he wrote the first volume of his *Huo* [Fire] trilogy.

The war cured Pa Chin's fits of depression. Fired by patriotism he described wartime Canton to a friend as follows: "This place is probably different from yours. Here there is neither courage nor cowardice. The residents do not love to die, but they are not afraid to die either. They treat death as a common event. If it visits them, they allow it to come into their houses without any fuss from the neighbors. One man dies, others continue to work. One house is destroyed, others continue to be inhabited. As soon as the blood on the balcony is washed away, the living walk on it again. Man falls, man bleeds — these are common sights. Even severed heads and limbs are not considered

---

17. *PCWC*, 10, *K'ung-su* [J'Accuse], pp. 22–23.

tragic. The dead are buried, the living continue to do their jobs — only working harder...."[18]

During the war years, Pa Chin traveled extensively throughout China. He made a number of trips to cities such as Changsha, Wuhan, Wuchow, and others, and he lived and worked in Canton, Kweilin, and Shanghai. On May 8, 1944, he married Miss Ch'en Yun-chen in Kweiyang. In May and June of 1944, the war situation deteriorated. Pressed by Japanese attacks, the Chinese army retreated in Hunan and Kwangsi, and on June 18, Changsha fell to the Japanese.

As a result, Pa Chin and his wife moved to Chungking. There they stayed until the war ended in 1945. Poor, they had to live in one small room, and saw many of their friends die of the rampaging tuberculosis. Pa Chin wrote a series of obituaries, collectively entitled *Huai-nien* [Reminiscences]. In its preface, he characterized his deceased friends as ordinary people, who "never did anything to harm others. They never cheated, they were humble and congenial, and responsibly did their work; they were poor, but they had rich hearts, and were sincere toward others ...."[19] In addition, he wrote three major works: *Ti-ssu ping-shih* [Ward Number Four], *Ch'i-yüan* [Leisure Garden], and *Han-yeh* [Cold Nights].

The Japanese surrendered in August 1945. But the victory did not bring much joy to Pa Chin. His feelings toward the victory were vividly expressed in his novel *Cold Nights* and in his dramatized essay, "Wu t'i" ["No Title"], written in 1946. Like the characters in *Cold Nights* and "No Title," Pa Chin was eager to leave Chungking; he returned to Shanghai two months later. His elder brother had been seriously ill and died in December 1945. In addition to being troubled by his

18. *PCWC*, 11, *Lü-t'u t'ung-hsün* [Letters on the Road], p. 13.

19. *PCWC*, 10, *Huai-nien* [Reminiscences], p. 3.

brother's death, he was also very much disenchanted with the post-war Nationalist government. In 1946, his output was limited to a few memorial essays in memory of departed friends. He resumed his post as editor for the Culture and Life Publishing Company in Shanghai and began to translate Kropotkin's *Speeches of a Rebel*. He continued to support anarchist activities in China and kept up his connections with anarchists abroad; he also showed a great interest in Christianity and often met with Father Monsterleet, a Belgian Jesuit, who was then writing a book about him. In 1947 he published *Cold Nights* and several short stories.

After the Communist victory in 1949, many writers gravitated to Peking or to Shanghai. Pa Chin remained in Shanghai. He was made a vice-chairman of the National Committee of the All-China Federation of Literary and Art Circles and of the All-China Writers' Association, a deputy from Szechwan Province to the National People's Congress, and a delegate to several international and political congresses. In March 1952, he led a group from the All-China Federation of Literary and Art Circles to Korea and spent seven months there; in August 1953, after the Armistice, he returned to Korea, this time by himself. In 1961 he attended the Emergency Meeting of the Afro-Asian Writers' Conference in Japan, and in 1962 participated in the Eighth Conference on the banning of Nuclear Weapons, also in Japan. In 1963 he visited North Vietnam. In addition, he traveled extensively within China and made a much publicized visit to a steel worker named Chiu Tsai-kung, who had been seriously burned while trying to protect public property.[20]

---

20. Chen Tan-chen, "Pa Chin the Novelist," *Chinese Literature*, No. 6 (Peking, 1963), pp. 84–92.

As a result of the Communist Party's rigid control over literature, beginning with the expanded Party-directed mass-criticism campaign in 1952 and followed by even more stringent controls over literature in 1954–55, few writers of the period before the Communist victory produced much. Ts'ao Yü, Hsia Yen, Yeh Sheng-tao, Hsieh Ping-hsin, and Mao Tun all quieted their revolutionary fires of the 1930s and early 1940s. Pa Chin wrote cautiously. His visits to Korea led to his writing about the Chinese who fought there in *Ying-hsiung ti ku-shih* [Stories of Heroes], which was published by the Foreign Languages Press of Peking under the title *Living Amongst Heroes*.

During the "cheng-feng" or "rectification of working style" campaigns in 1954 and 1955, many old writers were singled out for attack. Then the "Hundred Flowers Bloom" campaign began in 1956. In theory at least, the government invited writers to express their feelings on all subjects. At first reticent, the innocent writers soon expressed their frustrations with Party bureaucracy and other evils. A year later the government reversed its policy and punished those who had spoken out against the government.

Throughout all these campaigns, Pa Chin had been prudent. For example, during the "Great Leap Forward" movement of 1958, he promised to produce "one long novel, three medium novels and several translations in the course of a year."[21] But in April 1958, in a routine article written for *Wen-i pao*, he expressed more sympathy than regret for Howard Fast, the American writer who had recently broken with Communism. Consequently, Pa Chin was singled out for attack, particularly for his pre-1949 anarchist writings. The campaign against him was fully under way by October 1958, even though he had already publicly

21. Merle Goldman, *Literary Dissent in Communist China* (Cambridge: Harvard University Press, 1967), p. 244.

apologized for his indiscretion regarding Fast. The campaign against him subsided only after many readers had come to his defense.[22]

Under such circumstances it is understandable why Pa Chin would write in 1958 that he was totally unsatisfied with the creation of his romantic-anarchist hero in his first novel *Destruction*;[23] in 1961 he confessed that he had lived a life apart from the masses, had sat in his room with a few friends and fantasized about the world. He had failed to find a correct path to follow.[24] He also admitted his folly in believing that the pen could change society.[25] He said his style was not good because it had too many barbarisms, and that because of his translations he had adopted a writing style that seemed foreign in its sentence patterns. He further maintained that he had benefited greatly from studying the works of other Chinese writers such as Lu Hsün, Yeh Sheng-tao, Hsia Mien-tsun, Chu Tzu-ch'ing, and from his old-fashioned private tutors in Chengtu. And lastly, he expressed regret that he had not studied more Chinese classics and learned calligraphy properly.[26]

When Pa Chin prepared his collected works for publication, he changed the endings of several of them, excising references to anarchism; he denied that he had derived his pen name "Pa Chin" from the first and last syllables of Bakunin and Kropotkin's names. He also rationalized his acceptance of anarchism as follows:

> In the wake of the May Fourth Movement, when I was ready to accept new ideas, I found a brand-new world. I was a little frightened, yet I was

---

22. C. T. Hsia, *A History of Modern Chinese Fiction* (New Haven: Yale University Press, 1961), p. 640. See also Goldman, p. 263.
23. *PCWC*, 14, *Discussion*, p. 18.
24. *Ibid.*, p. 34.
25. *Ibid.*, pp. 36–37.
26. *Ibid.*, p. 173.

> overwhelmed by what I read. I tried to absorb everything. Every idea that I could put my hands on, I instantly swallowed. Anything that was new and progressive I loved; anything old and regressive I hated. My mind was simple and I lacked a sense of judgment. What I had read prior to that time were the *Four Books* and the *Five Classics*, and some Chinese and foreign fiction. So I accepted anarchism by reading Kropotkin's little books and other periodicals.... I was never able to give up anarchism. Maybe it was a subconscious way for me to cover up my weakness, my hesitation, and my doubts in order to live a life that was free and yet contradictory, leisurely and yet agonizing .... To tell the truth, I really looked for a leader who could give me guidance, but then I slowly got used to the life the anarchists advocated.[27]

During the Cultural Revolution (1966–1968), regular publications were suspended and old books confiscated or burned. Pa Chin's works were removed from bookstores and libraries and in some cases destroyed. Like other writers of his generation, he was again singled out for attack: for his petty bourgeois background, his failure to adopt a more definite revolutionary (read Communist) line in his writing, his lifelong association with anarchists, and even for alleged attacks on the thoughts of Mao Tse-tung. The attacks culminated in an article that appeared on February 26, 1968, in the newspaper *Wen-hui pao* of Shanghai. The article labeled him "The Big Literary Tyrant," and called him other names as well. A few months later, on June 20, 1968, Red Guards ransacked his home in Shanghai, destroying his art collection and his library, which contained an impressive collection of anarchist literature. Still unsatisfied with their treatment of him, the Red Guards dragged him to the People's Stadium, where he was made to kneel on broken glass and forced to confess his "sins." As insults mounted, an eyewitness reported that Pa Chin yelled: "You have your thoughts and I have mine. This is the fact, and you can't change it even if you

27. *PCWC*, 10, *Short Notes I*, pp. 12–13.

kill me." Soon afterwards he was put under house arrest.[28] Since the Cultural Revolution not much has been heard about him; he was believed to be working in Shanghai in 1975. In July 1977, he wrote an article for the *Wen-hui pao* in Shanghai revealing his persecution by the Gang of Four.[29]

Pa Chin's life mirrors the changes in twentieth-century China. Born during the transition period that led to the collapse of the Manchu regime and the establishment of the Republic of China, he was affected by the turmoil of the tens and twenties — student agitation, new cultural impulses and movements, increased foreign aggression, and the civil strife between the Nationalists and the Communists. He suffered and lived through the long Sino-Japanese War, and welcomed the victory of the Communists in 1949. The divided country which he loved was finally united but, ironically, under a government which denied freedom to individuals, a right which he cherished most dearly and sought to promote in his works.

In what he wrote before 1949, he was at least consistent in his artistic beliefs. From the very beginning, he was inspired by a sense of evangelical mission to do his best to help build a just society and a stronger China. He called himself a writer of conviction, and declared repeatedly that he was not an artist, that his message was more permanent than art, and that he would, if necessary to further his convictions, forsake his art without any compunction. He wrote for one purpose only — to arouse a hatred of "darkness" and a love of "light" and "truth" among his readers.

Consistent with that belief, in his early fiction he attacked what he considered evils of society: capitalism, exploitation of Chinese labor

---

28. Olga Lang (ed.), *Family* (New York: Doubleday Anchor Books, 1972), p. xxv.
29. *Central Daily News*, July 27, 1977.

by foreigners, and other themes. During the 1930s, his most productive period, he concentrated on his major theme: the evils in and the decline of the old family system. *Autumn in Spring* was a prelude to his most impressive achievement: the *Turbulent Stream* trilogy, the most comprehensive expatiation on the old family system yet written in modern China. *Family*, the first book of the trilogy, was well received, widely praised and frequently compared to the classic Chinese novel *Dream of the Red Chamber* in its wide range of characters and themes. In the 1940s, he returned to his interest in the family system in *Leisure Garden* and *Cold Nights*.

During the Sino-Japanese War, like many other writers of the time, he wrote about the activities of patriots both in short stories and in the *Fire* trilogy. In *Hsiao-jen, hsiao-shih* [Little People, Little Things] he robbed the war of its glamor and wrote about the "little people" exactly as they were. His pessimism about China grew as the long war dragged on, and was fully reflected in *Ward Number Four* and, particularly, in *Cold Nights*.

All through his life, he never wavered in his editorial mission regarding his country and his people. His writings reflected a sentimental journey from his optimism of the 1920s and 1930s to his despair of the 1940s.[30] There is no doubt that his major achievement lies in the comprehensive picture he painted of China during those twenty-odd years. It is an artist's personal record, and it correctly reflects those tumultuous years.

Emphasizing content and social message rather than artistic form, a number of Pa Chin's novels, though highly popular, are artistically

30. See Nathan Mao, "Pa Chin's Journey in Sentiment: From Hope to Despair," *Journal of the Chinese Language Teachers Association*, Vol. XI, No. 2 (May 1976), pp. 131–137.

weak, perhaps because they suffer from unconvincing attempts at realism, colorless revolutionaries, stereotyped characters, and a frequently wooden and monotonous style. However, one notable exception is the novel *Cold Nights*; it stands out as one of his masterpieces. It demonstrates an artistic maturity rarely seen in his previous works. Besides stressing the frightening aspects of a long war, he maintains the feeling of doom through his use of the imagery of dark and lonely nights and the change of seasons; he gives the reader a feeling of participating in the action through his use of scene; he presents the conflicts among the major characters through dialogue; and reveals the psyches of the major characters through monologue. All these devices contribute to the suffocating intensity of the novel while they deepen the reader's understanding of the members of a modern Chinese family during the darkest hours of the long war.

Readers of *Cold Nights* are likely to be overwhelmed by the consistent and persistent atmosphere of doom which is skillfully achieved by Pa Chin through the use of one principal image: night. Through thirty chapters and an epilogue, daytime scenes are limited to six chapters (3, 4, 5, 9, 17, and 25); and only eight (Chapters 11, 12, 13, 14, 20, 26, 27, and 29) contain both day and night scenes. The other seventeen (a majority of the chapters) are set at night.

To convey a feeling of doom, Pa Chin stresses gloominess, dimness, and darkness. Even during the daytime, the sun never shines, the sky remains gloomy, cloudy, and threatens rain. His nights are usually dark and cold, the settings dimly lit. The novel begins with a dark street scene which is soon replaced by the entrance of an apartment building. It is the dwelling of the protagonist Wang Wen-hsüan. The entrance is described as cave-like and a roundish red doorlight glows dimly. Wang's two-room apartment is subjected to frequent interruptions in the electric power, and when one occurs, Wang and his mother have to use a candle. The streets outside the apartment are also without light, or at best have a few isolated lights amidst a background of darkness.

If all the settings are dark or nearly dark, some of the characters in the novel, many of whom are unidentified, are shadowlike. They are the shadows crouching in the dark in Chapter 1, a handful of pedestrians moving hastily in the cold wind, the children who lie outside Wang's apartment in the cold, the refugees in the epilogue, or a neighbor woman, Mrs. Chang, holding a candle in her hand while walking up the stairs.

And then there are the noises of the night: the sound of rats chewing on the wooden floor, Mrs. T'ang Pai-ch'ing shrieking for her husband, a woman's tragic voice wailing for the spirit of a sickly child to come home, and every night the haunting voice of an old hawker selling hot water and fried rice-cakes.

Night is the time for troubled dreams. Wang has a series of them, beginning with one extensively described in Chapter 2, in which his wife Shu-sheng leaves him after an argument with his mother. The nightmare itself foreshadows the novel's ending. As the story progresses, Wang's body deteriorates physically, though his mind becomes ever more active. Lying in bed, he has many other nightmares. In each his wife runs away with someone, or he or his mother dies. It is at night or in the very early morning hours that Shu-sheng actually leaves Wang to go to Lanchow. Her departure marks the end of Wang's hopes and begins the last stage of his life. It is also at night that Mrs. T'ang Pai-ch'ing dies in childbirth, T'ang is killed by a truck, and Uncle Chung and Wang die in a hospital and at home respectively.

The dark and dismal settings do not merely serve as decorative backdrops to enhance the atmosphere of doom; they are also an important structural device, giving unity to the book. For instance, the first chapter is similar to the epilogue in its emphasis. Whereas Wang

(Chapter 1) hears disgruntled voices from dark corners of the street, a lonely shivering Shu-sheng (Epilogue) overhears passersby commenting and complaining about how little their life has improved since the Japanese surrender. The implication is clearly that misery drags on. Night and darkness dominate the entire book and typify the lives of many of its characters, particularly that of Wang Wen-hsüan.

In addition to using night as a principal image in the novel, Pa Chin uses the change of the seasons to mirror the inner condition of the central characters. The novel begins in the fall and ends in the fall, covering the cycle of one year. And fall is a season which suggests the withering of a dying relationship, as symbolized by Wang's frequent feelings of chill. Winter is the longest season in Pa Chin's bleak world. Throughout the almost endless winter, Wang, his mother, and his wife suffer continuously. During the winter, Wang discovers the seriousness of his illness, loses his job and his wife; his mother's resentment of her daughter-in-law increases and she worries about the future of her seriously ill son; and Shu-sheng agonizes about whether to go to Lanchow. Spring proves to be illusory. Wang's health fails to improve; the mother's hopes about her son's recovery prove to be false; and Shu-sheng, in leaving, vainly struggles after the happiness which has evaded her. Summer kills Wang. It is on a summer day that he dies; summer also brings total despair to his mother, who has lost not only her son but the sole means of her support. But it is once again in the fall that Shu-sheng returns to the city, only to find her husband dead and to become vaguely aware that she has been victimized by a romantic illusion. And another winter is coming, another season of pain and uncertainty, like the previous long winter in that two-room apartment with her husband, her mother-in-law, and her son.

In addition to utilizing to the full the images of night and the change of seasons to convey a sense of doom and the inner world of his characters, Pa Chin uses summary and scene for narration. His general method is to keep summary to the barest minimum, and to use scene to dramatize very intense moments, such as Shu-sheng's departure for Lanchow (Chapter 23) and Wang's mother keeping vigil by her son's bed (Chapter 30). Both scenes are extremely moving. The first describes an anxious Wang waiting for his wife to come home from a party on the eve of her departure, continues with Shu-sheng packing, and ends with their actual farewell. Its detailed description of the characters' every move and every thought helps to make it one of the most memorable and pathetic scenes in modern Chinese literature. The second vividly portrays a possessive mother's love for her son in her expressions of concern and her deepening sense of total despair.

In his use of scene, Pa Chin gives the reader a feeling of participating intensely in the action, and he uses dialogue not only to provide the reader a sense of immediacy, but also to show conflicts between and among the characters. Among the more notable examples of effective dialogue are the exchange of insults between Wang's mother and her daughter-in-law (Chapter 18). This scene clearly reveals the sharp differences between the values of traditional and modern Chinese women. Another example is the conversation between Wang and his wife in the fashionable International Café (Chapter 5) when Wang tries to convince his wife to return home with him after she has moved out. Their conversation discloses the depth of Wang's dependancy on his wife and her resentment of everything, including her job and family.

Another device used with great effectiveness is the internal monologue or "stream of consciousness." Pa Chin's type of monologue differs from that of James Joyce, Henry James, or Virginia Woolf. It is an organized monologue in which the mind presents reasoned and ordered thought, the "end-product" of the "stream of consciousness" rather than the disordered stream itself. One example of the use of this device takes place in Chapter 1, as Wang, coming out of an air-raid shelter, adds up in his mind an account of his family life. A second device Pa Chin uses to reveal the thoughts of his characters is the epistolary method, which brings the reader close to the thoughts and feelings of the character. For example, in a letter Shu-sheng writes to Wang, she fully reveals her heart and mind in an analysis of her non-productive relationship with her husband.[31] A third device used to reveal a character's unconscious is the recounting of dreams and fantasies. For instance, Wang's feeling of insecurity about his wife's attitude toward him, his need and love for her, his love for his mother, and his apprehensions about the future are all clearly revealed in the extended dream already referred to above (Chapter 2).

A great part of the achievement of *Cold Nights* lies in Pa Chin's portraits of Wang's mother, Wang's wife, and Wang himself. Wang's mother is a widow who raised and educated her son without any help. Deeply rooted in old traditions, she believes that a married woman should obey her husband, honor her mother-in-law, and spend most of her time at home doing housework. She sees in her daughter-in-law the living embodiment of a set of repugnant values diametrically opposed to hers. She dislikes Shu-sheng for not having insisted on a proper wedding ceremony when she married her son; she resents Shu-sheng's working at a bank and for being the one who can and does pay for her grandson's tuition; and she disapproves of Shu-sheng's dressing up "as a flower vase" and not doing much housework.

Her resentment of Shu-sheng's modern privileges barely conceals her unspoken desire to possess her son forever. Again and again, she tries to drive a wedge between her son and his wife by telling him that Shu-sheng won't stay with him and that Shu-sheng is no more than

31. See Chapter 26 in the translated text.

his mistress. But to Wang, she will forever be his good mother. She is shown mending her grandson's worn-out winter jacket, washing clothes in cold weather, doing all types of housework and worrying about her son's health. As he deteriorates physically from the ravages of tuberculosis, she stoops to do housework that few Chinese servants of the 1940s would touch. She scrubs, cleans, and cooks, prepares his medications, comforts him, and all the while hopes for his eventual recovery. But unconsciously and simultaneously, she is also aware of the advantage to be gained from his death, for then he will be hers forever. One of her wishes has been that he remain her young and uncorrupted child, and with his death he will fulfill her wish and make her victorious over her arch-opponent, Shu-sheng.

Caught in this struggle for the only male adult in the family is Shu-sheng. Pa Chin portrays her as a good but weak-willed woman. Thirty-four years old and attractive, she enjoys patronizing cafés and going dancing with her boss, activities too costly for her sick and whining husband to afford. And when she comes home from work, she finds her dingy two-room apartment, her hostile mother-in-law, her sickly husband, and her taciturn son (who plays a very minor role in the novel) all too unbearable. As a "new" woman, liberated from the shackles of the past, she wants the opportunity to explore whatever blessings life may offer. Seeking to fulfill herself and to end the interminable winter which typifies her dreary existence, she is both attracted to and repelled by her suave, rich superior, Manager Ch'en. His persistent interest in her offers both freedom and a new horizon. That her dream of a better life might be satisfied by association with Ch'en and by leaving her Chungking home to go to Lanchow suggests how limited her aspirations are. Here also lies the cause of the defeat by her mother-in-law. Oscillating between inner needs and external affairs, in the end she learns that she cannot accept Manager Ch'en's love and that she really loves her husband. But by that time it is too late, for her husband has been dead and buried for more than a month. Her life can only be viewed as a failure. She fails with her husband from her own shortcomings, for (along with her half-hearted desire to possess him) she lacks the capacity and the tenacity to take on her mother-in-law's challenges or to help carry the burden of her husband's anguished soul.

Wang Wen-hsüan is the center of this struggle between the two women. His father died when he was a child; as a result, he develops an attachment to his mother that colors his whole existence. Even though he loves his wife, he cannot belong to her completely while his mother lives, for as long as she is alive he cannot really love another woman. Being torn between mother and wife debilitates him. Without the inner strength or, perhaps the desire to choose one of the two, he relies on his obdurate stoicism to make living with himself possible. Willingly and knowingly, he permits, even urges, his wife to go to Lanchow, though he knows she will be going with another man, and he refuses to be a stumbling block to his wife's "pursuit of happiness." His masochism is intended to compensate for his failings as a son, for having subjected his mother to unnecessary grief; he unconsciously seeks his own death to repay her for his mostly imaginary misdeeds. For it is only in death that he can once again be completely his mother's son, undefiled and uncomplicated by a relationship with another woman.

Cold Nights is a mature piece of art. In it, Pa Chin has successfully used technical devices to illuminate the atmosphere, the moving scenes, the conflicts, and the inner thoughts of his characters. No one particular person is evil and there are no villains — only combinations of unfortunate circumstances that lead to the ultimate tragic ending. It seems that in addition to his realistic presentation of the grim realities in wartime Chungking, much of his achievement lies in his exploration of human motives and behavior. The conjunction of the above-mentioned factors has made *Cold Nights* one of his masterpieces.[32]

32. Since a Western reader may consider the novel extremely sentimental, it is important to point out that sentimentality has always been a characteristic feature of Chinese fiction and poetry and that what distinguishes the novel is the author's expression of true sentiments, and not his use of pathos.

Selected Bibliography

PRIMARY

(This list does not include Pa Chin's collected essays and translations. For a more detailed listing, see Olga Lang, *Pa Chin and His Writings*, pp. 341–353.)

Pa Chin hsüan-chi 巴金選集 [Pa Chin's Selected Works]. Shanghai: Chung-yang shu-tien, 1936.

Pa Chin hsüan-chi [Pa Chin's Selected Works]. Peking: K'ai-ming, 1951.

Pa Chin san-wen hsüan 巴金散文選 [Pa Chin's Selected Essays]. Peking: Hsin-hua, 1955.

Pa Chin tai-piao-tso hsüan 巴金代表作選 [Selections of Representative Works of Pa Chin]. Shanghai: Ch'üan ch'ui, 1951.

Pa Chin wen-chi 巴金文集 [Collected Works of Pa Chin]. 14 volumes. Peking: Jen-min wen-hsüeh, 1958–1962.

Pa Chin wen-chi [Collected Works of Pa Chin]. 14 volumes. Hong Kong: Nan-kuo ch'u-pan she, 1970. This is the most accessible edition. Texts differ slightly from the pre-1951 editions. Vol. 1: *Mieh-wang* 滅亡 [Destruction, 1927–1928]; *Hsin-sheng* 新生 [New Life, 1931, 1932]; *Ssu-ch'ü ti t'ai-yang* 死去的太陽 [The Setting Sun, 1930]; *Hai ti meng* 海的夢 [Dream on the Sea, 1932]; Vol. 2 : *Ch'un-t'ien li ti ch'iu-t'ien* 春天裏的秋天 [Autumn in Spring, 1932]; *Sha-ting* 砂丁 [The Antimony Miners, 1932]; *Hsüeh* 雪 [Snow, 1933]; *Li-na* 利娜 [Lina, 1934]; Vol. 3: *Wu* 霧 [Fog, 1931]; *Yü* 雨 [Rain, 1932], *Lei* 雷 [Thunder, 1933]; *Tien* 電 [Lightning, 1934]; Vol. 4: *Chia* 家 [Family, 1931]; Vol. 5: *Ch'un* 春 [Spring, 1938]; Vol. 6: *Ch'iu* 秋 [Autumn, 1940]; Vol. 7: *Fu-ch'ou* 復仇 [Revenge, 1929–1931]; *Kuang-ming* 光明 [Light, 1931]; *Tien-yi* 電椅 [The Electric Chair, 1931–1932]; Vol. 8: *Mo-pu* 抹布 [The Dustcloth, 1931–1932]; *Chiang-chün* 將軍 [The General, 1932–1933]; *Ch'en-mo* 沉默 [Deep Silence, 1934]; *Ch'en-lo* 沉落 [Sinking down, 1934]; *Shen, kuei, jen* 神鬼人 [God, Ghost, Man,

1934–1935; Vol. 9: *Ch'en-mo II* [Deep Silence II, 1934]; *Fa ti ku-shih* 髮的故事 [Story of Hair, 1936]; *Ch'ang-sheng t'a* 長生塔 [Pagoda of Long life, 1934–1936]; *Huan-hun ts'ao* 還魂草 [Grass of Resurrection, 1937–1941]; *Hsiao-jen, hsiao-shih* 小人小事 [Little People, Little Things, 1942–1945]; Vol . 10: *Yi* 憶 [Memories, 1933–1936]: *Tuan-chien* 短簡 *I* [Short Notes I, 1936]; *Sheng chih ch'an-hui* 生之懺悔 [Confessions of a Life, 1929–1934]; *Tien-ti* 點滴 [Drops, 1934–1935]; *Meng yü tsui* 夢與醉 [Dream and Inebriation, 1937]; *K'ung-su* 控訴 [J'Accuse, 1931–1937]; *Wu-t'i* 無題 [No Title, 1936–1940]; *Hei-t'u* 黑土 [Black Earth, 1939]; *Lung, hu, kou* 龍虎狗 [Dragon, Tiger, Dog, 1940–1941]; *Fei-yüan wai* 廢園外 [Behind a Desolate Garden, 1938–1942]; *Hui-nien* 懷念 [Reminiscences, 1938–1946]; *Ching-yeh ti pei-chü* 靜夜的悲劇 [Tragedy on a Quiet Night, 1945–1946]; Vol. 11: *Hai-hsing tsa-chi* 海行雜記 [Sea Voyage Notebook, 1927]; *Lü-t'u sui-pi* 旅途隨筆 [Random Notes of a Voyage, 1933–1934]; *Lü-t'u t'ung-hsün* 旅途通訊 [Letters on the Road, 1938–1939]; *Lü-t'u tsa-chi* 旅途雜記 [Travel Notebook, 1940–1942]; *Tuan-chien II* [Short Notes II, 1935–1937]; Vol. 12: *Huo* 火 [Fire, 1938–1940, 1941, 1943]; Vol. 13: *Ch'i-yüan* 憩園 [Leisure Garden, 1944]; *Ti-ssu ping-shih* 第四病室 [Ward Number Four, 1945]; Vol. 14: *Han-yeh* 寒夜 [Cold Nights, 1946]; *T'an tzu-chi ti ch'ung tso* 談自己的創作 [Discussion of My Creative Work, 1957–1961].

A Battle for Life: A Full Record of How the Life of Steel Worker Chiu Tsai-kang Was Saved in the Shanghai Kwangtze Hospital [I-ch'ang wan-chiu sheng-ming ti chan-tou 一場挽救生命的戰鬥]. Pa Chin *et al.* Tr. by Cheng Chi-yi and Shen Tzu-kao. Peking: Foreign Languages Press, 1959.

Li Ta-hai 李大海. Peking: Tso-chia ch'u-pan she, 1961.

Living Amongst Heroes. Peking: Foreign Languages Press, 1954.

Lo-ch'e shang 騾車上 [On the Mule Cart]. Hong Kong: Hsin-yüeh Publishing Company, 1959.

Ming-chu ho Yü-chi 明珠和玉姬 [Ming-chu and Yü-chi]. Peking: Chung-kuo shao-nien erh-t'ung ch'u-pan she, 1957.

Wo-men hui-chien liao P'eng Te-huai Ssu-ling yüan 我們會見了彭德懷司令員 [Our Meeting with Commander P'eng Te-huai]. Peking: Wen-hsüeh ch'u-pan she, 1953.

Ying-hsiung ti ku-shih 英雄的故事 [Stories of Heroes]. Shanghai: P'ing-ming ch'u-pan she, 1953.

SECONDARY

Anonymous. "The Collected Works of Pa Chin." In *Chinese Literature*, 1953, No. 4, pp. 117–120. Introduces Pa Chin's collected works (in 14 volumes).

Benedikter, Martin. "Un Racconto di Pa Chin: Cane." *In Cina* 6, pp. 88–89. Rome: Istituto italiana per il Medio ed Estremo Oriente, 1960. Brief note on Pa Chin.

Boorman, Howard C., and Howard, Richard C., eds. *Biographical Dictionary of Republican China*. 4 volumes. New York: Columbia University Press, 1967–1971. Vol. 2, pp. 297–299; Vol. 4, pp. 249–252. Useful as a general reference.

Briere, O. "Un Romancier Chinois Contemporarin: Pa Chin." In *Bulletin del' Universite l' Aurore*. Shanghai: Serie 3, 3.3. (1942). pp. 577–598. One of the earliest studies on Pa Chin.

Chang, Tang, tr. "Perseverance" ("Chien-ch'iang chan-shih"). In *Chinese Literature*, 1936, No. 6, pp. 84–92. Discusses Pa Chin's life and work after 1949.

Chung-yang jih-pao 中央日報 [Central Daily News]. Taiwan: Taipei. August 2, 1972 . Contains an anonymous article on the revival of interest in Pa Chin's work in Mainland China.

——. Taiwan: Taipei. July 27, 1977. Contains an anonymous article on Pa Chin's persecution by the "Gang of four."

Gibbs, Donald A., and Li Yun-chen. *A Bibliography of Studies and Transla-*

tions of Modern Chinese Literature, 1918–1942. Cambridge: Harvard University East Asian Research Center, 1975. Contains a section on Pa Chin, pp. 150–154.

Goldman, Merle. *Literary Dissent in Communist China.* Cambridge: Harvard University Press, 1967. Scholarly and well documented, it contains brief references to Pa Chin's life and work after 1949.

Granat, Diana. "Three Stories of France: Pa Chin and His Early Short Stories."Unpublished M.A. Thesis. University of Pennsylvania, 1972. Introduction too sketchy, but the translations of "Fang-tung t'ai-t'ai" ["Mrs. Landlady"], "Lo-po-erh hsien-sheng" [Mr. Robert"], and "Hao-jen" ["A Good Man"] are useful.

Hsia, C. T. *A History of Modern Chinese Fiction.* New Haven and London: Yale University Press, 1961. The best study of twentieth-century Chinese fiction. Includes an evaluation of Pa Chin's work.

Hsiao Ch'ien. *Etchings of a Tormented Age.* London: George Allen & Unwin Company, 1942. Concise and easy to read. Discusses Pa Chin's artistic beliefs and some of his early works.

Jen, Richard L., tr. "Star" ["Hsing"] in *T'ien Hsia Monthly*, 5.1 (August 1937), pp. 68–78; 5.2 (September 1937), pp. 193–207; 5.3 (October 1937), pp. 313–325; 5.4 (November 1937), pp. 404–414. Reprinted as *Star*. Shanghai: Shih-chieh ying-yu pien-yi she, 1947. No longer available.

Kalmer, J., tr. *Garten der Ruhe* [Leisure Garden]. Munich: G. Hauser, 1954.

Král, Oldřich. "Pa Chin's Novel 'The Family'." In *Studies in Modern Chinese Literature*, edited by Jaroslav Prusek, pp. 97–112. Berlin: Akademie-Verlag, 1964. Analysis somewhat superficial.

Lang, Olga. "Introduction" in *Family*, pp. vii-xxvi. New York: Doubleday Anchor Books, 1972. A most useful introduction to Pa Chin's life and work.

——. "Writer Pa Chin and His Time: Chinese Youth of the Transitional

Period." Unpublished Ph.D. Dissertation. Columbia University, 1962.

——. *Pa Chin and His Writings: Chinese Youth between the Two Revolutions.* Cambridge: Harvard University Press, 1967. Important study of Pa Chin's intellectual thought. Based on her doctoral dissertation.

Lechowska, T. "In Search of a New Ideal: The Metamorphoses of Pa Chin's Model Heroes." *ArOr*, 42 (1974), pp. 310–322. An interesting study of the ideals of some of Pa Chin's heroes whose idealism undergoes a continuous change as they move from oppression to freedom.

——. "Pa Chin" in *Dictionary of Oriental Literatures*, edited by Jaroslav Prusek. New York: Basic Books, 1974. Vol. I, pp. 135–136. A brief account of Pa Chin's life and work.

Lin, Man-shu, *et al. Chung-kuo tang-tai tso-chia hsiao-ch'uan* 中國當代作家小傳 [Biographies D'Auteurs Chinois Contemporarins]. Paris: Centre de publication Asie orientale de l'Universite Paris 7, 1976. pp. 46–47. In Chinese, a very succinct account of Pa Chin's life, including a bibliography of secondary sources on Pa Chin and his works.

Mao, Nathan K. *Pa Chin*. Boston: Twayne Publishers, 1978. A biographical-critical study of Pa Chin's life and his major short stories and novels.

——. "Pa Chin's Journey in Sentiment: From Hope to Despair." In *Journal of the Chinese Language Teachers Association*, Vol. XI, Number 2 (May 1975), pp. 131–137 . Traces Pa Chin's growing pessimism.

Ming-pao yüeh-k'an 明報月刊 [Ming-pao Monthly], Vol. 10, Number 11 (November 1975), pp. 10–11. Report on Pa Chin's nomination for the Nobel Prize in literature.

Mo, Chin-yi, tr. *Short Stories by Pa Chin, with English translations.* Hong Kong: Hui-t'ung shu-tien. Contains translations of "Fu-ch'ou" ["Revenge"], "Ch'u-lien " ["First Love"], and "Kou" ["Dog"].

Identical with *Short Stories by Pa Chin,* edited by Wen I. Shanghai: Chung-ying ch'u-pan she, 1941.

Monsterleet, Jean. *Pa Chin ti sheng-huo ho chu-tso* 巴金的生活和著作 [Pa Chin's L ife and Work]. Translated by Wang chi-wen. Shanghai: Wen-feng ch'u-pan she, 1950 .

Shapiro, Sidney, tr. *The Family (Chia)*. Peking: Foreign Languages Press, 1958. Reprinted by Doubleday Anchor Books, 1972, with supplemental parts translated by Lu Kuang-huan and introduction by Olga Lang. An abridged translation.

——. "A Moonlit Night" ["Yüeh-yeh"]. In *Chinese Literature*, 1962, No. 5, pp. 43–50.

Sheng, Hsien, tr. "We Shall Always Stand Together" (Chinese title not given). In *Chinese Literature,* 1961, No. 8, pp. 41–47.

Snow, Edgar. *Living China: Modern Chinese Short Stories*. London: George G. Harper & Co., Ltd., 1936. Contains a translation of "Kou" ["Dog"], pp. 174–180.

Tang, Sheng, tr. "When the Snow Melted" ("Hua-hsüeh ti jih-tzu"). In *Chinese Literature*, 1962, No. 5, pp. 50–63.

Wang, C. C., tr. "The Puppét Dead" (Excerpt: Chapter 34 of *Family*). In Wang's *Contemporary Chinese Stories*. New York: Columbia University Press, 1944, pp. 80–94. Excellent translation.

Wang, Yao. *Chung-kuo hsin wen-hsüeh shih-ko* 中國新文學史稿 [A Draft History of Modern Chinese Literature]. 2 volumes. Shanghai: Hsin wen-yi she, 1954. Biased but important.

Wong, Betty. "Pa Chin in His Middle Period as a Novelist. An Analysis of Characters in the *Torrent Trilogy* and *Fire*." Unpublished M.A. Thesis. Columbia University, 1967. Critical of Pa Chin's writing techniques.

Wong, Harriet, tr. "Dawn at Sea" ["Hai-shang ti jih-ch'u"]. In *Journal of Oriental Literature,* 2 (June 1948), p. 5.

Yeh, Mui Shang-lan, tr. "To a Cousin — Preface to the 10th edition of 'Family'." In *Renditions,* No. 4 (Spring, 1975), pp. 73–82.

Yu, Fan-chin, tr. "Photographs from Kamakura" ["Tsung lien-ts'ang tai-hui ti chao-p'ien"]. In *Chinese Literature,* 1963, No. 6, pp. 62–67.

Yü, Ssu-mu. *Tso-chia Pa Chin* 作家巴金 [Writer Pa Chin]. Hong Kong: Nankuo ch'u pan she, 1964. Lots of summaries, weak analysis.

本系列已出版書籍
Published Titles in the Series

《臺北人》*Taipei People* (2000)
白先勇 著　白先勇、葉佩霞 英譯
喬志高 主編
By Pai Hsien-yung
Translated by the Author and Patia Yasin
Edited by George Kao

《阿Q正傳》*The True Story of Ah Q* (2002)
《祝福及其他》*The New-Year Sacrifice and Other Stories* (2002)
《野草》*Wild Grass* (2003)
魯迅 著　楊憲益、戴乃迭 英譯
By Lu Xun
Translated by Yang Xianyi and Gladys Yang

《城南舊事》*Memories of Peking: South Side Stories* (2002)
林海音 著　殷張蘭熙、齊邦媛 英譯
By Lin Hai-yin
Translated by Nancy C. Ing and Chi Pang-yuan

《寒夜》*Cold Nights* (2002)
巴金 著　茅國權、柳存仁 英譯
By Pa Chin
Translated by Nathan K. Mao and Liu Ts'un-yan

《沈從文短篇小說選》*Selected Stories of Shen Congwen* (2004)
沈從文 著　金介甫 英譯
By Shen Congwen
Translated by Jeffrey C. Kinkley

《林家鋪子/春蠶》*The Shop of the Lin Family & Spring Silkworms* (2004)
茅盾 著　沙博理 英譯
By Mao Dun
Translated by Sidney Shapiro

《茶館》*Teahouse* (2004)
老舍 著　霍華 英譯
By Lao She
Translated by John Howard-Gibbon

《駱駝祥子》*Camel Xiangzi* (2005)
老舍 著　施曉菁 英譯
By Lao She
Translated by Shi Xiaojing

《染布匠的女兒：蕭紅短篇小說選》
The Dyer's Daughter: Selected Stories by Xiao Hong (2005)
蕭紅 著　葛浩文 英譯
By Xiao Hong
Translated by Howard Goldblatt

《雅舍小品選集・卷一》
From A Cottager's Sketchbook, vol. 1 (2005)
《雅舍小品選集・卷二》
From A Cottager's Sketchbook, vol. 2 (2006)
梁實秋 著　陳達遵 英譯
By Liang Shih-chiu
Translated by Ta-tsun Chen

《棋王》*The Chess Master* (2005)
阿城 著　詹納爾 英譯
By A Cheng
Translated by W.J.F. Jenner

《冷的文學：高行健著作選》
Cold Literature: Selected Works by Gao Xingjian (2005)
高行健 著　方梓勳、陳順妍 譯
By Gao Xingjian
Translated by Gilbert C. F. Fong and Mabel Lee

《周作人散文選》*Zhou Zuoren: Selected Essays* (2006)
周作人 著　卜立德 英譯
By Zhou Zuoren
Translated by David E. Pollard

《鴜鷺湖的憂鬱》*The Sorrows of Egret Lake* (2009)
端木蕻良 著　葛浩文、孔海立 英譯
By Duanmu Hongliang
Translated by Howard Goldblatt and Haili Kong